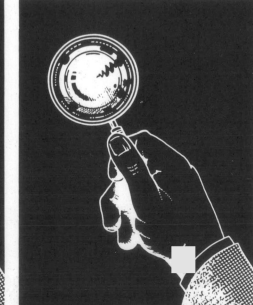

VINTAGE DETECTIVE STORIES

VINTAGE DETECTIVE STORIES

EDITED BY MIKE HIGGS

Galley Press

Selected by Mike Higgs primarily from an original compilation copyright
Dorothy L. Sayers and published 1930 by Victor Gollancz. Reasonable efforts
have been made to contact the original authors or their heirs and any ommission
in this respect is unintentional. However, any queries arising should be
forwarded to Patrick Hawkey & Company Ltd. for attention.

Sexton Blake story Copyright ©1987 IPC Magazines Ltd.

Published in this edition in 1987 by
Patrick Hawkey & Co. Ltd., Suite 411, 76 Shoe Lane, London EC4.
for GALLEY PRESS
an imprint of W.H. Smith & Son Ltd., Registered number 237811,
England, trading as W.H. Smith Distributors, St. John's House,
East Street, Leicester LE1 6NE.

ISBN 0 861 36617 4

Printed in England.

CONTENTS

THE TEA-LEAF
by Edgar Jepson & Robert Eustace

First published in 1925

Arthur Kelstern and Hugh Willoughton met in the Turkish bath in Duke Street, St. James's, and rather more than a year later in that Turkish bath they parted. Both of them were bad-tempered men, Kelstern cantankerous and Willoughton violent. It was, indeed, difficult to decide which was the worst-tempered; and when I found that they had suddenly become friends, I gave that friendship three months. It lasted nearly a year.

When they did quarrel they quarrelled about Kelstern's daughter Ruth. Wiloughton fell in love with here and she with him, and they became engaged to be married. Six months later, in spite of the fact that they were plainly very much in love with one another, the engagement was broken off. Neither of them gave any reason for breaking it off. My belief was that Willoughton had given Ruth a taste of his infernal temper and got as good as he gave.

Not that Ruth was at all a Kelstern to look at. Like the members of most of the old Lincolnshire families, descendants of the Vikings and the followers of Canute, one Kelstern is very like another Kelstern, fair-haired, clear-skinned, with light blue eyes and a good bridge to the nose. But Ruth had taken after her mother; she was dark, with a straight nose, dark-brown eyes of the kind often described as liquid, dark-brown hair, and as kissable lips as ever I saw. She was a proud, self-sufficing, high-spirited girl, with a temper of her own. She needed it to live with that cantankerous old brute Kelstern. Oddly enough, in spite of the fact that he always would try to bully her, she was fond of him; and I will say for him that he was very fond of her. Probably she was the only creature in the world of whom he was really fond. He was an expert in the application of scientific discoveries to industry; and she worked with him in his laboratory. He paid her five hundred a year, so that she must have been uncommonly good.

He took the breaking off the engagement very hard indeed. He would have it that Willoughton had jilted her. Ruth took it hard, too; her warm colouring lost some of its warmth; her lips grew less kissable and set in a thinner line. Willoughton's temper grew worse then ever; he was like a bear with a perpetually sore head. I tried to feel my way with both him and Ruth with a view to help bring about a reconciliation. To put it mildly, I was rebuffed. Willoughton swore at me; Ruth flared up and told me not to meddle in matters that didn't concern me. Nevertheless, my strong impression was that they were missing one another badly and would have been glad enough to come together again if their stupid vanity could have let them.

Kelstern did his best to keep Ruth furious with Willoughton. One night I told him—it was no busines of mine; but I never did give a tinker's curse for his temper—that he was a fool to meddle and had much better leave them alone. It made him furious of course; he would have it that Willoughton was a dirty hound and a low blackguard—at least those were about the mildest things he said of him. Given his temper and the provocation, nothing less could be expected. Moreover, he was looking a very sick man and depressed.

He took immense trouble to injure Willoughton. At his clubs, the Athenaeum, the Devonshire, and the Savile, he would display considerable ingenuity in bringing the conversation round to him; then he would declare that he was a scoundrel of the meanest type. Of course, it did Willoughton harm, though not nearly as much as Kelstern desired, for Willoughton knew his job as few engineers knew it; and it is very hard indeed to do much harm to a man who really knows his job. People have to have him. But of course it did him some harm; and Willoughton knew that Kelstern was doing it. I came across two men who told me that they had given him a friendly hint. That did not improve *his* temper.

An expert in the construction of those ferro-concrete buildings which are rising up all over London, he was as distinguished in his sphere as Kelstern in his. They were alike not only in the matters of brains and bad-temper; but I think that their minds worked in very much the same way. At any rate, both of them seemed determined not to change their ordinary course of life because of the breaking off of that engagement.

It had been the habit of both of them to have a Turkish bath, at the baths in Duke Street, at four in the afternoon on the second and last Tuesday in every month. To that habit they stuck. The fact that they must meet on those Tuesdays did not cause either of them to change his hour of taking his Turkish bath by the twenty minutes which would have given them no more than a passing glimpse of one another. They continued to take it, as they always had, simultaneously. Thick-skinned? They were thick-skinned. Neither of them pretended that he did not see the other; he scowled at him; and he scowled at him most of the time. I know this, for sometimes I had a Turkish bath myself at that hour.

It was about three months after the breaking off of the engagement that they met for the last time at that Turkish bath, and there parted for good. Kelstern had been looking ill for about six weeks;

there was a greyness and a drawn look to his face; and he was losing weight. On the second Tuesday in October he arrived at the bath punctually at four, bringing with him, as was his habit, a thermos flask full of a very delicate China tea. If he thought he was not perspiring freely enough, he would drink it after his bath. Willoughton arrived about two minutes later. Kelstern finished undressing and went into the bath a couple of minutes before Willoughton. They stayed in the hot room about the same tme; Kelstern went into the hottest room about a minute after Willoughton. before he went into it he sent for his thermos flask, which he had left in the dressing-room, and took it into the hot-test room with him.

As it happened, they were the only two people in the hottest room; and they had not been in it two minutes before the four men in the hot room heard them quarreling. They heard Kelstern call Willoughton a dirty hound and a low blackguard, among other things, and declare he would do him yet. Willoughton told him to go to the devil twice. Kelstern went on abusing him, and presently Willoughton fairly shouted: "Oh, shut up, you old fool! Or I'll make you!"

Kelstern did not shut up. About two minutes later Willoughton came out of the hottest room, scowling, walked through the hot room into the shampooing room, and put himself into the hands of one of the shampooers. Two or three minutes after that a man of the name of Helston went into the hottest room and fairly yelled. Kelstern was lying back on a couch, with the blood still flowing from a wound over his heart.

There was a devil of a hullabaloo. The police were called in; Willoughton arrested. Of course he lost his temper and, protesting furiously that he had had nothing whatever to do with the crime, abused the police. That did not incline them to believe him.

After examining the room and the dead body the detective-inspector in charge of the case came to the conclusion that Kelstern had been stabbed as he was drinking his tea. The thermos flask lay on the floor and some of the tea had evidently been spilt, for some tea-leaves—the tea in the flask must have been carelessly strained off the leaves by the maid who filled it—lay on the floor about the mouth of the empty flask. It looked as if the murderer had taken advantage of Kelstern's drinking his tea to stab him while the flask rather blocked his vision and prevented him from seeing what he would be at.

The case would have been quite plain sailing but for the fact that they could not find the weapon. It had been easy enough for Willoughton to take it into the bath in the towel in which he was draped. But how had he got rid of it? Where had he hidden it? A Turkish bath is no place to hide anything in. It is as bare as an empty barn—if anything barer; and Willoughton had been in the barest part of it. The police searched every part of it—not that there was much point in doing that, for Willoughton had come out of the hottest room and gone through the hot room into the shampooer's room. When Helston started shouting "Murder!" he had rushed back with the shampooers to the hottest room and there he had stayed. Since it was obvious that he had committed the murder, the shampooers and the bathers had kept their eyes on him. They were all of them certain that he had not left them to go the dressing-room; they would not have allowed him to do so.

It was obvious that he must have carried the weapon into the bath, hidden in the folds of the towel in which he was draped, and brought it away in the folds of that towel. He had laid the towel down beside the couch on which he was being shampooed; and there it still lay when they came to look for it, untouched, with no weapon in it, with no traces of blood on it. There was not much in the fact that it was not stained with blood, since Willoughton could have wiped the knife, or dagger, or whatever weapon he used, on the couch on which Kelstern lay. There were no marks of any such wiping on the couch; but the flood, flowing from the wound, might have covered them up. But why was the weapon not in the towel?

There was no finding that weapon.

Then the doctors who made the autopsy came to the conclusion that the wound had been inflicted by a circular, pointed weapon nearly three-quarters of an inch in diameter. It had penetrated rather more than three inches, and, supposing that its handle was only four inches long, it must have been a sizeable weapon, quite impossible to overlook. The doctors also discovered a further proof of the theory that Kelstern had been drinking tea when he was stabbed. Half-way down the wound they found two halves of a tea-leaf which had evidently fallen on to Kelstern's body, been driven into the wound, and cut in half by the weapon. Also they discovered that Kelstern was suffering from cancer. This fact was not published in the papers; I heard it at the Devonshire.

Willoughton was brought before the magistrates, and to most people's surprise did not reserve his defence. He went into the witness-box and swore that he had never touched Kelstern, that he had never had anything to touch him with, that he had never taken any weapon into the Turkish bath and so had had no weapon to hide, that he had never even seen any such weapon as the doctors described. He was committed for trial.

The papers were full of the crime; everyone was discussing it; and the question which occupied everyone's mind was: where had Willoughton hidden the weapon? People wrote to the papers to suggest that he had ingeniously put it in some place under everybody's eyes and that it had been overlooked because it was so obvious. Others suggested that, circular and pointed, it must be very like a thick lead-pencil, that it was a thick lead-pencil; and that was why the police had overlooked it in their search. The police had not overlooked any thick lead-pencil; there had been no thick lead-pencil to overlook. They hunted England through—Willoughton did a lot of motoring—to discover the man who had sold him the curious and uncommon weapon. They did not find the man who had sold it to him; they did not find a man who sold such weapons at all. They came to the conclusion that Kelstern had been murdered with a piece of steel, or iron, rod filed to a point like a pencil.

In spite of the fact that only Willoughton *could* have murdered Kelsten, I could not believe that he had done it. The fact that Kelstern was doing his best to injure him professionally and socially was by no means a strong enough motive. Willoughton was far too intelligent a man not to be very well aware that people do not take much notice of statements to the discredit of a man whom they need to do a job for them; and for the social injury he would care very little. Besides, he might very well injure, or even kill, a man in one of his tantrums; but his was not the kind of bad temper that plans a cold-blooded murder; and if ever a murder had been deliberately planned, Kelstern's had.

I was as close a friend as Willoughton had, and I went to visit him in prison. He seemed rather touched by my doing so, and grateful. I learnt that I was the only person who had done so. He was subdued and seemed much gentler. It might last. He discussed the murder readily enough, and naturally with a harassed air. he said quite franky that he did not expect me, in the circumstances, to believe that he had not committed it; but he had not, and he could not for the life of him conceive who had. I did believe that he had not committed it; there was something in his way of discussing it that wholly convinced me. I told him that I was quite sure that he had not killed Kelstern; and he looked at me as if he did not believe the assurance. But again he looked grateful.

Ruth was grieving for her father; but Willoughton's very dangerous plight to some degree distracted her mind from her loss. A woman can quarrel with a man bitterly without desiring to see him hanged; and Willoughton's chance of escaping hanging was not at all a good one. But she would not believe for a moment that he had murdered her father.

"No; there's nothing in it—nothing whatever," she said, firmly. "If Dad had murdered Hugh I could have understood it. He had reasons—or at any rate he had pursuaded himself that he had. But whatever reason had Hugh for murdering Dad? It's all nonsense to suppose that he'd mind Dad's trying all he knew to injure other people in that way, but they don't really injure them very much; and Hugh knows that quite well."

"Of course they don't; and Hugh wouldn't really believe that your father was injuring him much," I said. "But you're forgetting his infernal temper."

"No, I'm not," she protested. "He might kill a man in one of his rages on the spur of the moment. But this wasn't the spur of the moment. Whoever did it had worked the whole thing out and came along with the weapon ready."

I had to admit that that was reasonable enough. But who had done it? I pointed out to her that the police had made careful inquiries about everyone in the bath at the time, the shampooers and the people taking their baths, but they found no evidence whatever that anyone of them had at any time had any relations, except that of shampooer, with her father.

"Either it was one of them, or somebody else who just did it and got right away, or there'a a catch somewhere," she said, frowning thoughtfully.

"I can't see how there can possibly have been anyone in the bath, except the people who are known to have been there," said I. "In fact, there can't have been."

Then the Crown subpoenaed her as a witness for the prosecution. It seemed rather unnecessary and even a bit queer, for it could have found plenty of evidence of bad blood between the two men without dragging her into it. Plainly it was bent on doing all it knew to prove motive enough. Ruth worked her brain so hard trying to get to the bottom of the business that there came a deep vertical wrinkle just above her right eyebrow that stayed there.

On the morning of the trial I called for her after breakfast to drive her down to the New Bailey. She was pale and looked as if she had had a poor night's rest, and, naturally enough, she seemed to be suffering from an excitement she found hard to control. It was not like her to show any excitement she might be feeling.

She said in an excited voice: "I think I've got it!" and would say no more.

We had, of course, been in close touch with Willoughton's solicitor, Hamley; and he had kept seats for us just behind him. He wished to have Ruth to hand to consult should some point turn up on which she could throw light, since she knew more than anyone about the relations between Willoughton and her father. I had timed our arrival very well; the jury had just been sworn in. Of course, the Court was full of women, the wives of peers and bookmakers and politicians, most of them overdressed and overscented.

Then the judge came in; and with his coming the atmosphere of the court became charged with that sense of anxious strain peculiar to trials for murder. It was rather like the atmosphere of a sick room in a case of fatal illnes, but worse.

Willoughton came into the dock looking under the weather and very much subdued. But he was certainly looking dignified, and he said that he was not guilty in a steady enough voice.

Greatorex, the leading counsel for the Crown, opened the case for the prosecution. There was no suggestion in his speech that the police had discoverd any new fact. He begged the jury not to lay too much stress on the fact that the weapon had not been found. He had to, of course.

Then Helston gave evidence of finding that Kelstern had been stabbed, and he and the other three men who had been with him in the hot room gave evidence of the quarrel they had overheard between Willoughton and the dead man, and that Willoughton came out of the hottest room scowling and obviously furious. One of them, a fussy old gentleman of the name of Underwood, declared that it was the bitterist quarrel he had ever heard. None of the four of them could throw any light light on the matter of whether Willoughton was carrying the missing weapon in the folds of the towel in which he was draped; all of them were sure that he had nothing in his hands.

The medical evidence came next. In cross-examining the doctors who had made the autopsy, Hazeldean, Willoughton's counsel, established the fact quite definitely that the missing weapon was of a fair size; that its rounded blade must have been over half an inch in diameter and between three and four inches long. They were of the opinion that to drive a blade of that thickness into the heart a handle of at least four inches in length would be necessary to give a firm enough grip. They agreed that it might very well have been a piece of a steel, or iron, rod sharpened like a pencil. At any rate, it was certainly a sizeable weapon, not one to be hidden quickly or to disappear wholly in a Turkish bath. Hazeldean could not shake their evidence about the tea-leaf; they were confident that it had been driven into the wound and cut in half by the blade of the missing weapon, and that went to show that the wound had been inflicted while Kelstern was drinking his tea.

Detective-Inspector Brackett, who was in charge of the case, was cross-examined at great length about his search for the missing weapon. He made it quite clear that it was nowhere in that Turkish bath, neither in the hot rooms, nor the shampooing room, nor the dressing rooms, nor the vestibule, nor the office. He had had the plunge bath emptied, he had searched the roofs, though it was practically certain that the skylight above the hot room, not the hottest, had been shut at the time of the crime. In re-examination he scouted the idea of Willoughton's having had an accomplice who had carried away the weapon for him. He had gone into that matter most carefully.

The shampooer stated that Willoughton came to him scowling so savagely that he wondered what had put him into such a bad temper. In cross-examining him, Arbuthnot, Hazeldean's junior, made it clearer than ever that, unless Willoughton had already hidden the weapon in the bare hottest room, it was hidden in the towel. Then he drew from the shampooer the definite statement that Willoughton had set down the towel beside the couch on which he was shampooed; that he had hurried back to the hot rooms in front of the shampooer; that the shampooer had come back from the hot rooms, leaving Willoughton still in them dicussing the crime, to find the towel lying just as Willoughton had set it down, with no weapon in it and no trace of blood on it.

Since the inspector had disposed of the possibility that an accomplice had slipped in, taken the weapon from the towel, and slipped out of the bath with it this evidence really made it clear that the weapon had never left the hottest room.

Then the prosecution called evidence of the bad terms on which Kelstern and Willoughton had been. Three well-known and influential men told the jury about Kelstern's efforts to prejudice Willoughton in their eyes and the damaging statements he had made about him. One of them had felt it to be his duty to tell Willoughton about this; and Willoughton had been very angry. Arbuthnot, in cross-examining, elicited the fact that any damaging statement that Kelstern made about anyone was considerably discounted by the fact that everyone knew him to be in the highest degree cantankerous.

I noticed that during the end of the cross-examination of the shampooer and during this evidence Ruth had ben fidgeting and turning to look impatiently at the entrance to court, as if she were expecting someone. Then, just as she was summoned to the witness-box, there came in a tall, stooping grey-headed, grey-bearded man of about sixty, carrying a brown-paper parcel. His face was familiar to me, but I could not place him. He caught her eye and nodded to her. She breathed a sharp sigh of relief, and bent over and handed a letter she had in her hand to Willoughton's solicitor and pointed out the grey-bearded man to him. Then she went quietly to the witness box.

Hamley read the letter and at once bent over and handed it to Hazeldean and spoke to him. I caught a note of excitement in his hushed voice. Hazeldean read the letter and appeared to grow excited too. Hamley slipped out of his seat and went to the grey-bearded man, who was still standing just inside the door of the porch, and began to talk to him earnestly.

Greatorex began to examine Ruth; and naturally I turned my attention to her. His examination was directed also to show on what bad terms Kelstern and Willoughton had been. Ruth was called on to tell the jury some of Kelstern's actual threats. Then he questioned Ruth about her own relations with Willoughton and the breaking off of the engagement and its infuriating effect on her father. She admitted that he had been very bitter about it, and had told her that he was resolved to do his best to do Willoughton in. I thought that she went out of her way to emphasize this resolve of Kelstern's. It seemed to me likely to prejudice the jury still more against Willoughton, making them sympathize with a father's righteous indignation, and making yet more obvious that he was a dangerous enemy. Yet she would not admit that her father was right in believing that Willoughton had jilted her.

Hazeldean rose to cross-examine Ruth with a wholly confident air. He drew from her the fact that her father had been on excellent terms with Willoughton until the breaking off of the engagement.

Then Hazeldean asked: "Is it a fact that since the breaking off of your engagement the prisoner has more than once begged you to forgive him and renew it?"

"Four times," said Ruth.

"And you refused?"

"Yes," said Ruth. She looked at Willoughton queerly and added: "He wanted a lesson."

The Judge asked: "Did you intend, then, to forgive him ultimately?"

Ruth hesistated; then she rather evaded a direct answer; she scowled frankly at Willoughton, and said: "Oh, well, there was no hurry. He would always marry me if I changed my mind and wanted to."

"And did your father know this?" asked the Judge.

"No. I didn't tell him. I was angry with Mr. Willoughton," Ruth replied.

There was a pause. Then Hazeldean started on a fresh line.

In sympathetic accents he asked: "Is it a fact that your father was suffering from cancer in a painful form?"

"It was beginning to grow very painful," said Ruth sadly.

"Did he make a will and put all his affairs in order a few days before he died?"

"Three days," said Ruth

"Did he ever express an intention of committing suicide?"

"He said that he would stick it out for a little while and then end it all," said Ruth. She paused and added: "*And that is what he did do*."

One might almost say that the Court started. I think that everyone in it moved a little, so that there was a kind of rustling murmur.

"Will you tell the Court your reasons for that statement?" said Hazeldean.

Ruth seemed to pull herself together—she was looking very tired—the she began in quiet, even voice: "I never believed for a moment that Mr. Willoughton murdered my father. If my father had murdered Mr. Willoughton it would have been a different matter. Of course, like everybody else, I puzzled over the weapon; what it was and where it had got to. I did not believe that it was a pointed piece of a half-inch steel rod. If anybody had come to the Turkish bath meaning to murder my father and hide the weapon, they wouldn't have used one so big and difficult to hide, when a hat-pin would have done just as well and could be hidden more easily. But what puzzled me most was the tea-leaf in the wound. All the other tea-leaves that came out of the flask were lying on the floor. Inspector Brackett told me they were. And I couldn't believe that one tea-leaf had fallen on to my father at the very place above the heart at which the point of the weapon had penetrated the skin and got driven in by it. It was too much of a coincidence for me to swallow. But I got no nearer understanding it than anyone else."

She paused to asked if she might have a glass of water, for she had been up all night and was very tired. It was brought to her.

Then she went on in the same quiet voice: "Of course, I remembered that Dad had talked of putting an end to it; but no one with a wound like that could get up and hide the weapon. So it was impossible that he had committed suicide. Then, the night before last, I dreamt that I went into a laboratory and saw a piece of steel rod, pointed, lying on the table at which my father used to work."

"Dreams!" mumured Greatorex, a trifle pettishly, as if he was not pleased with the way things were going.

"I didn't think much of the dream, of course," Ruth went on. "I had been puzzling about it so hard for so long that it was only natural to dream about it. But after breakfast I had a sudden feeling that the secret was in the laboratory if I could only find it. I did not attach any importance to the feeling; but it went on growing stronger; and after lunch I went to the laboratory and began to hunt.

"I looked through all the drawers and could find nothing. Then I went round the room looking at everything and into everything, instruments and retorts and tubes and so on. Then I went into the middle of the floor and looked slowly round the room pretty hard. Against the wall, near the door, lying ready to be taken away, was a gas cylinder, I rolled it over to see what gas had been in it and found no label on it."

She paused to look round the Court as if claiming its best attention; then she went on: "Now that was very queer, because every gas cylinder must have a label on it—so many gases are dangerous. I turned on the tap of the cylinder and nothing came out of it. It was quite empty. Then I went to the book in which all the things which come in are entered, and found that ten days before Dad died he had had a cylinder of CO_2 and seven pounds of ice. Also he had had seven pounds of ice every day till the day of his death. It was the ice and the CO_2 together that gave me the idea CO_2, carbon dioxide, has a very low freezing-point—eighty degrees centigrade—and as it comes out of the cylinder and mixes with the air it turns into very fine snow; and that snow, if you compress it, makes the hardest and toughest ice possible. It flashed on me that Dad could have collected this snow and forced into a mould and made a weapon that would not only inflict that wound but would evaporate very quickly! Indeed, in that heat you'd have to see the wound inflicted to know what had done it."

She paused again to look round the Court at about as rapt a lot of faces as any narrator could desire. Then she went on: "I knew dioxide ice would make a hard, tough dagger, and it would evaporate quickly in the hottest room of a turkish bath and leave no smell because it is scentleess. So there wouldn't be any weapon. And it explained the tea-leaf, too. Dad had made a carbon dioxide dagger perhaps a week before he used it, perhaps only a day. And he had put it into the thermos flask as soon as he had made it. The thermos keep out the heat as well as the cold, you know. But to make sure that it couldn't melt at all, he kept the flask in ice till he was ready to use the dagger. It's the only way you can explain that tea-leaf. It came out of the flask sticking to the point of the dagger and was driven into the wound!"

She paused again, and one might almost say that Court heaved a deep sigh of relief.

"But why didn't you go straight to the police with this theory?" asked the Judge.
"But that wouldn't have been any good," she protested quickly. "It was no use my knowing it myself; I had to make other people believe it; I had to find evidence. I began to hunt for it. I felt in my bones that there was some. What I wanted to was the mould in which Dad compressed the carbon dioxide snow and made the dagger. I found it!"

She uttered the words in a tone of triumph and smiled at Willoughton; then she went on: "At least, I found bits of it. In the box into which we used to throw odds and ends, scraps of material, damaged instruments, and broken test tubes, I found some pieces of vulcanite; and I saw at once that they were bits of vulcanite container. I took some wax and rolled it into a rod about the right size, and then I pieced the container together on the outside of it—at least most of it—there are some small pieces missing. It took me nearly all night. But I found the most important bit—*the pointed end*!"

She dipped her hand into her handbag and drew out a black object about nine inches long and three-quarters of an inch thick, and held it up for everyone to see.

Someone, without thinking began to clap; and there came a storm of applause that drowned the voice of the Clerk calling for order.

When the applause died down, Hazeldean, who never misses the right moment said: "I have no more questions to ask the witness my lord," and sat down.

That action sccmcd to clinch it in my eyes, and I have no doubt it clinched it in the eyes of the jury.

The judge leant forward and said to Ruth in a rather shocked voice: "Do you expect the jury to believe that a well-known man like your father died in the act of deliberately setting a trap to hang the prisoner?"

Ruth looked at him, shrugged her shoulders, and said, with a calm acceptance of the facts of human nature one would expect to find only in a much older woman: "Oh, well, Daddy was like that. And he certainly believed he had very good reasons for killing Mr. Willoughton."

There was that in her tone and manner which made it absolutely certain that Kelstern was not only like that, but that he had acted according to his nature.

Greatorex did not re-examine Ruth; he conferred with Hazeldean. Then Hazeldean rose to open the case for the defence. He said that he would not waste the time of the Court, and that, in view of fact that Miss Kelstern had solved the problem of her father's death, he would only call one witness, Professor Mozley.

The grey-headed, grey-bearded, stooping man, who had come to the Court so late, went into the witness-box. Of course his face had been familiar to me; I had seen his portrait in the newspapers a dozen times. He still carried the brown-paper parcel.

In answer to Hazeldean's questions he stated that it was possible, not even difficult, to make a weapon of carbon dioxide hard enough and tough enough and sharp enough to inflict such a wound as that which caused Kelstern's death. The method of making it was to fold a piece of chamois leather into a bag, hold that bag with the left hand, protected by a glove, over the nozzle of a cylinder containing liquid carbon dioxide, and open the valve with the right hand. Carbon dioxide evaporates so quickly that its freezing-point, eighty degrees centigarde, is soon reached; and it solidifies in the chamois-leather bag as a deposit of carbon dioxide snow into a vulcanite continer of the required thickness, and ram it down with a vulcanite plunger into a rod of the required hardness. He added that it was advisable to pack the container in ice while filling it and ramming down the snow. Then put the rod into a thermos flask and keep it till it is needed.

"And you have made such a rod?" said Hazeldean.

"Yes," said the Professor, cutting the string of the brow-paper parcel. "When Miss Kelstern hauled me out of bed at half-past seven this morning to tell me her discoveries, I perceived at once that she had found the solution of the problem of her father's death, which had puzzled me considerably. I had breakfast quickly and got to work to make such a weapon myself for the satisfaction of the Court. Here it is."

He drew a thermos flask from the brown-paper, unscrewed the top of it, and inverted it. There dropped into his gloved hand a white rod, with a faint sparkle ot it, about eight inches long. He held it out for the jury to see, and said:

"This carbon dioxide ice is the hardest and toughest ice we know of; and I have no doubt that Mr. Kelstern killed himself with a similar rod. The difference between the rod he used and this is that his rod was pointed. I had no pointed vulcanite container; but the container that Miss kelstern pieced together is pointed. Doubtless Mr. Kelstern had it specially made, probably by Messrs. Hawkins and Spender."

He dropped the rod back into the thermos flask and screwed on the top.

Hazeldean sat down. Greatorex rose.

"With regard to the point of the rod, Professor Mozley, would it remain sharp enough to pierce the skin in that heat?" he asked.

"In my opinion it would," said the Professor. "I have been considering that point, and bearing in mind the facts that Mr. Kelstern would from his avocation be very deft with his hands, and being a scientific man would know exactly what to do, he would have a rod out of the flask and point in position in very little more than a second—perhaps less. He would, I think hold it in his left hand and drive it home by striking the butt of it hard with his right. The whole thing would ot take him two seconds. Besides, if the point of the weapon had melted the tea-leaf would have fallen off it."

"Thank you," said Greatorex, and turned and conferred with the Crown solicitors.

Then he said: "We do not propose to proceed the case, my Lord."

The foreman of the jury rose quickly and said: "And the jury doesn't want to hear anything more, my Lord. We're quite satisfied the prisoner isn't guilty."

"Very good," said the Judge, and he put the question formally to the jury, who returned a verdict of "Not guilty." He discharged Willoughton.

I came out of the Court with Ruth and we waited for Willoughton.

Presently he came out of the door and stopped and shook himself. Then he saw Ruth and came to her. They did not greet one another. She just slipped her hand through his arm; and they walked out of the New Baily together.

We made a good deal of noise, cheering them.

THE FACE IN THE DARK

by L.T. Meade & Robert Eustace

First published in 1903

I am an unmarried man with sufficient means to support myself in a quiet way. I enjoy a bachelor's life, am fond of dabbling in literature, write occasionally for the Press, possess a fair knowledge of science, and produce the best photographs of any amateur that I know. I have no present intention of marrying, but I am by no means unsociable. I like the company of my fellow-men, and go a good deal into Society. My name is Laurence Hyne, and I am thirty-two years of age.

In these days of intense living no man who is not a confirmed hermit can shut himself away from strong situations, from moments of danger, or from hours when the world seems more or less to totter beneath him. I, like others, have had my due share of adventures of one sort and another, and the one I am about to tell was by no means the least curious of those that occurred to me.

On the 18th of a very hot June, I went to the reception of some friends of mine, the Sitwells, who lived in Berkeley Square. This was always a brilliant function, and I knew that I should meet many of my friends there. On this occassion there was one in particular, a young fellow of the name of Granby Manners, whom I particulary wished to shake once more by the hand. I had known him as a boy, and as his mother had been my dearest and most valued friend, I took an interest in him. He was an open-handed, unselfish, clever lad, but was also one of the most nervous boys I had ever come across. His ideas were lofty and aspiring, but his nerves hampered him, and to such an extent that, when still quite a lad, not more than seventeen, he was ordered abroad, where he had resided under the care of a tutor ever since. Mrs. Manners had been a sort of elder sister to me—she had done me many good turns in life—had assisted me more than once, not only by her advice, but practically, and on her death-bed had charged me most emphatically to look after Granby, and if at any time I could do him a kindness, not to hesitate, for her sake, to do it.

"He is ten years your junior, don't forget that, Laurence," she said. "He knows little or nothing of English life. When the estate comes to him he will be surrounded by adventures—help him if you can."

I promised faithfully, and now the time had come, for Granby's mother and father were both dead—the boy inherited the old Croftwood estates, and had come home to attend to business matters.

On the day of the Sitwell's function I received a letter from Lady Willoughby, Granby's aunt. She wrote from Scotland.

"My nephew is in London," she wrote. "Pray find him out and write to me with regard to his appearance, his prospects, his present ideas of life. He was always a strange boy, and not at all a person to own a big estate like Croftwood Hall. I am unable to travel, as you know, but my dear sister told me on her death-bed that you had promised to be good to him. Pray do what you can and let me know."

Accordingly I went to the Sitwells primed in every way to see after young Manners. Mrs. Manners had had an unhappy life—her burden was a heavy one, so heavy that it had sent her to her grave before her time. The facts were these. Her husband was one of the worst men—a drunkard, reckless, fast, extravagant. There were rumours of even darker vices—of deeds committed that ought never to have seen the light of day. Some people said that the man was half insane. Well, he was dead, and the boy was not in the least like him.

I arrived at the Sitwells in good time. The house was already full of guests and very soon I ran up against young Manners. He had a bright face, a refined, elegant appearance, and an affectionate manner.

"I am glad to see you," he said to me. "This is quite like old times. Where can we go to have a long chat?"

"You must come to my rooms for that, Granby. But here—this terrace is empty for a few moments. Come and stand under this awning and let me look at you."

We went out through an open window and stood on a beautiful terrace screened by an awning and decked with chairs.

"You do look quite a man, Granby," I said. "Why, you must be two-and-twenty. Your hands must be pretty full of business now, my boy, with that big estate, and you the sole person to look after it."

"The fact is, Hyne," he answered, "I am so harried and rushed about that I have hardly a minute to call my own. I want to come to see you, and will at any hour you like to appoint."

"Here are two chairs," I said suddenly, for as he spoke I noticed the old nervous catch in his voice, and the quick movement of the head that spoke of a highly-strung system. "Sit down, won't you Granby. You have a big story to tell me. Let's begin to hear it at once."

"Well," he answered, "there's a great deal to say. My father has left things involved, but, of course, they *may* come all right; I can't say. Sometimes I fear—sometimes I hope. Anyhow, I shall know soon. What day is this—the 18th. I shall know, I must know, before the 24th."

"What do you mean by that?" I asked in astonishment.

"I will tell you presently. I could not in this crowd."

He glanced nervously behind him.

"Come and dine with me to-morrow night," was my answer.

His face lit up with pleasure. He was about to reply in the affirmative when some people came on to the terrace. They were two girls, both handsome and total strangers to me. I saw, however, that Granby knew them. His face flushed with vivid colour, and his eyes grew dark with delight. He greeted both girls, and especially the slighter and smaller of the two, with effusion.

"This is good," he said; "I was just talking to a special friend of mine. May I introduce you?"

A moment later I was shaking the hand and looking into the face of the brightest and most capable girl probably in the whole of England. her name was Angela Dickinson. She was the daughter of a well-known barrister, who would undoubtedly be appointed to a judgeship before long. She had only lately come out—had met Manners abroad; they were great chums. Oh, yes, it was good to see him again. They smiled at each other, and young Manners and Miss Angela Dickinson went off together; the other girl, whose name was Muriel, fell to my share to entertain.

"I am so glad we have met Mr. Manners and that he looks wo well," she said. "When we saw him at Naples he often appeared very much troubled. I am glad he has met an old friend in you."

"Yes," I replied. "I have known Granby since he was a little boy. His mother was one of my best friends. Granby had a sad childhood; his father—I suppose everyone knows about him."

She nodded and looked grave.

"The man is dead," I continued. "Let his ashes rest in peace. It seems to me, Miss Dickinson, that Manners's only fault is that he is extremely sensitive."

"I know that," she replied. "Angela and he are great friends."

I followed the direction of her eyes. The pair were standing closely together at the further end of the balcony.

"There is not a doubt that they care for each other," said Miss Muriel; "but up to the present no word has been spoken—at least to my father. I wish he would speak—his silence puts Angela in a strained position."

Soon afterwards I took my leave, going home to attend to some special business which was occupying me that night. Just as I was going downstairs young Manners bounded after me.

"May I come to-night instead of to-morrow night?" he said. "It doesn't matter about dinner. I want to talk things over with you."

I told him to come in about nine o'clock, and he nodded his acceptance.

Punctually to the hour he arrived, looking handsome and gentlemanly in his evening clothes. I offered him a pipe; he sat down and we both smoked in silence for a minute or two.

"Well," I said, suddenly—for I saw that it must be my business to lead the way—"I felt rather anxious about you when we sat together in the balcony; but Miss Dickinson has relieved all my fears. You are all right, Manners—I congratuate you most heartily on your future."

He wrung my hand but did not speak.

"I suppose the engagement will soon be announced?" I said, after a pause.

"Oh, we are not engaged, at least, not exactly. I'd give the world if it could be, but I don't see my way—there are difficulties, and monstrous ones. It is about those I want to talk to you."

"Well, speak up, old chap. I am interested in you from every point of view. Tell me everything and we will take counsel together."

He drew his chair close to mine.

"When were you last at Croftwood?" was his remark.

"Not for some years now—not since your mother's death. I grant the old place is gloomy, but nevertheless I love it. In your hands it will assume a very different appearance. You can rebuild and redecorate. You can cut down sufficient timber to give the place more air, and not such a crowded-up appearance. Croftwood Hall will be, I am sure, a lovely place in your reign, Manners, and Miss Angela is the very girl to make you happy there."

"I love the place," he answered—"it has been in our family for hundreds of years. Nevertheless I dread it very much. I had a terrible fright there and have never been the same since. Did you hear of it?"

"No," I answered, puzzled at his tone.

"It happened a long time ago now, and it was on account of that I was sent abroad. My mother and father were away at the time—my mother was ordered to the sea for her health. You know, of course, that the old place is supposed to be haunted?"

"Most old places are," I answered in some heat. "But really, Manners, at this time of day to talk of haunted houses means nonsense. No old family seat is complete without its ghost. But what of that—no one really believes in the unearthly visitant."

"Some people do," he said with a shudder. "Well, let me tell you. My father and mother were both away—my mother wanted me to go to her, but my father refused. You know what a brute he was."

"Hush," I said, "he is dead."

"Dead or alive, I must speak the truth—he was a brute. I dreaded and hated him, but I worshipped my mother. I was terribly put out at being left behind. I was a big lad—fifteen at the time, but I cried myself ill. The house was horribly lonely, and there were only two servants—old Tarring, the butler, who is still there, and the cook. Half the rooms were shut up. The days were terrible and the long evenings were enough to turn one's brain. I had not even a book to read, for my father had locked up the library. I had not a friend to speak to, there was not a young person anywhere within miles. My nervousness, always a big thing, got worse. I lost my sleep—I used to wander about the old house half the night. On one special night I was so bad that I could not eat any dinner, and afterwards I had a fit of shivering and fancied I saw things whenever I looked up. I rang for Tarring at last and begged of him, for God's sake, to keep me company. You know him, of course, a bent old party with a nose like a beak. He came up and looked into my face and said solemnly:

" 'Master Granby, if this goes on you will be mad soon.'

" 'What do you mean?' I asked, looking at him with terror.

" 'You have madness in your eyes, sir, and you inherit it—don't you forget that. There's that gentleman, your great-great-uncle, whose portrait is in the picture library and be warned. A young gentleman like you ought to be happy. He should come to his meals with appetite and sleep sound o'nights. Take my advice, sir, think no more about nerves or fancies, or they will be your undoing.'

"He went away, having positively refused to stay with me another moment, declaring that my face gave him the blues and that he preferred the cook's company in the kitchen. I thought I would go to bed and drown my terrors in sleep. I covered myself well up with the bedclothes, but I could not rest. You remember the picture gallery at Croftwood, don't you, Hyne?"

"Perfectly well," I replied.

"It is on the ground floor, and occupies almost the whole west wing of the house. It communicates with the chapel at one end and with the dining-hall on the other. I lay with my eyes wide open, my heart beating like a hammer, and my thoughts full of my mad great-uncle. Suddenly I remembered that his name was also Granby Manners. I took an unhealthy desire to look at his face. It could not be combated. I got up, and candle in hand went down through the old house. At last I found myself in the picture gallery. You know these deep embrasures near the mullioned windows?"

I nodded.

"The picture was at the end close to the old chapel. Just as I got up to it, I saw someone standing behind—someone in black—with a hood on. The whole thing was over in a minute' for I fainted away. But I remember now as distinctly as though it were only just happening, that the figure spoke with outstretched hands pointed at me and said:

" *'Granby Manners, you will die in this room!'*

"My screams must have brought old Tarring. I was taken to my bedroom, the doctor was summoned, and I was in bed in danger of brain fever for many weeks. My mother got better and returned home. When I saw her I told her exactly what had happened. She was full of sympathy and tenderness and love. She took immediate steps and I was sent abroad with a tutor. We went from one sunny land to another, and I began to forget my troubles and grew strong and healthy once again. Then came the terrible news of my mother's death—I should never see my darling more. I was striken to the earth—I resolved never to return to England. But two years after my father died, and the lawyers wrote and said that I must return home at once. I found the estate terribly involved, in short, the outlook is most gloomy."

"Have you told this strange story to Miss Dickinson?" I asked.

"I have. She knows everything. She knows that we cannot be engaged until things clear up a bit. If they never do, which is more than probable, I must give her up. Yes, I must, however hard it may be. As to the story of my mad ancestor, I do not think much about it. There has not been a second case of insanity in the family—so that goes for nothing; but I cannot ask Mr. Dickinson for Angela when I have no money to support her with."

"Surely that sound ridiculous," I said. "You, as owner of Croftwood Hall, must have plenty of money."

"That is the point, Hyne," he replied. "The complications are enormous. I will come to that presently; but as we are talking of nerves and fancies, may I tell you something else? You have heard, of course, of the Croftwood Elm?"

I nodded. He was alluding to an enormous elm, of great age, which grew by itself just within sight of the house. There was a superstition in the old place that a branch from this elm always fell before the owner's death.

"I was at Croftwood last week," continued Granby. "The gardeners were clearing away the great branch which had fallen from the elm two days before my father's death."

"Well," I said, "you are not going to think anything of that. I was merely a coincidence. Gales of wind will break off the branches of old trees to the end of time. Come, Manners, I am ashamed that you should pin your faith to such rubbish. But tell me, when are you going to Croftwood again?"

"To-morrow."

"What! To-morrow! May I come with you?"

"Would you come?"

His face lighted up with intense pleasure.

"That would be splendid," he said. "I can't tell you how I hate these visits. A great deal hangs on what takes place in the next few days. Poltimore will be there. He is the horrible man to whom the estate is mortgaged."

"Croftwood Hall mortgaged?" I cried.

"Yes, and up to the hilt. I shall be awfully glad to tell you. Of course, what I say is in confidence. I don't want the whole world to know that I am a pauper."

"You cannot be that," I answered; "but anyhow, you can trust me."

"I will tell you everything to-morrow," was his answer.

He rose as he spoke, and soon afterwards took his leave.

According to my appointment, I met the lad at Waterloo the following day. We reached Croftwood soon after six o'clock. It was a lovely day, bright and not too warm, and as we drove through the park the old trees in their summer greenery restored many memories to my mind.

"Here we are," cried Granby, as the dog-cart put us down at the porch, where the old butler was waiting to receive us.

A more decrepit, bent old man I had never seen. His hooked nose, his distorted, claw-like hands, gave him the appearance more of a bird of ill-omen than anything else. As he glanced with a fixed and by no means amiable expression from Granby to myself, I observed that his eyes were keen, bright, and sharp as a needle. Whatever else had happened to old Tarring, his intellect was still well to the fore. Tarring knew me, although he pretended to regard me as a total stranger, and evidently views me with small favour.

"Are there no letters?" asked Manners.

"The post won't be in just yet, sir."

"Well, Tarring, Mr. Hyne has come to stay with me. See that you get a room ready for him. Now, Hyne, let us have a stroll before dinner. Doesn't the place look lovely just now? By the way, you never have met Mr. Poltimore. He was a great friend of my father's. I will tell you how my affairs stand before we see him."

We strolled off through one of the gardens.

"The situation is far worse than you have any idea of," he began. "I will endeavour to explain. No one knows exactly what my father's life was, but there is no doubt that on a certain night he got into a most terrible affair in London. Nobody knows what he did, but it was necessary for him to have twenty thousand pounds in cash that night. It was that or suicide. He obtained the sum, how I don't know, from Mr. Poltimore, who is a rich jewel merchant in the city.

"In exchange for the money my father gave the man a document, all duly attested and witnessed—a sort of mortgage on Croftwood. It is to this effect. That Mr. Poltimore holds the place as security for his money, and the mortgager has to pay 10 per cent. on the loan. There are arrears of interest now amounting to ten thousand pounds. This sum has to be paid on Midsummer day, or, according to the mortgage, Mr. Poltimore seizes the property, which is worth not less than a hundred thousand pounds. But there is another and more terrible clause. It is this: even if the interest is paid regularly, I shall only have the place for my life, after that it passes altogether into Poltimore's hands, or into the hands of his heirs. If the arrears of interest can be paid by Midsummer day all will be well as far as I am concerned, but no child of mine can ever inherit the place. You must see for yourself that under such conditions I can't ask Angela to be my wife."

"I am not surprised," I answered. "But have you no reasonable hope that your lawyers will raise the money?"

"They say they will do their best. But it is by no means easy."

"Suppose they fail—have you no other means of getting the money?"

"No," he answered. "I once purchased some shares in a gold mine, and I think they will, in time, bring me in a lot of money, but of course it is all a speculation, and I don't suppose anyone would lend on the chance."

"I see," I replied. "And of course it is very much to Mr. Poltimore's advantage that you should not pay the interest on Midsummer day, for he would then have a place worth one hundred thousand pounds for twenty thousand."

"Quite so," was his reply.

Our stroll had led us by this time to the old elm tree.

"Ah," cried Manners, "look for yourself. Here is the place where the branch fell before my father's death."

We struck off across the grass towards the gnarled old tree.

"I thought they had cleared it away before now, but it is still there. How odd."

We were standing exactly under the tree, and a big branch, looking very fresh and green, lay beneath it at our feet. Granby's face turned white.

"Another branch," he cried. "What does this mean?"

"Nothing, except a fresh gale," was my answer.

"You don't understand," he replied impatiently. "A branch of the old elm always falls before the death of the owner. I am the present owner. What does this allude to?"

"Come away, and don't be nonsensical," were the words which crowded to my lips, but before I could utter them a bass voice, loud and ringing, sounded through the trees.

"Hullo!" it called.

I glanced up with relief at the interpretation, and saw a tall, heavily-built man in corduroys approaching us rapidly.

"Hullo, Granby," he cried. "Just come down, eh? How seedy you look—white as a turnip. What's the matter?"

"Nothing, thanks. Let me introduce you to my friend, Mr. Laurence Hyne, Mr. Poltimore.

Poltimore raised his hat. I thought I had never seen a more disagreeable face. He eyed me with small favour and turned again to the boy.

"Is your friend coming to stay?" he asked somewhat pointedly.

"Certainly. As my guest," said Granby, in a low tone.

Poltimore uttered a mocking laugh.

"Your guest, forsooth," he said. "By the way, have you had that letter?"

"No, but it may come by this evening's post."

"You will be out of suspense at least, after you have heard," said Poltimore.

He glanced round with a frown at me, and we turned towards the house. As we entered it, Tarring approached and handed Manners a letter in a blue envelope.

"Ah, here it is," he cried.

He turned aside to open it, his fingers shaking. Poltimore watched him with intense excitement.

"Well," he said impatiently, "what is the news?"

"Good news for you, Mr Poltimore," said Granby then. "There need be no secret," he continued, and he glanced from me to the other man. "The loan cannot be raised, therefore in four days this house is yours."

Poltimore raised his hand and brought it down again with great force on his thigh.

"It's an ill wind that blows nobody good." he said. "Upon my soul, I am sorry for you, lad, but I can't pretend that I'm not pleased on my own account at the turn events are taking. No offence to you, Mr. Hyne, but when the property comes into my hands I choose my own guests. You understand, sir. Now I'm off to the village. Don't wait dinner for me."

He went away with a great stride, banging the heavy oak door after him.

Manners turned to me. "Isn't he a brute?" he said. 'But for my sake you will try to endure him, Hyne."

"My dear lad, Poltimore is nothing to me, nothing whatever, except as far as you are concerned. But show me that letter. I don't believe that the worse can have happened."

"But it has," he answered, and he handed me the letter, the contents of which had so elated Mr. Poltimore.

I read it; it ran as follows:—

"DEAR SIR,—We regret to inform you that we cannot raise the money. The shares in the mine you hold are of no value as security. The estate will therefore pass to Mr. Poltimore on Midsummer day."

"But surely," I cried, "it would be possible to find twenty thousand pounds in order to let you keep the property. To tell you the truth, Manners, I don't believe in that extraordinary document your father signed. At least, I should like to have a good look at it. The estate is entailed."

"Yes; but he broke the entail."

"How so? How is that possible? He could not do it without your permission, and you were not of age."

"He sent me a paper to sign on my twenty-first birthday. I never even guessed what it was, and signed practically without reading, but now I am certain it was that, and I signed away my birthright."

I could not help feeling a sense of dismay, Manners had no more notion of business than an infant.

I thought hard during the remainder of that evening, and at last it suddenly occurred to me to consult no less a man than Mr. Dickinson, the father of Miss Angela. I determined to tell Granby of my resolution.

"You shan't want a friend at this juncture," I said. "If I had the money I would lend it to you with a heart and a half, and think myself well off, too," I added, "for Croftwood Hall is admirable security for any loan. But I have nothing like that amount at my command, so there is no good wasting time over that thought. The place, however, is worth saving, even if you had nothing to do with it. We don't want an old family place to get into the hands of a scoundrel of Poltimore's sort. Now I propose to go to London to-morrow, for there is, as you are aware, not a moment to lose, and when there I shall consult Dickinson."

"What?" cried Granby. "Angela's father?"

"The same."

He looked uncomfortable, started up, and began to pace the room. "You—would not surely tell him—about——?"

"You must leave that to me, my boy. Whatever happens, I must have an open hand. You cannot be worse off than you are now, and it would be impossible for Dickinson to despise you for loving his daughter."

The poor fellow covered his face with his hands and groaned.

"I am off in the morning to do what I can," I said. "In the meantime, stay here and await events."

I was sorry afterwards that I had not insisted on taking him with me: but how could I foretell the horrible future.

I reached home soon after eleven o'clock, and telephoned immediately to Dickinson to know if he could see me. I had a reply in the affirmative, and went to his chambers soon after noon.

"Come out and have lunch with me," he said heartily, "and then you can tell me what it is all about. Young Manners and the Croftwood estate! But surely that is a fine property?"

"It is if we can rescue it," I replied, "and it is for that purpose I want to consult you."

We lunched in his favourite coffee house off the Strand, and I told Dickinson as much as I thought necessary of the story. He was a middle-aged man, with a staid, reserved face. It was difficult to understand how he could be the sparkling and vivacious Angelan's father. He sat quietly after my communication had come to an end, then he said abruptly:

"Have you told me everything?"

I looked at him and resolved to trust him.

"There is one thing I have left out," I said. "It is this. Young Manners loves your youngest daughter as faithfully and truly as a man can love a woman. He would make her a good husband, and Croftwood is not to be despised."

"That is true," answered Dickinson. "I don't know what can be done, but I will consult my solicitor. If anyone can help you, Wantage is the man. Stay, I will give you a letter to take to him at once. You can explain matters more quickly than I could, and there isn't a moment to lose."

"The worst happens on Midsummer day, and this is the 20th. We have only four days."

He gave a low, significant whistle, then dashed off a few words to Wantage and put the letter into my hands.

Wantage was busy in his office in Lincoln's Inn. He was a little red-headed, freckled, elderly man, with a keen face, an observant eye, and manner which expressed nothing. He was very busy, as numerous clerks testified, but Dickinson's letter was *Open Sesame*, and I was allowed to see him almost immediately.

"A curious case," he said, after we had talked for over an hour. "Will you kindly leave me now, Mr. Hyne, and come back about this time to-morrow. I can give you my answer then—yes or no."

There was nothing for it but to comply. I spent the evening at my club, slept as best I could during the night that followed, and punctually to the moment was back with Wantage in the afternoon of the twenty-first. I was taken at once into his presence. He shut the door and locked it.

"I have not been idle since I saw you," he said to me. "I have been making enquiries with regard to those gold reefs. I have also heard several things by no means to Poltimore's credit. I do not believe that at the worst he can uphold his claim. It is my very firm impression that the law wants him, and sooner than he has any idea of. At any rate, one thing must be done—the cheque must be paid. I will let you have the amount. I heard, on the whole, favourable accounts with regard to those gold reefs. Croftwood is worth saving, the young man is worth rescuing. Now, if you will help me, the thing can be done."

"No fear of my not helping you," I answered cheefully. "I would almost cut off my right hand to help that boy."

"Thanks, Mr. Hyne," he said, gazing at me critically and almost with a quizzical expression. "You are a good friend."

"His mother was a good friend to me."

"Ah, I repsect you, Mr. Hyne. Well, this is your part in the matter. The cheque must be paid to you, and you must pay it to Poltimore. The lad himself must have nothing to do with it. You must accept Poltimore's letter of release. This is a matter for a lawyer, however, and if you are going down to Croftwood to-morrow I shall have pleasure in accompanying you. Poltimore may play tricks with Manners, and possibly also with you; but I do not think he will dare to try them on with me. Will you be ready to accompany me to Croftwood Hall to-morrow?"

"Certainly," I said.

We talked a little longer; matters were finally arranged, and I left in high spirits.

On my way home it occurred to me that I would wire to Granby.

I accordingly sent the following very cheerful message:

"All right. Money will be raised. Coming down with solicitor to-morrow. Cheer up—LAURENCE HYNE."

The rest of the day passed as usual. It was not until nine o'clock, just after I had returned from dining at my club, that all of a sudden it flashed upon me what a deadly and dangerous thing I had done in sending that wire to Granby. I sprang from my chair. Manners would, of course, tell Poltimore, and the man would be beside himself with rage and disappointment. Beyond doubt, Poltimore was in a most serious position; his own affairs were so critical that if he did not get relief soon, such as the Croftwood estate would furnish him with, he would go under, how deeply and how far I could not guess; but he would be submerged—ruined. As far as he was concerned, everything depended on whether young Manners was able to pay him by Midsummer day, or—great heavens! there was another alternative. Should Granby Manners *die* before Midsummer day, Poltimore would be equally safe—indeed, more safe than if the arrears of interest were paid. Then, beyond doubt, the estate would be his. He would be a rich man. Should Granby die, Poltimore would have attained the utmost height of his ambition. The position was too fearful to contemplate quietly. I, who had hoped to liberate the boy from all his troubles, had, by sending that telegram, in all possibility sealed his death warrant. Then there was that scoundrelly butler, a coward without a scrap of conscience. He had always hated the boy. I saw hatred in his eys when he greeted us both at Croftwood Hall. Yes, beyond doubt, Manners was in the gravest danger.

It was impossible for me to rest. Late as it was, I found myself ten minutes afterwards in a hansom cab. I had determined to catch the ten o'clock train for Waterloo. Not an instant's delay must keep me from the place. I would wire to Wantage in the morning. He could come down and the necessary business could be transacted. But I, in the meantime, would be on the spot to prevent mischeif.

I am not given to nervous fancies, but I must confess that during that railway journey to Croftwood station I had about as bad a time as a man often lives through. There was the lonely deserted house, steeped in all its superstitions; there was the supposed ghost; there was the villain who would stop at nothing; there was his tool, the old butler; and there was the boy himself, nervous, highly strung, innocent.

The train seemed to crawl—it stopped at every station. By the time I reached Croftwood station it was nearly one o'clock. There was no fly to be had—there was nothing for it but to finish my journey on foot. I knew my way well, and struck off along the country lanes at a brisk pace. The night was fine with a high wind. Scuds of broken cloud raced across the moon, giving alternate moments of bright light followed by darkness.

At last I turned up the avenue and finally reached the house. There was no light in any of the windows. I determined not to ring the bell, but to make my way round to the left under some close-growing shrubberies. I thought it extremely probable that I could enter by the old chapel, a place no longer used either for prayer or praise. No one would think of the chapel, or be concerned as to whether the heavy oak door was locked or not. I had observed that it was unlocked when with Granby two days ago. Now it yielded to my pressure. I went straight through the chapel. This led me into the picture gallery, at the further end of which was a secret door by which I could eventually reach Granby's room.

As I walked quickly down the long picture gallery, the greater part of which was in intense darkness, the windows having been all barred and bolted, I suddenly paused and listened. Something had broken the silence. What could it be? It sounded like low guttural breathing. My heart beat fast as I advanced, then it almost stopped, for hanging unsupported, and brought into relief by a long ray of moonlight which fell through a badly-fitting shutter, was a face within a few feet of my own. Oh God!—the face was *upside down*, while breath passed quickly between the anguished lips. It was the face of Granby.

This scene lasted for only a minute; before I could speak everything was changed—a bright light flooded the apartment, and Poltimore, a candle in his hand, approached from the dining hall end. Granby was hanging by his feet. I rushed at the villain—a desperate encounter took place.

"What is this, you scoundrel?" I shouted.

He swung me off with strength of a man nearly double my size, pushed the old butler towards me and dashed away. The latter I seized.

"Help me at once, Tarring," I cried, "or I'll wring your neck. Save Mr. Granby—what are you about, man? Be quick."

His face was ghastly, but he spoke no word. We worked quietly. A step-ladder stood behind us and a few moments later Manners lay upon the floor, still breathing, but unconscious.

"Go and fetch brandy," I cried.

The man disappeared and soon returned with a decanter and a glass. I poured a little down the boy's throat, and he opened his eyes.

A few hours later Granby was able to tell his own story.

"I got your telegram, and was nearly mad with joy," he said. "Poltimore found me holding it in my hand. He rushed at me, seized the sheet, and read the news. I shall never forget his face. It was just as though I were in Hades, and saw the face of a lost spirit. But before I had time to realise anything he had caught me in his powerful grip. He said something to Tarring, who was not far off and they carried me away with them to the picture gallery. I think I fainted, for when I came to myself I was tied by the ankles to that beam. What I lived through during the next awful hours I can never by any possibility explain."

The doctor when he arrived made it clear that death must have ensued in a very short time. This would have been caused by the enormous congestion of the brain. The cunningness of the mode of murder was made apparent when the doctor further said that after the boy died and the body was lowered down, there would not be the slightest trace apparent to anyone of what had happened.

Both Poltimore and Tarring were arrested, and are now undergoing a term of penal servitude.

As to Granby, his friends clustered round him, and the estate was put on a firm basis. he is about to marry Angela Dickinson in a short time. The shares in the gold reef have also turned out trumps, and the owner of Croftwood Hall will once more be a very rich man.

In the bright, calm, handsome fellow, who shows not a trace of fear or nervousness, who is happy of the happy, and gay of the gay, few would recognise the boy whom I was the means of rescuing from the most terrible death.

THE WRONG HOUSE

by E.W. Hornung

First published in 1899

My brother Ralph, who now lived with me on the edge of Ham Common, had come home from Australia with a curious affection of the eyes, due to long exposure to the glare out there, and necessitating the use of clouded spectacles in the open air. He had not the rich complexion of the typical colonist, being indeed peculiarly pale, but it appeared that he had been confined to his berth for the greater part of the voyage, while his prematurely grey hair was sufficient proof that the rigours of bush life had at last undermined an originally tough constitution. Our landlady, who spoilt my brother from the first, was much concerned on his behalf, and wished to call in the local doctor; but Ralph said dreadful things about the profession, and quite frightened the good woman by arbitrarily forbidding her ever to let a doctor inside her door. I had to apologise to her for the painful prejudices and violent language of "these colonists," but the old soul was easily mollified. She had fallen in love with my brother at first sight, and she never could do too much for him. It was owing to our landlady that I took to calling him Ralph, for the first time in our lives, on her beginning to speak of and to him as "Mr. Raffles."

"This won't do," said he to me. "It's a name that sticks."

"It must be my fault! She must have heard it from me," said I self-reproachfully.

"You must tell her it's the short for Ralph."

"But it's longer."

"It's the short," said he; "and you've got to tell her so." Henceforth I heard as much of "Mr. Ralph," his likes and his dislikes, what he would fancy and what he would not, and ah, what a dear gentleman he was, that I often remembered to say, "Ralph, old chap," myself.

It was an ideal cottage, as I said when I found it, and in it our delicate man became rapidly robust. Not that the air was also ideal, for, when it was not raining, we had the same faithful mist from November to March. But it was something to Ralph to get any air at all, other than night air, and the bicycle did the rest. We taught ourselves, and may I never forget our earlier rides, through and through Richmond Park when the afternoons were shortest, upon the incomparable Ripley Road when we gave a day to it. Raffles rode a Beeston Humber, a Royal Sunbeam was good enough for me, but he insisted on our both having Dunlop tyres.

"They seem the most popular brand. I had my eye on the road all the way from Ripley to Cobham, and there were more Dunlop marks than any other kind. Bless you, yes, they all leave their special tracks, and we don't want ours to be extra special; the Dunlop's like a rattlesnake, and the Palmer leaves telegraph-wires, but surely the serpent is more in our line."

That was the winter when there were so many burglaries in the Thames Valley from Richmond upward. It was said that the thieves used bicycles in every case, but what is not said? They were sometimes on foot to my knowledge, and we took a great interest in the series, or rather sequence of successful crimes. Raffles would often get his devoted old lady to read him the latest local accounts, while I was busy with my writing (much I wrote) in my own rooms.

We even rode out by night overselves, to see if we could not get on the tracks of the thieves, and never did we fail to find hot coffee on the hob for our return. We had indeed fallen upon our feet. Also, the misty nights might have been made for the thieves. But their success was not so consistent, and never so enormous, as people said, especially the sufferers, who lost more valuables than they had ever been known to possess. Failure was often the caitiffs' portion, and disaster once; owing, ironically enough, to that very mist which should have served them. But I am going to tell the story with some particularly, and perhaps some gusto, you will see why, who read.

The right house stood on high ground near the river, with quite a drive (in at one gate and out at the other) seeping past the steps. Between the two gates was a half-moon of shrubs, to the left of the steps a conservatory, and to their right the walk leading to the tradesmen's entrance and the back premises; here also was the pantry window, of which more anon. The right house was the residence of an opulent stockbroker who wore a heavy watch-chain and seemed fair game. There would have been two objections to it had I been the stockbroker. The house was one of a row, though a goodly row, and an army-crammer had established himself next door. There is a type of such institutions in the suburbs; the youths go about in knickerbockers, smoking pipes, except on Saturday nights, when they lead each other home from the last train. It was none of our business to spy upon these boys, but their manners and customs fell within the field of observation. And we did not choose the night upon which the whole row was likely to be kept awake.

The night that we did choose was as misty as even the Thames Valley is capable of making them. Raffles smeared vaseline over the plated parts of his Beeston Humber before starting, and our dear landlady cosseted us both, and prayed we might see nothing of the nasty burglars, not denying us the reward would be very handy to them that got it, to say nothing of the honour and glory. We had promised her a liberal perquisite in the event of our success, but she must not give other cyclists our idea by mentioning it to a soul. It was about midnight when we cycled through Kingston to Surbition, having trundled our machines across Ham Fields, mournful in the mists as those by Acheron, and so over Teddington Bridge.

I often wonder why the pantry window is the vulnerable point of nine houses out of ten. This house of ours was almost the tenth, for the window in question had bars or sorts, but not the right sort. The only bars that Raffles allowed to beat him were the kind that are let into the stone outside; those fixed within are merely screwed to the woodwork, and you can unscrew as many as necessary if you take the trouble and have the time. Barred windows are usually devoid of other fasteners worthy the name; this one was no exception to that foolish rule, and a push with a penknife did it business. I am giving householders some valuable hints, and perhaps deserving a good mark from the critics. These, in any case, are the points that I would see to, were I a rich stockbroker in a river-side suburb. In giving good advice, however, I should not have omitted to say that we had left our machines in the semi-circular shurbbery in front, or that Raffles had most ingeniously fitted our lamps with dark slides, which enabled us to leave them burning.

It proved sufficient to unscrew the bars at the bottom only, and then to wrench them to either side. Neither of us had grown stout with advancing years, and in a few minutes we had both wormed through into the sink, and hence to the floor. It was not an absolutely noiseless process, but once in the pantry we were mice, and no longer blind mice. There was a gas-bracket, but we did not meddle with that. Raffles went armed these nights with a better light than gas; if it were not immoral, I might recommend a dark-lantern which was more or less his patent. It was that handy invention, the electric torch, fitted by Raffles with a dark hood to fulfil the functions of a slide. I had held it through the bars while he undid the screws, and now he held it to the keyhole, in which a key was turned upon the other side.

There was a pause for consideration, and in the pause we put on our masks. It was never known that these Thames Valley robberies were all committed by miscreants decked in the livery of crime, but that was because until this night we had never even shown our masks. It was a point upon which Raffles had insisted on all feasible occasions since his furtive return to the world. To-night it twice nearly lost us everything—but you shall hear.

There is a forceps for turning keys from the wrong side of the door, but the implement is not so easy of manipulation as it might be Raffles for one preferred a sharp knife and the corner of the panel. You go through the panel because that is thinnest, of course in the corner nearest the key, and you use a knife when you can, because it makes least noise. But it does take minutes, and even I can remember shifting the electric torch from one hand to the other, before the aperture was large enough to receive the hand and wrist of Raffles.

He had at such times a motto of which I might have made earlier use, but the fact is that I have only once before described a downright burglary in which I assisted, and that without knowing it at the time. The most solemn student of these annals, cannot affirm that he has cut through many doors in our company, since (what was to me) the maiden effort to which I allude. I, however, have cracked only too many a crib in conjunction with A. J. Raffles, and at the crucial moment he would whisper "Victory or Wormwood Srubbs, Bunny!" or instead of Wormwood Scrubbs it might be Portland Bill. This time it was neither one nor the other, for with that very word "victory" upon his lips, they whitened and parted with the first taste of defeat.

"My hand's held?" gasped Raffles, and the white of his eyes showed all round the iris, a rarer thing than you may think.

At the same moment I heard the shuffling feet and the low excited young voices on the other side of the door, and a faint light shone round Raffles's wrist.

"Well-done, Beefy!"

"Hang on to him!"

"Good old Beefy!"

"Beefy's got him!"

"So have I—so have I!"

And Raffles caught my arm with his one free hand. "They've got me tight," he whispered. "I'm done."

"Blaze through the door," I urged, and might have done it had I been armed. But I never was. It was Raffles who monopolised that risk.

"I can't—it's the boys—the wrong house!" he whispered. "Curse the fog—it's done me. But you get out, Bunny, while you can; never mind me; it's my turn, old chap."

His one hand tightened in affectionate farewell. I put the electric torch in it before I went, trembling in every inch, but without a word.

Get out! His turn! Yes, I would get out, but only to come in again, for it was my turn—mine-not his. Would Raffles leave me held by a hand through a hole in a door? What he would have done in my place was the thing for me to do now. I began by diving head first through the pantry window and coming to earth upon all fours. But even as I stood up, and brushed the gravel from the palms of my hands and the knees of my knickerbockers, I had no notion what to do next. And yet I was half-way to the front door before I remembered the vile crape mask upon my face, and tore it off as the door flew open, and my feet were on the steps.

"He's into the next garden," I cried to a bevy of pyjamas with bare feet the young faces at either end of them.

"Who? Who?" said they, giving way before me.

"Some fellow who came through one of your windows head first."

"The other Johnny, the other Johnny," the cherubs chorused.

"Biking past—saw the light—why, what have you there?"

Of course it was Raffles's hand that they had, but now I was in the hall among them. A red-faced barrel of a boy did all the holding, one hand round the wrist, the other palm to palm, and his knees braced up against the panel. Another was rendering ostentatious but ineffectual aid, and three or four others danced about in their pyjamas. After all, they were not more than four to one. I had raised my voice, so that Raffles might hear me and take heart, and now I raised it again. Yet to this day I cannot account for my inspiration, that proved nothing less.

"Don't talk so loud," they were crying below their breath; "don't wake 'em upstairs, this is our show."

"Then I see you've got one of them," said I as desired. "Well, if you want the other you can have him too. I believe he's hurt himself."

"After him, after him!" they exclaimed as one.

"But I think he got over the wall——"

"Come on, you chaps, come on!"

And there was a soft stampede to the hall door.

"Don't all desert me, I say!" gasped the red-faced hero who held Raffles prisoner.

"We must have them both, Beefy!"

"That's all very well——"

"Look here," I interposed, "I'll stay by you. I've a friend outside, I'll get him too."

"Thanks awfully," said the valiant Beefy. The hall was empty now. My heart beat high.

"How did you hear them?" I inquired, my eye running over him.

"We were down having drinks—game o' nap—in there."

Beefy jerked his great head towards an open door, and the tail of my eye caught the glint of glasses in the firelight, but the rest of it was otherwise engaged.

"Let me relieve you," I said, trembling.

"No, I'm all right."

"Then I must insist."

And before he could answer, I had him round the neck with such a will that not a gurgle passed my fingers, for they were almost buried in his hot smooth flesh. Oh, I am not proud of it; the act was a vile as act could be; but I was not going to see Raffles taken, my one desire was to be the saving of him, and I tremble even now to think to what lengths I might have gone for its fulfilment. As it was I squeezed and tugged until one strong hand gave way after the other and came feeling round for me, but feebly because they had held on so long. And what do you suppose was happening at the same moment? The pinched white hand of Raffles, reddening with the returning blood, and with a clot of blood upon the wrist, was craning upward and turning the key in the lock without a moment's loss.

"Steady on, Bunny!"

And I saw that Beefy's ears were blue; but Raffles was feeling in his pockets as he spoke. "Now let him breathe," said he, clapping his handkerchief over the poor youth's mouth. An empty phial was in his other hand, and the first few stertorous breaths that the poor boy took were the end of him for the time being.

Oh, but it was villainous, my part especially, for he must have been far gone to go the rest of the way so readily. I began by saying I was not proud of this deed, but its dastardly character has come home to me more than ever with the penance of writing it out. I see in myself, at least my then self, things that I never saw quite so clearly before. Yet let me be quite sure that I would not do the same again. I had not the smallest desire to throttle this innocent lad (nor did I), but only to extricate Raffles from the most hopeless position he was ever in; and after all it was better than a blow from behind. On the whole, I will not alter a word, nor whine about the thing any more.

We lifted the plucky fellow into Raffles's place in the pantry, locked the door on him, and put the key through the panel. Now was the moment for thinking of ourselves, and again that infernal mask which Raffles swore by, came near the undoing of us both. We had reached the steps when we were hailed by a voice, not from without but from within, and I had just time to tear the accursed thing from Raffles's face before he turned.

A stout man with a blonde moustache was on the stairs, in his pyjamas like the boys.

"What are you doing here?" said he.

"There has been an attempt upon your house." said I, still spokesman for the night, and still on the wings of inspiration.

"Your sons——"

"My pupils."

"Indeed. Well, they heard it, drove off the thieves, and have given chase."

"And where do you come in?" enquired the stout man, descending.

"We were bicycling past, and I actually saw one fellow come head first through your pantry window. I think he got over the wall."

Here a breathless boy returned.

"Can't see anything of him," he gasped.

"It's true, then," remarked the crammer.

"Look at that door," said I.

But unfortunately the breathless boy looked also, and now he was being joined by other equally short of wind.

"Where's Beefy?" he screamed. "What on earth's happened to Beefy?"

"My good boys," exclaimed the crammer, "will one of you be kind enough to tell me what you've been doing, and what these gentlemen have been doing for you? Come in all, before you get your death. I see lights in the class-room, and more than lights. Can these be signs of a carouse?"

"A very innocent one, sir," said a well-set-up youth with more moustache than I have yet.

"Well, Olphert, boys will be boys. Suppose you tell me what happened, before we come to recriminations."

The bad old proverb was my first warning. I caught two of the youths exchanging glances under raised eye-brows. Yet their stout easy-going mentor had given me such a reassuring glance of sidelong humour, as between man of the world and man of the world, that it was difficult to suspect him of suspicion. I was nevertheless itching to be gone.

Young Olphert told his story with engaging candour. It was true that they had come down for an hour's nap and cigarettes; well, and there was no denying that was whisky in the glasses. The boys were now all back in their class-room, I think entirely for the sake of warmth; but Raffles and I were in knickerbockers and Norfolk jackets, and very naturally remained without, while the army-crammer (who wore bedroom slippers) stood on the threshold, with an eye each way. The more I saw of the man the better I liked and more I feared him. His chief annoyance thus far was, that they had not called him when they heard the noise, that they had dreamt of leaving him out of the fun. But he seemed more hurt than angry about that.

"Well, sir," concluded Olphert, "we left old Beefy Smith hanging on to his hand, and this gentleman with him, so perhaps he can tell us what happened next?"

"I wish I could," I cried, with all their eyes upon me, for I had had time to think. "Some of you must have heard me say I'd fetch my friend in form the road?"

"Yes, I did," piped an innocent from within.

"Well, and when I came back with him things were exactly as you see them now. Evidently the man's strength was too much for the boy's; but whether he ran upstairs or outside, I know no more than you do."

"It wasn't like that boy to run either way," said the crammer, cocking a clear blue eye on me.

"But if he gave chase!"

31

"It wasn't like him even to let go."

"I don't believe Beefy ever would," put in Olphert. "That's why we gave him the billet."

"He may have followed him through the pantry window," I suggested wildly.

"But the door's shut," put in a boy.

"I'll have a look at it," said the crammer.

And the key no longer in the lock, and the insensible youth within! The key would be missed, the door kicked in; nay, with the man's eye still upon me, I thought I could smell chloroform, I thought I could hear a moan, and prepared for either any moment. And how he did stare! I have detested blue eyes ever since, and blonde moustaches, and the whole stout easy-going type that is not such a fool as it looks. I had brazened it out with the boys, but the first grown man was too many for me, and the blood ran out of my heart as though there was no Raffles at my back. Indeed, I had forgotten him. I had so longed to put this thing through by myself! Even in my extremity it was almost a disappointment to me, when his dear cool voice fell like a delicious draught upon my ears. But its effect upon the others is more interesting to recall. Until now the crammer had the centre of the stage, but at this point Raffles usurped a place which was always his at will. People would wait for what he had to say, as these people waited now for the simplest and most natural thing in the world.

"One moment!" he had begun.

"Well?" said the crammer, relieving me of his eyes at last.

"I don't want to lose any of the fun——"

"Nor must you," said the crammer, with emphasis.

"But we've left our bikes outside, and mine's a Beeston Humber," continued Raffles. "If you don't mind, we'll bring 'em in before these fellows get away on them."

And out he went without a look to see the effect of his words, I after him with a determined imitation of his self-control. But I would have given something to turn round. I believe that for one moment the shrewd instructor was taken in, but as I reached the steps I heard him asking his pupils whether any of them had seen any bicycles outside.

That moment, however, made the difference. We were in the shrubbery, Raffles with his electric torch drawn and blazing, when we heard them kickng at the pantry-door, and in the drive with our bicycles before man and boys poured pell-mell down the steps.

We rushed our machines to the nearer gate, for both were shut, and we got through the and swung it home behind us in the nick of time. Even I could mount before they could reopen the gate which Raffles held against them for half an instant with unnecessary gallantry. But he would see me in front of him, and so it fell to me to lead the way.

Now, I have said that it was a very misty night (hence the whole thing) and also that these houses were on a hill. But they were not nearly on the top of the hill, and I did what I firmly believe that almost everybody would have done in my place. Raffles, indeed, said he would have done it himself, but that was his generosity, and he was the one man who would not. What I did was to turn in the opposite direction to the other gate, where we might so easily have been cut off, and to pedal for my life—up-hill!

"My God!" I shouted when I found it out.

"Can you turn in your own length?" asked Raffles, following loyally.

"Not certain."

"The stick to it. You couldn't help it. But it's the devil of a hill!"

"And here they come!"

"Let them," said Raffles, and brandished his electric torch, our only light as yet.

A hill seems endless in the dark, for you cannot see the end, and with the patter of bare feet gaining on us, I thought this one could have no end at all. Of course the boys could charge up it quicker than we could pedal, but I even heard the voice of their stout instructor growing louder through the mist.

"Oh, to think I've let you in for this!" I groaned, my head over the handle-bars, every ounce of my weight first on one foot and then on the other. I glanced at Raffles, and in the white light of his torch he was doing it all with his ankles, excactly as though he had been riding in a Gymkhana.

"It's the most sporting chase I was ever in," said he.

"All my fault!"

"My dear Bunny, I wouldn't have missed it for the world!"

Nor would he forge ahead of me, though he could have done so in a moment, he who from his boyhood, had done everything of the kind so much better than anybody else. No, he must ride a wheel's length behind me, and now we could not only hear the boys running, but breathing also. And then of a sudden I saw Raffles on my right striking with his torch; a face flew out of the darkness to meet the thick glass bulb with the glowing wire enclosed; it was the face of the boy Olphert, with his enviable moustache, but it vanished with the crash of glass, and the naked wire thickened to the eye like a tuning-fork struck red-hot.

I saw no more of that. One of them had crept up on my side also; as I looked, hearing him pant, he was grabbing at my left handle, and I nearly sent Raffles into the hedge by the sharp turn I took to the right. His wheel's length saved him. But my boy could run, was overhauling me again, seemed certain of me this time, when all at once the Sunbeam ran easily; every ounce of my weight with either foot once more, and I was over the crest of the hill, the grey road reeling out from under me as I felt for my brake. I looked back at Raffles. He had put up his feet. I screwed my head round still farther, and there were the boys in their pyjamas, their hands upon their knees, like so many wicket-keepers, and a big man shaking his fist. There was a lamp-post on the hill-top, and that was the last I saw.

We sailed down to the river, then on through Thames Ditton as far as Esher station, when we turned sharp to the right, and from the dark stretch by Imber Court came to light in Molesey, and were soon pedalling like gentlemen of leisure through Bushey Park, our lights turned up, and broken torch put out and away. The big gates had long been shut, but you can manoeuvre a bicycle through the others. We had no further adventures on the way home, and our coffee was still warm upon the hob.

"But I think it's an occasion for Sullivans" said Raffles, who now kept them for such. "By all my gods, Bunny, it's been the most sporting night we ever had in our lives! And do you know which was the most sporting part of it?"

"That up-hill ride!"

"I wasn't thinking of it."

"Turning your torch into a truncheon?"

"My dear Bunny! A gallant lad—I hated hitting him."

"I know," I said. "The way you got us out of the house!"

"No, Bunny," said Raffles, blowing rings. "It came before that, you sinner, and you know it!"

"You don't mean anything I did?" said I, self-consciously, for I began to see that this was what he did mean. And now at last it will also be seen why this story has been told with undue and inexcusable gusto; there is none other like it for me to tell; it is my one ewe-lamb in all these annals. But Raffles had a ruder name for it.

"It was the Apotheosis of the Bunny," said he, but in a tone I never shall forget.

"I hardly know what I was doing or saying," I said. "The whole thing was a fluke."

"Then," said Raffles, "It was the kind of fluke I always trusted you to make when runs were wanted."

And he held out his dear old hand.

THE CYPRIAN BEES

by Anthony Wynne

First published in 1924

Inspector Biles, of Scotland Yard, placed a small wooden box on the table in front of Dr. Hailey.

"There," he remarked in cheerful tones, "is a mystery which even you, my dear doctor, will scarcely be able to solve."

Dr. Hailey bent his great head, and examined the box with a lid, also of wood, was attached at one point by a nail. The lid rotated on this nail. He put out his hand to open it, but Biles checked that intention immediately.

"Take care!" he exclaimed; "there are three live bees in that box." He added, "There were four of them originally, but one stung a colleague of mine, who was incautious enought to pull the lid open without first finding out what it covered."

He leaned back in his chair, and drew a long whiff of the excellent cigar with which Dr. Hailey had supplied him. He remained silent, while a heavy vehicle went lumbering down Harley Street. Then he said:

"Last night, one of my men found the box lying in the gutter in Piccadilly Circus, just opposite the Criterion Theatre. He thought it looked peculiar, and brought it down to the Yard. We have a beekeeper of some distinction on the strength, and he declares that these insects are all workers, and that only a lunatic would carry them about in this fashion. Queens, it appears, are often transported in boxes."

Dr. Hailey raised his eyeglass and set it in his eye.

"So I have heard." He opened his snuff-box and took a large pinch. "You know, of course, my dear Biles," he added, "what this particular box contained before the bees were put into it?"

"No—I don't."

"Serum—either anti-diphtheria serum or one of the other varieties. Practically every manufacturer of this products uses this type of receptacle for them."

"H'm!" Biles leaned forward in his chair. "So that means that, in all probability, the owner of the bees is a doctor. How very interesting!"

Dr. Hailey shook his head.

"It doesn't follow," he remarked. "The box was perhaps left in a patient's house after its contents had been used. The patient may have employed it for its present purpose."

Biles nodded. He appeared to hesitate a moment; then he said:

"The reason why I troubled you was that, last night, a woman was found dead at the wheel of a motor car—a closed coupé—in Leicester Square. She had been stung by a bee just before death."

He spoke in quiet tones, but his voice nevertheless revealed the fact that the disclosure he was making had assumed great importance in his mind. He added:

"The body was examined by a doctor almost immediately. He observed the sting, which was in her forehead. The dead bee was recovered later, from the floor of the car."

As he spoke he took another box from his pocket and opened it. He held it out to the doctor.

"You will notice that there are rather unusual markings on the bee's body—these yellow rings. Our experts says that they indicate a special breed, the Cyprian, and that these insects are notoriously very ill-natured. The preculiar thing is that the bees in the wooden box are also Cyprian bees."

Dr. Hailey picked up a large magnifying glass which lay on the table beside him, and focussed it on the body of the insect. His knowledge of bees was not extensive, but he recognised that this was not the ordinary brown English Type. He set the glass down again, and leaned back in his chair.

"It is certainly very extraordinary," He declared. "Have your any theory?"

Biles shook his head. "None, beyond the supposition that the shock caused by the sting was probably the occasion for the woman's sudden collapse. She was seen to pull quickly to the side of the road, and stop the car, so she must have had a presentiment of what was coming. I suppose heart-failure might be induced by a sting?"

"It is just possible." Dr. Hailey took more snuff. "Once, long ago," he said, "I had personal experience of a rather similar case— that of a beekepper who was stung some years after he had given up his own apiary. He died in about five minutes. But that was a clear case of anaphylaxis.

"I don't understand."

Dr. Hailey thought a moment. "Anaphylaxis," he explained, "is the name given to one of the most amazing phenomena in the whole of medical science. If a human being receives an injection of serum or blood, or any extract or fluid from the animal body, a tremendous sensitiveness is apt to develope, afterwards, towards that particular substance. For example, an injection of the white of a duck's egg will, after the lapse of a week or so, render a man so intensely sensitive to this particular egg-white that, if a further injection is given, instant death may result.

"Even if a duck's egg is eaten, there may be violent sickness and collapse, though hen's eggs will cause no ill effect. Queerly enought, however, if the injection is repeated within, say, a day of its first administration no trouble occurs. For the sensitiveness to develop, it is essential that time should elapse between the first injection and the second one. Once the sensitiveness has developed it remains active for years. The beekeeper, whose death I happened to witness, had been stung before: but he had not been stung for a very long time.

"Good God!" Biles's face wore an expression of new interest. "So it is possible that this may actually be a case of—*murder*!"

He pronounced the word in tones of awe. Dr. Hailey saw that already his instincts as a man-hunter were quickening.

"It is just possible. But do not forget, my dear Biles, that the murderer using this method would require to give his victim a preliminary dose—by inoculation—of bee-poison, because a single sting would scarcely be enough to produce the necessary degree of sensitiveness. That is to say, he would require to exercise an amount of force which would inevitably defeat his purpose—*unless he happened to be a doctor.*"

"Ah! the wooden serum-box!" The detective's voice thrilled.

"Possibly. A doctor undoubtedly could inject bee-posion, supposing he possessed it, instead of ordinary serum, or of an ordinary vaccine. It would hurt a good deal—but patients expect inoculation to hurt them."

Biles rose. "There is no test, is there," he asked, "by which it would be possible to detect the presence of this sensitiveness you speak of in a dead body?"

"None."

"So we can only proceed by means of circumstantial evidence." He drew a sharp breath. "The woman has been identified as the widow of an artist named Bardwell. She had a flat—a luxurious one—in Park Mansions, and seems to have been well off. But we have not been able to find any of her relations so far." He glanced at his watch. "I am going there now. I suppose I couldn't persuade you to accompany me?"

Dr. Hailey's rather listless eyes brightened. For answer he rose, towering above the detective in the act.

"My dear Biles, you know that you can always persuade me."

The flat in Park Mansions was rather more, and yet rather less, than luxurious. It bespoke prodigality, but it bespoke also restlessness of mind—as thought its owner had felt insecure in her enjoyment of its comforts. The rooms were too full, and their contents were saved from vulgarity only be sheer carelessness of their bestowal. This woman seemed to have bought anything, and to have cared for nothing. Thus, in her dining-room, an exquisite Queen Anne sideboard was set cheek by jowl with a most horrible Victorian armchair made of imitation walnut. In the drawing-room there were flower-glasses of the noblest period of Venetian craftmanship, in which beauty was held captive in wonderful strands of gold, and beside these, shocking and obscene examples of "golden glass" ware from some a mental picture of the dead woman. He saw her, changeable, greedy, gaudy, yet with a certain instinctive charm—the kind of woman who, if she is young and beautiful, gobbles a man up. Women of that sort, his experience had shown him, were apt to drive their livers to despair with their extravagances or their infidelities. Had the owner of the bees embarked on his terrible course in order to secure himself against the mortification of being supplanted by some more attractive rival? Or was he merely removing from his path a woman of whom he had grown tired? In any case, if the murder theory was correct, he must have stood in the relationship to the dead girl of doctor to patient, and he must have possesed an apiary of his own.

A young detective, whom Biles introduced as Tadcaster, had already made a careful examination of that flat. He had found nothing, not even a photograph. Nor had the owners of neighbouring flats been able to supply an useful information. Mrs. Bardwell, it appeared, had had men friends who had usually come to see her after dark. They had not, apparently, been in the habit of writing to her, or, if they had, she had destroyed all their letters. During the last few weeks, she seemed to have been without a servant.

"So you have found nothing?" Biles's tones were full of disappointment.

"Nothing, sir—unless, indeed, this is of any importance."

Tadcaster held out a crumpled piece of paper. It was a shop receipt, bearing the name of *The Times* Book Club, for a copy of *The Love-Songs of Robert Browning*. There was no name on it.

Biles handed it to Dr. Hailey, who regarded it for a few moments in silence, and then asked:

"Where did you find this?"

The doctor's eyes narrowed.

"It does not strike me," he said, "that such a collection of poems would be likely to interest the owner of this flat."

He folded the slip, and put it carefully into his pocket-book. He added:

"On the other hand, Browning's love-songs do appeal very strongly to some women." He fixed his eyeglass and regarded the young detective. "You have not found the book itself, have you?"

"No, sir. There are a few novels in the bedroom, but no poetry of any kind."

Dr. Hailey nodded. He asked to be shown the collection, and made a detailed examination of it. The novels were all of the lurid, sex type. It was as he had anticipated. He opened each of the books, and glanced at the fly-leaves. They were all blank. He turned to Biles.

"I am ready to bet that Mrs. Bardwell did not pay that bill at the Book Club," he declared. "And I am ready to bet also that this book was not bought for her."

The detective shrugged his shoulders.

"Probably not," he said unconcernedly.

"Then, why should the receipt for it be lying in the room?"

"My dear doctor, how should I know? I suppose, because the man who possessed it chose to throw it away here."

The doctor shook his head.

"Men do not buy collections of love-songs for themselves, nor, for that matter, do women. They buy them—almost invariably—to give to people they are interested in. Everybody, I think, recognises that."

He broke off. A look of impatience came into Biles's face.

"Well?"

"Therefore, a man does not, as a rule, reveal to one woman the fact that he has made such a purchase on behalf of another. I mean, it is difficult to believe that any man on intimate terms with Mrs. Bardwell would have invited her jealousy by leaving such plain evidence of his interest in another woman lying about in her rooms. I assume, you see, that no man would give that poor lady this particular book."

Biles shrugged his shoulders. The point seemed to him immaterial. He glanced round the bedroom with troubled eyes.

"I wish," he declared, "that we had something to go on—something definite, leading towards some individual."

His words were addressed impartially to his subordinate and to Dr. Hailey. The former looked blank, but the doctor's expression was almost eager. He raised his eyeglass, and put in into his eye.

"My dear Bile," he said, "we have something definite to go on. I was about to suggest to you when you interrupted me that the receipt for the book probably fell from the pocket of the purchaser throught a hole in that pocket. Just as the little box containing the additional bees, which he had not found it necessary to release, was destined to fall later, when the man, having assured himself that an insect of unimpaired vigour was loose and on that wing, descended in Piccadilly Circus from Mrs. Bardwell's car."

He paused. The detective had turned to him, interested once more. The thought crossed Dr. Hailey's mind that it was a pity Biles had not been gifted by Providence with an appreciation of human nature as keen as his grasp of material circumstances. He allowed his eyeglass to drop, in a manner which proclaimed that he had shot his bolt. He asked:

"You have not, perhaps, taken occasion to watch a man receiving a shop receipt for goods he had just bought and paid for? Believe me, a spectacle full of instruction in human nature. The receipt is handed, as a rule, by a girl, and the man, as a rule, pushes it into his nearest pocket, because he does not desire to be so rude or so untidy as to drop it on the floor. Shyness, politeness, and tidiness, my dear Biles, are all prominent elements in our racial character."

Again he broke off, this time to take a pinch of snuff. The two detective watched that process with some impatience.

"A man with a hole in his coat-pocket—a hole not very large, yet large enough to allow a piece of crumpled paper to work its way out as the wearer of the coat strode up and down the floor of the room—is not that a clue? A doctor, perhaps, with, deep in his soul, the desire for such women as Mrs. Bardwell—cheap, yet attractive women——"

"I thought you expressed the opinion that he bought the love-songs for some other woman!" Biles snapped.

"Exactly. Some other woman sufficiently like Mrs Bardwell to attract him, though evidently possessed of a veneer of education to which Mrs. Bardwell could lay no claim." Dr. Hailey's large, kindly face grew thoughtful. "Has it to struck you," he asked, "That, though a man may not be faithful to any one woman, he is almost always faithful to a type? Again and again I have seen in first and second wives the same qualities of mind and appearance, both good and bad. Indeed, I would go so far as to say that our first loves and our last are kindred spirits, recognised and chosen by needs and desires which do not change, or change but little, throughout the course of life."

"Even so, my dear Hailey,"

Biles's look of perplexity had deepened. The doctor, however, was to eager to be discouraged.

"If Mrs. Bardwell was, in fact, murdered," he continued, "the figure of her murderer is not, I think, very difficult to visualise: a doctor in early middle life—because the dead woman is at least thirty—with a practice in the country, but the tastes of a townsman; a trifle careless of his clothes, since he tolerates holes in his pockets, a sentimental egoist, since he buys Browning's love-songs while plans of murder are turning over in his mind——" He broke off, and thought a moment. "It is probable that Mrs. Bardwell was an expensive luxury. Such women, too, fight like tigers for the possession of the men they rely on. Yet, though she had undoubtedly obtained a great, perhaps a terrible, hold on him, she had failed to make him marry her."

He turned to Biles, and readjusted his eyeglass.

"Why do you suppose," he asked, "Mrs. Bardwell failed to make this doctor marry her?"

"I have no idea." The detective's tones were crisp, almost to the point of abruptness.

Dr. Hailey moved across the room to a writing-table which stood near the window. He took a sheet of paper, and marked a small circle. He returned to the detectives, who stood watching him.

"Here is London," he said, pointing to the small circle, "and here is the country round it up to a distance of forty miles—that is to say, up to a two-hour journey by motor-car. As our doctor seems to make frequent visits to town, that is not, I think, too narrow a radius. Beyond about forty miles, London is no longer within easy reach."

He struck his pencil at two places through the circumference of the larger circle, marking off a segment.

"Here," he went on, "are the Surrey highlands, the area, within our district, where heather grows, and where, in consequence, almost everyone keeps bees."

He raised his head, and faced the two men, whose interest he seemed to have recaptured.

"It should not," he suggested, "be impossible to discover whether or not, within this area, there is a doctor in practice who keeps Cyprian bees, is constantly running up to London, wears an overcoat with a hole in one of the pockets, and lives apart from his wife."

"Good heavens!" Biles drew his breath sharply. His instincts as a man-hunter had reasserted themselves. He glanced at the doctor with an enthusiasm which lacked nothing of generosity. The younger detective, however, retained his somewhat critical expression.

"Why should the doctor be living apart from his wife?" he asked.

"Because, had she not left him as soon as he tired of her, he would probably have killed her long ago; and, in that case, he would almost certainly have married Mrs. Bardwell during the first flush of his devotion to her. I know these sensualists, who are also puffed up with literary vanity. Marriage possesses for them an almost incredible attractiveness."

He glanced at his watch as he spoke. The recollection of a professional appointment had come suddenly to his memory.

"If you are to follow up the clue, my dear Biles," he remarked, as he left the flat, "I hope you will let me know the result. *The Medical Directory* should serve as a useful starting-point."

Dr. Hailey was kept fully occupied during the next day, and was unable, in consequence, to pursue the mystery of the Cyprian bees any further. In the late afternoon, however, he rang up Inspector Biles at Scotland Yard. A voice, the tones of which were sufficiently dispirited, informed him that the whole of the home counties did not contain a doctor answering the description with which he had furnished the police.

"Mrs. Bardwell," Biles added, "kept a maid, who has been on holiday. She returned last night, and has now told us that her mistress received very few men at her flat, and that a doctor was not among the number. Of course, it is possible that a doctor may have called during the last fortnight, in the girl's absence. But, in the circumstances, I'm afraid we must look on the murder theory as rather far-fetched. After all, the dead woman possessed a car, and may have been in the country herself on the morning on which she was stung. Bees often get trapped in cars."

Dr. Hailey hung up the receiver, and took a pinch of snuff. He sat down in his big armchair, and closed his eyes that he might pass, in fresh review, the various scraps of evidence he had collected. If the dead woman had not received the doctor at her house, then the idea that they were on intimate terms could scarcely be maintained. In that case, the whole of his deductions must be invalidated. He got up and walked down Harley Street to *The Times* Book Club. He showed the receipt which he had retained, and asked if he might see the assistant who had conducted the sale. This girl remembered the incident clearly. It had occured about a week earlier. The man who had bought the volume of poems was accompanied by a young woman.

"Did you happen to notice," Dr. Hailey asked, "What his companion looked like?"

"I think she was very much 'made up'. She had fair hair; but I can't say that I noticed her carefully."

"And the Man?"

The girl shrugged her shoulders. "I'm afraid I don't remember him clearly. A business man, perhaps." She thought a moment. "He was a good deal older than she was, I should say."

Dr. Hailey left the shop, and walked back towards Harley Street. On one point, at least, he had not been mistaken. The purchaser of the *Love-songs* was a man, and he had bought them for a woman who was not Mrs. Bardwell. Biles had mentioned that this lady had auburn hair. Why should the man have visited Mrs. Bardwell so soon after making this purchase? He sighed. After all, why not? Biles was quite right in thinking that no jury in the world would listen to evidence the only basis of which was character-reading at second hand. He reached his door, and was about to let himself into the house when a cab drew up beside him. The young detective, Tadcaster, to whom Biles had introduced him at Park Mansions, got out.

"Can I see you a moment, doctor?" he asked.

They entered the house together, Tadcaster produced a letter from his pocket, and handed it to Dr. Hailey. It was a prescription written on Mrs. Bardwell's notepaper, and signed only with initials, which were nearly indecipherable.

"I found it after you had gone," the youngman explained. "It was dispensed, as you can see, by a local chemist. To-day I have seen him, and he says he has had other similar prescriptions to dispense. But he has no idea who the writer is. Mrs. Bardwell had the medicine a few days ago.

Dr. Hailey read the prescription, which was a simple iron tonic. The signature was illegible. He shook his head.

"This does not carry us much further, I'm afraid," he declared.

"You can't tell from the initials who the doctor is."

"No."

"In that case, I think we shall have to throw our hands in." Tadcaster's voice expressed considerable disappointment. It was obvious that he had hoped to make reputation out of the solution of the mystery. "Your reasoning yesterday," he added, "impressed me very much, sir, if I may say so."

Dr. Hailey inclined his head, but his eyes were vacant. So a doctor had called on the dead woman recently—and also, apparently, made earlier visits—a doctor, too, whose prescription were unfamiliar to the local chemist. He turned to the young detective.

"I have just heard from Biles," he said, "that the maid has come back. Do you happen to know if she has any recollection of these professional visits?"

"I asked her that myself. She says that she knows nothing about them."

Again the far-away look came to the doctor's eyes. The fact that the prescriptions were written on Mrs. Bardwell's notepaper showed that they had been given during an attendance at the flat. For what reason had the dead woman been at pains to hide her doctor's visits from her maid?

"Should I be troubling you very much," he said, "if I asked you to take me back to Park Mansions? I confess that I would like to ask that girl a few questions. A doctor can obtain information which is not likely to be imparted to any layman."

As they drove through the crowded streets, Dr. Hailey asked himself again the question which had caused him to embark on this fresh investigation. What reason had Mrs. Bardwell for hiding her need of medical attendance from her maid? Even supposing that her doctor was also her lover there seemed to be no sense in such a concealment. He opened his eyes and saw the stream of London's home-going population surging around the cab. Sweet-faced girls and splendid youths, mingled with women whose eyes told their story of disappointment, and men who wore pressing responsbility as an habitual expression. No wonder the police despaired of finding any one nameless human being in this vast tide of humanity, of hopes and fears, of desires and purposes!

The cab stopped. They entered the lift and came to the door of the flat. Tadcaster rang the bell. A moment later the door was opened by a young girl, who invited them to enter in tones which scarcely disguised the anxiety she apparently felt at the return of the police. She closed the door, and then led the way along the dim entrance corridor. She opened the door of the drawing-room.

As the light from the windows fell on her face, Dr. Hailey repressed an exclamation of amazement. He started, as though a new idea had sprung to his mind. A slight flush mounted to his cheeks. He raised his eyeglass and inserted it quickly in his eye.

"I have troubled you," he said to the girl, "because there are a few points about Mrs. Bardwell's health, before her fatal seizure, which I think you can help us to understand. I may say that I am a doctor, assisting the police."

"Oh, yes!"

The girl's voice was low. Her pretty, heavily powdered face seemed to drawn with anxiety, and her eyes moved restlessly from one man to the other. She raised her hand in a gesture of uneasiness, and clasped her brow, seeming to press her golden curls into the white flesh.

"Perhaps it might be better if I spoke to you alone?"

Dr. Hailey's tones were very gentle. He looked at Tadcaster as he spoke, and the detective immediately got up and left the room. Then he turned to the girl.

"Your mistress," he asked, "discharged you from her employment a fortnight ago?"

The girl started violently, and all the blood seemed to ebb from her cheeks. Wild fear stared at him from her big, lustrous eyes.

"No!"

"My dear girl, if I may say so, you have everything to gain, nothing to lose, by telling the truth."

He spoke coldly, yet there was a reassuring note in his voice. He saw fear give place a little to that quality of weakness which he had expected to find in her character—the quality which had attracted Mrs. Bardwell's lover, and which explained, in some subtle fashion, the gift of the *Love-Songs*. He repeated his question. The girl hung her head. She consented. He let his eyeglass fall.

"Because of your intimacy with a man she had been accustomed to look on as her own particular friend."

"Oh, no, no! It is not true!"

Again her eyes challenged him; she had thrown back her head, revealing the full roundness of her throat. The light gleamed among her curls. No wonder that this beauty had been able to dispossess her mistress!

"Listen to me." Dr. Hailey's face had grown stern. "You have denied that any doctor came to this flat—at least, so far as you know. As it happens, however, a number of prescriptions were dispensed for Mr. Bardwell by the local chemist; so that either she took great pains to hide from you the fact that she was calling in a doctor, or—You have not been speaking the truth."

"She did not tell me."

He raised his hand. "It will be easy," he said, "to get an answer to that question. If your mistress was really hiding her doctor's visits from you, she must have taken her prescriptions herself, personally, to the chemist. I shall find out from him later on whether or not that is so."

Again the girl's mood changed. She began to whimper, pressing a tiny lace handkerchief to her eyes in coquettish fashion.

Dr. Hailey drew a deep breath. He waited a moment before framing his next remark. Then he said:

"You realise, I suppose, that if a girl helps a man to commit a crime, she is as guilty as he is, in the eyes of the law."

"What do you mean?"

All her defences now were abandoned. She stood before him, abject in her terror, with staring eyes and trembling lips.

"That your presence her to-day proves you have had a share in this business. Why did you return to the flat?"

"Because—because——"

"*Because he—the man you are shielding—wanted to find out what the police were doing in the place?*"

"Oh, God, I am so frightened," she whispered.

"You have reason—to be frightened."

He led her to a chair, but suddenly she seemed to get her strength anew. Her grasp on his arm tightened.

"I didn't want him to do it," she cried, in tones of anguish. "I swear that. It was honest and above board, only he had her on his hands, and she had wasted so much of his money."

For the first time her voice rang true. She added:

"His wife cost a lot too, though she was not living with him. She died a month ago."

They stood facing one another. In the silence of the room, the ticking of an ornate little clock on the mantelshelf was distinctly audible.

Dr. Hailey leaned forward.

"His name?" he asked.

"No, I shall not tell you."

She had recaptured her feeble courage. it gleamed from her eyes, for an instant transforming even her weakness. The vague knowledge that she loved this man in her paltry, immoral way, came to him. He was about to repeat his demand, when the door of the room opened. Tadcaster came in with a small, leather-bound volume in his hand.

The girl uttered a shrill cry and sprang towards him; but Dr. Hailey anticipated that move. He held her firmly.

"It is the collection of Browning's *Love-Songs*," the detective said. "I found it lying open in the next room. There is an inscription signed 'Michael Cornwall.' "

He held the book out for the doctor's inspection, but Dr. Hailey's face had grown as pale, almost, as that of the girl by his side.

He repeated the name—"Michael Cornwall"—almost like a man in a dream.

The place was hidden among its trees. Dr. Hailey walked up the avenue with slow steps. The thought of the mission which had brought him to this lovely Hampstead house lay—as it had lain through all the hours of the night—like death on his spirits. Michael Cornwall, the well-known Wimpole Street bacteriologist, and he had been boys together at Uppingham. They were still acquaintances.

He came to the front door, and was about to ring the bell when the man he was looking for appeared round the side of the house, accompanied by an old man and a girl.

"Hailey—well I'm dashed!"

Dr. Cornwall advanced with outstretched hand. His deep, rather sinister eyes welcomed his colleague with an enthusiasm which was entirely unaffected. He introduced: "My uncle, Colonel Cornwall, and my cousin, Miss Patsy Cornwall, whom you must congratulate on having just become engaged," in his quick, staccato manner.

"We're just going round the garden," he explained, "and you must accompany us. And, after that, to luncheon. Whereupon my dear Hailey, if you have—as I feel you have—great business to discuss with me, we shall discuss it."

His bantering tones accorded well with his appearance, which had changed but little in the years. He was the same astute, moody, inordinately vain fellow who had earned himself, once a upon a time, the nickname of "The Lynx."

They strolled across the lawn, and came to a brick wall of that rich russet hue which only time and seasons can provide. Dr. Cornwall opened a door in the wall, and stood back for his companions to enter.

A sight of entrancing beauty greeted them, lines of fruit-trees in full blossom, as though the snows of some Alpine sunset had been spread, in all their glowing tints, on his English garden. Dr. Hailey, however, had no eyes for this loveliness. His gaze was fixed on a row of white-painted beehives which gleamed in the sunlight under the distant wall. Patsy Cornwall exclaimed in sheer wonder. Then a new cry of delight escaped her, as she detected, in a large greenhouse which flanked the wall, a magnificent display of scarlet tulips. She took Dr. Hailey, in whose eyes the melancholy expression seemed to have deepened, to inspect these, while her father and cousin strolled on up the garden path. She stood with him in the narrow gangway of the greenhouse, and feasted ecstatic eyes on the wonderful blossoms.

"Don't they make you wish to gather them all and take them away somewhere where there are no flowers?"

She turned to him, but he had sprung away from her side.

A cry, shrill and terrible, pierced the lazy silence of the morning. She saw her father and cousin fleeing back, pursued by an immense swarm of winged insects, toward the garden gate.

Blindly, frantically, they sought to ward off the dreadful onslaught. The old man stumbled, and would have fallen, had not his nephew caught him in his arms. She had a momentary glimpse of his face; it was as though she had looked on the face of Death.

"*The bees!*"

The words broke from Dr. Hailey's lips as a moan of despair. He had come to the closed door of the greenhouse, and seemed to be about to open it; but at the same moment one of the infuriated insects in delirious flight struck the glass pane beside him. Then another—and another—and another. He came reeling back towards the girl.

"Lie down on the gangway!" he shouted, at the highest pitch of his voice. "There may be a broken pane somewhere."

She turned her horror-stricken eyes to him.

"My father—oh, God!"

"Lie down for your life!"

He stood beside her, watching ready to strike if one of the bees succeeded in entering the greenhouse. Only once did he remove his straining eyes from this task. The sight which then greeted them wrought a fresh cry of horror from his lips.

The terrible swarm hung like a dust-cloud in the air above the garden gate, rising and falling in swift undulations, which caused the light to flash and scintillate on a myriad gilded bodies and shining wings. A faint, shrill piping came to his ears across the silence. The door in the wall was open, and the garden now quite empty.

Biles leaned forward.

"Mrs. Bardwell's maid has confessed that she rang up Dr. Cornwall immediately before luncheon this morning," he said. "She tried to communicate with him before, but he had gone to the country, to a case, overnight. He got her warning that the police suspected him of being responsible for her mistress's death, just after he had carried his second, victim, his uncle, in a dying condition, from the garden."

The detective struck a match, and relit his cigar. Dr. Hailey sat watching him with sorrowful eyes.

"Ten minutes later, as you know," he went on, "Cornwall blew his brains out. He had the wit to see that the game was up. He had been badly stung, of couse, but his long experience of the bees made this a less serious matter than it would have been in the case of an ordinary outsider. In any case, moreover, he had to accept that risk if his plan was to succeed."

Silence fell in the big consulting-room. Then the doctor remarked:

"Miss Cornwall has recently become engaged to be married?"

"Yes." Biles drew a long whiff. "That was the circumstance which made speed essential to her cousin's murderous plan. He was hopelessly in debt, as a result of Mrs. Bardwell's extravagance. Only his uncle's money, which is considerable, would have saved him. If Miss Cornwall married he must have lost all hope of obtaining it, and so of marrying the girl on whom he had set his fickel heart. I have ascertained that he insisted on inoculating both father and daughter against spring catarrh a month ago, and that the injections he gave them hurt them terribly. No doubt Mrs. Bardwell received a similar injection about the same time. Thus, for each of these three individuals, a bee-sting, on your showing, meant instant death."

Dr. Hailey inclined his head.

"The moment I saw the swarm, the truth flashed across my mind," he declared. "These Cyprian bees, as I have been at pains to find out, and as your bee-keeping friend told you, are exceedingly ill-natured. But no bee's unless they have been previously roused to a frenzy, ever attack at sight people who have not even approached their hives. It was all too clear, even in that first terrible moment, that the swarm was part of a carefully prepared plan."

The detective rose, and held out his hand.

"But for you, my dear friend," he said, "Miss Cornwall must inevitably have shared her fathers fate, and the most devilish murder of which I have ever so much as heard would, almost certainly, have gone unsuspected and unpunished."

PRINCE CHARLIE'S DIRK

by Eden Phillpotts

First published in 1926

When intellect is seated on a placid brow, honesty looks out of the eyes beneath, and humour lurks at the corners of the resolute mouth below, we are conscious that a man confronts us.

Such were the lineaments of John Ringrose, Detective-Inspector of New Scotland Yard; and to his portrait may be added dark hair on a big, broad head, and a small, well-knit, sturdy body of the middle size.

Though travelling to a new case, the matter did not occupy his mind at this juncture. He smoked his pipe and read industriously the pages of a weekly journal devoted to the culture of fruit. Already John dreamed of a garden, where should grow pears and apples, peaches and plums; but the time was not yet. He stood still on the threshold of his strange career and had been but recently promoted to an inspectorship.

The train pursued a leisurely way through rural scenery. It stopped near hamlets and at halts; then a guard called "Twamblcy," and John Ringrose, foldcd his railway rug, grippcd his largc suit-casc, and alighted.

An inspector of police was standing on the platform, and beside him a tall, fair young man clad in tweed knickerbockers. He had sloping shoulders and a slight stoop. His flaxen hair curled up round the rim of his cap and he gazed with an anxious expression out of blue and intelligent, though troubled, eyes. He was handsome in a conventional fashion, but revealed a temperament easily excited and lacking in balance. One had guessed him to be an artist of some sort. Ringrose approached the couple, introduced himself, and shook the policeman's hand.

"You'll be Mr. Inspector Burrows, no doubt," he said, "and I'm John Ringrose, from the Yard."

"And welcome," answered the other officer. He was a grey-bearded, tall man with dark brown eyes and a ruddy countenance.

"I'm thinking you'll eat a meal with me," said the elder, "and I'll tell what there is to tell from my point of view. This is Mr. Vincent Maydew, the nephew of the murdered lady."

John shook the hand extended to him, to find it delicate and feminine in his grasp. He was a student of hands and declared them eloquent of character.

"My respectful sympathy," he said. "A terrible shock, as such things must always be."

Vincent Maydew nodded.

"Thank you," he answered. "I wanted to see you half a minute. You'll need to be at Greystone a good bit, and it occurred to me you might find it more convenient to stop there. The village and the inn are best part of two miles from us, and should you prefer to stop at the house itself, we can make you comfortable."

The detective, who had kept his eyes on the speaker while listening to this invitation, expressed his thanks.

"Very considerate, Mr Maydew. It may prove the best course; but on the other hand it may not. The days are short and, for some things, we might gain if I was there; for others we might lose. Probably I'll find it better to do my work from the outside."

He looked at his watch.

"Half after noon," he said. "I'll have my talk with Inspector Burrows and be at Greystone at half-past two, if you please. Then we can settle the best course of action."

"Thank you," replied the youth. He nodded, bade both men "good-day," and strode off to a motor-bicycle standing outside the station.

When he was gone Mr. Burrows spoke.

"You won't want to go into the house for a day or two, if at all. It's an outside job in my opinion, though I can't give any deep reason for saying so, since there is not an outside clue of any sort or kind. But come and eat, and I'll tell you what there is to it on the surface."

A Ford car swiftly conveyed the men to Twambley, distant a mile from the station. A typical East Devon village was Twambley-in-the-Mire, picturesque, somnolent—the centre of a district where thatch still persisted and where many cottages twinkled with whitewashed or rosy-washed faces under old, moss-grown straw. Now the walls were bare of rose and jasmine, for the time was mid-January and red mud, rather than rustic beauty, triumphed over Twambley.

Leaving his Ford at the Constabulary Station, Inspector Burrows conveyed the vistor to an inn some hundred yards higher up the street, and there , at the Green Man, over a couple of very tough mutton chops, John learned what the other could tell him.

"Miss Mary Maydew," began the inspector, "was seventy-one years old—a maiden lady in good health. A common object of the countryside you might call her, for she'd lived at Greystone as long as any can remember. One brother she had still alive; but her father, Thomas Maydew—a London lawyer—had quarrelled with his son; and when Thomas died—I daresay half a century ago—he left his money and his estate to his daughter. And she's reigned at Greystone ever since. Her brother—John Maydew—paid her a visit once or twice a year—and it is understood she kept him, giving the man an income. About family particulars Mr. Vincent Maydew will tell you, and also Mr. Fosdike, the lawyer at Exeter.

"Greystone is a big, old-fashioned country house said to date from James I. I don't know whether that's true; but it don't matter. Miss Maydew lived in the west wing, where the kitchen premises lie behind the dwelling-rooms; but a good part of the place, including the big music and dancing hall, the library and museum combined, the billiard-room and, of course, a lot of bedrooms overhead, are shut up.

"The household is very small for a place that size. There's first the dead lady's companion, a Miss Forrester. She's been there a good few years—a very pretty and popular young woman, who has proved a sort of buffer between Miss Maydew and her tenants for a long time. Then there are William and Ann Jay, the butler and his wife. There's only the cook, besides them—an elderly widow woman, the sister of one of my own men. Jane Woodhouse she's called. Outside there's two gardeners and a gardener's boy. They only keep up a bit of garden round the west wing and, of course, the kitchen garden. The second gardener is also a mechanic and tends the electric light plant. He lives at the cottage the the entrance with his wife and two children.

"The staff waits on the old lady—or did so—and on Miss Forrester. There's no lady's maid and Mrs. Jay looked after Miss Maydew of a night, if she was poorly or wanted anything. But she seldom did, being the olf-fashioned, independent sort."

"And what of Mr. Vincent Maydew?" asked the listener.

"He comes and goes. He lives in London and is said to write books and go in for high art and so on. He's been at Greystone a good deal lately, off and on, and he was there when the fatal thing happened, two nights ago. All the inside details you'll get from him, Miss Forrester, and the Jays. And if you want independent information of the family and Miss Forrester, then William Jay can give it, for he's worked for the Maydews all his life and remembers Miss Maydew's father; while if there's anything you want to know about the Jays themselves, I can help you, because they're old friends of my wife and my own."

John made no attempt to hasten Inspector Burrows. He listened with close attention to his story, and abandoning a struggle with the leathery chops, turned to a large and promsing wedge of orange-coloured Cheshire cheese.

"Not a soul in the house was disturbed on the fatal night," continued the inspector; "but when Mrs. Jay took in Miss Maydew's early cut of tea, at half-past seven, she found the lady dead. She'd been stabbed under the left breast—just one deep, wicked wound, that when to the heart and must have killed instantly, so Doctor Forbes says. The bedclothes had been dragged off her and the knife driven home. There was no struggle and not a thing out of its place. Her bedroom window was open two inches at the top, but that it always would be, winter and summer, and the blind was up as usual, because the last thing the old lady did at night, before she got into bed, was to pull up the blind.

"There was no disorder and nothing unusual anywhere, and not a trace in the room, or passage, or house next morning, to show an intruder. Nor was there a sign of a weapon.

"The doctor judged the old woman had been dead since midnight, or not much later, for she was stone cold when he got to her; but it was a cold night and she being a thin creature, and lying bare like that no doubt the heat soon left her body after the life left it.

"Outside the window there was nothing to show—not a scratch on the window-ledge or bare wall round about, and not a touch upon the flower-bed that runs along the ground beneath. I, myself, conducted that examination and can testify from long experience that none of the little marks, inevitable if there had been entry or exit from the window, were there. Neither inside nor outside did we find a shadow of a clue."

"And yet you said, when we met, that this is certainly an outside job?"

"I do say so—for the reason that it can't have been an inside one. Everybody in that house is beyond suspicion. You can take each and turn him, or her, inside out and you'll find no excuse why they should have killed the old woman. At least, no cause that's known to me, or anybody here. There may be plenty of information waiting for you at Greystone, but, on the face of it, one can see no motives in any case. Miss Maydew was very rich, and all in that house lived by her. Her companion loses her job now; and, unless Vincent Maydew keeps on the old staff, Jay and his wife and Mrs. Woodhouse will be out of very good employment."

"Vincent Maydew's the heir, then?"

"So I'm given to understand. There's only him and his uncle interested, and William Jay knows for a fact—or did, when he mentioned the family to me six weeks ago in conversation—that the young man was the heir and not John Maydew, the dead lady's brother. However, that may be all different now. You'll find out in due course."

"And the household all happy and pulling together comfortably?"

"So far as I know. I wouldn't say Jay liked Miss Forrester. What their difference was I never heard, but he gave me the impression that he was a bit jealous of her power over the old woman. And old servant might feel like that if he'd been used to first place and she'd taken the lead and been trusted and consulted more than him."

"So he might."

"Don't imagine there was any quarrel, however, because I'm in a position to say there was not. William didn't, perhaps, like Miss Forrester's power over the mistress; but he never said a word against the young woman herself. In fact, she's exceedingly popular at Twambley—a parish worker and an understanding, kindly young creature. Also a beauty—out of the common handsome."

"And you found nothing, inspector?"

"Not a solitary thing, Ringrose. Not a spot; not a shirt-button. Somebody went into that room and killed the old woman with a blow; then he left that sleeping house. Nothing was found open next morning—bolts and bars all in their places. The murderer got clean away with it and not a trace of him remained behind."

"And you honestly believe the people in the house had nothing to do with it?"

"Emphatically. It's purely a matter of motive. If it's true, as Jay thinks, that Mr. Vincent Maydew is the heir, then you may say he might be glad for his aunt to die; but no sane man can imagine he would hasten the death of one who willed him so well. Besides, look at him; listen to him. He's not that sort. And everybody else in the house and on the staff is a loser by Miss Maydew's death."

John Ringrose said little; but he perceived that the local man was speaking and arguing on what might be very insufficient knowledge. The situation had yet to be revealed, and he suspected that his course of action would lie along no conventional path and depend upon no material clues. Already, with a strange added sense for which he was famous, the young detective's intuition told him that Mr. Burrows was not within sight of the needful preliminary line of thought.

And hour later John drove out to Greystone and beheld a large, undistinguished house, a portion of which was in occupation. He proceeded on routine lines, studied the face of the murdered woman in her coffin, and beheld an austere, bleak countenance that even death had been powerless to soften.

The inquest was fixed for the following day, and Ringrose proceeded with preliminaries, leaving his first examination of the living until daylight failed. The theatre of the crime offered no complications. From the large main hall of Greystone, a flight of shallow stairs ascended to the first storey, and at the extreme west end of this corridor Miss Maydew had her private apartments. They consisted of a bedroom and boudoir leading out of it. Other bedrooms extended along the broad passageway of the first floor and faced south, while a service staircase opened not far from the corner occupied by the dead woman and descended to the kitchen premises on the ground floor. Immediately beneath Miss Maydew's bedroom was the dining-room—a comparatively small chamber used for that purpose. The deceased lady had entertained but little and the larger public apartments were all closed.

Two others had slept on the upper floor upon the night of the murder. Miss Juanita Forrester occupied a bedroom distant but three doors from her employer's chamber; while Vincent Maydew always chose the same apartment when visiting his aunt—an eastern-facing room at the other end of the main corridor. Eight empty rooms separated his apartment from Miss Forrester's. The servants slept in the rear of the house, Jay and his wife occupying one north-facing room, while the bedroom of Mrs. Woodhouse was not far distant.

The whole radius of occupation, as compared with the total bulk of the house, was absurdly restricted. Half a dozen persons only inhabited a mansion that might have furnished accommodaton for half a hundred.

Ringrose, having inspected the chamber of the crime and the adjacent boudoir, made a tour of the house and met Miss Forrester and the domestic servants. Juanita Forrester, to whom Mr. Maydew introduced him over a cup of tea, offered a challenge during the first five minutes of their meeting. She was dark and, so she told him, very much like her Spanish mother. "A poor copy," she said. Her parents were no more, and her father's death leaving the young woman penniless, she was forced to earn her own living. An advertisement had attracted her, and on visiting Miss Maydew, then in search of a new companion, she satisfied the stern old lady and obtained the post.

The girl's remarkable frankness, contrasted with Vincent Maydew's obvious distress, impressed Ringrose at this brief preliminary interview. Juanita was a pretty woman, typically Spanish. She displayed a small and perfect figure, with a pale, oval face and immense wealth of black hair pile over her white forehead and supported by a black tortoiseshell comb. Her eyes were marvellous, and John had never seen such a pair; while her full-lipped but firm mouth and perfect little nose completed a countenance of unusual beauty.

Her expression was placid, yet not devoid of pride, and her gaze direct and steadfast. She revealed no particular sorrow at the disaster and was self-contained but deeply interested.

"I never liked Miss Maydew," she said, speaking in level and unemotional tones. "She was a bitter, unkind old woman, with no milk of human kindness in her. A tyrant, and used her power unjustly. But for circumstances which Mr. Maydew will give you I should long since have left her. No companion ever stayed here as long as I. But it served my purpose to remain, for personal reasons concerning which there need be no secrecy. These you will hear."

"In your relations with the lady you can form no conlusions as to the reason for her death, nor think of anything to help me?" askded Ringrose, but she shook her head.

"I understand what you mean. I answered many of her letters, but was not in her secrets—if she had any. I don't think she had. She was direct and open in all her dealings—cruelly so sometimes. She loved power. I did what I could, in my very small way, for tenants, and often helped them with her. I'm afraid many humble people rather hated her, for she was hard and grasping; but it is impossible for me to point to anybody who hated her enough to kill her. Twambley people are all easy-going and law-abiding in my experience,"

"You can form no theory of this murder?"

"None, Mr. Ringrose. Vincent and I have tried hard to do so. So has Mr. Burrows; so has Mr. Mainprice, the bailiff; so has William, the butler. Perhaps William and his wife, Ann, knew her better than anybody."

"Apart from the possibility," continued Vincent Maydew, "there are the facts. Inspector Burrows thinks it was somebody from outside, since nobody from inside can be suspected. But how did they get in, and, still more difficult to understand, how did they get out again and leave no window or door open to show it?"

They explained the geography of the house, while Ringrose listened with interest. Juanita was sagacious and logical. No personal sorrow confused her clarity. She appeared profoundly interested but utterly unmoved, while her companion, the fair young man, made no attempt to hide his mangled emotions. It was not, however, the death of his aunt which caused his obvious anxiety and concern. He spoke of her with pity, but without regret. The secrets of his uneasiness remained to be learned. Their first interview extended only over a cup of tea, but it decided Ringrose in a main particular. He determined to come to Greystone and operate from within. His decision was not, however, imparted to Maydew until he had seen the indoor servants.

Mr Jay proved a commonplace little man, with a dull, putty-coloured face, white whiskers, a dry, old-maidish manner, a sharp, long nose, and a high forehead. People said he had framed himself upon his mistress. But while servile to his betters, he was suspected of tyranny behind the scenes. He proved voluble, and John discovered that in the kitchen, as above stairs, interest in the crime was great, though sorrow for the sufferer little. Only Mrs Jay appeared to feel the catastrophe, but in her case self-pity had loosened tears. She it was who had found her dead mistress and suffered from the shock of that horrible experience. She was a thin, grey-haired woman, nervous and irresponsible.

William, in measured phrases and with a sort of dry unction, told his tale; but when asked if his knowledge of Miss Maydew and her affairs sufficed to inspire a threory, or prompt to suggestions, he could only shake his head.

"To me it's a bigger puzzle than it might be to most," said Mr. Jay, "because of my inner knowledge. It happens that me and Inspector Burrows are old friends, and so he went into it with me pretty deep. We don't agree and, while my heart is with him, if you understand, my head is not."

"You're in a dilemma about it?"

"That's the word. This thing was done either from inside or from outside, Mr. Detective. So far so good. But there's everything to show it couldn't have been done from inside, and yet again there's everything to show it couldn't have been done from outside."

"Suppose we assume it was done from outside—with help from inside?"

"A clever thought, and it would do away with one difficulty, but not the other. If it was done with help from outside, that argues that somebody in the house would deliberately have lent a hand to murder Miss Maydew, and from that to doing the deed wouldn't be far. The will would be there. There's five people might have let a murderer in and showed him where she was, and let him out after he'd killed her without waking the rest. Strictly speaking, there's four, because husband and wife are one, and it would have been as difficult for me to leave my partner without waking her as it would have been for her to leave me, sleeping as we do in a four-post bed.

"Take 'em one by one. Mr. Vincent Maydew will tell you about the family complications, because that's no business of mine, and what I might hear, or not hear, when waiting on the family, is beside the question. But as to him, you could swear on your oath he wouldn't kill a fly, let alone his aunt, whatever she'd done to vex him. He's not even a sportsman—all for poetry and art and so on—a bit of a namby, to say it kindly. He'd think twice before he'd kill a wasp, let alone an old woman. Then there's Miss Juanita Forrester, been here four years. She's foreign on her mother's side, no doubt— Spanish—but no fellow-creature ever won the affection of a place like what she has done at Greystone and all round about. A heart of gold, you may say, and never did any man, woman, or child quarrel with the gentle creature."

"You couldn't," declared Mrs. Jay. "Wonderful human she is for such a young thing. Many a time she's showed pity for me and Jane, the cook, when Miss Maydew sent out hard, beastly, bullying messages. She's brought 'em, as in duty bound, but she's taken the edge off 'em. And everybody— Mr. Mainprice, the bailiff, included—will tell you she's everlasting on the side of kindness and gentleness. She's only stopped with such an employer for her wages and a comfortable home, I reckon."

"That's the point" added William. "That lets her out, just as it lets me and my wife and Jane out. We all suffered Miss Maydew because we had our living to earn and weren't likely to kill the goose that laid the golden eggs. So you may take it in reason that none of us would have done it, nor yet help to do it, even if we was built to be criminals. But where are we, then? Up against the fact it weren't done from inside, or with help from inside. And yet, when Burrows says it was done from outside, I'm in a position to swear that not a bolt, or bar, or window-catch was out of place. Master himself went round with me when my wife brought the fatal news."

"You regard Mr. Maydew as your master now, then?" asked the detective.

"Yes, sir; Mr Vincent is the master, so far as we yet know."

Ringrose did not press him further.

"I'm coming to stop here for the present," he said, and the butler and his wife expressed satisfaction at the fact. He then spoke with Mrs. Woodhouse, the cook, and found her chatty, civil, and indifferent. Jane was a big, amiable woman of handsome presence and well-mannered. She had no opinions on the subject, but appeared chiefly interested concerning her late mistress' fate in the world to come.

"I'm a religious creature," she explained, "and I'm fearing that a hard case like Miss Maydew, cut off so sudden, may wake up to a very sharp reminder in the next world. However, thank Heaven, there's pardon for all there. But you'd say she'll take a lot of forgiving when the Books be opened."

Ringrose announced his determination to stay at Greystone presently, and Vincent Maydew accepted it without demur. Of all beneath that roof, the present master of it seemed most downcast and perturbed. Now the day was done and John Ringrose returned to Twambley beside Inspector Burrows, who had arrived with his car.

John declared himself as at present without light and, leaving the inspector after a second cup of tea, carried his suit-case up to Greystone and found a room prepared for him.

He dined with Maydew and Miss Forrester, and after the lady had left them, the young man took Ringrose to a small study, gave him a good cigar, and prepared to tell his part of the story.

Vincent Maydew spoke clearly, yet with a measure of nervousness and even dread. His mind was fretted and his concern appeared to rise from private thoughts, rather than out of the narrative he unfolded for the detective's ear.

"The situation is simple now," he said, "thanks to an extraordinary coincidence. My uncle, John Maydew, died three days ago—a natural death. I only heard the fact by this morning's post. But I will come to what that means in a moment. The situation a week ago was this. There were then three of my family living. Now I alone remain. I enjoyed my aunt's confidence and respect, for though she did not much value my literary work, she knew me to be a serious man and a steady one. I was her heir, while her brother received from her an allowance of one thousand a year and no more. This she intended to continue for his life. They were quite friendly, and Uncle John visited his sister twice a year; but he was a bachelor and she held her allowance enough for him, because she knew that he did nothing, and she hated an idle man, even if he were old. That Uncle John was intemperate and unwise she did not know, for he was very careful to conceal the fact when he came to see her.

"So things stood, and then came the complication.

"I fell in love with Juanita—Miss Forrester—and could not see why on earth I should not win her, when I found my love returned. Juanita, however, believed—rightly as time proved—that my aunt would object to such an engagement. However, I was not prepared to wait for ever, and after a secret betrothal extending over more than a year, I told my future wife that there was no rational ground for further delay. We loved each other with absolute devotion, and, while only a companion to Miss Maydew, she was my life to me.

"A week ago I informed Aunt Mary that I proposed to wed Juanita as soon as she could find another companion to suit her. The result was appalling. I need not go over the fearful row, but I was accused of every sort of crime, and Miss Maydew absolutely declined to sanction the engagement. Juanita pleaded in vain. The old woman blamed her bitterly enough; but me she attacked with that ferocious and venomous temper common to her when the least incident threatened her convenience, or crossed her will. She told me plainly that she should disinherit me if I took Juanita from her, and at last a succession of violent scenes culminated with Juanita finally on my side.

"What man could do less? My aunt was sound as a bell and good at least for another ten years. I expressed my sorrow, but was firm. Then she sent for her lawyer, Mr. Fosdike, from Exeter, and made a new will, leaving all her property to her brother.

"On the morning which found her dead, I was leaving Greystone for good, and Juanita, at my wish, was remaining until it pleased my aunt to dismiss her. Of course, I stopped when we heard the terrible news. And now Fate has willed this extraordinary sequel. My uncle never lived to know that Miss Maydew had done. He was actually dead a few hours before she did it. There was no bequest of the residue of Miss Maydew's fortune. She had made an absolute bequest of everything to John Maydew; but that, of course, becomes inoperative, because he predeceased her. As her next-of-kin, therefore, everything passes to me."

The young man stopped and sighed.

"That's all there is to tell, I think; and whether it will help you I know not."

"It is very possible that it may," answered Ringrose. "At any rate, after the inquest and a search round to-morrow, I'll see Miss Maydew's lawyer and the new will. You never know where you may get a ray of light. At any rate, the legal position is clear. Owing to the death of John Maydew before his sister signed, the bequest to him lapses and falls into the residue. But you say there is none, so, as next-of-kin, you stand extactly where you did, and her purpose to cut you out was defeated. Thank you for this lucid summary. And now tell me what's biting you, as the Ameicans say. This shocking affair naturally saddens you, especially as relations were so badly strained at the finish; but there's more to your distress than that."

Maydew stared and flushed; then he recovered himself.

"You are mistaken. I'm all right. Nothing but natural concern and sorrow for this awful mystery troubles me. I can't let a passing estrangement come between me and the long memory of the past. She was hard and difficult, but I had little cause to hate her, and at the worst I never actually hated her. I was only deeply distressed that I had to run counter to her wishes."

Ringrose did not pursue the subject.

"So much the better; I'm glad I was wrong," he said. "I only thought you might be hiding something you held not pertinent to the case; but don't do that, Mr. Maydew. The most unexpected and apparently trivial facts often contain the kernel of the nut."

"I can undertand they might," answered the other. "Be very sure, if anything occurs to me as remotely useful, you shall be the first to know it."

"You are, of course, in complete understanding with Miss Forrester?"

"Complete and absolute," replied Vincent. "We are one, heart and soul."

"Tell me exactly when you heard of your uncle's death, and from whom."

"This morning, by the first post. The news was somewhat delayed, as Uncle John's lawyers were not informed of his death until twenty-four hours after it had happened. They had, of course, already heard of this murder through the newspapers, and for another day didn't know whom to write to. Then Uncle John's landlady told them about me, and they wrote to me at Greystone, directing the letter to be forwarded if I were not here."

He took the letter of which he spoke from a pocket-book and handed it to his visitor.

The detective scanned the note and returned it.

They chatted for another half-hour and then John Ringrose decided that he would go to bed. Their attitude was cordial on the elder's side, restrained and somewhat inconsequent on the part of his host. But Maydw presently conducted the visitor to his apartment, expressed hopes that all was as he desired it, and asked him if he would breakfast in his own room or join Juanita and himself. Ringrose preferred the latter course.

"Let me breakfast with you," he said. "And the later the better."

"Nine too early?"

"That will do exceedingly well," answered the detective, who had made private plans for the morning.

He was up and dressed at six, and as the light increased had worked industriously through the silent house for an hour and more before any domestic appeared. Neither the upper floor nor the scene of the murder occupied him; he devoted the early hours of a grey and very cold morning to examination of the dwelling-rooms. There were no bulbs in the electric sconces, but he opened shutters and conducted a general investigation, which ended at a huge apartment devoted to books and containing glass cases, wherein were stored a mixed collection of curiosities from all lands.

The great chamber lay deserted and deep in dust. A gallery lifted some feet above the top of the bookshelves, ran round the walls, and the place was lighted from a lantern of frosted glass in the roof.

Ringrose readily perceived that the bygone head of the family was responsible for a collection which had suffered neglect since his departure. He examined the receptacles with mild astonishment at the heterogeneous curios assembled within them; then something arrested him and he stopped and bent over a show-case situated immediately beneath the central dome. Not a curiosity, but a missing one, had challenged his attention. Care and patience marked the collection and everything was labelled, while to many objects were attached information concerning them. Thus an empty card immediately arrested the eye. Something had disappeared from its place, and the enquirer was concerned to know what. The lid of the glass showcase opened to his touch and he drew forth a card and read the few words neatly printed upon it. They proved exceedingly significant.

The empty place had held a dirk, "Once the authentic property of Prince Charlie."

John Ringrose restored the card to its place. He observed that the vanished weapon had been fastened to the card with a piece of pink tape, and that the tape had been cut to liberate it. A fragent only remained. The discovery ended his present investigation within doors. The dawn had broken, the sky was burning redly to the East, and he presently let himself through a French window in the disused great drawing-room, and strolled the terrace. A clue so simple and direct as the missing dirk created natural mistrust. John told himself that such things do not happen. He suspected an ingenious attempt to hoodwink him, but could not feel sure, since the possibility that he would examine the contents of the old and neglected collection with close care must have seemed doubtful to any interested in his actions. Moreover, an explanation might be immediately forthcoming, did he seek it from the household.

At breakfast he met his host and Juanita. The girl was pale and dressed in black, and the young man appeared if possible more anxious than on the preceding day. Miss Forrester, however, showed no perturbation. She was frankly interested in the inquest, timed for noon, and she asked John various questions concerning the procedure of the enquiry.

He said nothing of his morning's work within the house, and studied the man and woman carefully. His unique gift, to bring a human touch into every relation with his fellow-creatures, served the detective as usual. He found the tension relax and soon established himself in friendly relations with Juanita. She interested him least, however, for her complete self-possession, and a certain directness of speech and thought were obviously natural and not assumed. The young woman made no pretence of sorrow, and John perceived that, like himself, she was secretly a little puzzled by her sweetheart. Their common affection neither attempted to conceal. They were passionately in love, but while the course of events and the sequel to the tragedy now meant certain happiness for Juanita, she indicated in some subtle fashion that she could not fathom Vincent Maydew's profound depression.

Ringrose perceived this and it interested him. That the young man should be agitated and even oppressed by the terrible event that had lifted his problems off his shoulders was not strange, but why such sustained melancholy and obvious anxiety? There was a mystery here whose significance, John already suspected, would, if explained, help him upon his way.

Of one thing the detective was now secretly assured: the crime, if not actually committed by a member of the dead woman's household, had been assisted from within. That the assassin had come from without remained a probability, but he had not worked without help, and Ringrose felt already confident that a large measure of the truth might be known to somebody with whom he had already spoken. As yet he associated none of them more than another with the commission of the deed, but began to believe that, if anybody in reality knew anything at all, it was Vincent Maydew.

After breakfast he examined the upper floor with close scrutiny, and visited not only each of the occupied chambers, but also those for many years disused. The result of these investigations John kept to himself, and, of course, he pursued them alone. But they presented him with two interesting discoveries: the splintered edge of a broken board in the floor of Juanita Forrester's bedroom cupboard, and a piece of pink tape.

The inquest, conducted in the great drawing-room, pursued its way and threw no light, unless upon the mind of the detective, who silently attended it. The coroner, a sagacious and capable man, ruled his court with tact and sympathy. Each witness gave an explicit account from his or her own point of view. But Miss Forrester's evidence proved the most interesting. With absolute frankness she revealed the inner situation of those chiefly concerned—her lover and herself—and related the family quarrel and the attitude of the dead woman to her nephew's announcement of his engagement. She told all that Ringrose had heard on the previous evening from Vincent Maydew, and John was not dead to the deep attention with which the young man listened while his sweetheart spoke. It appeared that she had been nearer to the heart of the tragedy than anybody imagined.

"After that terrible conflict between Mr. Maydew and his aunt", said Juanita, "I could not sleep and on the night of Miss Maydew's death I was faced with another sleepless night, because Mr. Vincent was leaving that day. At two o'clock in the morning I left my room, lighted a candle, and went down into the library for something to read, that I might distract my mind and get to sleep. I found a book; and then I left the great library and went into the small one, used as a dining-room. From the sideboard I took some biscuits and poured myself out a glass of port wine from the decanter. I ate the biscuits, drank the wine, and went upstairs again with my book.

"It was then, just as I reached the corridor at the top of the great flight of stairs, that I thought I heard a sound in the passage, at the far end, near Miss Maydew's corner of the corridor. It was a sound like the quiet shutting of a door. I left my book on a console table, that stands opposite the top of the staircase, and went to Miss Maydew's door. Everything was quiet, and I then opened the swing door on the opposite side of the corridor, which gives upon the service staircase. I went to the top of the service staircase and listened, but heard nothing. I half fancied I saw the glimmer of a light below, but I was holding my own candle all the time and could not be sure the light came from another. I blew out my own candle, but the light—if light there was—had vanished. Everything was quite silent and quite dark.

"I stood for a few moments listening, then went back to bed with my book. I must have gone to sleep reading it, for when I was called, Ann—Mrs. Jay—laughed at me and said I had forgotten to turn out the electric light. She had, of course, not been to her mistress then. She always called me first."

The coroner put various questions upon this evidence, but Juanita had nothing to add to it, and its value appeared negative, since both the sound and the light were an impression rather than a conviction in her mind.

Ringrose perceived that Maydew showed signs of relief when his sweetheart's tetimony and examination concluded. The young man himself had little to say, save that on hearing the news he had risen instantly and hunted the house with William. The servants only reported what the police already knew.

Mr. Fosdike, Miss Maydew's lawyer, spoke as to the new will and, when opportunity offered, agreed to let John Ringrose see the document on the following day. The police reiterated their belief that the murder had been committed from outside, though not a trace of evidence existed to support it; but the staff stood on friendly terms with members of the Force, and the coroner pointed out that there existed nobody within Greystone who could have gained any advantage from Mary Maydew's death save, indeed, Vincent Maydew. Vincent himself admitted how on the night of the murder, he was ignorant of his uncle's end, and still imagined that he had lost all. Ringrose observed that the young man created no suspicion in the minds of the jury, or the police by this statement.

The inquest was adjourned for a fortnight and the proceedings terminated.

It was reserved for the detective's next private interview with his host to quicken interest at last and create for John a sensation far beyond any that his business had, as yet, brought him. That, however, did not come till night.

During the afternoon he again busied himself in the house, yet, for personal reasons, kept severely aloof from the chief occupants. He was now in doubt before a curious conflict of clues and spent most of his time with the Jays, accepting the house-keeper's invitation to tea and listening to the old woman's conversation. He also visited the library and museum a second time for his own purpose and, discovering a second dirk fixed to a card, which recorded its historical interest, removed the weapon, wrapped it up in his pocket handkerchief, and presently returning to the chamber on the ground floor, where the dead woman lay, again examined the body.

IIe left thc housc after dark and called upon the local practitioner—a Dr. Forbes, who had given evidence of the death wound at the inquest.

He was back at Greystone in time for dinner, at which meal Vincent Maydew appeared more silent than on the previous night. He ate little, but drank rather heavily. It was evident that Juanita felt increased anxiety on his account, and desired private speech with Ringrose. The meal ended, he prepared to give her the opportunity she sought, but then became aware that Vincent Maydew had marked her wish. It was easy for the girl's lover to frustrate any possible private interview at this moment, and he took care to do so.

Explaining that he wanted some immediate conversation with the detective, Vincent drew John away to the small sitting-room, and when coffee and liqueurs were served and Ringrose had lighted a cigar, Maydew locked the door and plunged into a hurried narrative. He was very pale; his drink had made him perspire and he mopped his face as he spoke.

"Mr. Ringrose," began the young man, "I can stand this no longer. I have something to say to you, and I have something to offer you. I'm not so much concerned for myself as another; that's why I want to couple a big proposal with what I have to tell you. Do not feel annoyed—I implore you to keep an open mind. When you recognise my situation your humanity will at least prevent you from being angry with me—or anybody. I have no right to ask for the least sacrifice of principle from you, and it lies entirely in your power to ignore my suggestion; but I know you are too generous not to understand it, and far too acute not to see that I plead for another rather than myself."

He stopped a moment, but Ringrose did not speak. Then Maydew confessed to the crime.

"I killed my aunt in a moment of stark aberration. The deed is done, and I am faced with the consequences; but all that matters now is this: that I insist upon leaving the sequel in your hands. Do you gather my meaning Mr. Ringrose?"

The detective regarded him without speech for a moment. Then he spoke.

"I think so; but you had better make it clearer."

"In a word, then, I yielded to a passing wave of irrational hate against the old woman who had treated me so damnably, and feeling assured that the world would be better without her, I destroyed her. Some devil played with me, and I committed a cowardly and infernal crime on the spur of passion, convinced that I did evil that good might come. The irony of the situation when I heard my uncle was dead you will appreciate. I worked swiftly, yet believed that I had laid my plans so perfectly that discovery must prove impossible. Now I know otherwise. I know you will presently discover the truth, and so confess to save you any more trouble."

Ringrose summoned a picture to his mind and smiled internally. It was a vision that must have appeared very inappropriate to any beholder less subtle than himself. He saw a hen partridge pretending to be wounded and fluttering clumsily along the ground, to distract an enemy from her chickens. But a moment later this theory of the situation was clouded, for the young man made swift and complete response to the obvious challenge now offered.

"You say you killed the old lady, Mr. Maydew. Can you prove it?" asked John, and his question met instant answer, for rising, Maydew proceeded to a small desk, unlocked it, and then moved an invisible spring which revealed a secret drawer. Within this receptacle lay an object wrapped in paper, and he now handed the parcel to Ringrose.

"I killed Mary Maydew with that dirk," he said quietly. "I took it from the museum—the collection made by my grandfather. It is a dagger which is supposed to have been the property of Prince Charlie. I had meant, of course, to put it back in its place. You will see the card from which I took it if you examine the large central case in the library."

Ringrose examined the weapon. The haft was of chased silver, the head, a huge golden cairngorm that shone and sparkled. The blade was of blue steel, and blood had dried upon it.

"You would soon have proved me guilty," continued the criminal quietly. "I quickly saw that my fancied security was vain. And the revelation of what such work as this means to the sinner is so terrible that, if I had to consider myself alone, I should have either confessed within twenty-four hours of the crime, or destoyed myself. But the situation is terribly complicated for me by a fellow-creature. I could escape my own sufferings by death, and my remorse would end with my life; but if my life ends, another precious and innocent life will practically end with it. Knowledge of the truth must assuredly kill Juanita. It is not that I should lose her; the point seems to be this: that her life is ruined if this becomes known, and so the innocent suffers far more terribly than it is possible for the guilty to do. Life to me, you understand, is henceforth a punishment rather than a boon, I should already have ended my existence but for the thought of her agony. For her sake only I am stripping the truth naked and putting myself in your hands."

The listener showed less concern than might have been expected before a situation so tragical.

"And what follows?" he asked.

"What follows is this, Mr. Ringrose. To me it appears an ethical question, and so I hope and pray it may appear to you. That the righteous should suffer for the guilty is a commonplace. No man can sin as I have sinned and endure the consequences alone. Many innocent persons are called to a punishment they did not deserve, and my one thought at present—my one resolve—is to save others from the consequences of my crime to the best of my power. That may be done by myself in every case save one. The servants will receive money and adequate pensions in any case. They lose nothing; but, if the truth becomes known, then a punishment that is far worse than the sentence of death falls on Juanita. Only for her I plead. Do believe that. Life, even with her, must not be incomparably more terrible for me than swift and merciful death. But for her sake I plead to live because the truth would destroy her and cover that guiltless head with shame. Her temperament is such that knowledge of this thing would bring a measure of agony impossible to describe. Her reason might well to succumb to it; or, unable to face an appalling situation, she might take her own life. She is made of precious stuff, Mr. Ringrose, and rather than that she should be called to drink this cup, I would live—for her sake alone."

The other listened intently. He studied every word and every gesture that accompanied it. He indicated that he felt much impressed.

"You ask me to respect your secret and condone your crime?" he said, when the young man ceased.

"For the human reason that I have given. For my unfortunate girl alone. I should not beg for my own sake. I have no wish to live now. You know I have spoken the truth. I am only concerned to do right, and Juanita's life is a thousand times more precious to the world than mine. Rather than that she shall be destroyed, I am prepared to live; and seeing that justice—a justice above any law of man—cries out for Juanita, I implore you to meet me. I would press the ethical side upon you, Mr. Ringrose. Your duty lies on another plane, and no doubt you do it as a rule, sternly regardless of consequences; but you are not a machine only; you are a man of genius, and I have seen enough of you to know that humanity means much to you."

"Granted; but duty often clashes with inclination," replied John, taking another cigar. "An action may have two sides and looks wrong from one aspect, right from another. For the sake of argument, suppose I fail to solve this case, I am perhaps doing a humane thing—a thing which might, or might not, be justified on strictly moral grounds; but I am none the less being false to myself and my employers. And that is not all. Failure in a case, which already began to resolve its difficulties pretty swiftly, means a great deal more than a doubtful hope that I may have done rightly by pretending to fail. It means that punishment for your crime falls on me also. I fail where I ought to succeed; I deliberately permit a black mark to be scored against me where it matters most—at Headquarters. I celebrate my promotion to a detective-inspectorship by a very inefficient piece of work. Perhaps that situation had not occurred to you?"

"It had. I recognise it. I recognised it from the first. I have imagination to see how this must look in your professional eyes, and had you been a different sort of man I should have felt the case was hopeless. But you revealed a heart and a deep human sense of sympathy. That is what I am coming to now. You concede that for the sake of the innocent, the crime might reasonably be concealed, and you know that concealment is by no means a blessing or boon to the criminal. The rights and wrongs of concealment do not eliminate each other and leave the situation doubtful. Everything points to the fact that concealment in this case is the highest justice and brings the greatest good to the innocent. That only leaves your personal position; and I venture to think that the wrong your reputation undoubtedly suffers—the actual injustice done to you by concealment may be regarded purely as a matter of business."

Ringrose nodded.

"It is a point of view," he said.

"One case in your career amounts to little," argued Maydew, with increasing hope. "Everybody knows that you are an extraordinary man, and probably your next mystery will be solved with such speed and brilliance that this affair must quickly be forgotten. So confident I am of that, and so sure that failure in this affair cannot really harm anything but your natural self-esteem, that I feel it in no sense a slight or reflection upon your honour to make it a question of money. I insist again that this is no selfish bargain. My crime will never torment me less than now; but even legal justice should be rightly concerned with the welfare of the innocent before the destruction of the guilty. I am a rich man and if, knowing that the highest, purest honour and justice are on your side, you can reduce your own loss in the matter to a financial figure, I should indeed thank Heaven."

For a full minute John Ringrose made no reply. He smoked with his eyes on the blood-stained knife lying on the table before him. Maydew rose after his appeal and wandered the room restlessly.

"Sit down and light your cigar," began the detective at length. "These are interesting and illuminating things you tell me. There is nothing like breadth of vision and, be it as it may, I respect your confidence and admit the strength of your position on strictly ethical grounds. But what is your view on my side? What sort of solatium should you judge may fairly be offered for my obvious loss of credit?"

"I leave it to you, Mr. Ringrose."

"They say every man has his price. One must weigh the advantage of permanent improvement to one's income, against depreciation of one's credit in business."

"A transitory depreciation; but don't speak of having your price, Mr. Ringrose; I couldn't buy you and I well know it. The sole question is, can Juanita's life tempt you? Her very existence is involved. I offer a perfectly reasonable deal that reflects in no way at all on your character—or, I would argue, on mine either."

Mr. Maydew rose, returned to his private desk and produced a cheque-book, while unseen the detective suffered his features to relax into a genial grin. The smile relieved him; but his face was again composed when his host returned to the lamplight.

"I have arranged with Mr. Fosdike," he said, "to have access to capital as it may be required; but I imagine a transaction of this magnitude must be carried out with considerable caution."

"I think so. There is no hurry. There are ways of doing these things. I only need your cheque as evidence of good faith. I shall not, of course, cash it. You may pay me the sum at issue in another way later—with foreign bonds to bearer, or securities you can privately make over. For the moment your cheque will merely be a guarantee of indebtedness."

Mr. Maydew took up his pen.

"Name the figure, then."

"Shall we say ten thousand?"

A wave of thankfulness which he was quite powerless to hide, brought fleeting colour to the young man's face. It seemed that the weight of his sufferings already began to lighten, despite his recent assurance that they never would.

"No," he said, "we will not say ten thousand; we will say twenty thousand, Mr. Ringrose."

"You are generous."

"I am only just. May I never write a cheque with more deep a sense of obligation than I write this one."

He drew the cheque and pushed it across the table.

"I am in your hands," he said, "and the welfare of one who is far more to me than my life lies also in your hands."

"I perfectly understand. You need feel no more anxiety, either on her behalf or your own. The future should prove absolutely clear for you both, Mr. Maydew; but we have none the less got to consider the present from my point of view. There are a few little considerations. We must cover our tracks, for the benefit of those who might not appreciate the high ethical standpoint that has determined our course of action. Your task is quite simple. I shall be busy here—no doubt fruitlessly—poking about and following up clues and so forth; but the clue you so naturally regard as of supreme significance and which you have made me a present of, must return to its accustomed place, and be a clue no more. That is all I require from you. Cleanse it carefully and to-night, when everybody has retired, return it to the central cabinet from which you say you took it."

He picked up the cheque, ran his eye over it, and doubled it up and put it in his pocket.

"And now good-night, Mr. Maydew, and may you sleep in peace."

"I shall sleep as I have not slept for many days," replied the other, shaking the hand extended with warm pressure; and then, as though conscious that his relief was exaggerated, he relapsed and strove to conceal it.

"My own sufferings remain," he declared, "but they must be lessened by the assurance that my future wife will not be called to suffer."

"Time is a great healer," answered Ringrose drily. Concealing the dirk, Vincent Maydew rang for spirits, and having spent another half-hour together, the men separated for the night. But Maydew's work was not yet done. Alone in his own room he cleansed the knife with soap and water and, at two o'clock in the morning, restored it to its place. He was strangely careless of details, however, and fastened it back upon the card with a piece of brown twine.

Though not a religious man, the young fellow spent full twenty mintues on his knees before finally sinking to sleep; but his prophecy of a good night was not fulfilled, and dawn had broken before an exhausted mind permitted him to slumber.

On the following day Ringrose spent some hours in Exeter and proceeded as though his private meeting with young Maydew had not taken place. He was apparently anxious to learn more than either Vincent Maydew or his betrothed could tell him, and the old family lawyer found himself invited to give all particulars concerning the making of the new will.

"She was an obdurate client," said Mr. Fosdike, a bald, big man with clean-shaven and pendulous cheeks, "and though I understood her, I was usually powerless to influence her. Fiery people, as a rule, between their conflagrations, are reasonable, and will undo in sane moments what they did when 'outside themselves,' as we say. Miss Maydew, however, was both short-tempered and obstinate. She would do unjust things in a rage and stick to them afterwards for pride. A sort of insensate vanity—common in men, but rather rare in women—always made her cleave to a decision, however mistaken. One could not shake her. It was a foolish boast of hers that she had never found the need to apologise in her life! So the new will would most certainly have stood had she lived. I prepared it at her wish. She might have made another will later and appointed someone else her legatee instead of John Maydew, her brother; but she would never have forgiven Vincent Maydew or restored him to his position as residuary legatee. He had crossed her; and those who crossed my client were never pardoned."

"You prepared this new will and went down yourself with it?" asked Ringrose, considering the document.

"That is so. One had to watch things with the lady. Any failure on my part to comply with her demands would have meant speedy loss of a valuable estate. She was quite capable of taking Greystone out of my hands at a moment's warning; and had she done that, nothing on earth would ever have induced her to restore the conduct of her affairs to me."

"There was no secret about this will?"

"None whatever. She told her nephew that he must choose between her and her companion, and gave him exactly twelve hours in which to do so. She could keep in a passion longer than anybody I have ever known. It is an exhausting ordeal for most people; but Miss Maydew seemed to burn with an incandescent rage which failed to consume her dreadful energy. The will, as you see, was exceedingly brief. Before she signed it, I reminded her of various bequests and certain obligations—directions from her late father—which were handed down in the existing will; but all she said was they they could wait and be restored by codicils, if she so wished.

" 'Life is uncertain,' she declared in her icy voice—a voice that always made you feel as though the window were open and an east wind blowing. 'Life is uncertain, and I cannot sleep until this mater is determined and my nephew, Vincent Maydew, aware of his situation." At a later date she intended to reconsider a few minor points from her former will, which she had not opened for some years; but for the moment all she was concerened with was the blow to Vincent. That struck, and her brother installed as legatee, she grew calmer. By the irony of chance, as you know, her brother predeceased her, and was actually dead before the will came to be signed. Thus the thing she felt chiefly concerned to do was not done, and Maydew, I am glad to say, is not disinherited. Indeed, he is a gainer."

"Who is Alfred Warner?" asked John Ringrose, with his eyes on the will.

"My clerk. He went down with the document when all was done, and he and William Jay attested Miss Maydew's signature."

"Was the former will destroyed?"

"She had specially directed me to preserve it, that she might read in on a future occasion. It embraced certain injunctions handed down by her late father and had to do with the development of the property and other points which it was only right the future heir respected, whomsoever he might be."

"Exactly," said John. "And now, of course, this will goes before Vincent Maydew, and he will respect its provisions. I will ask you to let me see it."

"Most certainly. It can hardly bear on the crime, however."

"On the contrary, I have reason to think it might."

The lawyer fetched it and his visitor spent half an hour in careful study of the document. He made no comment whatever.

His scrutiny completed, John turned to a decanter of sherry and two glasses which had stood at his elbow since the beginning of their conversation. He broke a biscuit and the lawyer poured out two glasses of wine.

"We shall meet again," said the visitor; "and it is my earnest hope that, before we do so, I may have proceeded and found definite clues to this crime. I thank you. You may have assisted me more than you guess."

"Nothing would give me greater satisfaction," declared the other; "but I confess I see no ray of light. You will probably find the criminal outside Greystone, if Providence wills that he should be discovered."

"A crime is not a conjuring trick, Mr. Fosdike. It often appears to defy natural laws and argue supernatural interference with reality. But the police never permit any supernatural theory either to challenge or defeat them. We argue that the seemingly impossible means only that the clue, or pass key, to the mystery is withheld, and we seek steadfastly and untiringly for that. When we fail to find it the unknown conjurer escapes us—perhaps to play his trick again. Sometimes we only catch him the second or third time. I am, however, far from feeling that I shall fail to find both the trick and the trickster in this case."

"Do you anticipate a long inquiry?"

"I do not. I am disposed to believe I may be successful inside a week or ten days. But if I fail within that time I shall probably fail altogether."

The detective took his leave and presently lunched alone. A chance spectator would have marked upon his face neither perturbation nor anxiety. Amusement at private thoughts and a hearty appetite were the natural indications of a mind at peace. Presently he visited the cathedral and listened to the anthem.

Vincent Maydew was gone to London that he might see after the funeral arrangements of his uncle, while two days later the burial of Mary Maydew would take place. But Ringrose found plenty to occupy him on returning that night to Greystone. Indeed, the case forced itself upon his attention, for he found Juanita Forrester anxious to have some conversation while her sweetheart was absent, and William Jay had also something remarkable to communicate.

At tea-time the girl invited John to take his meal with her and when they were alone she explained her care.

"I saw Vincent off this morning," she told him. "After you had gone to Exeter he started on his motor-bicycle to ride up by the road the way he best likes over Salisbury Plain. But I am a good deal bothered, Mr. Ringrose. He is taking this dreadful affair in a manner I cannot at all understand. One knows that he must be harrowed and shaken—such a sensitive being as he is—but, as I tried to point out to him, he had no power to prevent the tragedy, and he certainly did not precipitate it in any way. After all, for him, dear fellow, there are very obvious compensations. I daren't tell him so, of course; he'd think it a flippant, cruel, and heartless attitude. Perhaps it is. But when you consider how bitterly Miss Maydew attacked him and how actively she tried to prevent him from enjoying what should have been lawfully his in the future—then I, for one, cannot feel very overwhelmed with grief before his wonderful escape. It would be humbug if I pretended that it was. Yet Vincent is overwhelmped. The crime has had a most extraordinary effect upon him, and I was more conscious of it than ever this morning."

"How so, Miss Forrester?"

"There's something happened to him. It's almost as if his character was changed. He'a aloof, abstracted. He stares through you rather than at you. He's not cold exactly—not really changed to me, but changed in himself; and the change does involve a different attitude, even to me. And a change of that sort can only have been produced by some tremendous shock. I know him so well and feel sure of it."

"He's said nothing definite?"

"No, he hasn't mentioned his aunt's death to me since the inquest. But the situation now existing, which might have been expected to challenge all his powers of concentration and energy, leaves him apparently indifferent. He wants to get away. He actually spoke as though he might not return to his aunt's funeral! There was something almost reckless in his talk. He said that perhaps he should break his neck on Salisbury Plain and snuff out the last of the family. I was rather shocked, but he spoke as though it might be the best thing that could happen for everybody. Have you known a tragedy like this actually unseat a man's reason?"

"Never, Miss Forrester. There must be something here you don't understand."

"Have you observed anything strange?"

"Since you ask me, I can honestly say that I have. There are undoubtedly reasons for Mr. Maydew's profound preoccupaiton. He has confided in me up to a point, and be sure I shall respect his confidence. I have, I believe, already set his mind at rest in sundry particulars."

"If you discover the murderer it might go far to calm him," she answered. "I know one thing: that he is tremendously concerned to get to the bottom of poor Miss Maydew's death."

"We must not give up hope yet. Be sure I shall spare no pains to solve the problem, though it certainly looks difficult still."

She changed the subject suddenly.

"I noticed a curious thing in my bedroom cupboard to-day," she said. "I was turning out some dresses to find one I'm going to dye black, and I noticed on the floor of the cupboard a streak of white wood. A splinter, some inches long, must have been torn from the floor of the cupboard. Now I felt positive that was something new, because it impressed my mind as strange. So I examined it, and I found a floorboard, so that it was easily lifted. I lifted it and found a hold underneath—an empty hole. It seems to mean nothing, but it must have been done by somebody, for some purpose, and I thought I'd mention it. Did you do it yourself, perhaps, when you were examining my bedroom?"

"No," he answered, "I did not do it; but I have already found what you describe. A receptacle was made there by pulling up a short board, and in the operation a splinter broke from the old deal and left a conspicuous streak of new wood. Beneath, as you say, is a receptacle."

"Made on purpose?"

"No. The hole beneath was natural."

"Did you find anything it it, Mr. Ringrose?"

"Nothing that appears to be very interesting. Ony a few inches of pink tape."

"How extraordinary! Might I see them?"

John complied at once, and, taking his pocket-book from his breast, soon placed the tape in Juanita's hands.

She could make nothing of it, however.

"It's old and grubby," she said. "It might have been there a hundred years, I should think."

"Yes, it well might. Yet somehow I associated it with the case."

"How extraordinary, Mr. Ringrose. In what way?"

"Indirectly; but the fact is too isolated as yet to be of immediate value. A case, Miss Forrester, is often like an American Cross Word Puzzle. Thick darkness hangs over one light, and, cudgel your brains as you will, you cannot trace any correspondence between the given definition and the wanted word. But presently, as other words are guessed and fitted into their places—behold! without any effort on your part, the wanted word suddenly appears. You have it without guessing at all. And so, perhaps, with this shabby fragment of pink tape. I may meant nothing and lie outside problem altogether, but it may meant something quite important. Obviously an attempt has been made to create a hiding-place in your dress cupboard. But for the splinter we should not have perceived it. The splinter is very curious. I would give a great deal to find that splinter."

"I never thought to look for it," she said.

"You wouldn't but I did—without success. To return to Mr. Maydew. If may advise, so not let any strangeness that he may reveal alter your attitude to him. Treat him as usual. He is, as you say, an amazingly sensitive man, an artist, and his nerves are abnormally developed probably. You can best help him by igonoring the oddity of manner or wildness of speech. Time will restore his balance.

Meanwhile, don't mention this subject—the cupboard—to him, or anybody. Be sure to remember that."

Juanita thanked the detective, and, true to herself, strove to show him that she sympathised with his own difficulties and had imagination to realise the painful nature of his work in life. She was gracious and kindly, and in a man himself gracious and kindly, her attitude found ready appreciation and response. Already he shared the accepted opinion of Miss Forrester, and when he had left her he might have been expected to balance her sweet nature against the dark secret overhanging the soul of the man she loved, and mourn for both. But no gravity darkened John Ringrose, as he sat presently in the kitchen with Mrs. Jay and the cook, smoked a pipe and listened to their theories of the crime. Jane Woodhouse was indifferent, but the elder woman suffered from reaction.

"You miss her, though she was hard and a driver," confessed Ann. "I told Mr. Maydew so this morning, and he understood, same as he understands everything. 'Yes,' he said, 'you'll miss her, Ann, same as the old convicts they kept in chains missed the irons when they were struck off.'"

"A very good simile, ma'am, no doubt," answered John.

Then he heard that William desired to speak with him, and when he had smoked his pipe he joined the butler, who was cleaning plate in his pantry.

John found Mr. Jay full of a curious little discovery. "It may be nought," he said, "or it may mean a lot. We people are not in a position to tell what's useful and what's useless; you are. It's like this. Have you cast your eyes round the library, Mr. Ringrose?"

"Yes, William. I've had a pretty good look round everything in there."

"You would. And you noticed a pretty knife or two in the show-cases, I expect?"

"I took special note of them. There are two Scottish dirks, and there are other daggers from the East. They interested me above a bit, and you'll understand why. I've satisfied myself, with the doctor's assurance, that pretty well any one of those knives might have done the deed."

"Ah! Trust you! And its about one of the knives—a Scottish dirk, sir—that I wanted to speak. No doubt you see things about 'em that's hid from me; but I see one thing about one of them that's hid from you."

"Good, William! What is it?"

"Just this. I don't say I'm very well up in the collection, or anything like that. Miss Maydew cared not a button for books or curiosities; but she cared for cleanliness, and it was my job once a month to run over that room, dust the backs of the books, and polish the glass of the show-cases. So I got to know roughly what was in them—the cases, not the books. And I happened to be familiar with the middle case, because the cream of my late master's collection was in it. That Scot's dirk—and I'll take my oath of it—was fastened to its card with a piece of pink tape 'The Prince Charlie' dirk, Mr. Ringrose. There's no manner of doubt about that. I wouldn't say anybody in this house can substantiate the statement, but I'm prepared to swear to it."

"What of it, William?"

"This: that since the murder, the dirk is fastened to its card with a bit of common book twine, uncoloured. That dirk has been out of the case unknown to me, and now it's back; but the pink tape's gone, and a piece of ordinary string has taken its place."

Ringrose showed deep interest.

"That most certainly means something," he replied. "Show me the dirk. Can you describe the former pink tape exactly?"

"You can see the like in the case," answered the old man. "There's a lot of curios tied to their cards with similar stuff."

Mr. Jay lighted a lamp and groaned while doing so.

"I've hurt my arm," he explained, "and got a boil forming on it that gives me pain."

"How did you do that?" asked John, for it was his curious custom to let no statement of any sort or kind go unquestioned, when it came from an interesting person.

"Couldn't tell you more than the dead. I felt pain there a fortnight ago—woke with it, but saw nought but a flea-bite as it seemed. Then it got worse, and my wife's poulticing it."

"Don't let it get worse. A bite's often poisonous. Let your doctor see it."

"I reckon I will" answered Mr. Jay; then Ringrose took the lamp from him and they repaired to the library. The case was soon open and the dirk in the detective's hand. He took it by the blade, then studied the pink tape on other specimens.

"You can form no idea where this string came from?" he asked, but William was unable to say.

"There's nothing distinct to my eye about it," he replied.

"If I remove it, will it be missed?" inquired John.

"Not a chance. Nobody ever looks in these cases."

"There may be finger-prints," exclaimed Ringrose. "That's why I avoid the handle. Thank you, William. Now we'd better separate. I'll look after this knife for the present. Don't mention the subject to anybody."

They parted and the visitor retired to his room, not again appearing until, at Miss Forrester's wish, he dined with her. William waited upon them, but the conversation was turned to the future and devoted to general subjects. Juanita showed concern for the Butler's hurt, of which she knew, and repeated John's advice. Indeed, she urged him to delay no longer, and when the meal was ended, Mr. Jay presently donned a thick coat and left the house.

On the following morning he reported that Dr. Forbes had lanced his arm, and that he felt much better in consequence.

In the course of that day Vincent Maydew returned home and, during the evening, he and the detective very vitally advanced their private understanding. But the course of the conversation was little to have been expected.

At dinner, John announced his intention of soon leaving Greystone, and when the meal was ended, the two men departed to the little study as before. Juanita went with them. She remained but half an hour, then retired, and as she kissed her sweetheart and bade him "good-night," the watcher observed a shadow deepen on the man's face and understood it. Miss Forrester was also concious of the darkness that still held Vincent Maydew; indeed, she voiced it as she shook John's hand.

"Cheer him up if you can, Mr. Ringrose, for I am powerless to do so," she said, and the elder smiled upon her, while Vincent stared.

"I will make a great effort," promised John, and then, the girl gone, he shut the door he had opened for her and returned to his armchair.

"Mend the fire," he said; "you're in for a pretty long sitting, my friend."

He lighted his cigar and then regarded the melancholy youth before him with an expression in which amusement and deep sympathy were blended.

Maydew spoke first and blurted a piece of information. "That knife's gone out of the museum," he said. "For some infernal reason I was prompted to look at it again to-night before dinner. I went for a book to the library—or said I did—and turning to look at the darned thing, discovered that it had been taken off the card."

Ringrose nodded.

"I took it," he answered.

"Why?"

"I want it. I want to keep it, that I may add it to an interesting little private collection. You'll say you've given me enough, no doubt."

He tapped his breast.

"Twenty thousand pounds sounds good, Mr. Maydew. But I want Prince Charlie's dirk, too, and I guess you'll have no further use for it."

The other flinched before humour he felt intolerable.

"Keep it," he answered, "and leave us as soon as you reasonably can."

"Thank you. That's my intention. But there are vital points to clear to-night."

"You mean the money? Well, in a few months, or possibly less, I will hand you bearer bonds for the full amount."

"Excellent! But there's another interesting little complication I've got to break to you. I think I know who really murdered Miss Maydew."

Agony convulsed John's hearer. Vincent glared and for a moment could not speak; but the other was quick to spare him all needless torture. He rose, poured a stiff whisky, added but a splash of soda from a siphon, and took command.

"Drink and listen. It was not Miss Forrester. She is as innocent as yourself, my friend."

The sufferer stiffened and grew deadly pale; his eyes rolled up and he was about to faint; but relief took another turn. He had already drunk at the other's command. Now he relaxed; his heart leapt and he burst into tears. John, knowing that all was well, patted his shoulder, spoke comforting words, then left Maydew to recover. Indeed, he was moved himself, and though his eyes twinkled, they were dim. Silence fell on them; as Maydew regained self-control and looked longingly at the door, his visitor spoke.

"Yes, I know what you want to do, young fellow. You want to bolt to her and throw yourself on your knees at her feet, and ask her forgiveness, and tell her you're the most unworthy dog that ever loved a rare girl who was too good for him. But that's a scene you must play in your own heart and nowhere on this earth. Now listen to me. Sit still, light a cigarette, or something, and believe that you're out of the wood. You've got to heed me, and then I've got to heed you; and then you may be allowed to go to bed. As for Miss Forrester, she has had a good deal to endure lately and has stood under a pretty dark shadow, though, thank Heaven, her blessed innocence never allowed her to feel the cloud. Anybody else might have wondered at your misery, and for that matter she did; but she little guessed the reason and she never must—remember that. However, we'll come to her. Now I start."

John put down his cigar and perceived his listener was collected and in a condition to follow the argument with a mind at rest.

"When you told me that you had killed Miss Maydew," he began, "you told me a great deal more than the fact. Utterly ignorant as you probably are of criminal psychology—like most of the other writing chaps who invent murder stories—you overlooked certain very obvious indications of your own character which you had already presented to me. I'd studied you very carefully long before your confession. You will never commit a murder, Mr. Maydew. You can take it from me your talents will never rise to that. William was perfectly right when he told me you would find it hard to kill a wasp, let alone an old woman. Moreover, you are highly intelligent—an intellectual man—the last who would be likely to let any futile passion for revenge obscure your outlook, or run you into a capital crime. A Slav, or Latin 'intellectual' might; not an Anglo-Saxon. Our 'high-brows' are a meek and mild crew, except with the pen.

"Beyond that you are naturally honest. You lied badly, obviously, absurdly. Had you been already under my suspicion as the probable murderer of Miss Maydew, I should have let you out after your confession. But, of course, a great deal more than evidence of your own innocence accompanied your statement. I knew in two minutes that you never killed your aunt; but somebody had certainly done so, and what did you do? You made it exceedingly clear that you knew, or thought you knew, the culprit!

"What followed? Your terror was laid bare under my eyes and your suspicion appeared. There only existed one person in the world for you who would create such confusion. For none else on God's earth would you have been prepared to take on your shoulders a crime of this magnitude, or confess it to me. Love blinds in more ways than one. It actually blinded you in the vital particular of your sweetheart's innocence; and that, of course, proved that evidence of the most terrific character confronted you. Only such evidence could have forced you to your conviction against years of devotion and experience and love. You'll tell me about that presently. A secret between us for ever, remember; but a secret that it will be essential I should know for the satisfaction of the law.

"The evidence that convinced your reason against your heart must have been prodigious, for it conquered reality, as doubtless it was meant to do. You know Juanita Forrester better than anybody else in the world. You shared the common knowledge of her extraordinary distinction—her rare warm heart—her generosity—her sympathy with all who were unhappy or downtrodden. I've heard it echoed on every side, from the baliff to the bootboy. And beyond that, you knew her inner soul and had won her confidence and worship. From you nothing was hidden; yet where the rest of the world scorned the possibility of evil breathed in connection with her name, you found yourself convinced that she was a murderess! That's interesting and shows how, as I said just now, love blinds in more ways than one. It's because love, like conscience, makes us cowards, Mr. Maydew."

He paused for a moment, but lifted his hand for silence when the other was about to speak.

"Listen a little longer, We've nearly done with the first act," continued John. "Well, I knew, while you told your story, that you were innocent, but believed your sweetheart guilty. I felt tempted then and there to undeceive you, so far as your attempt to delude me was concerned; but business is business and I saw, of course, that the truth might be as your secret terror prompted you to fear. I could not yet feel positive that you were mistaken; and so I fell in with your transparent little plot, named my price, and took your money. It was understood that I should pretend to work and presently throw up the sponge and retire beaten. The interesting and original thing is that I might actually have retired beaten had it not been for your efforts to choke me off! They were, of course, full of invaluable information.

"I obeyed you, save in one particular. Instead of pretending to work, I did work, and my work swiftly convinced me that your fears were folly. I longed to tell you, boy. The hardest thing in the case was to keep my mouth shut to you and let you go on thinking that the girl you loved was a murderess even for one hour. But I'll be frank. I couldn't trust you. It was better you wilted a little longer and left her wondering. Because, you see, your Juanita was safe enough. She puzzled and she troubled, but nothing to hurt; while somebody else, who mattered a great deal more than either of you, had to receive my respectful consideration; and that was the doer of the deed. One didn't want to create any uneasiness in that quarter."

"Good heavens! You knew?"

"No; I guessed; but I didn't know. But after I'd seen Mr. Fosdike, the lawyer, I began to feel tolerably sure. Now hear what you can do to help me."

"How should I help? I wish I could."

"Tell me exactly what made you so terribly sure that your sweetheart, and nobody else, had killed Miss Maydew. I attach the very greatest importance to this information, so take your time and give me every detail."

Vincent Maydew collected his thoughts and then spoke. "I come out of this darned badly," he began.

"Not so badly as you tried to, however."

"The facts are these. After my Aunt Mary declared her intentions against me, Juanita and I sat tight for a day or two and hoped that she would change her mind, grow calmer and allow reason to work with her. However, she never changed her mind, and reason was not he strong suit at any time. She sent for Fosdike and told us, on the night of her death, that she had made a new will and left everything to her brother. When she had gone to bed and before I went upstairs to pack before an early start on the following day, Juanita, for once in her life was really angry. She cut loose and cried out that the old woman was a monster and dead to every decent human feeling. Her abstract sense of justice prompted her, rather than her indignation for me, or her own personal disappointment. She railed against Miss Maydew and declared that she would leave her instantly and never see her again. She had actually planned to leave the house on the following morning with me, and she thought me rather mean for pleading against such a natural action. We differed, but we didn't quarrel. I looked ahead and still hoped that a thing done in anger might be cancelled presently, if neither of us took any hasty step to make a change of front impossible. Juanita at last allowed me to persuade her. She consented to stop, at least for a time, and await events. Then she went to bed."

"One moment. When you speak of a 'personal disappointment' for Miss Forrester, you mean that, under the old will, she enjoyed a considerable bequest, while the new will contained no mention of her?"

"Yes; at dinner, when she told us what she had done, my aunt specially mentioned to Juanita that she had withdrawn her promised legacy. The amount I do not know, neither did Juanita, but she had reason to believe it handsome."

"It was ten thousand pounds," said Mr. Ringrose.

"Was it' Well, I'm probably wrong when I speak of 'personal disappointment,' for my girl certainly did not think of herself that night. She only thought of justice and the wicked wrong to me after long years of steadfast support to my aunt, and my patience and consideration and so on. I had really tried to win the old woman, and had studied her pleasure in a thousand ways. They say every artist has a good slice of feminine make-up in him, and, at any rate, I thought I understood Aunt Mary and could sympathise with her difficulties of character and see the best side of her. When the smash came, Juanita remembered these things and they made her furious on my account. She went to bed angry—honestly angry—and my mind was left acutely conscious of such an extraordinary fact. Her Spanish blood, no doubt, and her intense love for justice.

"The next thing is this. She went to bed and so did I; but I couldn't sleep. I was terribly upset by the disaster of the day, and tossed and turned and troubled hour after hour and cudgelled my wits in vain to find some rational and intelligent way of saving the situation. Somewhere about two o'clock I thought I heard a noise in the passage, rose and looked out—just in time to see Juanita enter her room, carrying a candle in one hand and something else in the other I could not make out. I guessed that, like myself, she was sleepless, and I felt half inclined to go and see her. I wish that I had done so. It might have saved me many appalling hours. But I did not, and I had forgotten the incident entirely before the shock of the morning's tragedy until she mentioned it to me many hours later.

"Then she told me exactly what she told the coroner at the inquest—how she had gone to get a book and something to eat and drink; and how she thought a sound came from the corridor near Miss Maydew's door. She had been strange during the hours after the discovery—or so it seemed to me. A calmness and indifference that appeared foreign to her as I understood her followed the evil news.

She showed no great sorrow and hardly any surprise. But there was something. I felt almost as though she found herself under the weight of a dread akin to my own—as though, perhaps, the horrible thought crossed her mind that I might be responsible! At any rate, she avoided me—doubtless in reality from a delicate feeling that I might prefer to be alone at such a time—but I was unbalanced and full of vague fears.

"Thus when opportunity came something inspired me to go into Juanita's room, when she was out of the house, and make such an examination as would doubtless presently be made by the law. I did so and found nothing to cause uneasiness until I came to the cupboard. There I found evidence of something—a splinter broken off old wood—a sort of thing to catch the eye, Ringrose. Closer search showed that a board had been displayed, and I found no difficulty in lifting it—an old, solid plank not more than three feet long. Underneath it was some white, thin material huddled up in a ball. I pulled this out, and as I did so Prince Charlie's dirk fell out of it. The thing was obviously one of Juanita's nightgowns, and the right wrist was soaked in blood.

"At that moment my mind moved queerly. It seemed that the truth was a thing of the past—that I had known for an eternity how my aunt died. I was only concerned with Juanita, and I sat on the ground and stared at the blood-stained knife and nightgown and explained to myself that my sweetheart had suffered an awful fit of temporary insanity, had done this thing and hidden the evidence, then probably forgotten all about it. I wove a theory and my mind moved as quickly as our minds move in dreams. I passed through vast arguments all tending in one direction, and after what seemed a lapse of hours I woke, as it were, wondering that nobody had come to find me. As a matter of fact, no more than five minutes had passed since I made the discovery. I restored the board to its place and took the evidence of the tragedy to my own room. And that night, when alone in this study after the household had retired, I burned the nightdress, destroying every fragment of it, and I locked up the dirk in my private desk.

"By now I had proved conclusively to myself that the deed must have been prompted by some strange freak of atavism in Juanita—an impulse awakended by my wrongs—not her own. I suspected that, in a sort of walking trance, she had done a deed which her maternal ancestors might have condoned, or themsleves committed readily enough. She had remembered the museum and obtained the knife. I guessed that I had seen her returning with it, and that at a later hour she had unconciously committed the crime, concealed the evidence, slept and awakened to suppose she had dreamed the deed—if, indeed, it remained in her memory at all. You can see how my devotion quickened my mind to explain what seemed so terribly certain.

"So it stood next day, and contact with Juanita convinced me that she knew nothing of the horrible event. To tell her what I knew as unthinkable, for she would have insisted on making the facts public. I resolved to the dumb, therefore; but I delayed too long in a very vital particular. My first action should have been to cleanse the knife and return it to the place from which I knew it had come. This I intended to do, but two things happended on the following morning. The post brought the news that Uncle John was dead, and I guessed at once this fact destroyed the new will; then, early after breakfast, Inspector Burrows arrived and asked me if I would meet your train and invite you to stop at Greystone. He held that desirable and, though a detective in the house was the very last thing I desired, I dared not say so without rousing suspicions in the policeman's mind.

"No opportunity to visit the library secretly occured until the time had come to go to the station. I went on my motorbicycle, met you, and invited you to Greystone. I didn't think you were coming. I meant, however, to get the knife back, and that night determined to secure the card from the museum so that nothing should appear to be missing. I had meant to go after everybody was asleep in the small hours, and judged that to move the card would be as safe as to return the knife. But on going to bed I slept like the dead and didn't wake up till the first glimmer of dawn. I started at once for the card, but it was too late. You were actually in the museum, and unseen by you, from the gallery, I observed you at the centre case and saw you read the empty card. Then I cleared out, leaving you unaware that I'd seen your action."

Ringrose nodded.

"I can pretty well guess the rest," he said.

"Nobody will ever guess what the next twenty-four hours meant to me," replied the young man. "I suffered the torments of hell, for I knew, as surely as I was alive, that you would get to the bottom of it with such a clue. You somehow inspired me with an infernal certainty that Juanita was doomed sooner or later. Not reason, but terror, for you had no real clue. But my nerve was gone, and at last I determined upon taking the blame and cutting the ground from under your feet by confessing to the murder myself. It seemed a safe way to look from your point of view. You didn't give me a chance to appreciate it, for that matter. You decieved me into thinking that I had deceived you."

"What we call a double-cross, Mr. Maydew."

"Nothing matters now," replied the younger; "but I thought I'd got you, and the money had done the trick. I ought to apologise, I suppose, but by Heaven! you've earned the money all right in your own way."

The elder smiled.

"Now it's my turn," he said. "I haven't much imagination maybe, yet quite enough to see how this looked to you and what a cleft stick you found yourself in. You argued very well, and being a literary man with a poetic turn of mind, you did pretty much what one might have expected. But you're no actor, Mr. Maydew, and as I've told you, your own yarn stultified itself. I knew what you were after, and that reduced the problem. You thought your sweetheart had done the deed—that was clear. The next thing for me to do was to find out if you were right. I found out you were wrong. That's where intuition came in. A dangerous thing intuition—if you use it to fight against reason, as so many clever people often do—but a mighty useful gift in its place.

"The problem was to find out whether any motive existed for the murder of Miss Maydew in her companion's mind. Did Miss Forrester gain by it? If you and she had hear of John Maydew's death before the murder, then one saw at once that a good deal was gained. But neither of you had heard. Therefore, to kill her mistress was to lose any future chance of changing the situation for the better. Such an act could only be performed by a certain type of character. It argued a tempest of uncontrolled passion and a lust for immediate revenge at any cost. Nothing more unlikely to overtake Miss Forrester seemed possible. Her attitude to the affair was quite in keeping with the situation. She pretended nothing she did not feel. She continued to be herself. Her only cause for distraction, apart from the natural horror or such an event, was your behaviour. She knew you so well, and she could not understand the way you took it, especially after you learned the will was inoperative owing to your uncle having died before it was made. That puzzled her very much and she told me so. Then she discovered the loose board in her dress cupboard and showed it to me. I, of course, had seen it for myself long before, and showed her the piece of tape I had taken from it—the tape from the card in the museum as it turned out. That you had overlooked with the other more terrible clues in your hand.

"I was quite sure that she knew nothing whatever. She's the sort of girl whose native quality looks our of her wonderful eyes. To kill an old woman for revenge was absolutely beyond her power, even if she'd been born a Borgia. What followed? Why, that somebody unknown had been at amazing pains to plant the crime on Miss Juanita. I guessed at once where you had probably found the knife. But what had led you to search for it, or imagine she was involved, I did not know until you told me.

"The knife, then, was put there—to be found—not by you, but by those who would presently search Greystone; and the splinter was deliberately torn off the board to challenge attention. Without that accident, the floor of the cupboard would not have arrested any eye.

"So I found the fun really beginning, from my point of view. And there, if you please, I'll stop to-night. The first act's ended. To-morrow will see the second act played, and you have told me important things that should help in certain rather vital particulars. I must fit your information into its place and see whether it supports my present theory, or if at any point it upsets it. I hope not, and I think not. Meantime, be at rest and feel neither shame for your falsehoods nor fear for the future. I may be right, or I may be entirely mistaken; but after the funeral to-morrow it is quite possible, with a pinch of luck, that the second and third acts can both be played."

Ringrose shook the lover's hand, and with many expressions of graditude and thanksgiving, Vincent Maydew bade him goodnight.

The following day brought the funeral of Miss Maydew, and large numbers, attracted by curiosity rather than esteem, crowded the little country churchyard. For human beings will go far and take no little pains to look at the outside of a coffin wherein lies a murdered man or woman.

Vincent and Juanita attended the ceremony, while the whole of the Greystone staff were also present. Inspector Burrows and his constables found enough to do to regulate the traffic and preserve decency; while Ringrose availed himself of a house practically empty to pursue certain investigations inspired by young Maydew's last statement and his own deductions upon it.

For more than an hour Greystone was deserted, save for a caretaker in the kitchen and John himself. He had purposely offered to remain and promised Maydew to watch the front of the premises while they should be empty. His purpose, however, demanded absolute secrecy, and, to ensure it, he entered the kitchen five minutes after the last coach had left the front door, and bade the under-gardener, left in charge, to convey a telegram for him to the post-office. The young man raised no demure, since it was understood that Ringrose now ruled. Glad enough to leave the deserted mansion, the youth set out, and was gone three parts of an hour.

And on the return of the little funeral party, Ringrose left the house for Twambley and enjoyed a long interview with Inspector Burrows.

He returned in the afternoon and sought the society of Vincent and Juanita, after chatting with the servants and hearing from them all particulars of the funeral and the sightseers.

All the staff appeared cheerful. Indeed, the very house seemed to have gained a new and more exhilerating atmosphere with the departure of its defunct mistress. Again the trio took their dinner together, and the meal, despite the melancholy business of that day, showed Vincent Maydew in a happier mood.

He alluded to the affairs of his uncle, not mentioned until then. John Maydew had died somewhat suddenly of physical mischief resulting from intemperance. His death had not surprised his physician, and his affairs presented no complication save a body of debt, which his nephew had made immediate arrangements to cancel. Two days later would see his funeral, and young Maydew proposed to attend it.

Later in the evening John and his host took their way to the little study, and the detective, after half an hour in the united company of the lovers, begged Juanita to retire.

"I don't like to separate you," he said, "but I'm off to-morrow morning, and I must have a serious talk with Mr. Maydew to-night. You go to bed, Miss Forester, and go to sleep."

Juanita kissed Vincent, and he opened the door for her. Then he returned and expressed regret that his guest was about to depart so soon.

"Your theory has broken down, I suppose," he said. "I hated the sight of you till yesterday, Ringrose, but now I love the sight of you, and I want you to promise to be my friend."

"A promise I'll make and keep," replied the other heartily enough. "But I've not gone yet, and my theory has not broken down, and several rather startling things are going to happen before I'm off to-morrow. You're in for another bad night. However, there's no escape from that."

He looked at his watch.

"Dr. Forbes will be here in ten minutes or so; but we'll get on from where we left off yesterday. A lot has happened to me since then."

"Dr. Forbes? Why have you sent for him?" asked the other.

"Because, unless I miss my guess, somebody's going to want him badly before very long."

"Not Juanita?"

"No, no! I hope Miss Forrester will sleep soundly and not wake up till to-morrow morning. And I think she will. You've taken a tidy lot off her mind by coming back to your old cheerful self. Now follow me as closely as you can. Last night we had only finished with you and your sweetheart, but there were three persons open to suspicion in the house besides yourself and Miss Forrester. And all three, by the way, had spoken to me with the warmest affection and regard for her. Well, what about these three old servants associated with Greystone for a great many years? I put it to myself this way. There had been a big thing happen in the house, and William, waiting at table and enjoying the confidence of all concerned, knew all about the row and the consequence. Through him, his wife, and Jane, the cook, would also know about it. He'd heard of the quarrel and knew it was a grim reality, for he'd been one of the witnesses to the new will.

"I had a chat with him on that subject and found him, though full of talk about every other matter, reticent as to that. He'd known what was in the will, because his mistress had told him; but he'd not, of course, read the will when he attested Miss Maydew's signature. Asked by me whether Miss Forrester was interested in the new will, he replied that he had no idea. All he could say was that Miss Maydew had disinherited you.

"I'd already intended to see Mr. Fosdike and study both the old will and the new, and I did so two days ago and found out an exceedingly interesting fact. You had told me that Miss Forrester was remebered in the earlier will, and I informed you of the amount last night. She was to have had ten thousand pounds, and there were other legacies under the first will. Among them————"

Ringrose was interrupted, for Williams opened the door and announced Dr. Forbes. The physician entered, beat some snow off his overcoat and demanded to know the purpose of the message that brought him; but he was not immediately answered. Maydew bade William fetch spirits and syphons, and when he had done so and withdrawn, both men turned to the detective.

"It's like this, doctor," explained John. "A weak heart is a weak heart, and there's a weak heart beating in the breast of somebody in this house to-night. That same heart is going to get a very ugly shock at exactly ten-thirty. That's within half an hour from the present time. The shock will be severe and I'm a merciful sort of man, so I judged you would be better on the spot, and left the note for you accordingly. Now let me finish what I was saying to Mr. Maydew, please. You brought your bag, I see."

"I did, Ringrose," replied Forbes.

"Thank you. I was telling Mr. Maydew about his aunt's former will. She'd remembered one or two old people in it at the direction of her late father; and some of these had already received their bequests and were eliminated by codicil. But four legates remained, including Miss Forrester, while in the new will all four had been ommitted. The point of interest was, first, the size of the legacies, secondly, the fact that the legatees must know their money had gone. William and his wife, Ann, were down for five thousand pounds jointly; Mrs. Woodhouse, the cook, got one thousand."

"How do you know that they knew they were out?" asked Maydew.

"For the best of reasons. William was brought in to witness the testator's signature. He knew that he and his wife were in the old will for five thousand, for he told Miss Forrester so long ago; but now he knew that since he witnessed her will, he could be no longer in it. Moreover it was so exceedingly short that he might have read it if it wasn't actually covered when he signed. And Fosdike says it was not, and I doubt not he read every word.

"Now what might a facer like that have done for William? He was a self-controlled man before his betters, but I found that, behind the scenes, he had a devil of a temper and ruled with a rod of iron. His heart's groggy and it was understood as a sort of unwritten law by his wife and Jane that he must never be crossed. Even with me he had some ado, when I bothered him, to be civil. There is temper in his eyes. I began to see light. Things happened—and, as I looked at the growing theory, it developed.

"In a case of this sort the detective, if he's wise, will attempt to get into the skin of the suspected person and consider the situation from his point of view. Here was William quietly going on with his life; but, assuming he'd had a hand in this affair, how was he thinking and feeling? Well, obviously he must have been the most puzzled man on God's earth. For how did things look to him? He'd been devilish careful to say nothing but what was true touching Miss Forrester. He'd absolved her and his new master; he'd also whitewashed his wife and the cook, and, of course, himself, in a logical and reasonable fashion. But assuming, for argument's sake, that, in a sudden fury to be revenged on her, he'd killed the old woman, who'd robbed him of his legacy at a stroke, then what had he done afterwards?

"What he had apparently done was to plant the weapon and other evidence in Miss Forrester's bedroom at the first opportunity following the crime. That argued careful preparation. He had to make that cubby hole in the cupboard, and he had to be free to do it. Nothing was easier. He could have spent an hour in her bedroom any day, when she was out and his wife and Jane down below. That William did; but whether he got a nightdress actually prepared before the murder or after, we don't know yet. I think after. At any rate, the point is that, in that disordered house on the morning after the murder, he had fifty opportunities to slip into Miss Forrester's room and plant the clues. And here's a side question for you, doctor. What's wrong with Mr. Jay at this moment?"

"He's got a large tumour on his left forearm."

"Could you say what produced it?

"Impossible now—poison of some sort."

"A good, deep cut might have done it?"

"Yes, if the wound had suppurated."

"Then I'll go on."

"Now I'm William," continued Ringrose. "I've killed Miss Maydew and worked off the incriminating evidence where it can't well be missed by the police, though it will look as if it had been carefully hidden, of course. And what next? I—as William—find first that my manufactured evidence has been apparently overlooked by the professional detective altogether; and then I find it's gone! I am now in a quandary. But light is presently thrown on my darkness. I find the dirk back in the museum. That proves to my mind that John Ringrose did not discover it, but somebody else did. That must leave William horribly mystified; but, of course, he's powerless and daren't pretend he knows anything. He was quite clever about it, however, and called my attention to Prince Charlie's dirk and the new piece of string; but that was all he could do. Since then, no doubt, he's been living in hope that I was on a wrong tack. And he's very glad I've failed and am leaving tomorrow."

Vincent Maydew stared.

"Jay!" he cried.

"Yes. An ingenious man, but a ferocious temper was always simmering under that restrained exterior, and Fate unfortunately liberated it. He probably killed the old woman for revenge—perhaps told her so before he struck; but the plot to involve Miss Forrester, shows far more than mere passion and hate under a cruel disappointment. He's a bad old devil under his skin. I'll forgive anybody who forfeits his life for the luxury of a murder; but it's hard to forgive one who played the game as William played it and then wanted to have cake and eat it, too, at an innocent woman's expense.

"The nightdress solved the problem, Mr. Maydew. You see what it told me? Perhaps not; but it was this. William had got the hiding-place in Miss Forrester's bedroom ready before he wanted it, no doubt. But what was going into it? The dirk, of course, and the bit of tape. But with the actual murder came another inspiration. The nightdress. And why? In my mind's eye I saw Mr. Jay commit the crime. It was short business. He'd slip out of his bed, do the deed and be back under five minutes. But what happened? The blood. He found his pyjama jacket sleeve red. That gave him the inspiration. So, when you told me of the nightdress and the red, right sleeve, I thought of William's pyjamas. They might have gone the way of the nightdress and be burned, or they might not. I happened to remember they were not. When you were at the funeral and the house was empty, I looked for them—where? Not in William's bedroom, but in his wife's work-basket. I'd seen her mending a pyjama jacket, you see. William had met with an accident and burned the right sleeve—so she explained and so no doubt he told her. But, after the nightdress story, I knew that he'd cut away the right sleeve and burned the edge of the cut. I fitted in. He's wearing the pyjama jacket again—with the right sleeve mended.

"And one more sweet touch. I found the splinter! I found it in William's morning jacket. But not in the pocket. He'd put it in the breast pocket when he broke the board, and been much surprised, no doubt, to find it gone later when he came to destroy it. And why did he find it gone? Because it had dropped through a hole in the lining and was at the bottom edge of the coat safe and sound. He'd put on his best for the funeral, and his coat was hanging on a peg behind his bedroom door. Feeling the lower pocket, I touched something hard in the lining and in half a minute the splinter was in my hand. Things will slip down from a worn pocket like that. I've known it happen to myself.

"So there you are. He killed her for revenge, because she'd forgotten the legacy and ruled him out; though Mr. Fosdike thinks she quite meant to put him and his wife and Jane back afterwards; and he plotted to land Miss Forrester when the deed was done. It's clever murder enough in its little way, and he had some good touches. The most masterly thing he did was to praise Miss Forrester so heartily. The temptation to drop a word of doubt in my ear must have been considerable, but he withstood it. And now Burrows and the constable ought to be at the back door."

As Vincent explained these things for the benefit of a bewildered doctor, there came a muffled scream in the passage and the men rose. A moment later Jane Woodhouse rushed into the room.

"The police!" she cried. "Mr Burrows and my brother-in-law have just come in and arrested William for the murder, and he's fallen lumpus in a faint, and Ann's going mad!"

"Your bag, doctor," suggested John, and a moment later all hastened to the kitchen.

They found the police striving to restore William Jay, only to hear from Dr. Forbes that the little man had passed beyond reach of law, or physic.

At his wholly unexpected arrest he had leapt from his chair and in half a minute succumbed. Dr. Forbes quickly found that the widow needed all his care.

To John Ringrose's satisfaction, Ann Jay, an hour later, was able to add a measure of testimony to the circumstantial evidence responsible for her husband's death. She had been fully conscious that his mind was clouded and, by many bitter blasphemous speeches, he had indirectly led her to fear that he was involved in the crime. He had lived to appreciate its futility and to know that his legacy was safe with Vincent Maydew. Asked concerning her husband's wound, she explained it.

"He told me a knife fell from a shelf and stabbed him," she said; but Ringrose perceived the bearing of this incident and knew the wound self-inflicted.

"He wanted blood for the nightdress which he'd taken from Miss Forester's chest of drawers," he explained to Inspector Burrows, the doctor, and Maydew, when they were along; "and there was no tap to turn on but his own. He cut himself, therefore, and he cut pretty deep. Then the wound gave trouble and didn't heal."

John Ringrose left Twambley on the following morning and spoke a last few words to Vincent Maydew before he did so. "I shall be down again for the inquest when it finishes," he said, "and then all's cleared up. Meantime, one thing. On your life never breathe a word of what you've been through to Miss Forrester. The facts she has got to know, of course; but the inference, that has given you such a hell of a time, must be hidden from her forevermore. That's easy. Your gloom was caused by the horrible discovery that somebody was plotting against her—no more than that."

"Trust me there. I'd rather die than that she should hear what I feared. And—you—how can I thank you, Ringrose?"

"Why should you? I'll take one of those cigars, please, for the journey. And I'll say one thing more. Believe me, I was never better pleased to cut a knot than this. Here, by the way, is your cheque."

He handed it to Vincent, who pressed it back upon him.

"At least keep that. I'd thankfully double it. You've saved two lives."

Mr Ringrose laughed, folded the cheque into a spill, walked to the fire, and thrust it in. Then he lighted his cigar with it.

"I can burn money as well as the best, you see!" he said. "There's Mr. Burrows and the Ford coming up the drive. My respects to your lady. And bear up—bear up! Good-bye, my lad, and Heaven bless you both."

THE EPISODE OF THE BLACK DIAMOND

A Sexton Blake Adventure

First published in 1920

Blake had just received a curt message over the telephone from his friend, Inspector Purvis, to the effect that Canon Wimberley, the cousin and heir to Lord Wayne, of the Henge, had been found dead in his library under suspicious circumstances.

"I wish you would run down and have a look at things," Purvis had concluded. "The Canon was found by the servants early this morning. I went to the house myself shortly after nine. The doctor declares that he died of snake bite, probably about two in the morning. The canon was a naturalist of considerable ability, and a well-known authority on British birds; but the servants declare positively that though he had many pets in the garden at the back of the deanery, there was never such a thing as a snake amongst them.

"The whole affair is a bit of a puzzle. I would go down with you, but I got bowled over by a cab on my way back to the Yard, and have to lay up for a bit; so if you can, I would rather you handled the case than any of our men."

Blake was busy when the message came through; but as the deanery was only a short distance away, he promised Purvis to look round as soon as possible.

The house was a large, old-fashioned building of red brick, dating back to Queen Anne, standing in a quiet narrow by-street of Chelsea. It had a big, and, for London, an extremely pretty garden, shut in by high walls on all sides, and was an ideal home for a man of studious habits.

On presenting his card and explaining his errand, Blake was at once shown into the library by the elderly butler. It was a pleasant, spacious room, overlooking the garden. Canon Wimberley, besides being a man of refined tastes, and a student, had also possessed a considerable private income, and the room bore evidence of his appreciation of the fact.

Rare and costly first editions lined the bookshelves. There were some beautiful specimens of Glissonier's marvellous leather work, richly gilt, fine bronzes, and one or two exceptional marbles. The one jarring note was a plain deal table placed near one of the windows, which had evidently been used for experimental and taxidermal work.

Blake glanced round him slowly, taking in the details one by one, and then turned to the waiting manservant.

"Who was it who first discovered the body?" he asked.

"One of the maids, sir; but I heard her shriek—I was in the dining-room—and came at once, guessing that something was amiss."

"What time was that?"

"About seven o'clock, sir."

"Describe to me, please, as nearly as you can what you saw."

"Well, sir, the first thing I noticed was that the lights were still on—even the one with the green shade on the working table over there, where the master used to do his stuffing of birds and things. Then I looked down and saw the master himself lying on the floor, just here, sir. He was all twisted up, as though he were in pain, and he was sort of swollen like. I ran to him, but the moment I touched him I knew he was dead. I telephoned at once for Dr Harborough—a friend of his, sir, who always attended him—and by his advice I also sent for the police."

"With the exception of the body itself, nothing has been touched, I take it?"

"Nothing at all, sir. The maid was coming in to do the room when she cried out. Besides, we all of us had very strict orders about disturbing any papers or anything on the worktable."

"I understand. I see that he must have been at work last night, for there is a dismembered skeleton of a bird of some sort still on the table. Now, if you will show me the way, I should like to go upstairs."

"Very good, sir. This way, please."

The old servant led Blake up the broad staircase to the death chamber, and there left him.

The doctor's verdict was correct, beyond all doubt. Blake had seen too many cases of snake bite to question it for an instant. Moreover, there were two small punctured wounds in the right hand, one on the ball of the thumb, the other in the palm.

Blake examined these carefully with a puzzled expression, for the two punctures were quite three inches apart, and their relative positions needed explanation.

Even supposing that, unknown to the servants, the canon had had in his possession a poisonous snake, an accidental bite through careless handling would not have presented that appearance. The punctures would have been close together, with barely an inch between them.

Returning to the library he began to make a detailed investigation of the room in the hopes of discovering something which might serve him as a starting point. He met with no very great success, however. The one thing he did discover was that early on the previous day Canon Wimberley had received a small parcel through the post, for in the waste-paper basket was a piece of brown paper, the creases of which showed that it had been wrapped round an oblong box measuring about eight inches by four. This cover only bore two stamps, so clearly the box could not have contained anything so heavy as a live snake capable of inflicting a fatal bite.

Blake rang the bell for the manservant, and showed him the creased paper.

"Do you happen to know what was in the box that this was wrapped round?" he asked. "By the postmark it seems to have arrived some time early yesterday morning."

The old man looked at it doubtfully.

"The master used to get such a lot of queer things sent him, sir," he answered. "People from all parts of the country were always sending him birds, and beetles, and such like. You see, sir, they knew he took an interest in them things."

"Yes, I understand; but in the case of this particular parcel—try and think."

"There was a parcel come yesterday, sir. I took it in myself, because it was too big for the letter-box. Ah, yes; I remember now! The master was busy at the time. He just opened it and glanced at the contents. They were just a few small bones—there they are on his work-table now. He emptied 'em out himself and handed me the box to throw away."

"That will do for the present, then, thank you."

The man withdrew, and Blake turned to examine the bird bones, but with little hope of discovering anything from them.

There was one point, however, which lent them some importance. It was practically certain that Canon Wimberley had been studying them at the time of, or shortly before his death.

The structure of the bones was rather peculiar, most of them being slender and light, but very strong. The skull was fairly long-beaked, with a slight downward curve at the end, and two of the wing bones were fractured in a curious manner, rather as if they had been broken deliberately instead of accidentally.

Suddenly he gave vent to a sharply-suppressed exclamation, and snatched a pair of powerful tweezers from the box of implements on the table. In the hollow of the bone he was holding he had detected a foreign body of some kind. What it was he was scarcely able to see, so cunningly was it concealed.

He inserted the sharp-pointed tweezers, and getting a good grip, gave a wrench. The obstacle came away readily enough. It was nearly three-qarters of an inch long, and the upper end was as fine and sharp as a needle. It was slightly curved, and down the back of the whole length of it ran a minute, almost imperceptible, groove. At the lower end was a sort of socket, to which still adhered a small, wrinkled morsel of tough skin.

Blake laid it down, releasing it from the grip of the tweezers, and whistled softly to himself. A single glance had been sufficient to tell him what it was, and the manner of Canon Wimberley's death. He had died of snake-bite, and the object which Blake had withdrawn from the hollow cavity of the bone was a full-grown rattlesnake's tooth, poison bag and all complete. There was no mistaking it. The case was one of cold-bloodied and deliberate murder, carefully planned and thought out.

Whatever the motive, the method was clear enough. The murderer was aware of the canon's craze for ornithology, and had sent him, through the post, the bones of a bird that was certainly out of the common and sure to arouse his interest.

The trap had been laid with diabolical cunning. The construction of a rattlesnake's tooth is peculiar, and lent itself well to the scheme. In a sort of socket at the back of the top of the fang is a small poison sack of tough membrane about the size of a pea. When the snake strikes, this sack of compressed, and the poison is squirted down the tiny groove in the tooth into the small punctured wound made by the point. A very slight pressure is sufficient to bring this about. The wound itself is scarcely more than a pinprick, and the pain of it at the moment, comparatively speaking, insignificant.

The murderer had extracted the tooth and sack from a live snake, presumably under an anaesthetic, and inserted it in the fractured bone so that the needle-point of the fang just projected below the poison sack. Blake discovered that the man had placed a small wad of cork to form a resisting surface in handling the bone, It was practically a certainty that sooner or later the fingers must come in contact with that fine and almost invisible point; a slight pressure on it, sufficient to penetrate the skin, would mean, in a man of the canon's age, death.

The device explained satisfactorily the otherwise unaccountable distance between the two punctures in the canon's hand.

It was evident that whilst examining the fracture with its jagged end, either his thumb or palm had pressed on the end of the tooth. He must undoubtedly have felt the prick of it but, suspecting nothing, had probably imagined that it was caused by the splintered bone itself, and continuing his work had incurred a second scratch.

The idea that there was any danger in two such insignificant little wounds would not have entered his head till an hour, or possibly two hours, later, when the virus, having done its work, gripped him suddenly, and wrapped him in a spasm of pain so severe that he was unable even to ring for assistance.

Blake picked up the fang again gingerly with the tweezers, and replaced it in the hollow of the bone, which he put aside.

Then he wrote out several telegrams, prepaying the replies in each case, and bade the manservent send them off. They were addressed to the various best-known dealers in wild animals.

A rattlesnake is by no means a common sight in England; possible not one person in five thousand has ever set eyes on one, even in a Zoo. The murderer must have obtained his through a dealer, and Blake had every hope that one or other of his telegrams would be productive of results.

Whilst waiting for the answers, he went upstairs once more to search for a possible clue to the motive.

The canon was successor to his cousin, Lord Wayne, but the latter was the younger man by nearly a score of years, and the canon's chance of practical succession was so remote that it became a factor which could be eliminated from the problem.

He searched the dead man's clothes, in hopes of finding some scrap of writing—a note, a letter, an address—anything which might suggest a new train of thought, but found nothing beyond a few unimportant memoranda.

In despair, he turned to the body, lying so quietly beneath its coverings in the still, silent room, and here at last he made a discovery. Round the neck hung a thin, black silk cord, from which depended a small silver crucifix and a silver key.

He detached the key carefully, and balanced it in the palm of his hand, feeling instinctively that in some way this key, which the dead man had kept so carefully hidden from sight, was connected with the mystery of the crime.

He glanced round the room, but there was nothing there which such a key seemed likely to fit, so he want back to the library.

He set to work systematically, but it was a long time before he found what he was looking for. Still, he found it at last—an antique silver casket at the back of the bottom shelf of a big buhl cabinet full of curios. The workmanship, though, was similar to that of the key, and, from the design, he judged it to be the handiwork of a Mexican Indian.

To open the cabinet was a simple matter. The casket itself would have proved much the harder task without a key, for the lock was cunningly devised, on the same principle as a Chinese padlock, which would puzzle any expert's skeleton key.

Inside the casket lay some papers, and on the top of them a slip of pasteboard about the size of a visiting-card, yellow and grimy with age. It contained no inscription, but in the centre was printed a black, diamond-shaped patch, similar to the ace of diamonds in a pack of playing cards as regards shape and size.

He turned from it to the packet of papers in the bottom of the box. These were carefully tied up in an outer wrapping with a piece of tape, and sealed.

On the outside was written in faded ink: "Only to be opened after my death."

Blake hesitated for an instant, wondering whether he ought to hand the packet over intact to the executors. The urgency of the case, however, induced him to set aside his scruples, on the off-chance that he might find some clue as to the motive of the crime.

He slid off the outer wrapping, and commenced to read. The first page bore the date, 1870, and began as follows:

"This is an account of a chapter in my life unknown to any of my dear friends and relatives here in England, and to save them pain I do not wish the facts to be revealed till after they, and I also, have passed the way of all flesh.

"Two years ago—in 1868, in fact—just after I finally came down from Oxford, and before I had any thought of taking up the career which now lies before me—the Church—it was arranged that I should travel for a while and see something of the world. Having visited most of the capitals of Europe, I went to the States, and from there drifted down into Mexico.

"During my stay in Mexico City I interested myself in politics to a certain extent, and was appalled by the intolerable tyranny of a certain high official of the State—a tyranny that amounted almost to brutality, so far as the poorer classes of the community were concerned.

"His actions offended my sense of justice to such an extent that one evening at a supper-party, in the company of many young Spaniards and Mexicans, I was carried away by my enthusiasm for his deposition, and emphatically announced my intention of joining any society that had the tyrant's overthrow at heart.

"It was then that I first heard of the society known as the 'Black Diamond,' an old-established circle of extreme political agitators, about which there was a good deal of mystery, and of which everyone was talking more or less wildly, and without accurate knowledge. I was curious, as was everyone else, and, though I did not know it at the time, there were three members of the society present at the supper in question.

"After the party broke up, however, these three men, who could see that I felt bitterly on the subject, came to me and asked me if I would really like to join.

" 'Of course I should,' I replied. I knew them for the wildest and most reckless of a wild set, but I did not intend to draw back.

" 'It may cost you your life,' said one of them. " 'And if you flinch from obeying the rules it certainly will. Perhaps, as you're an Englishman, you will be afraid to take the risk?'

"That nettled me, and made me more determined than ever.

" 'I'm not afraid of anything," I retorted angrily. Englishmen were by no means popular in Mexico at that time.

" 'Very well, then,' they answered. 'There is to be a meeting tomorrow night. We will call here for you, and, if you still wish it, you shall be elected.'

"What followed I will relate as briefly as possible. I went through some form of initiation, which even here I cannot write down, and took the oath, not realising what a terrible thing I was doing. Imagine my horror, therefore, when I found that I had joined a mad and criminal society which was practically a murder club!

"The procedure was as follows: The members, some forty in number, sat round a long table, and cards of a corresponding number was put into a bag and shaken. All these cards were blank except one, which was marked with a black diamond. The drawer of the black card was bound by his oath to kill the object of the society's hate—who at the time was the tyrant I mention—within seven days, the chosen one being himself condemned to die if for any reason he failed to fulfil his oath. The mad, pitiful, foolishness of it all!

"By ill-fortune—or, as I fancy, by deft manipulation—I drew the fatal black card that very first night. I flung it down on the table, and, in the midst of a wild uproar, declared that nothing on earth should compel me to commit murder; though they might try to kill me if they liked.

"Then I left them. The next morning the black card which I had thrown down was returned to me in a sealed envelope by a messenger. That same afternoon I fled from the city, and as soon as possible from America. Twice since than I have received threatening letters, here at home in England; but for the past year I have heard nothing, and hope that the infamous society has been broken up. I have written this confession to show into what criminal folly rashness and bad companions may lead a young man, and to ease my conscience of a burden which still lies heavy upon it, before entering upon that sacred calling in which I pray heaven I may make amends for the past.

"(Signed) CHARLES WIMBERLEY."

Blake laid the papers down, and stared out through the window at the garden beyond.

"Forty years ago," he muttered. "The thing's impossible! And yet, after all, nothing's impossible; and there seems to be no other conceivable motive. A Mexican—especially one who has probably gone to the bad—has curious ideas, and will wait for half a generation to secure his aim."

He was still staring through the window, lost in thought, when the butler entered with three yellow envelopes on a salver.

Blake took them and tore them open hurriedly. The first two proved unsatisfactory, the third, from a dealer whose name is known all over the world, turned out to be more to the point, however.

"Sold two of the variety you mention to an elderly man giving name of Anderson last week. Man who sold them will wait on you nine tonight."

Blake had had many dealings with the sender of the telegram, who, from the length of his reply, clearly understood that the matter was urgent.

He crumpled up the reply, and thrust it into his pocket. Then he replaced the papers in the casket, locked it, collected the boxes and the wrapping-paper, and returned to his rooms.

The man mentioned in the telegram, whose name was Mitchell, turned up punctually.

"The governor thought I'd better come up and see you, sir, as he guessed that there was probably something amiss, and you might want to ask a few questions."

"Quite right, Mr Mitchell. I'm much obliged. It is you, I understand, who had the selling of the snakes?"

"Yes, sir. The boss was away, and I was in charge. It was last Thursday when this man Anderson, as he called himself, came in—a small, neat figure of a man, very dapper and well-dressed, little grey beard carefully trimmed, and a waxed moustache, very black eyes and eye-brows, and spoke with a strong foreign accent. We get most sorts down our way in the course of business, and learn to size 'em up. This chap was a Spaniard, or from Mexico or Brazil; for all that he called himself Anderson."

Blake's eyes gleamed.

"What sort of age?"

"Well, sir, it's a bit hard to say. He'd got himself up a bit, and didn't look much more than fifty five; but when it came to moving he seemed a bit older—past sixty a goodish bit."

"What did he ask for?"

"Just came prowling about, as most of 'em do, said he'd like to have a look round if there was no objection. I showed him all the newest lots we'd got in, and then he asked, careless-like, whether we had any snakes ever. He'd got a friend who was interested in snakes, and collected 'em.

"It so happened we'd just got some rattlers in off a Savannah beat. He perked up when I showed them to him, and said he'd buy a couple. I offered to send them on, but he said no; he's take 'em if I could put 'em in a safe box. I did that easy enought, with some milk, and told him how to keep 'em warm and feed 'em. Then he paid me, and gave me half-a-crown to fetch him a hansom."

"They hadn't had their fangs drawn, I suppose?"

"You bet not, sir. Spitting poison all over the glass lid of the box they were when you stirred 'em up."

"You didn't note the number of the cab, or the address given?"

"No, sir; but after he'd gone I found this, sir. He'd left his cigarette-case behind. I showed it to the boss, and he locked it away for me; didn't know where to send it."

He produced a packet wrapped in tissue-paper form his pocket, and handed it over. Blake undid it carefully, and disclosed a large, flat, cigarette-case, with the monogram "Y. M." or "M. Y." engraved on it. Holding it by the edges, he examined it with a lens.

"I think this is going to be worth a five-pound note to you, Mitchell. I'll keep it for the present; there's nothing more, thank you. Goodnight."

Three days later Inspector Purvis called on Blake at his rooms. He was limping slightly, but seemed otherwise little the worse for his accident.

"Well, Mr. Blake," he said, "what of the Wimberley affair? I was hoping to have heard from you."

"I am ready to help you to arrest Cannon Wimberley's murderer whenever you please," replied Blake.

Purvis whistled.

"Murder, is it? Are you sure? I though there was something queer about the business; but I hadn't got as far as that."

"I have," said Blake curtly. "I dined at the same table with the man last night, and spoke to him."

Purvis whistled again softly.

"Who's your man. I'll get a warrant out at once, and be back in half an hour."

"Senor Manuel Yturbe," said Blake, "connected with one of the best-known families in Mexico. I'll drive down with you."

An hour later they dismissed the cab in front of a well-appointed block of flats, and Purvis followed Blake to the second floor. A silent-footed, foreign-looking manservant admitted them. Blake pushed past him unceremoniously, and entered the sitting-room.

An elderly, dapper-looking man was seated before a wood fire, smoking an excellent cigar.

"There is your man," said Blake. "Mr. Yturbe, this is Inspector Purvis, of Scotland yard. He has come to arrest you for the murder of Canon Wimberley."

Yturbe had half-risen to his feet in surprise as they entered. He re-seated himself, however, and continued to smoke placidly.

"I presume you have some proof of your accusation," he said, with a marked accent.

Blake laid some photographs on the table, also the cigarette-case, and the bird bones.

"They are here," he said sharply. "I discovered that Canon Wimberley received a parcel on the morning of his death; in that parcel were these bones. You will see here, Purvis, that rattlesnake's tooth was ingeniously inserted so that the point just projected, anyone handling this bone unsuspectingly was nearly certain to receive an injection of the virus. Canon Wimberley received two, and death resulted.

"I wired to various dealers, and discovered that a foreigner, giving the name of Anderson, recently bought two snakes and took them away with him. He was careless enough to leave behind him this cigarette-case bearing the initials 'M. Y.'

"I photographed the case, having carefully dusted it over with powder, and obtained this result: there are three distinct sets of finger-prints. Those marked **A** were made by a man named Mitchell, these others marked **B** are his master's; the others—nine in all—were made by the owner of the case.

"I also discovered a confession written a long time ago by the canon, concerning a certain society in Mexico—a murder club called the 'Black Diamond.' The canon joined this, and, discovering the truth, broke his oath.

"The members were all men of position, so I looked about for a Mexican or Spaniard—whose description and initials I already knew—possessing a well-known name. I applied to the Mexican Legation, and, as a result, one of the secretaries pointed out to me that Senor Manuel Yturbe had recently come to town, and usually dined at one of the more exclusive restaurants.

"He told me in confidence that as a young man this Yturbe had been very wild, and a bad lot, a noted duellist, and was now, though past sixty, little more than a professional gambler, and was believed to have been the organiser of the long-extinct 'Black Diamond Society.' I went the round of the restaurants, and soon discovered my man. The next night I dined at the same table with him, having privately told the waiter to carefully preserve the glass he drank out of, and keep it for me. This was done. Subsequently I powdered that also, and photographed it; here is the result. You can see for yourself that the finger-prints are identical.

"He bought the snakes, prepared his diabolical trap, and, after all these years, deliberately murdered the canon out of sheer malice!"

Yturbe rose to his feet slowly.

"Monsieur is very ingenious," he said, with a sneer. "If it is any satisfaction to him to know it. I once had the honour of being the president of the society he named. This Wimberley broke his oath, and for years I tried to find him. I did not know till recently that he had entered the Church. Having discovered him, I did not choose that his lack of faith or courage should go unpunished. Therefore I did what I have done. But if you think I will permit arrest—No! Look, senors!"

He whipped out a long, keen-bladed knife, set the hilt on the table, and before they could stop him, fell heavily forward on to the point. He only moved once again.

THE END

THE MYSTERIOUS DEATH IN PERCY STREET

by Baroness Orczy

First published in 1908

THE MYSTERIOUS DEATH IN PERCY STREET

Miss Polly Burton had had many an argument with Mr. Richard Frobisher about that old man in the corner, who seemed far more interesting and deucedly more mysterious than any of the crimes over which he philosophised.

Dick thought, moreover, that Miss Polly spent more of her leisure time now in that A.B.C. shop than she had done in his own company before, and told her so, with that delightful air of sheepish sulkiness which the male creature invariably wears when he feels jealous and won't admit it.

Polly liked Dick to be jealous, but she liked that old scarecrow in the A.B.C. shop very much too, and though she made sundry vague promises from time to time to Mr. Richard Frobisher, she nevertheless drifted back instinctively day after day to the teashop in Norfolk Street, Strand, and stayed there sipping coffee for as long as the man in the corner chose to talk.

On this particular afternoon she went to the A.B.C. shop with a fixed purpose, that of making him give her his views of Mrs. Owen's mysterious death in Percy Street.

The facts had interested and puzzled her. She had had countless arguments with Mr. Richard Frobisher as to the three great possible solutions of the puzzle—"Accident, Suicide, Murder?"

"Undoubtedly neither accident nor suicide," he said drily.

Polly was not aware that she had spoken. What an uncanny habit that creature had of reading her thoughts!

"You incline to the idea, then, that Mrs. Owen was murdered. Do you know by whom?"

He laughed, and drew forth the piece of string he always fidgeted with when unravelling some mystery.

"You would like to know who murdered that old woman?" he asked at last.

"I would like to hear your views on the subject," Polly replied.

"I have no views," he said drily. "No one can know who murdered the woman, since no one ever saw the person who did it. No one can give the faintest description of the mysterious man who alone could have committed that clever deed, and the police are playing a game of blind man's buff."

"But you must have formed some theory of your own," she persisted.

It annoyed her that the funny creature was obstinate about this point, and she tried to nettle his vanity.

"I suppose that as a matter of fact your original remark that 'there are no such things as mysteries' does not apply universally. There is a mystery—that of the death in Percy Street, and you, like the police, are unable to fathom it."

He pulled up his eyebrows and looked at her for a minute or two.

"Confess that that murder was one of the cleverest bits of work accomplished outside Russian diplomacy," he said with a nervous laugh. "I must say that were I the judge, called upon to pronounce sentence of death on the man who conceived the murder, I could not bring myself to do it. I would politely request the gentleman to enter our Foreign Office—we have need of such men. The whole *mise en scène* was truly artistic, worthy of its *milieu*—the Rubens Studios in Percy Street, Tottenham Court Road.

"Have you ever noticed them? They are only studios by name, and are merely a set of rooms in a corner house, with the windows slightly enlargd, and the rents charged accordingly in consideration of that additional five inches of smokey daylight, filtering through dusty windows. On the ground floor there is the order office of some stained glass works, with a workshop in the rear, and on the first floor landing a small room allotted to the caretaker, with gas, coal, and fifteen shillings a week, for which princely income she is deputed to keep tidy and clean the general aspect of the house.

"Mrs. Owen, who was the caretaker there, was a quiet, respectable woman, who eked out her scanty wages by sundry—mostly very meagre—tips doled out to her by impecunious artists in exchange for promiscuous domestic services in and about the respective studios.

"But if Mrs. Owen's earnings were not large, they were very regular, and she had no fastidious tastes. She and her cockatoo lived on her wages; and all the tips added up, and never spent, year after year, went to swell a very comfortable little account at interest in the Birkbeck Bank. This little account had mounted up to a very tidy sum, and the thrifty widow—or old maid—no one ever knew which she was—was generally referred to by the young artists of the Rubens Studios as a 'lady of means.' But this is a digression.

"No one slept on the premises except Mrs. Owen and her cockatoo. The rule was that one by one as the tenants left their rooms in the evening they took their respective keys to the caretaker's room. She would then, in the early morning, tidy and dust the studios and the office downstairs, lay the fire and carry up coals.

80

"The foreman of the glass works was the first to arrive in the morning. He had a latchkey, and let himself in, after which it was the custom of the house that he should leave the street door open for the benefit of the other tenants and their visitors.

"Usually, when he came at about nine o'clock, he found Mrs. Owen busy about the house doing her work, and he had often a brief chat with her about the weather, but on this particular morning of February 2nd he neither saw nor heard her. However, as the shop had been tidied and the fire laid, he surmised that Mrs. Owen had finished her work earlier than usual, and thought no more about it. One by one the tenants of the studios turned up, and the day sped on without any one's attention being drawn noticeably to the fact that the caretaker had not appeared upon the scene.

"It had been a bitterly cold night, and the day was even worse; a cutting north-easterly gale was blowing, there had been a great deal of snow during the night which lay quite thick on the ground, and at five o'clock in the afternoon, when the last glimmer of the pale winter daylight had disappeared, the confraternity of the brush put palette and easel aside and prepared to go home. The first to leave was Mr. Charles Pitt; he locked up his studio and, as usual, took his key into the caretaker's room.

"He had just opened the door when an icy blast literally struck him in the face; both the windows were wide open, and the snow and sleet were beating thickly into the room, forming already a white carpet upon the floor.

"The room was in semi-obscurity, and at first Mr. Pitt saw nothing, but instinctively realising that something was wrong, he lit a match, and saw before him the spectacle of that awful and mysterious tragedy which has ever since puzzled both police and public. On the floor, already half covered by the drifting snow, lay the body of Mrs. Owen face downwards, in a nightgown, with feet and ankles bare, and these and her hands were of a deep purple colour; whilst in a corner of the room, huddled up with the cold, the body of the cockatoo lay stark and stiff."

"At first there was only talk of a terrible accident, the result of some inexplicable carelessness which perhaps the evidence at the inquest would help to elucidate.

"Medical assistance came too late; the unfortunate woman was indeed dead, frozen to death, inside her own room. Further examination showed that she had received a severe blow at the back of the head, which must have stunned her and caused her to fall, helpless, beside the open window. Temperature at five degrees below zero had done the rest. Detective Inspector Howell discovered close to the window a wrought-iron gas bracket, the height of which corresponded exactly with the bruise at the back of Mrs. Owen's head.

"Hardly however had a couple of days elapsed when public curiosity was whetted by a few startling headlines, such as the halfpenny evening papers alone know how to concoct.

" 'The mysterious death in Percy street.' 'Is it Suicide or Murder?' 'Thrilling details—Strange developments.' 'Sensational Arrest.'

"What had happened was simply this:

"At the inquest a few certainly very curious facts connected with Mrs. Owen's life had come to light, and this had led to the apprehension of a young man of very respectable parentage on a charge of being concerned in the tragic death of the unfortunate caretaker.

"To begin with, it happened that her life, which in an ordinary way should have been very monotonous and regular, seemed, at any rate latterly, to have been more than usually chequered and excited. Every witness who had known her in the past concurred in the statement that since October last a great change had come over the worthy and honest woman.

"I happen to have a photo of Mrs. Owen as she was before this great change occurred in her quiet and uneventful life, and which led, as far as the poor soul was concerned, to such disastrous results.

"Here she is to the life, added the funny creature, placing the photo before Polly—"as respectable, as stodgy, as uninteresting as it is well possible for a member of your charming sex to be; not a face, you will admit, to lead any youngster to temptation or to induce him to commit a crime.

"Nevertheless, one day all the tenants of the Rubens Studios were surprised and shocked to see Mrs. Owen, quiet, respectable, Mrs. Owen, sallying forth at six o'clock in the afternoon, attired in an extravagent bonnet and a cloak trimmed with imitaton astrakhan which—slightly open in front— displayed a gold locket and chain of astonishing proportions.

"Many were the comments, the hints, the bits of sarcasm levelled at the worthy woman by the frivolous confraternity of the brush.

"The plot thickened when from that day forth a complete change came over the worthy caretaker of the Rubens Studios. While she appeared day after day before the astonished gaze of the tenants and the scandalised looks of the neighbours, attired in new and extravagent dresses, her work was hopelessly neglected, and she was always 'out' when wanted.

"There was, of course, much talk and comments in various parts of the Rubens Studios on the subject of Mrs. Owen's 'dissipations.' The tenants began to put two and two together, and after a very little while the general consensus of opinion became firmly established that the honest caretaker's demoralisation coincided week for week, almost day for day, with young Greenhill's establishment in No. 8 Studio.

"Everyone had remarked that he stayed much later in the evening than any one else, and yet no one presumed that he stayed for purposes of work. Suspicions soon rose to certainty when Mrs. Owen and Arthur Greenhill were seen by one of the glass workmen dining together at Gambia's Restaurant in Tottenham Court Road.

"The workman, who was having a cup of tea at the counter, noticed particularly that when the bill was paid the money came out of Mrs. Owen's purse. The dinner had been sumptuous—veal cutlets, a cut from the joint, dessert, coffee and liqueurs. Finally the pair left the restaurant apparently very gay, young Greenhill smoking a choice cigar.

"Irregularities such as these were bound sooner or later to come to the ears and eyes of Mr. Allman, the landlord of the Rubens Studios; and a month after the New Year, without further warning, he gave her a week's notice to quit his house.

"'Mrs. Owen did not seem the least bit upset when I gave her notice,' Mr. Allman declared in his evidence at the inquest; 'on the contrary, she told me that she had ample means, and had only worked lattery for the sake of something to do. She added that she had plenty of friends who would look after her, for she had a nice little pile to leave to anyone who would know how "to get the right side of her."

"Nevertheless, in spite of this cheeful interview, Miss Bedford, the tenant of No. 6 Studio, had stated that when she took her key to the caretaker's room at 6.30 that afternoon she found Mrs. Owen in tears. The caretaker refused to be comforted, nor would she speak of her trouble to Miss Bedford.

"Twenty-four hours later she was found dead.

"The coroner's jury returned an open verdict, and Detective-Inspector Jones was charged by the police to make some enquiries about young Mr. Greenhill, whose intimacy with the unfortunate woman had been universally commented upon.

"The detective, however, pushed his investigations as far as the Birkbeck Bank. There he discovered that after her interview with Mr. Allman, Mrs. Owen had withdrawn the money she had on deposit, some £800, the result of twenty-five years' saving and thrift.

"But the immediate result of Detective-Inspector Jones's labours was that Mr. Arthur Greenhill, lithographer, was brought before the magistrate at Bow Street on the charge of being concerned in the death of Mrs. Owen, caretaker of the Rubens Studios, Percy Street.

"Now that magisterial enquiry is one of the few interesting ones which I had the misfortune to miss," continued the man in the corner, with a nervous shake of the shoulders. "But you know as well as I do how the attitude of the young prisoner impressed the magistrate and police so unfavourably that, with every new witness brought forward, his position became more and more unfortunate.

"Yet he was a good-looking, rather coarsely built young fellow, with one of those awful Cockney accents which literally make one jump. But he looked painfully nervous, stammered at every word spoken, and repeatedly gave answers entirely at random.

"His father acted as lawyer for him, a rough-looking elderly man, who had the appearance of a common country attorney rather than of a London solicitor.

"The police had built up a fairly strong case against the lithographer. Medical evidence revealed nothing new: Mrs. Owen had died from exposure, the blow at the back of the head not being sufficiently serious to cause anything but temporary disablement. When the medical officer had been called in, death had intervened for some time; it was quite impossible to say how long, whether one hour, or five, or twelve.

"The appearance and state of the room, when the unfortunate woman was found by Mr. Charles Pitt, were again gone over in minute detail. Mrs. Owen's clothes, which she had worn during the day, were folded neatly on a chair. The Key of her cupboard was in the pocket of her dress. The door had been slightly ajar, but both the windows were wide open; one of them, which had the sash-line broken, had been fastened up most scientifically with a piece of rope.

"Mrs. Owen had obviously undressed preparatory to going to bed, and the magistrate very naturally soon made the remark how untenable the theory of an accident must be. No one in their five senses would undress with a temperature at below zero, and the windows wide open.

"After these preliminary statements the cashier of the Birbeck was called and he related the caretaker's visit at the bank.

" 'It was then about one o'clock,' he stated. 'Mrs. Owen called and presented a cheque to self for £827, the amount of her balance. She seemed exceedingly happy and cheerful, and talked about needing plenty of cash, as she was going abroad to join her nephew, for whom she would in future keep house. I warned her about being sufficiently careful with so large a sum, and parting from it injudiciously, as women of her class are very apt to do. She laughingly declared that not only was she careful of it in the present, but meant to be so for the far-off future, for she intended to go that very day to a lawyer's office to make a will.'

"The cashier's evidence was certainly startling in the extreme, since in the window's room no trace of any kind was found of any money; against that, two of the notes handed over by the bank to Mrs. Owen on that day were cashed by young Greenhill on the very morning of her mysterious death. One was handed in by him to the West End Clothiers Company, in payment for a suit of clothes, and the other he changed at the Post Office in Oxford Street.

"After that all the evidence had of necessity to be gone through again on the subject of young Greenhill's intimacy with Mrs. Owen. He listened to it all with an air of the most painful nervousness, his cheeks were positively green, his lips seemed dry and parched, for he repeatedly passed his tongue over them, and when Constable E18 deposed that at 2 a.m. on the morning of February 2nd he had seen the accused and spoken to him at the corner of Percy Street and Tottenham Court Road, young Greenhill all but fainted.

"The contention of the police was that the caretaker had been murdered and robbed during that night before she went to bed, that young Greenhill had done the murder, seeing that he was the only person known to have been intimate with the woman, and that it was, moreover, proved unquestionably that he was in the immediate neighbourhood of the Rubens Studios at an extraordinarily late hour of the night.

"His own account of himself, and of that same night, could certainly not be called very satisfactory. Mrs. Owen was a relative of his late mother's, he declared. He himself was a lithographer by trade, with a good deal of time and leisure on his hands. He certainly had employed some of that time in taking the old woman to various places of amusement. He had on more than one occasion suggested that she should give up menial work, and come and live with him, but, unfortunately, she was a great deal imposed upon by her nephew, a man of the name of Owen, who exploited the good-natured woman in every possible way, and who had on more than one occasion made severe attacks upon her savings at the Birbeck Bank.

"Severely cross-examined by the prosecuting counsel about this supposed relative of Mrs. Owen, Greenhill admitted that he did not know him—had, in fact, never seen him. He knew that his name was Owen, and that was all. His chief occupation consisted in sponging on the kind-hearted old woman, but he only went to see her in the evenings, when he presumably knew that she would be alone, and invariably after all the tenants of the Rubens Studios had left for the day.

"I don't know whether at this point it strikes you at all, as it did both magistrate and counsel, that there was a direct contradiction in this statement and the one made by the cashier of the Birkbeck on the subject of his last conversation with Mrs. Owen. 'I am going abroad to join my nephew, for whom I am going to keep house,' was what the unfortunate woman had said.

"Now Greenhill, in spite of his nervousness and at times contradictory answers, strictly adhered to his point, that there was a nephew in London, who came frequently to see his aunt.

"Anyway, the savings of the murdered woman could not be taken as evidence in law. Mr. Greenhill senior put the objection adding: 'There may have been two nephews,' which the magistrate and the prosecution were bound to admit.

"With regard to the night immediately preceding Mrs. Owen's death, Greenhill stated that he had been with her to the theatre, had seen her home, and had had some supper with her in her room. Before he left her, at 2 a.m., she had of her own accord made him a present of £10, saying: 'I am a sort of an aunt to you, Arthur, and if you don't have it, Bill is sure to get it.'

"She had seemed rather worried in the early part of the evening, but later on she cheered up.

" 'Did she speak at all about this nephew of hers or about her money affairs?' asked the magistrate.

"Again the young man hesitated, but said, 'No! she did not mention either Owen or her money affairs.'

"If I remember rightly," added the man in the corner, "for recollect I was not present, the case was here adjourned. But the magistrate would not grant bail. Greenhill was removed looking more dead than alive—though every one remarked that Mr. Greenhill senior looked determined and not the least worried. In the course of his examination on behalf of his son, of the medical officer and one or two other witnesses, he had very ably tried to confuse them on the subject of the hour at which Mrs. Owen was last known to be alive.

"He made a very great point of the fact that the usual morning's work was done throughout the house when the inmates arrived. Was it conceivable, he argued, that a woman would do that kind of work overnight, especially as she was going out to the theatre, and therefore would wish to dress in her smarter clothes? It certainly was a very nice point levelled against the prosecution, who promptly retorted: Just as conceivable as that a woman in those circumstances of life should, having done her work, undress beside an open window at nine o'clock in the morning with the snow beating into the room.

"Now it seems that Mr. Greenhill senior could produce any amount of witnesses who could help to prove a conclusive *alibi* on behalf of his son, if only some time subsequent to that fatal 2 a.am the murdered woman had been seen alive by some chance passer-by.

"However, he was an able man and an earnest one, and I fancy the magistrate felt some sympathy for his strenuous endeavours on his son's behalf. He granted a week's adjournment, which seemed to satisfy Mr. Greenhill completely.

"In the meanwhile the papers had talked of and almost exhausted the subject of the mystery in Percy Street. There had been, as you no doubt know from personal experience, innumerable arguments on the puzzling alternatives:

"Accident?

"Suicide?

"Murder?

"A week went by, and then the case against young Greenhill was resumed. of course the court was crowded. It needed no great penetration to remark at once that the prisoner looke more hopeful, and his father quite elated.

"Again a great deal of minor evidence was taken, and then came the turn of the defence. Mr. Greenhill called Mrs. Hall, confectioner, of Percy Street, opposite the Rubens Studios. She deposed that at 8 o'clock in the morning of February 2nd, while she was tidying her shop window, she saw the caretaker of the Studios opposite, as usual, on her knees, her head and body wrapped in a shawl, cleaning her front steps. Her husband also saw Mrs Owen, and Mrs. Hall remarked to her husband how thankful she was that her own shop had tiled steps, which did not need scrubbing on so cold a morning.

"Mr Hall, confectioner, of the same address, corroborated this statement, and Mr. Greenhill, with absolute triumph, produced a third witness, Mrs. Martin, of Percy Street, who from her window on the second floor had, at 7.30 a.m., seen the caretaker shaking mats outside her front door. The description this witness gave of Mrs. Owen's get-up, with the shawl round her head, coincided point by point with that given by Mr. and Mrs. Hall.

"After that Mr. Greenhill's task became an easy one; his son was at home having his breakfast at 8 o'clock that morning—not only himself, but his servants would testify to that.

'The weather had been so bitter that the whole of that day Arthur had not stirred from his own fireside. Mrs. Owen was murderd after 8 a.m. on that day, since she was seen alive by three people at that hour, therefore his son could not have murdered Mrs. Owen. The police must find the criminal elsewhere, or else bow to the opinion originally expressed by the public that Mrs. Owen had met with a terrible untoward accident, or that perhaps she may have wilfully sought her own death in that extraordinary and tragic fashion.

"Before young Greenhill was finally discharged, one or two witnesses were again examined, chief among these being the foreman of the glassworks. He had turned up at Rubens Studios at 9 o'clock, and been in business all day. He averred positively that he did not specially notice any suspicious-looking individual crossing the hall that day. 'But,' he remarked with a smile, 'I don't sit and watch every one who goes up and down the stairs. I am too busy for that. The street door is always left open; any one can walk, in up or down, who knows the way.'

"That there was a mystery in connection with Mrs. Owen's death—of that the police have remained perfectly convinced; whether young Greenhill held the key of that mystery or not they have never found to this day.

"I could enlighten them as to the cause of the young lithographer's anxiety at the magisterial inquiry, but, I assure you, I do not care to do the work of the police for them. Why should I? Greenhill will never suffer from unjust suspicions. He and his father alone—besides myself—know in what a terribly tight corner he all but found himself.

"The young man did not reach home till nearly five o'clock that morning. His last train had gone; he had to walk, lost his way, and wandered about Hampstead for hours. Think what his position would have been if the worthy confectioners of Percy Street had not seen Mrs. Owen 'wrapped up in a shawl, on her knees, doing the front steps.'

"Moreover, Mr. Greenhill senior is a solicitor, who has a small office in John Street, Bedford Row. The afternoon before her death Mrs. owen had been to that office and had there made a will by which she had left all her savings to young Arthur Greenhill, lithographer. Had that will been in other paternal hands, it would have been proved, in the natural course of such things, and one other link would have been added to the chain which nearly dragged Arthur Greenhill to the gallows— 'the link of a very strong motive.'

"Can you wonder that the young man turned livid, until such time as it was proved beyond a doubt that the murdered woman was alive hours after he had reached the safe shelter of his home.

"I saw you smile when I used the word 'murdered,'" continued the man in the corner, growing quite excited now that he was approaching the *dénouement* of the story. "I know that the public, after the magistrate had discharged Arthur Greenhill were quite satisfied to think that the mystery in Percy Street was a case of accident—or suicide."

"No," replied Polly, "there could be no question of suicide for two very distinct reasons."

He looked at her with some degree of astonishment. She supposed that he was amazed at her venturing to form an opinion of her own.

"And may I ask what, in your opinion, these reasons are?" he asked very sarcastically.

"To begin with, the question of money," she said— "has any more of it been traced so far?"

"Not another £5 note," he said with a chuckle; "they were all cashed in Paris during the Exhibition, and you have no conception how easy a thing that is to do; at any of the hotels or small *agents de change*."

'That nephew was a clever blackguard," she commented.

"You believe, then in the existence of that nephew?"

"Why should I doubt it? Some one must have existed who was sufficiently familiar with the house to go about in it in the middle of the day without attracting any one's attention."

"In the middle of the day?" he said with a chuckle.

"Any time after 8.30 in the morning."

"So you, too, believe in the 'caretaker, wrapped up in a shawl,' cleaning her front step?" he queried.

"But——"

"It never struck you, in spite of the training your intercourse with me must have given you, that the person who carefully did all the work in the Rubens Studies, laid the fires and carried up the coals, merely did it in order to gain time, in order that the bitter frost might really and effectually do its work, and Mrs. Owen be not missed until she was truely dead."

"But——" suggested Polly again.

"It never struck you that one of the greatest secrets of succesful crime is to lead the police astray with regard to the time when the crime was committed. That was, if you remember, the great point in the Regent's Park murder.

"In this case the 'nephew,' since we admit his existence, would—even if he were ever found, which is doubtful—be able to prove as good an *alibi* as young Greenhill."

"But I don't understand——"

"How the murder was committed?" he said eagerly, "Surely you can see it all for yourself, since you admit the 'nephew'—a scamp, perhaps—who sponges on the good-natured woman. He terrorises and threatens her, so much so that she fancies her money is no longer safe even in the Birkbeck Bank. Women of that class are apt at times to mistrust the Bank of England. Anyway, she withdraws her money. Who knows what she meant to do with it in the immediate future?

"In any case, she wishes to secure it after her death to a young man whom she likes, and who has known how to win her good graces. That afternoon the nephew begs, entreats for more money; they have a row; the poor woman is in tears, and is only temporarily consoled by a pleasant visit at the threatre.

"At 2 o'clock in the morning young Greenhill parts from her. Two minutes later the nephew knocks at the door. He comes with a plausible tale of having missed his last train, and asks for 'a shake down' somewhere in the house. The good-natured woman suggests a sofa in one of the studios, and then quietly prepares to go to bed. The rest is very simple and elementary. The nephew sneaks into his aunt's room, finds her standing in her nightgown; he demands money with threats of violence; terrified, she staggers, knocks her head against the gas bracket, and falls on the floor stunned, while the nephew seeks for her keys and takes possession of the £800. You will admit that the subsequent *mise en scène*—is worthly of a genius.

"No struggle, not the usual hideous accessories round a crime. Only the open windows, the bitter north-easterly gale, and the heavily falling snow—two silent accomplices, as silent as the dead.

"After that the murderer, with perfect presence of mind busies himself in the house, doing the work which will ensure that Mrs. Owens shall not be missed, at any rate, for some time. He dusts and tidies; some few hours later he even slips on his aunt's skirt and bodice, wraps his head in a shawl, and boldy allows those neighbours who are astir to see what they believe to be Mrs. Owen. Then he goes back to her room, resumes his normal appearance, and quietly leaves the house."

"He may have been seen."

"He undoubtedly *was* seen by two or three people, but no one thought anything of seeing a man leave the house at that hour. It was very cold, the snow was falling thickly, and as he wore a muffler round the lower part of his face, those who saw him would not undertake to know him again."

"That man was never seen nor heard of again?" Polly asked.

"He has disappeared off the face of the earth. The police are searching for him, and perhaps some day they will find him—then society will be rid of one of the most ingenious men of the age.

He had paused, absorbed in meditation. The young girl also was silent. Some memory too vague as yet to take a definite form was persistently haunting her—one thought was hammering away in her brain, and playing havoc with her nerves. That thought was the inexplicable feeling within her that there was something in connection with that hideous crime which she ought to recollect, something which—if she could only remember what it was—would give her the clue to the tragic mystery, and for once ensure her triumph over this self-conceited and sarcastic scarecrow in the corner.

He was watching her through his great bone-rimmed spectacles, and she could see the knuckles of his bony hands, just above the top of the table, fidgeting, fidgeting, fidgeting, till she wondered if there existed another set of fingers in the world which could undo the knots his lean ones made in the tiresome piece of string.

Then suddenly—*à propos* of nothing, Polly *remembered*—the whole thing stood before her, short and clear like a vivid flash of lightning—Mrs. Owen lying dead in the snow beside her open window; one of them with a broken sash-line, tied up most scientifically with a piece of string. She remembered the talk there had been at the time about this improvised sash-line.

That was after young Greenhill had been discharged, and the question of suicide had been voted an impossibility.

Polly remembered that in the illustrated papers photographs appeared of this wonderfully knotted piece of string, so contrived that the weight of the frame could but tighten the knots, and thus keep the window open. She remembered that people deduced many things from the improvised sash-line, chief among these deductions being that the murderer was a sailor—so wonderful, so complicated, so numerous were the knots which secured that window-frame.

But Polly know better. In her mind's eye she saw those fingers, rendered doubly nervous by the fearful cerebral excitement, grasping at first mechanically, even thoughtlessly, a bit of twine with which to secure the window; then the ruling habit strongest through all, the girl could see it; the lean and ingenious fingers fidgeting, fidgeting with that piece of string, tying knot after knot, more wonderful, more complicated, than any she had yet witnessed.

"If I were you," she said, without daring to look into that corner where he sat, "I would break myself of the habit of perpetually making knots in a piece of string."

He did not reply, and at last Polly ventured to look up—the corner was empty, and through the glass door beyond the desk, where he had just deposited his few coppers, she saw the tails of his tweed coat, his extraordinary hat, his meagre, shrivelled-up personality, fast disappearing down the street.

Miss Polly Burton (of the *Evening Observer*) was married the other day to Mr. Richard Frobisher (of the *London Mail*). She has never set eyes on the man in the corner from that day to this.

A HAPPY
SOLUTION
by Raymund Allen

First published in 1916

The portmanteau, which to Kenneth Dale's strong arm had been little more than a feather-weight on leaving the station, seemed to have grown heavier by magic in the course of the half-mile that brought him to Lord Churt's country house. He put the portmanteau down in the porch with a sense of relief to his cramped arm, and rang the bell.

He had to wait for a few minutes, and then Lord Churt opened the door in person. His round, rubicund face, that would hardly have required any make-up to present an excellent "Mr Pickwick," beamed a welcome. "Come in, my dear boy, come in. I'm delighted to see you. I wish you a merry Christmas."

It was Christmas Eve, and his manner was bubbling over with the kindliness appropriate to the season. He seized the portmanteau and carried it into the hall.

"I am my own footman and parlour-maid and everything else for the moment. Packed all the servants off to a Christmas entertainment at the village school and locked the doors after 'em. My wife's gone, too, and Aunt Blaxter."

"Ah! Norah?" Kenneth inquired.

"Ah! Norah!" Churt answered, with a friendly clap on Kenneth's shoulder. "Norah's the only person that really matters, of course she is, and quite right too. Norah stayed in to send off a lot of Christmas cards, and I fancy she is still in her room, but she must have disposed of the cards, because they are in the letter-bag. She would have been on the the look-out for you, no doubt, but your letter said you were not coming."

"Yes, I know. I thought I couldn't get away, but to-day my chief's heart was softened, and he said he would manage to do without me till the day after to-morrow. So I made a rush for the two-fifteen, and just caught it."

"And here you are as a happy suprise for your poor, disappointed Norah—and for us all," he added, genially.

"I hope you approve of my *fiancée*," Kenneth remarked, with a smile that expressed confidence as to the answer.

"My dear Kenneth," Churt replied, "I can say with sincerity that I think her both beautiful and charming. We were very glad to ask her here, and her singing is a great pleasure to us." He hesitated for a moment before continuing. "You must forgive us cautious old people if we think the engagement just a little bit precipitate. As Aunt Blaxter was saying to-day, you can't really know her very well on such a short acquaintance, and you know nothing at all of her people."

Kenneth mentally cursed Aunt Blaxter for a vinegar-blooded old killjoy, but did not express any part of the sentiment aloud.

"We must have another talk about your great affair later," Churt went on. "Now come along to the library. I am just finishing a game of chess with Sir James Winslade, and then we'll go and find where Miss Norah is hiding."

He stopped at a table in the passage that led from the hall to the library, and took a bunch of keys out of his pocket. "She was sending you a letter, so there can be no harm in our rescuing it out of the bag." He unlocked the private letter-bag and turned out a pile of letters on to the table, muttering an occasional comment as he put them back, one by one, in the bag, in his search for the letter he was looking for. "Aunt Emma—ah, I ought to have written to her to; must write for her birthday instead. Mrs Dunn—same thing there, I'm afraid Red Cross—hope that won't get lost; grand work, the Red Cross. Ah, here we are: 'Kenneth Dale, Esq., 31, Valpy Street, London S. W.' " He tumbled the rest of the letters back into the bag and re-locked it. "Put it in your pocket and come along, or Winslade will think I am never coming back."

He was delayed a few moments longer, however, to admit the servants on their return from the village, and he handed the bag to one of them to be taken to the post-office.

In the library Sir James Winslade was seated at the chess-board, and Churt's private secretary, Gornay, a tall, slender figure, with a pale complexion and dark, clever eyes, was watching the game.

The secretary greeted Kenneth rather frigidly, and turned to Churt. "Have the letters gone to post yet?"

"Yes; did yo want to send any?"

"Only a card that I might have written," Gornay answered, "but it isn't of any consequence"; and he sat down again beside the chess-players.

Churt had the black pieces, black nominally only, for actually they were the little red pieces of a travelling board. He appeared to have got into difficulties, and, greatly to the satisfaction of

Kenneth, who was impatient to go in quest of Norah, the game came to an end after a few more moves.

"I don't see any way out of this," Churt remarked, after final, perplexed survey of the position. "You come at me, next move, with queen or knight, and, either way, I am done for. It is your game. I resign."

"A lucky win for you, Sir James," Gornay observed.

"Why lucky?" Winslade asked. "You told us we had both violated every sound principle of development in the opening, but could Black have done any better for the last few move?"

"He can win the game as the pieces now stand," Gornay answered.

He proved the statement by making a few moves on the board, and then replaced the pieces as they had been left.

"Well, it's your game fair and square, all the same," Churt remarked good-humouredly. "I should never have found the right reply for myself."

Gornay continued to study the board with attention, and his face assumed an expression of keenness, as though he had discovered some fresh point to interest him in the position. At the moment Kenneth merely chafed at the delay. It was an hour or so later only that the secretary's comments on the game assumed for him a vital importance that made him recall them with particularity.

"If the play was rather eccentric sometimes, I must say it was bold and dashing enough on both sides," Gornay commented. "For instance, when Lord Churt gave up his knight for nothing, and when you gave him the choice of taking your queen with either of two pawns at your queen's knight's

WHITE.

BLACK.

Black to play and win.

sixth." He turned to Churt. "Possibly you might have done better to take the queen with the bishop's pawn instead of with the rook's."

"I daresay, I daresay," Churt replied. "I should have probably got into a mess, whatever I played. But come along, now, all of you , and see if we can find some tea."

Kenneth contrived, before entering the drawing-room, to intercept Norah for an exchange of greetings in private, and her face was still radiant with the delight of the unexpected meeting as they entered the room.

After tea Sir James carried off the secretary to keep him company in the smoking-room, and Churt turned to Norah. "You must sing one of the Christmas carols you promised us, and then you young folk may go off to the library to talk over your own private affairs. I know you must both be longing to get away from us old fogies."

"Thank you, Lord Churt, for 'old fogie,' on behalf of your wife and myself," Aunt Blaxter commented, with a mild sarcasm that somehow failed of its intended playful effect. But Norah had sat down at once to the piano, and her voice rang out in a joyous carol before he could frame a suitable reply.

A second carol was asked for, that the others might join in, and in the course of it Kenneth's hand came upon the letter in his pocket. He was opening the envelope as Norah rose from the piano. Her eye caught her own handwriting and she blushed very red. "Be careful, Ken. Don't let anything fail out!" she cried in alarm.

Thus warned, he drew the letter out delicately, being careful to leave in the envelope a little curl of brown hair, a lover's token that she would have been shy to see exposed to the eyes of the others. But, in his care for this, a thin bit of paper fluttered from the fold of the letter to the carpet, and all eyes instinctively followed it. It was a Bank of England note for a thousand pounds.

Kenneth looked at Norah in wonder, but got no enlightenment. Then at Lord Churt, as the bare possibility occurred to his mind that, in a Christmas freak of characteristic generosity, he might have somehow contrived to get in enclosed with her letter. But Churt's dumbfounded expression was not the acting of any genial comedy. His hands trembled as he put on his glasses to compare an entry in his pocket-book with the number on the note. He was the first to break the amazed silence. "This is a most extra-ordinary thing. This is the identical bank-note that I put into the Red Cross envelope this afternoon as my Christmas gift, the very same that I got for the purpose of sending anonymously and that you ladies were interested to inspect at breakfast time."

Each looked at the others for an explanation, till all eyes settled on Norah, as the person who might be expected to give one.

Churt, looked vexed and troubled, Aunt Blaxter severely suspicious, as she saw that the girl remained silent, with a face that was losing its colour. "As the note was found in a letter sent by Norah, she should be the natural person to explain how it got there," she remarked.

"I haven't the remotest notion how it got there," Norah replied. "I can only say that I did not put it there, and that I never saw it again since breakfast time, until it dropped out of my letter a few moments ago."

"Very strange," Aunt Blaxter remarked, drily. Kenneth turned upon her hotly. "You don't suggest that Norah stole the note, I imagine!"

"My dear people," Churt intervened soothingly, "do let us keep our heads cool, and not have any unpleasant scene."

Kenneth still glared. "If Norah had put the note into this envelope, she would have referred to it in her letter. I suppose you will accept my word that she doesn't."

"Read out the postcript, Ken," Norah requested. "Miss Blaxter may like to suggest that it refers to the note." The girl looked at her with a face that was now blazing with anger, and Kenneth read out: "P.S. Don't let anybody see what I am sending you!" It had not occurred to him that it could be taken as anything but a jesting reference to the lock of hair, the note of exclamation at the end giving the effect of "As though I should ever dream you would," or some equivalent. The matter was growing too serious for any shamefacedness, and he produced the lock of hair in explanation. It was cruel luck, he reflected, that the unfortunate postcript should be capable of misconstruction. He had counted on Norah's making a triumphant conquest of the Churt household, and it was exceedingly galling to find her, instead, exposed to an odious suspicion. Aunt Blaxter's demeanour was all that more maddening that he could think of no means to prove its unreasonableness. He looked gratefully at Lady Churt, as her gentle voice gave the discussion a fresh turn. "How long has Mr. Gornay been with us?" she asked her husband.

Churt looked shocked. "My dear, we musn't make any rash insinuations in a matter of this kind. What possible motive could Gornay have for putting the note into Norah's letter, if he meant to steal it? Besides, my evidence clears him."

"Would you mind telling us what you did with the note after you showed it at the breakfast table this morning?" Kenneth asked.

"I'll tell you exactly," Churt answered. "When it had made the round of the breakfast table, I put it back in my pocket-book and kept it in my pocket till this afternoon. It was while we were playing chess that I remembered that the bag would be going to post earlier than usual, and I put the note in the Red Cross envelope with the printed address and stuck it down and put it into the bag. I came straight back to the library, and I remember being surprised at the move I found Winslade had played because he was offering me his queen for nothing. Just at that moment it occurred to my mind that Norah had probably already put her letters into the bag, and that, if so, I might as well lock it at once, for fear of forgetting to do so later. I looked at the chess-board for a few minutes, standing up, and then went and found that Norah's letters were in the bag, and I locked it, and came back and took Winslade's queen."

"But I don't quite see what all that has to do with Mr. Gornay or how it clears him." Lady Churt remarked.

"Why, my dear, whoever took the note out of one envelope, and put it into the other must have done so in the few minutes between my two visits to the bag. It was the only time that the letter was in the bag without its being locked. And during that time Gornay was watching the chess, so it can't have been him."

"Was he in the library all the time you were playing?" Kenneth asked.

"I can't say that," Churt replied. "I don't think he was I didn't notice particularly. But I am positive that he did not enter or leave the room while I was standing looking at Winslade move, and he must have been there when Winslade offered his queen and when I took it, because he was commenting on those very moves after the game was finished, and suggesting that I might have done better to take with the other pawn. You heared him yourself."

"Yes," Kenneth answered. "I follow that. But there is such a thing as picking a lock, you know."

"The makers guarantee that it can't be done to this one," Churt answered, "and the key has always been in my possession, so he couldn't have had a duplicate made, even if there had been any time."

Norah interposed in a voice that trembled with indignation. "In short, Lord Churt, you think the evidence conclusive against the only other person, except Sir James Winslade, who was in the house. I have only my word to give against it."

"It is worth all the evidence in the world," Kenneth cried, and she thanked her champion with a bright glance.

"Lady Churt is quite right," Kennneth went on. "I'd stake my life it was that sneaking Gornay. Have him in here now, and see if his face doesn't show his guilt when I call him a thief."

"Not for the world!" Churt exclaimed, aghast. "We should have a most painful scene. This is no case for rash precipitancy." He assumed the air of judicial solemnity with which, from the local bench, he would fine a rascal five shillings who ought to have gone down for six months. "I entirely refuse to entertain any suspicion of anybody under this roof, guests, servants, or anyone else. It will probably turn out that some odd little accident has occurred, that will seem simple enough when it is explained. On the other hand, it is just conceivable that some evil-disposed person from outside should have got into the house, though I confess I can't understand the motive of their action if they did. In any case, I feel it my duty, for the credit of my household, to have the matter cleared up by the proper authority."

"What do yo mean by the proper authority?" Lady Churt asked. "I didn't think the local police were very clever that time when poor Kelpie got stolen?"

The Aberdeen terrier at her feet looked up at the sound of his name, and Churt continued: "I shall telephone to Scotland Yard. If Shapland is there, I am sure he would come down at once in his car. He could be here in less than two hours. Until he, or somebody else, arrives I beg that none of you say a word about this affair to anyone who is not now present in this room."

"Quite the most proper course," Aunt Blaxter observed. "It is only right that guilt should be brought home to the proper person, *whoever* that person may be."

With a tact of which Kenneth had hardly thought him capable, Churt turned to Norah. "I have no doubt Shapland will clear up the mystery for us satisfactorily. Meantime, my dear girl, you and I find ourselves in the same boat, for there is only my word for it that I ever put the note into the Red Cross envelope at all."

The kindness of his manner brought the tears to her eyes, and Kenneth took her away to the library.

"Fancy their thinking I was a thief—a thief, Ken—a common mean *thief!*"

"Nonsense, my darling girl," he said. "Nobody could believe any such rubbish."

"That odious Aunt Blaxter does, at any rate. She as good as said so." She sat down in a chair, and began to grow calmer, while he paced about the room, angry but thoughtful.

"I was glad I had you to stick up for me, Ken, and Lord Churt is an old dear."

"He's a silly old dear, all the same," He answered. "He has more money than he knows what to do with, but fancy fluttering a thousand-pound note through the Christmas post, to get lost among all the robins and good wishes!"

They were interrupted at this point by the entry of Gornay.

"I am not going to stay," he said, in answer to their not very welcoming expressions. "I have only come to ask a quite small favour. I am having a great argument with Sir James about character-reading from handwriting, and I want specimens from people we both know. Any little scrap will do."

Kenneth took up a sheet of note-paper from a writing table and wrote, "All is not gold that glitters," and Norah added below, "Birds of a feather flock together." It seemed the quickest way to get rid of him.

Gornay looked at the sheet with a not quite satisfied air. "I would *rather* have had something not written specially. Nobody ever writes quite naturally when they know that it is for the sort of purpose. You haven't got an old envelope, or something like that?"

Neither could supply what he wanted, and he went off, looking a little disappointed.

"I wonder whether that was really what he wanted the writing for," Kenneth remarked, suspiciously. "He's a quick-witted knave. Look how sharp he was to see the right move in that game of chess. It wasn't very obvious.

The chess-board was lying open on the table, where Churt had left it before ta. He glanced at it, casually at first, and then with growing interest. He took up one of the pieces to examine it, then re-placed it, to do the same with others, his manner showing all the time an increasing excitement.

"What is it, Ken?" Norah asked.

"Just a glimmer of something." He dropped into a chair. "I want to think—to think harder than ever in my life."

He leant forward, with his head resting on his hands, and she waited in silence till, after some minutes, he looked up.

"Yes, I begin to see light—more than a glimmer. He's a subtle customer, is Mr. Gornay, oh, very subtle!" He smiled, partly with the pleasure of finding one thread of a tangled web, partly with admiration for the cleverness that had woven it. "Would you like to know what he was really after when he came in here just now?"

"Very much," she answered. "But do you mean that he never had any argument with Sir James?"

"Oh, I daresay he had the argument all right—got it up for the occasion; but what he really wanted was this." He took out of his pocket the envelope in which the bank-note had been discovered. "The character-reading rot was not a bad shot at getting hold of it, and probably his only chance. But no, friend Gornay, you are not going to have that envelope—not for the thousand pounds you placed in it!"

"Do explain, Ken," Norah begged.

"I will presently," he answered, "but I want to piece the whole jigsaw together. There is still the other difficulty."

He dropped his eyes to the hearthrug again, and began to do his thinking aloud for her benefit. "Churt's reasoning is that Gornay must have been in here, watching the game, at the only time when the letters could have been tampered with, because he knew afterwards the move that was played just at the end. But why might not Winslade have told him about those two moves while Churt was letting me in at the front door? That would solve the riddle. I should have thought Winslade would have been too punctilious to talk about the game while his opponent was out of the room, but I'll go and ask him. I needn't tell him the reason why I want to know."

He came back almost immediately. "No, there was no conversation about the game while Churt was out of the room. Very well. Try the thing the other way round. Assume—as I think I can prove—that Gornay did tamper with the letters, the question is how could he tell that those two moves had been played?"

He took up the chess-board again and looked at it so intently and so long that, at last, Norah grew impatient.

"My dear boy, what *can* you be doing, poring all this time over the chess?"

"I have a curious sort of chess problem to solve before the Sherlock Holmes man turns up from Scotland Yard. Follow this a moment. If there was any way by which Gornay could find out that the two important moves had been played, without being present at the time and without being told, then Churt's argument goes for nothing doesn't it?"

"Clearly; but what other way was there? Did he look in through the window?"

"I think we shall find it was something much cleverer than that. I think I shall be able to show that he could infer that those two moves had been played, without any other help, from the position of the pieces as they stood at the end of the game; as they stand on the board now." he again bent down over the board. "White plays queen to queen's knight's sixth, not taking anything, and Black takes the queen with the rook's pawn; those are the two moves."

For nearly another half-hour Norah waited in loyal silence watching the alternations of his face as if brightened with the light of comprehension and clouded again with fresh perplexity.

At last he shut up the board and put it down, looking profoundly puzzled.

"Can it not be proved that the queen must have been taken at that particular square?" Norah inquired.

"No," he answered. "It might equally have been a rook. I can't make the matter out. So many of the jigsaw bits fit in that I know I must be right, and yet there is just one little bit that I can't find. By Jove!" he added, suddenly starting up, "I wonder if Churt could supply it?"

He was just going off to find out when a servant entered the room with a message that Lord Churt requested their present in his study.

The conclave assembled in the study consisted of the same persons who, in the drawing-room, had witnessed the discovery of the bank-note, with the addition of Shapland, the detective from Scotland Yard. Lord Churt presided, sitting at the table, and Shapland sat by his side, with a face that might have seemed almost unintelligent in its lack of expression but for the roving eyes, that scrutinised in turn the other faces present.

Norah and Kenneth took the two chairs that were left vacant and, as soon as the door was shut, Kenneth asked Churt a question.

"When you played your game of chess with Sir James Winslade this afternoon, did he give you the odds of the queen's rook?"

Everyone, except Norah and the sphinx-like detective, whose face gave no clue to his thoughts, looked surprised at the triviality of the question.

"I should hardly have thought this was a fitting occasion to discuss such a frivolous matter as a game of chess," Aunt Blaxter remarked sourly.

"I confess I don't understand the relevance of your question," Churt answered. "As a matter of fact, he did give me those odds."

"Thank God!" Kenneth exclaimed, with an earnestness that provoked a momentary sign of interest from Shapland.

"I should like to hear what Mr. Dale has to say about this matter," he remarked. "Lord Churt has put me in possession of the circumstance.

"I have an accusation to make against Lord Churt's private secretary, Mr. Gornay. Perhaps he had better be present to hear it."

"Quite unnecessary, quite unnecessary," Churt interposed. "We will not have any unpleasant scenes if we can help it."

"Very well," Kenneth continued. "I only thought it might be fairer. I accuse Gornay of stealing the thousand-pound bank-note out of the envelope addressed to the Red Cross and putting it into a letter addressed to me. *I accuse him of using colourless ink, of a kind that would become visible after a few hours, to cross out my address and substitute another*, the address of a confederate, no doubt."

"You must be aware, Mr. Dale," Shapland observed, "that you are making a very serious allegation in the presence of witnesses. I presume you have some evidence to support it?"

Kenneth opened the chess-board. "Look at the stains on those chess pieces. They were not there when the game was finished. They were there, not so distinctly as now, about an hour ago. Precisely those pieces, and only those, are stained that Gornay touched in showing that Lord Churt might have won the game. If they are not stains of invisible ink, why should they grow more distinct? If they are invisible ink, how did it get there, unless from Gornay's guilty fingers?"

He took out of his pocket the envelope of Norah's letter, and a glance at it brought a look of triumph to his face. He handed it to Shapland. "The ink is beginning to show there, too. It seems to act more slowly on the paper than on the polish of the chess-men."

"It is a difference of exposure to the air," Shepland corrected.

"The envelope has been in your pocket. If we leave it there on the table, we shall see presently whether your deduction is sound. Meanwhile, if Mr. Gornay was the guilty person, how can you account for his presence in the library at the only time when a crime could have been committed?"

"By denying it," Kenneth answered. "What proof have we that he was there at that particular time?"

"How else could he know the moves that were played at that time?" Shapland asked.

Kenneth pointed again to the chess-board. "From the position of the pieces at the end of the game. Here it is. I can prove, from the position of those pieces alone, *provided the same was played at this odds of queen's rook*, that White must, in the course of the game, have played his queen to queen's knight's sixth, not making a capture, and that Black must have taken it with the rook's pawn. If I can draw those inferences from the position, so could Gornay. We known how quickly he can think out a combination for the way in which he showed that Lord Churt could have won the game, when it looked so hopeless that he resigned."

The detective, fortunately, had an elementary knowledge of chess sufficient to enable him to follow Kenneth's demonstration.

"I don't suggest," Kenneth added, when the accuracy of the demonstration was admitted, "that he planned this *alibi* before-hand. It was a happy afterthought, that occurred to his quick mind when he saw that the position at the end of the game made it possible. What he relied on was the invisible ink trick, and that would have succeeded by itself, if I hadn't happened to turn up unexpectedly in time to intercept my letter from Norah."

While Kenneth was giving this last bit of explanation, Shapland had taken up the envelope again. As he had foretold, exposure to the air had brought out the invisible writing so that, although still faint, it was already legible. Only the middle line of the address, the number and name of the street, had been struck out with a single stroke, and another number and name substituted. The detective handed it to Churt. "Do you recognise the second handwriting, my lord?"

Churt put on his glasses and examined it. "I can't say that I do," he answered, "but it is not that of Mr. Gornay." He took another envelope out of his pocket-book, addressed to himself in his secretary's hand, and pointed out the dissimilarity of the two writings. Norah cast an anxious look at Kenneth, and Aunt Blaxter one of her sourest at the girl. The detective showed no surprise.

"None the less, my lord, I think it might forward our investigation if you would have Mr. Gornay summoned to this room. I don't think you need be afraid that there will be any scene," he added, and, for an instant, the faintest of smiles flitted across his lips.

Churt rang the bell and told the servant to ask his secretary to come to him.

"Mr. Gornay left an hour ago, my lord. He was called away suddenly and doesn't expect to see his grandmother alive."

"Poor old soul! On Christmas Eve, too!" Churt muttered, sympathetically, and this time Shapland allowed himself the indulgence of a rather broader smile.

"I guessed as much," he observed, "when I recognised the handwriting in which the envelope had been redirected, or I should have taken the precaution of going to fetch the gentleman, whom you know as Mr. Gornay, myself. He is a gentleman who is known to us at the Yard by more than one name, as well as by more than one handwriting, and now that we have so fortunately discovered his present whereabouts I can promise you that he will soon be laid by the heels. Perhaps Lord Churt will be kind enough to have my car ordered and to allow me to use his telephone."

"But you'll stay to dinner?" Churt asked. "It will be ready in a few minutes, and we shall none of us have time to dress."

"I am much obliged, my lord, but Mr. Dale has done my work for me here in a way that any member of the Yard might be proud of, and now I must follow the tracks while they are fresh. It may not prove neccessary to trouble you any further about this matter, but I think you are likely to see an important development in the great Ashfield forgery case reported in the newspapers before very long."

"Well," Churt observed, "I think we may all congratulate ourselves on having got this matter cleared up without any unpleasant scenes. Now we shall be able to enjoy our Christmas. I call it a happy solution, a very happy solutions."

His face beamed with relief and good-humour as he once more produced his pocket-book. "Norah, my dear, you must accept and old man's apology for causing you a very unpleasant afternoon; and you must accept this as well. No, I shall not take a refusal, and it will be much safer to send a *cheque* to the Red Cross."

The solution of the end-game given in this story, and the proof that a white queen must have been taken by the pawn at Q Kt 3, is given on page 285.

SIR GILBERT MURRELL'S PICTURE

by Victor Whitechurch

First published in 1912

SIR GILBERT MURRELL'S PICTURE

The affair of the goods truck on the Didcot and Newbury branch of the Great Western Railway was of singular interest, and found a prominent place in Thorpe Hazell's note-book. It was owing partly to chance, and partly to Hazell's sagacity, that the main incidents in the story were discovered, but he always declared that the chief interest to his mind was the unique method by which a very daring plan was carried out.

He was staying with a friend at Newbury at the time, and had taken his camera down with him, for he was a bit of an amateur photographer as well as book-lover, though his photos generally consisted of trains and engines. He had just come in from a morning's ramble with his camera slung over his shoulder, and was preparing to partake of two plasmon biscuits, when his friend met him in the hall.

"I say, Hazell," he began, "you're just the fellow they want here."

"What's up?" asked Hazell, taking off his camera and commencing some "exercises."

"I've just been down to the station. I know the station-master very well, and he tells me an awfully queer thing happened on the line last night."

"Where?"

"On the Didcot branch. It's a single line, you know, running through the Berkshire Downs to Didcot."

Hazell smiled, and went on whirling his arms round his head. "Kind of you to give me the information," he said, "but I happen to know the line. But what's occurred?"

"Well, it appears a goods-train left Didcot last night bound through to Winchester, and that one of the waggons never arived here at Newbury."

"Not very much in that," replied Hazell, still at his "exercises," "unless the waggon in question was behind the brake and the couplings snapped, in which case the next train along might have run into it."

"Oh no. The waggon was in the middle of the train."

"Probably left in a siding by mistake," replied Hazell.

"But the station-master says that all the stations along the line have been wired to, and that it isn't at any of them."

"Very likely it never left Didcot."

"He declares there is no doubt about that."

"Well, you begin to interest me," replied Hazell, stopping his whirligigs and beginning to eat his plasmon. "There may be something in it, though very often a waggon is mislaid. But I'll go down to the station."

"I'll go with you, Hazell, and introduce you to the station-master. He has heard of your reputation."

Ten minutes later they were in the station-master's office, Hazell having re-slung his camera.

"Very glad to meet you," said that functionary, "for this affair promises to be mysterious. *I* can't make it out at all."

"Do you know what the truck contained?"

"That's just where the bother comes in, sir. It was valuable property. There's a loan exhibition of pictures at Winchester next week, and this waggon was bringing down some of them from Leamington. They belong to Sir Gilbert Murrell—three of them I believe—large pictures, and each in a separate packing-case."

"H'm—this sounds very funny. Are you *sure* the truck was on the train?"

"Simpson, the brakesman, is here now, and I'll send for him. Then you can hear the story in his own words."

So the goods-guard appeared on the scene. Hazell looked at him narrowly, but there was nothing suspicious in his honest face.

"I know the waggon was on the train when we left Didcot," he said in answer to enquiries, "and I noticed it at Upton, the next station, where we took a couple off. It was the fifth or sixth in front of my brake. I'm quite certain of that. We stopped at Compton to take up a cattle-truck, but I didn't get out there Then we ran right to Newbury, without stopping at the other stations, and then I discovered that the waggon was not on the train. I thought very likely it might have been left at Upton or Compton by mistake, but I was wrong, for they say it isn't there. That's all I know about it, sir. A rum go, ain't it?"

"Extraordinary!" exclaimed Hazell. "You must have made a mistake."

"No, sir, I'm sure I haven't."

"Did the driver of the train notice anything?"

98

SIR GILBERT MURRELL'S PICTURE

"No, sir."

"Well, but the thing's impossible," said Hazell. "A loaded waggon couldn't have been spirited away. What time was it when you left Didcot?"

"About eight o'clock sir."

"Ah!—quite dark. You noticed nothing along the line?"

"Nothing, sir."

"You were in your brake all the time, I suppose?"

"Yes, sir—while we were running."

At this moment there came a knock at the station-master's door and a porter entered.

"There's a passenger train in just from the Didcot branch," said the man, "and the driver reports that he saw a truck loaded with packing-cases in Churn siding."

"Well, I'm blowed!" exclaimed the brakesman. "Why, we ran through Churn without a stop—trains never do stop there except in camp time."

"Where is Churn?" asked Hazell, for once at a loss.

"It's merely a platform and a siding close to the camping ground between Upton and Compton," replied the station-master, "for the convenience of troops only, and very rarely used, except in the summer, when soldiers are encamped there."

"I should very much like to see the place, and as soon as possible," said Hazell.

"So you shall," replied the station-master. "A train will soon start on the branch. Inspector Hill shall go with you, and instruction shall be given to the driver to stop there, while a return train can pick you both up."

In less than an hour Hazell and Inspector Hill alighted at Churn. It is a lonely enough place, situated in a vast, flat basin of the Downs, scarcely relieved by a single tree, and far from all human habitation, with the exception of a lonely shepherd's cottage some half a mile away.

The "station" itself is only a single platform, with a a shelter and a solitary siding, terminating in what is know in railway language as a "dead-end"—that is, in this case, wooden buffers to stop any trucks. This siding runs off the single line of rail at points from the Didcot direction of the line.

And in this siding was the lost truck, right against the "dead-end," filled with three packing-cases, and labelled "Leamington at Winchester, via Newbury." There could be no doubt about it at all. But how it had got there from the middle of a train running through without a stop was a mystery even to the acute mind of Thorpe Hazell.

"Well," said the inspector, when they had gazed long enough at the truck, "we'd better have a look at the points. Come along."

There is not even a signal-box at this primitive station. The points are actuated by two levers in a ground frame, standing close by the side of the line, one lever unlocking and shifting the same points.

"How about these points?" said Hazell as they drew near. "You only use them so occasionally that I suppose they are kept out of action?"

"Certainly," replied the inspector. "A block of wood is bolted down between the of the point rail and the main rail, fixed as a wedge—ah! there it is, you see, quite untouched; and the levers themselves are locked—here's the keyhole in the ground frame. This is the strangest thing I've ever come across, Mr. Hazell."

Thorpe Hazell stood looking at the points and levers, sorely puzzled. They *must* have been worked to get that truck in the siding, he knew well. But how?

Suddenly his face lit up. Oil evidently had been used to loosen the nut of the bolt that fixed the wedge of wood. Then his eyes fell on the handle of one of the two levers, and a slight exclamation of joy escaped him.

"Look," said the inspector at that moment, "it's impossible to pull them off," and he stretched out his hand towards a lever. To his astonishment Hazell seized him by the collar and dragged him back before he could touch it.

"I beg you pardon," he exclaimed, "hope I've not hurt you, but I want to photograph those levers first, if you don't mind."

The inspector watched him rather sullenly as he fixed his camera on a folding tripod stand he had with him, only a few inches from the handle of one of the levers, and took two very careful photographs of it.

"Can't see the use of that, sir," growled the inspector. But Hazell vouchsafed no reply.

"Let him find it out for himself," he thought.

Then he said aloud:

"I fancy they must have had that block out, inspector—and it's evident the points must have been set to get the truck where it is. How it was done is a problem, but, if the doer of it was anything of a regular criminal, I think we might find *him*."

"How?" asked the puzzled inspector.

"Ah," was the response, "I'd rather not say at present. Now, I should very much like to know whether those pictures are intact?"

"We shall soon find that out," replied the inspector, "for we'll take the truck back with us." And he commenced undoing the bolt with a spanner, after which he unlocked the levers.

"H'm—they work pretty freely," he remarked as he pulled one. "Quite so," said Hazell, "they've been oiled recently."

There was an hour or so before the return train would pass, and Hazell occupied it by walking to the shepherd's cottage.

"I am hungry," he explained to the woman there, "and hunger is Nature's dictate for food. Can you oblige me with a couple of onions and a broomstick?"

And she talks to-day of the strange man who "kept a swingin' o' that there broomstick round 'is 'ead and then eat them onions as solemn as a judge."

The first thing Hazell did on returning to Newbury was to develop his photographs. The plates were dry enough by the evening for him to print one or two photos on gaslight-paper and to enclose the clearest of them with a letter to a Scotland Yard official whom he knew, stating that he would call for an answer, as he intended returning to town in a couple of days. The following evening he received a note from the station-master, which read:

"DEAR SIR,—I promised to let you know if the pictures in the cases on that truck were in any way tampered with. I have just received a report from Winchester by which I understand that they have been unpacked and carefully examined by the Committee of the Loan Exhibition. The Committee are perfectly satisfied that they have not been damaged or interfered with in any way, and that they have been received just as they left the owner's hands.

"We are still at a loss to account for the running of the waggon on the Churn siding or for the object in doing so. An official has been down from Paddington, and, at his request, we are not making the affair public—the goods having arrived in safety. I am sure you will observe confidence in this matter."

"More mysterious than ever," said Hazell to himself, "I can't understand it at all."

The next day he called at Scotland Yard and saw the official. "I've had no difficulty with your little matter, you'll be glad to hear," he said. "We looked up our records and very soon spotted the man."

"Who is he?"

"His real name is Edgar Jeffreys, but we know him under several aliases. He's served four sentences for burglary and robbery—the latter daring theft from a train, so he's in your line, Mr. Hazell. What's he been up to, and how did you get that print?"

"Well," replied Hazell, "I don't quite know yet what he's been doing. But I should like to be able to find him if anything turns up. Never mind how I got the print—the affair is quite a private one at present, and nothing may come of it."

The official wrote an address on a bit of paper and handed it to Hazell.

"He's living there just now, under the name of Allen. We keep such men in sight, and I'll let you know if he moves."

When Hazell opened his paper the following morning he gave a cry of joy. And no wonder, for this is what he saw:

"MYSTERY OF A PICTURE

"Sir Gilbert Murrell and the Winchester Loan Exhibition
"An Extraordinary Charge

"The Committee of the Loan Exhibition of Pictures to be opened next week at Winchester are in a state of very natural excitement brought about by a strange charge that has been made against them by Sir Gilbert Murrell.

"Sir Gilbert, who lives at Leamington, is the owner of several very valuable pictures, among them being the celebrated 'Holy Family', by Velazquez. This picture, with two others, was despatched by him from Leamington to be exhibited at Winchester, and yesterday he journeyed to that city in order to make himself satisfied with the hanging arrangements, as he had particularly stipulated that 'The Holy Family' was to be placed in a prominent position.

"The picture in question was standing on the floor of the gallery, leaning against a pillar, when Sir Gilbert arrived with some representatives of the Committee.

"Nothing occurred till he happened to walk behind the canvas, when he astounded those present by saying that the picture was not his at all, declaring that a copy had been substituted, and stating that he was absolutely certain on account of certain private marks of his at the back of the canvas, which were quite indecipherable, and which were now missing. He admitted that the painting itself in every way resembled his picture, and that it was the cleverest forgery he had every seen; but a very painful scene took place, the hanging Committee stating that the picture had been received by them from the railway company just as it stood.

"At present the whole affair is a mystery, but Sir Gilbert insisted most emphatically to our correspondent, who was able to see him, that the picture was certainly not his, and said that, as the original is extremely valuable, he intends holding the Committee responsible for the substitution which, he declares, has taken place."

It was evident to Hazell that the papers had not, as yet, got hold of the mysterious incident at Churn. As a matter of fact, the railway company had kept that affair strictly to themselves, and the loan Committee knew nothing of what had happened on the line.

But Hazell saw that enquiries would be made, and determined to probe the mystery without dealy. He saw at once that if there was any truth in Sir Gilbert's story the substitution had taken place in that lonely siding at Churn. He was staying at his London flat, and five minutes after he had read the paragraph had called a hansom and was being hurried off to a friend of his who was well known in art circles as a critic and art historian.

"I can tell you exactly what you want to know," said he, "for I've only just been looking it up, so as to have an article in the evening papers on it. There was a famous copy of the picture of Velazquez, said to have been a controversy among the respective owners as to which was the genuine one—just as there is to-day about a Madonna belonging to a gentleman at St. Moritz, but which a Vienna gallery also claims to possess.

"However, in the case of 'The Holy Family,' the dispute was ultimately settled once and for all years ago, and, undoubtedly, Sir Gilbert Murrell held the genuine picture. What became of the copy no one knows. For twenty years all trace of it has been lost. There—that's all I can tell you. I shall pad it out a bit in my article, and I must get to work on it as once. Good-bye!"

"One moment—where was the copy last seen?"

"Oh! the old Earl of Ringmere had it last, but when he knew it to be a forgery he is said to have sold it for a mere song, all interest in it being lost, you see."

"Let me see, he's a very old man, isn't he?"

"Yes—nearly eighty—perfect enthusiast on pictures still though."

"Only *said* to have sold it," muttered Hazell to himself, as he left the house; "that's very vague—and there's no knowing what these enthusiasts will do when they're really bent on a thing. Sometimes they lose all sense of honesty. I've known fellows actually rob a friend's collections of stamps or butterflies. What if there's something in it? By George, what an awful scandal there would be. It seems to me that if such a scandal were prevented I'd be thanked all round. Anyhow, I'll have a shot at it in spec. And I *must* find out how that truck was run off the line."

When once Hazell was on the track of a railway mystery he never let a moment slip by. In an hour's time, he was at the address given him at Scotland Yard. On his way there he took a card from his case—a blank one— and wrote on it, "From the Earl of Ringmere." This he put into an envelope.

"It's a bold stroke," he said to himself, "but, if there's anything in it, it's worth trying."

So he asked for Allen. The woman who opened the door looked at him suspiciously, and said she didn't think Mr. Allen was in.

"Give him this enevelope," replied Hazell. In a couple of minutes she returned, and asked him to follow her.

A short, wiry-looking man, with sharp, evil-looking eyes, stood in the room waiting for him and looking at him suspiciously.

"Well," he snapped, "what is it—what do you want?"

"I come on behalf of the Earl of Ringmere. You will know that when I mention Churn," replied

Hazell, playing his trump card boldly.

"Well," went on the man, "what about that?"

Hazell wheeled round, locked the door suddenly, put the key in his pocket, and then faced his man. The latter darted forward, but Hazell had a revolver pointing at him in a twinkling.

"You—detective!"

"No, I'm not—I told you I came on behalf of the Earl—that looks like hunting up matters for his sake, doesn't it?"

"What does the old fool mean?" asked Jeffreys.

"Oh! I see you know all about it. Now listen to me quietly, and you may come to a little reason. You changed that picture at Churn the other night."

"You seem to know a lot about it," sneered the other, but less defiantly.

"Well, I do—but not quite all. You were foolish to leave your traces on that lever, eh?"

"How did I do that?" exclaimed the man, giving himself away.

"You'd been dabbling about with oil, you see, and you left your thumb-print of the handle. I photographed it, and they recognised it at Scotland Yard. Quite simple."

Jeffreys swore beneath his breath.

"I wish you'd tell me what you mean," he said.

"If I have, I'm not going to take any risks. I told the old man so. He's worse than I am—he put me up to getting the picture. Let him takes his chance when it comes out. I suppose he wants to keep his name out of if—thay's why you're here."

"Your're not quite right. Now, just listen to me. You're a villain, and you deserve to suffer; but I'm acting in a purely private capacity, and I fancy I can get the original picture back to its owner that it will be better for all parties to hush this affair up. Has the old Earl got it?"

"No, not yet," admitted the other, "he was too artful. But he knows where it is, and so do I."

"Ah—now you're talking sense! Look here! You make a clean breast of it, and I'll take it down on paper. you shall swear to the truth of your statement before the commissioner for oaths—he need not see the actual confession. I shall hold this in case it is necessary; but, if you help me to get the picture back to Sir Gilbert, I don't think it will be."

After a little more conversation, Jeffreys explained. Before he did so, however, Hazell had taken a bottle of milk and a hunch of wholemeal bread from his pocket, and calmly proceeded to perform "exercises" and then to eat his 'lunch" while Jeffreys told the following story:

"It was the old Earl who did it. How he got hold of me doesn't matter; perhaps I got hold of him— maybe I put him up to it—but that's not the question. He'd kept that forged picture of his in a lumber room for years, but he always had his eye on the genuine one. He paid a long price for the forgery, and he got to think that he *ought* to have the original. But there, he's mad on pictures.

"Well, as I say, he kept the forgery out of sight and let folk think he'd sold it, but all the time he was in hopes of getting it changed somehow for the original.

"Then I came along and undertook the job for him. There were three of us in it, for it was a ticklish business. We found out by what train the picture was to travel—that was easy enought. I got hold of a key to unlock the ground frame, and the screwing off of the bolt was a mere nothing. I oiled the points well so that the thing should work as I wanted it to.

"One pal was with me—in the siding, ready to clap on the side-brake when the truck was running in. I was to work the points, and my other pal, who had the most awkward job of all, was on the goods train—under a tarpaulin in a truck. He had two lengths of very stout rope with a hook at each end of them.

"When the train left Upton, he started his job. Goods trains travel very slowly, and there was plenty of time. Counting from the back brake-van, the truck we wanted to run off was No. 5. First he hooked No. 4 truck to No. 6, fixing the hook at the side of the end of both trucks, and having the slack in his hand, coiled up.

"Then, when the train ran down a bit of a decline, he uncoupled No. 5 from No. 4, standing on No. 5 to do it. That was easy enough, for he'd taken a coupling staff with him; then he paid out the slack till it was tight. Next he hooked the second rope from No. 5 to No. 6, uncoupled No. 5 from No. 6, and paid out the slack of the second rope.

"Now you can see what happened. The last few trucks of the train were being drawn by a long rope reaching from No. 4 to No. 6, and leaving a space in between. In the middle of this space No. 5 ran, drawn by a short rope from No. 6. My pal stood on No. 6, with a sharp knife in his hand.

"The rest was easy. I held the lever, close by the side of the line, coming forward to it as soon as the engine passed. The instant the space appeared after No. 6 I pulled it over, and No. 5 took the siding points, while my pal cut the rope at the same moment.

"Directly the truck had run by and off I reversed the lever so that the rest of the train following took the main line. There is a decline before Compton, and the last four trucks came running down to the main body of the train, while my pal hauled in the slack and finally coupled No. 4 to No. 6 when they came together. He jumped from the train as it ran very slowly into Compton. That's how it was done."

Hazell's eyes sparkled.

"It's the cleverest thing I've heard of on the line," he said.

"Think so? Well, it wanted some handling. The next thing was to unscrew the packing-case, take the picture out of the frame and put the forgery we'd bought with us in its place. That took us some time, but there was no fear of interruption in that lonely part. Then I took the picture off—rolling it up first—and hid it. The old Earl insisted on this. I was to tell him where it was, then he was going to wait for a few weeks and get it himself."

"Where did you hide it?"

"You're sure you're going to hush this up?"

"You'd have been in charge long ago if I were not."

"Well, there's a path from Churn to East Ilsley across the downs, and on the right hand of that path is an old sheep well—quite dry. It's down there. You can easily find the string if you look for it—fixed near the top."

Hazell took down the man's confession, which was duly attested. His conscience told him that perhaps he ought to have taken stronger measures.

"I told you I was merely a private individual," said Hazell to Sir Gilbert Murrell. "I have acted in a purely private capacity in bringing you your picture."

Sir Gilbert looked from the canvas to the calm face of Hazell.

"Who are you, sir?" he asked.

"Well, I rather aspire to be a book-collector; you may have read my little monogram on *Jacobean Bindings*?"

"No," said Sir Gilbert, "I have not had that pleasure. But I must enquire further into this. How did you get this picture? Where was it—who——?"

"Sir Gilbert," broke in Hazell, "I could tell you the whole truth, of course. I am not in any way to blame myself. By chance, as much as anything else, I discovered how your picture had been stolen and where it was."

"But I want to know all about it. I shall prosecute—I——"

"I think not. Now, do you remember where the forged picture was seen last?"

"Yes; the Earl of Ringmere had it—he sold it."

"Did he?"

"Eh?"

"What if he kept it all this time?" said Hazell, with a peculiar look.

There was a long silence.

"Good heavens!" exclaimed Sir Gilbert at length. "You don't mean *that*. Why, he has one foot in the grave—a ver old man—I was dining with him only a fortnight ago."

"Ah! Well, I think you are content now, Sir Gilbert?"

"It is terrible—terrible! I have the picture back, but I wouldn't have the scandal known for worlds."

"It never need be," replied Hazell. "You will make it all right with the Winchester people?"

"Yes—yes—even if I have to admit I was mistaken, and let the forgery stay through the exhibition."

"I think that would be the best way," replied Hazell, who never regretted his action.

"Of course, Jeffreys ought to have been punished," he said to himself; "but it was a clever idea—a clever idea!"

"May I offer you some lunch?" asked Sir Gilbert.

"Thank you; but I am a vegetarian, and——"

"I think my cook could arrange something; let me ring."

"It is very good of your, but I ordered a dish of lentils and a salad at the station restaurant. But if you will allow me just to go through my physical training ante-luncheon exercises here, it would save me the trouble of a more or less public display at the station.''

"Certainly," replied the rather bewildered baronet; where upon Hazell threw off his coat and commenced whirling his arms like a windmill.

"Digestion should be considered *before* a meal," he explained.

THE ACE OF TROUBLE

by Hedley Barker

First published in 1925

It must have been unbearable for Herbert Dawlish to reflect that, had the waitress not been slack, he would never have committed murder.

Dawlish had just ten minutes to spare, and he was feeling infernally hungry. So he dropped into an A.B.C. and called for a cup of tea and a bath bun. The waitress dawdled, and Herbert Dawlish fidgeted impatiently. He must have taken out his watch at least ten times in five minutes. When at last his tea and bath bun arrived, he had two minutes in which to bolt it down and catch the train for Herne Bay.

He rushed on to the platform just as the train was pulling out. His lips tightened with annoyance as he realised that he couldn't possibly reach the saloon. This meant that he would miss the "coasters," and his game of cards.

The train gathered speed. Dawlish gripped his bag, and ran, realising that he would be lucky now to catch it at all. However, he managed with a flying leap to land (amid the yells of railway officials) on the footboard of the rear coach. He clung there for a moment, panting, then opened the door and subsided with a gasp on the seat.

The man opposite regarded Herbert Dawlish with interest. He was a flashy sort of person with a gold horsehoe in his tie, and aggressively square shoes. He said the usual things that people do say on these occasions—narrow shave, not so easy to run at Dawlish's time of life, and so forth. He also launched into a protracted and lurid reminiscence which had to do with one Sam Biggs, who, being denied the luck which had attended Mr. Dawlish, fell between the footboard and the platform.

" 'Orrible sight. I never want to see another like it."

Herbert Dawlish, far as distant Jupiter in that moment from murderous intent, gazed upon the man he was going to murder. He never suffered fools gladly, and this fellow seemed a particularly priceless specimen. However, when the man suggested a game of cards, Dawlish brightened considerably. He had a passion for cards, and he fell in eagerly with the proposal.

"I have a pack here," he said diving into his pocket. There his fingers came in contact with something hard, and he pulled it out with an embarrassed smile. He said, jocularly, laying an automatic pistol on the table:

"Don't be alarmed. I'm no gunman. I bought this in town today. You see, I belong to the Herne Bay rifle club, and they've just started a revolver class. Fascinating sport."

The other nodded.

"May I?" he said, and, picking up the weapon examined it with the eye of an expert. "Dandy little gun," was his comment. "Loaded, too, by gosh!"

"Er—yes. I brought some cartridges along. It's quite safe. The catch is on. Now, what shall we play? Do you happen to know Soixante-six? It's an ideal game for two."

"Swa—?"

"In other words, sixty-six. It's a kind of—"

"Right, govenor! I got you. Sixty-six. Yers. Used to play it over the other side at Vimmy Ridge—"

"Cut, will you?"

Herbert Dawlish dealt.

"What about stakes?" he mumured with a swift, appraising glance at the other's ensemble.

"Oh, five bob a time."

Dawlish was surprised. This was a good deal higher than he was used to, but he guessed he could hold his own, anyway. He dealt the cards in bundles of three and two. Play began.

Now, it very soon became obvious to Dawlish that this fellow with the horseshoe had handled cards before. He had that nifty method of shuffling and dealing which involves a flourishing and crackling of the cards. He licked his thumbs. The pasteboards flew from his nimble fingers like greased lightning.

Dawlish paid out. Five—ten—fifteen—thirty-five—fifty. He lost six pounds. A dull flush tinted his high cheekbones. He fortified himself with a long pull from his pocket-flask, clenched his teeth, and concentrated grimly.

Long before the train had reached Chatham that six pounds had become forty-six. Dawlish was plunging madly to retrieve his losses. A ghastly fear contracted his heart. He had lost much—very much more than he could afford to lose. It was quarter day, and he had calls to meet which must be met out of his money that he was losing.

At seventy pounds Herbert Dawlish leant back and wiped the sweat from his forehead with a shaky hand. He was pale, and the corners of his mouth were out of his control. A very unpleasant sight indeed.

"I am afraid," he muttered, "that I can't go on. I've lost every penny."

The nifty man stopped short in the midst of a tune he was whistling.

"That a fact? Hard luck, mate. Good game, though eh? 'Ammer and tongs."

"Look here," said Dawlish abjectly. "I—it's a queer thing to ask, but—could you let me have that money back? For a little while, I mean. I would repay you, later. But, just no, I—I——"

The nifty man had been staring at Dawlish in blank surprise. Now he suddenly guffawed.

"Well, that's rich," he observed. "I'll tell the missus that when I gits 'ome. She'll cry 'er eyes out, that she will. No, matey. Napoo. I ain't the Salvation Army 'Ome."

"Let me explain," begged Dawlish in agony. "You don't understand. It's like this——"

"Aw, shove a boot in it, ole feller. You oughtn't never to 'ave come out without yer nurse. Hey! What the——"

"Put up your hands," said Dawlish, staring wickedly from behind his automatic. "Right up!"

Even then, Dawlish had no notion of murder. He merely wanted to scare the fellow into parting with the money. He was frantic. He positively daren't go home and face his wife with a story of seventy pounds lost. But, firearms are dangerous things to play with. The nifty man's eyes narrowed. He made a sudden spring. And Dawlish, closing his eyes pulled the trigger.

Death is shockingly quick and sudden. In one brief second Dawlish was saddled with a corpse. There wa a grim blue hole in the middle of its forehead, and it had sagged slackly on the floor like a sack of something. Dawlish commanded himself with an effort, and began to think of ways and means.

He was about to bundle the body out of the carriage on to the permanent way when he caught sight of the wrist-watch. An inspiration caused him to alter the time of this watch to five-fifty. He counted on the watch stopping when the crash came, and a watch stopped at five-fifty (unless the body were found immediatly) would point to the fact of the man's having travelled down by an earlier train.

This done, he opened the carriage-door, looked cautiously ahead, and behind, then, with the train doing about forty, shoved out the remains of the nifty man.

Venner, the Scotland Yard man, was in the eight-forty to town on the following morning. He and two other greeted Dawlish with ribald cries, as usual. These four had played cards on the up journey every day (barring holidays) for ten years.

"Come along, you old blighter—the cards," they cried. "Where were you loafing last night, by the way?"

"Late," said Dawlish. "had to run for it. Seen the paper? This murder on the five-ten?"

Smith, who was sorting out Dawlish's cards, nodded.

"Poor devil's all bashed about," he said. "Face practically gone, they say. Not that he'd feel that, I suppose. You heard anything about it, Venner, apart from what the papers give?"

Venner smiled quietly.

"I hear a good deal," he said, "that I'm not allowed to tell. As a matter of fact, I viewed the body about two or three hours after the murder. They rushcd me up by car from Herne Bay."

"I say," said Smith "look here, old Dawlish, You've only got half a pack here. The ace of trouble's missing."

Smith always called the ace of spades the ace of trouble, because spades stood for trouble in the fortune-tellers jargon.

"I expect it's in my pocket," said Dawlish.

But he was spared the trouble of searching by Venner. The man from the Yard looked suddenly grave as he pulled out a card from his own pocket.

"No," he said. "Here it is, unless I'm mistaken."

He laid the ace of spades on the table—the ace which had been missing from that same pack.

"Yes, that's it by Jove!" cried Smith. "Where the devil did you get it, you old card-sharper?"

Venner turned and looked at Dawlish. Then he laid a hand on his arm

"Dawlish," he said, "this hurts like blazes. But I've got to do it. You're arrested. *That ace of spades was found up the sleeve of the murdered man*."

THE HANOVER COURT MURDER

by Sir Basil Thomson

First published in 1925

A whole week had passed since Mr. Pepper—and the small boy—had spoilt, Mr. Cohen's scheme; and no one had come near the office. My Chief spent the time in perfecting his scientific apparatus which had not been called into use since my short association with him. It was therefore with immense satisfaction that an opportunity for exercising Mr. Pepper's higher art was thrown into my way.

An acquaintance at my club, finding me in the smoking-room when other people were working, took the chair opposite to mine and said, "By the way, Jones, I hear that you dabble in detective work; that you have discovered a wonderful Yankee who wipes the eye of Scotland Yard. Why don't you make your name by solving this Hanover Court case?"

"I've never heard of it."

"No, it hasn't got into the papers yet, but it will."

He had himself heard of it only that morning. His landlord had a sister who let lodgings in Hanover Court. She had opened the luggage of a tenant who had gone abroad owing rent and had been horrified by finding in one of the trunks what appeared to be the remains of a dismembered human body. She had run at once to her brother, who consulted my friend as to what she ought to do. He took the usual course of advising that she should report the matter to the police, but, as far as he knew, she had not yet done so because she had made the discovery only that morning at breakfast time. He gave me her address.

I seized my hat and took a taxi to Hanover Court. I found the poor landlady wringing her hands. "You heard of the case through my brother, sir? Well, I am glad that you've come in time. I was just going off to the police, but it will ruin my business to have the police messing about the house, asking me a lot of questions and calling in the Coroner. They would make me appear as a witness at the inquest and the papers would publish the address. Then what chance would there be of the best class of people taking rooms where there's been a murder? It is not respectable. Now if you'll take away the trunk and take all responsibility I shall breathe freely. Of course, if there *has* been a murder I must stand by it, but you will ferret it all out and I hope that I shall hear no more about it."

I agreed to everything on the condition that she gave me all the information she possessed. She showed me the trunk which stood on the landing of the second floor. I opened it with trembling fingers. It contained a number of packages wrapped in dirty newspaper and enveloped in part of what appeared to be an old army blanket. I satisfied myself that they contained bones, probably human bones, and with her assistance carried the trunk downstairs for removal to our office. In the meantime she told me the story of her lodger.

"He was what they call an eccentric, sir—always going off without notice and writing letters asking me to reserve his room and take care of his luggage. He always sent me money for the rent while he was away. He would write from all sorts of places—Naples, Egypt, Athens, and one letter I had came from Peru. I never knew him pack anything for his journeys. All he said was that he was called away on business and would I be sure and feed his cat?"

"You haven't told me his name, Mrs. Auger."

"To tell your the truth, I had almost forgotten it. We always called him 'The Doctor' because when he came to me five years ago he said something about being in the medical profession. But his real name was Allen—Henry Allen."

"That sounds English enough."

"Oh, there was nothing foreign about him except his hair. He never seemed to get it cut—his hair and his eccentricity—for foreigners *are* eccentric, don't you think so, Mr. Meddlesome-Jones? His age? Well, that would be hard to say—something between thirty-five and fifty, I should say."

"Had he no friends, no visitors?"

"That's the peculiar thing. He had none. No, I am wrong there. About three years ago a lady did call and ask for Dr. Allen. I asked her what name I should give. She said, 'Don't trouble; just tell me what floor he's on, and I'll find him myself.' And up she walked, but of course he must have heard her voice. She soon came down again and said he wasn't there. Then I went up myself, and of course there he was, hiding under the bed. He said nothing to me, but I can't help thinking that that lady was his wife. She never came again, not to my knowledge."

"Did he get no letters?"

"Yes, once a month, always on the 2nd unless it was a Sunday, there would be a fat registered letter addressed 'Henry Allen, Esq.'—no doctor on the envelope. I think it was from a bank, but I don't remember which. He never had a meal in the house, not even his breakfast, but he used to bring back a little meat for his cat. Where did he go all day? Well sir, that's more than I can tell you. On weekdays I would hear him coming downstairs regular at nine—I could have set my clock by him. If he passed me he would say 'Good morning,' but nothing else. On Sundays he would lie in bed all the morning, and go out punctually at twelve. Oh, he was eccentric, but not the sort to commit a cold-blooded murder; for it is cold-blooded, Mr. Meddlesome-Jones, whatever you may say, to cut up a person into little bits like that, now isn't it? He had no books in his room and he didn't leave a scrap of writing behind him. What he did all day is a mystery to me."

"When did you see him last?"

"It would be back in April. Yes, it is just three months. He just walked out of the house as usual and when I went up to do his room I found that he had packed everything away in his trunks. 'Off again, I suppose,' I said to myself, and I was right—only this time I had no letter and he hadn't paid me for the room. I didn't think very much of that—he had been behind with the rent before. I thought that the money would come. But then as the weeks went by and I had no letter I began to get anxious and I thought I had better see what he had left behind him. There wasn't a scrap of writing in any of the trunks—only old clothes and—and what you saw."

"But the letters from the bank?"

"That's the peculiar thing. Whenever he went off those letters stopped coming. There hasn't been a letter since he left. Do you think he can have committed suicide after the murder?"

"We have got to find out first if there has been a murder, Mrs. Auger. I suppose there has been no one missing in the neighbourhood?"

She thought for some moments and then shook her head. "But I'm sure that lady who came to see him was his wife," he said.

"Why?"

"Well, she had a masterful, disagreeable way with her and he got under the bed to hide from her. A man would never do that with anybody except his wife." I forebore to evoke any confidences of Mrs. Auger's own experience of the married state.

"And if she was his wife, what then?"

"Why, it might be her that's in the trunk."

The taxi driver knew nothing of what his burden contained. For an extra shilling he helped me upstairs with it into the office where my Chief's face became a mark of interrogation until the man was gone. Then I told him the story and opened the trunk. I never saw him so much moved before. He laid the bones out on the table as if they were jewels, I noticed that desiccated flesh was adhering to some of them; it was quite inoffensive. At the bottom of the trunk was the skull carefully wrapped in newspaper by itself. We carried them into the laboratory and cleared a table for them. While he was arranging them in order I committed to paper what Mrs Auger had told me.

Now, if my Chief had a fault it was that he tried to do too much himself rather than call in the expert. My instinct would have been to call in a surgeon or an anatomist and let him express his opinion on the bones, but when I ventured to suggest this my Chief flew up in the air. "What does your surgeon know of plastic reconstruction?" he said, and not knowing what plastic reconstruction was I said that I didn't know. "Well," he said, "I am going to show you.

It was a great opportunity for me. When I was admitted to the laboratory the bones were disposed on the table like a complete skeleton. My Chief's first words were disconcerting. "Some of the bones are missing," he said, "but the curious thing is that the body was deformed. That ought to make our work easier, but it is a very remarkable case. This woman had the left leg three inches shorter than the right and the right arm two inches shorter than the left. She must have had a very odd appearance.

"We'll soon see what she looked like," said my Chief, confidently, as he manipulated was in a pan of warm water. The skull was secured in a wooden vice clamped to the table. With extraordinary dexterity he pinched off little cones from the lump of wax in the pan, warmed them over a spirit lamp, and stuck them all over the skull. Very gradually he began to build up a face; and after an hour's work it became under his skilled manipulation a human face certainly, but a face that one could only see in a nightmare. With her bodily deformities in addition she might have made a good living at a show.

"There," he said, "is the murdered woman as she was in life." I had it on the tip of my tongue to say, "Then she deserved to die," but I restrained myself in time, and I suggested that Mrs. Auger should be called to the office to identify her with Mrs. Allen. But my Chief thought that the time had not come for that. "Let us find the murderer and confront him with his victim," he said. "In nine cases out of ten he is so startled that he makes a full confession."

"And if he does, what then? Surely we should have to hand him over to the police."

"Yes," he mused, "but in a case of felony it is the duty of any citizen to arrest the felon. You will make the arrest; I will call in the reporters, and then we will ring up your wonderful Scotland Yard." There was the most subtle irony in his tone. He covered the remains with a sheet, and we sat down to consider the best way of finding Henry Allen. I was for advertising in the Agony Columns of *The Times*, the *Daily Telegraph* and the *Daily Mail*. "Henry Allen. Come back and all will be forgiven."

"He would plead at his trial that he had been promised a free pardon."

"Then why not something like this? 'If Henry Allen, late of 17 Hanover Court, will communicate with Pepper and Jones, Adelphi, London, he will hear of something to his advantage.'" My Chief snorted with contempt; I feared that it might be because for the first time I had dared to couple our two names.

"Do you really suppose that a man who goes in daily fear that his crime will be discovered would reply to an advertisement?"

"Well, you see them in the newspapers every day when lawyers want to get hold of a man. Someone must reply to them or they wouldn't put them in."

"No, Mr. Meddleston-Jones; if we use the newspapers we will proceed in quite a different way. I have there (he pointed to his card index cabinet) the names and addresses of the principal newspapers of every country in the world—daily and weekly. We would prepare a little news paragraph, a snappy little thing of how an Englishman named Henry Allen, had been named as residuary legatee to an eccentric lady who died leaving a million and a half, and that when the sole executor, Mr. Pepper (there was no mention of 'Meddleston-Jones' in the proposed paragraph) wrote to the happy legatee he found that he had gone abroad leaving no address and the letter was returned by the Post Office. Under the provisions of the will, if Henry Allen fails to claim his legacy within six months, the whole of the money goes to found a Home for Starving Cats in London. We would have this translated into every language and sent out through one of the press agencies. Everyone likes to read about unclaimed money."

"Wouldn't you be inundated with false claimants?"

"All the better. We would confront them all with the corpse first, then with Mrs. Auger, and they would be glad to get away alive."

It seemed to me to be a very dilatory method of procedure, but my Chief must have adopted it because a week or so later reporters connected with the press agency began to hang about the office and stop me in the street. This annoyed my Chief very much. If appeared that he had made a confidential arrangement with the head of the Agency, that the paragraph should not be released to any newspaper in the United Kingdom, because he would have to confess that there was no eccentric millionaire lady in the case at all. But the paragraph must have appeared in foreign newspapers because later we received begging letters from abroad. An Englishwoman wrote from Leghorn to say that if Henry Allen failed to appear, there were more starving cats in Leghorn than there could possibly be in London, that they kept her awake at night by their me-owing, and that she would be glad to establish a home for them if she might have part of the money. A man signing himself 'Henry Allen' wrote from Cooktown in Queensland, asking for the expenses necessary for him to come to England to establish his claim. Another wrote from Salt Lake City to say that though he was known locally as Richard Doherty, he was satisfied that as his mother's name was Allen he was the person named in the will, and he would be thankful if a payment could be made on account; and a lady, writing from Buenos Ayres in the name of Mary Allen, claimed the legacy on the ground that when she was a girl her schoolfellows always called her 'Henry.' But of the real Henry Allen not a word.

My Chief was becoming impatient. He was engaged on several cases at the time and the remains of the murdered woman, taking up nearly half the laboratory, were in his way. He had added chestnut hair to his reconstruction of the head, and colour to the cheeks; in her reconstructed state she must certainly have been very trying to live with, even when covered with a sheet. One morning he said to me, "Mr. Meddleston-Jones, we are not getting on with this Allen case. Why don't you bring the landlady down to identify the victim? Then we might get on."

Mrs. Auger did not take at all kindly to my suggestion. She reminded me that our agreement was that she should not be troubled with the case any more, and I had some difficulty in getting her to the office. When I drew back the sheet she uttered a piercing scream and fell into a chair. "Oh! My heart!" she sobbed. "My poor heart!" and she tried to clutch that organ in her anatomy.

"You recognise her, Mrs. Auger? Is she like the wife?"

"She is like nothing on earth," she gasped, "and after seeing her I shall be ill for a week." It was a great disappointment.

I persuaded my Chief at last to take a photograph of the head, and give it to an illustrated daily paper for circulation as a missing person about whom information was desired. He took the photograph, but ten minutes before I started with it for the newspaper office in Fleet Street, an event occurred which entirely changed the course of our enquiry. Mrs. Auger reappeared.

She produced a picture postcard, bearing the Genoa postmark, from Henry Allen himself, saying that he would be in London within the week. "And now," she said, "what am I to say to him when he asks for his trunk? I can't say that the police have taken it, can I? You had better pack up all those bones in the newspapers just as he left them and bring back the trunk." To this proposition, of course, my Chief would not agree. He pointed out that, according to the law, Mrs. Auger herself was bound to arrest him as soon as he set foot in her house.

"Arrest him?" she exclaimed aghast. "How can a woman arrest a man?"

"The law knows no difference between men and women, Mrs. Auger," I said. "Women serve on juries; there are women police. All you have to do is to lay your hand on his shoulder and say, 'Henry Allen, I arrest you for the wilful murder of a woman unknown, and I must caution you that anything you say will be taken down in writing, and will be used against you at your trial.' Then write down what he says, lock him up in his room, and telephone to Mr. Pepper, Central 1202."

"I could never do such a thing. Mr. Meddlesome-Jones, were he a murderer three times over. You'll have to do this yourself."

I looked at Mr. Pepper and Mr. Pepper looked at me. It seemed to me that this was the moment for calling in the regular police who are paid for doing these things, but I did not dare to say so. I had an uncomfortable feeling that I had read somewhere about a man being charged as an accessory after the fact, and I had a horrible presentiment that Pepper and I would find ourselves standing in the dock at the Old Bailey. We dismissed Mrs. Auger with some difficulty on the plea that we had to consider our position. There were still four days before us. Mr. Pepper was equally perturbed. The only solution which he could suggest was that I should wait at Mrs. Auger's door day after day and as soon as Allen appeared accost him, and induce him to come to the office to be confronted with his victim. We would then be guided by events. If he displayed signs of guilt we might go so far as to telephone to the police. It was the first time I had ever known him to contemplate lowering his dignity as a scientific detective, and I honoured him for it though I cannot say that I liked the rôle he had assigned to me. An extraordinary coincidence saved me. I owed my rescue to the same club acquaintance who had first introduced me to the man whom I shall continue to regard as the greatest detective of the age.

My friend was lunching at a table for two. As I passed him he sprang up and introduced me to his guest, a middle-aged man with a beard turning grey, and asked me to join them. In the course of conversation it appeared that his guest was the head of a well-known medical school in London, and that he was as the moment of my appearance relating an unpleasant incident at the school. My friend asked him to begin the story again. "Mr. Meddleston-Jones," he was good enough to say, "is the very man to advise you. He is associated with the best detective brains in London, besides being himself a man of very wide experience in crime." It was rather oddly expressed, but my friend meant well.

"But I don't want to call in the police—at any rate until we know more."

"Bless you, Mr. Meddleston-Jones has no connection with Scotland Yard. He is an amateur'—if I may say so—a brilliant amateur."

Thus reassured, the doctor told his story. A young man, an assistant to the custodian of the anatomical school, had disappeared two days before. His character was exemplary; he handled no money; as far as the custodian knew, he had no private worries. He had put away the 'subjects' on the Monday evening and had remarked to the custodian that he thought it looked like rain. At eight next morning he should have returned to work for he was always punctual. It was a busy day and when the students arrived at ten everything was late; some of them complained to him, the doctor, that if their 'subjects' were not arranged for them, they could not expect to do well in the approaching examination. He sent for the custodian, and it was thus for the first time that he learned that John was missing. They sent to his home to enquire the cause; he had not been home. The whole day passed without news of him. The obvious course was to report his disappearance to the police, but, as we could easily understand, it would be very disturbing to the young minds of the students then in the throes of preparing for examination, and destructive to the morale of the establishment to have detectives pratically in charge of the place, questioning everybody and poking their noses into every part of the building. He wished to avoid it if possible. But there was one solution that had occurred to him—he scarcely liked to breathe it—which would make the intervention of the police inevitable—if the poor lad had been the victim of foul play, in the building itself—then—

"But why should you suspect that?"

"Well, I don't quite know. Perhaps it was that when I was going my rounds a few evenings ago I heard loud words coming from the laboratory. All the students had left for the day. I went to the door and I heard the custodian speaking very sharply to the boy, and he was answering much in the same tone. It was one of those quarrels about the details of duty in which a principal had better not interfere, and I went away. But I confess that if left a disagreeable impression on my mind. The custodian always seemed to me an excellent servant—been with us for years—but he his short-tempered and I confess that his language on that occasion was rather a shock to me. Perhaps his duties tend to make a man callous."

"But there is a wide gap between bad language and murder."

"I know, I know. Only it occurred to me—I may be unduly imaginative—that for a man in his position—alone in the building with this boy till a late hour, there are so many facilities for disposing of a body—the furnace and so forth—it is nothing more than a vague suspicion."

We were silent for some time, leaving our food untasted. Then my friend said, "Why don't you ask Jones to go back with you? He could look over the place and tackle the porter in a way you could not. Let him represent himself as employed to find the missing boy."

"Will you?" said the doctor, turning to me. "It would take a great load off my mind, but I scarcely liked to suggest it."

We wasted no further time over luncheon. The doctor had his car waiting and drove me to the school. "If you don't mind," I said, "I should like you to introduce me to the custodian and leave him to show me round. I can put the necessary questions to him as we go. It will seem less formal and official." This being precisely what the doctor wanted, he took me straight to the laboratory, where a middle-aged man was moving about in his shirt sleeves. "Stokes," he said, "this is Mr. Meddleston-Jones, who is enquiring into the disappearance of young Sopwith. He would like you to show him round the premises. I'll leave him with you." He shook hands with me and disappeared.

Stokes seemed quite glad to see me. "We had better not disturb the students in the operating-room, sir. They'll all be gone at five and in the meantime we can go over the basement. Queer business, this of young Sopwith. A better lad never stepped, but I had noticed lately that things had been going wrong with him. He had lost interest in his work."

"Had he anything on his mind?"

"That's just what I think. From things he let drop I think he was gone on some young woman who wouldn't have him. One day he said, 'What's the least that a young couple could live on in London, Mr. Stokes?' And when I named two pound a week, he just fell to pieces, as if I'd crushed him. He's never been the same lad since they refused him for the Army. This is where they bring them in, sir."

"Bring what in?"

"The subjects," he said, in some surprise. We were in a vaulted tunnel in the basement. "And this is the boiler house." A furnace was glowing behind a red hot door.

"Whose duty is it to stoke the boiler?"

"That's just it, sir. It was young Sopwith's duty, but latterly he neglected it and it fell upon me. The same with the packing."

"The packing?"

"Yes, packing the subjects into the coffins. Here is the packing room." We were in a vaulted cellar. One one side was a pile of rough deal coffins stained black, on the other trays of bones and skulls with dried flesh adhering to them. "They come down here from the operating-room like that, sir, and it was young Sopwith's duty to sort them out into some sort of body for each coffin; that is to say, he was supposed to be careful that, as far as he could, there should be only one head, two arms and two legs in each coffin before it was nailed up and taken to the cemetery, but he was very careless latterly and I've had to see to it myself."

"You mean he mixed up the bodies?"

"Oh, no one could help doing that, sir. You can't keep them distinct, but we keep a register of the names and each coffin has the name of one of the subjects tacked on to it for funeral purposes. But of course it may not be their remains. Probably there is something belonging to ten or a dozen in each coffin."

While we were holding this cheerful conversation I was leaning on an enormous wooden box in the outer cellar. I ventured on a question.

"When they bring in the—the subjects, what is done with them?"

"If you will stand over there, sir, I'll show you. You are leaning on them." I must have startled him by the speed of my movements. "Oh, they won't bite, sir," he said, smiling, as he lifted the heavy lid. I peeped over his shoulder. There are racks lay ten human bodies, old and young, stiff, nude, and white, the debris of humanity, the homeless, and friendless, who lead their lives in the London workhouses and probably are sorry to leave them in spite of the misery they have known. In their death they do more for humanity than they have ever done in life, by furnishing material for each fresh generation of surgeons to work upon. "We keep them fresh by injecting formalin," he said, pointing to a wound in the neck of one of the corpses. He shut down the lid and looked at his watch. "The students will be gone now, sir", he said. "I'll take you to the dissecting-room." He led the way upstairs to a large room with high windows that ran the length of the building. A dozen tables, each covered with a sheet, held the subjects that were in the hands of students. One attracted my attention on account of its great bulk in comparison with the rest. The sheet scarcely sufficed to cover it. "Oh that. That's a young elephant that died in the Zoo. One of the students who is sure of his final had a fancy for it."

At the end of the room were a number of iron doors labelled "Head", "Arm", "Leg", "Pelvis", and so on. I asked Stokes what was in them, for they were a possible hiding-place for the body of the missing youth. He threw open one of the iron doors disclosing iron racks, on which human remains were disposed in various stages of dissection.

"It's these that make our job of 'assembling' so difficult downstairs. There's perhaps the arms of twenty people in there and there'll be twenty heads in the next cupboard but one. But it has to be like this so that a student can take up his work just where he left off."

Something had caught my attention and I was scarcely listening. These human arms with disiccated flesh adhering to the bones. Where had I seem them? Then it came to me with a flash—the remains of the murdered woman in our office. I turned to Stokes.

"Do you ever lose any of these bodies?"

"Oh, now and again a student will take away a hand or foot in his bag to work on at home, but if he did such a thing without reporting it to me there'd be trouble, sir. You see, they can't get past my system of booking in and out. I make 'em all sign for what they have. You, for instance, sir, suppose you were a new student. You come to me and say, 'Stokes, have you got a knee for me to-day?' 'Yes,' I says, 'but you'll have to sign for a whole leg.' And then you slip it into your bag and walk away with it. Then, the next morning you says, 'Stokes, I think I'll work at the wrist and hand to-day. Have you got a nice fore-arm?' I look at my book and I say, 'Mr. Meddleston-Jones, not another bit do you get until I see that leg you had yesterday.'" He became silent and thoughtful. "Mind you, I don't say that I've never had them get by me. There was that Allen, for instance—I'll have something to say to *him* when he comes back, if he ever does."

"Tell me about Allen," I said, trying hard to keep my voice even and steady.

"Oh, you should ask the Principal about him. He'd have plenty to tell you. He got away with a whole body from me last year—more than a body—and I didn't find it out till I was going over my books afterwards. Cunning? I never knew a man to beat him. I'll tell you how he did it. On a Monday he'd ask for a head, and just before five I'd see him go to that locker with the head in his hand. Of course, I thought he'd put it back. On Tuesday I'd get a note from him to say he'd been called away. Would I keep the same head for him? He'd be away perhaps a week, and then he'd ask for an arm and so it went on. It wasn't for weeks that I found out what he'd been doing, and then it was too late: he'd gone abroad. He was always doing that—playing fast and loose with the institution. I can't understand why the Principal lets him come back time after time. Well, if he comes back after this he'll have some questions to answer. I've got them all booked up and I'd know them anywhere. Look here, sir, a page all to himself."

He turned over the leaves of his ledger and there, under the name of Henry Allen, were the entries, "June 20th. Head No. 128, male. July 2nd. Forearm No. 43, female," and so on.

"Would you know your—your specimens again if you saw them?"

"Know them? Yes, and could swear to every one of them. When Allen had a subject I put my private mark on it, so there should be no mistake. It's a theft, that's what it is, to say nothing of the trouble it meant for me if I couldn't make up the number of the funerals."

I asked him whether the Principal was still in the building. If so I must see him before he left. He looked at his watch.

"You'll just catch him if you are quick, sir. He leaves sharp at six. It's the second door on the left as you go down the passage."

I was just in time; the Doctor was brushing his hat. "Well," he said, "any daylight?"

"I think I have cleared up one thing: young Sopwith has not been murdered on the premises."

"And you think?"

"I think that you should report him to Scotland Yard as missing, giving his home address. It may be a case of suicide." (I was justified next morning when Sopwith's body was found in the Thames, with a letter in the pocket addressed to the object of his affections.) "But I came to ask you about another matter altogether. You had a student named Henry Allen!"

He threw down his hat and lifted his hands to Heaven. "Henry Allen! Has that fellow turned up again? I never met such a man in my life before. The most charitable view that one can take of Allen is to say that he was mad. Why, that man has been on our books for six years. He passed all his intermediate tests brilliantly, and I used to think that he would carry all before him in his final. Then, on the eve of the examination I would get a note from him saying that he was called abroad on business and we might see nothing of him for six months. I don't know whether it was stage fright or simply a love of roving; perhaps a little of both. He was a good deal older than the ordinary run of pupils, and was an interesting person if one got him to talk. But he made no friends here. He paid his fees regularly and worked hard. You should get Stokes to tell you about him. He accuses him of stealing some of his subjects."

"And I think he is right about that. But I can get them back for you if you think it worth while. I know where they are."

"Is there anything in London that you don't know? Of course, we'd like them back."

"Can Stokes come and identify them?"

"Of course he can. Arrange it with him—anytime you like. And now I must be off—one of these horrible early public dinners. I cannot thank you enough for coming."

I found Stokes in the laboratory just sitting down to his tea. "Let me get you a cup, sir. A drop of tea helps one through the evening." He pushed back the place containing a human eye to make room for my cup, and I found my appetite had left me. I declined the tea, but we talked while he ate and drank. It was a creepy sort of place, this laboratory: bottles from ceiling to floor all alike and all containing the intimate machinery of the human machine—the watch-springs of the human body— bleached and half-floating in yellowish liquid. They did not disturb Stokes' appetite in the least.

"You said just now that you could identify the—er—specimens that Allen took away."

"Try me, sir."

"That's exactly what I want to do if you'll come with me now."

"You know where they are!" he exclaimed in astonishment.

"I'll go whenever you like."

It was past seven when we reached the office, but a light showing beneath the door proved that my Chief was still there. I asked Stokes to wait on the landing till I called him.

"I've been thinking over that Henry Allen case. Mr. Meddleston-Jones," said my Chief before I could speak. "I've been waiting for you all the afternoon. I am now satisfied that in Allen we have got Jack the Ripper. That woman in there is one of his victims." I was so much taken aback that I forgot all about Stokes. "Yes," my Chief continued, "everything points to it—the man's personal habits—his secretiveness—his sudden disappearances. When you arrest him bear in mind that he has a knife about him."

"Don't say any more, Mr. Pepper, till you've heard what I've got to tell you. I have a man here who says he can identify the bones. They are surgical specimens which Allen stole from him." I have never seen a face so transfigured with noble indignation. After all, I was belittling one of the most important cases in his experience.

"Bring him in," he said faintly, and he lighted up the laboratory, into which I led Stokes. My Chief threw back the sheet while I watched Stokes. His was not usually an expressive face. First his eyes grew very round: then his whole frame was shaken with some strong emotion. He seemed quite unable to speak. When at last he found his voice it came harsh and loud. He picked up a thigh bone and said, "You are right, sir; they're ours right enough. Here's my private mark," and he showed me "128" scratched in minute figures on the bone. He looked hard at the face, and again his sturdy frame was shaken by a convulsive movement that began quite low down in his body and seemed to deprive him of speech. If his face had not been so impassive. I should have said that his emotion was supposed laughter. When at last he had recovered command of his voice he said, "You've made a fine woman of No. 48, but what about his beard? He had a long grey beard when he was with us." I did not dare to look at my Chief.

"I think," I said very gently, "that Mr. Stokes had better take the bones away with him. They belong to his medical school, where Henry Allen was a student. They were, in fact, stolen, and the authorities may wish to prosecute." My Chief made no sign, and Stokes began to pack up the specimens in the trunk.

"When Mr. Henry Allen comes home," he said, "and asks for his trunk, you might refer him to the Principal, if you don't mind." He took one long look at the head before he wrapped it up. "I wouldn't damage this wax-work for the world: we'll put it in our Museum." As I was helping him down the stairs with the trunk, he said, "Your friend must have been puzzled by the different sizes of the bones. One arm and one leg belonged to women."

"He was a little puzzled. He thought that the murdered woman was deformed."

"I suppose he didn't happen to notice that she had three hands. I see that he had put one of them where a foot was missing."

When I reached Mrs. Auger's door a man was ringing the bell. He was a thin, hunted-looking creature of about thirty, with three days' growth of beard. The door opened as I came up and Mrs. Auger said, "Oh, Mr. Allen, where *have* you been?"

"I've been to Lisbon," he said in a weak voice.

I laid my hand firmly on his shoulder and said, "Henry Allen, you are wanted at the Medical School to explain why you are unlawfully in possession of certain anatomical specimens which are their property and I must caution you that anything you say will be taken down in writing and used against you at your trial." He turned very white and Mrs. Auger collapsed on her own doorstep.

But the Principal declined to prosecute.

THE ENGLISH FILTER

by Bechhofer Roberts

First published in 1926

I am unlikely ever to forget the visit that my friend, A. B. C. Hawkes, the scientist, and I paid to Rome. "A. B. C.," as I always call him, had let only one man know we were coming—his old acquaintance, Professor Castagni, the bacteriologist. We were astonished, therefore, to find at least a hundred people awaiting us at the station.

Castagni introduced many of them, a lengthy business, and I was amused to discover that his instinctive Italian love of pageantry had apparently caused him to marshal representatives of every branch of learning in the city. I found myself, for example, walking to the hotel with an elderly historian on one side, who knew a little French and less English, and delivered himself of an uninterrupted flow of words in both languages, while at the other ear was a still older professor of philosophy who spoke only Italian—of which tongue I am ignorant, although this did not seem to prevent his addressing me in it.

Hawkes, in the inevitable grey frock-coat and sponge-bag trousers, with a rose in his buttonhole, was submerged in an excited crowd, from whom there arose a Babel of welcome and congratulation. Our arrival was a comic triumph.

The moment we reached our hotel, however, they all bowed, shook our hands, and withdrew.

"What a nerve-racking experience, A. B. C.," I commented, as my friend and I reached our rooms.

"And, of course, the one man I do want to meet wasn't there," Hawkes replied.

I asked who this was.

"Ribotta, the physicist," A. B. C. said. "He must be an old man now, and, I confess, I had never rated him very highly. but just lately he's published some really very remarkable papers on atomic magnetism. How he's managed to make up fifty years leeway in his work, I don't pretend to know. But that is what I've come to Rome to find out."

There was a tap at the door, and a young Italian entered.

"My name is Dorsi, Professor Castagni's assistant," he said in perfect English. "The professor wishes me to act as your guide here in Rome."

"That is most kind of you both," said Hawkes with assumed gratification. "But really, I mustn't trouble you."

"It is truly a pleasure. I appreciate the honour of coming into contact with so famous a man of science. Of course, if yo wish to rest now after you journey, I will wait for you downstairs."

A. B. C. smiled resignedly.

"What my friend Johnstone and I really want," he said, "is an early lunch. I see it's just twelve—perhaps we may indulge our appetites. You will lunch with us, Mr. Dorsi, I trust?"

Our guest proved a sympathetic and intelligent young man. Educated partly in England, he has a sound knowledge of our language and tastes. I could see that Hawkes liked him as well as I did.

"Now, Mr. Dorsi," said A. B. C., as the waiter served the coffee and we lit our cigars. "You tell me that I may expect to be able to pay my formal call on Professor Castagni at three o'clock. Right! The only other visit I am anxious to make is to Professor Ribotta. His latest work interest me profoundly."

"That will be very simple," said Dorsi. "If you like, we can go there now—he is sure to be in his laboratory. And while you are there, gentleman, I should advise yo to talk to his assistant as well."

"You are trying to tell me something," remarked A. B. C., with a shrewed glance.

The Italian smiled.

"The facts are these, professor," he commenced.

"Holy Darwin! Don't call me 'professor'!" cried A. B. C. "Anything but that! The word suggests all the academic foibles I most detest—vanity, pedantry, untidiness, petty jealousies, and tyranny!"

"You must excuse this outburst, Mr. Dorsi," I laughed. "It is a form of address that always rouses his tempestuous nature."

Dorsi stole a humorous glance at the scientist's flaming red hair and smiled more broadly.

"Well, then, Mr. Hawkes," he began again—("that's better!" murmured A. B. C.)—"I am perhaps being indiscreet, but your time is too valuable to be wasted. Professor Ribotta—I emphasise the title in this case—is not responsible for the theories you speak of. He takes the credit for them, but it is due to his assistant, Mr. Lavorello. You know the stupid system we have in our Continental universities—promotion goes by seniority, and a position may be held for life, or at least to a very advanced age, by any old man who does not wish to retire on a pension. That is the case of Professor Ribotta. He holds a chair for which, however well he may have filled it thirty years ago, he is to-day quite unqualified. You will see this for yourselves. But Lavorello—ah, there is a young man of the first quality, an experimenter without rival in all Italy, a scientific genius."

"I have heard such cases before," said A. B. C. "I shall make a point of getting into touch with him. Thank you for your friendly advice. Shall we be going?"

The three of us set out for Ribotta's laboratory, which we found in an old part of the city, near the Pantheon. The entrance was remote from the main portion of the institute, and Dorsi told us that it led to Ribotta's and his assistant's rooms only.

The porter inside took off his cap to us and led us into a small room which, Dorsi told me, was the preserve of the laboratory attendant. It was dark and confined; the remains of a meal lay on the table and a couple of dirty overalls hung on a hook on th wall.

We stopped before another door, on which the porter knocked.

It was opened to us by Ribotta himself, to whom Dorsi swiftly explained who we were. The professor, an old man with a flowing beard and piercing eyes, then invited us to enter. He greeted A. B. C. effusively, led us to his desk, and motioned to us to sit down. He leaned forward in his chair, holding a hand to his ear.

"You do? Well, no matter; I prefer to speak English. Oh, I am very fond of England. Forty years ago I was a Cambridge under your great professors." He mentioned some famous names. "They taught me much—but I see you are too young to know them. I have not been in England since then, but I still have my great love for English things. I have many beautiful English things in my laboratory. I will call my assistant; he shall show them to you. Lavorello! Lavorello! Ah, he does not hear me. No matter, I will send the attendant to him. Carlo!" he called.

"That wretched attendant," the garrulous old man went on, "I cannot make him obey me. He attends only to Mr. Lavorello's work; he leaves my laboratory dirty. When he comes, he will hear from me. And now I will call my assistant myself."

He pounded on a door at the other side of the room. We heard a chair pushed back and the slamming of a door. Through an unglazed, barred window that gave on to a corridor—apparently the only ventilation of the room, for all the other windows were tightly closed—we saw a man pass.

Ribotta tittered. "You think it odd, perhaps," he said. "My assistant is in the next room, but he cannot come in through the connecting door. Ah, this is done on purpose. I do not want anybody to come into the room. So I locked that door twenty years ago, and it has remained locked ever since. He must come in the way you came, the only entrance. And that has a Yale lock, so that nobody can come in except myself and the attendant, unless I let them in myself. Only he and I have keys. Even the porter I never allow to enter. I want quiet, and in this way I get it. Ah, there must be Lavorello!"

He motioned to Dorsi, and our guide slipped across to unfasten the door. A young man entered, keen and dark, but very fleshy for his age—a point, we afterwards discovered, on which he was rather sensitive. I looked at him with interest, for he was the brilliant youth whose work had brought Hawkes to Rome.

"Sit down, Lavorello, sit down," cried Ribotta. "But no, I want you to show my English guests the great things that have come here from their country. First give them a glass of water from my filter."

Without a word the young man went over to a large glass tank, uncovered at the top and with some kind of filter and tap attached. It was one of the most noticeable objects in the peculiarly bare room. He filled a glass from it and and brought this to us. Ribotta held it under Hawkes's nose.

"Taste!" he said, "What beautiful clear water! Rome water is not good to drink, but out of my English filter—ah, then one may drink with pleasure and safety. Lavorello, empty this ashtray and give me some matches!"

Expressionately Lavorello obeyed. Then Ribotta told him to get the cigars out of a drawer, and the old man offered them to A. B. C., Dorsi, and me—we refused them—and lit one of the rank things himself. He did not trouble to offer one to Lavorello, I noticed.

"Now you have seen the filter," he rattled on. "Next you must see the English microscope. Lavorello, bring the microscope and show it to Professor Hawkes."

It was, even as I could see, a very ordinary piece of laboratory apparatus, but the old man gloated over it as if it were a marvel.

"Very interesting indeed," murmured A. B. C.; "but have you any new results in your work on magnetism, sir?"

"No, I have not them here at the moment. I do not make the experiments myself these days; I leave them to the young men. Lavorello shall show you them in his laboratory. It is good work—I showed him how it should be done. The brains are mine; the hand is his. That is how it should be, is it not?"

For politeness' sake, we agreed.

"Do have another glass of water. Professor Hawkes. No? Ah, but it is good, thanks to my English filter. Your friend, then? Oh, you must! Lavorello, bring another glass of water! Quickly! If you drank more of this water, Lavorello, you would not be so fat! There is no water like this in Rome."

It tasted to me like any other water, but I thought it incumbent on me to express loud admiration.

"We must not take up any more of your time, sir," said Hawkes, rising from his chair. "With your permission, we shall just glance at Mr. Lavorello's work, and then we must be going away."

"Delighted to have seen you professor," said Ribotta, shaking our hands. "I am always glad to welcome foreign scientists to my laboratory, especially from England. Lavorello, you are to show these gentlemen your work—*our* work—so that they may see that we old men can still keep pace with the young. Ah, but first give me some more matches."

As we left the laboratory through the little ante-room, the attendant hurried in. He was, I noticed, a sinister-looking fellow, the sort of man one would instinctively avoid on a dark night. He went past us into the professor's room, the door of which he opened with his pass-key, and we heard the old man greet him with a storm of angry words.

The corridor led us round towards Lavorello's room. Dorsi in a whisper called my attention to the cupboards and bookcases that were placed against the doors leading to the rest of the building—another example of Ribotta's insitence upon isolation. As we passed the barred window, we saw the attendant standing by the desk, gazing at the professor with a malicious glance. The old man was shouting and gesticulating, but, as he heard us go by, he turned and waved.

We reached Lavorello's laboratory, the whole atmosphere of which was very different from the old professor's, and A. B. C. and he were soon bent in eager interest over note-books and curves, with an occasional reference to some proof-sheets that lay on the table.

They forgot all about Dorsi and myself. The subject was far beyond either of us and we passed the time chatting.

"It's pretty clear," Dorsi said, after a long and bitter attack upon the old man in the next room, "with whom Mr. Hawkes finds himself more at home.'

I sympathised with his denunciation of Ribotta's selfishness, his ridiculous pride in the very ordinary filter and microscope, and his bullying treatment of Lavorello, but, as a stranger, I thought it best not to be drawn into the expression of an opinion, and I looked round for an opportunity to change the subject.

"Hallo," I said, thankfully, "here is something I do understand a little about."

I walked over to a cabinet in the corner of the room, in which were ranged objects that I recognised as Italian and Greek-Italian antiques. There were coins and little statuettes and rings and toys and other trifles.

Lavorello happened to see us gazing at his collection. He smiled and unlocked the door of the cabinet.

"A hobby of mine," he said to me. "My country—I am a Sicilian, you know—is especially rich in such things."

"What are these?" asked Dorsi, pointing to some small white objects, which were familiar with me.

"Knucklebones," answered Lavorello, "with which I suppose our ancestors used to play. The queer glasses behind them are for another game, *cottabos*; and those square things on the same shelf are *tesserae*, the counterparts of modern dice."

A. B. C. called him back to the papers and Dorsi and I discussed the customs of the ancients and their survivals in modern times.

It was a long time before Hawkes was ready to leave. Then the three of us took leave of Lavorello and tip-toed along the corridor so as not to attract Ribotta's attention, for we had no desire to be called in to hear another harangue. We glanced in through the barred opening and saw him at his desk, with his beloved filter beyond him underneath the clock. Fortunately he was absorbed in a newspaper and did not notice us past.

"Shades of Cavendish!" whispered A. B. C. "It's three o'clock already!"

We hurried past the porter's lodge, to whose occupant the laboratory attendant was declaiming fiercely.

"The attendant's opinion of Ribotta," A. B. C. said to me when we got outside, "is not much higher than our own, I'm afraid. If my knowledge of Italian, or at least of the Roman dialect, is not in error, he was expressing a wish that the old professor might be devoured by hungry wolves. He added that, if they or some similar agents of destiny did not perform this necessary action, he himself would have to attend to it. I must confess, after comparing Ribotta's and Lavorello's capacity, I have some sympathy with the attendant's desire."

"Lavorello is a good man, is he?" I smiled.

"First rate," said my friend. "A brilliant, ingenious brain with a magnificent grasp of scientific possibilities! If he has a fault, it's a tendency to rush at conclusions, to go the short way to a result when a longer and more patient method would be more suitable. But he'll go far! It's a crying shame that he should be held back by that old charlatan. And for the latter to steal the credit of Lavorello's researches is an insult to science."

For a moment Hawkes's round, good-natured face looked quite angry, but his usual smile soon reappeared.

We made a short call on Castagni, and spent the rest of the afternoon in the Forum. Not only did we visit the usual sights there, but, as honoured guests, we were invited to view various collections and excavations not open to the general public.

For once I was able to display more knowledge than Hawkes, and, to his mock awe, I traced resemblances between some of the exhibits and various specimens I had unearthed on the more successful of my archaeological expeditions in England. A. B. C. was in his element, however, with some ancient scientific instruments, and his identification of their uses has now, I understand, been officially adopted. I learned from the director of the excavations that Lavorello had performed a similar service at the time of some earlier discoveries.

We were to meet Dorsi for dinner at the "Ulpia," which he recommend as the most picturesque restaurant in the city. We found it in an ancient basilica, whose curved brick walls, arching to the roof, made a curious and sombre background for the bright napery and electric lights. The blend of old and new—so typical of Rome—was carried down to the smallest details; the lamps, for example, were fixed in amphorae of antique form, and the menu was rolled like an old parchment scroll. The place amused us, and we settled down patiently to await our guest.

An hour after the agreed time we despaired of his arrival and decided to begin. At ten o'clock, just as we were about to leave, he came in.

"Forgive my absence," he said, "but a terrible thing as happened. Professor Ribotta has been murdered!"

"Murdered!" I exclaimed.

"He was found poisoned in his laboratory this afternoon," Dorsi went on. A pallid smile flickered on his lips as he added, "The posion was apparently administered in the filter of which he was so proud."

"Who did it?" A. B. C. asked.

"The attendant has disappeared, and the police are in search of him. the chief of police is in the laboratory now, and, as you were among the last people to see the professor alive, he wishes to interrogate you. He was going to send to your hotel, but I volunteered to come here and fetch you."

We called for the bill and left the restaurant in silence. We walked through the warm night to the laboratory, and found it ablaze with lights. A group of men were standing in the dead man's room, among them Lavorello and the porter, both much moved.

The body had been removed to a neighbouring mortuary for examination. They told us that the professor had been found sitting upright at his desk, just as we had seen him as we tip-toed out that same afternoon. Tightly grasped in his hand was a glass of water, of which he had drunk perhaps half; and his eyes were fixed in a rigid stare.

The chief of police asked Hawkes a string of questions, writing the replies in a note-book.

"There seems no doubt," Dorsi said to me, "that the attendant is the villain. We all heard the

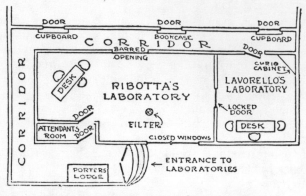

PLAN OF PROFESSOR RIBOTTA'S LABORATORY

quarrel and the threats he uttered against the old man. He, the attendant, was seen to leave the building a few minutes after three o'clock; in fact, he did not go back into the laboratory after we left. Lavorello says that at a quarter past five, on his way out to the baths that he visits every afternoon to try to reduce his weight, he spoke to Ribotta through the barred window from the corridor. The porter confirms that Lavorello went out at that time. Now comes the important evidence; at half-past five the attendant came in—not too sober, the porter thinks, and still muttering threats against the old man—and entered his little room, through which alone, as you know, it is possible to enter his laboratory.

"He came out ten minutes later and has not been seen since. At six o'clock, twenty minutes after the attendant went away, the porter knocked on the inner door to give the professor a message. Alarmed at receiving no reply, he went round to the barred window and called to him. When he saw that the old gentleman did not move, he called some students who were passing by. They had, of course, to smash down the door to enter, and they discovered Ribotta dead with the glass in his hand."

I was considering these facts when a stir outside was followed by the appearance of a couple of policeman with the attendant.

The villain was even more unprepossessing than before; he was both drunk and frightened.

The chief of police told him that he was suspected of causing the professor's death, and the man, moistending his parched lips, vehemently denied the charge. Ordered to account for his movements that afternoon, he said the professor had driven him past endurance and he had gone away in a temper. He thought this must have been about three o'clock.

He went to a wine-shop and had some drinks and then made up his mind to go home to his village, a few miles out of the city, but on his way he remembered that he had left some personal belongings in his room and came back to fetch them. After making a parcel of them, he said, he went away again, without entering the laboratory at all. Then he took the tram to his home, where the police had just arrested him.

He repeatedly denied that he had gone into the professor's laboratory during his short return. He had, he insisted, stayed in his own little room and made his parcel.

Asked whether he had not uttered threats against the professor's life earlier in the afternoon, he at first said he had not. But, confronted with the evidence of the porter and ourselves, he had to admit that in the heat of his anger he might have done so.

His account in other respects certainly tallied with the previous statements. But the damning facts

124

remained that only he and the dead man had keys to the laboratory and that he had admittedly been in the ante-room between the time Ribotta was last seen alive—by Lavorello, at a quarter past five—and the time of his being found dead at six o'clock.

Suddenly the chief turned to the porter. "And you?" he said. "Did you enter the laboratory during that period?" A. B. C. interpreted all this to me.

"The professor never permitted me inside," answered the porter. "And I had no key. No one had a key, not even Signor Lavorello, except the professor and the attendant."

"Perhaps the professor opened the door to somebody else, or the murderer had provided himself with a third key?"

"Even so," was the reply, "my lodge is opposite the door of the ante-room, and I should have seen anyone enter it. Nobody did. There is no other entrance to the laboratory."

The chief went round the room examining it. As he showed us, there was indeed no other entrance than by the door from the attendant's room. The door to Lavorello's room was still bolted, and it was clear that it had not been opened. The dust on the skylight and on the windows proved that they, too, had not been tampered with. As for the window to the corridor, the bars were firmly fixed in the mortar; a baby could not have climbed between them.

We were asked to accompany the part to the mortuary. A sheet was reverently pulled back and the dead man's face revealed. I watched the attendant. He shuddered and crossed himself surreptitiously. One might have said that his very emotion testified to his guilt.

The unnatural rigidity of the dead man's features seemed to interest Hawkes. He took a glass from his pocket and intently examined the staring eyes for some minutes. Then he entered upon a conversation with the doctors in a corner of the room, where they were working.

When the rest of us went out, glad to leave the presence of death, A. B. C. did not immediately follow. Dorsi and I waited outside, after seeing the prisoner removed, protesting violently, by the police. My friend came out at last.

"Gentlemen," he said, "you must excuse me. Johnstone, take Mr. Dorsi back to the hotel and entertain him—and Mr. Lavorello too, if he will accompany you. I am going to help with the medical examination."

"What a gruesome idea!" I said.

"My erudite friend," he replied, "you ought to know my interest in the border-line between physics and physiology. Good night." And he hurried back inside the mortuary.

We walked to the hotel, discussing the terrible event.

"I suppose," I said, "It is certain the poor man was poisoned?"

"Of that there is no doubt," said Dorsi. "The doctors suspected it from the first, and Mr. Hawkes, who seems to know everything, agrees with them. They all think it is a poison of the strychnine class, although probably not strychnine itself."

"It ought to be easy to find where the attendant procured it," I suggested.

"In England it might be," smiled Lavorello, "but not, I fear, in Rome. However, as no one but the attendant could possibily have entered and dropped it in the filter, and question where he obtained it hardly seems to matter."

"Can it possibly have been introduced through the walls or the roof or the windows?" I asked.

"Impossible," said Dorsi. "Stupid and deaf as the old man was, he was very keen-sighted, and, sitting at his desk with the filter right in front of him, he would have noticed any attempt to tamper with it. Besides, how on earth could anyone have done so, when it was in the very middle of the room?"

I had to admit that they were right.

They would not come in with me, and we parted at the entrance to my hotel. I sat in my room for some time, but I saw nothing to shake my conviction that the attendant was guilty. This seemed established beyond the possibility of doubt.

Hawkes did not return all that night, nor was he in the hotel when I left it the next morning to visit St. Peter's and one of the Vatican galleries. I lunched in a little restaurant near the Cathedral and returned to the hotel in the middle of the afternoon.

I found A. B. C. waiting for me. From his look I guessed that he had spent the whole night on his researches.

"Well, what news?" he asked.

"I look to you for that, A. B. C." I replied. "Has the attendant confessed?"

"Not yet; but things are very black against him."

"You look tired," I said. "Why don't you lie down for a while?"

"I am a little fatigued," he admitted. "Between you and me, Ribotta dead presents more scientific interest than he did alive, but he is equally wearying in both states. I fear you will think that remark in bad taste, I don't think I'll lie down, however. What would you say to taking a Turkish bath—a Roman bath, I suppose I ought to call it here? Our full-bodied friend Lavorello patronizes the baths every afternoon, it seems, like the lover of antique Roman customs that he is, and I have arranged to visit one of them with him to-day. I hope you will accompany us."

I readily agreed, and we drove off to the laboratory and picked up Lavorello. We took the opportunity to glance in at the dead man's room, and I confirmed my impressions of the case. Nobody could possibly have entered it except through the attendant's room.

The three of us were soon in the baths enjoying the delights that Lavorello, lying on a slab near us, assured us were the daily pleasures of the ancient Romans. His admiration for my friend was so evident, and he addressed his conversation so exclusively to him, that A. B. C. seemed to fear that I was being unduly relegated to the background.

"Cease to emulate the modest violet, friend Johnstone," he smiled. "Discourse to use upon topics suitable to the occasion. An archaeologist like you ought to welcome the society of a fellow-enthusiast like Mr. Lavorello—Professor Lavorello, I suppose his friends will call him now. Expound to us, my able adjutant, the pastimes of antique Roman society in the baths they frequented."

"Surely, A. B. C.," I said, "Mr. Lavorello is better qualified than I? His collection shows him to be a specialist."

"I doubt it," said Hawkes. "He has been to busy, I am sure, adequately to interest himself in the subject; is that not so, Lavorello?"

"Oh, I don't know," replied Lavorello; "I have found time in my leisure moments to study it with a certain thoroughness."

"Theory, theory, all is theory!" A. B. C. scoffed. "I'll wager for example, that you, Lavorello, couldn't even tell me the right way to hold those old knucklebones that are in your cabinet.

"Surely knucklebones are played to-day pretty much as they ever were?" said the Italian. "The simplest and yet the most difficult game is to toss them one after the other in the air and to endeavour to catch the whole set—three or five—on the back of your hand. It is difficult, but after long practice I found I could do it."

"So you have joined practice to theory after all," said A. B. C. "I apologise for my unworthy doubts. Now, Johnstone, I give you one more chance to retrieve you reputation as an archaeologist. Tell me some other game that the ancient played on such occasions as these—and in such prodigious heat as this."

"That's easy," I said. "I was reminded of it yesterday. Mr. Lavorello has the instruments in his cabinet. It is the old game of *cottabos*."

"Oh, how do you play that, friend Lavorello?"

"I am afraid," replied he, laughing, "knowledge stops short at knucklebones. As you hinted, I am not a universal genius."

"Now, splendid Johnstone, cover yourself with glory! Tell us how the royal and ancient game of *cottabos* was played."

"As far as I remember," I said, "the players amused themselves with it at drinking parties. The aim of the game was to throw wine from a specially-shaped glass in such a way that the liquid travelled through the air without scattering. This was done, according to German scholars, who know everything about everything, by a particular twirling movement imparted to the glass. The object was to sink a little metal saucer floating in a sunken tank by casting the wine into it. Isn't that right, Mr. Lavorello?"

Just at that moment Dorsi entered, smiling at the sight of us three in our scanty attire.

"What stifling heat!" he said. "You sent for me, Mr. Hawkes?"

"Yes," said A. B. C. "I wanted you to know that I have discovered the murderer of Professor Ribotta."

"You have?" we exclaimed, in one breath.

"I thought, sir, the police arrested him yesterday," said Dorsi.

"No, dear Dorsi, no. The attendant had no hand in the crime."

"But it was proved——" I began.

"It was proved, my intelligent compatriot, that the attendant entered the building a half-past five for a few minutes. The corpse was not discovered till six, and so it was taken for granted that the man had entered the professor's room and dropped the poison in the filter."

"Exactly," I said.

"But when I saw the corpse," A. B. C. went on, "I was struck at once by the peculiar red discoloration of the eyes. There is a certain obscured poison of the strychnine class which produces this effect. If also produces almost instantaneouse death. As you know, the eye is like a camera, with the retina at the back like a sensitive plate, on which the different pictures are continually formed. Now, this poison makes the lens lose its transparency, with the result that no light enters, and the eyeball becomes like a camera with the shutter closed.

"It occurred to me, therefore, that the picture that was cast on the retina at the moment of death might have persisted. Of course, we should not perceive this picture direct. I thought, however, that it might be possible, as it were, to develop the image. The doctors agreed to allow me to try. I will not give you details of the method, for they are not particularly pleasant to hear. We were not successful with the first eye; the work was more difficult than I had suspected. But from the second I got a blurred picture—not a studio photograph, perhaps, but sufficient for our purpose. That picture told me all I wanted to know."

"What did it show?" I asked.

"Just the clock on the wall, on which, as I took the trouble to observe this afternoon, the rays of the afternoon sun fall. Now that photograph on the dead man's retina, which was the last thing he saw in this life, showed with clearness that, at the moment of his death, the hands of the clock stood at exactly five o'clock!"

"Five o'clock," cried Dorsi. "Then the attendant had not yet returned!"

"Before he came back on that unfortunate visit to his room," said A. B. C. solemnly, "the professor was already dead."

"But nobody else had entered the laboratory," I objected.

"And nobody had!" said A. B. C. "That what made me so curious about the game of *cotabos*. You see, a really skilled player, standing in the corridor with the proper kind of glass, might well throw the poison through the barred window into the filter. It would be difficult, I admit, but a practised hand could achieve it. The professor at his desk would not notice the liquid passing across the room."

A choking sound came from the slab where Lavorello lay. he was gasping as if unable to draw his breath. A. B. C. strode across to him and spoke softly but distinctly in his ear, while Dorsi and I watched with a terrible suspicion in our minds.·

"Lavorello," said Hawkes, sternly, "*you* understand!"

The young scientist groaned and fought for air. Then a sudden agitation of his body threw him off the slab on to the floor. Dorsi and I rushed to raise him, but A. B. C. waved us back.

"It's too late," he said. "I knew his heart was weak—he was foolish to use these hot rooms. The heat of the bath, the strain of his recent crime, and the knowledge that it had been detected have killed him. I must confess that this was my reason for staging this little scene here. We may now be able to avert a very nasty scandal; whereas, if it had come to a public trail——" He shook his head. "Yes, he was a great experimenter, was young Lavorello, but his ambition was too great for him. A true scientist should await results, not force them, even when a stupid, vain old man stands in the way."

THE MYSTERY OF MARIE ROGÊT

by Edgar Allan Poe

First published in 1842

There are ideal series of events which run parallel with the real ones. They rarely coincide. Men and circumstances generally modify the ideal train of events, so that it seems imperfect, and its consequences are equally imperfect. Thus with the Reformation; instead of Protestantism came Lutheranism.—NOVALIS. *Moral Ansichten.*

There are few persons, even among the calmest thinkers, who have not occasionally been startled into a vague yet thrilling half-credence in the supernatural, by *coincidences* of so seemingly marvellous a character that, as *mere* coincidences, the intellect has been unable to receive them. Such sentiments—for the half-credences of which I speak have never the full force of *thought*— such sentiments are seldom thoroughly stifled unless by reference to the doctrine of chance, or, as it is technically termed, the Calculus of Probabilities. Now this Calculus is, in its essence, purely mathematical; and thus we have the anomaly of the most rigidly exact in science applied to the shadow and spirituality of the most intangible in speculation.

The extraordinary details which I am now called upon to make public, will be found to form, as regards sequence of time, the primary branch of a series of scarcely intelligible *coincidences*, whose secondary or concluding branch will be recognised by all readers in the late murder of Mary Cecilia Rogers, at New York.

When, in an article entitled, *The Murders in the Rue Morgue*, I endeavoured, about a year ago, to depict some very remarkable features in the mental character of my friend, the Chevalier C. Auguste Dupin, it did not occur to me that I should ever resume the subject. This depicting of character constituted my design; and this design was thoroughly fulfilled in the wild train of circumstances brought to instance Dupin's indiosyncrasy. I might have adduced other examples, but I should have proven no more. Late events, however, in their surprising development, have startled me into some further details, which will carry with them the air of extorted confession. Hearing what I have lately heard, it would be indeed strange should I remain silent in regard to what I both heard and saw long ago.

Upon the winding up of the tragedy involved in the deaths of Madame L'Espanaye and her daughter, the Chevalier dismissed the affair at once from his attention, and relapsed into his old habits of moody reverie. Prone, at all times, to abstraction, I readily fell in with his humour; and continuing to occupy our chambers in the Faubourg Saint Germain, we gave the Future to the winds, and slumbered tranquilly in the Present, weaving the dull world around us into dreams.

But these dreams were not altogether uninterrupted. It may readily be supposed that the part played by my friend, in the drama at the Rue Morgue, had not failed of its impression upon the fancies of the Parisian police. With its emissaries, the name of Dupin had grown into a household word. The simple character of those inductions by which he had disentangled the mystery never having been explained even to the Prefect, or to any other individual than myself, of course it is not surprising that the affair was regarded as little less than miraculous, or that the Chevalier's analytical abilities acquired for him the credit of intuition. His frankness would have led him to disabuse every inquirer of such prejudice; but his indolent humour forbade all further agitation of a topic whose interest to himself had long ceased. It thus happened that he found himself the cynosure of the political eyes; and the cases were not few in which attempt was made to engage his services at the Prefecture. One of the most remarkable instances was that of the murder of a young girl named Marie Rogêt.

This event occurred about two years after the atrocity in the Rue Morgue. Marie, whose Christian and family name will at once arrest attention from their resemblance to those of the unfortunate "cigar-girl", was the only daughter of the widow Estelle Rogêt. The father had died during the child's infancy, and from the period of his death, until within eighteen months before the assasination which forms the subject of our narrative, the mother and daughter had dwelt together in the Rue Pavée Saint Andrée; Madame there keeping a *pension*, assisted by Marie. Affairs went on to thus until the latter had attained her twenty-second year, when her great beauty attracted the notice of a perfumer, who occupied one of the shops in the basement of the Palais Royal, and whose custom lay chiefly among the desperate adventurers infesting that neighbourhood. Monsieur Le Blanc was not unaware of the advantages to be derived from the attendance of the fair Marie in his perfumery; and his liberal proposals were accepted eagerly by the girl, although with somewhat more of hesitation by Madame.

The anticipations of the shopkeeper were realised, and his rooms soon became notorious through the charms of the sprightly *grisette*. She had been in his employ about a year, when her admirers were thrown into confusion by her sudden disappearance from the shop. Monsieur Le Blanc was unable to account for her absence, and Madame Rogêt was distracted with anxiety and terror. The public papers immediately took up the theme, and the police were upon the point of making serious investigations, when, one morning, after the lapse of a week, Marie, in good health, but with a somewhat saddened air, made her reappearance at her usual counter in the pefumery. All inquiry, except that of a private character, was, of course, immediately hushed. Monsieur Le Blanc professed total ignorance, as before. Marie, with Madame replied to all questions, that the last week had been spent at the house of relation in the country. Thus the affair died away, and was generally forgotten; for the girl, ostensibly to relieve herself from the impertinence of curiosity, soon bade a final adieu to the perfumer, and sought the shelter of her mother's residence in the Rue Pavée Saint Andrée.

It was about five months after his return home, that her friends were alarmed by her sudden disappearance for the second time. Three days elapsed, and nothing was heard of her. On the fourth her corpse was found floating in the Seine, near the shore which is opposite the Quartier of the Rue Saint Andrée, and at a point not very far distant from the secluded neighbourhood of the Barrière de Roule.

The atrocity of this murder (for it was at once evident that murder had been committed), the youth and beauty of the victim, and, above all, her previous notoriety, conspired to produce intense excitement in the minds of the sensitive Parisians. I can call to mind no similar occurrence producing so general and so intense an effect. For several weeks, in the discussion of this one absorbing theme, even the momentous political topics of the day were forgotten. The Prefect made unusual exertions; and the powers of the whole Parisian police were, of course, tasked to the utmost extent.

Upon the first discovery of the corpse, it was not supposed that the murderer would be able to elude, for more than a very brief period, the inquisition which was immediately set on foot. It was not until the expiration of a week that it was deemed necessary to offer a reward; and even then this reward was limited to a thousand francs. In the meantime the investigation proceeded with vigour, if not always with judgment, and numerous individuals were examined to no purpose; while, owing to the continual absence of all clue to the mystery, the popular excitement greatly increased. At the end of the tenth day it was thought advisable to double the sum originally proposed; and, at length, the second week having elapsed without leading to any discoveries, and the prejudice which always exists in Paris against the police having given itself in several serious *emeutes*, the Prefect took it upon himself to offer the sum of twenty thousand francs "for the conviction of the assissin", or, if more than should prove to have been implicated, "for the conviction of any one of the assassins". In the proclamation setting forth this reward, a full pardon was promised to any accomplice who should come forward in evidence against his fellow; and to the whole was appended, wherever it appeared, the private placard of a committee of citizens, offering ten thousand francs, in addition to the amount proposed by the Prefecture. The entire reward thus stood at no less than thirty thousand francs, which will be regarded as an extraordinary sum when we consider the humble condition of the girl, and the great frequency, in large cities, of such atrocities as the one described.

No one doubted now that the mystery of this murder would be immediately brought to light. But although, in one or two instances, arrests were made which promised elucidation, yet nothing was elicited which could implicate the parties suspected; and they were dischaged forthwith. Strange as it may appear, the third week from the discovery of the body had passed, and passed without any light being thrown upon the subject, before even a rumour of the events which had so agitated the public mind reached the ears of Dupin and myself. Engaged in researches which had absorbed our whole attention, it had been nearly a month since either of us had gone abroad, or received a visitor, or more than glanced at the leading political articles in one of the daily papers. The first intelligence of the murder was brought us by G——, in person. He called upon us early in the afternoon of the thirteenth of July 18——, and remained with us until late in the night. He had been piqued by the failure of all his endeavours to ferret out the assasins. His reputation—so he said with a peculiarly Parisian air—was at stake. Even his honour was concerned. The eyes of the public were upon him; and there was really no sacrifice which he would not be willing to make for the development of the mystery. He concluded a somewhat droll speech with a compliment upon what he was pleased to term the *tact* of Dupin, and made him a direct and certainly a liberal proposition, the precise nature of which I do not feel myself at liberty to disclose, but which has no bearing upon the proper subject of my narrative.

The compliment my friend rebutted as best he could, but the proposition he accepted at once, although its advantages were altogether provisional. This point being settled, the Prefect broke forth at once into explanations of his own views, interspersing them with long comments upon the evidence; of which latter we were not yet in possession. He discoursed much and, beyond doubt, learnedly; while I hazarded an occasional suggestion as the night wore drowsily away. Dupin, sitting steadily in his accustomed arm-chair, was the embodiment of respectful attention. He wore spectacles, during the whole interview; and an occasional glance beneath their green glasses sufficed to convince me that he slept not the less soundly, because silently, throughout the seven or eight leaden-footed hours which immediately preceded the departure of the Prefect.

In the morning, I procured, at the Prefecture, a full report of all the evidence elicited, and, at the various newspaper offices, a copy of every paper in which, from first to last, had been published any decisive information in regard to this sad affair. Freed from all that was positively disproved, the mass of information stood thus:

Marie Rogêt left the residence of her mother, in the Rue Pavée St. Andrée, about nine o'clock in the morning of Sunday, June the 22nd, 18—. In going out, she gave notice to a Monsieur Jacques St. Eustache, and to him only, of her intention to spend the day with an aunt, who resided in the Rue des Drômes. The Rue des Drômes is a short and narrow but populous thoroughfare, not far from the banks of the river, and at a distance of some two miles, in the most direct course possible, from the *pension* of Madame Rogêt. St. Eustache was the accepted suitor of Marie, and lodged, as well as took his meals, at the *pension*. He was to have gone for his bethrothed at dusk, and to have escorted her home, In the afternoon, however, it came on to rain heavily; and, supposing that she would remain at her aunt's (as she had done under similar circumstances before), he did not think it necessary to keep his promise. As night drew on, Madame Rogêt (who was an infirm old lady, seventy years of age) was heard to express a fear "that she should never see Marie again"; but this observation attracted little attention at the time.

On Monday it was ascertained that the girl had not been to the Rue des Drômes; and when the day elapsed without tidings of her, a tardy search was instituted at several points in the city and its environs. It was not, however, until the fourth day from the priod of her disappearance that anything satisfactory was ascertained respecting her. On this day (Wednesday, the 25th of June) a Monsieur Beauvais, who, with a friend, had been making inquiries for Marie near the Barrière du Roule, on the shore of the Seine which is opposite the Rue Pavée St. Andrée, was informed a corpse had just been towed ashore by some fishermen, who had found it floating in the river. Upon seeing the body, Beauvais, after some hesitation, identified it as that of the perfumery-girl. His friend reocgnised it more promptly.

The face was suffused with dark blood, some of which issued from the mouth. No foam was seen, as in the case of the merely drowned. There was no discoloration in the cellular tissue. About the throat were bruises and impressions of fingers. The arms were bent over on the chest, and were rigid. The right hand was clenched; the left partially open. On the left wrist were two circular excoriations, apparently the effect of ropes, or of a rope in more than one volution. As part of the right wrist, also, was much chafed, as well as the back. In bringing the body to the shore the fishermen had attached to it a rope, but none of the excoriations had been effected by this. The flesh of the neck was much swollen. There were no cuts apparent, or bruises which appeared the effect of the blows. A piece of lace was found tied so tighly around the neck as to be hidden from sight; it was comletely buried in the flesh, and was fastened by a knot which lay just under the left ear. This alone would have sufficed to produce death. The medical testimony spoke confidently of the virtuous character of the deceased. She had been subjected, it said, to brutal violence. The corpse was in such condition when found that there could have been no difficulty in its recognition by friends.

The dress was much torn and otherwise disordered. In the outer garment, a slip, about a foot wide, had been torn upward from the bottom hem to the waist, but not torn off, was wound three times around the waist, and secured by a sort of hitch in the back. The dress beneath the frock was of fine muslin; and from this a slip eighteen inches wide had been torn entirely out—torn very evenly and with great care. It was found around her neck, fitting loosely, and secured with a hard knot. Over this muslin slip and the slip of lace the strings of a bonnet were attached, the bonnet being appended. The knot by which the strings of the bonnet were fastened was not a lady's, but a slip of sailors knot.

After the recognition of the corpse, it was not, as usual, taken to the Morgue (this formality being superfluous), but hastily interred not far from the spot at which it was brought ashore. Through the exertions of Beauvais, the matter was industriously hushed up, as far as possible; and several days had elapsed before any public emotion resulted. A weekly paper, however, at length took up the theme; the corpse was disinterred, and a re-examination instituted; but nothing was elicited beyond what has been already noted. The clothes, however, were now submitted to the mother and friends of the deceased and fully identified as those worn by the girl upon leaving home.

Meantime, the excitement increased hourly. Several individuals were arrested and discharged. St. Eustache fell especially under suspicion; and he failed, at first, to give an intelligible account of his whereabouts during the Sunday on which Marie left home. Subsequently, however, he submitted to Monsieur G—affidavits, accounting satisfactorily for every hour of the day in question. As time passed and no discovery ensued, a thousand contradictory rumours were circulated, and journalists busied themselves in *suggestions*. Among these, the one which attracted the most notice, was the idea that Marie Rogêt still lived—that the corpse found in the Seine was that of some other unfortunate. It will be proper that I submit to the reader some passages which embody the suggestion alluded to. These passages are *literal* translations from *L'Etoile*, a paper conducted, in general, with much ability.

"Madamoiselle Rogêt left her mother's house on Sunday morning, June the 22nd, 18—, with the ostensible purpose of going to see her aunt, or some other connection in the Rue des Drômes. From that hour, nobody is proved to have seen her. There is no trace or tidings of her at all . . . .Now, though we have no evidence that Marie Rogêt was in the land of the living after nine o'clock on Sunday, June the 22nd, we have proof that, up to that hour, she was alive. on Wednesday noon, at twelve, a female body was discovered afloat on the shore of the Barrière du Roule. This was, even if we presume that Marie Rogêt was thrown into the river within three hours after she left her mother's house, only three days from the time she left her home—three days to an hour. But it is folly to suppose that the murder, if murder was committed on her body could have been consummated soon enough to have enabled her murderers to throw the body into the river before midnight. Those who are guilty of such horrid crimes choose darkness rather than light. . . . Thus we see that if the body found in the river *was* that of Marie Rogêt, it could only have been in the water two and a half days, or three at the outside. All experience has shown that drowned bodies, or bodies thrown into the water immediately after death by violence, require from six to ten days for sufficient decomposition to take place to bring them to the top of the water. Even where a cannon is fired over a corpse, and it rises before, at least, five or six days' immersion, it sinks again, if left alone. Now, we ask what was there in this case to cause a departure from the ordinary course of nature? . . . If the body had been kept in its mangled state on shore until Tuesday night, some trace would be found on shore of the murderers. It is a doubtful point, also, whether the body would be so soon afloat, even were it thrown in after having been dead two days. And, furthermore, it is exceedingly improbable that any villains who had committed such a murder as is here supposed, would have thrown the body in without weight to sink it, when such a precaution could have so easily been taken."

The editor here proceeds to argue that the body must have been in water "not three days merely, but, at least, five times three days," because it was so far decomposed that Beauvais had great difficulty in recognising it. This latter point, however, was fully disproved. I continue the translation:

"What,, then, are the facts on which M. Beauvais says that he has no doubt the body was that of Marie Rogêt? He ripped up the gown sleeve, and says he found marks which satisfied him of the identity. The public generally supposed those marks to have consisted of some description of scars. He rubbed the arm and found *hair* upon it – something as indefinite, we think as can readily be imagined – as little conclusive as finding an arm in the sleeve. M. Beauvais did not return that night, but sent word to Madame Rogêt, at seven o'clock, on Wednesday evening, that an investigation was still in progress respecting her daughter. If we allow that Madame Rogêt, from her age and grief, could not go over (which is allowing a great deal), there certainly must have been some one who would have thought it worth while to go over and attend the investigation, if they thought the body was that of Marie. Nobody went over. There was nothing said or heard about the matter in the Rue Pavée St. Andreé, that reached even the occupants of the same building. M. St. Eustache, the lover and intended husband of Marie, who boarded in her mother's house, deposes that he did not hear of the discovery of the body of his intended until the next morning, when M. Beauvais came into his chamber and told him of it. For an item of news like this, it strikes us it was very coolly received."

In this way the journal endeavoured to create the impression of an apathy on the part of the relatives of Marie, inconsistent with the supposition that these relatives believed the corpse to be hers. Its insinuations amount to this: that Marie, with the connivance of her friends, had absented herself from the city for reasons involving a charge against her chastity; and that these friends upon the discovery of a corpse in the Seine, somewhat resembling that of the girl, had availed themselves of the opportunity to impress the public with the belief of her death. But *L'Etoile* was again overhasty. It was distinctly proved that no apathy, such as was imagined, existed; that the old lady was exceedingly feeble, and so agitated as to be unable to attend to any duty; that St. Eustache, so far from receiving the news coolly, was distracted with grief, and bore himself so frantically, that M. Beauvais prevailed upon a friend and relative to take charge of him, and prevent his attending the examination at the disinternment. Moreover, although it was stated by *L'Etoile*, that the corpse was re-interred at the public expense, that an advantageous offer of private sepulture was absolutely declined by the family, and that no member of the family attended the ceremonial; although, I say, all this was asserted by *L'Etoile* in furtheance of the impression it designed to convey – yet *all* this was satisfactorily disproved. In a subsequent number of the paper, an attempt was made to throw suspicion upon Beauvais himself. The editor says:

"Now, then, a change comes over the matter. We are told that, on one occasion, while a Madame B——was at Madame Rogêt's house, M. Beauvais, who was going out, told her that a *gendarme* was expected there, and that she, Madame B——, must not say anything to the *gendarme* until he returned, but let the matter be for him. . . . In the present posture of affairs M. Beauvais appears to have the whole matter locked up in his head. A single step cannot be taken without M. Beauvais, for go which way you will, you run against him . . . . For some reason he determined that nobody shall have anything to do with the proceedings but himself, and he has elbowed the male relatives out of the way, according to their representations, in a very singular manner. He seems to have been very much averse to permitting the relatives to see the body."

By the following fact, some colour was given to the suspicion thus thrown upon Beauvais. A visitor at his office, a few days prior to the girl's disappearance, and during the absence of its occupant, had observed a *rose* in the key-hole of the door, and the name "Marie" inscribed upon a slate which hung near at hand.

The general impression, so far as we were enabled to glean it from the newspapers, seemed to be that Marie had been the victim of a *gang* of desperadoes—that by these she had been borne across the river, maltreated, and murdered. *Le Commerciel*, however, a print of extensive influence, was earnest in combating this popular idea. I quote a passage or two from its columns:

"We are persuaded that pursuit has hitherto been on a false scent so far as it has been directed to the Barrière du Roule. It is impossible that a person so well known to thousands as this young woman was, should have passed three blocks without someone having seen her; and any one who saw her would have remembered it, for she interested all who knew her. It was when the streets were full of people, when she went out . . . It is impossible that she could have gone to the Barrière du Roule, or to the Rue des Drômes, without being recognised by a dozen persons; yet no one has come forward who saw her outside her mother's door, and there is no evidence except the testimony concerning her *expressed intentions*, that she did go out at all. Her gown was torn, bound round her, and tied; and by that body was carried as a bundle. If the murder had been committed at the Barrière du Roule, there would have been no necessity for any such arrangement. The fact that the body was found floating near the Barrière is no proof as to where it was thrown into the water. . . . A piece of one of the unfortunate girl's petticoats, two feet long and one foot wide, was torn out and tied under her chin around the back of her head, probably to prevent screams. This was done by fellows who had no pocket-handkerchief."

A day or two before the Prefect called upon us, however, some important information reached the police, which seemed to overthrow, at least, the chief portion of *Le Commerciel's* argument. Two small boys, sons of a Madame Deluc, while roaming among the woods near the Barrière du Roule, chanced to penetrate a close thicket, within which were three or four large stones, forming a kind of seat with a back and footstool. On the upper stone lay a white petticoat; on the second, a silk scarf. A parasol, gloves, and a pocket-handkerchief were also here found. The handkerchief bore the name "Marie Rogêt." Fragments of dress were discovered on the brambles around. The earth was trampled, the bushes were broken, and there was every evidence of a struggle. Between the thicket and the river, the fences were found taken down, and the ground bore evidence of some heavy burden having been dragged along it.

A weekly paper, *Le Soliel*, had the following comments upon this discovery—comments which merely echoed the sentiment of the whole Parisian press:

"The things had all evidently been there at least three or four weeks; they were all mildewed down hard with the action of the rain, and stuck together with mildew. The grass had grown around and over some of them. The silk on the parasol was strong, but the threads of it were run together within. The upper part, where it had been doubled and folded, was all mildewed and rotten, and tore on its being opened . . . The pieces of her frock torn out by the bushes were about three inches wide and six inches long. One part was the hem of the frock, and it had been mended; the other piece was part of the skirt, not the hem. They looked like strips torn off, and were on the thorn bush, about a foot from the ground.

. . . There can be no doubt, therefore, that the spot of this appalling outrage has been discovered."

Consequent upon this discovery, new evidence appeared, Madame Deluc testified that she keeps a roadside inn not far from the bank of the river, opposite the Barrière du Roule. The neighbourhood is secluded—particularly so. It is the usual Sunday resort of blackguards from the city, who cross the river in boats. About three o'clock, in the afternoon of the Sunday in question, a young girl arrived at the inn accompanied by a young man of dark complexion. The two remained here for some time. On their departure, they took the road to some thick woods in the vicinity. Madame Deluc's attention was called to the dress worn by the girl, on account of its resemblance to one worn by a deceased relative. A scarf was particularly noticed. Soon after the departure of the couple, a gang of miscreants made their appearance, behaved boisterously, ate and drank without making payment, followed in the route of the young man and girl, returned to the inn about dusk, and re-crossed the river as if in great haste.

It was soon after dark, upon this same evening, that Madame Deluc, as well as her eldest son, heard the screams of a female in the vicinity of the inn. The screams were violent but brief. Madame D. recognised not only the scarf which was found in the thicket, but the dress which was discovered upon the corpse. An omnibus driver, Valence, now also testified that he saw Marie Rogêt cross a ferry on the Seine, on the Sunday in question, in company with a young man of dark complexion. He, Valence, knew Marie, and could not be mistaken in her identity. The articles found in the thicket were fully identified by the relatives of Marie.

The items of evidence and information thus collected by myself, from the newspapers, at the suggestion of Dupin, embraced only one more point – but this was a point of seemingly vast consequence. It appears that, immediately after the discovery of the clothes as above described, the lifeless or nearly lifeless body of St. Eustache, Marie's betrothed, was found in the vicinity of what all now supposed the scene of the outrage. A phial labelled "laudanum", and emptied, was found near him. His breath gave evidence of the poison. He died without speaking. Upon his person was found a letter, briefly stating his love for Marie, with his design of self-destruction.

"I need scarcely tell you," said Dupin, as he finished the perusal of my notes, "that this is a far more intricate case than that of the Rue Morgue; from which it differs in one important respect. This is an *ordinary*, although an atrocious, instance of crime. There is nothing peculiarly *outré* about it. You will observe that, for this reason, the mystery has been considered easy when for this reason it shoud have been considered difficult of solution. Thus, at first, it was thought unnecessary to offer a reward. The myrmidons of G—— were able at once to comprehend how and why such an atrocity *might have been* committed. They could picture to their imaginations a mode—many modes—and a motive—many motives; and because it was not impossible that either of these numerous modes and motives *could* have been the actual one, they have taken it for granted that one of them *must*. But the ease with which these variable fancies were entertained, and the very plausibility which each assumed, should have been understood as indicative rather of the difficulties than of the facilities which must attend elucidation. I have therefore observed that it is by prominences above the plane of the ordinary, that reason feels her way, if at all, in her search for the true, and that the proper question in cases such as this is not so much 'what has occurred?' as 'what has occurred that has never occurred before?' In the investigations at the house of Madame L'Espanaye, the agents of G—— were discouraged and confounded by that very *unusualness* which, to a properly regulated intellect, would have afforded the surest omen of success; while this same intellect might have been plunged in despair at the ordinary character of all that met the eye in the case of the perfumery-girl, and yet told of nothing but easy triumph to the functionaries of the Prefecture.

"In the case of Madame L'Espanaye and her daughter, there was, even at the beginning of our investigation, no doubt that murder had been committed. The idea of suicide was excluded at once. Here, too, we are freed, at the commencement, from all supposition of self-murder. The body found at the Barrière du Roule was found under such circumstances as to leave us no room for embarrassment upon this important point. But it has been suggested that the corpse discovered is not that of the Marie Rogêt for the conviction of whose assassin, or assassins, the reward is offered, and respecting whom, solely, our agreement has been arranged with the Prefect. We both know this gentleman well. It will not do to trust him too far. If, dating our inquiries from the body found, and then tracing a murderer, we yet discover this body to be that of some other individual than Marie; or if, starting from the living Marie, we find her, yet find her unassassinated—in either case we lose our labour; since it is Monsieur G—— with whom we have to deal. For our own purpose, therefore, if not for the purpose of justice, it is indispensable that our first step should be the determination of the identity of the corpse with the Marie Rogêt who is missing.

"With the public the arguments of *L'Etoile* have had weight; and that the journal itself is convinced of their importance would appear from the manner in which it commences one of its essays upon the subject—'Several of the morning papers of the day,' it says, 'speak of the *conclusive* article in Monday's *Etoile*'. To me, this article appears conclusive of little beyond the zeal of its inditer. We should bear in mind that, in general, it is the object of our newspapers rather to create a sensation—to make a point—than to further the cause of truth. The latter end is only pursued when it seems coincident with the former. The print which merely falls in with ordinary opinion (however well founded this opinion may be) earns for itself no credit with the mob. The mass of the people regard as profound only him who suggests *pungent contradictions* of the general idea. In ratiocination, nor less than in literature, it is the *epigram* which is the most immediately and the most universally appreciated. In both, it is of the slowest order of merit.

"What I mean to say is, that it is the mingled epigram and melodrame of the idea, that Marie Rogêt still lives, rather than any true plausibility in this idea, which have suggested it to *L'Etoile*, and secured it a favourable reception with the public. Let us examine the heads of this journal's argument; endeavouring to avoid the incoherence with which it is originally set forth.

"The first aim of the writer is to show, from the brevity of the interval between Marie's disappearance and the finding of the floating corpse, that this corpse cannot be that of Marie. The reduction of this interval to its smallest possible dimension, becomes thus, at once, an object with the reasoner. In the rash pursuit of this object, he rushes into mere assumption at the outset. 'It is folly to suppose,' he says, 'that the murder, if murder was committed on her body, could have been consummated soon enough to have enabled her murderers to throw the body into the river before midnight.' We demand at once, and very naturally, *why?* Why is it folly to suppose that the murder was committed *within five minutes* after the girl's quitting her mother's house? Why is it folly to suppose that the murder was committed at any given period of the day? There have been assassinations at all hours. But, had the murder taken place at any moment between nine o'clock in the morning of Sunday and a quarter before midnight, there would still have been time enough 'to throw the body into the river before midnight.' This assumption, then, amounts precisely to this—that the murder was not committed on Sunday at all—and, if we allow *L'Etoile* to assume this, we may permit it any liberties whatever. The paragraph beginning 'It is folly to suppose that the murder, etc.,' however it appears as printed in *L'Etoile*, may be imagined to have existed actually *thus* in the brain of the inditer: 'It is folly to suppose that the murder, if murder was committed on the body, could have been committed soon enough to have enabled her murderers to throw the body into the river before midnight; it is folly, we say, to suppose all this, and to suppose at the same time (as we are resolved to suppose), that the body was *not* thrown in until *after* midnight'—a sentence sufficiently inconsequential in itself, but not so utterly preposterous as the one printed.

"Were it my purpose," continued Dupin, "merely to *make out a case* against this passage of *L'Etoile's* argument, I might safely leave it where it is. It is not, however, with *L'Etoile* that we have to do, but with the truth. The sentence in question has but one meaning, as it stands; and this meaning I have fairly stated; but it is material that we go behind the mere words for a idea which these words have obviously intended, and failed to convey. It was the design of the journalists to say that at whatever period of the day or night of Sunday this murder was committed, it was improbable that the assassins would have ventured to bear the corpse to the river before midnight. And herein lies, really, the assumption of which I complain. It is assumed that the murder was committed at such a position, and under such circumstances, that *the bearing it* to the river became necessary. Now, the assassination might have taken place upon the river's brink, or on the river itself; and, thus, the throwing the corpse in the water might have been resorted to at any period of the day or night, as the most obvious and most immediate mode of disposal. You will understand that I suggest nothing here as probable, or as coincident with may own opinion. My design, so far, has no reference to the *facts* of the case. I wish merely to caution you against the whole tone of *L'Etoile's suggestion*, by calling your attention to its *ex-parte* character at the outset.

"Having prescribed thus a limit to suit its own preconceived notions; having assumed that, if this were the body of Marie, it could have been in the water but a very brief time, the journal goes on to say:

" 'All experience has shown that drowned bodies, or bodies thrown into the water immediately after death by violence, require from six to ten days for sufficient decomposition to take place to bring them to the top of the water. Even when a cannon is fired over a corpse, and it rises before at least five of six days' immersion, it sinks if let alone.'

"These assertions have been tacitly received by every paper in Paris, with the exception of *Le Moniteur*. This latter print endeavours to combat that portion of the paragraph which has reference to 'drowned bodies' only, by citing some five or six instances in which the bodies of individuals known to be drowned were found floating after the lapse of less time than is insisted upon by *L'Etoile*. But there is something excessively unphilosophical in the attempt, on the part of *Le Moniteur*, to rebut the general assertion of *L'Etoile*, by a citation of particular instances militating against that assertion. Had it been possible to adduce fifty instead of five examples of bodies found floating at the end of two or three days, these fifty examples could still have been properly regarded only as exceptions to *L'Etoile*'s rule, until such time as the rule itself should be confuted. Admitting the rule (and this *Le Moniteur* does not deny, insisting merely upon its exception), the argument of *L'Etoile* is suffered to remian in full force; for this argument does not pretend to involve more than a question of the *probability* of the body having risen to the surface in less than three days; and this probability will be in favour of *L'Etoile*'s position until the instances so childishly adduced shall be sufficient in number to establish an antagonistical rule.

"You will see at once that all argument upon this head should be urged, if at all, against the rule itself; and for this end we must examine the *rationale* of the rule. Now the human body, in general, is neither much lighter nor much heavier than the water of the Seine; that is to say, the specific gravity of the human body, in its natural condition, is about equal to the bulk of fresh water which it displaces. The bodies of fat and fleshy persons, with small bones, and of women generally, are lighter than those of the lean and large-boned, and of men; and the specific gravity of the water of a river is somewhat influenced by the presence of the tide from the sea. But, leaving this tide out of the question, it may be said that *very* few human bodies will sink at all, even in fresh water, *of their own accord*. Almost any one, falling into a river, will be enabled to float, if he suffer the specific gravity of the water fairly to be adduced in comparison with his own—that is to say, if he suffer his whole person to be immersed, with as little exception as possible. The proper position for one who cannot swim, is the upright position of the walker on land, with the head thrown fully back, and immersed; the mouth and nostrils alone remaining above the surface. Thus circumstanced, we shall find that we float without difficulty and without exertion. It is evident, however, that the gravities of the body, and of the bulk of water displaced, are very nicely balanced, and that a trifle will cause either to preponderate. An arm, for instance, uplifted from the water, and thus deprived of its support, is an additional weight sufficient to immerse the whole head, while the accidental aid of the smallest piece of timber will enable us to elevate the head so as to look about. Now, in the struggles of one unused to swimming, the arms are invariably thrown upward, while an attempt is made to keep the head in its usual perpendicular position. The result is the immersion of the mouth and nostrils, and the inception, during efforts to breathe while beneath the surface, of water into the lungs. Much is also received into the stomach, and the whole body becomes heavier by the difference between the weight of the air originally distending these cavities, and that of the fluid which now fills them. This difference is sufficient to cause the body to sink, as a general rule; but it is insufficient in the cases of individuals with small bones and an abnormal quantity of flaccid or fatty matter. Such individuals float even after drowning.

"The corpse, being supposed at the bottom of the river, will there remain until, by some means, its specific gravity again becomes less than that of the bulk of water which it displaces. This effect is brought about by decomposition, or otherwise. The result of decomposition is the generation of gas, distending the cellular tissues and all the cavities, and giving the *puffed* appearance which is so horrible. When this distension has so far progressed that the bulk of the corpse is materially increased without a corresponding increase of *mass* or weight, its specifc gravity becomes less than that of the water displaced, and it forthwith makes its appearance at the surface. But decomposition is modified by innumerable circumstances—is hastened or retarded by innumeralbe agencies; for example, by the heat or cold of the season, by the mineral impregnation of purity of the water, by its depth or shallowness, by its currency or stagnation, by the temperament of the body, by its infection or freedom from disease before death. Thus it is evident that we can assign no period, with anything like accuracy, at which the corpse shall rise through decomposition. Under certain conditions this result would be brought about within an hour; under others it might not take place at all. There are chemical infusions by which the animal frame can be preserved *for ever* from corruption; the bichloride of mercury is one. But, apart from decomposition, there may be, and very usually is, a generation of gas within the stomach, from the acetous fermentation of vegetable matter (or within other cavities from other causes), sufficient to induce a distension which will bring the body to the surface. The effect produced by the firing of a cannon is that of simple vibration. This may either loosen the corpse from the soft mud or ooze in which it is embedded, thus permitting it to rise when other agencies have already prepared it for so doing: or it may overcome the tenacity of some putrescent portions of the cellular tissues, allowing the cavities to distend under the influence of the gas.

"Having thus before us the whole philosophy of this subject, we can easily test by it the assertions of *L'Etoile*. 'All experience shows,' says this paper, 'that drowned bodies, or bodies thrown into the water immediately after death by violence, require from six to ten days for sufficient decomposition to take place to bring them to the top of the water. Even when a cannon is fire over a corpse, and it rises before at lease five or six days' immersion, it sinks again if let alone.'

"The whole of this paragraph must now appear a tissue of inconsequence and incoherence. All experience does *not* show that 'drowned bodies' *require* from six to ten days for sufficient depcomposition to take place to bring them to the surface. Both necessarily must be indeterminate. If, moreover, a body has risen to the surface through firing of cannon, it will *not* 'sink again if let along,' until decomposition has so far progressed as to permit the escape of the generated gas. But I wish to call your attention to the distinction which is made between 'drowned bodies,' and 'bodies thrown into water immediately after death by violence.' Although the writer admits the distinction, he yet includes them all in the same category. I have shown how it is that the body of a drowning man becomes specificially heavier than its bulk of water, and that he would not sink at all, except for the struggle by which he elevates his arms above the surface, and his gasps for breath while beneath the surface—gasps which supply by water the place of the original air in the lungs. But these struggles and these gasps would not occur in the body 'thrown into the water immediately after death by violence.' Thus, in the latter instance, *the body, as a general rule, would not sink at all*—a fact of which *L'Etoile* is evidently ignorant. When decomposition had proceeded to a very great extent—when the flesh had in a great measure left the bones—then, indeed,but not *till* then, should we lose sight of the corpse.

"And now what are we to make of the argument, that the body found could not be that of Marie Rogêt, because, three days only having elapsed, this body was found floating? If drowned being a woman, she might never have sunk; or, having sunk, might have reappeared in twenty-four hours or less. But no one supposes her to have been drowned; and, dying before being thrown into the river, she might have been found floating at any period afterward whatever.

" 'But,' says *L'Etoile*, 'if the body had been kept in its mangled state on shore until Tuesday night, some trace would be found on shore of the murderers.' Here it is at first difficult to perceive the intention of the reasoner. He means to anticipate what he imagines would be an objection to his theory—viz.: that the body was kept on shore two days, suffering rapid decomposition—*more* rapid than if immersed in water. He supposes that, had this been the case, it *might* have appeared at the surface on the Wednesday, and think that *only* under such circumstances it could have so appeared. He is accordingly in haste to show that it *was not* kept on shore; for, if so, 'some trace would be found on shore of the murderers.' I presume you smile at the *sequitur*. You cannot be made to see how the mere *durations* of the corpse on the shore could opeate to *multiply traces* of the assassins. Nor can I.

" 'And furthermore it is exceedingly improbable,' continues our journal, 'that any villains who had committed such a murder as is here supposed, would have thrown the body in without weight to sink it, when such a precaution could have so easily been taken.' Observe, here, the laughable confusion of thought! No one—not even *L'Etoile*—disputes the murder committed *on the body found*. The marks of violence are too obvious. It is our reasoner's object merely to show that this body is not Marie's. He wishes to prove that *Marie* is not assassinated—not that the corpse was not. Yet his observation proves only the latter point. Here is a corpse without weight attached. Murderers, casting it in, would not have failed to attach a weight. Therefore it was not thrown in by murderers. This is all which is proved, if anything is. The questions of identify is not even approached, and *L'Etoile* has been at great pains merely to gainsay now what it has admitted only a moment before. 'We are perfectly convinced,' it says, 'That the body found was that of a murdered female.'

"Nor is this the sole instance, even in this division of his subject, where our reasoner unwittingly reasons against himself. His evident object, I have already said, is to reduce, as much as possible, the interval between Marie's disappearance and the finding of the corpse. Yet we find him *urging* the point that no person saw the girl from the moment of her leaving her mother's house. 'We have no evidence,' he says, 'that Marie Rogêt was in the land of the living after nine o'clock on Sunday, June the 22nd.' As his argument is obviously an *ex-parte* one, he should, at least, have left this matter out of sight; for had any one been known to see Marie, say on Monday, or on Tuesday, the interval in question would have been much reduced, and, by his own ratiocination, the probability much diminished of the corpse being that of the *grisette*. It is, nevertheless, amusing to observe that *L'Etoile* insists upon its point in the full belief of its furthering its general argument.

"Re-peruse now that portion of this argument which has reference to the identification of the corpse by Beauvais. In regard to the *hair* upon the arm, *L'Etoile* has been obviously disingenuous. M. Beauvais, not being an idiot, could never have urged in identification of the corpse, simply *hair upon its arm*. No arm is *without* hair. The *generality* of the expression of *L'Etoile* is a mere perversion of the witness' phraseology. He must have spoken of some *peculiarity* in this hair. It must have been a peculiarity of colour, of quantity, of length, or of situation.

" 'Her foot,' says the journal, 'was small—so are thousands of feet. Her garter is no proof whatever—nor is her shoe—for shoes and garters are sold in packages. The same may be said of the flowers in her hat. One thing upon which M. Beauvais strongly insists is, that the clasp on the garter found had been set back to take it in. This amounts to nothing; for most women find it proper to take a pair of garters home and fit them to the size of the limbs they are to encircle, rather than to try them in the store where they purchase.' Here it is difficult to suppose the reasoner in earnest. Had M. Beauvais, in his search for the body of Marie, discovered a corpse corresponding in general size and appearance to the missing girl, he would have been warranted (without reference to the question of habiliment at all) in forming an opinion that his search had been successful. If, in addition to the point of general size and contour, he had found upon the arm a peculiar hairy appearance which he had observed upon the living Marie, his opinion might have been justly strengthened; and the increase of positiveness might well have been in the ratio of the peculiarity, or unusualness of the hairy mark. If the feet of Marie being small, those of the corpse were also small, the increase of probability that the body was that of Marie would not be an increase in a ratio merely arithmetical, but in one highly geometrical, or accumulative. Add to all this shoes such as she had been known to wear upon the day of her disappearance, and, although these shoes may be 'sold in packages', you so far argument the probability as to verge upon the certain. What, of itself, would be no evidence of identity, becomes, through its corroborative position, proof most sure. Give us then, flowers in the hat corresponding to those worn by the missing girl, and we seek for nothing further. If only *one* flower, we seek for nothing further—what then if two or three, or more? Each successive one is multiple evidence—proof not *added* to proof, but multiplied by hundreds or thousands. Let us now discover, upon the deceased, garters such as the living used, and it is almost folly to proceed. But these garters are found to be tightened, by the setting back of a clasp, in just such a manner as her own had been tightened by Marie shortly previous to her leaving home. It is now madness or hypocrisy to doubt. What *L'Etoile* says in respect to this abbreviation of the garters being an unusual occurrence, shows nothing beyond its own pertinacity in error. The elastic nature of the clasp-garter is self-demonstration of the *unusualness* of the abbreviation. What is made to adjust itself, must of necessity require foreign adjustment but rarely. It must have been by an accident, in its strictest sense, that these garters of Marie needed the tightening described. They alone would have amply established her identity. But it is not that the corpse was found to have the garters of the missing girl, or found to have her shoes, or her bonnet, or the flowers of her bonnet, or her feet, or a peculiar mark upon the arm, or her general size and appearance—it is that the corpse had each, and *all collectively*. Could it be proved that the editor of *L'Etoile really* entertained a doubt, under the circumstances, there would be no need, in his case, of a commission *de lunatico inquirendo*. He has thought it sagacious to echo the small talk of the lawyers, who, for the most part, content themselves with echoing the rectangular precepts of the courts. I would here observe that very much of what is rejected as evidence by a court is the best of evidence to the intellect. For the court, guided itself by the general principles—of evidence—the recognised and *booked* principles—is averse from swerving at particular instances. And this steadfast adherence to principle, with rigorous disregard of the conflicting exception, is a sure mode of attaining the *maximum* of attainable truth, in any long sequence of time. The practice, *enmasse*, is therefore philosophical; but it is not the less certain that it engenders vast individual error.

"In respect to the insinuations levelled at Beauvais, you will be willing to dismiss them in a breath. You have already fathomed the true character of this good gentlemen. He is a *busy-body*, with much of romance and little of wit. Any one so constituted will readily so conduct himself, upon occasion of *real* excitement, as to render himself liable to suspicion on the part of the over-acute, or the ill-disposed. M. Beauvais (as it appears from your notes) had some personal interviews with the editor of *L'Entoile*, and offended him by venturing an opinion that the corpse, notwithstanding the theory of the editor, was, in sober fact, that of Marie. 'He persists,' says the paper, 'in asserting the corpse to be that of Marie, but cannot give a circumstance, in addition to those which we have commented upon, to make others believe.' Now, without re-adverting to the fact that stronger evidence 'to make others believe,' could *never* have been adduced, it may be remarked that a man may very well be understood to believe, in a case of this kind, without the ability to advance a single reason for the belief of a second party. Nothing is more vague than impressions of individual identity. Each man recognises his neighbour, yet there are few instances in which any one is prepared *to give a reason* for his recognition. The editor of *L'Etoile* had no right to be offended at M. Beauvais' unreasoning belief.

"The suspicious circumstances which invest him, will be found to tally much better with my hypothesis of *romantic busy-bodyism*, than with the reasoner's suggestion of guilt. Once adopting the more charitable interpretation, we shall find no difficulty in comprehending the rose in the key-hole; the 'Marie' upon the slate; the 'elbowing the male relatives out of the way'' the 'aversion to permitting them to see the body'; the caution given to Madame B———, that she must hold no conversation with the *gendarme* until his (Beauvais') return; and, lastly, his apparent determination, 'that nobody should have anything to do with the proceedings except himself.' It seems to me unquestionable that Beauvais was a suitor of Marie's; that she coquetted with him; and that he was ambitious of being thought to enjoy her fullest intimacy and confidence. I shall say nothing more upon this point; and, as the evidence fully rebuts the assertion of *L'Etoile*, touching the matter of *apathy* on the part of the mother and other relatives—an apathy inconsistent with the supposition of their believing the corpse to be that of the perfumery-girl—we shall now proceed as if the question of *identity* were settled to our perfect satisfaction."

"And what," I here demanded, "do you think of the opinions of *Le Commerciel*?"

"That in spirit they are more worthy of attention than any which have been promulgated upon the subject. The deductions from the premises are philosophical and acute; but the premises, in two instances, at least, are founded in imperfect observation. *Le Commerciel* wishes to intimate that Marie was seized by some gang of low ruffians not far from her mother's door. 'It is impossible,' it urges, 'that a person so well known to thousands as this young woman was, should have passed three blocks without some one having seen her.' This is the idea of a man long resident in Paris—a public man—and one whose walks to and fro in the city have been mostly limited to the vicinity of the public offices. He is aware that he seldom passes so far as a dozen blocks from his own *bureau*, without being recognised and accosted. And, knowing the extent of his personal acquaintance with others, and of others with him, he compares his notoriety with that of the perfumery-girl, finds no great difference between them, and reaches at once the conclusion that she, in her walks, would be equally liable to recognition with himself in his. This could only be the case were her walks of the same unvarying methodical character, and within the same *species* of limited region as are his own. He passes to and fro, at regular intervals, within a confined periphery, abounding in individuals who are led to observation of his person through interest in the kindred nature of his occupation with their own. But the walks of Marie may, in general, be supposed discursive. In this particular instance, it will be understood as most probable that she proceeded upon a route of more than average diversity, from her accustomed ones. The parallel which we imagine to have existed in the mind of *Le Commerciel* would only be sustained in the event of the two individuals traversing the whole city. In this case, granting the personal acquaintances to be equal, the chances would be also equal that an equal number of personal recontres would be made. For my own part, I should hold it not only as possible, but as far more than probable, that Marie might have proceeded, at any given period, by any one of the many routes between her own residence and that of her aunt, without meeting a single individual whom she knew, or by whom she was known. In viewing this question in its full and proper light, we must hold steadily in mind the great disproportion between the personal acquaintances of even the most noted individuals in Paris, and the entire population of Paris itself.

"But whatever force there may still appear to be in the suggestion of *Le Commerciel*, will be much diminished when we take into consideration *the hour* at which the girl went abroad. 'It was when the streets were full of people,' says *Le Commerciel*, 'that she went out'. But not so. It was at nine o'clock in the morning. Now at nine o'clock of every morning in the week, *with the exception of Sunday*, the streets in the city are, it is true, thronged with people. At nine on Sunday, the populace are chiefly within doors *preparing for church*. No observing person can have failed to notice the peculiarly deserted air of the town, from about eight until ten on the morning of every Sabbath. Between ten and eleven the streets are thronged, but not at so early a period as that designated.

"There is another point at which there seems a deficiency of *observation* on the part of *Le Commerciel*. 'A piece,' it says, 'of one of the unfortunate girl's petticoats, two feet long, and one foot wide, was torn out and tied under her chin, and around the back of her head, probably to prevent screams. This was done by fellows who had no pocket-handkerchief.' Whether this idea is or is not well founded, we will endeavour to see hereafter; but by 'fellows who have no pocket-handkerchiefs,' the editor intends the lowest class of ruffians. these, however, are the very description of people who will always be found to have handkerchiefs even when destitute of shirts. You must have had occasion to observe how absolutely indispensable, of late years, to the thorough blackguard, has become the pocket-handkerchief."

"And what are we to think," I asked, "of the article in *Le Soleil*?"

"That it is a vast pity its inditer was not born a parrot—in which case he would have been the most illustrious parrot of his race. He has merely repeated the individual items of the already published opinion; collecting them, with a laudable industry, from this paper and from that. 'Things had all *evidently* been there,' he says, 'at least three or four weeks, and there can be *no doubt* that the spot of this appalling outrage has been discovered.' The facts here re-stated by *Le Soleil* are very far indeed from removing my own doubts upon this subject, and we will examine them more particularly hereafter in connection with another division of the theme.

"At present we must occupy ourselves with other investigations. You cannot fail to have remarked the extreme laxity of the examination of the corpse. To be sure, the question of identity was readily determined, or should have been; but there were other points to be ascertained. Had the body been in any respect *despoiled*? Had the deceased any articles of jewellery about her person upon leaving home? if so, had she any when found? These are important questions utterly untouched by the evidence; and there are others of equal moment, which have met with no attention. We must endeavour to satisfy ourselves by personal enquiry. The case of St. Eustache must be re-examined. I have no suspicion of this person; but let us proceed methodically. We will ascertain beyond a doubt the validity of the *affidavits* in regard to his whereabouts on the Sunday. Affidavits of this character are readily made matter of mystification. Should there be nothing wrong here, however, we will dismiss St. Eustache from our investigations. His suicide, however corroborative of suspicion, were there found to be deceit in the affidavits, is, without such deceit, in no respect an unaccountable circumstance, or one which need cause us to deflect from the line of ordinary analysis.

"In that which I now propose, we will discard the interior points of this tragedy, and concentrate our attention upon its outskirts. Not the least usual error in investigations such as this is the limiting of enquiry to the immediate, with total disregard of the collateral or circumstantial events. It is the mal-practice of the courts to confine evidence and discussion to the bounds of apparent relevancy. Yet experience has shown, and a true philosophy will always show, that a vast, perhaps the larger portion of truth arises from the seemingly irrelevant. It is through the spirit of this principle, if not precisely through its letter, that modern science has resolved to *calculate upon the unforeseen*. But perhaps you do not comprehend me. The history of human knowledge has so uninterruptedly shown that to collateral, or incidental, or accidental events we are indebted for the most numerous and most valuable discoveries, that it has at length become necessary, in prospective view of improvement, to make not only large, but the largest, allowances for inventions that shall arise by chance, and quite out of the range of ordinary expectation. It is no longer philosophical to base upon what has been a vision of what is to be. *Accident* is admitted as a portion of the substructure. We make chance a matter of absolute calculation. We subject the unlooked-for and unimagined to the mathematical *formulæ* of the schools.

"I repeat that it is more than fact that the *larger* portion of all truth has sprung from the collateral; and it is but is accordance with the spirit of the principle involved in this fact that I would divert enquiry, in the present case, from the trodden and hitherto unfruitful ground of the event itself to the contemporary circumstances which surround it. While you ascertain the validity of the affidavits, I will examine the newspapers more generally than you have as yet done. So far, we have only reconnoitred the field of investigation; but it will be strange, indeed, if a comprehensive survey, such as I propose, of the public prints will not afford us some minute points which shall establish a *direction* for inquiry."

In pursuance of Dupin's suggestion, I made scrupulous examination of the affair of the addidavits. The result was a firm conviction of their validity, and of the consequent innocence of St. Eustache. In the meantime my friend occupied himself, with what seemed to me a minuteness altogether objectless, in a scrutiny of the various newpaper files. At the end of a week he placed before me the following extracts:

"About three years and a half ago, a disturbance very similar to the present was caused by the disappearance of this same Marie Rogêt from the *parfumerie* of Monsieur Le Blanc, in the Palais Royal. At the end of a week, however, she re-appeared at her customary *comptoir*, as well as ever, with the exception of a slight paleness not altogether usual. It was given out by Monsieur Le Blanc and her mother that she had merely been on a visit to some friend in the country; and the affair was speedily hushed up. We presume that the present absence is a freak of the same nature, and that, at the expiration of a week or, perhaps, of a month, we shall have her amoung us again."—*Evening Paper*, Monday, June 23rd.

"An evening journal of yesterday refers to a former mysterious disappearance of Mademoiselle Rogêt. It is well known that, during the week of her absence from Le Blanc's *parfumerie*, she was in the company of a young naval officer much noted for his debaucheries. A quarrel, it is supposed, providentially led to her return home. We have the name of the Lothario in question, who is at present stationed in Paris, but for obvious reasons, forbear to make it public."—*La Mercure*, Tuesday morning, June 24th.

"An outrage of the most atrocious character was perpetrated near the city the day before yesterday. A gentleman, with his wife and daughter, engaged about dusk, the services of six young men, who were idly rowing a boat to and fro near the banks of the Seine to convey him across the river. Upon reaching the opposite shore the three passengers stepped out, and had proceeded so far so to be beyond the view of the boat, when the daughter discovered that she had left in it her parasol. She returned for it, was seized by the gang, carried out into the stream, gagged, brutally treated, and finally taken to the shore at a point not far from that at which she had originally entered the boat with her parents. The villians have escaped for the time, but the police are upon their trail, and some of them will soon be taken."—*Morning Paper*, June 25th.

"We have received one or two communications, the object of which is to fasten the crime of the late atrocity upon Mennais, but as this gentleman has been fully exonerated by a legal inquiry, and as the arguments of our several correspondents appear to be more zealous than profound, we do not think it advisable to make them public."—*Morning Paper*, June 28th.

"We have received several forcibly written communications, apparently from various sources, and which go far to render it a matter of certainty that the unfortunate Marie Rogêt has become a victim of the city upon Sunday. Our own opinion is decidedly in favour of this supposition. We shall endeavour to make room for some of these arguments hereafter."—*Evening Paper*, Tuesday, June 31st.

"On Monday, one of the bargemen connected with the revenue service saw an empty boat floating down the Seine. Sails were lying in the bottom of the boat. The bargemen towed it under the barge office. The next morning it was taken from thence without the knowledge of any of the officers. The rudder is now at the barge office."—*La Diligence*, Thursday, June 26th.

Upon reading these various extracts, they not only seemed to me irrelevant, but I could perceive no mode in which any one of them could be brought to bear upon the matter in hand. I waited for some explanation from Dupin.

"It is not my present design," he said, "to *dwell* upon the first and second of these extracts. I have copied them chiefly to show you the extreme remissness of the police, who, as far as I can understand from the Prefect, have not troubled themselves, in any respect, with an examination of the naval officer alluded to. Yet it is mere folly to say that between the first and second disappearance of Marie there is no *supposable* connection. Let us admit the first elopement to have resulted in a quarrel between the lovers, and the return home of the betrayed. We are now prepared to view a second *elopement* (if we *know* that an elopement has again taken place) as indicating a renewal of the betrayer's advances rather than as the result of new proposals by a second individual—we are prepared to regard it as a 'making up' of the old *amour*, rather than as the commencement of a new one. The chances are ten to one, that he who had once eloped with Marie would again propose an elopement, rather than that she to whom proposals of elopement had been made by one individual, should have them made to her by another. And here let me call your attention to the fact that the time elapsing between the first ascertained and the second supposed elopement is a few months more than the general period of the cruises of our men-of-war. Had the lover been interrupted in his first villainy by the necessity of departure to sea, and had he seized the first moment of his return to renew the base designs not yet altogether accomplished—or not yet altogether accomplished by *him*? Of all these things we know nothing.

"You will say, however, that, in the second instance, there was *no* elopement as imagined. Certainly not—but are we prepared to say that there was not the frustrated design? Beyond St. Eustache and perhaps Beauvais, we find no recognised, no open, no honourable suitors of Marie. Of none other is there anything said. Who then, is the secret lover, of whom the relatives (*at least most of them*) know nothing, but whom Marie meets upon the morning of Sunday, and who is so deeply in her confidence, that she hesitates not to remain with him until the shades of the evening descend, amid the solitary groves of the Barrière du Roule? Who is that secret lover, I ask, of whom, at least, *most* of the relatives know nothing? And what means the singular prophecy of Madame Rogêt on the morning of Marie's departure—'I fear that I shall never see Marie again.'

"But if we cannot imagine Madame Rogêt privy to the design of elopement, may we not at least suppose this design entertained by the girl? Upon quitting home, she gave it to be understood that she was about to visit her aunt in the Rue des Drômes, and St. Eustache was requested to call for her at dark. Now, at first glance, this fact strongly militates against my suggestion; but let us reflect. That she *did* meet some companion, and proceed with him across the river, reaching the Barrière du Roule at so late an hour as three o'clock in the afternoon, is known. But in consenting so to accompany this individual (*for whatever purpose—to her mother known or unknown*), she must have thought of her expressed intention when leaving home, and of the surprise and suspicion aroused in the bosom of her affianced suitor, St. Eustache, when, calling for her, at the hour appointed, in the Rue des Drômes, he should find that she had not been there, and when, moreover, upon returning to the *pension* with this alarming absence from home. She must have thought of these things, I say. She must have foreseen the chagrin of St. Eustace, the suspicion of all. She could not have thought of returning to brave this suspicion; but the suspicion becomes a point of trivial importance to her, if we suppose her *not* intending to return.

"We may imagine her thinking thus—'I am to met a certain person for the purpose of elopement, or for certain other purposes known only to myself. It is necessary that there be no chance of interruption—there must be a sufficient time given us to elude pursuit—I will give it to be understood that I shall visit and spend the day with my aunt at the Rue des Drômes—I will tell St. Eustache not to call for me until dark—in this way, my absence from home for the longer possible period, without causing suspicion or anxiety, will be accounted for, and I shall gain more time than in any other manner. If I bid St. Eustache call for me at dark, he will sure not to call before; but if I wholly neglect to bid him call, my time for escape will be diminished, since it will be expected that I return the earlier, and my absence *at all*—if I had in contemplation merely a stroll with the individual in question—it would not be my policy to bid St. Eustache call; for, calling, he will be *sure* to ascertain that I have played him false—a fact of which I might keep him for ever in ignorance, by turning before dark, and by then stating that I had been to visit my aunt in the Rue des Drômes. But, as it is my design *never* to return—or not for some weeks—or not until certain concealments are effected—the gaining of time is the only point about which I need give myself any concern.'

"You have observed, in your notes, that the most general opinion in relation to this sad affair is, and was from the first, that the girl had been the victim of a *gang* of blackguards. Now, the popular opinion, under certain conditions, is not to be disregarded. When arising of itself— when manifesting itself in a strictly spontaneous manner—we should look upon it as anologous with that *intuition* which is the idiosyncrasy of the individual man of genius. In ninety-nine cases from the hundred I would abide by its decision. But it is important that we find no palpable traces of *suggestion*. The opinion must be rigorously *the public's own*; and the distinction if often exceedingly difficuly to perceive and to maintain. In the present instance, it appears to me that this 'public opinion,' in respect to a *gang*, has been superinduced by the collateral event which is detailed in the third of my extracts. All Paris is excited by the discovered corpse of Marie, a girl young beautiful, and notorious. This corpse is found, bearing marks of violence, and floating in the river. But it is now made known that, at the very period, or about the very period, in which it is supposed that the girl was assasinated, an outrage similar in nature to that endured by the deceased, although less in extent, was perpetrated, by a gang of young ruffians, upon the person of a second young female. Is it wonderful that the one known atrocity should influence the popular judgment in regard to the other unknown? This judgment awaited direction, and the known outrage seemed so opportunely to afford it! Marie, too, was found in the river; and upon this very river was this known outrage committed? The connection of the two events had about it so much of the palpable, that the true wonder would have been a *failure* of the populace to appreciate and seize it. But, in fact, the one atrocity. known to be so committed, is, if anything, evidence that the other committed at a time nearly coincident, was *not* so committed. it would have been a miracle indeed, if, while a gang of ruffians were perpetrating, at a given locality, a most unheard-of wrong, there should have been another similar gang, in a similar locality, in the same city, under the same circumstances, with the same means and appliances, engaged in a wrong of precisely the same aspect, at precisely the same period of time! Yet in what, if not in this marvellous train of coincidence, does the accidentally *suggested* opinion of the populace call upon us to believe?

"Before proceeding further, let us consider the supposed scene of the assassination, in the thicket at the Barrière du Roule. This thicket, although dense, was in the close vicinity of a public road. Within were three or four large stones forming a kind of seat with a back and a footstool. On the upper stone was discovered a white petticoat; on the second, a silk scarf. A parasol, gloves, and a pocket-handkerchief were also here found. The handkerchief bore the name 'Marie Rogêt.' Fragments of dress were seen on the branches around. The earth was trampled, the bushes were broken and there was every evidence of a violent struggle.

"Notwithstanding the acclamation with which the discovery of this thicket was received by the press, and unanimity with which it was supposed to indicate the precise scene of the outrage, it must be admitted that there was some very good reason for doubt. That it *was* the scene, I may or I may not believe—but there was excellent reason for doubt. Had the *true* scene been, as *le Commerciel* suggested, in the neighbourhood of Rúe Pavée St. Andrée, the perpetrators of the crime, supposing them still resident in Paris, would naturally have been stricken with terror at the public attention thus acutely directed into the proper chanell; and, in certain classes of minds, there would have arisen, at once a sense of the necessity of some exertion to redivert the attention. And thus, the thicket of the Barrière du Roule having been already found might have been naturally entertained. There is no real evidence, although *Le Soleil* so supposes, that the articles where they were found might have been naturally entertained. There is no real evidence, although *Le Soliel* so supposes, that the articles discovered had been more than a few days in the thicket; where is much circumstantial proof that they could not have remained there , without attracting attention, during the twenty days elapsing between the fatal Sunday and the afternoon upon which they were found by the boys. 'They were all *mildewed* down hard,' says *Le Soleil*, adopting the opinions of its predecessors, 'with the action of the rain and stuck together from *mildew*. The grass had grown around and over some of them. The silk of the parasol was strong, but the threads of it were run together within. The upper part, where it had been doubled and folded, was all *mildewed* and rotten, and tore on being opened.' In respect to the grass having 'grown around and over some of them,' it is obvious that the fact could only have been ascertained from the words, and thus from the recollections, of two small boys; for these boys removed the articles and took them home before they had been seen by a third party. But the grass will grow, especially in warm and damp weather (such as was that of the period of the murder), as much as two or three inches in a single day. A parasol lying upon a newly turfed ground, might, in a single week, be entirely concealed from sight by the upspringing grass. And touching that *mildew* upon which the editor of *Le Soleil* so pertinaciously inists, that he employs the word no less than three times in the brief paragraph just quoted, is he really unaware of the nature of this mildew? Is he to be told that it is one of many classes of fungus, of which the most ordinary feature is its upspringing and decadence within twenty-four hours?

"Thus we see, at a glance, that what has been most triumphantly adduced in support of the idea that the articles had been 'for at least three or four weeks' in the thicket, is most absurdly null as regards any evidence of that fact. On the other hand, it is exceedingly difficult to believe that these articles could have remained in the thicket specified for a longer period than a single week—for a longer period than from one Sunday to the next. Those who know anything of the vicinity of Paris, know that extreme difficulty of finding *seclusion*, unless at a great distance from its suburbs. Such a thing as an unexplored or even an unfrequently visited recess, amid its woods or groves, is not for a moment to be imagined. Let any one who, being at heart a lover of nature, is yet chained by duty to the dust and heat of this great metropolis—let any such one attempt, even during the week-days, to slake his thirst for solitude amid the scenes of natural loveliness which immediately surround us. At every second step, he will find the growing charm dispelled by the voice and personal intrusion of some ruffian or party of carousing blackguards. He will seek privacy amid the densest foliage all in vain. Here are the very nooks where the unwashed most abound—here are the temples most desecrate. With sickness of the heart the wanderer will flee back to the polluted Paris as to a less odious because less incongruous sink of pollution. But if the vicinity of the city is so beset during the working days of the week, how much more so on the Sabbath! It is now especially that, released from the claims of labour, or deprived of the customary opportunities of crime, the town blackguard seeks the precincts of the town, not through love of the rural, which in his heart he despises, but by way of escape from the restraints and conventionalities of society. He desires less the fresh air and the green trees, than the utter *licence* of the country. Here at the roadside inn, or beneath the foliage of the woods, he indulges, unchecked by any eye except those of his boon companions, in all the mad excess of a counterfeit hilarity—the joint offspring of liberty and of rum. I say nothing more than what must be obvious to every dispassionate observer, when I repeat that the circumstances of the articles in question haveing remained undiscovered, for a longer period than from one Sunday to another, in *any* thicket in the immediate neighbourhood of Paris, is to be looked upon as little less than miraculous.

"But there are not wanting other grounds for the suspicion that the articles were placed in the thicket with the view of diverting attention from the real scene of the outrage. And, first, let me direct your notice to the *date* of the discovery of the articles. Collate this with the date of the fifth extract made by myself from the newspapers. You will find that the discovery followed, almost immediately, the urgent communications sent to the evening paper. These communications, although various, and apparently from various sources, tended all to the same point—viz., the directing of attention to a *gang* as the perpetrators of the outrage, and to the neighbourhood of the Barrière du Roule as its scene. Now, here, of course, the situation is not that, in consequence of these communications, or of the public attention by them directed, the articles were found by the boys; but the suspicion might and may well have been, that the articles were not *before* found by the boys, for the reason that the articles had not before been in the thicket; having been deposited there only at so late a period as at the date, or shortly prior to the date of the communications, by the guilty authors of these communications themselves.

"This thicket was a singular—an exceedingly singular one. It was unusually dense. Within its naturally walled enclosure were three extraordinary stones, *forming a seat with a back and a footstool*. And this thicket, so full of art, was in the immediate vicinity, *within a few rods*, of the dwelling of Madame Duluc, whose boys were in the habit of closely examining the shrubberies about them in search of the bark of the sassafras. Would it be a rash wager—a wager of one thousand to one—that a *day* never passed over the heads of these boys without finding at least one of them ensconced in the umbrageous hall, and enthroned upon its natural throne? Those who would hesitate at such a wager, have either never been boys themselves, or have forgotten the boyish nature. I repeat—it is exceedingly hard to comprehend how the articles could have remianed in this thicket undiscovered, for a longer period than one or two days; and that thus there is good ground for suspicion, in spite of the dogmatic ignorance of *Le Soleil*, that they were, at a comparatively late date, deposited where found.

"But there are still other and stronger reasons for believing them so deposited, than any which I have as yet urged. And, now, let me beg you notice to the highly articial arrangement of the articles. On the *upper* stone lay a white petticoat; on the *second*, a silk scarf; scattered around were a parasol, gloves, and a pocket-handkerchief bearing the name 'Marie Rogêt.' Here is just such an arrangement as would *naturally* be made by a not over-acute person wishing to dispose the articles *naturally*. But it is by no means a *really* natural arrangement. I should rather have looked to see the things *all* lying on the ground and trampled underfoot. In the narrow limits of that bower, it would have been scarcely possible that the petticoat and scarf shold have retained a position upon the stones, when subjected to the brushing to and fro of many struggling person. 'There was evidence,' it is said, 'of a struggle; and the earth was trampled, the bushes were broken,'—but the petticoat and the scarf are found deposited as if upon shelves. 'The pieces of the frock torn out by the bushes were about three inches wide and six inches long. One part was the hem of the frock, and it had been mended. They *looked like strips torn off.*' Here, inadvertently, *Le Soleil* has employed an exceedingly suspicious phrase. The pieces, as described, do indeed 'look like strips torn off'; but purposely and by hand. It is one of the rarest of accidents that a piece is 'torn off' from any garment such as is now in question, but the agency *of a thorn*. From the very nature of such fabrics, a thorn or nail becoming entangled in them tears them rectangularly—divides them into two longitudinal rents, at right angles with each other, and meeting at an apex where the thorn enters—but it is scarcely possible to conceive the piece 'torn off.' I never so knew it, nor did you. To tear a piece *off* from such fabric, two distinct forces, in different directions, will be, in almost every case, required. If there be two edges to the fabric—if, for example, it be a pocket-handkerchief, and it is desired to tear from it a slip, then, and then only, will the one force sever the purpose. But in the present case the question is of a dress, presenting but one edge. To tear a piece from the interior, where no edge is presented, could only be effected by a miracle through the agency of thorns, and no *one* thorn could accomplish it. But, even where an edge is presented, two thorns will be necessary, operating, the one in two distinct directions, and the other in one. And this in the supposition that the edge is unhemmed. If hemmed, the matter is nearly out of the question. We thus see the numerous and great obstacles in the way of pieces being 'torn off' through the simple agency of 'thorns'; yet we are required to believe not only that one piece but that many have been so torn. 'And one part,' too, '*was the hem of the frock*!' Another piece was '*part of the skirt, not the hem,*'—that is to say, was torn completely out, through the agency of thorns, from the unedged interior of the dress! These, I say, are things which one may well be pardoned for disbelieving; yet, taken collectedly, they form, perhaps, less of reasonable ground for suspicion, than the one startling circumstance of the articles having been left in the thicket at all, by any *murders* who had enought precaution to think of removing the corpse. You will not have apprehended me rightly, however, if you suppose it my design to *deny* this thicket as the scene of the outrage. There might have been a wrong *here*, or, more possibly, an accident at Madame Deluc's. But, in fact, this is a point of minor importance. We are not engaged in an attempt to discover the scene, but to produce the perpetrators of the murder. What I have adduced, notwithstanding the minuteness with which I have adduced it, has been with the view, first, to show the folly of the positive and headlong assertions of *Le Soleil*, but secondly and chiefly, to bring you, by the most natural route, to a further contemplation of the doubt whether this assassination has, or has not, been the work of a *gang*.

"We will resume this question by mere allusion to the revolting details of the surgeon examined at the inquest. It is only necessary to say that his published *inferences*, in regard to the number of the ruffians, have been properly ridiculed as unjust and totally baseless, by all the reputable anatomists of Paris. Not that the matter *might not* have been as inferred, but that there was no ground for the inference:—was there not much for another?

"Let us reflect now upon 'the traces of a struggle'; and let me ask what these traces have been supposed to demonstrate. A gang. But do they not rather demonstrate the absence of a gang? What *struggle* could have taken place—what struggle so violent and so enduring as to have left its 'traces' in all directions—between a weak and defenceless girl and the *gang* of ruffians imagined? The silent grasp of a few rough arms and all would have been over. The victim must have been absolutely passive at their will. You will here bear in mind that the arguments used against the thicket as the scene, are applicable, in chief part, only against it as the scene of an outrage committed by *more than a single individual*. If we imagined but *one* violator, we can conceive, and thus only conceive, the struggle of so violent and so obstinate a nature as to have left the 'traces' apparent.

"And again. I have already mentioned the suspicion to be excited by the fact that the articles in question were suffered to remain *at all* in the thicket where discovered. It seems almost impossible that these evidences of guilt should have been accidentally left where found. There was sufficient presence of mind (it is supposed) to remove the corpse; and yet a more positive evidence than the corpse itself (whose features might have been quickly obliterated by decay), is allowed to lie conspicuously in the scene of the outrage—I allude to the handkerchief with the *name* of the deceased. If this was accident, it was not the accident *of a gang*. We can imagine it only the accident of an individual. Let us see. An individual has committed the murder. He is alone with the ghost of the departed. He is appalled by what lies motionless before him. The fury of his passion is over, and there is abundant room in his heart for the natural awe of the deed. His is none of that confidence which the presence of numbers inevitably inspires. He is *alone* with the dead. He trembles and is bewildered. Yet there is a necessity for disposing of the corpse. He bears it to the river, and leaves behind him the other evidences of his guilt; for it is difficult, if not impossible, to carry all the burthen at once, and it will be easy to return for what is left. But in his toilsome journey to the water his fears redouble within him. The sounds of life encompass his path. A dozen times he hears or fancies he hears the step of an observer. Even the very ligths from the city bewilder him. Yet, in time, and by long and frequent pauses of deep agony, he reaches the river's brink, and disposes of his ghastly charge—perhaps through the medium of a boat. But *now* what treasure does the world hold—what threat of vengeance could it hold out—which would have power to urge the return of that lonely murderer over that toilsome and perilous path, to the thicket and its blood-chilling recollections? He returns *not*, let the consequences be what they may. He *could* not return if he would. His sole thought is immediate escape. He turns back *for ever* upon those dreadful shrubberies, and flees as from the wrath to come.

"But how with a gang? Their number would have inspired them with confidence; if, indeed, confidence is ever wanting in the breast of the arrant background; and of arrant blackguards alone are the supposed *gangs* ever constituted. Their number, I say, would have prevented the bewildering and unreasoning terror which I have imagined to paralyse the single man. Could we suppose an oversight in one, or two, or three, this oversight would have been remedied by a fourth. They would have left nothing behind them; for their number would have enabled them to carry *all* at once. There would have been no need of *return*.

"Consider now the circumstance that, in the outer garment of the corpse when found, 'a slip, about a foot wide, had been torn upward from the bottom hem to the waist, wound three times round the waist, and secured by a sort of hitch in the back.' This was done with the obvious design of affording a *handle* by which to carry the body. But would any *number* of men have dreamed of resorting to such an expedient? To three or four, the limbs of the corpse would have afforded not only a sufficient but the best possible hold. The device is that of a single individual; and this brings us to the fact that 'between the thicket and the river the rails of the fences were found taken down, and the ground bore evident traces of some heavy burden having been dragged along it.' But would a *number* of men have put themselves to the superfluous trouble of taking down a fence, for the purpose of dragging through it a corpse which they might have *lifted over* any fence in an instant? Would a *number* of men have so *dragged* a corpse at all as to have left evident *traces* of the dragging?

"And here we must refer to an observation of *Le Commercial*; an observation upon which I have already, in some measure, commented. 'A piece,' says this journal, 'of one of the unfortunate girl's petticoats was torn out and tied under her chin, and around the back of her head, probably to prevent screams. This was done by fellows who had no pocket-handkerchiefs.'

"I have before suggested that a genuine blackguard is never *without* a pocket-handkerchief. But it is not to this fact that I now specially advert. That it was not through want of a handkerchief for the purpose imagined by *Le Commerciel*, that this bandage was emplyed, is rendered apparent by the handkerchief left in the thicket; and that the object was not 'to prevent screams' appears also, from the bandage having been employed in preference to what would so much better have answered the purpose. But the language of the evidence speaks of the strip in question as 'found around the neck, fitting loosely, and secured with a hard knot.' These words are sufficiently vague, but differ materially from those of *Le Commerciel*. The slip was eighteen inches wide, and therefore, although of muslin, would form a strong band when folded or rumpled longitudinally. And this rumpled it was discovered. My interference is this: The solitary murderer, having borne the corpse for some distance (whether from the thicket ot elsewhere) by means of the bandage *hitched* around its middle, found the weight, in this mode of procedure, too much for his strength. He resolved to drag the burthen—the evidence goes to show that it *was* dragged. With this object in view, it became necessary to attach something like a rope to one of the extemities. It could be best attached about the neck, where the head would prevent its slipping off. And not the murderer bethought him, unquestionably, of the bandage about the loins. He would have used this, but for its volution about the corpse, the *hitch* which embarassed it, and the reflection that it had not been 'torn off' from the garment. It was easier to tear a new slip from the petticoat. He tore it, made it fast about the neck, and so *dragged* his victim to the brink of the river. That this 'bandage,' only attainable with trouble and delay, and but imperfectly answering its purpose—that this bandage was employed *at all*, demonstrates that the necessity for its employment sprang from circumstances arising at a period when the handkerchief was no longer attainable—that is to say, arising, as we have imagined, after quitting the thicket (if the thicket it was), and on the road between the thicket and the river.

"But the evidence, you will say, of Madame Deluc (!) points especially to the presence of *a gang* in the vicinity of the thicket, at or about the epoch of the murder. This I grant. I doubt if there were not a *dozen gangs*, such as described by madame Deluc, in and about the vicinity of the Barrière du Roule at *or about* the period of this tragedy. But the gang which has drawn upon itself the pointed animadversion, although the somewhat tardy and very suspicious evidence of Madame Deluc, is the *only* gang which is represented by that honest and scrupulous old lady as having eaten her cakes, and swallowed her brandy, without putting themselves to the trouble of making her payment. *Et hinc illæ iræ?*

"But what *is* the precise evidence of Madame Deluc? 'A gang of miscreants made their appearance, behaved boisterously, ate and drank without making payment, followed in the route of the young man and the girl, returned to the inn *about dusk*, and re-crossed the river as if in great haste.'

"Now, this 'great haste' very possibly seemed *greater* haste in the eyes of Madame Deluc, since she dwelt lingeringly and lamentingly upon her violated cakes and ale—cakes and ale for which she might still have entertained a faint hope of compensation. Why, otherwise, since it was *about dusk*, should she make a point of the *haste*? It is no cause for wonder, surely, that a gang of blackguards should make *haste* to get home when a wide river is to be crossed in small boats, when storm impends, and when night *approaches*.

"I say *approaches*; for the night had *not yet arrived*. It was only *about dusk* that the indecent haste of these 'miscreants' offended the sober eyes of Madame Deluc. But we are told that it was upon this very evening that Madame Deluc, as well as her eldest son, 'heard the screams of a female in the vicinity of the inn.' And in what words does Madame Deluc designate the period of the evening at which these screams were heard? 'It was *soon after dark*,' she says. But 'soon after dark' is at least *dark*; and '*about dusk*' is as certainly daylight. Thus it is abundantly clear that the gang quitted the Barrière du Roule *prior* to the screams overheard (?) by Madame Deluc. And although, in all the many reports of the evidence, the relative expressions in question are distinctly and invariably employed just as I have employed them in this conversation with yourself, no notice whatever of the gross discrepancy has, as yet, been taken by any of the public journals, or by any of the myrmidons of police.

"I shall add but one to the arguments against *a gang*; but this *one* has, to my own understanding at least, a weight altogether irresistible. Under the circumstances of large reward offered, and full pardon to any king's evidence, it is not to be imagined, for a moment, that some member of a *gang* of low ruffians, or of any body of men, would not long ago have betrayed his accomplices. Each one of a gang, so placed, is not so much greedy of reward, or anxious for escape, as *fearful of betrayal*. He betrays eagerly and early that *he may not himself be betrayed*. That the secret has not been divulged is the very best of proof that it is, in fact, a secret. The horrors of this dark deed are known only to *one*, or two, living human beings, and to God.

"Let us sum up now the meagre yet certain fruits of our long analysis. We have attained the idea either of a fatal accident under the roof of Madame Deluc, or of a murder perpetrated in the thicket at the Barrière du Roule, by a lover, or at least by an intimate and secret associate of the deceased. The associate is of swarthy complexion. This complexion, the 'hitch' in the bandage, and the 'sailor's knot' with which the bonnet-ribbon is tied, point to a seaman. His companionship with the deceased—a gay but not abject young girl—designates him as above the grade of the common sailor. Here the well-written and urgent communications to the journals are much in the way of corroboration. The circumstances of the first elopement, as mentioned by *Le Mercurie*, tends to blend the idea of this seaman with that of the 'naval officer' who is first known to have led the unfortunate into crime.

"And here, most fitly, comes the consideration of the continued absence of him of the dark complexion. Let me pause to observe that the complexion of this man is dark and swarthy; it was no common swarthiness which constituted the *sole* point of resemblance, both as regards Valence and Madame Deluc. But why is this man absent? Was he murdered by the gang? If so, why are there only *traces* of the assassinated *girl*? The scene of the two outrages will naturally be supposed identical. And where is his corpse? The assassins would most probably have disposed of both in the same way. But it may be said that this man lives, and is deterred from making himself known through dread of being charged with the murder. This consideration might be supposed to operate upon him now—at this late period—since it has been given in evidence that he was seen with Marie, but it would have had no force at the period of the deed. The first impulse of an innocent man would have been to announce the outrage, and to aid in identifying the ruffians. This *policy* would have suggested. He had been seen with the girl. He had crossed the river with her in an open ferry-boat. The denouncing of the assassins would have appeared, even to an idiot, the surest and sole means of relieving himself from suspicion. We cannot suppose him, on the night of the fatal Sunday, both innocent himself and incognisant of an outrage committed. Yet only under such circumstances is it possible to imagine that he would have failed, if alive, in the denouncement of the assassins.

"And what means of multiplying and gathering distinctness as we proceed. Let us sift to the bottom this affair of the first elopment. Let us know the full history of 'the officer,' with his present circumstances, and his wheareabouts at the precise period of the murder. Let us carefully compare with each other the various communications sent to the evening paper, in which the object was to inculpate *a gang*. This done, let us compare these communications, both as regards style and MS., with those sent to the morning paper, as a previous period, and insisting so vehemently upon the guilt of Mennais. And, all this done, let us again compare these various communications with the known MSS. of the officer. Let us endeavour to ascertain, by repeated questionings of Madame Deluc and her boys, as well as of the omnibus-driver, Valence, something more of the personal appearance and bearing of the 'man of dark complexion.' queries, skilfully directed, will not fail to elicit, from some of these parties, information on this particular point (or upon others)—information which the parties themselves may not even by aware of possessing. And let us now trace *the boat* picked up by the bargeman on the morning of Monday the twenty-third of June, and which was removed from the bargeoffice, without the cognisance of the officer in attendance, and *without the rudder*, at some period prior to the discovery of the corpse. With a proper caution and perseverance we shall infallibly trace this boat; for not only can the bargeman who picked it up identify it, but the *rudder is at hand*. The rudder *of a sail boat* would not have been abandoned without enquiry, by one altogether at ease in heart. And here let me pause to insinuate a question. There was no *advertisement* of the picking up of this boat. It was silently taken to the barge-office, and as silently removed. But its owner or employer—how *happened* he, at so early a period on Tuesday morning, to be informed, without the agency of advertisement, of the locality of the boat taken up on Monday, unless we imagine some connection leading to cognisance of its minute interests—its petty local news?

"In speaking of the lonely assassin dragging his burden to the shore, I have already suggested the probability of his availing himself *of a boat*. Now we are to understand that Marie Rogêt *was* precipitated from a boat. This would naturally have been the case. The corpse could not have been trusted to the shallow waters of the shore. The peculiar marks on the back and shoulders of the victim tell of the bottom ribs of the boat. That the body was found without weight is also corroborative of the idea. If thrown from the shore a weight would have been attached. We can only account for its absence by supposing the murderer to have neglected the precaution of supplying himself with it before pushing off. In the act of consigning the corpse to the water he would unquestionably have noticed his oversight; but then no remedy would have been at hand. Any risk would have been preferred to a return to that accursed shore. Having rid himself of his ghastly charge, the murderer would have hastened to the city. There, at some obscure wharf, he would have leaped on land. But the boat, would he have secured it? He would have been in too great haste for such things as securing a boat. Moreover, in fastening it to the wharf, he would have felt as if securing evidence against himself. His natural though would have been to cast from him, as far as possible, all that held connection with his crime. He would not only have fled from the wharf, but he would have cast it adrift. Let us pursue our fancies.—In the morning, the wretch is stricken with unutterable horror at finding that the boat has been picked up and detained at a locality which he is in the dialy habit of frequenting—at a locality, perhaps, which his duty compels him to frequent. The next night, *without daring to ask for the rudder*, he removes it. Now *where* is that rudderless boat? Let it be one of our first purposes to discover. With the first glimpse we obtain of it, the dawn of our success shall begin. This boat shall guide us, with a rapidity which will surprise even ourselves, to him who employed it in the midnight of the fatal Sabbath. Corroboration will rise upon corroboration, and the murderer will be traced."

THE MYSTERY OF THE MARIE ROGÊT

[For reasons which we shall not specify, but which to many readers will appear obvious, we have taken the liberty of here omitting, from the MSS. placed in our hands, such portion as details the *following up* of the apparently slight clue obtained by Dupin. We feel it advisable only to state, in brief, that the result desired was brought to pass; and that the Prefect fulfilled punctually, although with reluctance, the terms of his compact with the Chevalier. Mr. Poe's article concludes with the following words.—*Eds.*[1]

It will be understood that I speak of coinicidences and *no more*. What I have said above upon this topic must suffice. In my own heart there dwells no faith in praeter-nature. That Nature and its God are two, no man who thinks will deny. That the latter, creating the former, can, at will, control or modify it, is also unquestionable. I say "at will"; for the question is of will, and not, as the insanity of logic has assumed, of power. It is not that the Deity *cannot* modify His laws, but that we insult Him in imagining a possible necessity for modification. In their origin these laws were fashioned to embrace *all* contingencies which *could* lie in the Future. With God all is *Now*.

I repeat, then, that I speak of these things only as of coincidences. And further: in what I relate it will be seen that between the fate of the unhappy Mary Cecilia Rogers, so far as that fate is known, and the fate of one Marie Rogêt, up to a certain epoch in her history, there has existed a parallel in the contemplation of whose wonderful exactitude the reason becomes embrassed. I say all this will be seen. But let it not for a moment be supposed that, in proceeding with the sad narrative of Marie from the epoch just mentioned, and in tracing to its *dénouement* the mystery which enshrouded her, it is my covert design to hint at an extension of the parallel, or even to suggest that the measures adopted in Paris for the discovery of the assassin of a *grisette*, or measures founded in any similar ratiocination, would produce any similar result.

For, in respect to the latter branch of the supposition, it should be considered that the most trifling variation in the facts of the two cases might give rise to the most important miscalculations, by diverting thoroughly the two courses of events; very much as, in arithmetic, an error which, in its own individuality, may be inappreciable, produces at length, by dint of multiplication at all points of the precess, a result enormously at variance with truth. And, in regard to the former branch, we must not fail to hold in view that the very Calculus of Probabilities to which I have referred, forbids all idea of the extension of the parallel—forbids it with a positiveness strong and decided just in proportion as this parallel has already long-drawn and exact. This is one of those anomalous propositions which, seemingly, appealing to thought altogether apart from the mathematical, is yet one which only the mathematician can fully entertain. Nothing, for example, is more difficult than to convince the merely general reader that the fact of sixes having been thrown twice in succession by a player at dice, is sufficient cause for betting the largest odds that sixes will not be thrown in the third attempt. A suggestion to this effect is usually rejected by the intellect at once. It does not appear that the two throws which have been completed, and which lie now absolutely in the Past, can have influence upon the throw which exists only in the Future. The chance for throwing sixes seems to be precisely as it was at any ordinary time—that is today, subject only to the influence of the various other throws which may be made by the dice. And this is a reflection which appears so exceedingly obvious that attempts to controvert it are received more frequently with a derisive smile than with anything like respectful attention. The error here involved—a gross error redolent of mischief—I cannot pretend to expose within the limits assigned me at present; and with the philosophical it needs no exposure. It may be sufficient here to say that it forms one of an infinite series of mistakes which arise in the path of Reason through her propensity for seeking truth *in detail*.

[1] Of *Snowden's Lady's Companion*.

THE BLUE
SEQUIN
by Austin Freeman

First published in 1909

Thorndyke stood looking up and down the platform with anxiety that increased as the time drew near for the departure of the train.

"This is very unfortunate," he said, reluctantly stepping into an empty smoking compartment as the guard executed a flourish with his green flag. "I am afraid we have missed our friend." He closed the door, and, as the train began to move, thrust his head out of the window.

"Now I wonder if that will be he," he continued. "If so, he has caught the train by the skin of his teeth, and is now in one of the rear compartments."

The subject of Thorndyke's speculations was Mr. Edward Stopford, of the firm of Stopford & Myers, of Portugal Street, solicitors, and his connection with us at present arose out of a telegram that had reached our chambers on the preceding evening. It was reply-paid, and ran thus:

"Can you come here to-morrow to direct defence? Important case. All costs undertaken by us.—STOPFORD & MYERS."

Thorndyke's reply had been in the affirmative, and early on this present morning a further telegram—evidently posted overnight—had been delivered:

"Shall leave for Woldhurst by 8.25 from Charing Cross. Will call for you if possible.—EDWARD STOPFORD."

He had not called, however, and, since he was unkown personally to us both, we could not judge whether or not he had been among the passengers on the platform.

"It is most unfortunate," Thorndyke repeated, "for it deprives us of that preliminary consideration of the case which is so invaluable." He filled his pipe thoughtfully, and, having made a fruitless inspection of the platform at London Bridge, took up the paper that he had bought at the bookstall, and began to turn over the leaves, running his eye quickly down the columns, unmindful of the journalistic baits in paragraph or article.

"It is a great disadvantage," he observed, while still glancing through the paper, "to come plump into an inquiry without preparation—to be confronted with the details before one has a chance of considering the case in general terms. For instance———"

He paused, leaving the sentence unfinished, and as I looked up inquiringly I saw that he had turned over another page, and was now reading attentively.

"This looks like our case, Jervis," he said presently, handing me the paper and indicating a paragraph at the top of the page. It was quite brief, and was headed "Terrible Murder in Kent," the account being as follows:

"A shocking crime was discovered yesterday morning at the little town of Woldhurst, which lies on the branch line from Halbury Junction. The discovery was made by a porter who was inspecting the carriages of the train which had just come in. On opening the door of a first-class compartment, he was horrified to find the body of a fashionably dressed woman stretched upon the floor. Medical aid was immediately summoned, and on the arrival of the divisional surgeon, Dr. Morton, it was ascertained that the woman had not been dead more than a few minutes.

"The state of the corpse leaves no doubt that a murder of a most brutal kind has been perpetrated, the cause of death being a penetrating wound of the head, inflicted with some pointed implement, which must have been used with terrible violence, since it has perforated the skull and entered the brain. That robbery was not the motive of the crime is made clear by the fact that an expensively fitted dressing-bag was found on the rack, and the dead woman's jewellery, including several valuable diamond rings, was untouched. It is rumoured that an arrest has been made by the local police."

"A gruesome affair," I remarked, as I handed back the paper, "but the report does not give us much information."

"It does not," Thorndyke agreed, "and yet it gives us something to consider. Here is a perforating wound of the skull, inflicted with some pointed implement—that is, assuming that it is not a bullet wound. Now, what kind of implement would be capable of inflicting such an injury? How would such an implement be used in the confined space of a railway-carriage, and what sort of person would be in possession of such an implement? These are preliminary questions that are worth considering, and

I commend them to you, together with the further problems of the possible motive—excluding robbery—and any circumstances other than murder which might account for the injury."

"The choice of suitable implements is not very great," I observed.

"It is very limited, and most of them, such as a plasterer's pick or a geological hammer, are associated with certain definite occupations. You have a note-book?"

I had, and, accepting the hint, I produced it and pursued my further reflections in silence, while my companion, with his notebook also on his knee, gazed steadily out of the window. And thus he remained, wrapped in thought, jotting down an entry now and again in his book, until the train slowed down at Halbury Junction, where we had to change on to a branch line.

As we stepped out I noticed a well-dressed man hurrying up the platform from the rear and eagerly scanning the faces of the few passengers who had alighted. Soon he espied us, and, approaching quickly, asked, as he looked from one of us to the other:

"Dr. Thorndyke?"

"Yes." replied my colleague, adding, "And you, I presume, are Mr. Edward Stopford?"

The solicitor bowed. "This is a dreadful affair," he said, in an agitated manner. "I see you have the paper. A most shocking affair. I am immensely relieved to find you here. Nearly missed the train, and feared I should miss you."

"There appears to have been an arrest," Thorndyke began.

"Yes—my brother. Terrible business. Let us walk up the platform; our train won't start for a quarter of an hour yet."

We deposited our joint Gladstone and Thorndyke's travelling-case in an empty first-class compartment, and then, with the solicitor between us, strolled up to the unfrequented end of the platform.

"My brother's position," said Mr. Stopford, "fills me with dismay—but let me give you the facts in order, and you shall judge for yourself. This poor creature who has been murdered so brutally was a Miss Edith Grant. She was formerly an artist's model, and as such was a good deal employed by my brother, who is a painter—Harold Stopford, you know, A.R.A. now————"

"I know his work very well, and charming work it is."

"I think so, too. Well, in those days he was quite a youngster—about twenty—and he became very intimate with Miss Grant, in quite an innocent way, though not very discreet; but she was a nice, respectable girl, as most English models are, and no one thought any harm. However, a good many letters passed between them, and some little presents, amongst which was a beaded chain carrying a locket, and in this was fool enough to put his portrait and the inscription, 'Edith, from Harold.'

"Later on, Miss Grant, who had a rather good voice, went on the stage, in the comic opera line, and, in consequence, her habits and associates change somewhat; and, as Harold had meanwhile become engaged, he was naturally anxious to get his letters back, and especially to exchange the locket for some less compromising gift. The letters she eventually sent him, but refused absolutely to part with the locket.

"Now, for the last month Harold has been staying at Halbury, making sketching excursions into the surrounding country, and yesterday morning he took the train to Shinglehurst, the third station from here, and the one before Woldhurst.

"On the platform here he met Miss Grant, who had come down from London, and was going on to Worthing. They entered the branch train together, having a first-class compartment to themselves. It seems she was wearing his locket at the time, and he made another appeal to her to make an exchange, which she refused, as before. The discussion appears to have become rather heated and angry on both sides, for the guard and a porter at Munsden both noticed that they seemed to be quarrelling; but the upshot of the affair was that the lady snapped the chain, and tossed it together with the locket to my brother, and they parted quite amiably at Shinglehurst, where Harold got out. He was then carrying his full sketching kit, including a large holland umbrella, the lower joint of which is an ash staff fitted with a powerful steel spike for driving into the ground.

"It was about half-past ten when he got out at Shinglehurst; by eleven he had reached his pitch and got to work, and he painted steadily for three hours. Then he packed up his traps, and was just starting on his way back to the station, when he was met by the police and arrested.

"And now, observe the accumulation of circumstantial evidence against him. He was the last person seen in company with the murdered woman—for no one seems to have seen her after they left Munsden; he appeared to be quarrelling with her when she was last seen alive, he had a reason for possibly wishing for her death, he was provided with an implement—a spiked staff—capable of inflicting the injury which caused her death, and, when he was searched, there was found in his possession the locket and the broken chain, apparently removed from her person with violence.

"Against all this is, of course, his known character—he is the gentlest and most amiable of men—and his subsequent conduct—imbecile to the last degree if he had been guilty; but, as a lawyer, I can't help seeing that appearances are almost hopelessly against him."

"We won't say 'hopelessly,'" replied Thorndyke, as we took our places in the carriage, "though I expect the police are pretty cocksure. When does the inquest open?"

"To-day at four. I have obtained an order from the coroner for you to examine the body and be present at the post-mortem."

"Do you happen to know the exact position of the wound?"

"Yes; it is a little above and behind the left ear—a horrible round hole, with a ragged cut or tear running from it to the side of the forehead."

"And how was the body lying?"

"Right along the floor, with the feet close to the off-side door."

"Was the wound on the head the only one?"

"No; there was a long cut or bruise on the right cheek—a contused wound the police surgeon called it, which he believes to have been inflicted with a heavy and rather blunt weapon. I have not heard of any other wounds or bruises."

"Did anyone enter the train yesterday at Shinglehurst?" Thorndyke asked.

"No one entered the train after it left Halbury."

Thorndyke considered these statements in silence, and presently fell into a brown study, from which he roused only as the train moved out of Shinglhurst station.

"It would be about here that the murder was committeed," said Mr. Stopford; "at least, between here and Woldhurst."

Thorndyke nodded rather abstractedly, being engaged at the moment in observing with great attention the objects that were visible from the windows.

"I notice," he remarked presently, "a number of chips scattered about between the rails, and some of the chair-wedges look new. Have there been any platelayers at work lately?"

"Yes," answered Stopford, "they are on the line now, I believe—at least, I saw a gang working near Woldhurst yesterday, and they are said to have set a rick on fire; I saw it smoking when I came down."

"Indeed; and this middle line of rails is, I suppose, a sort of siding?"

"Yest; they shunt the goods trains and empty trucks on to it. There are the remains of the rick—still smouldering, you see."

Thorndyke gazed absently at the blackened heap until an empty cattle-truck on the middle track hid it from view. This was succeeded by a line of goods-waggons, and these by a passenger coach, one compartment of which—a first-class—was closed up and sealed. The train now began to slow down rather suddenly, and a couple of minutes later we brought up in Woldhurst station.

It was evident that rumours of Thorndyke's advent had preceded us, for the entire staff—two porters, an inspector, and the stationmaster—were waiting expectantly on the platform, and the latter came forward, regardless of his dignity, to help us with our luggage.

"Do you think I could see the carriage?" Thorndyke asked the solicitor.

"Not the inside sir," said the stationmaster, on being appealed to. "The police have sealed it up. You would have to ask the inspector."

"Well, I can have a look at the outside, I suppose?" said Thorndyke.

And to this the stationmaster readily agreed, and offered to accompany us.

"What other first-class passengers were there?" Thorndyke asked.

"None, sir. There was only one first-class coach, and the deceased was the only person in it. It has given us all a dreadful turn, this affair has," he continued, as we set off up the line. "I was on the platform when the train came in. We were watching a rick that was burning up the line and a rare blaze it made, too; and I was just saying that we should have to move the cattle-truck that was on the mid-track, because, you see, sir, the smoke and sparks were blowing across, and I thought it would frighten the poor beasts. And Mr. Felton he don't like his beasts handled roughly. He says it spoils the meat."

"No doubt he is right," said Thorndyke. "But now, tell me, do you think it is possible for any person to board or leave the train on the off-side unobserved? Could a man, for instance, enter a compartment on the off-side at one station and drop off as the train was slowing down at the next, without being seen?''

"I doubt it," replied the stationmaster. "Still, I wouldn't say it is impossible."

"Thank you. Oh, and there's another question. You have a gang of men at work on the line, I see. Now, do those men belong to the district?"

"No, sir; they are strangers, every one, and pretty rough diamonds some of 'em are. But I shouldn't say there was any real harm in 'em. If you was suspecting any of 'em of being mixed up in this————"

"I am not," interrupted Thorndyke rather shortly. "I suspect nobody; but I wish to get all the facts of the case at the outset."

"Naturally, sir," replied the abashed official; and we pursued our way in silence.

"Do you remember, by the way," said Thorndyke, as we approached the empty coach, "whether the off-side door of the compartment was closed and locked when the body was discovered?"

"It was closed, sir, but not locked. Why, sir, did you think————"

"Nothing, nothing. The sealed compartment is the one, of course?"

Without waiting for a reply, he commenced his survey of the coach, while I gently restrained our two companions from shadowing him, as they were disposed to do.

The off-side footboard occupied his attention specially, and when he had scrutinised minutely the part opposite the fatal compartment he walked slowly from end to end with his eyes but a few inches from its surface, as though he was searching for something.

Near what had been the rear end he stopped and drew from his pocket a piece of paper; then, with a moistened finger tip he picked up from the footboard some evidently minute object, which he carefully transferred to the paper, folding the latter and placing it in his pocket-book.

He next mounted the footboard, and, having peered in through the window of the sealed compartment, produced from his pocket a small insufflator or powder-blower, with which he blew a stream of impalpable smoke-like powder on to the edges of the middle window, bestowing the closest attention on the irregular dusty patches in which it settled, and even measuring one on the jamb of the window with a pocket-rule.

At length he stepped down, and, having carefully looked over the near-side footboard, announced that he had finished for the present.

As we were returning down the line, we passed a working man, who seemed to be viewing the chairs and sleepers with more than casual interest.

"That, I suppose, is one of the platelayers?" Thorndyke suggested to the stationmaster.

"Yes, the foreman of the gang," was the reply.

"I'll just step back and have a word with him, if you will walk on slowly." And my colleague turned back briskly and overtook the man, with whom he remained in conversation for some minutes.

"I think I see the police inspector on the platform," remarked Thorndyke, as we approached the station.

"Yes, there he is," said our guide. "Come down to see what you are after, sir, I expect." Which was doubtless the case, although the officer professed to be there by the merest chance.

"You would like to see the weapon, sir, I suppose?" he remarked, when he had introduced himself.

"The umbrella-spike," Thorndyke corrected. "Yes, if I may. We are going to the mortuary now."

"Then you'll pass the station on the way; so, if you care to look in, I will walk up with you."

This proposition being agreed to, we all proceeded to the police-station, including the stationmaster, who was on the very tiptoe of curiosity.

"There you are, sir," said the inspector, unlocking his office, and ushering us in. "Don't say we haven't given every facility to the defence. There are all the effects of the accused, including the very weapon the deed was done with."

"Come, come," protested Thorndyke; "we mustn't be premature."

He took the stout ash staff from the officer, and, having examined the formidable spike through a lens, drew from his pocket a steel calliper-guage, with which he carefully measured the diameter of the spike, and the staff to which it was fixed.

"And now," he said, when he had made a note of the measurements in his book, "we will look at the colour-box and the sketch. Ha! a very orderly man, your brother, Mr. Stopford. Tubes all in their places, palette-knives wiped clean, palette cleaned off and rubbed bright, brushes wiped—they ought to be washed before they stiffen—all this is very significant."

He unstrapped the sketch from the blank canvas to which it was pinned, and, standing it on a chair in a good light, stepped back to look at it.

"And you tell me that that is only three hours' work!" he exclaimed, looking at the lawyer. "It is a really marvellous achievement."

"My brother is a very rapid worker," replied Stopford dejectedly.

"Yes, but this is not only amazingly rapid; it is in his very happiest vein—full of spirit and feeling. But we musn't stay to look at it longer."

He replaced the canvas on its pins, and having glanced at the locket and some other articles that lay in a drawer, thanked the inspector for his courtesy and withdrew.

"That sketch and the colour-box appear very suggestive to me," he remarked, as we walked up the street.

"To me also," said Stopford gloomily, "for they are under lock and key, like their owner, poor old fellow."

He sighed heavily, and we walked on in silence.

The mortuary-keeper had evidently heard of our arrival, for he was waiting at the door with the key in his hand, and, on being shown the coroner's order, unlocked the door, and we entered together.

But, after a momentary glance at the ghostly, shrouded figure lying upon the slate table, Stopford turned pale and retreated, saying that he would wait for us outside with the mortuary-keeper.

As soon as the door was close and locked on the inside, Thorndyke glanced curiously round the bare whitewashed building.

A stream of sunlight poured in through the skylight, and fell upon the silent form that lay so still under its covering-sheet, and one stray beam glanced into a corner by the door, where, on a row of pegs and a deal table, the dead woman's clothing was displayed.

"There is something unspeakably sad in these poor relics, Jervis," said Thorndyke, as we stood before them. "To me they are more tragic, more full of pathetic suggestion, than the corpse itself. See the smart, jaunty hat, and the costly skirts hanging there, so desolate and forlorn; the dainty *lingerie* on the table, neatly folded—by the mortuary-man's wife, I hope—the little French shoes and open-work silk stockings. How pathetically eloquent they are of harmless, womanly vanity, and the gay, careless life, snapped short in the twinkling of an eye. But we must not give way to sentiment. There is another life threatened, and it is in our keeping."

He lifted the hat from its peg and turned it over in his hand. It was, I think, what is called a "picture-hat"—a huge, flat, shapeless mass of gauze and ribbon and feather, spangled over freely with dark-blue sequins dropped off in little showers when the hat was moved.

"This will have been worn tilted over on the left side," said Thorndyke, "judging by the general shape and the position of the hole."

"Yes," I agreed. "Like that of the Duchess of Devonshire in Gainsborough's portrait."

"Exactly."

He shook a few of the sequins into the palm of his hand, and, replacing the hat on its peg, dropped the little discs into an envelope, on which he wrote, "From the hat," and slipped it into his pocket. Then, stepping over to the table, he drew back the sheet reverently and even tenderly from the dead woman's face, and looked down at it with grave pity.

It was a comely face, white as marble, serene and peaceful in expression, with half-closed eyes, and framed with a mass of brassy yellow hair; but its beauty was marred by a long linear wound, half cut, half bruise, running down the right cheek from the eye to the chin.

"A handsome girl," Thorndyke commented—"a dark-haired blonde. What a sin to have disfigured herself so with that horrible peroxide."

He smoothed the hair back from her forehead, and added: "She seems to have applied the stuff last about ten days ago. There is about a quarter of an inch of dark hair at the roots. What do you make of that wound on the cheek?"

"It looks as if she had struck some sharp angle in falling, though, as the seats are padded in first-class carriages, I don't see what she could have struck."

"No. And now let us look at the other wound. Will you note down the description?"

He handed me his note-book, and I wrote down as he dictated:

"A clean-punched circular hole in the skull, and inch behind and above margin of left ear—diameter, an inch and seven-sixteenths; starred fracture of parietal bone; membranes perforated, and brain entered deeply; ragged scalp-wound, extending forward to margin of left orbit; fragments of gauze and sequins in edges of wound. That will for the present. Dr. Morton will give us further details if we want them.''

He pocketed his callipers and rule, drew from the bruised scalp one or two loose hairs, which he placed in the envelope with the sequins, and, having looked over the body for other wounds or bruises (of which there were none), replaced the sheet, and prepared to depart.

As we walked away from the mortuary, Thorndyke was silent and deeply thoughtful, and I gathered that he was piecing together the facts that he had acquired.

At length Mr. Stopford, who had several times looked at him curiously, said:

"The post-mortem will take place at three, and is now only half-past eleven. What would you like to do next?''

Thorndyke, who, in spite of his mental preoccupation, had been looking about him in his usual keen, attentive way, halted suddenly.

"Your reference to the post-mortem,'' said he, "reminds me that I forgot to put the ox-gall into my case.''

"Ox-gall!'' I exclaimed, endeavouring vainly to connect this substance with the technique of the pathologist. "What were you going to do with————''

But here I broke off, remembering my friend's dislike of any discussion of his methods before strangers.

"I suppose,'' he continued, "there would hardly be an artist's colourman in a place of this size?''

"I should think not,'' said Stopford. "But couldn't you get the stuff from a butcher? There's a shop just across the road.''

"So there is,'' agreed Thorndyke, who had already observed the shop. "The gall ought, of course, to be prepared, but we can filter it ourselves—that is, if the butcher has any. We will try him, at any rate.''

He crossed the road towards the shop, over which the name "Felton'' appeared in gilt lettering, and, addressing himself to the proprietor, who stood at the door, introduced himself and explained his wants.

"Ox-gall?'' said the butcher. "No, sir, I haven't any just now; but I am having a beast killed this afternoon, and I can let you have some then. In fact,'' he added, after a pause, "as th matter is of importance, I can have one killed at once if you wish it.''

"That is very kind of you,'' said Thorndyke, "and it would greatly oblige me. Is the beast perfectly healthy?''

"They're in splendid condition, sir. I picked them out of the herd myself. But you shall seem them—ay, and choose the one that you'd like killed.''

"You are really very good,'' said Thorndyke warmly. "I will just run into the chemist's next door, and get a suitable bottle, and then I will avail myself of your exceedingly kind offer.''

He hurried into the chemist's shop, from which he presently emerged, carrying a white paper parcel; and we then follwed the butcher down a narrow lane by the side of this shop.

It led to an enclosure containing a small pen, in which were confined three handsome steers, whose glossy black coats contrasted in a very striking manner with their long, greyish-white, nearly straight horns.

"These are certainly very fine beasts, Mr. Felton,'' said Thorndyke, as we drew up beside the pen, "and in excellent condition, too.''

He leaned over the pen and examined the beasts critically, especially as to their eyes and horns; then, approaching the nearest one, he raised his stick and bestowed a smart tap on the underside of the right horn, following it by a similar tap on the left one, a proceeding that the beast viewed with stolid surprise.

"The state of the horns,'' explained Thorndyke, as he moved on to the next steer, "enables one to judge, to some extent, of the beast's health.''

"Lord bless you, sir,'' laughed Mr. Felton, "they haven't got no feeling in their horns, else what good'ud their horns be to 'em?''

Apparently he was right, for the second steer was as indifferent to a sounding rap on either horn as the first.

Nevertheless, when Thorndyke approached the third steer, I unconsciously drew near to watch; and I noticed that, as the stick struck the horn, the beast drew back in evident alarm, and that when the blow was repeated, it became manifestly uneasy.

"He don't seem to like that,'' said the butcher. "Seems as if———— Hullo, that's queer!''

Thorndyke had just brought his stick up against the left horn, and immediatley the beast had wince and started back, shaking his head and moaning.

There was no, however, room for him to back out of reach, and Thorndyke, by leaning into the pen, was able to inspect the sensitive horn, which he did with the closest attention, while the butcher looked on with obvious perturbation.

"You don't think there's anything wrong with this beast, sir I hope," said he.

"I can't say without a further examination," replied Thorndyke. "It may be the horn only that is affected. If you will have it sawn off close the head, and sent up to me at the hotel, I will look at it and tell you. And, by way of preventing any mistakes, I will mark it and cover it up, to protect it from injury in the slaughterhouse."

He opened his parcel and produced from it a wide-mouthcd bottle labelled "Ox-gall," a sheet of gutta-percha tissue, a roller bandage, and a stick of sealing-wax.

Handing the bottle to Mr. Felton, he encased the distal half of the horn in a covering by means of the tissue and the bandage, which he fixed securely with the sealing-wax.

"I'll saw the horn off and bring it up to the hotel myself, with the ox-gall," said Mr. Felton. "You shall have them in half an hour."

He was as good as his word, for in half an hour Thorndyke was seated at a small table by the window of our private sitting-room in the Black Bull Hotel.

The table was covered with newspaper, and on it lay the long grey horn and Thorndyke's travelling-case, now open and displaying a small microscope and its accessories.

The butcher was seated solidly in an armchair waiting, with a half-suspicious eye on Thorndyke, for the report; and I was endeavouring by cheerful talk to keep Mr. Stopford from sinking into utter despondency, though I, too, kept a furtive watch on my colleague's rather mysterious proceedings.

I saw him unwind the bandage and apply the horn to his ear, bending it slightly to and fro.

I watched him as he scanned the surface closely through a lens and observed him as he scraped some substance from the pointed end on to a glass slide, and, having applied a drop of some reagent, began to tease out the scraping with a pair of mounted needles.

Presently he placed the slide under the microscope, and, having observed it attentively for a minute or two, turned round sharply.

"Come and look at this Jervis," said he.

I wanted to second bidding, being on tenderhooks of curiosity, but came over and applied my eye to the instrument.

"Well, what is it?" he asked.

"A multipolar nerve corpuscle—very shrivelled, but unmistakable."

"And this?"

He moved the slide to a fresh spot.

"Two pyramidal nerve corpuscles and some portions of fibres.'

"And what do you say the tissue is?"

"Cortical brain substance, I should say, without a doubt."

"I entirely agree with you. And that being so," he added, turning to Mr. Stopford, "we may say that the case for the defence is practically complete."

"What, in heaven's name, do you mean?" exclaimed Stopford, starting up.

"I mean that we can now prove when and where and how Miss Grant met her death. Come and sit down here, and I will explain. No, you needn't go away, Mr. Felton. We shall have to subpoena you. Perhaps," he continued, "we had better go over the facts and see what they suggest. And first we note the position of the body, lying with the feet close to the off-side door, showing that, when she fell, the deceased was sitting, or more probably standing, close to the door. Next there is this."

He drew from his pocket a folded paper, which he opened, displaying a tiny blue disc.

"It is one of the sequins with which here hat was trimmed, and I have in this envelope several more which I took from the hat itself.

"This single sequin I picked up on the rear end of the off-side footboard, and its presence there makes it nearly certain that at some time Miss Grant had put her head out of the windown on that side.

"The next item of evidence I obtained by dusting the margins of the off-side window with a light powder, which made visible a greasy impression three and a quarter inches long on the sharp corner of the right-hand jamb (right-hand from the inside, I mean).

"And now as to the evidence furnished by the body: The wound in the skull is behind and above the left ear, is roughly circular, and measures one inch and seven-sixteenths at most, and a ragged scalp-wound runs from it towards the left eye. On the right cheek is a linear contused wound three and a quarter inches long. There are no other injuries.

"Our next facts are furnished by this."

He took up the horn and tapped it with his finger, while the solicitor and Mr. Felton stared at him in speechless wonder.

"You notice it is a left horn, and you remember that it was highly sensitive. If you put your ear to it while I strain it, you will hear the grating of a fracture in the bony core.

"Now look at the pointed end, and you will see several deep scratches running lengthwise, and where those scratches end the diameter of the horn is, as you see by this calliper-gauge, one inch and seven-sixteenths. Covering the scratches is a dry blood-stain, and at the extreme tip is a small mass of a dried substance which Dr. Jervis and I have examined with the microscope and are satisfied is brain tissue."

"Good God!" exclaimed Stopford eagerly. "Do you mean to say——"

"Let us finish with the facts, Mr. Stopford," Thorndyke interrupted. "Now, if you look closely at that blood-stain, you will see a short piece of hair stuck to the horn, and through this lens you can make out the root-bulb. It is a golden hair, you notice, but near the root it is black, and our calliper-gauge shows us that the black portion is fourteen sixty-fourths of an inch long.

"Now, in this enevelope are some hairs that I removed from the dead woman's head. They also are golden hairs, black at the roots, and when I measure the black portion I find it to be fouteen sixty-fourths of an inch long. Then, finally, there is this."

He turned the horn over and pointed to a small patch of dried blood. Embedded in it was a blue sequin.

Mr. Stopford and the butcher both gazed at the horn in silent amazement; then the former drew a deep breath and looked up at Thorndyke.

"No doubt," said he, "you can explain this mystery, but for my part I am utterly bewildered, though you are filling me with hope."

"And yet the matter is quite simple," returned Thorndyke, "even with these few facts before us, which are only a selection from the body of evidence in our possession. But I will state my theory, and you shall judge."

He rapidly sketched a rough plan on a sheet of paper, and continued:

"These were the conditions when the train was approaching Woldhurst: Here was the passenger-coach, here was the burning rick, and here was a cattle-truck. This steer was in that truck. Now my hypothesis is that at the time Miss Grant was standing with her head out of the off-side window, watching the burning rick. Her wide hat, worn on the left side, hid from her view the cattle-truck which she was approaching, and then this is what happened."

He sketched another plan to larger scale.

"One of the steers—this one—had thrust its long horn out through the bars. The point of that horn struck the deceased's head, driving her face violently against the corner of the window, and then, in disengaging, ploughed its way through the scalp, and suffered a fracture of its core from the violence of the wrench. This hypothesis is inherently probable, it fits all the facts, and those facts admit of no other explanation."

The solicitor sat for a moment as though dazed; then he rose impulsively and seized Thorndkye's hands.

"I don't know what to say to you," he exclaimed huskily, "except that you have saved my brother's life, and for that may God reward you !"

The butcher rose from his chair with a slow grin.

"It seems to me," said he, "as if that ox-gall was what you might call a blind, eh, sir?"

And Thorndyke smiled an inscrutable smile.

When we returned to town on the following day we were a party of four, which included Mr. Harold Stopford.

The verdict of "Death by misadventure," promptly returned by the coroner's jury, had been shortly followed by his release from custody, and he now sat with his brother and me, listening with rapt attention to Thorndyke's analysis of the case.

"So, you see," the latter concluded, "I had six possible theories of the cause of death worked out before I reached Halbury, and it only remained to select the one that fitted the facts. And when I had seen the cattle-truck, had picked up that sequin, had heard the description of the steers, and had seen the hat and the wounds, there was nothing left to do but the filling in of details.''

"And you never doubted my innocence?'' asked Harold Stopford.

Thorndyke smiles at his quondam client.

"Not after I had seen your colour-box, and your sketch,'' said he, "to say nothing of the spike.''

THE CLEVER COCKATOO

by E.C. Bentley

First published in 1914

"Well, that's my sister," said Mrs. Lancey, in a low voice. "What do you think of her, now you've spoken to her?"

Philip Trent, newly arrived from England, stood by his hostess within the loggia of an Italian villa looking out upon a prospect of such loveliness as has enchanted and enslaved the Northern mind from age to age. Before the villa lay a long paved terrace, and by the balustrade of it a woman stood looking out over the lake and conversing with a tall, grey-haired man.

"Ten minutes is rather a short acquaintance," Trent replied. "Besides, I was attending rather more to her companion. Mynheer Scheffer is the first Dutchman I have met on social terms. One thing about Lady Bosworth is clear to me, though. She is the most beautiful thing in sight, which is saying a good deal."

Mrs Lancey laughed.

"But I want you to take a personal interest in her, Philip; it means nothing, I know, when you talk like that. I care a great deal about Isabel; she is far more to me than any other woman. That's rather rare between sisters, I believe. And it makes me wretched to know that there's something wrong with her."

"Yes her health, do you mean? One wouldn't think so."

"Yes, but I fear it is that."

"Is it possible?" said Trent. "Why, Edith, the woman has the complexion of a child and the step of a racehorse and eyes like jewels. She looks like Atalanta in blue linen."

"Did Atalanta marry an Egyptian mummy?" enquired Mrs. Lancey.

"It is true," said Trent thoughtfully, "that Sir Peregrine looks rather as if he had been dug up somewhere. But I think he owes much of his professional success to that. People like a great doctor to look more or less unhealthy."

"Perhaps they do; but I don't think the doctor's wife enjoys it very much. Isabel is always happiest when away from him—if he were here now she would be quite different from what you see. You know, Philip, their marriage hasn't been a success—I always knew it wouldn't be."

Trent shrugged his shoulders.

"Let us drop the subject, Edith. Tell me why you want me to know about Lady Bosworth having something the matter with her. I'm not a physician."

"No; but there's something very puzzling about it, as you will see; and you are clever at getting at the truth about things other people don't understand. Now, I'll tell you no more. I only want you to observe Bella particularly at dinner this evening, and tell me afterwards what you think. You'll be sitting opposite to her, between me and Agatha Stone. Now go and talk to her and the Dutchman."

"Scheffer's appearance interests me," remarked Trent. "He has a face curiously like Frederick the Great's and yet there's a difference—he doesn't look quite as if his soul were lost for ever and ever."

"Well, go and ask him about it," suggested Mrs. Lancey.

When the party of seven sat down to dinner that evening, Lady Bosworth had just descended from her room. Trent perceived no change in her; she talked enthusiastically of the loveliness of the Italian evening, and joined in a conversation that was general and lively. It was only after some ten minutes that she fell silent, and that a new look came over her face.

Little by little all animation departed from it. Her eyes grew heavy and dull, her red lips were parted in a foolish smile, and to the high, fresh tint of her cheek there succeeded a disagreeable pallor.

All charm, all personal force had departed. It needed an effort to recall her quaint, vivacious talk of an hour ago, now that she sat looking vaguely at the table before her, and uttering occasionally a blank monosyllable in reply to the discourse that Mr. Scheffer poured into her ear. It was not, Trent told himself, that anything abnormal was done. It was the staring fact that Lady Bosworth was not herself, but someone wholly of another kind, that opened a new and unkwown spring of revulsion in the recesses of his heart.

An hour later Mrs. Lancey carried Trent off to a garden-seat facing the lake.

"Well?" she said quietly.

"It's very strange, and rather ghastly," he answered, nursing his knee. "But if you hand't told me it puzzled you, I should have thought it was easy to find an explanation."

"Drugs, you mean?" He nodded. "Of course everybody must think so. George does, I know. It's horrible!" declared Mrs. Lancey, with a thump on the arm of the seat. "Agatha Stone began hinting at it after the first few days. Gossiping cat! She loathes Isabel, and she'll spread it round everywhere that my sister is a drug-fiend. Philip, I asked her point blank if she was taking anything that could account for it. She was much offended at that; told me I had known her long enough to know she never had done and never would do such a thing. And though Isabel has her faults, she's absolutely truthful."

Trent looked on the ground. "Yes; but you may have heard—"

"Oh, I know! They say that kind of habit makes people lie and deceive who never did before. But, you see, she is so completely herself, except just at this time. I simply couldn't make up my mind to disbelieve her. And, besides, if Bella is peculiar about anything, it's clean, wholesome, hygienic living. She has every sort of carbolicky idea. She never uses scent or powder or any kind of before-and-after stuff, never puts anything on her hair; she is washing herself from morning till night, but she always uses ordinary yellow soap. She never touches anything alcoholic, or tea, or coffee. You wouldn't think she had that kind of fad to look at her and her clothes; but she has; and I can't think of anything in the world she would despise more than dosing herself with things."

"How long has it been going on?"

"This is the seventh evening. I entreated her to see a doctor; but she hates the idea of being doctored. She says it's sure to pass off and that it doesn't make any difference to her general health. George, who has always been devoted to her, only talks to her now with an effort. Randolph Stone is just the same; and two days before you arrived the Illingworths and Captain Burrows both went earlier than they had intended—I'm certain, because this change in Isabel was spoiling their visit for them."

"She seems to get on remarkably well with Scheffer," remarked Trent.

"I know—it's extraordinary, but he seems more struck with her than ever."

"Well, he is; but in a lizard-hearted way of his own. He and I were talking just now after you left the dining-room. He spoke of Lady Bosworth in a queer, semi-scientific sort of way, saying she was very interesting to a medical man like himself. You didn't tell me he was one."

"I didn't know. George calls him an anthropologist, and disagrees with him about the races of Farther India. It's the one thing George does know something about, having lived there twelve years governing the poor things. They took to each other at once when they met last year, and when I asked him to stay here he was quite delighted. He only begged to be allowed to bring his cockatoo, as it could not live without him."

"Strange pet for a man," Trent observed. "He was showing off its paces to me this afternoon. Well, it seems he's greatly interested in these attacks of hers. He has seen nothing quite like them. But he is convinced the thing is due to what he calls a toxic agent of some sort. As to what, or how, he is absolutely at a loss."

"Mr. Scheffer really is a wonderful person," the lady said. "He's lived for years among the most appalling savages in Dutch New Guinea, doing scientific work for this Government, and according to George they treat him like a sort of god. He's most attractive and quite kind really, I think, but there's something about him that makes me afraid of him."

"What is it?"

"I think it is the frosty look in his eyes," replied Mrs. Lancey, drawing her shoulders together in a shiver.

"Perhaps that is the feeling about him in Dutch New Guinea," said Trent. "Did you tell me, Edith, that your sister began to be like this the very first evening she came here?"

"Yes. And it had never happened before, she declares."

"She came out from England with the Stones, didn't she?"

"Only the last part of the journey. They got on the train at Lucerne."

Trent looked back into the drawing-room at the wistful face of Mrs. Stone, who was playing piquet with her host. She was slight and pretty, with large, appealing eyes that never lost their melancholy, though she was always smiling.

"You say she loathes Lady Bosworth," he said. "Why?"

"Well, I suppose it's mainly Bella's own fault," confessed Mrs. Lancey, with a grimace. "You may as well know, Philip—you'll soon find out, anyhow—the truth is she *will* flirt with any that she doesn't actively dislike. She's so brimful of life she can't hold herself in—or she won't, rather; she says there's no harm in it, and she doesn't care if there is. Several times she has practised on Randolph, and, although he's a perfectly safe old donkey if there ever was one, Agatha can't bear the sight of her."

"She seems quite friendly with her," Trent observed.

Mrs. Lancey produced through her delicate nostrils a sound that expressed a scorn for which there were no words.

"Well, what do you make of it, Philip?" his hostess asked, at length. "Myself, I simply don't know what to think. These queer fits of her frighten me horribly. There's one dreadful idea, you see, that keeps occurring to me. Could it, perhaps, be"—Mrs. Lancey lowered her already low tone—"the beginning of insanity?"

He spoke reassuringly. "Oh, I shouldn't cherish that fancy. There are other things much more likely and much less terrible. Look here, Edith, will you try to arrange certain things for tomorrow, without asking my why? And don't let anybody know I asked you to do it—not even George. Until later on, at least. Will you?"

"How exciting!" Mrs. Lancey breathed. "Yes, of course, mystery-man. What do you want me to do?"

"Do you think you could manage things to-morrow so that you and I and Lady Bosworth could go out in the motor-boat on the lake for an hour or two in the evening, getting back in time to change for dinner—just the three of us and the engineer?"

She pondered. "Then the three of us could run down in the boat to San Marmette—it's a lovely little place—and be back before seven. In this weather it's really the best time of day for the lake."

"That would do admirably, if you could work it. And one thing more—if we do go as you suggest, I want you privately to tell your engineer to do just what I ask him to do—no matter what it is."

Mrs. Lancey worked it without difficulty. At five o'clock the two ladies and Trent, with a powerful young man of superb manners at the steering-wheel, were gliding swiftly southward, mile after mile, down the long lake. They landed at the most picturesque, and perhaps the most dilapidated and dirtiest, of all the lakeside villages, where, in the tiny square above the landing-place, a score of dusky infants were treading the measures and chanting the words of one of the immemorial games of childhood. While Mrs. Lancey and her sister watched them in delight, Trent spoke rapidly to the young engineer, whose gleaming eyes and teeth flashed understanding.

Soon afterwards they strolled through San Marmette, and up the mountain road to a little church, half a mile away, where a curious fresco could be seen.

It was close on half-past six when they returned, to be met by Guiseppe, voluble in excitement and apology. It appeared that while he had been fraternising with the keeper of the inn by the landing-place certain *triste individui* had, unseen by anyone, been tampering maliciously with the engine of the boat, and had poured handfuls of dust into the delicate mechanism. Mrs. Lancey, who had received a private nod from Trent, reproved him bitterly for leaving the boat, and asked how long it would take to get the engine working again.

Guiseppe, overwhelmed with contrition, feared that it might be a matter of hours. Questioned, he said that the public steamer had arrived and departed twenty minutes since; the next one, the last of the day, was not due until after nine. Their excellences could at least count on getting home by that, if the engine was not ready sooner. Questioned farther, he said that one could telephone from the post-office, and that food creditably cooked was to be had at the *trattoria*.

Lady Bosworth was delighted. She declared that she would not have missed this occasion for anything. She had come to approve highly of Trent, who had made himself excellent company, and she saw her way to being quite admirable, for she was in dancing spirits.

It was a more than cheerful dinner that they had under a canopy of vine-leaves on a tiny terrace overlooking the lake. Twilight came on unnoticed, and soon afterwards appeared the passenger-boat, by which, Giuseppe advising it, they decided to return. It was as they sought for places on the crowded upper deck that Mrs. Lancey put her hand in Trent's arm. "There hasn't been a sign of it all the evening," she whispered. "What does that mean?"

"It means," murmured Trent, "that Lady Bosworth was prevented, by the merest accident, from dining at home in the ordinary way."

It was not until the following afternoon that Trent found an opportunity of being alone with his hostess in the garden.

"She is perfectly delighted at having escaped it last night," said Mrs. Lancey. "She says she knew it would pass off, but she hasn't the least notion how she was cured. Nor have I."

"She isn't," replied Trent. "Last night was only a beginning, and we can't get her unexpectedly stranded for the evening every day. The next move can be made know, if you consent it. Lady Bosworth will be out until this evening, I believe?"

"She's gone shopping in the town. What do you want to do?"

"I want you to take me up to her room, and there I want you to look very carefully through everything in the place—in every corner of every box and drawer and bag and cupboard—and show me anything you find that might—"

"I should hate to do that!" Mrs. Lancey interrupted him, her face flushing.

"You would hate much more to see your sister again this evening as she was every evening before last night. Look here, Edith; the position is simple enough. Every day, about seven, Lady Bosworth goes into that rooom in her normal stateto dress for dinner. Every day she comes out of it apparently as she went in, but turns queer a little later. Now is ther any other place than that room where the mischief could happen?"

Mrs. Lancey frowned dubiously. For a few moments she stood carefully boring a hole in the gravel with one heel. Then, "Come along," she said, and led the way toward the house.

"Unless we take the floor up," said Mrs. Lancey, seating herself emphatically on the bed in her sister's room twenty minutes later, "there's nowhere else to look. I've taken everything out and pried into every hole and corner. There isn't a single lockable thing that is locked. There isn't a bottle or phial or pill-box of any sort to be found. So much for your suspicions. What interests you about that nail-polishing pad? You must have seen one before, surely."

"This ornamental design on hammered silver is very beautiful and original," replied Trent, abstractedly. "I have never seen anything quite like it."

"The same design is on the whole of the toilet-seat," Mrs. Lancey observed tartly, "and it shows to least advantage on the manicure things. You are talking rubbish; and yet," she added slowly, "you are looking rather pleased with yourself."

Trent turned round slowly. "I'm only thinking. Whose are the rooms on each side of this, Edith?"

"This side, the Stones's; that side, Mr. Scheffer's."

"Then I will go for a walk all alone and think some more. Good-bye."

Trent was not in the house when, three hours later, a rousing tumult broke out on the upper floor. Those below in the loggia heard first a piercing scream, then a clatter of feet on parquet flooring, then more sounds of feet, excited voices, other screams of harsh, inhuman quality, and a lively scuffling and banging. Mr. Scheffer, with a volley of guttural words of which it was easy to gather the general sense, headed the rush of the company upstairs.

"Gisko! Gisko!" he shouted, at the head of the stairway. There was another ear-splitting screech, and the cockatoo came scuttling and fluttering out of Lady Bosworth's room, pursued by three vociferating women servants. The bird's yellow crest was erect and quivering with agitation; it screetched furious defiance again as it leapt upon its master's outstretched wrist.

"Silence, devil!" exclaimed Mr. Scheffer, seizing it by the head and shaking it violently. "I know not how to apologise, Lancey," he declared. "The accursed bird had somehow slipped from his chain away. I left him in my room secure just before we had tea."

"Never mind, never mind!" replied his host, who seemed rather pleased than otherwise with this small diversion. "I don't suppose he's done any harm beyond frightening the women. Anything wrong, Edith?" he asked, as they approached the open door of the bedroom, to which the ladies had already hurried. Lady Bosworth's maid was telling a voluble story.

"When she came in just now to get the room ready for Isabel to dress," Mrs. Lancey summarised, "she suddenly heard a voice say something, and saw the bird perched on top of the mirror, staring at her. It gave her such a shock that she dropped the watercan and fled; then the other girls came and helped her, trying to drive it out. They hadn't the sense to send for Mr Scheffer."

"Apologise, carrion!" commanded Gisko's master. The cockatoo uttered a string of Dutch words in a subdued croak. "He says he asks one thousand pardons, and he will sin no more," Mr. Scheffer translated. "Miserable brigand! Traitor!"

Lady Bosworth hurried out of her room.

"I won't here the poor thing scolded like that," she protested. "How was he to know my maid would be frightened? He looks so wretched! Take him away, Mr. Scheffer, and cheer him up."

It was half an hour later that Mrs. Lancey came to her husband in his dressing-room.

"I must say Bella was very decent about Scheffer's horrid bird," she began. "Do you know what the little fiend had done?"

"No, my dear. I thought he had confined himself to frightening the maid out of her skin."

"Not at all. He had been having the time of his life. Bella saw at once that he had been up to mischief, but she pretended there was nothing. Now it turns out he has bitten the buttons off two pairs of gloves, chewed up a lot of hair-pins, and spoiled her pretty little manicure set. He's torn the lining out of the case, the silver handles are covered with beak-marks, two or three of the things he seems to have hidden somewhere, and the polishing-pad is a ruin."

"It's too bad!" declared Mr. Lancey, bending over a shoe.

"I believe you're laughing, George," said his wife coldly.

He began to do so audibly. "You must admit it's funny to think of the bird going solemnly through a programme of mischief like that. I wish I could have been the little beggar at it. Well, we shall have to get Bella a new nail-outfit. I'm glad she held her tongue about it just now."

"Why?"

"Because, my dear, we don't ask people to the house to make them feel uncomfortable—especially foreigners."

"Bella wasn't thinking of your ideal of hospitality. She held her tongue because she's taken a fancy to Scheffer. But, George, how do you suppose the little pest got in? The window was shut, and Hignett declares the door was too, when she went to the room."

"Then I expect Hignett deceives herself. Anyway, what does it matter? What I am anxious about is your sister's little peculiarity. As I've told you, I don't at all like the look of her having been quite normal yesterday evening, the one evening when she was away from the house by accident. I really am feeling miserably depressed, Edith. What I'm dreading now is a repetition of the usual ghastly performance tonight."

But neither that night, nor any night after, was that performance repeated. Lady Bosworth, free now of all apprehension, renewed and redoubled the life of the little company. And the lips of Trent were obstinately sealed.

Three weeks later Trent·was shown into the consulting-room of Sir Peregrine Bosworth. The famous physician was a tall, stooping man of exaggerated gauntness, narrow-jawed, and high-nosed. He was courteous of manner and smiled readily; but his face was set in unhappy lines.

"Will you sit down, Mr. Trent?" said Sir Peregrine. "You wrote that you wished to see me upon a private matter concerning myself. I am at a loss to imagine what it can be, but, knowing your name, I had no hesitation in making an appointment."

Trent inclined his head. "I am obliged to you, Sir Peregrine. The matter is really important, and also quite private—so private that no person whatever knows the material facts besides myself. I won't waste words. I have lately been staying with the Lanceys, whom you know, in Italy. Lady Bosworth was also a guest there. For some days before my arrival she had suffered each evening from a curious attack of lassitude and vacancy of mind. I don't know what it is. Perhaps you do."

Sir Peregrine, immovably listening, smiled grimly. "The description of symptoms is a little vague. I have heard nothing of this, I may say, from my wife."

"It always came on at a certain time of the day, and only then. That time was a few minutes after eight, at the beginning of dinner. The attack passed off gradually after two hours or so."

The physician laid his clenched hand on the table between them. "You are not a medical man, Mr. Trent, I believe. What concern have you with all this?" His voice was coldly hostile now.

"Lots," answered Trent briefly. Then he added, as Sir Peregrine got to his feet with a burning eye, "I know nothing of medicine, but I cured Lady Bosworth."

The other sat down again suddenly. His open hands fell upon the table and his dark face became very pale. "You—" he began with difficulty.

"I and no other, Sir Peregrine. And in a curiously simple way. I found out what was causing the trouble, and without her knowledge I removed it. It was—oh, the devil!" Trent exclaimed in a lower tone. For Sir Peregrine Bosworth, with a brow gone suddenly white and clammy, had first attempted to rise and then sunk forward with his head on the table.

Trent, who had seen such things before, hurried to him, pulled his chair from the table, and pressed his head down to his knees. Within a minute the stricken may was leaning back in his chair. He inspired deeply from a small bottle he had taken from his pocket.

"You have been overworking, perhaps," Trent said. "Something is wrong. I think I had better not—"

Sir Peregrine had pulled himself together. "I know very well what is wrong with me, sir," he interrupted brusquely. "It is my business to know. That will not happen again. I wish to hear what you have to say, before you leave this house."

"Very well." Trent took a tone of colourless precision. "I was asked by Lady Bosworth's sister, Mrs. Lancey, to help in trying to trace the source of the disorder which attacked her every evening. I need not decribe the signs of it, and I will not trouble you with an account of how I reasoned on the matter. But I found out that Lady Bosworth was, on these occasions, under the influence of a drug, which had the effect of lowering her vitality and clogging her brain, without producing stupefaction or sleep; and I was led to the conclusion that she was administering this drug to herself without knowing it."

He paused, and felt in his waistcoat pocket. "When Mrs. Lancey and I were making a search for something of the kind in her room, my attention was caught by the fine workmanship of a manicure set on the dressing-table. I took up the little round box meant to contain nail-polishing paste, admiring its shape and decoration, and on looking inside it found it half-full of paste. But I have often watched the process of beautifying finger-nails, and it seemed to me that the stuff was of a depper red than usual pink confection; and I saw next that the polishing-pad of the set, though well-worn, had never been used with paste, which leaves a sort of dark incrustation on the pad. Yet it was evident that the paste in the little box had been used. It is useful sometimes, you see, to have a mind that notices trifles. So I jumped to the conclusion that the paste that was not employed as nail-polish was employed for some other purpose; and when I reached that point I simply put the box in my pocket and went away with it. I may say that Mrs. Lancey knew nothing of this, or what I did afterwards."

"And what was that?" Sir Peregrine appeared now to be following the story with an ironic interest.

"Naturally, knowing nothing of such matters I took it to the place that called itself 'English Pharmacy' in the town, and asked the proprietor what the stuff was. He looked at it, took a little on his finger, smelt it, and said it was undoubtedly lip-salve.

"It was then I remembered how, when I saw Lady Bosworth during one of her attacks, her lips were brilliantly red, though all the colour had departed from her face. That had struck me as very odd, because I am a painter, and naturally I could not miss an abnormality like that. Then I remembercd another thing. One evening, when Lady Bosworth, her sister, and myself were prevented from returning to the house for dinner, and dined at a country inn, there had been no signs of her trouble; but I had noticed that she moistened her lips again and again with her tongue."

"You are observant," remarked Sir Peregrine dispassionately and again had recourse to his smelling-bottle.

"You are good enough to say so," Trent replied, with a wooden face. "On thinking these things over, it seemed to me probably that Lady Bosworth was in the habit of putting on a little lip-salve when she dressed for dinner in the evening; perhaps finding that her lips at that time of day tended to become dry, or perhaps not caring to use it in daylight, when its presence would be much more easily detected. For I had learned that she made some considerable parade of not using any kind of cosmetics or artificial aids to beauty; and that, of course, accounted for her carrying it in a box meant for manicure-paste, which might be represented as merely a matter of cleanliness, and at any rate was not to be classed with paint and powder. It was not pleasant to me to have surprised this innocent little deception; but it was as well that it did so, for I soon ascertained beyond doubt that the stuff had been tampered with.

"When I left the chemist's I went and sat in a quiet corner of the Museum grounds. There I put the least touch of the salve on my tongue, and awaited results. In five minutes I had lost all power of connected thought or will; I no longer felt any interest in my own experiment. I was conscious. I felt no discomfort, and no loss of power of movement. Only my intelligence seemed to be paralysed. For an hour I was looking out upon the world with the soul of an ox, placid and blank."

Trent now opened his fingers and showed a little round box of hammered silver, with a delicate ornamentation running round the lid. It was about the bigness of a pill-box.

"It seemed best to me that this box should simply disappear, and in some quite natural, unsuspicious way. Merely to remove the salve would have drawn Lady Bosworth's attention to it and set her guessing. She did not suspect the stuff as yet, I was fully convinced; and I thought it well that the affair of her seizures should remain a mystery. Your eyes ask why. Just because I did not want a painful scandal in Mrs. Lancey's family—we are old friends, you see. And now here I am with the box, and neither Lady Bosworth nor any other person has the smallest inkling of its crazy secret but you and I."

He stopped again and looked in Sir Peregrine's eyes. They remained fixed upon him with the gaze of a statue.

"It was plain, of course," Trent continued, "that someone had got at the stuff immediately before she went out to Italy, or immediately on her arrival. The attacks began on the first evening there, two hours after reaching the house. Therefore any tampering with the salve after her arrival was practically impossible. When I asked myself who should have tampered with it before Lady Bosworth left this house to go out to Italy, I was lead to form a very unpleasant conjecture."

Sir Peregrine stirred in his chair. "You had been told the truth—or part of the truth—about our married life, I suppose?"

Trent inclined his head. "Three days ago I arrived in London and showed a little of this paste to a friend of mine who is an expert analyst. He has sent me a report, which I have here." He handed an envelope across the table. "He was deeply interested in what he found, but I have not satisfied his curiosity. He found the salve to be evenly impregnated with a very slight quantity of a rare alkaloid body called 'purvisine'. Infinitesimal doses of it produce the effects on the human organism which he describes, as I can testify, with considerable accuracy. It was discovered, he notes, by Henry Purvis twenty-five years ago; and you will remember, Sir Peregrine, what I only found out by inquiry—that you were assistant to Purvis about that time in Edinburgh, where he had the Chair of medical jurisprudence and toxicology."

He ceased to speak, and there was a short silence. Sir Peregrine gazed at the table before him. Once or twice he drew breath deeply, and at length began to speak calmly.

"I shall not waste words," he said, "in trying to explain fully my state of mind or my action in this matter. But I will tell you enough for your imagination to do the rest. My feeling for my wife was an infatuation from the beginning, and is still. I was too old for her. I don't think now that she ever cared for me greatly; but she was too strong-minded ever to marry a wealthy fool. By the time we had been married a year I could no longer hide from myself that she had an incurable weakness for philandering. She has surrendered to it with less and less restraint, and without any attempt to deceive me on the subject. If I tried to tell you what torture it has been to me, you wouldn't understand. The worst was when she was away from me, staying with her friends. At length I took the step you know. It was undeniably an act of baseness, and we will leave it at that, if you please. If you should ever suffer as I do, you will modify your judgment upon me. I knew of my wife's habit, discovered by you, of using lip-salve at her evening toilette. On the night before her departure I took what was in that box and combined it with a preparation of the drug purvisine. The infinitesimal amount which would pass into the mouth after the application of the salve was calculated to produce for an hour or two the effects you have described, without otherwise doing any harm. But I knew the impression that would be produced upon normal men and women by the sight of anyone in such a state. I wanted to turn her attractiveness into repulsiveness, and I seemed to have succeeded. I was mad when I did it. I have been aghast at my own action ever since. I am glad it has been frustrated. And now I should like to know what you intend to do."

Trent took up the box. "If you agree, Sir Peregrine, I shall drop this from Westminster Bridge tonight. And so long as nothing of the sort is practised again, the whole affair shall be buried. Yours is a wretched story, and I don't suppose any of us would find our moral fibre improved by such a situation. I have no more to say."

He rose and moved to the door. Sir Peregrine rose also and stood with lowered eyes, apparently deep in thought.

"I am obliged to you, Mr. Trent," he said, formally "I may say, too, that your account of your proceedings interested me deeply. I should like to ask a question. How did you contrive that the box should disappear without its owner seeing anything remarkable in its absence?"

"Oh, easily," Trent replied, his hand on the door-knob. "After experimenting on myself, I went back to the house beore tea-time, when no one happened to be in. I went upstairs to a room where a cokatoo was kept—a mischievous brute—took him off his chain, and carried him into Lady Bosworth's room. There I put him on the dressing-table, and teased him a little with the manicure things to interest him in them. Then I took away one of the pairs of scissors, so that the box shouldn't be the one thing missing, and left him shut in there to do his worst, while I went out of the house again. When I went he was ripping out the silk lining of the case, and had chewed up the silver handles of the other things. In the riot that took place when he was found, the disappearance of the little box and scissors became a mere detail. Certainly Lady Bosworth suspected nothing.

"I suppose," he added, thoughtfully "that occasion would be the only time a cockatoo was of any particular use."

And Trent went out.

THE ABSENT MINDED COTERIE

by Robert Barr

First published in 1906

Some years ago I enjoyed the unique experience of pursuing a man for one crime, and getting evidence against him of another. He was innocent of the misdemeanour, the proof of which I sought, but was guilty of another most serious offence, yet he and his confederates escaped scot free in circumstances which I now purpose to relate.

You may remember that in Rudyard Kipling's story, *Bedalia Herodsfoot,* the unfortunate woman's husband ran the risk of being arrested as a simple drunkard, at a moment when the blood of murder was upon his boots. The case of Ralph Summertrees was rather the reverse of this. The English authorities were trying to fasten upon him a crime almost as important as murder, while I was collecting evidence which proved him guilty of an action much more momentous than that of drunkenness.

The Englilsh authorities have always been good enough, when they recognise my existence at all, to look down upon me with amused condescension. If to-day you ask Spenser Hale, of Scotland Yard, what he thinks of Eugène Valmont, that complacent man will put on the superior smile which so well becomes him, and if you are a very intimate friend of his, he may draw down the lip of his right eye, as he replies:

"Oh, yes, a very decent fellow, Valmont, but he's a Frenchman", as if, that said, there was no need of further inquiry.

Myself, I like the English detective very much, and if I were to be in a *mêlée* to-morrow, there is no man I would rather find beside me than Spenser Hale. In any situation where a fist that can fell an ox is desirable, my friend Hale is a useful companion, but for intellectuality, mental acumen, finesse— ah, well! I am the most modest of men, and will say nothing.

It would amuse you to see this giant come into my room during an evening, on the bluff pretence that he wishes to smoke a pipe with me. There is the same difference between this good-natured giant and myself as exists between that strong black pipe of his and my delicate cigarette, which I smoke feverishly when he is present, to protect myself from the fumes of his terrible tobacco. I look with delight upon the huge man, who, with an air of the utmost good humour, and a twinkle in his eye as he thinks he is twisting me about his finger, vainly endeavours to obtain a hint regarding whatever case is perplexing him at that moment. I baffle him with the case that an active greyhound eludes the pursuit of a heavy mastiff, than at last I say to him with a laugh:

"Come, *mon ami* Hale, tell me all about it, and I will help you if I can."

Once or twice at the beginning he shook his massive head, and replied the secret was not his. The last time he did this I assured him that what he said was quite correct, and then I related full particulars of the situation in which he found himself, excepting the names, for these he had not mentioned. I had pieced together his perplexity from scraps of conversation in his half-hour's fishing for my advice, which, of course, he could have had for the plain asking. Since that time he has not come to me except with cases he feels at liberty to reveal, and one or two complications I have happily been enabled to unravel for him.

But, staunch as Spense Hale holds the belief that no detective service on earth can excel that centring in Scotland Yard, there is one department of activity in which even he confesses that Frenchmen are his master, although he somewhat grudgingly qualifies his admission by adding that we in France are constantly allowed to do what is prohibited in England. I refer to the minute search of a house during the owner's absence. If you read that excellent story, entitled *The Purloined Letter,* by Edgar Allan Poe, you will find a record of the kind of thing I mean, which is better than any description I, who have so often taken part in such a search, can set down.

Now, these people among whom I live are proud of their phrase, "The Englishman's house is his castle", and into that castle even a policeman cannot penetrate without a legal warrant. This may be all very well in theory, but if you are compelled to march up to a man's house, blowing a trumpet, and rattling a snare drum, you need not be disappointed if you fail to find what you are in search of when all the legal restrictions are complied with. Of course, the English are a very excellent people, a fact to which I am always proud to bear testimony, but it must be admitted that for cold common sense the French are very much their superiors. In Paris, if I wish to obtain an incriminating document, I do not send the possessor a *carte postale* to inform him of my desire, and in this procedure the French people sanely acquiesce. I have known men who, when they go out to spend an evening on the boulevards, toss their bunch of keys to the concierge, saying:

"If you hear the police rummaging about while I'm away, pray assist them, with an expression of my distinguished consideration."

I remember while I was a chief detective in the service of the French Government being requested to call at a certain hour at the private hotel of the Minister for Foreign Affairs. It was during the time that Bismarck meditated a second attack upon my country, and I am happy to say I was then instrumental in supplying the Secret Bureau with documents which mollified that iron man's purpose, a fact which I think entitled me to my country's gratitude, not that I ever even hinted such a claim when a succeeding ministry forgot my services. The memory of a republic, as has been said by a greater man than I, is short. However, all that has nothing to do with the incident I am about to relate. I merely mention the crisis to excuse a momentary forgetfulness on my part which in any other country might have been followed by serious results to myself. But in France—ah, we understand those things, and nothing happened.

I am the last person in the world to give myself away, as they say in the great West. I am usually the calm, collected Eugène Valmont whom nothing can perturb, but this was a time of great tension, and I had become absorbed, I was alone with the minister in his private house, and one of the papers he desired was in his bureau at the Ministry for Foreign Affairs; at least, he thought so, and said:

"Ah, it is in my desk at the bureau. How annoying! I must send for it!"

"No, Excellency," I cried, springing up in a self-oblivion the most complete, "it is here." Touching the spring of a secret drawer, I opened it, and taking out the document he wished, handed it to him.

It was not until I met his searching look, and saw the faint smile on his lips, that I realised what I had done.

"Valmont," he said quietly, "on whose behalf did you search my house?"

"Excellency," I replied in tones no less agreeable than his own, "to-night at your orders I pay a domiciliary visit to the mansion of Baron Dumoulaine, who stands high in the estimation of the President of the French Republic. If either of those distinguised gentlemen should learn of my informal call and should ask me in whose interests I made the domiciliary visit, what is it you wish that I should reply?"

"You should reply, Valmont, that you did it in the interests of the Secret Service."

"I shall not fail to do so, Excellency, and in answer to your question just now, I had the honour of searching this mansion in the interests of the Secret Service of France".

The Minister for Foreign Affairs laughed; a heartly laugh that expressed no resentment.

"I merely wished to compliment you, Valmont, on the efficiency of your search, and the excellence of your memory. This is indeed the document which I thought was left in my office."

I wonder what Lord Landsdowne would say if Spenser Hale showed an equal familiarity with his private papers! But now that we have returned to our good friend Hale, we must not keep him waiting any longer.

I well remember the November day when I first heard of the Summertrees case, because there hung over London a fog so thick that two or three times I lost my way, and no cab was to be had at any price. The few cabmen then in the streets were leading their animals slowly along, making for their stables. It was one of those depressing London days which filled me with ennui and a yearning for my own clear city of Paris, where, if we are ever visited by a slight mist, it is at least clean, white vapour, and not this horrible London mixture saturated with suffocating carbon. The fog was too thick for any passer to read the contents bills of the newspapers plastered on the pavement, and as there were probably no races that day the newsboys were shouting what they considered the next most important event—the election of an American President. I bought a paper and thrust in into my pocket. It was late when I reached my flat, and, after dining there, which was an unusual thing for me to do, I put on my slippers, took an easy-chair before the fire, and began to read my evening journal. I was distressed to learn that the eloquent Mr. Bryan had been defeated. I knew little about the silver question, but the man's oratorical powers had applealed to me, and my sympathy was aroused because he owned many silver mines, and yet the price of the metal was so low that appratetly he could not make a living through the operation of them. But of course, the cry that he was a plutocrat, and a reputed millionaire over and over again, was bound to defeat him in a democracy where the average voter is exceeding poor and not comfortably well-to-do as is the case with our peasants in France. I always took great interest in the affairs of the huge republic to the west, having been at some pains to inform myself accurately regarding its politics, and although, as my readers know, I seldom quote anything complimentary that is said of me, nevertheless, an American client of mine once admitted that he never knew the true inwardness—I think was the phrase he used—of American politics until he heard me discourse upon them. But then, he added, he had been a very busy man all his life.

I had allowed my paper to slip to the floor, for in very truth the fog was penetrating even into my flat, and it was becoming difficult to read, notwithstanding the electric light. My man came in, and announced that Mr. Spenser Hale wished to see me, and, indeed, any night, but especially when there is rain or fog outside, I am more pleased to talk with a friend than to read a newspaper.

"Mon Dieu, my dear Monsieur Hale, it is a brave man you are to venture out in such a fog as is abroad to-night."

"Ah, Monsieur Valmont," said Hale with pride, "you cannot raise a fog like this in Paris!"

"No. There you are supreme," I admitted, rising and saluting my visitor, then offering him a chair.

"I see you are reading the latest news", he said, indicating my newspaper. "I am very glad that man Bryan is defeated. Now we shall have better times."

I waved my hand as I took my chair again. I will discuss many things with Spenser Hale, but not American politics; he does not understand them. It is a common defeat of the English to suffer complete ignorance regarding the internal affairs of ther countries.

"It is surely an important thing that brought you out on such a night as this. The fog must be very thick in Scotland Yard."

This delicate shaft of fancy completely missed him, and he answered stolidly:

"It's thick all over London, and, indeed, throughout most of England."

"Yes, it is," I agreed, but he did not see that either.

Still a moment later he made a remark which, if it had come from some people I know, might have indicated a glimmer of comprehension.

"You are a very, very clever man, Monsieur Valmont, so all I need say is that the question which brought me here is the same as that on which the American election was fought. Now, to a countryman, I should be compelled to give further explanation, but to you, monsieur, that will not be necessary."

There are times when I dislike the crafty smile and partial closing of the eyes which always distinguishes Spenser Hale when he places on the table a problem which he expects will baffle me. If I said he never did baffle me, I would be wrong, of course, for sometimes the utter simplicity of the puzzles which trouble him leads me into an intricate involution entirely unnecessary in the circumstances.

I pressed my finger tips together, and gazed for a few moments at the ceiling. Hale had lit his black pipe, and my silent servant placed at his elbow the whisky and soda, then tip-toed out of the room. As the door closed my eyes came from the ceiling to the level of Hale's expansive countenance.

"Have they eluded you?" I asked quietly.

"Who?"

"The coiners."

Hale's pipe dropped from his jaw, but he managed to catch it before it reached the floor. Then he took a gulp from the tumbler.

"That was just a lucky shot," he said.

"Parfaitement," I replied carelessly.

"Now, own up, Valmont, wasn't it?"

I shrugged my shoulders. A man cannot contradict a guest in his own house.

"Oh, stow that!" cried Hale impolitely. He is a trifle prone to strong and even slangy expressions when puzzled. "Tell me how you guessed it."

"It is very simple, *mon ami*. The question on which the American election was fought is the price of silver, which is so low that it has ruined Mr. Bryan, and threatens to ruin all the farmers of the west who possess silver mines on their farms. Silver troubled America, ergo silver troubles Scotland Yard."

"Very well, the natural inference is that some one has stolen bars of silver. But such a theft happened three months ago, when the metal was being unloaded from a German steamer at Southampton, and my dear friend Spenser Hale ran down the thieves very cleverly as they were trying to dissolve the marks off the bars with acid. Now crimes do not run in series, like the numbers in roulette at Monte Carlo. The thieves are men of brains. They say to themselves, "What chance is there successfully to steal bars of silver while Mr. Hale is at Scotland Yard? Eh, my good friend?"

"Really, Valmont," said Hale, taking another sip, "sometimes you almost persuade me that you have reasoning powers."

"Thanks, comrade. Then it is not a *theft* of silver we have now to deal with. But the American election was fought on the *price* of silver. If silver had been high in cost, there would have been no silver question. So the crime that is bothering you arises through the low price of silver, and this suggests that it must be a case of illicit coinage, for there the low price of metal comes in. You have, perhaps, found a more subtle illegitimate act going forward than heretofore. Some one is making your shillings and your half-crowns from real silver, insteead of from baser metal, and yet there is a large profit which has not hitherto been possible through the high price of silver. With the old conditions you were familiar, but this new element sets at nought all your previous formulae. That is how I reasoned the matter out."

"Well, Valmont, you have hit it. I'll say that for you; you have hit it. There is a gang of expert coiners who are putting out real silver money, and making a clear shilling on the half-crown. We can find no trace of the coiners, but we know the man who is shoving the stuff."

"That ought to be sufficient," I suggested.

"Yes, it should; but it hasn't proved so up to date. Now I came to-night to see if you would do one of your French tricks for us, right on the quiet."

"What French trick, Monsieur Spenser Hale?" I inquired with some asperity, forgetting for the moment that the man invariably became impolite when he grew excited.

"No offence intended," said this blundering officer, who really is a good-natured fellow, but always puts his foot in it, and then apologises. "I want some some one to go through a man's house without a search warrant, spot the evidence, let me know, and then we'll rush the place before he has time to hide his tricks."

"Who is this man, and where does he live?"

"His name is Ralph Summertrees, and he lives in a very natty little bijou residence, as the advertisements call it, situated in no less a fashionable street than Park Lane."

"I see. What has aroused your suspicions against him?"

"Well, you known, that's an expensive district to live in; it takes a bit of money to do the trick. This Summertrees has no ostensible business, yet every Friday he goes to the United Capital Bank in Piccadilly, and deposits a bag of swag, usually all siver coin."

"Yes, and this money?"

"This money, so far as we can learn, contains a good many of these new pieces which never saw the British Mint."

"It's not all the new coinage, then?"

"Oh, no, he's a bit too artful for that, You see, a man can go round London, his pockets filled with new coinage five-shilling pieces, buy this, that, and the other, and come home with his change in legitimate coins of the realm—half-crowns, florins, shillings, sixpences, and all that."

"I see. Then why don't you nab him one day when his pockets are stuffed with illegitimate five-shilling pieces?"

"That could be done, of course, and I've thought of it, but, you see, we want to land the whole gang. Once we arrested him, without knowing where the money came from, the real coiners would take flight."

"How do you know he is not the real coiner himself?"

Now poor Hale is as easy to read as a book. He hesitated before anwereing this question, and looked confused as a culprit caught in some dishonest act.

"You need not be afraid to tell me," I said soothingly after a pause. "You have had one of your men in Mr. Summertrees's house, and so learned that he is not the coiner. But your man has not succeeded in getting you evidence to incriminate other people."

"You've about hit it again, Monsieur Valmont. One of my men has been Summertrees's butler for two weeks, but, as you say, he has found no evidence."

"Is he still butler?"

"Yes."

"Now tell me how far you have got. You know that Summertrees deposits a bag of coin every Friday in the Piccadilly bank, and I suppose the bank has allowed you to examine one or two of the bags."

"Yes, sir, they have, but, you see, banks are very difficult to treat with. They don't like detectives bothering round, and whilst they do not stand out against the law, still they never answer any more questions than they're asked, and Mr. Summertrees has been a good·customer at the United Capital for many years."

"Haven't you found out where the money comes from?"

"Yes, we have; it is brought there night after night by a man who looks like a respectable city clerk, and he puts it into a large safe, of which he holds the key, this safe being on the ground floor, in the dining-room."

"Haven't you followed the clerk?"

"Yes. He sleeps in the Park Lane house every night, and goes up in the morning to an old curiosity shop in Tottenham Court Road, where he stays all day, returning with his bag of money in the evening."

"Why don't you arrest and question him?"

"Well, Monsieur Valmont, there is just the same objection to his arrest as to that of Summertrees himself. We could easily arrest both, but we have not the slightest evidence against either of them, and then, although we put the go-betweens in clink, the worst criminals of the lot would escape."

"Nothing suspicious about the old curiosity shop?"

"No. It appears to be perfectly regular."

This game has been going on under your noses for how long?"

"For about six weeks."

"Is Sumertrees a married man?"

"No."

"Are there any women servants in the house?"

"No, except that three charwomen come in every morning to do up the rooms."

"Of what is his household comprised?"

"There is the butler, then the valet, and last, the French cook."

"Ah," cried I, "the French cook! This case interests me. So Summertrees has succeeded in completely disconcerting your man? Has he prevented him going from top to bottom of the house?"

"Oh, no, he has rather assisted him than otherwise. On one occasion he went to the safe, took out the money, had Podgers—that's my chap's name—help him to count it, and then actually sent Podgers to the bank with the bag of coin."

"And Podgers has been all over the place?"

'Yes.'

"Saw no signs of a coining establishment?"

"No. It is absolutely impossible that any coining can be done there. Besides, as I tell you, that respectable clerk brings him the money."

"I suppose you want me to take Podger's position?"

"Well, Monsieur Valmont, to tell you the truth, I would rather you didn't. Podgers had done everything a man can do, but I thought if you got into the house, Podgers assisting, you might go through it night after night at your leisure."

"I see. That's just a little dangerous in England. I think I should prefer to assure myself the legitimate standing of being the amiable Podger's successor. You say that Summertrees has no business?"

"Well, sir, not what you might call a business. He is by way of being an author, but I don't count that any business."

"Oh, an author, is he? When does he do his writing?"

"He locks himself up most of the day in his study."

"Does he come out for lunch?"

"No; he lights a little spirit lamp inside, Podgers tells me, and makes himself a cup of coffee, which he takes with a sandwich or two."

"That's rather frugel fare for Park Lane."

"Yes, Monsieur Valmont, it is, but he makes it up in the evening, when he has a long dinner with all them foreign kickshaws you people like, done by his French cook."

"Sensible man! Well, Hale, I see I shall look forward with pleasure to making the acquaintance of Mr. Summertrees. Is there any restriction on the going and coming of your man Podgers?"

"None in the least. He can get away either night or day."

"Very good, friend Hale, bring him here to-morrow, as soon as our author locks himself up in his study, or rather, I should say, as soon as the respectable clerk leaves for Tottenham Court Road, which I should guess, as you put it, is about half an hour after his master turns the key of the room in which he writes."

"You are quite right in that guess, Valmont. How did you hit it?"

"Merely a surmise, Hale. There is a good deal of oddity about that Park Lane house, so it doesn't surprise me in the least that the master gets to work earlier in the morning than the man. I have also a suspicion that Ralph Summertrees knows perfectly well what the estimable Podgers is here for."

"What makes you think that?"

"I can give no reason except that my opinion of the acuteness of Summertrees has been gradually rising all the while you were speaking, and at the same time my estimate of Podgers's craft has been as steadily declining. However, bring the man here tomorrow, that I may ask him a few questions."

Next day, about eleven o'clock, the ponderous Podgers, hat in hand, followed his chief into my room. His broad, impassive, immobile smooth face gave him rather more the air of a genuine butler than I had expected, and this appearance, of course, was enhanced by his livery. His replies to my questions were those of a well-trained servant who will not say too much unless it is made worth his while. All in all, Podgers exceeded my expectations, and really my friend Hale had some justification for regarding him, as he evidently did, a triumph in his line.

"Sit down, Mr. Hale, and you, Podgers."

The man disregarded my invitation, standing like a statue until his chief made a motion; then he dropped into a chair. The English are great on discipline.

"Now, Mr. Hale, I must first congratulate you on the make-up of Podgers. It is excellent. You depend less on artificial assistance than we do in France, and in that I think you are right."

"Oh, we know a bit over here, Monsieur Valmont," said Hale, with pardonable pride.

"Now then, Podgers, I want to ask you about this clerk. What time does he arrive in the evening?"

"At prompt six, sir."

"Does he ring, or let himself in with a latchkey?"

"With a latchkey, sir."

"How does he carry the money?"

"In a little locked leather satchel, sir, flung over his shoulder."

"Does he go direct to the dining-room?"

"Yes, sir."

"Have you seen him unlock the safe and put in the money?"

"Yes, sir."

"Does the safe unlock with a word or a key?"

"With a key, sir. It's one of the old-fashioned kind."

"Then the clerk unlocks his leather money bag?"

"Yes, sir.

"That's three keys used within as many minutes Are they separate or in a bunch?"

"In a bunch, sir."

"Did you ever see your master with this bunch of keys?"

"No, sir."

"You saw him open the safe once, I am told?"

"Yes, sir."

"Did he use a separate key, or one of a bunch?"

Podgers slowly scratched his head, then said:

"I don't just remember, sir."

"Ah, Podgers, you are neglecting the big things in that house. Sure you can't remember?"

"No, sir."

"Once the money is in and the safe locked up, what does the clerk do?"

"Goes to his room, sir."

"Where is this room?"

"On the third floor, sir?"

"Where do you sleep?"

"On the fourth floor with the rest of the servants, sir?"

"Where does the master sleep?"

"On the second floor, adjoining his study."

"The house consists of four stories and a basement, does it?"

"Yes, sir."

"I have somehow arrived at the suspicion that it is a very narrow house. Is that true?"

"Yes, sir."

"Does the clerk ever dine with your master?"

"No, sir. The clerk don't eat in the house at all, sir."

"Does he go away before breakfast?"

"No, sir."

"No one takes breakfast to his room?"

"No, sir."

"What time does he leave the house?"

"At ten o'clock, sir."

"When is breakfast served?"

"At nine o'clock, sir."

"At what hour does your master retire to his study?"

"At half-past nine, sir."

"Locks the door on the inside?"

"Yes, sir."

"Never rings for anything during the day?"

"Not that I know of, sir."

"What sort of a man is he?"

Here Podgers was on familiar ground, and he rattled off a description minute in every particular.

"What I meant was, Podgers, is he silent, or talkative, or does he get angry? Does he seem furtive, suspicious, anxious, terrorised, calm, excitable, or what?"

"Well, sir, he is by way of being very quiet, never has much to say for himself; never saw him angry, or excited."

"Now, Podgers, you've been at Park Lane for a fortnight or more. You are a sharp, alert, observant man. What happens there that strikes you as unusual?"

"Well, I can't exactly say, sir," replied Podgers, looking rather helplessly from his chief to myself, and back again.

"Your professional duties have often compelled you to enact the part of butler before, otherwise you wouldn't do it so well. Isn't that the case?"

Podgers did not reply, but glanced at his chief. This was evidently a question pertaining to the service, which a subordinate was not allowed to answer. However, Hale said at once:

"Certainly. Podgers has been in dozens of places."

"Well, Podgers, just call to mind some of the other households where you have been employed, and tell me any particulars in which Mr Summertree's establishment differs from them."

Podgers pondered a long time.

"Well, sir, he do stick to writing pretty close."

"Ah, that's his profession, you see, Podgers. Hard at it from half-past nine till towards seven, I imagine?"

"Yes, sir."

"Anything else, Podgers? No matter how trivial."

"Well, sir, he's fond of reading too; leastways, he's fond of newspapers."

"When does he read?"

"I've never seen him read 'em, sir; indeed, so far as I can tell, I never knew the papers to be opened, but he takes them all in, sir."

"What, all the morning papers?"

"Yes, sir, and all the evening papers too."

"Where are the morning papers placed?"

"One the table in his study, sir."

"And the evening papers?"

"Well, sir, when the evening papers come, the study is locked. They are put on a side table in the dining-room, and he takes them upstairs with him to his study."

"This has happened every day since you've been there?"

"Yes, sir."

"You reported that very striking fact to your chief, of course?"

"No, sir, I don't think I did," said Podgers, confused.

"You should have done so. Mr. Hale would have known how to make the most of a point so vital."

"Oh, come now, Valmont," interrupted Hale, "you're chaffing us. Plenty of people take in all the papers!"

"I think not. Even clubs and hotels subscribe to the leading journals only. You said *all*, I think, Podgers?"

"Well, *nearly* all, sir."

"But which is it? There's a vast difference."

"He takes a good many, sir."

"How many?"

"I don't just know, sir."

"That's easily found out, Valmont," cried Hale, with some impatience, "if you think it really important."

"I think it so important that I'm going back with Podgers myself. You can take me into the house, I suppose, when you return?"

"Oh, yes, sir."

"Coming back to these newspapers for a moment, Podgers. What is done with them?"

"They are sold to the ragman, sir, once a week."

"Who takes them from the study?"

"I do, sir."

"Do they appear to have been read very carefully?"

"Well, no, sir; leastways, some of them seem never to have been opened, or else folded up very carefully again."

"Did you notice that extracts have been clipped from any of them?"

"No, sir."

"Does Mr. Summertrees keep a scrapbook?"

"Not that I know of, sir."

"Oh, the case is perfectly plain," said I, leaning back in my chair, and regarding the puzzled Hale with that cherubic expression of self-satisfaction which I know is so annoying to him.

"*What's* perfectly plain?" he demanded, more gruffly perhaps than etiquette would have sanctioned.

"Summertrees is no coiner, nor is he linked with any band of coiners."

"What is he, then?"

"Ah, that opens another avenue of inquiry. For all I know to the contrary, he may be the most honest of men. On the surface it would appear that he is a reasonably industrious tradesman in Tottenham Court Road, who is anxious that there should be no visible connection between a plebeian employment and so aristocratic a residence as that in Park Lane."

At this point Spenser Hale gave expression to one of those rare flashes of reason which are always an astonishment to his friends.

"That is nonsense, Monsieur Valmont," he said, "the man who is ashamed of the connection between his business and his house is one who is trying to get into Society, or else the women of his family are trying it, as is usually the case. Now Summertrees has no family. He himself goes nowhere, gives no entertainments, and accepts no invitations. He belongs to no club, therefore to say that he is ashamed of his connection with the Tottenham Court Road shop is absurd. He is concealing the connection for some other reason that will bear looking into."

"My dear Hale, the goddess of Wisdom herself could not have made a more sensible series of remarks. Now, *mon ami*, do you want my assistance, or have you enough to go on with?"

"Enough to go on with? We have nothing more than we had when I called on you last night."

"Last night, my dear Hale, you supposed this man was in league with coiners. To-day you know he is not."

"I know you *say* he is not."

I shrugged my shoulders, and raised by eyebrows, smiling at him.

"It is the same thing, Monsieur Hale."

"Well, of all the conceited——" and the good Hale could get no further.

"If you wish my assistance, it is yours."

"Very good. Not to put too fine a point upon it, I do."

"In that case, my dear Podgers, you will return to the residence of our friend Summertrees, and get together for me in a bundle all of yesterday's morning and evening papers that were delivered to the house. Can yo do that, or are they mixed up in a heap in the coal cellar?"

"I can do it, sir. I have instructions to place each day's papers in a pile by itself in case they should be wanted again. There is always one week's supply in the cellar, and we sell the papers of the week before to the rag man."

"Excellent. Well, take the risk of abstracting one day's journals, and have them ready for me. I will call upon you at half-past three o'clock exactly, and then I want you to take me upstairs to the clerk's bedroom in the third story, which I suppose is not locked during the daytime?"

"No, sir, it is not."

With this the patient Podgers took his departure. Spenser Hale rose when his assistant left.

"Anything further I can do?" he asked.

"Yes; give me the address of the shop in Tottenham Court Road, Do you happen to have about you one of those new five-shilling pieces which you believe to be illegally coined?"

He opened his pocket-book, took out the bit of white metal, and handed it to me.

"I'm going to pass this off before evening," I said, putting it in my pocket, "and I hope none of your men will arrest me."

"That's all right," laughed Hale as he took his leave.

At half-past three Podgers was waiting for me, and opened the front door as I came up the steps, thus saving me the necessity of ringing. The house seemed strangly quiet. The French cook was evidently down in the basement, and we had probably all the upper part to ourselves, unless Summertrees was in his study, which I doubted. Podgers led me directly upstairs to the clerk's room on the third floor, walking on tiptoe, with an elephantine air of silence and secrecy combined, which struck me as unnecessary.

"I will make an examination of this room," I said. "Kindly wait for me down by the door of the study."

The bedroom proved to be of respectable size when one considers the smallness of the house. The bed was all nicely made up, and there were two chairs in the room, but the usual washstand and swing-mirror were not visible. However, seeing a curtain at the farther end of the room, I drew it aside, and found, as I expected, a fixed lavatory in an alcove of perhaps four feet deep by five in width. As the room was about fifteen feet wide, this left two-thirds of the space unaccounted for. A moment later, I opened a door which exhibited a closet filled with clothes hanging on hooks. This left a space of five feet between the clothes closet and the lavatory. I though at first that the entrance to the secret stairway must have issued from the lavatory, but examining the boards closely, although they sounded hollow to the knuckles, they were quite evidently plain matchboarding, and not a concealed door. The entrance to the stairway, therefore, must issue from the clothes closet. The right hand wall proved similar to the matchboarding of the lavatory as far as the casual eye or touch was concerned, but I saw at once it was a door. The latch turned out to be somewhat ingeniously operated by one of the hooks which held a pair of old trousers. I found that the hook, if pressed upward, allowed the door to swing outward, over the stairhead. Descending to the second floor, a similar latch let me in to a similar clothes closet in the room beneath. The two rooms were identical in size, one directly above the other, the only difference being that the lower room door gave into the study, instead of into the hall, as was the case with the upper chamber.

The study was extremely neat, either not much used, or the abode of a very methodical man. There was nothing on the table except a pile of that morning's papers. I walked to the farther end, turned the key in the lock, and came out upon the astonished Podgers.

"Well, I'm blowed!" exclaimed he.

"Quite so," I rejoined, "you've been tiptoeing past an empty room for the last two weeks. Now, if you'll come with me, Podgers, I'll show you how the trick is done."

When he entered the study, I locked the door once more, and led the assumed butler, still tiptoeing through force of habit, up the stair into the top bedroom, and so out again, leaving everything exactly as we found it. We went down the main stair to the front hall, and there Podgers had my parcel of papers all neatly wrapped up. This bundle I carried to my flat, gave one of my assistants some instructions, and left him at work on the papers.

I took a cab to the foot of Tottenham Court Road, and walked up that street til I came to J. Simpson's old curiosity shop. After gazing at the well-filled windows for some time, I stepped aside, having selected a little iron crucifix displayed behind the pane; the work of some ancient craftsman.

I knew at once from Podgers's description that I was waited upon by the veritable respectable clerk who brought the bag of money each night to Park Lane, and who I was certain was no other than Ralph Summertrees himself.

There was nothing in his manner differing from that of any other quiet salesman. The price of the crucifix proved to be seven-and-six, and I threw down a sovereign to pay for it.

"Do you mind the change being all in silver, sir?" he asked, and I answered without any eagerness, although the question aroused a suspicion that had begun to be allayed:

"Not in the least."

He gave me half-a-crown, three two-shilling pieces, and four separate shillings, all the coins being well-worn silver of the realm, the undoubted inartistic product of the reputable British Mint. This seemed to dispose of the theory that he was palming off illegitimate money. He asked me if I were interested in any particular branch of antiquity, and I replied that my curiosity was merely general, and exceedingly amateurish, whereupon he invited me to look round. This I proceeded to do, while he resumed the addressing and stamping of some wrapped-up pamphlets which I surmised to be copies of his catalogue.

He made no attempt either to watch me or to press his wares upon me. I selected at random a little inkstand, and asked it price. It was two shillings, he said, whereupon I produced my fraudulent five-shilling piece. He took it, gave me the change without comment, and the last doubt about his connection with coiners flickered from my mind.

At this moment a young man came in, who, I saw at once, was not a customer. He walked briskly to the farther end of the shop, and disappeared behind a partition which had one pane of glass in it that gave an outlook towards the front door.

"Excuse me a moment," said the shopkeeper, and he followed the young man into the private office.

As I examined the curious heterogeneous collection of things for sale, I heard the clink of coins being poured out on the lid of a desk or an uncovered table, and the murmur of voices floated out to me. I was now near the entrance of the shop, and by a sleight-of-hand trick, keeping the corner of my eye on the glass pane of the private office, I removed the key of the front door without a sound, and took an impression of it in wax, returning the key to its place unobserved. At this moment another young man came in, and walked straight past me into the private office. I heard him say:

"Oh, I beg pardon, Mr. Simpson. How are you, Rogers?"

"Hallo, Macpherson," saluted Rogers, who then came out, bidding good-night to Mr. Simpson, and departed whistling down the street, but not before he had repeated his phrase to another young man entering, to whom he gave the name of Tyrrel.

I noted these three names in my mind. Two others came in together, but I was compelled to content myself with memorising their features, for I did not learn their names. These men were evidently collectors, for I heard the rattle of money in every case; yet here was a small shop, doing apparently very little business, for I had been within it for more than half an hour, and yet remained the only customer. If credit were given one collector would certainly have been sufficient, yet five had come in, and had poured their contributions into the pile Summertrees was to take home with him that night.

I determined to secure one of the pamphlets which the man had been addressing. They were piled on a shelf behind the counter, but I had no difficulty in reaching across and taking the one on top, which I slipped into my pocket. When the fifth young man went down the street Summertrees himself emerged, and this time he carried in his hand the well-filled locked leather satchel, with the straps dangling. It was now approaching half-past five, and I saw he was eager to close up and get away.

"Anything else you fancy, sir?" he asked me.

"No, or rather yes and no. You have a very interesting collection here, but it's getting so dark I can hardly see."

"I close at half-past five, sir."

"Ah, in that case," I said, consulting my watch, "I shall be pleased to call some other time."

"Thank you, sir," replied Summertrees quietly, and with that I took my leave.

From the corner of an alley on the other side of the street I saw him put up the shutters with his own hand, then he emerged with overcoat on, and the money satchel slung across his shoulder. He locked the door, tested it with his knuckles, and walked down the street, carrying under one arm the pamphlets he had been addressing. I followed him some distance, saw him drop the pamphlets into the box at the first post office he passed, and walk rapidly towards his house in Park Lane.

When I returned to my flat and called in my assistant, he said:

"After putting to one side the regular advertisements of pills, soap, and what not, here is the only one common to all the newpapers, morning and evening alike. The advertisements are not identical, sir, but they have two points of similarity, or perhaps I should say three. They all profess to furnish a cure for absentmindedness; they all ask that the applicant's chief hobby shall be stated, and they all bear the same address: Dr. Willoughby, in Tottenham Court Road."

"Thank you," said I, as he placed the scissored advertisements before me.

I read several of the announcements. They were all small, and perhaps that is why I had never noticed one of them in the newspapers, for certainly they were odd enough. Some asked for lists of absent-minded men, with the hobbies of each, and for these lists, prizes of from one shilling to six were offered. In other clippings Dr. Willoughby professed to be able to cure absent-mindedness. There were no fees, and no treatment, but a pamphlet would be sent, which, if it did not benefit the receiver, could do no harm. The doctor was unable to meet patients personally, nor could he enter into correspondence with them. The address was the same as that of the old curiosity shop in Tottenham Court Road. At this juncture I pulled the pamphlet from my pocket, and saw it was entitled *Christian Science and Absent Mindedness*, by Dr Stamford Willoughby, and at the end of the article was the statement contained in the advertisements, that Dr. Willoughby would neither see patients nor hold any correspondence with them.

I drew a sheet of paper towards me, wrote to Dr. Willoughby alleging that I was a very absent-minded man, and would be glad of his pamphlet, adding that my special hobby was the collecting of first editions. I then signed myself, "Alport Webster, Imperial Flats, London, W."

I may here explain that it is often necessary for me to see people under some other name than the well-known appellation of Eugène Valmont". There are two doors to my flat, and on one of these is painted, "Eugène Valmont"; on the other there is a receptacle, into which can be slipped a sliding panel bearing any *nom de guerre* I choose. The same device is arranged on the ground floor, where the names of all the occupants of the building appear on the right-hand wall.

I sealed, addressed, and stamped my letter, than told my man to put out the name of Alport Webster, and if I did not happen to be in when any one called upon that mythical person, he was to make an appointment for me.

It was nearly six o'clock next afternoon when the card of Angus Macpherson was brought in to Mr Alport Webster. I recognised the youngman at once as the second who had entered the little shop carrying his tribute to Mr. Simpson the day before. He held three volumes under his arm, and spoke in such a pleasant, insinuating sort of way, that I knew at once he was an adept in his profession of canvasser.

"Will you be seated, Mr Macpherson? In what can I serve you?"

He placed the three volumes, backs upward, on my table.

"Are you interested at all in first editions, Mr Webster?"

"It is the one thing I am interested in," I replied; "but unfortunately they often run into a lot of money."

"That is true," said Macpherson sympathetically, "and I have here three books, one of which is an exemplification of what you say. This one costs a hundred pounds. The last copy that was sold by auction in London brought a hundred and twenty-three pounds. This next one is forty pounds, and the third ten pounds. At these prices I am certain you could not duplicate three such treasures in any book shop in Britain."

I examined them critically, and saw at once that what he said was true. He was still standing on the opposite side of the table.

"Please take a chair, Mr. Macpherson. Do you mean to say you go round London with a hundred and fifty pounds worth of goods under your arm in this careless way?"

"I run very little risk, Mr. Webster. I don't suppose any one I meet imagines for a moment there is more under my arm than perhaps a trio of volumes I have picked up on the fourpenny box to take home with me."

I lingered over the volume for which he asked a hundred pounds, than said, looking across at him:

"How came you to be possessed of this book, for instance?"

He turned upon me a fine, open countenance, and answered without hesitation in the frankest possible manner:

"I am not in actual possession of it, Mr. Webster. I am by way of being a connoisseur in rare and valuable books myself, although, of course, I have little money with which to indulge in the collection of them. I am acquainted, however, with the lovers of desirable books in different quarters of London. These three volumes, for instance, are from the library of a private gentleman in the West End. I have sold many books to him, and he knows I am trustworthy. He wishes to dispose of them at something under their real value, and has kindly allowed me to conduct the negotiation. I make it by business to find out those who are interested in rare books, and by such trading I add considerably to my income."

"How, for instance, did you learn that I was a bibliophile?" Mr. Macpherson laughed genially.

"Well, Mr. Webster, I must confess that I chanced it. I do that very oftern. I take a flat like this, and send in my card to the name on the door. If I am invited in, I ask the occupants the question I asked you just now: "Are you interested in rare editions?" If he says no, I simply beg pardon and retire. If he says yes, then I show my wares."

"I see," said I, nodding. What a glib young liar he was, with that innocent face of his, and yet my next question brought forth the truth.

"As this is the first time you have called upon me, Mr. Macpherson, you have no objection to my making some further inquiry, I suppose. Would you mind telling me the name of the owner of these books in the West End?"

"His name is Mr. Ralph Summertrees, of Park Lane."

"Of Park Lane? Ah, indeed."

"I shall be glad to leave the books with you, Mr. Webster, and if you care to make an appointment with Mr. Summertrees, I am sure he will not object to say a word in my favour."

"Oh, I do not in the east doubt it, and should not think of troubling the gentleman."

"I was going to tell you," went on the young man, "that I have a friend, a capitalist, who, in a way, is my supporter; for, as I said, I have little money of my own. I find it is often inconvenient for people to pay down any considerable sum. When, however, I strike a bargain, my capitalist buys the book, and I make an arrangement with my customer to pay a certain amount each week, and so even a larger purchase is not felt, as I make the instalments small enough to suit my client."

"You are employed during the day, I take it?"

"Yes, I am a clerk in the City."

Again we were in the blissful realms of fiction!

"Suppose I take this book at ten pounds, what instalment should I have to pay each week?"

"Oh, what you like, sir. Would five shillings be too much?"

"I think not."

"Very well, sir, if you pay me five shillings now, I will leave the book with you, and shall have pleasure in calling this day week for the next instalment."

I put my hand into my pocket, and drew out two half-crowns, which I passed over to him.

"Do I need to sign any form or undertaking to pay the rest?"

The young man laughed cordially.

"Oh, no, sir, there is no formality necessary. You see, sir, this is largely a labour of love with me, although I don't deny I have my eye on the future. I am getting together what I hope will be a very valuable connection with gentlemen like yourself who are fond of books, and I trust some day that I may be able to resign my place with the insurance company and set up a choice little business of my own, where my knowledge of values in literature will prove useful."

And then, after making a note in a little book he took from his pocket, he bade me a most graceful good-bye and departed, leaving me cogitating over what it all meant.

Next morning two articles were handed to me. The first came by post and was a pamphlet on *Christian Science and Absent Mindedness*, exactly similar to the one I had taken away from the old curiosity shop; the second was a small key made from my wax impression that would fit the front door of the same shop—a key fashioned by an excellent anarchist friend of mine in an obscure street near Holborn.

That night at ten o'clock I was inside the old curiosity shop, with a small storage battery in my pocket, and a little electric glow lamp at my buttonhole, a most useful instrument for either burglar or detective.

I had expected to find the books of the establishment in a safe, which, if it was similar to the one in Park Lane, I was prepared to open with the false keys in my possession or to take an impression of the keyhole and trust to my anarchist friend for the rest. But to my amazement I discovered all the papers pertaining to the conern in desk which was not even locked. The books, three in a number, were the ordinary day book, journal, and ledger referring to the shop; book-keeping of the older fashion; but in a portfolio lay half a dozen foolscap sheets, headed "Mr. Roger's List," "Mr. Machpherson's," "Mr. Tyrrel's," the names I had already learned, and three others. These lists contained in the first column names; in the second column, addresses; in the third, sums of money; and then in the small, square places following were amounts ranging from two-and-sixpence to a pound. At the bottom of Mr. Machpherson's list was the name of Alport Webster, Imperial Flats, £10; then in the small, square place, five shillings. These six sheets, each headed by a canvasser's name, were evidently the record of current collections, and the innocence of the whole thing was so apparent that if it were not for my fixed rule never to believe that I am at the bottom of any case until I have come on something suspicious, I would have gone out empty-handed as I came in.

The six sheets were loose in a thin portfolio, but standing on a shelf above the desk were a number of fat volumes, one of which I took down, and saw that it contained similar lists running back several years. I noticed on Mr. Macpheson's current lists the name of Lord Semptam, an eccentric old nobleman whom I knew slightly. Then turning to the list immediatly before the current one the name was still there; I traced it back through list after list until I found the first entry, which was no less than three years previous, and there Lord Semptam was down for a piece of furniture costing fifty pounds, and on that account he had paid a pound a week for more than three years, totalling a hundred and seventy pounds at the least, and instantly the glorious simplcity of the scheme dawned on me, and I became so interested in the swindle that I lit the gas, fearing my little lamp would be ex-haused before my investigation ended, for it promised to be a long one.

In several instances the intended victim proved shrewder than old Simpson had counted upon, and the word "Settled" had been written on the line carrying the name when the exact number of instalments was paid. But as these shrewd persons dropped out, others took their places, and Simpson's dependence on their absent-mindedness seemed to be justified in nine cases out of ten. His collectors were collecting long after the debt had been paid. In Lord Semptam's case, the payment had evidently become chronic, and the old man was giving away his pound a week to the suave Machperson two years after his debt had been liquidated.

From the big volume I detached the loose leaf, date 1893, which recorded Lord Semptam's purchase of a carved wood table for fifty pounds, and on which he had kept paying a pound a week from that time to the date of which I am writing, which was November 1896. This single document taken from the file of three years previous, was not likely to be missed, as would have been the case if I had selected a current sheet. I nevertheless made a copy of the names and addresses of Machperson's present clients; then, carefully extinguished the gas, and went out of the shop, locking the door behind me. With the 1893 sheet in my pocket I resolved to prepare a pleasant little surprise for my suave friend Macpherson when he called to get his next instalment of five shillings.

Late as was the hour when I reached Trafalgar Square I could not deprive myself of the felicity of calling on Mr. Spenser Hale, who I knew was then on duty. He never appeared at his best during of-fice hours, because of officialism stiffened his stalwart frame. Mentally he was impressed with the importance of his position, and added to this he was not then allowed to smoke his big, black pipe and terrible tobcco. He received me with the curtness I had been taught to expect when I inflicted myself upon him at his office. He greeted me abruptly with:

"I say, Valmont, how long do you expect to be on this Job?"

"What job?" I asked mildly.

"Oh, you know what I mean: the Summertrees affair."

"Oh, *that*!" I exclaimed, with surprise, "The Summertrees case is already completed, of course. If I had known you were in a hurry, I should have finished up everything yesterday, but as you and Podgers, and I don't know how many more, have been at it sixteen or seventeen days, if not longer, I thought I might venture to take as many hours, as I am working entirely alone. You said nothing about haste you know."

"Oh, come now, Valmont, that's a bit thick. Do you mean to say you have already got evidence against the man?"

"Evidence absolute and complete."

"The who are the coiners?"

"My most estimable friend, how often have I told you not to jump at conclusions? I informed you when you first spoke to me about the matter that Summertrees was neither a coiner nor a confederate of coiners. I secured evidence sufficient to convict him of quite another offence, which is probably unique in the annals of crime. I have penetrated the mystery of the shop, and discovered the reason for all those suspicious actions which quite properly set you on his trail. Now I wish you to come to my flat next Wednesday night at a quarter to six, prepared to make an arrest.''

"I must know who I am to arrest, and on what counts."

"Quite so, *mon ami* Hale; I did not say you were to make an arrest, but merely warned you to be prepared. If you have time now to listen to the disclosures, I am quite at your service. I promise you there are some original features in the case. If, however, the present moment is inopportune, drop in on me at your convenience, previously telephoning so thay you may know wether I am there or not, and thus your valuable time will not be expended purposely.''

With this I presented to him my most courteous bow, and although his mystified expression hinted a suspicion that he thought I was chaffing him, as he would call it, official dignity dissolved somewhat, and he intimated his desire to hear all about then and there. I had succeeded with perplexed brow, and at last ejaculated he would be blessed.

"This young man," I said in conclusion, "will call upon me at six on Wednesday afternoon, to receive his second five shillings. I propose that you, in your uniform, shall be seated there with me to receive him, and I am anxious to study Mr. Macpherson's countenance when he realises he has walked in to confront a policeman. If you will then allow me to cross-examine him for a few moments, not after the manner of Scotland Yard, with a warning lest he incriminate himself, but in the free and easy fashion we adopt in Paris, I shall afterwards turn the case over to you to be dealt with at your discretion."

"You have a wonderful flow of language, Monsieur Valmont," was the officer's tribute to me. "I shall be on hand at a quarter to six on Wednesday."

"Meanwhile," said I, "kindly say nothing of this to any one. We must arrange a complete surprise for Macpherson. That is essential. Please make no move in the matter at all until Wednesday night."

Spenser Hales, much impressed, nodded acquiescence, and I took a polite leave of him.

The question of lighting is an important one in a room such as mine, and electricity offers a good deal of scope to the ingenious. Of this fact I have taken full advantage. I can manipulate the lighting of my room so that any particular spot is bathed in brilliancy, while the rest of the space remains in comparative gloom, and I arranged the lamps so that the full force of their rays impinged against the door that Wednesday evening, while I sat on one side of the light table in semi-darkness and Hale sat on the other, with alight beating down on him from above which gave him the odd, sculptured look of a living statue of Justice, stern and triumphant. Any one entering the room would be first dazzled by the light, and next would see the gigantic form of Hale in the full uniform of his order.

When Angus Macpherson was shown into this room he was quite visibly taken aback, and paused abruptly on the threshold, his gaze riveted on the huge policeman. I think his first purpose was to turn and run, but the door closed behind him, and he doubtless heard, as we all did, the sound of the bolt being thrust in its place, thus locking him in.

"I-I beg your pardon," he stammered, "I expected to meet Mr. Webster."

As he said this, I pressed the button under my table, and was instantly enshrouded with light. A sickly smile overspread the countenance of Machperson as he caught the sight of me, and he made a very creditable attempt to carry off the situation with nonchalance.

"Oh, there you are, Mr. Webster; I did not notice you at first."

It was a tense moment. I spoke slowly and impressively.

"Sir perhaps you are not unaquainted with the name of Eugène Valmont."

He replied brazenly:

"I am sorry to say, sir, I never heard of the gentleman before."

At this came a most inopportune "Haw-haw" from that blockhead Spenser Hale, completely spoiling the dramatic situation I had elaborated with such thought and care. It is little wonder the English possess no drama, for they show scant appreciation of the sensational moments in life.

"Haw-haw," brayed Spenser Hale, and at once reduced the emotional atmosphere of a fog of commonplace. However what is a man to do? He must handle the tools with which it pleases Providence to provide him. I ignored Hale's untimely laughter.

"Sit down, sir," I said to Machperson, and he obeyed.

"You have called on Lord Semptam this week," I continued sternly.

"Yes, sir."

"And collected a pound from him?"

"Yes, sir."

"In October, 1893, you sold Lord Semptam a carved antique table for fifty pounds?"

"Quite right, sir."

"When you were here last week you gave me Ralph Summertrees as the name of a gentleman living in Park Lane. You knew at the time that this man was your employer?"

Macpherson was now looking fixedly at me, and on this occasion made no reply. I went on calmly:

"You also knew tha Summertrees, of Park Lane, was identical with Simpson, of Tottenham Court Road?"

"Well, sir," said Macpherson, "I don't exactly see what you're driving at, but it's quite usual for a man to carry on a business under an assumed name. There is nothing illegal about that."

"We will come to the illegality in a moment, Mr. Macpherson. You, and Rogers and Tyrrel, and three others, are confederates of this man Simpson."

"We are in his employ; yes, sir, but no more confederates than clerks usually are."

"I think, Mr. Macpherson, I have said enough to show you that the game is, what you call, up. You are now in the presence of Mr. Spenser Hale, from Scotland Yard, who is waiting to hear your confession."

Here the stupid Hale broke in with his:

"And remember, sir, that anything you say will be——"

"Excuse me, Mr. Hale," I interrupted hastily, "I shall turn over the case to you in a very few moments, but I ask you to remember our compact, and to leave it for the present entirely in my hand. Now, Mr. Macpherson, I want your confession, and I want it at once."

"Confession: Confederates?" protested Macpherson with admirably simulated surprise. "I must say you use extraordinary terms, Mr.—Mr.——What did you say the name was?"

"Haw-haw," roared Hale. "His name is Monsieur Valmont."

"I implore you, Mr. Hale, to leave this man to me for a very few moments. Now, Macpherson, what have you to say in your defence?"

"Where nothing criminal has been alleged, Monsieur Valmont, I see no necessity for defence. If you wish me to admit that somehow you have acquired a number of details regarding our business, I am perfectly willing to do so, and to subscribe to their accuracy. If you will be good enough to let me know of what you complaint, I shall endeavour to make the point clear to you if I can. There has evidently been some misapprehension, but for the life of me, without further explanation, I am as much in a fog as I was on my way coming here, for it is getting a little thick outside."

Macpherson certainly was conducting himself with great descretion, and presented, quite unconsciously, a much more diplomatic figure than my friend, Spenser Hale, sitting stiffly opposite me. His tone was one of mild expostulation, mitigated by the intimation that all misunderstanding speedily would be cleared away. To outward view he offered a perfect picture of innocence, neither protesting too much nor too little. I had, however, another surprise in store for him, a trump card, as it where, and played it down on the table.

"There!" I cried with vim, "have you ever seen that sheet before?"

He glanced at it without offering to take it in his hand.

"Oh, yes" he said, "that has been abstracted from our file. It is what I call my visiting list."

"Come, come sir," I cried sternly, "you refuse to confess, but I warn you we know all about it. You never heard of Dr. Willoughby, I suppose?"

"Yes, he is the author of the silly pamphlet on Christian Science."

"You are in the right, Mr. Macpherson; on Christian Science and Absent-Mindedness."

"Possibly. I haven't read it for a long while."

"Have you ever met this learned doctor, Mr. Macpherson?"

"Oh, yes. Dr. Willoubhy is the pen-name of Mr. Summertrees. He believes in Christian Science and that sort of thing, and writes about it."

"Ah, really. We are getting your confession bit by bit, Mr. Macpherson. I think it would be better to be quite frank with us."

"I was just going to make the same suggestion to you, Monsieur Valmont. If you will tell me in a few words exactly what is your charge against either Mr. Summertrees or myself, I will know then what to say."

"We charge you, sir, with obtaining money under false pretences, which is a crime that has landed more than one distinguished financier in prison."

Spenser Hale shook his fat forefinger at me, and said:

"Tut, tut, Valmont; we mustn't threaten, we mustn't threaten, you know;" but I went on without heeding him.

"Take, for instance, Lord Semptam. You sold him a table for fifty pounds, on the instalment plan. He was to pay a pound week, and in less than a year the debt was liquidated. But he is an absent-minded man, as all your clients are. That is why you came to me. I had answered the bogus Willoughby's advertisement. And so you kept on collecting and collecting for something more than three years. Now do yo understand the charge?"

Mr. Macpherson's head during this accusation was held slightly inclined to one side. At first his face was clouded by the most clever imitation of anxious concentration of mind I had ever seen, and this was gradually cleared away by the dawn of awakening perception. When I had finished, an ingratiating smile hovered about his lips.

"Really, you know," he said, "that is rather a capital scheme. The absent-minded league, as one might call them. Most ingenious. Summertrees, if he had any sense of humour, which he hasn't, would be rather taken by the idea that his innocent fad for Christian Science had led him to be suspected of obtaining money under false pretences. But, really, there are no pretensions about the matter at all. As I understand it, I simply call and receive the money through the forgetfulness of the person on my list, but where I think you would have both Summertrees and myself, if there was anything in your audacious theory, would be an indictment for conspiracy. Still, I quite see how the mistake arises. You have jumped to the conclusion that we sold nothing to Lord Semptam except that carved table three year ago. I have pleasure in pointing out to you that his lordship is a frequent customer of ours, and has had many thing from us at one time or another. Sometimes he is in our debt; sometimes we are in his. We keep a sort of running contract with him by which he pays us a pound a week. He and several other customers deal on the same plan, and in return for an income that we can count upon, they get the first offer of anything in which they are supposed to be interested. As I have told you, we call these sheets in the office our visiting lists, but to make the visiting lists complete you need what we term our encyclopaedia. We call it that because it is in so many volumes; a volume for each year, running back I don't know how the amount stated on this visiting list. These figures refer to the page of the encyclopaedia for the current year, and on that page is noted the new sale, and the amount of it, as it might be set down, say, in a ledger."

"That is a very entertaining explanation, Mr. Macpherson. I suppose this encyclopaedia, as you call it, is in the shop at Tottenham Court Road?"

"Oh, no, sir. Each volume of the encyclopaedia is self-locking.

These books contain the real secret of our business, and they are kept in the safe at Mr. Summertree's house in Park Lane. Take Lord Semptam's account, for instance. You will find in faint figures under a certain date, 102. If you turn to page 102 of the encyclopaedia for that year, you will then see a list of what Lord Semptam has bought, and the prices he was charged for them. It is really a very simple matter. If you will allow me to use your telephone for a moment, I will ask Mr. Summertrees, who has not yet begun dinner, to bring with him here the volume for 1893, and, within a quarter of an hour, you will be perfectly satisfied that everything is quite legitimate."

I confess that the young man's naturalness and confidence staggered me, the more so as I saw by the sarcastic smile on Hale's lips that he did not believe a single word spoken. A portable telephone stood on the table, and as Macpherson finished his explanation, he reached over and drew it towards him. The Spencer Hale interfered.

"Excuse *me*," he said, "I'll do the telephoning. What is the call number of Mr. Summertrees?"

"140 Hyde Park."

Hale at once called up Central, and presently was answered from Park Lane. We heard him say:

"Is this the residence of Mr. Summertrees? Oh, is that you, Podgers? Is Mr. Summertrees in? Very well. This is Hale. I am in Valmont's flat—Imperial Flats—you know. Yes, where you went with me the other day. Very well, go to Mr. Summertrees, and say to him that Mr. Macpherson wants the encyclopaedia for 1983. Do you get that? Yes, encyclopaedia. Oh, he'll understand what it is. Mr. Macpherson. No, don't mention my name at all. Just say Mr. Macpherson wants the encyclopaedia for the year 1983, and that you are to bring it. Yes, you may tell him that Mr. Mcpherson is at Imperial Flats, but don't mention my name at all. Exactly. As soon as he gives you the book, get into a cab, and come here as quickly as possible with it. If Summertrees doesn't want to let the book go, then tell him to come with you. If he won't do that, place him under arrest, and bring both him and the book here. All right. Be as quick as you can; we're waiting."

Macpherson made no protest against Hale's use of the telephone; he merely sat back in his chair with a resigned expression on his face which, if painted on canvas, might have been entitled "The Falsely Accused." When Hale rang off, Macpherson said:

"Of course you know your own business best, but if your man arrests Summertrees, he will make you the laughing-stock of London. There is such a thing as unjustifiable arrest, as well as getting money under false pretences, and Mr. Summertrees is not the man to forgive an insult. And then, if you will allow me to say so, the more I think over your absent-minded theory, the more absolutely grotesque it seems, and if the case ever gets into the newspapers, I am sure, Mr. Hale, you'll experience and uncomforable half-hour with your chiefs at Scotland Yard."

"I'll take the risk of that, thank you," said Hale stubbornly.

"Am I to consider myself under arrest," enquired the young man.

"No, sir."

"Then, if you will pardon me, I shall withdraw. Mr. Summertrees will show you everything you wish to see in his books, and can explain his business much more capably than I, because he knows more about it; therefore, gentlemen, I bid you goodnight.

"No, you don't. Not just yet awhile," exclaimed Hale, rising to his feet simultaneously with the young man.

"Then I *am* under arrest," protected Macpherson.

"You're not going to leave this room until Podgers brings that book."

"Oh, very well," and he sat down again.

And now, as talking is dry work, I set out something to drink, a box of cigars, and a box of cigarettes. Hale mixed his favourite brew, but Macpherson, shunning the wine of his country, contented himself with a glass of plain mineral water, and lit a cigarette. Then he awoke my high regard by saying pleasantly as if nothing had happened:

"While we are waiting, Monsieur Valmont, may I remind you that you owe me five shillings?"

I laughed, took the coin from my pocket, and paid him, whereupon he thanked me.

"Are you connected with Scotland Yard, Monsieur Valmont?" asked Macpherson, with the air of a man trying to make conversation to bridge over a tedious interval; but before I could reply, Hale blurted out:

"Not likely!"

"You have no official standing as a detective, then, Monsieur Valmont?"

"None whatever," I replied quickly, thus getting in my oar ahead of Hale.

"That is a loss to our country," pursued this admirable young man, with evident sincerity.

I began to see I could make a good deal of so clever a fellow if he came under my tuition.

"The blunders of our police," he went on, "are something deplorable. If they would but take lessons in strategy, say, from France, their unpleasant duties would be so much more acceptable performed, with much less discomfort to their victims."

"France," snorted Hale in derision, "why, they call a man guilty there until he's proven innocent."

"Yes, Mr. Hale, and the same seems to be the case in Imperial Flats. You have quite made up your mind that Mr. Summertrees is guilty, and will not be content until he proves his innocence. I venture to predict that you will hear from him before long in a manner that may astonish you."

Hale grunted and looked at his watch. The minutes passed very slowly as we sat there smoking, and at last even I began to get uneasy. Macpherson, seeing our anxiety, said that when he came in the fog was almost as thick as it hand been the week before, and that there might be some difficulty in getting a cab. Just as he was speaking the door was unlocked from the outside, and Podgers entered, bearing a thick volume in his hand. This he gave to his superior, who turned over its pages in amazement, and then looked at the back, crying:

"*Encyclopaedia of Sport,* 1893! What sort of a joke is this, Mr. Macpherson?"

There was a pained look on Mr. Macpherson's face as he reached forward and he took the book. He said with a sigh:

"If you had allowed me to telephone, Mr. Hale, I should have made it perfectly plain to Summertrees what was wanted. I might have known this mistake was liable to occur. There in increasing demand for out-of-date books of sport, and no doubt Mr. Summertrees thought this was what I meant. There is nothing for it but to send your man back to Park Lane and tell Mr. Summertrees that what we want is the locked volume of accounts for 1893, which we call the encyclopaedia. Allow me to write an order that will bring it. Oh, I'll show what I have written before your man takes it," he said, as Hale stood ready to look over his shoulder.

On my notepaper he dashed off a request such as he had outlined, and handed it to Hale, who read it and gave it to Podgers.

"Take that to Summertrees, and get back as quickly as possible. Have you a cab at the door?"

"Yes, sir."

"Is it foggy outside?"

"Not so much, sir, as it was an hour ago. No difficulty about the traffic now, sir."

"Very well, get back as soon as you can."

"Podgers saluted, and left with the book under his arm. Again the door was locked, and again we sat smoking in silence until the stillness was broken by the tinkle of the telephone. Hale put the receiver to his ear.

"Yes, this is the Imperial Flats. Yes. Valmont. Oh, yes; Macpherson is here. What? Out of what? Can't hear you. Out of print. What, the encyclopaedia's out of print? Who is that speaking? Dr. Willoughby; thanks."

Macpherson rose as if he would go to the telephone, but instead (and he acted so quietly that I did not notice what he was doing until the thing was done), he picked up the sheet which he called his visiting list, and walking quite without haste, held it in the glowing coals of the fire-place until it disappeared in a flash of flame up the chimney. I sprang to my feet indignant, but too late to make even a motion towards saving the sheet. Macpherson regarded us both with the self-deprecatory smile which had several times lighted up his face.

"How dared you burn that sheet?" I demanded.

"Because, Monsieur Valmont, it did not belong to you; because you do not belong to Scotland Yard; because you stole it; because you had no right to it; and because you have no official standing in this country. If it had been in Mr. Hale's possession I should not have dared, as you put it, to destroy the sheet, but as this sheet was abstracted from my master's premises by you, an entirely unauthorised person, whom he would have been justified in shooting dead if he had found you housebreaking and you had resisted him on his discovery, I took the liberty of destroying the document. I have always held that these sheets should not have been kept, for, as has been the case, if they fell under the scrutiny of so intelligent a person as Eugène Valmont, improper inferences might have been drawn. Mr. Summertrees, however, persisted in keeping them, but made this concession, that if I ever telegraphed him or telephoned him the word 'Encyclopaedia', he would at once burn these records, and he, on his part, was to telegraph or telephone to me "The *Encyclopaedia* is out of print," whereupon I would know that he had succeeded.

"Now, gentlemen, open this door, which will save me the trouble of forcing it. Either put me formally under arrest, or cease to restrict by liberty. I am very much obliged to Mr. Hale for telephoning, and I have made no protest to so gallant a host as Monsieur Valmont is, because of the locked door. However, the farce is now terminated. The proceedings I have sat through were entirely illegal, and if you will pardon me, Mr. Hale, they have been a little too French to go down here in old England, or to make a report in the newspapers that would be quite satisfactory to your chiefs. I demand either my formal arrest, or the unlocking of that door."

In silence I pressed a button, and my man threw open the door. Macpherson walked to the threshold, paused, and looked back in Spenser Hale, who sat there silent as a sphinx.

"Good-evening, Mr. Hale."

There being no reply, he turned to me with the same ingratiating smile:

"Good-evening, Monsieur Eugène Valmont," he said, "I shall give myself the pleasure of calling next Wednesday at six for my five shillings."

THE SECRET OF THE SINGULAR CIPHER

by F.A.M. Webster

First published in 1925

"Modern murders are merely disgusting." The exclamation burst involuntarily from my lips, as I threw down the morning paper. I had been reading the account of a more than usually revolting case, in which the murderer , a married man, had killed a wretched girl, who had trusted to him and whose condition would have made it awkward for him to face the consequences of their infatuation without breaking up his normal home life.

Old Ebbie regarded me with a quizzical smile. It was evident that he had already studied the column which had attracted my interest.

"I fancy that case cuts deeper than you imagine," he said. "Later on it will undoubtedly transpire that the man was in financial difficulties and had exhausted the resources of the girl he killed. You may remember that he was already on touch with another young woman, who had money of her own, even before he had disposed of the body of his first victim."

"All that you say may be perfectly true," I agreed, "but it does not alter the fact that those elements of mystery and unexpected motive, such as came to light in the case of The Man Who Sold Jewels, have been lacking from the affairs which have come our way of late."

Before my companion could answer, the telephone bell rang sharply from the hall. A moment later Jenkin entered the room.

"Inspector Wilson would like to speak to you on the telephone, sir."

Ole Ebbie's smile broadened as he left the room.

"Get your hat and coat, Hicks," he called presently; "there's a job for us in Mayfair."

At the entrance to Bulstrode Mansions a big constable received us.

"The inspector will be pleased if you will go up to No. 16, gentleman," he sakd.

We found our old frient Wilson seated at a small table in the dining-room, tapping his teeth with the butt end of his pencil and staring at a queer assortment of odds and ends. A note-book was open before him. In the corner of the room was sinister-looking shape covered with a sheet. A number of playing-cards were scattered across the dinner-table, and there was an empty glass beside the half-empty decanter of whisky.

"Good of you to come along so promptly," he greeted us. "I was just cataloguing the contents of the dead man's pockets."

"Anything interesting?" queried Old Ebbie.

"Oh, I don't know. At first sight the whole case looks clear enough. And yet there are one or two unusual features. The tenant of this flat is a fellow called Gilmour; he seems to have arrived from abroad a few months back, but nothing whatever is known of his antecedents of present business in England. Judging from his name, I should say the dead man, Christiernsson, was a Swede."

"If you know his name the Swedish Consulate ought to be able to help you."

"Yes, if Christiernsson really is his name."

"Why the doubt?"

Wilson stroked his chin reflectively. "Well, you see, the tenant of No. 17, across the landing, who called himslef Humphries, committed suicide a week ago with a shot-gun; which, it is true, rendered his face pretty well unrecognisable, and now a dead man, who has not been dead more than twelve hours, turns up here in Gilmour's flat with a knife struck through his heart."

"But why the confusion about the names?" asked Ebbie.

"The caretaker is prepared to swear that the man over there under the sheet is Humphries, but just take a look at his visiting-cards."

He picked up a small silver card-case from among the odds and ends on the table and handed it to Ebbie. Each card bore the fantastic inscription, "Linka Dobrowolski Christiernsson." Old Ebbie slipped one into his pocket before handing back the card-case.

"Well, let me hear your theory," he said.

The inspector indicated the whole room with a comprehensive gesture of his hand.

"You see the playing-cards,"he said, "the empty glass and the half-empty decanter, the contents of which I will have analysed as soon as possible. Doesn't it occur to you that Gilmour lured Humphries, or Christiernsson, or whatever his name was, here, fleeced him—perhaps drugged him—and then made an end of him?"

"Humph, and where is the man with the many names supposed to have hidden himself during the week that has gone?"

"Ah, there you have me!" admitted Wilson.

"I rather thought as much," smiled Ebbie. "Well, let's have a look round the place, anyway."

"But won't you examine the dead man first?"

"No, I'd rather sense the atmosphere before I see the victim."

For the best part of half an hour Ebbie prowled about the flat. He looked into linen-baskets and drawers, examined bedding and furniture, and paid particular attention to the larder and kitchen. From time to time he shot out a trite sentence.

"Now why the deuce should a man use four sets of pyjamas and two pairs of sheets in a week?" he ejaculated, as he peered from the full linen-basket to the open laundry-book he had taken from a hook on the kitchen dreser. Or, again, "Doesn't it strike you, Wilson, that someone has been searching pretty hard for something in this flat? Surely Gilmour wouldn't be put to the necessity of ransacking his own place so thoroughly?"

"That's as may be," replied Wilson bluntly; "the fact remains that Gilmour has bolted."

"And since he is not here to excuse himself, he must, *ipso facto*, be held to accuse himself, eh?"

Ebbie crossed the room and pulled back the sheet which covered the body. The countenance was serenely calm and there was not the slightest sign that a struggle had taken place. Ebbie opened the man's coat, vest, and shirt and scrutinised the wound.

"Whoever did this deed held the knife flat on the palm of his hand and thrust if forward," he said. "Englishmen never use a knife that way and seldom kill a man in cold blood with steel; any criminolgist will tell you that."

He examined the dead man's features with close attention.

"This fellow," he said, "was neither Tcheco-Slovakian, Pole, nor Swede."

Ebbie brought the visiting-card out of his pocket.

"All these three names are surnames," he said. "Linka is Tcheco-Slovakian, Dobrowolski is Polish, and, as you yourself pointed out, Christiernsson is Swedish. Now let us see if we can find what the murderer wanted so badly and which we can only hope he failed to secure."

Through and through that flat we hunted, long after the body had been removed. When every possible hiding place had been exhausted Old Ebbie turned his attention to the very food in the larder and there, in the centre of a loaf of bread which I would have sworn had never been tampered with, he discovered, a tiny note-book. It was filled with a jumble of apparently incoherent phrases and meaningless words.

Wilson, after one glance through the pages, made no objection to Ebbie taking charge of the book for the time being.

Twice during that night I awakened and went through into the dining-room of our flat in Victoria. My comrade was still seated at the table, the little note-book, a pencil and writing-pad were before him and all the floor was littered with sheets of paper, upon which he had inscribed figures and characters which to me appeared to have no meaning.

Once he looked up and spoke to me.

"I reckon Humphries, or whatever his name was, knew that he was near his end when he hid his note-book in the loaf," he said, "and the careful way he did it proves that he wasn't hurried. I've been all night working on every sort of possible and impossible cipher. I fancy this case would come a whole lot clearer if we could understand what is written in the pages of this note-book."

"Perhaps Humphries had a drink and played patience with those cards we saw on the table, to help keep his nerves steady, while he waited," I suggested.

Ebbie turned that over in his mind for some moments before he spoke.

"No, I don't think Humphries drank the whisky," he said, at last; "but you've set me thinking about those cards. Did you notice there were no ash-trays on the table and no tobacco ash on the carpet or in the hearth? There was a cigarette-case in the dead man's pocket, and his nicotine-stained fingers testify that he was a heavy smoker. I fancy he'd have smoked had he played cards with Gilmour, or even by himself."

At breakfast-time Wilson arrived.

"By gad, Mr. Entwistle," he exclaimed; "this business is getting devilish deep and sinister. We have traced Gilmour to Paddington; he left there, dressed in rough clothing, by the five o'clock train yesterday morning. Last night he hid in a Portsmough doss-house. When the police went there this morning, they learned that there had been a most unholy fight in the night, and that the man who had shared Gilmour's room was dead; they thought it was Gilmour at first; because; by some chance, he had changed beds with the other fellow, who was knifed."

"That strikes me as being very significant," said Old Ebbie. 'And what became of Gilmour?"

"He's vanished again. We don't think he could have got aboard a ship, but a motor-cycle has been stolen, and we are hoping to catch him somewhere out on the open moors."

"I'd dearly like a few words with him when he does turn up," said Old Ebbie. "In the meantime, I think you are barking up the wrong tree, Wilson, if you imagine that Gilmour did the murder. Everything I have seen so far points to the fact that he had probably given Humphries, *alias* Christiernsson, shelter since the night upon which the former is supposed to have committed suicide."

"But why on earth should the man wish to practise such a deception?" I interrupted.

"I fancy friend Humphries was pretty hard pressed; he probably had a secret that certain people were anxious to prevent him from passing on. Of course, the suicide would provide a perfect blind. No doubt he hoped that his persecutors would believe they had scared him into doing it."

"But surely it would be very difficult to arrange?"

"Difficult, yes, but not impossible. Have you forgotten the Bouverie Case, and our visit to the Surrey side of the Thames? I showed you then how easily a dead body can be procured, if you know how to go about it."

"Come out in the open, Mr. Entwistle," invited the inspector. "What's at the back of your mind?"

"I hate to theorise," Old Ebbie answered, "but, for once in a way, I'm willing to humour you. My own feeling is that Humphries, or Christiernsson, was up against some secret force, and that, having arranged his own apparent death, he either went to Gilmour for shelter, or the latter stumbled into the business and offered him protection, or at any rate a hiding place. Gilmour, of course, continued to go out and about in the normal way, while his strange guest lay hid. One night, I fancy, Gilmour came home to his flat and found Humphries dead on the floor, and evident signs that the whole place had been pretty thoroughly searched. He must then have found himself in a remarkably awkward situation. He would see at once that, with all due deference to you, Wilson, no C.I.D. man would believe his fantastic story. He may, therefore, have cleared out to avoid arrest. On the other hand, I have a sort of feeling that he probably knew something of the causes that led up to Humphries' murder, and he would, equally of course, appreciate how dangerous was the knowledge he had acquired."

"And those playing-cards on the table, and the empty whisky glass?"

"I fancy Gilmour would have needed a peg to steady his nerves after the shock of finding the dead body; but I frankly admit that I do not at present see the significance of the cards scattered all over the table. I'm certain someone left them there for a specific purpose. What that purpose was we should probably know if we could find the key to the pages of that little note-book that was hidden in the loaf of bread."

Wilson hesitated a moment.

"I'm bound to admit," he said, "that the bottom has rather fallen out of the fleecing theory. I've got on to Gilmour's bankers, through the owners of Bulstrode Mansions, and it seems that he is, comparatively speaking, a rich man."

"Good," answered Ebbie. "By the way, can you furnish me with a photography of Humphries?"

"A post-mortem one," said Wilson; "we had it taken to compare with others in the Black Museum."

"And you could not find its counterpart, eh?"

"No; neither his features nor his finger-prints are recorded with us."

"Let me have a copy of the portrait," said Ebbie, "perhaps I may have better luck."

When the picture came he studied it for a long time.

"You'd hardly believe that chap was dead," he said at last. "Just look at those eyes, Hicks. Is it only my imagination, or is there in them the light of the certain knowledge of success? By heavens, there's something about this little fellow's face that appeals enormously to me."

Next morning, as we walked down to the Foreign Office, my companion dropped his hand on my arm.

"We're going to try a very long shot in the dark, my friend," he said; "but, as you ought to know by this time, no chance is so small that one can afford to overlook it. I was up at Bulstrode Mansions again last night; the porter tells me some queer, foreign-looking customers have been trying to get permission to look over Gilmour's flat, and he is half inclined to think that an attempt was made to force the lock yesterday afternoon when he was off duty."

At the Foreign Office Lord Arlen of Ashurst granted us an immediate interview. He listened attentively to all that Old Ebbie had to say, then touched a bell.

"This is a bit out of my depth, Mr. Entwistle," he said, as we waited; " but I fancy the Permanent Secretary will be very glad to have a chat with you."

Sir Claude Ducane made no effort to conceal his interest. At the sight of the photograph which Ebbie laid down on the table a gasp escaped him.

"This man was one of the best of our Secret Service agents," he said. "You say he is dead? We had lost sight of him for months. His one bad fault was that he would always work alone. More often than not he found things out, but he never let us have a hint of what was going on until he had the whole thing cut and dried and ready to place before us complete in every detail. God alone knows what he was after this time; but, as you say, I very much doubt if Gilmour killed him."

"Do you happen to have the key to the cipher he used, Sir Claude?"

"No, that was another of his mysteries. He absolutely refused to employ any of the conventional ciphers, or to give us the key to the one he had himself invented."

"But surely he must have foreseen the possibility of just such a tradegy as has occurred?"

"He most certainly did. In fact, he told me more than once that if ever he was caught out before he could communicate with us he would leave a hint, that any clever man could read, as to the key to the cipher. But why do you ask?"

Old Ebbie produced the little note-book and laid it on the table beside the photograph. For a while the Permanent Secretary turned over the pages before handing the book back with a hopeless gesture.

"I can make absolutely nothing of it," he said.

That night, as Old Ebbie sat poring over the pages of the notebook, and covering sheet after sheet of notepaper with figures, I suddenly interrupted him.

"Do you know, Ebbie," I said, "I can't get out of my mind the picture of that poor devil sitting there in the silent flat, terrified to go outside to meet his fate, but yet man enough to play a game of patience while death stole nearer to him step by step."

"How the devil you know he did play patience?" asked Old Ebbie, thoroughly irritated by my thoughtless interruption of his work.

"We, what on earth did he put the cards on the table for?" I answered with equal acerbity.

Old Ebbie, got slowly to his feet, staring at me with fascinated eyes.

"What else did he put the cards on the table for?" he repeated very slowly, and his hand stole up to his waistcoat pocket, from which he withdrew Christiernsson's visiting-card. "Lord, what a blind fool I've been! And now, for goodness sake, Hicks, stop chattering. I've got some hard thinking and ciphering to do."

Upon this very pointed hint I left him and took myself off to bed. About four o'clock in the morning he awakened me. By the light of the candle he carried I saw that his eyes were blazing with excitement. "Come into the dining-room," he said eagerly. "I've just about got this business straightened last."

"Do you mean that you've found the key to the cipher?" I asked eagerly.

"Well, I think you found it," he answered; "but I've worked it out. You kept on harping on about the playing-cards on the table, and that set me thinking of the visiting-cards in the silver case. I remembered what Sir Claude had told us about Humphries having promised to leave a clue that a clever man could follow; but, somehow, I couldn't envisage your picture of the poor chap playing patience. Then, again, the three names on the visiting-card neither hung together, because they are all surnames belonging to different nationalities, nor seemed to fit the dead man. We knew, indeed, from Sir Claude that they were not his. I began to wonder if they were the key to the cipher. It looked likely, but the letters in those three names number thirty, and there are only twenty-six letters in the English alphabet. On the other hand, it did not appear likely that so subtle a fellow as the dead Humphries would be satisfied with a simple, corresponding alphabetical-numerical cipher.

"For hours on end I puzzled over the orthographical aspect of the business. I was pretty well sure that the grammar of letters wasn't going to help me very much; so I turned my attention to the grammar of sounds. It struck me quite suddenly that the vowels are five in number, and the consonants twenty-five, the latter divided roughly into eleven mutes and fourteen spirants. If you look at this paper, you will see how I have set out the three names which are engraved on the visiting card.

L — a	D — g	C — y
I — e	O — j	H — zh
N — i	B — d	R — z
K — o	R — b	I — th (as in bathe)
A — u	O — k	S — v
	W — ch (as in church)	T — w
	O — t	I — h
	L — p	E — sh
	S — ng	R — s
	K — n	N — th (as in bath)
	I — m	S — f
		S — wh
		O — r
		N — l

"It took a bit of working out, but finally I got at it by grading the mutes into flat, sharp, and nasal sounds, and the spirants into flat, sharp, and trilled sounds. Even so, deciphering the writing in the note-book was a terrible job, because the same letters occur several times in the code words; but the difficulty was not insuperable, only laborious; one had to leave blanks and try all possible corresponding letters to get the complete words."

So far his keen eyes had shone with the artist's joy of accomplishment, but now they took on a haunted, desperate look.

"The Bolsheviks are at the back of this business, Hicks," he said. "There is a plot to wreck the big power station at Alton Heath, thereby creating more unemployment and stirring up further trouble among the labouring classes. There is also mention of a plan to dispose of the people's leader, in such a way that it must enevitably appear that the assassination was planned in a high quarter.

"You may quite well argue that the plant and the man can be protected, and that, in any case, no one would believe that MacReady had been deliberately put out of the way at the investigation of the leaders of the accredited government; but the notes make no mention of the dates upon which these tragedies are to occur. Nor is there any indication of the names or whereabout of the real conspirators. We may save the power station and MacReady but what guarantee is there that even if we prevent these disasters, more serious measures will not be taken against us?"

"Yes, I see all that," I answered, "and you will, of course, hand over this information to Scotland Yard and the Foreign Office; but it still does not account for the disappearance of Gilmour."

"No," agreed Old Ebbie. "I'm very anxious to meet that young gentleman. I fancy he must be a pretty far-seeing sort of person. He may, as I suggested to Wilson, have bolted in a panic when he realised that, firstly, no police official would believe what, on the face of it, must have appeared a highly improbable story, and, secondly, he undoubtedly shared some of the dead Secret Service man's knowledge. He would, therefore, be well aware that his life is in danger at the hands of the men who did not hesitate to kill Humphries and who, I shrewdly suspect, tried to do away with Gilmour himself in the Portsmouth doss-house to which he fled.

"If we can find Gilmour I rather fancy we shall get those missing dates we want; and it's just possible he may be able also to tell us something about the people who are at the back of this hellish plot. Anyway, we'll lodge such information as we have in the right quarters and then get down to Portsmouth. We may be able to pick up his trail. If my deductions are correct he will not have left the country."

The owner of the Portsmouth doss-house turned out to be an old chanty man, who had sailed the Seven Seas when wind-jammers were in fashion; and a very shrewd old fellow he proved himself to be.

"The man who was here the night of the big fight, when Jake was killed; what sort of a man was he, you ask? Well, I'd say just an or'nary sailorman, sir. A gentleman? No, not by any manner of means; just an or'nary fo'castle sort of fellow, such as I've sailed with hundreds an' hundreds o' voyages."

"Humph," growled Old Ebbie, "we're up against a pretty tough proposition. I'll bet you this chap Gilmour knows all about camouflage and has hunted big game more than half his life. According to what that old sailorman said he hasn't bothered to change his appearance, only his circumstances. He's literally faded into his new atmosphere, just as a wild creature fades into its natural background. If we do find him you'll see that he is not playing his assumed part, he'll be actually living it. Do you see what I mean? The real secret of disguise is not make-up or anything of that sort, but the ability to convince yourself that you actually are, for the time being, what you wish other people to take you for. This chap won't slip up anywhere, and I can tell you that it is going to be devilish hard to find him. Personally I'm going to keep my eyes skinned for the opposition, they probably know more than we do and may lead us to our man."

For the next week we hung around Portsmouth, hired a motorcar and journeyed farther afield; but had no luck at all. Then, by a strange chance, we heard of some curious happenings over Devon way. The whole story was so unusual that a local correspondent had sent it up to one of the London papers, and the editor had given it a paragraph and a catchy headline.

It appeared that a tramp had come to back door of a moorland farm and had begged a night's shelter. He had, however, offered to pay for his supper. The farmer was away from home, but his wife had given the man a jug of cider, half a loaf and some cheese, and had told him that he might sleep in an empty hayloft. Half-way through the night the woman was awakened by a terrific explosion and had rushed to the window to discover the barn where the tramp had slept going up to the sky in lurid flames.

"It's another long shot," said Old Ebbie, as he handed me the paper, "but that reads to me remarkably as though our man transferred himself to Devonshire."

The car we were using was a big, powerful Bentley, which would make short work of the distance. Before we started Ebbie sent a wire to Wilson.

At Moretonhampstead, close to the farm-house where the barn had been destroyed, it seemed to me that we were at last getting on to a fairly hot trail.

The landlord joined us in a glass of punch after supper and Old Ebbie handled him admirably.

"I see from the papers you've had quite a sensation in these parts," said my comrade.

"So a lot of volks seems to think," answered the old fellow, as he treated us to a shrewd stare.

"Um! Half the town's been out to see the farm, I suppose," said Ebbie.

"Oh that, that's nuthin'. It's the likes of you vurriners that comes pryin' an' questionin' that we'm don't like," said the landlord.

"We're not asking questions, my good man," said Ebie indifferently. "I happened to read about the explosion in the morning paper and naturally thought the matter, being of a purely local nature, would interest you."

"Aye, an' a lot of other volks besides, seemin'ly," grumbled the innkeeper. "Girt big car cooms here to-day and a rare vine lot of questions I did have to answer before I could satisfy the gentlemen. Real vurriners they was, I raickon, an' no Englishmen at all, by that same token."

"I think," said Old Ebbie to me, as we sought our rooms that night, "that we will go to the high beacons to-morrow morning, taking with us our field-glasses. I wonder what sort of a car our host's 'vurriners' were driving."

"That should be easy enough to ascertain," I answered, and so it proved.

Soon after dawn Old Ebbie roused me out, and long before breakfast time we were hidden on a high hill, with our own car safe from observation in a sheltered glen. Our glasses paralleled the landscape; but for a long time no sign of human movement was to be seen. Then suddenly we sighted a solitary man moving as much in cover as possible, across the moorland. Presently a row of widely-separated figures, spaced for all the world like gamebeaters, appeared above the horizon of a far ridge, approaching also in our direction.

Old Ebbie shut his glasses with a snap.

"If that is our man and he follows his present route," he said, "he will reach us before the hunt overtakes him,"

For myself, I lay on my stomach, with the binoculars screwed to my eyes and an ever-increasing thrill of excitement running through me. At last Old Ebbie dropped his hand on my shoulder.

"Slip down and get the engine running," he said. "Turn the car round ready to break for the open as soon as I've got Gilmour."

Another quarter of an hour passed before I heard them stumbling down the hillside towards me. At the same moment a shout rang out from the crest of the tor, followed quickly by the sharp whip of a revolver shop, but the range was extreme, and no whine of a passing bullet followed. For a second the rough-looking fellow clad in home-spun hesitated.

"You've got to take us on trust, Mr Gilmour," said Old Ebbie. "If you won' do that, then your attentive friends on the sky-line are bound to get you, and I fancy the information you have is going to be pretty badly needed at Scotland Yard."

With a weary gesture tha man climbed into the back seat, followed by Ebbie, and I opened up my throttle. The great car leaped forward, just as the pursuit came pouring down the hill. Next day we found outselves once more in Sir Claude Ducane's luxurious office, where Inspector Wilson and the Permanent Secretary were eagerly awaiting us, but long before that Gilmour had told us his story.

"I got your wires, Mr. Entwistle," the inspector greeted us; "the second one set things buzzing, and we caught the whole bunch as they were making for the coast. Bolsheviks they were, and I fancy that what Mr. Gilmour is going to tell us will serve to keep them out of mischief for some time to come. Can you tell us, sir, who actually committed the murder at your flat?"

"I'm afrad not," Gilmour answered. "Mr. Entwistle has told me this theories, and all I can do is confirm them. It is true that I did shelter poor Humphries, but he told me very little of what was going on. I knew that he was in great danger; I had moreover, caught a glimpse of the ruffians who were hanging around the mansions, and I knew that some terrible thing was planned for the end of the month.

"Whe I came home that night and found Humphries dead, and myself likely to arrested for his murder, I made up my mind to get on the track of those fellows and to find out what was going forward. I found their headquarters in the very heart of the most desolate part of Devon. I got the fullest sort of proofs necessary. Here they are ." He threw a wallet on the table. "but when I tried to break back for London I found myself ringed in whichever I tried to get out, and I'm convinced they'd have got me and settled me but for the luck of Mr. Entwistle being there to pull me out yesterday morning."

"Luck, eh?" muttered Wilson beneath his breath "I only wish I'd got half his sort of luck!.

COINCIDENCE
by J. Storer Clouston

First published in 1920

CHAPTER 1
MR. WICKLEY'S STORY

"If it wasn't for lucky coincidences," said Carrington, "many a gentleman in ginger and broad arrows would be a highly respected citizen. They're done in again and again by the most infernal flukes. The most baffling mystery—yes, I really think I may call it absolutely the most insoluble-looking that has ever come my way—was solved by what semed like a mere series of extraordinary coincidences."

" Do you mean they weren't really coincidences?" somebody asked.

"There was one real coincidence. The rest was a curuious but not at all an unnatural result of quite an ordinary affair—a county dinner, in fact."

After that we simply had to get the story out of him

"I was asked as a guest to the Devorsetshire Association's Annual Dinner in London (you can guess which county it really was for yourselves). There was nothing very remarkable in that, for I get asked to all sorts of dinners. I had to reply to the toast of the guests, and there was nothing very remarkable in that either, for I'm always getting let in for after-dinner speaking—when they don't want a very serious oration. In consequence everybody—or at all events most of the people there—discovered who I was; which was a very natural consequence.

"Again, it was very natural that natives of Devorsetshire and people connected with the county who hadn't seen each other for years, should happen to meet on such an occasion. And if any one, or any two, or any three of them wanted advice in a ticklish mater, it was extremely natural that they should think of the eloquent gentleman who had replied for the guests.

"If you bear all this in mind, you'll see how things fell out, though on the surface it looked as if some capricious elf had taken over the duties of destiny.

"Well, to come to our muttons. The very next morning a card with the name of 'Mr. R. C. Wickley' was handed in to me, and in a moment Mr. Wickley himself walked into my room. He had reddish hair, a somewhat receding forehead, curiously suspicious eyes, and a prize-fighting jowl. It doesn't sound a very promising description, and yet somehow or other the man was distinctly likeable. For one thing, he had a pleasant smile, and for another, the look of one who has seen a good bit of trouble and yet hasn't let his tail down; also he was unmistakably a gentleman.

" 'I saw you last night at the Devorset dinner, Mr. Carrington,' he began, 'and I thought you looked the sort of man who might help me, and who could be trusted.'

"This was not merely flattering, but it was said with an air of really meaning it and of badly wanted some one he could trust, that roused my interest at once.

" 'What I am going to tell you,' he went on, 'must be *absolutely* confidential. Your business is a purely private agency, isn't it? You don't give thigs away to the police?'

"You may imagine that this roused my interest still more.

"If you come to me confidentially I give nothing away to anybody.'

" 'Not even murder?'

"I tell you frankly I hesitated. I had never had such a question put to me before.

" 'It would depend on the circumstances,' I said.

"He looked at me and thought for a moment.

" 'I'll risk it,' he said, and plunged into this yarn.

" 'I'm a Devorset man originally,' said he, 'but I've lived a lot abroad and had a pretty mixed career. I'm going to make no bones about anything, and I may tell you candidly that there was one particular part of my life that I want to forget and don't want other people to know. It isn't the part I'm going to tell you about, but if partly accounts for it.

" 'Eleven years ago an old uncle of mine died, and as he hadn't left a will I came into his property in Devorset. It included an old manor-house of the smaller type and quite a nice bit of mixed covert shooting—rough but good sport, and it suited me down to the ground. I came home, settled down on the place, and hoped my troubles were at an end. Being a hilly, wooded part of the county I hadn't many neighbours—in fact I couldn't raise enough guns to shoot my coverts properly, but that was the only disadvantage. Things being as they had been, I didn't like meeting too many people, for fear some one should turnup who knew what I didn't want known.

" 'Were you married, by the way?' I asked.

" 'No. I'm not much of a ladies' man and have never missed a wife. I was quite contented, in fact, till things began to go wrong, and I may tell you absolutely honestly, Mr. Carrington, that why they began to go wrong has always been a complete mystery to me. In fact, as you'll see presently, the whole thing has been more like a nightmare than a bit of ordinary life.

" 'My nearest neighbour was a man Spencer, "Toddy" Spencer they called him, a fellow with a handsome wife but no children, pots of money, and quite a big country house. He was a wealthy stockbroker and bought the place himself, largely for the shooting. As he was always keen for an extra gun, and so was I, we struck up quite a friendship to begin with and I saw a good bit of them. The wife was a trifle too go-ahead for my own taste—though most men would probably have been keen about her; but Toddy Spencer himself seemed quite a nice fellow, in spite of being rather a sulky-looking chap and obviously with a devil of a temper. like a lot of fellows of his type, he did himself a little too well, both in the eating or drinking line; though I never saw him actually the worse for liquor.

" 'At first, the Spencers used to come down to Devorsetshire only for part of the year, and then they settled down there for good; though Toddy himself always spent at least two or three days in the week in London on business. He was one of several partners in a very big firm, I may mention.

" 'Well, after about two and a half years, during which we had been excellent neighbours, the first mystery began. For some unkown reason Spencer suddenly took a violent dislike to me. In fact, dislike is too mild a term. The man hated me.'

" 'How did he show it?' I asked.

" 'Wouldn't shoot with me, stopped me and my tenants from using a path through his grounds, blackguarded me behind my back, and insulted me to my face. This low-class swine of a stockbroker! A man without birth or breeding or any conncection with the county before he bought the place! A damned *nouveau riche*!'

"It was quite evident that though Mr. Wickley didn't look particularly aristocratic, he was a gentleman with a very sensitive family pride. In fact, the mere recollection of Mr. Spencer's behaviour was making him boil afresh.

" 'I won't trouble you with all the details, for his final performance made the rest seem like nothing. I gave him a bit of my own mind, I may mention, which finally put an end to all relations . . .'

" 'What did you say to him?' I asked.

" 'What I thought,' he answered briefly, and I guessed that what Mr. Wickley though had probably made Mr. Spencer sit up pretty sharply. 'Well, anyhow, things had gone like this for months, and were past speaking terms, when one day I got a note from him. I can't remember the exact words, for I threw the thing straight into the fire, but this was the gist of it.He had discovered a black mark against me, and gave me the choice of exposure, or leaving the county and selling my place to him.'

" 'One moment,' I interrupted, for I saw that my visitor wanter to hurry over this part. 'I don't want to press you to tell me anything you prefer not to, but in order to understand this extraordinary ultimatum I must ask you one or two questions. Was this "black mark"—er—pretty serious?'

"He hesitated for an instant, and I saw how suspicious those eyes of his could look. Then he answered, and I saw how doggedly that jowl of his could set.

" 'It was nothing I could actually suffer for—by the law, I mean. I had suffered already. But it had an ugly name, and I don't suppose many people would have been keen to speak to me again. You don't need to know the name, do you?"

" 'No,' I said. 'In fact I had rather not. I only wanted to be sure that it actually did give him the leverage he seems to have assumed it gave him. How did he find this out?'

"Wickley shook his head.

" 'I don't know. He could have found out in one or two ways, if he set to work to find things out about me. And he obviously did.'

" 'Why did he want to buy your place?'

" 'Simply because he hated me, and knew that was the way to hit me hardest. He didn't want more land or an extra house.'

" 'I see,' I said. 'Go ahead.

" 'Well, after that note came I want you to understand, Mr. Carrington, that things happened right on end, one after the other, without giving me time to cool down or think quietly. I had a lot woodland on my place, and was rather keen about forestry. It was a hobby of Spencer's, and he had started me, and, curiously enough, the pruning-knife I was carrying that afternoon was a present from him. He got one for himself and one for me. I picked it up and took it with me simply automatically, because I had been carrying it every day lately. But I was thinking of nothing but that note.

" 'Imagine what it meant for me! To hand over a place my family had owned for four hundred years—hand it over to this unspeakable bounder, lose everything worth having, and clear out of the county—imagine what it meant! As to the other alternative, I felt I would rather shoot myself first. Perhaps I don't express myself very well, Mr. Carrington, but I daresay you can more or less understand.'

"His words may have been restrained, but his face was working and his eyes blazing, just as they must have been when he set out on that walk. I did understand, and told him so. He seemed pleased, and for a moment almost smiles. And then his face set, and he went on—

" 'Without thinking where I was going I wandered about the Lords knows where, but, anyhow, at last I headed for a certain wood where I had been doing some pruning before. It was just on the boundary of the two properties. In fact, the stream that formed the boundary ran through it. It was a winter afternoon, and growing a little dusky by this time. I entered the wood—all the time, mind you, without realising where I was or what I was doing—and then about ten paces from the outer edge of it I pulled up dead. Spencer was standing, half leaning against a tree, with his back to me!'

"Wickley stopped for an instant, and looked at me hard.

" 'I am trusting you with everything!' he said.

" 'I know you are.'

"He moistened his lips and went on—

" 'The sound of the running water had drowned my footsteps. It still drowned them as I took three more steps, and then let him have it in the broad of his back with the pruning knife. I remember striking sort of slanting and downwards so as to give the curbed knife a chance. I'm pretty strong, and it did give it a chance. It went in up to the handle and stopped there. He fell on his face without a sound or a struggle. I had seen dead men before, and I knew he was one. And then, suddenly, I realised what I had done.'

"He paused and licked his lips afresh.

" 'How long ago was this?'

" 'Eight years,' he said.

" 'Eight years!' I exclaimed. 'but I never remember hearing—'

" 'Wait a bit,' said he. 'The interesing part of the story hasn't begun yet.'

"I wondered what his idea of an *un*-interesting story was, but I said nothing, and he went on—

" 'I don't mind confessing that I lost my head—or anyhow my nerve utterly. I remember I could only say one thing to myself—"I didn't know what I was doing!" I hurried home and made no attempt to seem cool. I got out my car, drove it myself at break-neck speed to the station, and simply left it standing outside. I took the first train to London, and made so little effort to hide what I was feeling, that everybody who saw me stared. I got to London late in the evening, and wandered about the streets all night. In the morning I still kept wandering, trying to avoid newspapers and posters. Then I suddenly got desperate and bought a paper. There was nothing about the murder in it. So I bought another and then another, till I had bought six papers, but still there was nothing. And then I got reckless. I went straight off to the Hotel Metropole in Northumberland Avenue, the place where both Spencer and I generally stayed when we wanted an hotel in London, ordered a room and went straight to bed.'

"He paused for a moment again, and I couldn't help observing:

" 'Your story is interesting enough now, Mr. Wickley.'

" 'Wait! he said. 'I haven't come to the interesing part yet.'

" 'I slept almost all day,' he continued, 'and when I woke up in the late afternoon my head was pretty clear again. And, Heavens! I was afraid now! I dressed very quickly, and then sat in my room waiting for some one to come for me. And then I suddenly got reckless again, walked out into the corridor, and boldly went down to the lift. I stepped out of the lift, and was crossing the hall, when out of the corner of my eye I seemed to see someone I knew. I looked round, and as I'm a living sinner, Carrington, there was Toddy Spencer sitting in an armchair looking at me!'

"He stopped abruptly and added—

" '*That's* the interesting part.'

"And I had to confess he was right.

" 'What did you do?' I asked.

" 'Simply stared at him, just as he was staring at me, only he wasn't staring quite so hard. And then he suddenly spoke to me in quite a friendly voice, almost nervously infact. I answered him in just the same tone, and there we were talking together in the hall of the Metropole as if nothing had happened at all.'

" 'What did you talk about?'

" 'The weather, I think, and we each made the pretty obvious remark that the other seemed to have come up from Devorsetshire. We exchanged about half a dozen sentences or so, and then we each nodded, and I went out.'

" 'I'm not a murderer after all!' was my first thought, and for half an hour I was happy as a boy.

" 'And then the whole thing began to come back to me—Spencer standing in the woods—the way he fell—everything. I simply *couldn't* have imagined it! And yet equally I couldn't have imagined talking to Spencer in the Metropole. I stayed three days in London hesitating, and then I simply had to go back and see for myself.'

"Again he stopped abrupty and asked—

" 'Now what's your impression so far, Mr. Carrington?'

" 'That you were overwrought, and imagined—or else dreamt—the murder scene.'

"Wickley's voice sank.

" 'I went back to that wood, very cautiously, and taking care that nobody was about—and there was a freshly filled-in grave there. Some one had been buried, very roughly and hurriedly, and not very deep. Who was it?'

'I thought he was going to answer the question himself, but instead he waited for me to speak.

" 'Do you mean to say you never discovered?'

"He shook his head.

" 'It's an absolute mystery to me! Nobody in the neighbourhood apparently was missing. Nothing was ever said, or whispered, or rumoured, of a murder. Nothing more ever happened. I couldn't possilby live on in that place. I let the house, but not the shooting—because I didn't want people to be going through that wood, and I've been a wanderer for eight years. Last week I came to London and met a cousin who persuaded me to go to the Devorset dinner last night. And there I saw Spencer again, for the first time since we parted in the Metropole. That started the whole thing again in my mind. And then when I heard you were a private inquiry agent, I suddenly decided to end the suspense and come to you. I want you to find out what happened—who that man was.'

"I thought for a minute or two.

" 'You have only mentioned three people,' I said. 'It obviously wan't yourself, and it wasn't Spencer. The third was his wife.'

" 'It certainly wasn't her. It was a man. Besides, she is still alive.'

" 'Then I have absolutely nothing to start upon. What made you think it was Spencer?'

" 'I knew his overcoat and his felt hat.'

" 'That was all you had to go upon?'

" 'It was a man of the same height. Besides, who else would be in that spot wearing Spencer's coat and hat?'

" 'Or a coat and hat like them.'

" 'Identically the same! I can still see them quite distinctly.'

" 'You say it was getting dark?'

" 'Dusky; but then I was within a yard of him.'

"I was silent for a little longer, and then I said—

" 'I must think it over, Mr. Wickley. Leave me your address.'

"He left me thinking very hard, I can assure you."

CHAPTER 2
THE STOCKBROKER'S WIFE

Carrington lit a fresh cigarette and began the second part of his story.

"Wickley left my office only a little before my usual lunch hour, and I sat on over my fire for some time, thinking, but not seeing a ray of light. That made me rather late in getting back after lunch, and when I came in my clerk handed me a card and told me a gentleman was waiting in my room. On the card I read the name, 'Mr. A. D. Spencer.'

"When I glanced up from it and caught my clerk's eye, I could see that he evidently thought I had done myself too well at lunch. I suppose I had been standing for the whole of five minutes gazing at that card. The appearance of Mr. Spencer immediately on top of Mr. Wickley seemed a thing hardly in the course of nature. I began to wonder whether there was some sort of a conspiracy between the two men. I tried to see in advance what line this man Spencer was going to take. And then I recovered my wits and walked into my room.

"I found a heavy-looking man of rather above middle height, clean-shaven, with a blue chin, baggy eyes, and very black hair. He had the skin of a man who, as Wickley said, did himself a little too well, and I could also quite believe that he could be a sulky ill-tempered devil if things went wrong.

" 'We didn't exactly meet last night, Mr. Carrington,' he began, and there was quite a dash of geniality about the man when he made the effort, 'but I was at the Devorset dinner and heard you speak. I also came across an old acquaintance there. Meeting him set me worrying about an old problem, and seeing you put it into my head to come and consult you on the matter.'

"And then I realised that ther was no consipiracy at all, nor even any very extraordinry coincidence, but, as I told you at the start, just a series of quite natural events that had produced this startling result. My second thought was—'What a bit of luck! The solution to the insoluble problem walks into my office!' However, you'll see how far out I was there.

" 'Of course you'll understand that this is strictly confidential,' said he.

" 'Naturally,' I said; and noted that though he was evidently keen on secrecy, he didn't show the same extreme anxiety as Wickley.

" 'Well,' he said, 'I'll begin my story eleven years back. Or perhaps I should first mention that some years before that I had puchased an estate in Devorset. I'm a stockbroker, by the way: Spencer, Spencer & Ludeman is my firm, and I'm the senior partner. Eleven years ago an old fellow in the neighbourhood Wickley died, and his nephew came into the property and settled down next door to me. By next door I mean rather under a couple of miles away; but we had no other neighbours—of that class, I mean—within six or seven miles, and we didn't know them either. Consequently Wickley and I saw a lot of one another and became very friendly.'

" 'What sort of a fellow was he? 'I inquired, with my most truth-seeking expression.

" 'I wish you had noticed him at the dinner last night,' said he, 'and you'd have understood better what kind of a proposition he was. A reddish-haired, heavy-chinned sort of fellow, with queer eyes, and the word "past" stamped all over him.'

" 'What do you mean exactly?'

" 'Well, I mean that he *had* a past, and I soon began to guess as much from his very appearance and manner, though at first I only felt vaguely that there was something unusual about him. I may mention that he isn't the kind of person one would naturally suspect of a shady record, for the Wickleys are a very good old Devorset family, and if family pride would keep people straight, well, it ought to have kept him. He didn't show that feature either to begin with, but you'll see in a minute the sort of too-good-for-a-damned-stockbroker gentleman he was. My place was about twice the size of his, I may add, and he was deuced glad to have many days shooting with me as he could get. Some precious rotten days he gave me in exchange; but of course shooting with a two-penny-halfpenny squire was always an honour!'

"This speech naturally didn't prejudice me much in favour of Mr. Spencer. Little though he realised it, he was making me look at things more and more from Wickley's point of view—bad hat though Mr. W. may have been, and respectable as Mr. S. no doubt was.

" 'I am coming to a very painful part of my story now, Mr. Carrington,' he continued. 'In fact it's so infernally unpleasant that it has kept me from telling the facts to a living soul up to this moment. I had a wife, in fact she's legally my wife still, and I was very fond of her. I can assure you on that point—I was desperately fond of her! She was an uncommonly beautiful girl. She was on the stage at one time, I may say, and might have gone very far on her looks alone, but I married he and took her away from it. She was a lady by birth, but she hadn't a penny, and it was love marriage pure and simple—love marriage on my part at least, for I don't believe she ever really loved me. We had no children, either, and that was a fatal mistake.'

"He paused to get over an unpleasant business as quickly as possible, we began to drift apart pretty fast. I still loved her to distraction—in a way; but we both had tempers and she led me the devil of a dance, and it was cat and dog half the time. When I bought this place in Devorset, she kicked at living there permanently—too slow for her. She'd stay for some months and we'd have house parties and so on, and then back to town again. And then all of a sudden she quite changed round. Perfectly agreeable to living all the year in the country she became now, so we gave up out flat in town and settled in Doverset; even though it meant her being a good bit by herself, for I generally had to spend part of my week in town for business reasons.'

" 'Then, like a thunderclap, came the suspicion that there was something behind this change of tune. One needn't go into all the details, but several little things made me morally certain that Elise was being unfaithful to me. We were having worse rows than usual at that time, and in one shindy I charged her with it. In order to hit me back hard she actually admitted it!'

" 'In order to hit you hard?' I interrupted. 'Are you sure she meant it?'

" 'Perfectly, because she got in a funk afterwards, when her temper cooled, and tried to unsay it and back out. Besides, the little things on which I had based my suspicions had convinced me already. And now I had her word for it!

"Spencer was quite carried away by his own story by this time, and I could judge exactly the kind of dangerous revengeful man he was.

" 'The only question was, who was the man? And ther couldn't be any question about that either. Wickley was the only possibility!'

" 'Ah!' I exclaimed, and he looked at me sharply. 'Go on,' I said, 'I begin to see the position now.'

"I saw it a lot clearer than he had any notion of. This of course accounted for Wickley's first mystery—the sudden hatred of Spencer for his neighbour.

" 'There could be no doubt about it,' said he. 'He was the only man in the neighbourhood of our own position in life whom we knew in the very least intimately. And he lived inside of two miles from us. Six miles away there was a fat fellow of fifty with a wife and large family—a dull bore of a fellow. Seven miles away were two maiden ladies. Nine miles away was an invalid of seventy. Those were the only alternatives, and we scarcely ever saw any of them. Besides, I had grown more and more convinced that Wickley had something shady in the background. I knew him now to be a blackguard!'

" 'Knew?' I repeated. 'But had you any proof?'

" 'When there are no possible alternatives that's proof enough! Besides, I soon got proof of his character. I made inquiries about him—set an agency on to his track, and I discovered'—he paused and hesitated for an instant—'well, I need only say that he would never have been received in any decent society—he had done ti——' Again he broke off and the scowl lifted a little from his face. 'But the man had suffered for his sins, and it had really nothing to do with my story except that it gave me a hold over him. I was mad with anger and I determined to use it.'

" 'Had nothing else passed between you?' I ventured to ask, for I remembered Wickley's version and I suspected Spencer was skipping a bit.

" 'Oh well,' he admitted, 'I may as well allow that I had shown him pretty plainly that I didn't want to have anything more to do with him. We had one open row, and that was when he showed me what a damned high and mighty aristocratic snob he was. "Gentlemen aren't grown in two days out of dirty stockbroking mushrooms!" Those were his actual words!'

"I must confess that I had scarcely given Mr. Wickley credit for such powers of invective, and I realised now to what a pitch of fury the two of them had roused one another.

" 'As I was saying,' he went on, 'I was quite beside myself with rage by this time, and I did a damned silly thing. I wrote to him threatening to show him up if he didn't clear out of the place. I even went the length of telling him he must sell me his property. That was simply to crush his pride, of course.

" 'You called it "silly," ' I said. 'That seems hardly the adjective.'

" 'Wait a bit and you'll see why,' said he. 'I must tell you first that I was trying hard to catch my wife all this time having to go up to town two or three days a week and leave her to play the devil with that fellow nearly drove me demented. On the other hand, it gave me a chance of catching her napping. One of my servants was watching her for me, but I think Elise must have suspected him. . . .'

" 'Him'? I said. 'Do you mean your butler?'

" 'It was my chauffeur as a matter of fact; a smart young fellow. He came to me one day and told me he suspected what was up and offered to watch her. I paid him well for it, but though he said Wickley was often hanging round my place, he never found anything definite against my wife. I tried my own hand at it too, by coming back from town when she didn't expect me, but they were cunning as Satan. I never caught them.

" 'But to come to the climax of the affiar: I wrote that letter to Wickley from my London office, and then the sudden thought struck me that I would come straight home myself. He wouldn't expect me, seeing the address on the letter, and he would probably see my wife at once about it. That's how I argued. When I got home my wife was out, nobody knew where. My suspicions became a practical certainty. I took my gun and I set out in the direction of his house. I'm telling you everything quite candidly, Mr. Carrington. I was just approaching the boundary of the two properties when I saw him coming towards me, as I thought. I slipped behind a tree and watched him. He turned into a wood that lies just on the boundary, and I stood for a short while like a man in hell!'

"Mr. Spencer took out his handkerchief and passed it across his face. As for me, I never was more fascinated in my life. To think of hearing the other half of Wickley's story like this! In a moment Spencer went on—

" 'I yielded to temptation, Mr. Carrington. I felt sure that he and my wife were in that wood, and I meant to kill one or both—Wickley certainly. I made a little detour, entered the wood, crossed a stream that forms the boundary, and suddenly I saw him. He was lying dead on his face, with a huge blood stain all over his back!'

" 'Wickley was?' I exclaimed.

" 'I had just seen him go into the wood. Who else could it be? But I didn't go near the body. I simply turned tail and hurried home as fast as I could walk, It took me all my time to keep at a walk and not to run! And now do you see what a silly performance that threatening letter was? It had come on top of other foolishness, for I had used my tongue pretty freely about the fellow. And now he was lying murdered and I had been seen leaving my house with a gun, and probably had been seen going in that very direction! Also, I knew in my heart I had meant to kill him. Lord, what a shock I got! You may think me a fool to have felt like that. . . .'

" 'I don't in the very least,' I assured him in all sincerity.

" 'Well, that's how I did feel. I may add as some excuse for my next performance that this trouble had been leading me to drink a bit too much, and my nerve wasn't at its best. Anyhow when I got home I didn't wait in the house longer than to order the car; and then as a finishing touch, the chauffeur couldn't be found, and so I couldn't get to the station in time to catch the last train that evening! I had hired from the station when I arrived, so as to give no warning of my coming, but the car had gone back, and there I was landed. However, I didn't wait in my house—I simply couldn't do it. I tramped off to a little local pub, slept the night there, and went back to town in the morning. And now comes a bit of the story that you probably won't believe, Mr. Carrington.'

" 'I believe everything you tell me,' I said.

" 'I had a room at the Hotel Metropole at that time. On the same afternoon, soon after I had got back to London, I was sitting in the hall with a bundle of evening papers, looking for some news of Wickley's murder, when what do you think? Wickley himself stepped out of the lift and walked across the hall under my nose!'

" 'He looked at me expectantly, and I tried to seem dumbfounded. I must have succeeded pretty well, for he seemed satisfied.

" 'It is absolute gospel truth,' he said. 'Just as he was passing, he spotted me, and do you know, the extraordinary thing was that all signs of enmity seemed to have left the man! As for me, I was so thankful to see him alive, I could have embraced him. We exchanged a few ordinary remarks in a perfectly friendly way, and then he walked out of the hotel. I haven't seen him from that moment till last night at the dinner, and it was meeting him again that tuned me up to doing what of course I always should have done. I want this mystery cleared up, Mr. Carrington. I want to know who that man was lying dead in the wood.'

"He stopped, and I realised with a shock that Spencer's story had done absolutely nothing to solve Wickley's mystery. I had counted confidently on its cracking the nut, but instead it simply presented me with the same mystery over again.

" 'You never discovered who it was?'

"He shook his head.

" 'Never to this day. I can only tell you that nobody is known to have been murdered, or even missing, in Devorset at that time. But I'm afraid that won't help you very much.'

" 'Tell me what you did, and your wife did, immediately afterwards.'

" 'I funked going back for three or four days. My nerves were utterly rattled. When I got home, my wife had left, cleared right out, and we have never lived together again since. Before leaving she told our housekeeper that she sacked Martin, the chauffeur—no, Marwell, that was his name. Presumably she sacked him because she had discovered he had been spying on her. Of course she had no business to do it on her own account, but I didn't care by that time. In fact I was rather glad to be rid of him; He knew to much about the miserable business. She left a short note for me, only a line or two. I can remember it by heart. "This is absolutely the end of it. We must never meet again. I have done my best for you. Be grateful to me for that."

" 'What did she mean?' I asked.

"He shook his head.

"I haven't the least ideal. A woman's way of getting in the last word and claiming to be in the right, I suppose.'

" 'And have you ever met again?'

" 'Never.'

"I fell very thoughtful. Dim ideas were beginning to float across my mind, but very mistily and tentatively.

" 'Have you lived there at all since then?'

" 'No. I let the place at once. And Wickley let his too. Neither of us have lived in Devorset since.'

" 'Did you by any chance lose an overcoat about that time?'

"Spencer stared at me very hard.

" 'Lose an overcoat?' He repeated. 'No—or rather yes, now I come to think of it. I used to have rather a nice Burberry, which must have gone missing just about that time. I remember wondering what had become of it, though such trifles didn't worry me much then.'

" 'And a felt hat?'

"He stared again and then thought again.

" 'Possibly; but I had several felt hats. and one might have gone astray without my noticing it, especially in the state of mind I was in. Why do you ask?'

" 'Just a vague ideal I had . It was getting towards dusk, you say, when you saw the body in the wood?'

" 'I don't think I said so, but it was.'

" 'Well, I'll think over the whole story,' I told him, and Mr. Spencer shook hands and walked off."

CHAPTER 3
THE LOST ENGINEER

"Now," said Carrington, "we come to the one really remarkable coincidence. There was present at that Devorset dinner a man with an unsolved riddle lying on dusty shelf at the back of his memory, and he wasn't a Devorset man either, but a guest like myself. He was a fellow Tuke, a London solicitor; he knew the man who was acting as my own host that night, and so I made his acquantance at the dinner and had quite a yarn with him. Furthermore, Tuke's host knew Spencer and introduced Tuke to him. It was Tuke's two meetings with Spencer and myself that brought him to my office a couple of days later, and one can trace cause and effect just as in the cases of Wickley's and of Spencer's visits to me. But it was an extraordinary chance that Tuke, with that riddle on the dusty shelf, should have happened to be at the dinner at all. Here you get the work of the sprite who seemed to be acting for Destiny."

"He was a nice, gentlemanly, solid-looking man was Tuke, and didn't suggest anything very exciting when he sat down and told me he had come to see me professionally. But when he said that it was the meeting with Spencer which had reminded him of an unsolved, half-forgotten mystery, I assure you I pricked up my ears.

" 'About nine years ago,' he began 'a poor girl came to me with a very queer story, and a very sad story too it was. She was a Mrs. Borham, or thought she was—a pretty slender young thing of barely twenty-one, full of pluck, but with the marks of pain and worry stamped too clearly on her face for any one with any observation to miss. And this was the story she told me.

" 'She was the daughter of an impecunious half-pay Naval Officer and was staying with some relatives at Dover when she met Reginald Borham, if that was his real name, which I should think is very doubtful. He was a man of about twenty-five or twenty-six, a mechanical engineer by profession, remarkaby good-looking, with the manners and address of a gentleman, and a most romantic tale of high-born relations who had disowned him owing to his refusal to marry an heiress whom he did not love. It was a cock-and-bull story if ever there was one, but as he professed to having fallen in love with this poor girl, and as she certainly fell in love with him, she swallowed it whole, and to make a long story short, married him.

" 'Reading between the lines of her story, and interpreting it by what I was able to pick up about the man, he seems to have married her simply because she wouldn't succumb to his advances otherwise. She was unusually attractive, and he was evidently carried away by her for the moment very completely, for it wasn't his usual procedure with women by any means. As a rule he specialised in married ladies, and lived either on their bounty or on blackmail. In fact he was the worst type of animal that goes about on two legs, a creature vicious to the core, without a rag of honour to cover him or an ounce of compunction in his heart. Such animals ought to be shot at sight!

" 'He actually had an engineer's training, plenty of brains, and considerable aptitude for mechanical work, and at the moment was connected with some Admiralty job at Dover, but within three months of his marriage he deserted his work and his wife and vanished into space. I traced another woman in connection with his flight, but she lost sight of him too, and as his employers strongly suspected his honesty, they didn't make any effort to trace him. In fact every man he has been connected with has been thankful to see the last of him, and every woman has bitterly regretted she ever met him.

" 'The poor young wife came up to London and determined to make her own living. She had no money, her people had strongly disapproved of the marriage, and things weren't pleasant at home. Have no business training of any kind and being passionately fond of children, she took on the job of nursemaid in the house of some people she knew, and there she was in dark-blue uniform and bonnet, wheeling a parambulator about the Park and the streets of Bayswater when I made her acquaintance.

" 'Well, now I'm coming to the part where I want your detective mind to follow me very closely, Mr. Carrington. Just ask any question you like if things don't seem clear. It was about a year after her marriage, and she had been nearly nine months on this job, when she was wheeling her pram one day along a quiet street in the neighbourhood of the Edgware Road. Suddenly on the opposite pavement she spied her husband walking rather quickly in the opposite direction, with a lady at his side! They never glanced across the street, and of course it would never have entered the blackguard's head to suspect that a nursemaid wheeling a pram could be his wife; but she, on the other hand, studied them carefully and described them to me exactly.

" 'Borham himself was got up immaculately as the young man about town—silk hat fashionably tilted backwards, morning coat, black and white striped trousers, patent boots with yellow tops, and all the rest of it. The lady had extremely golden hair, a face which even her rival admitted was remarkably pretty, with long eyelashes and very red lips, decidedly of the actress type. Mrs. Borham described her; and as for her dress and hat, she protrayed those so exactly that we were able to identify the lady afterwards through them alone. Of course I can't remember a single item, but anyhow she was very smartly and extremely expensively rigged out.

" 'Mrs. Borham stopped short on the opposite pavement and bent over her charge as a nurse might naturally do, but her eyes were following the couple across the way, and she was prepared to wheel round the follow them when they were safely past. However, they didn't go very much farther. There was quiet hotel in this street, one of the type which probably does a pretty mixed sort of business, but with a very large smart-looking motor-car standing in front of it. She was struck at once, she said, with the contrast beween the car and the hotel. Borham and the lady glanced over their shoulders as if to see that the coast was clear, and then turned into the hotel.

" 'Imagine the poor girl's feelings as she watched this performance! Fortunately she had heaps of pluck and resource and she determined to see the affair through, so she crossed the street and paced backwards and forwards for almost half an hour, taking care never to come near enough to the hotel to be seen from the windows. Unfortunately she was just about at the farther end of her beat when the lady reappeared, and she didn't even see her actually come out of the hotel. In fact, when Mrs. Borham looked round, the lady was on the pavement just about to get into the car that was standing by the kerb, and the only person with her was the chauffeur, who was just at her back. He opened the door of the car, she got in, and then off they went.'

" 'Never came out at all. His wife waited and waited in that street, but there was not a sign of him.'

" ' Could he have come out before the lady, while his wife happened to be walking away from the hotel?'

" 'She declared it was quite impossible, for she kept constantly glancing over her shoulder. No; for some reason or other he must have remained in the hotel till after his wife went away. Conceivably he had spotted her.'

" 'Was the chauffeur with the car before the lady came out?'

" ' It seemed a curious thing, but Mrs. Borham declared that there was no one with the car. Presumably the man was in the hotel having a drink. You see he would have a long wait, and his mistress would hardly be in a position to wig him for it, considering that he could scarcely help seeing what she was up to.'

" ' I see. Well, what happened next?'

" 'Just before leaving, Mrs. Borham wheeled her pram right past the hotel, and when she was passing the door her eye was caught by an envelope lying in the gutter immediately opposite. On the of chance that the lady had dropped it while getting into the car, she picked it up. It turned out to be empty, but on the outside was written, "Mr. J. Marwell, c/o A. D. Spencer, Esq.," and then followed an address at some well-known Kensington flats. Next morning she came to me with her story and the envelope.'

" 'Dropped by a chauffeur, I suppose?'

" 'By Jove, you're quite right! I put the matter into the hands of an inquiry agent, and found that Mrs. Spencer corresponded to the account of the mysterious lady, and one of her costumes tallied exactly with Mrs. Borham's description. Also Spencer's chauffeur was named Marwell.

" 'And Borham?'

" 'Ah, now we come to the most mysterious and extraordinary part of the whole business. Not a single trace was ever seen or heard of Borham again! I admit there was difficulties in the way of tracing him. There was obviously no use in tackling Mrs. Spencer direct, for she would simply have denied everything. We might have threatened her with exposure, but Mrs. Borham wouldn't hear of a public scandal, for in all probability exposure would have meant the Divorce Court for Mrs. Spencer, with Borham's name and history brought into the business. The people at the hotel denied all knowledge of the whole affair. It was that sort of an hotel, you see. My agent tried Marwell, but he was like a clam. And nobody connected with the Spencers, whom we could get hold of, seemed to have even heard of Mr. Borham.

" 'As a final and complete checkmate, the Spencers very shortly afterwards gave up their flat in town, and settled down on an estate he had purchased in Devorset. Our only remaining chance of getting at Borham had been by watching Mrs. Spencer, and now, of course, that was gone.'

" 'Has Mrs. Borham never heard anything of her husband again?'

" 'Not from that day to this. I heard from her about six months ago. Apparrently some other man was wanting to marry her, but that vanished blackguard, Borham, stood in the way. She asked what I should advise? Well, I gave her the best advice I could, but I had to confess that the man had beaten us completely. And now, Mr. Carrington, can you suggest any possible step that might be taken?'

"I thought for a minute or two, and then I said—

" 'You can tell Mrs. Borham that her husband has been dead for eight years.'

"Tuke stared at me very hard indeed.

" 'But—how do you know?' he exclaimed.

" 'Borham was Marwell,' I said, 'and Marwell met the fate he deserved—very suddenly.' "

"After Tuke left me I made certain other inquiries, and here's the true history of the vanished Borham, *alias* Marwell, from the time he went down to Devorset with the Spencers.

"Mrs Spencer was infatuated with the scoundrel, and the scoundrel had Mrs. Spencer under his thumb. His latest enterprise, just before he first met her, had been in connection with a fraudulent motor company. You'll remember, of course, that he ws a useful engineer, and he was a man who would stoop to anything, and stick at nothing. He applied for the job of Spencer's chauffeur, and Mrs. S. saw that he got the billet, without rising the faintest suspicion in her husband's mind. Then he started this double life of young blood and chauffeur, always changing clothes at that hotel.

"The next thing was the warning given them by the efforts of Tuke's agent (who must have been a bit of an ass) to bribe Marwell to give away Borham! Hence the move to Devorset, where they thought they would have an absolutely free hand, and in a very short time the scoundrel found himself in clover. Mrs. Spencer had her scene with her husband, and knew he suspected Wickley. She told Marwell *alias* Borham, whereupon the man—without telling her—hit upon the ingenious device of going to Spencer and offering to shadow his wife. He thus had three sources of income: his pay as chauffeur, together with various perquisites that he didn't stick at picking up—honestly or otherwise, his payments from Spencer for acting as spy, and any amount of odd sums from the infatuated woman. Also he lived in comfort, and had a beautiful women devoted to him. And with Spencer's suspicions all directed at the wrong man (and Marwell assisted in this) the game seemed safe as houses.

"After a time, however, one small fly got into the ointment—though it seemed only a trifle. Under yet a third name, he started an intrigue with the daughter of a respectable farmer some miles away, and then began to get in a funk of driving his mistress about in the car more than he could help. He belonged to that class of man who seems able to tell an infatuated woman anything without breaking the spell, and he actually had the audacity to tell her this, and suggest meetings in the woods about the place, instead of taking her afield. She provided him with a coat and hat of her husband's, so that he might pass as Spencer himself if any one caught a glimpse of them; for Spencer was know to come and go constantly between London and his country house, and was also known to be often wandering about his woods when he was at home. And now Destiny prepared at last to clear the earth of the pest."

Carrington rose and planted himself before the fire, looking down upon the three of us who were listening to him; and suddenly and very impressively came to the *dénoûment* of his tale.

"One evening at dusk she came a little late to a rendezvous in a certain wood. It was just across the boundary, so as to add to the chances of not being interrupted—Destiny had seen to that. There she found him stark dead on his face, with the handle of a pruning-knife sticking out of his back. She had thought her husband was in town, but guessed instantly he had come back—and guessed rightly. She thought she recognised his pruning-knife (he had bought two, and given one to Wickley, you'll remember)—and this time she guessed wrong.

"She hurried back to the house half demented, and found her husband had actually been home, and now had fled. And then she was quite certain who had done the deed. What should she do? Hide her own shame, save her husband's neck, and smother the scandal! That woman actually took a spade, and in the dark, in the lonely wood found a bit of loose soil, and got the body hidden somehow. The next evening, she had the nerve to go down again and pile more earth on top, and meanwhile she told the housekeeper that Marwell had been sacked. Nobody else in the house had liked him, and nobody worried what had become of him. And then she wrote that note of her husband—'I have done by best for you. Be grateful to me for that,' and left the house for ever."

"How did you find all those details?" we asked.

"Well, to begin by giving myself a little pat on the back, I came to a pretty correct conclusion at the end of Spencer's story. One man alone had disappeared from the neighbourhood, and that was the chauffeur Marwell. He was said to have been sacked within the next day or two, but he couldn't be found immediately after the murder when his master wanted the car. I judged him to be an obvious rascal from his offer to spy upon the wife. Also I know that there was nobody in her own station of life who could possibly have been Mrs. Spencer's lover. Finally, I had learnt that one of Spencer's coats had been abstracted, which not only accounted for the unknown victim being mistaken for Spencer, but pointed to his having been a member of the household. I suspected something very like the truth, but of course one needed more facts."

"Then came Tuke with his story which confirmed my suspicion, and told me almost everything. And finally, I hunted down Mrs. Spencer, and made her tell me the rest of the story."

"And did you tell any of them the whole truth?"

"Only Wickley. I couldn't give his secret away to anybody else. But I told him everything. Whether it consoled the poor devil or not I don't know, but I assured him he was simply and instrument selected by Fate to rid the world of an unspeakable blackguard."

THE EBONY
BOX
by Mrs. Henry Wood

First published in 1890

THE EBONY BOX

In one or two of the papers already written for you, I have spoken of "Lawyer Cockermuth," as he was usually styled by his fellow-townspeople at Worcester. I am now going to tell of something that happened in his family: that actually did happen and is no invention of mine.

Lawyer Cockermuth's house stood in the Foregate Street. He had practised in it for a good many years; he had never married, and his sister lived with him. She had been christened Betty; it was a more common name in those days than it is in these. There was a younger brother named Charles. They were tall, wiry men with long arms and legs. John, the lawyer, had a smiling, homely face; Charles was handsome, but given to be choleric.

Charles had served in the militia once, and had been ever since called Captain Cockermuth. When only twenty-one he married a young lady with a good bit of money; he had also a small income of his own; so he abandoned the law, to which he had been bred, and lived as a gentleman in a pretty little house on the outskirts of Worcester. His wife died in the course of a few years leaving him with one child, a son, named Philip. The interest of Mrs Charles Cockermuth's money would be enjoyed by her husband until his death, and then would go to Philip.

When Philip left school he was articled to his uncle, Lawyer Cockermuth, and took up his abode with him. Captain Cockermuth (who was a restless disposition, and fond of roving) gave up his house then and went travelling about. Philip Cockermuth was a very nice steady young fellow, and his father was liberal to him in the way of pocket-money, allowing him a guinea a week. Every Monday morning Lawyer Cockermuth handed (for his brother) to Philip a guinea in gold; the coin being in use then. Philip spent most of this in books, but he saved some of it; and by the time he was of age he had sixty golden guineas put aside in a small round box of carved ebony. "What are you going to do with it, Philip?" asked Miss Cockermuth, as he brought it down from his room to show her. "I don't know what yet, Aunt Betty," said Philip, laughing. "I call it my nest-egg."

He carried the little black box (the sixty guineas quite filled it) back to his chamber and put it back into one of the pigeon-holes of the old-fashioned bureau which stood in the room, where he always kept it, and left it there, the bureau locked as usual. After that time, Philip put his spare money, now increased by a salary, into the Old Bank; and it chanced that he did not again look at the ebony box of gold, never supposing but that it was safe in its hiding-place. On the occasion of his marriage some years later, he laughingly remarked to Aunt Betty that he must now take his box of guineas into use; and he went up to fetch it. The box was not there.

Consternation ensued. The family flocked upstairs; the lawyer, Miss Betty, and the captain—who had come to Worcester for the wedding, and was staying in the house—one and all put their hands into the deep, dark pigeon-holes, but failed to find the box. The captain, hot-tempered man, flew into a passion and swore over it; Miss Betty shed tears; Lawyer Cockermuth, always cool and genial, shrugged his shoulders and absolutely joked. None of them could form the slightest notion as to how the box had gone or who was likely to have taken it, and it had to be given up as a bad job.

Philip was married the next day, and left his uncle's house for good, having taken one out Barbourne way. Captain Cockermuth felt very sore about the loss of the box, he strode about Worcester talking of it, and swearing that he would send the thief to Botany bay if he could find him.

A few years more yet, and poor Philip became ill. Ill of the disorder which had carried off his mother—decline. When Captain Cockermuth heard that his son was lying sick, he being (as usual) on his travels, he hastened to Worcester and took up his abode at his brother's—always his home on these visits. The disease was making very quick progress indeed; it was what is called "rapid decline". The captain called in all the famed doctors of the town—if they had not been called before: but there was no hope.

The day before Philip died, his father spoke to him about the box of guineas. It had always seemed to the captain that Philip must have, or ought to have, *some* notion of how it went. And he put the question to him again, solemnly, for the last time.

"Father," said the dying man—who retained all his faculties and his speech to the very end—"I declare to you that I have none. I have never been able to set up any idea at all upon the loss, or attach suspicion to a soul, living or dead. The two maids were honest; they would not have touched it; the clerks had no opportunity of going upstairs. I had always kept the key safely, and you know that we found the lock of the bureau had not been tampered with.

Poor Philip died. His widow and four children went to live at a pretty cottage on Malvern Link—upon a hundred pounds a year, supplied to her by her father-in-law. Mr Cockermuth added the best part of another hundred. These matters settled, Captain Cockermuth set off on his rovings again, considering himself hardly used by Fate at having his limited income docked of nearly half its value.

And yet some more years passed on.

This much has been by way of introduction to what has to come. It was best to give it.

Mr. and Mrs. Jacobson, our neighbours at Dyke Manor, had a whole colony of nephews, what with brothers' sons and sisters' sons; of nieces also; batches of them would come over in relays to stay at Elm Farm, which had no children of its own. Samson Dene was the favourite nephew of all; his mother was sister to Mr. Jacobson, his father was dead. Samson Reginald Dene he was christened, but most people called him "Sam." He had been articled to the gentleman who took to his father's practice; a lawyer in a village in Oxfordshire. Later, he had gone to a firm in London for a year, had passed, and then came down to his uncle at Elm Farm, asking what he was to do next. For, upon his brother-in-law's death, Mr Jacobson had taken upon himself the expenses of Sam, he eldest son.

"Want to know what you are to do now, eh?" cried old Jacobson, who was smoking his evening pipe by the wide fire of the dark-wainscoted, handsome dining-parlour, one evening in February. He was a tall, portly man with a fresh-coloured, healthy face; and not, I dare say, far off sixty years old. "What would you like to do?—what is your own opinion upon it, Sam?"

"I should like to set up in practice for myself, uncle."

"Oh, indeed! In what quarter of the globe, pray?"

"In Worcester. I have always wished to practise at Worcester. It is the assize town: I don't care for pettifogging places: one can't get on in them."

"You'd like to emerge all at once into a full-blown lawyer there? That's your notion, is it, Sam?"

Sam made no answer. He knew by the tone his notion was being laughed at.

"No, my lad. When you have been in some good office for another year or two maybe, then you might think about setting up. The office can be in Worcester if you like."

"I am hard upon twenty-three, Uncle Jacobson. I have as much knowledge of law as I need."

"And as much steadiness also, perhaps?" said old Jacobson.

Sam turned as red as the table-cover. He was a frank-looking, slender young fellow of middle height, with fine wavy hair almost a gold colour and worn of a decent length. The present fashion—to be cropped as if you were a prison-bird and to pretend to like it so—was not favoured by gentlemen in those days.

"You may have been acquiring a knowledge of law in London, Sam; I hope you have; but you've been kicking up your heels over it. What about those sums of money you've more than once got out of your mother?"

Sam's face was a deeper red that the cloth now. "Did she tell you of it, uncle?" he gasped.

"No, she didn't; she cares too much for her graceless son to betray him. I chanced to hear of it, though."

"One has to spend so much in London," murmured Sam, in lame apology.

"I dare say! In my past days, sir, a young man had to cut his coat according to his cloth. We didn't rush into all kinds of random games and then go out to our fathers or mothers to help us out of them. Which is what you've been doing, my gentleman."

"Does aunt know?" burst out Sam in a fright, as a step was heard on the stairs.

"I've not told her," said Mr. Jacobson, listening—"she is gone into the kitchen. How much is it that you've left owing in London, Sam?"

Sam nearly choked. He did not perceive this was just a random shot: he was wondering whether magic had been at work.

"Left owing in London?" stammered he.

"That's what I asked. How much? And I mean to know. 'Twon't be of any use your fencing about the bush. Come! tell it in a lump."

"Fifty pounds would cover it all, sir," said Sam, driven by desperation into the avowal.

"I want the truth, Sam."

"That is the truth, uncle, I put it all down in a list before leaving London; it comes to just under fifty pounds."

"How could you be so wicked as to contract it?"

"There has not been much wickedness about it," said Sam miserably, "indeed there hasn't. One gets drawn into expenses unconsciously in the most extraordinary manner up in London. Uncle Jacobson, you may believe me or not, when I say that until I added it up, I did not think it amounted to twenty pounds in all."

"And then you found it to be fifty! How do you propose to pay this?"

"I intend to send it up by instalments, as I can."

"Instead of doing which, you'll get into deeper debt at Worcester. If it's Worcester you go to."

"I hope not, uncle. I shall do my best to keep out of debt. I mean to be steady."

Mr. Jacobson filled a fresh pipe, and lighted it with a spill from the mantlepiece. He did not doubt the young fellow's intentions; he only doubted his resolution.

"You shall go into some lawyer's office in Worcester for two years, Sam, when we shall see how things turn out," said he presently. "And, look here, I'll pay these debts of yours myself, provided you promise me not to get into trouble again. There, no more"—interrupting Sam's grateful looks—"your aunt's coming in."

Sam opened the door for Mrs. Jacobson. A little pleasant-faced woman in a white net cap, with small flat silver curls under it. She carried a small basket lined with blue silk, in which lay her knitting.

"I've been looking to your room, my dear, to see that all's comfortable for you," she said to Sam, as she sat down by the table and the candles. "That new housemaid of ours is not altogether to be trusted. I suppose you've been telling your uncle all about the wonders of London?"

"And something else, too," put in old Jacobson gruffly. "He wanted to set up in practice for himself at Worcester: off-hand, red-hot!"

"Oh dear!" said Mrs. Jacobson.

"That's what the boy wanted, nothing less. No. Another year or two's work in some good house, to acquire stability and experience, and then he may talk about setting up. It will be all for the best, Sam; trust me."

"Well, uncle, perhaps it will." It was of no use for him to say perhaps it won't: he could not help himself. But it was a disappointment.

Mr. Jacobson walked over to Dyke Manor the next day, to consult the Squire as to the best lawyer to place Sam with, himself suggesting their old friend Cockermuth. He described all Sam's wild ways (it was how he put it) in that dreadful place, London, and the money he had got out of amidst its snares. The Squire took up the matter with his usual hearty sympathy, and quite agreed that no practitioner in the law could be so good for Sam as John Cockermuth.

John Cockermuth proved to be agreeable. He was getting to be an elderly man then, but was active as ever, saving when a fit of the gout took him. He received young Dene in his usual cheery manner, upon the day appointed for his entrance, and assigned him his place in the office next to Mr. Parslet. Parslet had been there more than twenty years; he was, so to say, at the top and tail of all the work that went on in it, but he was not a qualified solicitor. Samson Dene was qualified, and could therefore represent Mr. Cockermuth before the magistrates and what not, of which the old lawyer expected to find the benefit.

"Where are you going to live?" he questioned of Sam that first morning.

"I don't know yet, sir. Mr. and Mrs. Jacobson are about the town now, I believe, looking for lodgings for me. Of course they couldn't let *me* look; they'd think I should be taken in," added Sam.

"Taken in and done for," laughed the lawyer. "I should not wonder but Mr Parslet could accommodate you. Can you, Parslet?"

Mr. Parslet looked up from his desk, his thin cheeks flushing. He was small and slight, with weak brown hair, and had a patient, sad sort of look in his face and in his meek, dark eyes.

James parslet was one of those men who are said to spoil their own lives. Left alone early, he was looked after by a bachelor uncle, a minor canon of the cathedral, who perhaps tried to do his duty by him in a mild sort of manner. But young Parslet liked to go his own ways, and they were not very good ways. He did not stay at any calling he was put to, trying first one and then another; either the people got tired of him, or he of them. Money (when he got any) burnt a hole in his pocket, and his coats grew shabby and his boots dirty. "Poor Jamie Parslet! how he has spoilt his life!" cried the town, shaking its pitying head at him: and thus things went on till he grew to be nearly thirty years of age. Then, to the public astonishment, Jamie pulled up. He got taken on by Lawyer Cockermuth as copying clerk at twenty shillings a week, married, and became as steady as Old Time. He had been nothing but steady from that day to this, had forty shillings a week now, instead of twenty, and was ever a meek, subdued man, as if he carried about with him a perpetual repentance for the past, regret for the life that might have been. He lived in Edgar Street, which is close to the cathedral, as every one knows, Edgar Tower being at the top of it. An old gentleman attached to the cathedral had now lodged in his house for ten years, occupying the drawing-room floor; he had recently died, and hence Lawyer Cockermuth's suggestion.

Mr. Parslet looked up. "I should be happy to, sir", he said; "if our rooms suited Mr Dene. Perhaps he would like to look at them?"

"I will," said Sam. "If my uncle and aunt do not fix on any for me."

Is there any subtle mesmeric power, I wonder, that influences things unconsciously? Curiously to say, at this very moment Mr. and Mrs. Jacobsen were looking at these identical rooms. They had driven into Worcester with Sam very early indeed, so as to have a long day before them, and when breakfast was over at the inn, took the opportunity, which they very rarely got, of slipping into the cathedral to hear the beautiful ten o'clock service. Coming out the cloister way when it was over, and so down Edgar Street, Mrs. Jacobson espied a card in a window with "Lodgings" on it. "I wonder if they would suit Sam?" she cried to her husband.

"Edgar Street is a nice, wide, open street, and quiet. Suppose we look at them?"

A young servant-maid, called by her mistress "Sally", answered the knock. Mrs. Parslet, a capable, bustling woman of ready speech and good manners, came out of the parlour, and took the visitors to the floor above. They liked the rooms and they liked Mrs. Parslet; they also liked the rooms and they liked the moderate rent asked, for respectable country people in those days did not live by shaving one another; and when it came out that the house's master had been clerk to Lawyer Cockermuth for twenty years, they settled the matter off-hand, without the ceremony of consulting Sam. Mrs. Jacobson looked upon Sam as a boy still. Mr. Jacobson might have done the same but for the debts made in London.

And all this, you will say, has been yet more explanation; but I could not help it. The real thing begins now, with Sam Dene's sojourn In Mr. Cockermuth's office, and his residence in Edgar Street.

The first Sunday of his stay there, Sam went out to attend the morning service in the cathedral, congratulating himself that that grand office stood so conveniently near, and looking, it must be confessed, a bit of a dandy, for he had put a little bunch of spring violets into his coat, and "button-holes" were quite out of the common way then. The service began with the Litany, the earlier service of prayers being held at eight o'clock. Sam Dene has not yet forgotten that day, for it is no imaginary person I am telling you of, and never will forget it. The Reverand Allen Wheeler chanted, and the prebendary in residence (Somers Cocks) preached. While wondering when the sermon (a very good one) would be over, and thinking it rather prosy, after the custom of young men, Sam's roving gaze was drawn to a young lady sitting in the long seat opposite to him on the other side of the choir, whose whole attention appeared to be given to the preacher, to whom her head was turned. It is a nice face, thought Sam; such a sweet expression in it. It really was a nice face, rather pretty, gentle and thoughtful, a patient look in the dark brown eyes. She had on a well-worn dark silk, and straw bonnet; all very quiet and plain; but she looked very much of a lady. Wonder if she sits there always? thought Sam.

Service over, he went home, and was about to turn the handle of the door to enter (looking another way) when he found it turned for him by some one who was behind and had stretched out a hand to do it. Turning quickly, he saw the same young lady.

"Oh, I beg your pardon," said Sam, all at sea; "did you wish to come in here?"

"If you please," she answered—and her voice was sweet and her manner modest.

"Oh," repeated Sam, rather taken aback at the answer. "You did not want me, did you?"

"Thank you, it is my home," she said.

"Your home?" stammered Sam, for he had not seen the ghost of any one in the house yet, saving his landlord and landlady and Sally. "Here?"

"Yes. I am Maria Parslet."

He stood back to let her enter; a slender, gentle girl of middle height; she looked about eighteen, Sam thought (she was that and two years on to it), and he wondered where she had been hidden. He had to go out again, for he was invited to dine at Lawyer Cockermuth's, so he saw no more of the young lady that day; but she kept dancing about in his memory. And somehow she so fixed herself in it, and as the time went on so grew in it, and at last so filled it, that Sam may well hold that day as a marked day—the one that introduced him to Maria Parslet. But that is anticipating.

On the Monday morning all his ears and eyes were alert, listening and looking for Maria. He did not see her; he did not hear a sound of her. By degrees he got to learn that the young lady was resident teacher in a ladies' school hard by; and that she was often allowed to spend the whole day at home on Sundays. One Sunday evening he ingeniously got himself invited to take tea in Mrs. Parslet's parlour, and thus became acquainted with Maria; but his opportunities for meeting her were rare.

There's not much to tell of the first twelvemonth. It passed in due course. Sam Dene was fairly steady. He made a few debts, as some young men, left to themselves, can't help making—at least, they'd tell you they can't. Sundry friends of Sam's in Worcester knew of this, and somehow it reached Mr. Cockermuth's ears, who gave Sam a word of advice privately.

This was just as the first year expired. According to agreement, Sam had another year to stay. He entered upon it with inward gloom. On adding up his scores, which he deemed it as well to do after his master's lecture, he again found that they amounted to far more than he had thought for, and how he should contrive to pay them out of his own resources he knew no more than the man in the moon. In short he could not do it; he was in a fix; and lived in perpetual dread of its coming to the ears of his uncle Jacobson.

The spring assize, taking place early in March, was just over; the judges had left the town for Stafford, and Worcester was settling down again to quietness. Miss Cockermuth gave herself and her to handmaidens a week's rest—assize time being always a busy and bustling period at the lawyer's, no end of chance company looking in— and then the house began its spring cleaning, a grand institution with our good grandmothers, often lasting a couple of weeks. This time, at the lawyer's house, it was to be a double bustle; for visitors were being prepared for.

It had pleased Captain Cockermuth to write word that he should be at home for Easter; upon which, the lawyer and his sister decided to invite Philip's widow and her children also to spend it with them; they knew Charles would be pleased. Easter Day was very early indeed that year, falling at the end of March.

To make clearer what's coming, the house had better have a word or two of description. You entered from the street into a wide passage; no steps. On the left was the parlour and general sitting-room; in which all meals were usually taken. It was a long, low room, its two rather narrow windows looking upon the street, the back of the room being a little dark. Opposite the door was the fireplace. On the other side the passage, facing the parlour-door, was the door that opened to the two rooms (one front, one back) used as the lawyer's offices. The kitchens and staircase were at the back of the passage, a garden lying beyond; and there was a handsome drawing-room on the first floor, not much used.

The house, I say, was in a commotion with the spring cleaning, and the other preparations. To accommodate so many visitors required contrivance: a bedroom for the captain, a bedroom for his daughter-in-law, two bedrooms for the children. Mistress and maids held momentous consultations together.

"We have decided to put the three little girls in Philip's old room, John," said Miss Betty to her brother, as they sat in the parlour after dinner on the Monday evening of the week preceding Passion Week; "and little Philip can have the small room off mine. We shall have to get in a child's bed, though; I can't put the three little girls in one bed; they might get fighting. John, I do wish you'd sell that old bureau for what it will fetch."

"Sell the old bureau!" exclaimed Mr. Cockermuth.

"I'm sure I should. What good does it do? Unless that bureau goes out of the room, we can't put the extra bed in. I've been in there half the day with Susan and Ann, planning and contriving, and we find it can't be done any way. Do let Ward take it away, John; there's no place for it in the other chambers. He'd give you a fair price for it, I dare say."

Miss Betty had never cared for this piece of furniture, thinking it more awkward than useful; she looked eagerly at her brother, awaiting his decision. She was the elder of the two; tall, like him; but whilst he maintained his thin, wiry form, just the shape of an upright gas-post with arms, she had grown stout with no shape at all. Miss Betty had dark, thick eyebrows and an amiable red face. She wore a "front" of brown curls with a high and dressy cap perched above it. This evening her gown was of soft twilled shot-green silk, a white net kerchief was crossed under its body, and she had on a white muslin apron.

"I don't mind," assented the lawyer, as easy in disposition as Miss Betty was; "it's no use keeping it that I know of. Send for Ward and ask him, if you like, Betty."

Ward, a carpenter and cabinet-maker, who had a shop in the town and sometimes bought second-hand things, was sent for by Miss Betty on the following morning and he agreed, after some chaffering, to buy the old bureau. It was the bureau from which Philip's box of gold had disappeared—but I dare say you have understood that. In the midst of all this stir and clatter, just as Ward betook himself away after concluding the negotiaton, and the maids were hard at work above stairs with mops and pails and scrubbing-brushes, the first advance-guard of the visitors unexpectedly walked in: Captain Cockermuth.

Miss Betty sat down in an access of consternation. She could do nothing but stare. He had not been expected for a week yet; there was nothing ready and nowhere to put him.

"I wish you'd take to behaving like a rational being, Charles!" she exclaimed. "We are all in a mess; the rooms upside down, and the bedside carpets hanging out at the windows."

Captain Cockermuth said he did not care for bedside carpets, he could sleep anywhere—on the brewhouse-bench, if she liked.

He quite approved of selling the old bureau, when told it was going to be done.

Ward had appointed five o'clock that evening to fetch it away. They were about to sit down to dinner when he came, five o'clock being the hour for late dinners then in ordinary life. Ward had brought a man with him and they went upstairs.

Miss Betty, as carver, sat at the top of the dining-table, her back to the windows, the lawyer in his place at the foot, Charles between them facing the fire. Miss Betty was cutting off the first joint of a loin of veal when the bureau was heard coming down the staircase with much bumping and noise.

Mr. Cockermuth stepped out of the dining-room to look on. The captain followed: being a sociable man with his fellow-towns people, he went to ask Ward how he did.

The bureau came down safely, and was lodged at the foot of the stairs; the man wiped his hot face, while Ward spoke with Captain Cockermuth. It seemed quite a commotion in the usual quiet dwelling. Susan, a jug of ale in her hand, which she had been to the cellar to draw, stood looking on from the passage; Mr. Dene and a younger clerk, coming out of the office just then to leave for the evening, turned to look on also.

"I suppose there's nothing in here, sir?" cried Ward, returning to business and the bureau.

"Nothing, I believe," replied Mr. Cockermuth.

"Nothing at all," called out Miss Betty through the open parlour-door. "I emptied the drawers this morning."

Ward, a cautious man and honest, drew back the lid and put his hand in succession into the pigeon-holes, which had not been used since Philip's time. There were twelve of them; three above, and three below on each side, and a little drawer that locked in the middle. "Halloa!" cried Ward, when his hand was in the depth of one of them: "here's something."

And he drew forth the lost box. The little ebony box with all the gold in it.

Well now, that was a strange thing, Worcester thinks so, those people who are still living to remember it, to this day. How it was that the box had appeared to be lost and was searched for in vain over and over again, by poor Philip and others; and how it was that it was now recovered in this easy and natural manner, was never explained or accounted for. Ward's opinion was that the box must have been put in, side upwards, that it had in some way stuck to the back of the deep, narrow pigeon-hole, which just about held the box in width, that those who had searched took the box for the back of the hole when their fingers touched it, and that the bumping of the bureau now in coming downstairs had dislodged the box and brought it forward. As a maker of bureau's, Ward's opinion was listened to with deference. Any way, it was a sort of theory, serving passably well in the absence of any other. But who knew? All that was certain about it was the fact; the loss and the recovery after many years. It happened just as here described, as I have already said.

Sam Dene had never heard of the loss. Captain Cockermuth perfectly beside himself with glee, explained it to him. Sam laughed as he touched with his forefinger the closely packed golden guineas, lying here so snug and safe, offered his congratulations, and walked home to tea.

It chanced that on that especial Tuesday evening, matters were at sixes and sevens in the parslets' house, Sally had misbehaved herself and was discharged in consequence; and the servant engaged in her place, who was to have entered that afternoon, had not made her appearance When Sam entered, Maria came out of the parlour, a pretty blush upon her face. And to Sam the unexpected sight of her, it was not often he got a chance of it, and the blush and the sweet eyes came like a gleam of Eden, for he had grown to love her dearly. Not that he had owned it to himself yet.

Maria explained. Her school had broken up for the Easter holidays earlier than it ought, one of the girls showing symptoms of measles; and her mother had gone out to see what had become of the new servant, leaving a request that Mr. Dene would take his tea with them in the parlour that evening, as there was no one to wait on him.

Nothing loth, you may be sure, Mr. Dene accepted the invitation, running up to wash his hands, and give a look at his hair, and running down in a trice. The tea-tray stood in readiness on the parlour-table, Maria sitting behind it. Perhaps she had given a look at *her* hair, for it was quite more lovely, Sam thought, more soft and silken than any hair he had even seen. The little copper kettle sang away on the hob by the fire.

"Will papa be long, do you know?" began Maria demurely, feeling shy and conscious at being thus thrown along into Sam's company." I had better not make the tea until he come in."

"I don't know at all," answered Sam. "He went out on some business for Mr. Cockermuth at half-past four, and was not back when I left. Such a curious thing has just happened up there, Miss Parslet!"

"Indeed! What is it?"

Sam entered on the narrative. Maria, who knew all about the strange loss of the box, grew quite excited as she listened. "Found!" she exclaimed. "Found in the same bureau! And all the golden guineas in it!"

"Every one," said Sam: "as I take it. They were packed right up to the top!"

"Oh, what a happy thing!" repeated Maria, in a fervent tone that rather struck Sam, and she clasped her fingers into one another, as one sometimes does in pleasure or in pain.

"Why do you say that, Miss Parslet?"

"Because papa—but I do not think I ought to tell you," added Maria, breaking off abruptly.

"Oh, yes you may. I am quite safe, even if it's a secret. Please do."

"Well," cried the easily persuaded girl, "papa has always had an uncomfortable feeling upon him ever since the loss. He feared that some people, knowing he was not well off, might think perhaps it was he who had stolen upstairs and taken it."

Sam laughed at that.

"He has never *said* so, but somehow we have seen it, my mother and I. It was altogether so mysterious a loss, you see, affording no clue as to *when* it occurred, that people were ready to suspect anything, however improbable. Oh, I am thankful it is found!"

The kettle went on singing, the minutes went on flitting, and still nobody came. Six o'clock struck out from the cathedral as Mr. Parslet entered. Had the two been asked the time, they might have said it was about a quarter-past five. Golden hours fly quickly; fly on angels' wings.

Now it chanced that whilst they were at tea, a creditor of Sam's came to the door, one Jonas Badger. Sam went to him: and the colloquy that ensued might be heard in the parlour. Mr. Badger said (in quite a fatherly way) that he really could not be put off any longer with promises; if his money was not repaid to him before Easter he should be obliged to take steps about it, should write to Mr. Jacobson, of Elm farm, to begin with. Sam returned to the tea-table with a wry face.

Soon after that, Mrs. Parslet came in. The delinquent servant in her rear. Next, a friend of Sam's called, Austin Chance, whose father was a solicitor in good practice in the town. The two young men, who were very intimate and often together, went up to Sam's room above.

"I say, my good young friend," began Chance, in a tone that might be taken for jest or earnest, "don't you go and get into any entanglement in that quarter."

"What d'you mean now?" demanded Sam, turning the colour of the rising sun.

"I mean Maria Parslet," said Austin Chance, laughing. "She's a deuced nice girl; I know that; just the one a fellow might fall in love with unawares. But it wouldn't do, Dene."

"Why wouldn't it do?"

"Oh, come now, Sam, you know it wouldn't. Parslet is only a working clerk at Cockermuth's."

"I should like to know what has put the thought in your head?" contended Sam. "You had better put it out again. I've never told you I was falling in love with her; or told herself, either. Mrs. Parslet would be about me, I expect, if I did. She looks after her as one looks after gold."

"Well, I found you in their room, having tea with them, and——"

"It was quite by accident, an exceptional thing," interrupted Sam.

"Well," repeats Austin, "you need not put your back up, old fellow; a friendly warning does no harm. Talking of good, Dene, I've done my best to get up the twenty pounds you wanted to borrow of me, and I can't do it. I'd let you have it with all my heart if I could; but I find I am harder up than I thought for."

Which was all true. Chance was as good-natured a young man as ever lived, but at this early stage of his life he made more debts than he could pay.

"Badger has just been here, whining and covertly threatening," said Sam. "I am to pay up in a week, or he'll make me pay—and tell my uncle, he says, to begin with."

"Hypocritical old skinflint!" ejaculated Chance, himself sometimes in the hands of Mr. Badger—a worthy gentleman who did a little benevolent usury in a small and quiet way, and took his delight in accommodating safe young men. A story was whispered that young M., desperately hard-up, borrowed two pounds from him one Saturday night, undertaking to repay it, with two pounds added on for interest, that day month; and when the day came and M. had not got the money, or was at all likely to get, he carried off a lot of his mother's plate under his coat to the pawnbroker's.

"And there's more besides Badger's that is pressing," went on Dene. "I must get money from somewhere, or it will play the very deuce with me. I wonder whether Charley Hill could lend me any?"

"Don't much think so. You might ask him. Money seems scarce with Hill always. Has a good many ways for it, I fancy."

"Talking of money, Chance, a lot has been found at Cockermuth's to-day. A box full of guineas that has been lost for years."

Austin Chance stared. "You don't mean that box of guineas that mysteriously disappeared in Philip's time?"

"Well, they say so. It is a small, round box of carved ebony, and it is stuffed to the brim with old guineas. Sixty of them, I hear."

"I can't believe it's true; that *that's* found."

"Not believe it's true, Chance! Why, I saw it. Saw the box found, and touched the guineas with my fingers. It has been hidden in an old bureau all the time," added Sam, and he related the particulars of the discovery.

"What an extraordinary thing!" exclaimed young Chance: "The queerest start I ever heard of." And he fell to musing.

But the "queer start," as Mr. Austin Chance was pleased to designate the resuscitation of the box, did not prove to be a lucky one.

II

The sun shone brightly on Foregate Street, but did not yet touch the front windows on Lawyer Cockermuth's side of it. Miss Betty Cockermuth sat near one of them in the parlour, spectacles on nose, and hard at work unpicking the braid of some very old woolen curtains, green once, but now faded to a sort of dingy brown. It was Wednesday morning, the day following the wonderful event of finding the box, lost so long, full of its golden guineas. In truth though of it as anything less than marvellous.

The house-cleaning, in preparation for Easter and Easter's visitors, was in full flow to-day, and would be for more than a week to come; the two maids were hard at it above. Ward, who did not disdain to labour with his own hands, was at the house, busy at some mysterious business in the brew-house, coat off, shirt-sleeves stripped up to elbow, plunging at that moment something or other into the boiling water of the furnace.

"How I could have let them remain up so long in this state. I can't think," said Miss Betty to herself, arresting her employment, scissors in hand, to regard the dreary curtains. She had drawn the table towards her from the middle of the room, and the heavy work was upon it. Susan came in to impart some domestic news.

"Ward says there's a rare talk in the town about the finding of that box, missis," cried she, when she had concluded it. "My; how bad them curtains look, now they're down!"

Servants were on more familiar terms with their misstress in those days without meaning, or showing, any disrespect; identifying themselves, as it were, with the family and its interests. Susan, a plump, red-cheeked young woman turned thirty, had been housemaid in her present place for seven years. She had promised a baker's head man to marry him, but never could be got to fix the day. In winter she'd say to him, "Wait till summer"; and when summer came, she'd say, "Wait till winter." Miss Betty commended her prudence.

"Yes," said she now, in answer to the girl, "I've been wondering how we could have kept them up so long; they are not fit for much, I'm afraid, save the rag-bag. Chintz will make the room look much nicer."

As Susan left the parlour, Captain Cockermuth entered it, a farmer with him who had come in from Hallow to the Wednesday's market. The captain's delighted excitement at the finding of the box had not at all subsided; he had dreamt of it, he talked of it, he pinned every acquaintance he could pick up this morning and brought him in to see the box of gold. Independently of its being a very great satisfaction to have had the old mysterious loss cleared up, the sixty guineas would be a huge boon to the captain's pocket.

"But how was it that none of you ever found it, if it remained all this while in the pigeon-hole?" cried the wondering farmer, bending over the little round box of guineas, which the captain placed upon the table open, the lid by its side.

"Well, we didn't find it, that's all I know; or poor Philip, either," said Captain Cockermuth.

The farmer took his departure. As the captain was showing him to the front-door, another gentleman came bustling in. It was Thomas Chance, the lawyer, father of the young man who had been the previous night with Samson Dene. He and Lawyer Cockermuth were engaged together just then in some complicated, private, and very disagreeable business, each acting for a separate client, who were the defendant against a great wrong—or what they thought was one.

"Come in, Chance, and take a look at my box of guineas, resuscitated from the grave," cried the captain, joyously. "You can go into the office to join afterwards."

"Well, I've hardly time this morning," answered Mr. Chance, turning, though, into the parlour and shaking hands with Miss Betty. "Austin told me it was found."

Now it happened the Lawyer Cockermuth came then into the parlour himself, to get something from his private desk-table which stood there. When the box had been discussed, Mr. Chance took a letter from his pocket and placed it in his brother practitioner's hands.

"What do you think of that?" he asked. "I got it by post this morning."

"Think! why, that it is of vital importance," said Mr. Cockermuth when he had read it.

"Yes; not doubt of that. But what is to be our next move in answer to it?" asked the other.

Seeing they were plunging into business, the captain strolled away to the front-door, which stood open all day, for the convenience of those coming to the office, and remained there whistling, his hands in his pockets, on the look out of somebody else to bring in. He had put the lid on the box of guineas, and left the box on the table.

"I should like to take a copy of the letter," said Mr. Cockermuth to the other lawyer.

"Well, you can take it," answered Chance. "Mind who does it, though—Parselt, or somebody else that's confidential. Don't let it go into the office."

"You are wanted, sir," said Mr. Dene, from the door.

"Who is it?" asked his master.

"Mr. Chamberlain. He says he is in a hurry."

"I'm coming. Here, Dene!" he called out as the latter was turning away: and young Dene came back again.

"Sit down here, now, and take a copy of this letter," cried the lawyer, rapidly drawing out and opening the little writing-desk table that stood against the wall at the back of the room. "Here's pen, ink and paper, all ready: the letter is confidential, you perceive."

He went out of the room as he spoke, Mr. Chance with him; and Sam Dene sat down to commence his task, after exchanging a few words with Miss Betty, with whom he was on good terms.

"Charles makes as much fuss over this little box as if it were filled with diamonds from Golconda, instead of guineas," remarked she, pointing with her scissors to the box, which stood near her on the table, to direct the young man's attention to it.

"I don't know how many folks he has not brought in already to have a look at it."

"Well, it was a capital find, Miss Betty; one to be proud of," answered Sam, settling to his work.

For some little time nothing was heard but the scratching of Mr. Dene's pen and the clicking of Miss Betty's scissors. Her task was nearing completion. A few minutes more, and the last click was given, the last bit of the braid was off. "And I'm glad of it," cried she aloud, flinging the end of the curtain on the top of the rest.

"This braid will do again for something or other," considered Miss Betty, as she began to wind it upon an old book. "It was put on fresh only three or four years ago. Well brushed, it will look almost like new."

Again Susan opened the door. "Miss Betty, here's the man come with the chintz: five or six rolls of it for you to choose from," cried she. "Shall he come in here?"

Miss Betty was about to say Yes, but stopped and said No, instead. The commotion of holding up the chintzes to the light, to judge of their different merits, might disturb Mr. Dene; and she knew better than to interrupt business.

"Let him take them to the room where they are to hang, Susan; we can judge best there."

Tossing the braid to Susan, who stood waiting at the door, Miss Betty hastily took up her curtains, and Susan held the door open for her mistress to pass through.

Choosing chintz for window-curtains takes some time; as everybody knows whose fancy is erratic. And how long Miss Betty and Susan and the young man from the chintz-mart had been doubting and deciding and doubting again, did not quite appear, when Captain Cockermuth's voice was heard ascending from below.

"Betty! Are you upstairs, Betty?"

"Yes, I'm here," she called back, crossing to the door to speak. "DO you want me, Charles?"

"Where have you put the box?"

"What box?"

"The box of guineas."

"It is on the table."

"It is not on the table. I can't see it anywhere."

"It was on the table when I left the parlour. I did not touch it. Ask Mr. Dene where it is: I left him there."

"Mr. Dene's not here. I wish you'd come down."

"Very well; I'll come in a minute or two," concluded Miss Betty, going back to the chintzes.

"Why, I saw that box on the table as I shut the door after you had come out, ma'am," observed Susan, who had listened to the colloquy.

"So did I," said Miss Betty; "it was the very last thing my eyes fell on. If young Mr. Dene finished what he was about and left the parlour, I dare say he put the box up somewhere for safety. I think, Susan, we must fix upon this light pea-green with the rose-buds running up it. It matches the paper: and the light coming through it takes quite a nice shade."

A little more indecision yet; and yet a little more, as to whether the curtains should be lined, or not, and then Miss Cockermuth went downstairs. The captain was pacing the passage to and fro impatiently.

"Now then, Betty, where's my box?"

"But how am I to know where the box is, Charles, if it's not on the table?" she remonstrated, turning in the parlour, where two friends of the captain's waited to be regaled with the sight of the recovered treasure. "I had to go upstairs with the young man who brought the chintzes; and I left the box here"—indicating the exact spot on the table. "It was where you left it yourself. I did not touch it at all."

She shook hands with the visitors. Captain Cockermuth looked gloomy—as if he were at sea and had lost his reckoning.

"If you had to leave the room, why didn't you put the box up?" asked he. "A box full of guineas shouldn't be left alone in an empty room."

"But Mr. Dene was in the room; he sat at the desk there, copying a letter for John. As to why didn't I put the box up, it was not my place to do so that I know of. You were about yourself, Charles—only at the front-door, I suppose."

Captain Cockermuth was aware that he had not been entirely at the front-door. Two or three times he had crossed over to hold a chat with acqaintances on the other side the way; had strolled with one of them nearly up to Salt Lane and back. Upon catching hold of these two gentlemen, now brought in, he had found the parlour empty of occupants and the box not to be seen.

"Well, this is a nice thing—that a man can't put his hand upon his own property when he wants to, or hear where it is!" grumbled he. "And what business on earth had Dene to meddle with the box?"

"To put it in safety—if he did meddle with it, and a sensible thing to do," retorted Miss Betty, who did not like to be scolded unjustly. "Just like you, Charles, making a fuss over nothing! Why don't you go and ask young Dene where it is?"

"Young Dene is not in. And John's not in. Nobody is in but Parslet; and he does not know anything about it. I must say, Betty, you manage the house nicely!" concluded the captain, ironically, giving way to his temper.

This was, perhaps the reader may think, commotion enough "over nothing," as Miss Betty put it. But it was not much as compared with the commotion which set in later. When Mr. Cockermuth came in, he denied all knowledge of it, and Sam Dene was impatiently waited for.

It was part two o'clock when he returned, for he had been home to dinner. The good-looking young fellow turned in at the front door with a fleet step, and encountered Captain Cockermuth, who attacked him hotly, demanding what he had done with the box.

"Ah," said Sam, lightly and coolly, "Parslet said you were looking for it." Mr. Parslet had in fact mentioned it at home over his dinner.

"Well, where is it?" said the captain. "Where did you put it?"

"I?" cried young Dene. "Not anywhere. Should I be likely to touch the box, sir? I saw the box on the table while I was copying a letter from Mr. Cockermuth; that's all I know of it."

The captain turned red, and pale, and red again. "Do you mean to tell me to my face, Mr. Dene, that the box is *gone*?"

"I'm sure I don't know," said Sam in the easiest of all easy tones. "It seems to be gone."

The box was gone. Gone once more with all its golden guineas. It could not be found anywhere; in the house or out of the house, upstairs or down. The captain searched frantically, the others helped him, but no trace of it could be found.

At first it was impossible to believe it. That this self-same box should mysteriously have vanished a second time, seemed to be too marvellous for fact. But it was true.

Nobody would admit a share in the responsibility. The captain left the box safe amidst (as he put it) a room full of people: Miss Betty considered that she left it equally safe, with Mr. Dene seated at the writing-table, and the captain dodging (as *she* put it) in and out. Mr. Cockermuth had not entered the parlour since he left it, when called to Mr Chamberlain, with whom he had gone out. Sam Dene reiterated that he had not meddled with the box; no, nor thought about it.

Sam's account, briefly given, was this. After finishing copying the letter, he closed the little table-desk and pushed it back to its place against the wall, and had carried the letter and the copy into the office. Finding Mr. Cockermuth was not there, he locked them up in his own desk, having to go to the Guildhall upon some business. The business there took up some time, in fact until past one o'clock, and he then went home to dinner.

"And did you consider it right, Sam Dene, to leave a valuable box like that on the table, unguarded?" demanded Captain Cockermuth, as they all stood together in the parlour, after questioning Sam; and the captain had been looking so fierce and speaking so sharply that it might be thought he was taking Sam for the thief, off-hand.

"To tell the truth, captain, I never thought of the box," answered Sam. "I might not have noticed that the box was in the room at all but for Miss Betty's drawing my attention to it. After that, I grew so much interested in the letter I was copying (for I know all about the cause, as Mr. Cockermuth is aware, and it was curious news) that I forgot everything else."

Lawyer Cockermuth nodded to confirm this. The captain went on:

"Betty drew your attention to it, did she? Why did she draw it? In what way?"

"Well, she remarked that you made as much fuss over that box as if it were filled with diamonds," replied the young man, glad to pay out the captain for his angry and dictatorial tone. But the captain was in truth beginning to entertain a very ominous suspicion.

"Do you wish to deny, Samson Dene, that my sister Betty left that box on the table when she quitted the room?"

"Why, who does?" cried Sam. "When Miss Betty says she left the box on the table, of course she did leave it. She must know. Susan, it seems also saw that it was left there."

"And you could see that box of guineas standing stark staring on the table, and come out of the room and leave it to its fate!" foamed the captain. "Instead of giving me a call to say nobody was on guard here!"

"I didn't see it," returned Sam. "There's no doubt it was there, but I did not see it. I never looked towards the table as I came out, that I know of. The table, as I dare say you remember, was not in its usual place; it was up there by the window. The box had gone clean out of my thoughts."

"Well, Mr. Dene, my impression is *that you have got the box*," cried the angry captain.

"Oh, is it!" returned Sam, with supreme good humour, and just the least suspicion of a laugh. "A box like that would be uncommonly useful to me."

"I expect, young man, the guineas would!"

"Right you are, captain."

But Captain Cockermuth regarded this mocking pleasantry as particularly ill-timed. *He believed the young man was putting it on to divert suspicion from himself.*

"Who did take the box?" questioned he. "Tell me that."

"I wish I could, sir."

"How could the box vanish off the table unless it was taken, I ask you?"

"That's a puzzling question," coolly rejoined Sam. "It was too heavy for the rats, I expect."

"Oh, dear, but we have not rats in the house," cried Miss Betty.

"I wish we had, "I'm sure—and could find the box in their holes."

She was feeling tolerably uncomfortable. Placid and easy in a general way, serious worry always upset her considerably.

Captain Cockermuth's suspicions were becoming certainties. The previous night, when his brother had been telling him various items of news of the old town, as they sat confidentially over the fire after Miss Betty had gone to bed, Mr. Cockermuth chanced to mention the fact that young Dene had been making a few debts. Not speaking in any ill-natured spirit, quite the contrary, for he liked the young man amazingly. Only a few, he continued; thoughtless young men would do so; and he had given him a lecture. And then he laughingly added the information that Mr. Jacobson had imparted to him twelve months ago, in their mutual friendship—of the debts Sam had made in London.

No sensible person can be surprised that Charles Cockermugh recalled this now. It rankled in his mind. Had Sam Dene taken the box of guineas to satisfy these debts contracted during the past year at Worcester? It looked like it. And the longer the captain dwelt on it, the more and more likely it grew to look.

All the afternoon the search was kept up by the captain. Not an individual article in the parlour but was turned inside out; he wanted to have the carpet up. His brother and Sam Dene had returned to their work in the office as usual. The captain was getting to feel like a raging bear; three times Miss Betty had to stop him in a dreadful fit of swearing; and when dinner-time came he could not eat. It was a beautiful slice of Severn salmon, which had its price, I can tell you, in Worcester then, and minced veal, and a jam tart, all of which dishes Charles Cockermuth especially favoured. But the loss of the sixty guineas did away with his appetite. Mr. Cockermuth, who took the loss very cooly, laughed at him.

The laughing did not mend the captain's temper: neither did the hearing that Sam Dene had departed for home as usual at five o'clock. Had Sam been innocent, he would at least have come to the parlour and inquired whether the box was found, instead of sneaking off home to tea.

Fretting and fuming, raging and stamping, disturbing the parlour's peace and his own, strode Charles Cockermuth. His good-humoured brother John bore it for an hour or two, and then told him he might as well go outside and stamp on the pavement for a bit.

"I will," said Charles. Catching up his hat, saying nothing to anybody, he strode off to see the sergeant of police—Dutton—and laid the case concisely before him: The box of guineas was on the table where his sister sat at work; her work being at one end, the box at the other. Sam Dene was also in the room, copying a letter at the writing-table. Miss Betty was called upstairs; she went, leaving the box on the table. It was the last thing she saw as she left the room; the servant, who had come to call her, also saw it standing there. Presently young Dene also left the room and the house; and from that moment the box was never seen.

"What do you make of that, Mr. Dutton?" summed up Captain Cockermuth.

"Am I to understand that no other person entered the room after Mr. Dene quitted it?" inquired the sergeant.

"Not a soul. I can testify to that myself."

"Then it looks as though Mr. Dene must have taken the box."

"Just so," assented the complainant, triumphantly. "And I shall give him into custody for stealing it."

Mr. Dutton considered. His judgment was cool; the captain's hot. He thought there might be ins and outs in this affair that had not yet come to the surface. Besides that, he knew young Dene, and did not much fancy him the sort of individual likely to do a thing of this kind.

"Captain Cockermuth," said he, "I think it might be best for me to come up to the house and see a bit into the matter personally, before proceeding to extreme measures. We experienced officers have a way of turning up scraps of evidence that other people would never look at. Perhaps, after all, the box is only mislaid."

"But I tell you it's *lost*," said the captain. "Clean gone. Can't be found high or low."

"Well, if that same black box is lost again, I can only say it is the oddest case I ever heard of. One would think the box had a demons inside it."

"No, sergeant, you are wrong there. The demon's inside him that took it. Listen while I whisper something in your ear—that young Dene is over head and ears in debt: he has debts here, debts there, debts everywhere. For some little time now, as I chance to know, he has been at his very wits' end to think where or how he could pick up some money to satisfy the most pressing; fit to die of fear, lest they should travel to the knowledge of his uncle at Elm Farm."

"*Is* it so?" exclaimed Mr. Dutton, severely. And his face changed, and his opinion also. "Are you sure of this, sir?"

"Well, my informant was my brother; so you may judge whether it is likely to be correct or not," said the captain. "But, if you think it best to make some inquiries at the house, come with me and do so."

They walked to Foregate together. The sergeant looked a little at the features of the parlour, where the loss had taken place, and heard what Miss Betty had to say, and questioned Susan. This did not help the suspicion thrown on Sam Dene, saving in one point—their joint testimony that he and the box were left alone in the room together.

Mr. Cockermuth had gone out, so the sergeant did not see him: but, as he was not within doors when the loss occurred, he could not have aided the investigation in any way.

"Well, Dutton, what do you think now?" asked Captain Cockermuth, strolling down the street with the sergeant when he departed.

"I confess my visit has not helped me much," said Dutton, a slow-speaking man, given to be cautious. "If nobody entered the room between the time when Miss Cockermuth left it and you entered it, why then, sir, there's only young Dene to fall back upon."

"I tell you nobody did enter it," cried the choleric captain; "or *could*, without my seeing them. I stood at the front-door. Ward was busy at the house that morning, dodging perpetually across the top of the passage, between the kitchen and brew-house: he, too, is sure no stranger cold have come in without being seen by him."

"Did you see young Dene leave the room, sir?"

"I did. Hearing somebody come out of the parlour, I looked round and saw it was young Dene with some papers in his hand. He went into the office for a minute or two, and then passed me, remarking, with all the impudence in life, that he was going to the town hall. He must have had my box in his pocket then."

"A pity but you had gone into the parlour at once, captain," remarked the sergeant. "If only to put the box in safety—provided it was there."

"But I thought it was safe. I thought my sister was there. I did go in almost directly."

"And you never stirred from the door—from first to last?"

"I don't say that. When I first stood there I strolled about a little, talking wiht one person and another. *But I did not stir from the door after I saw Sam Dene leave the parlour*. And I do not think five minutes elapsed before I went in. Not more than five, I am quite certain. What are you thinking about Dutton?—you don't seem to take me."

"I take you well enough sir, and all you say. But what is puzzling me in the matter is this; strikes me as strange, in fact: that Mr. Dene should do the thing (allowing that he has done it) in so open and barefaced a manner, laying himself open to immediate suspicion. Left alone in the room with the box by Miss Betty, he must know that if, when he left it, the box vanished with him, only one inference would be drawn. Most thieves exercise some caution."

"Not when they are as hard up as Dene is. Impudence with them is the order of the day, and often carries luck with it. Nothing risk, nothing win, they cry, and they *do* risk—and win. Dene has got my box, sergeant."

"Well, sir, it looks dark against him; almost *too* dark; and if you decide to give him into custody, of course we have only too— Good-evening, Badger!"

They had strolled as far as the Cross, and were standing on the wide pavement in front of St. Nicholas' Church, about to part, when that respectable gentleman, Jonas Badger, passed by. A thought struck the captain. He knew the man was a money-lender in a private way.

"Here, Badger, stop a minute," he hastily cried. "I want to ask you a question about young Dene—my brother's clerk, you know. Does he owe you money?—Much?"

Mr. Badger, wary by nature and by habit, glanced first at the questioner and then at the police-sergeant, and did not answer. Whereupon Captain Cockermuth, as an excuse for his curiosity, plunged into the history of what had occurred: the finding of the box of guineas yesterday and the losing it again to-day, and the doubt of Sam.

Mr. Badger listened with interest; for the news of that marvellous find had not yet reached his ears. He had been shut up in his office all the morning, very busy over his account-books; and in the afternoon had walked over to Kempsey, where he had a client or two, getting back only in time for tea.

"That long-lost box of guineas come to light at last!" he exclaimed. "What an extraordinary thing! And Mr. Dene is suspected of—— Why, good gracious!" he broke off in fresh astonishment, "I have just seen him with a guinea in his pocket!"

"Seen a guinea in Sam Dene's pocket!" cried Captain Cockermuth, turning yellow as the gas-flame under which they were standing.

"Why yes, I have. It was——"

But there Mr. Badger came to a full stop. It had suddenly struck him that he might be doing harm to Sam Dene; and the rule of his life was not to harm any one, or to make an enemy, if his own interest allowed him to avoid it.

"I won't say any more, Captain Cockermuth. It is no business of mine."

But here Mr. Sergeant Dutton came to the fore. "You must, Badger. You must say all you know that bears upon the affair; the law demands it of you. What about the guineas?"

"Well, if you force me to do so—putting it in that way," returned the man, driven into a corner.

Mr Badger had just been down to Edgar Street to pay another visit to Sam. Not to torment him; he did not do that more than he could help; but simply to say he would accept smaller instalments for the liquidation of his debt—which of course meant giving to Sam a longer time to pay the whole in. This evening he was admitted to Sam's sitting-room. During their short conversation, Sam, searching impatiently for a pencil in his waistcoat-pocket, drew out with it a few coins in silver money, and one coin in gold. Mr. Badger's hungry eyes saw that it was an old guinea. These particulars he now imparted.

"What did he *say* about the guinea?" cried Captain Cockermuth, his own eye glaring.

"Not a word," said Badger; "Neither did I. He slipped it back into his pocket."

"I hope you think there's some proof to go upon *now*," were Charlies Cockermuth's last words to the police-officer as he wished him good-night.

On the following morning, Sam Dene was apprehended, and taken before the magistrates. Beyond being formally charged, very little was done; Miss Betty was in bed with a sick headache, brought on by the worry, and could not appear to give evidence so he was remanded on bail until Saturday.

I'm sure you might have thought all his rick-yards were on fire by the way old Jacobson came bursting in. It was Saturday morning, and we were at breafast at Dyke Manor. He had run every step of the way from Elm Farm, two miles nearly, not having patience to wait for his gig, and came in all excitement, the *Worcester Herald* in his hand. The Squire started from his chair; Mrs. Todhetley, then in the act of pouring out a cup of coffee, let if flow over on to the tablecloth.

"What on earth's amiss, Jackson?" cried the Squire.

"Ay, what's amiss," stuttered Jacobson in answer; "*this* is amiss," holding out the newspaper. "I'll prosecute the editor as sure as I'm a living man. It is a conspiracy got up to sell it; a concocted lie. It can't be anything else, you know, Todhetley. And I want you to go off with me to Worcester. The gig's following me."

When we had somewhat collected our senses, and could look at the newspaper, there was the account as large as life. Samson Reginald Dene had been had up before the magistrates on Thursday morning on a charge of stealing a small box of carved ebony, containing sixty guineas in gold, from the dwelling house of Lawyer Cockermuth; and he was to be brought up again that day, Saturday, for examination.

"A preety thing this is to see, when a man opens his weekly newspaper at his breakfast-table?" gasped Jacobson, flicking the report with his angry finger. "I'll have the law of them—accusing *my* nephew of such a thing as that! You'll go with me, Squire!"

"Go! of course I'll go!" returned Squire, in his hot partisanship. "We were going to Worcester, any way; I've things to do there. Poor Sam! Hanging would be too good for the printers of that newspaper, Jacobson."

Mr. Jacobson's gig was heard driving up to the gate at railroad speed; and soon our own carriage was ready. Old Jacobson sat with the Squire, I behind with Giles; the other groom, Blossom, drove. Tod in the gig; and away we went in the blustering March wind. Many people, farmers and others, were on the road, riding or driving to Worcester market.

Well, we found it was true. And not the mistake of the newspaper: they had but reported what passed before the magistrates at the town hall.

The first person we saw was Miss Cockermuth. She was in a fine way, not knowing what to think or believe, and sat in the parlour in that soft green gown of twilled silk (that might have been a relic of the silk made in the time of the Queen of Sheba), her cap and front all awry. Rumour said old Jacobson had been a sweetheart of hers in their young days; but I'm sure I don't know. Any way they were very friendly with one another, and she sometimes called him "Frederick." He sat down by her on the horsehair sofa, and we took chairs.

She recounted the circumstances (ramblingly) from beginning to end. Not that the end had come yet by a long way. And—there it was, she would up, when the narrative was over: the box had disappeared, just for all the world as mysteriously as it disappeared in the days gone by.

Mr. Jacobson had listened patiently. He was a fine, upright man, with a healthy colour and bright dark eyes. He wore a blue frock-coat to-day with metal buttons, and top-boots. As yet he did not see how they had got grounds for accusing Sam, and he said so.

"To be sure," cried the Squire. "How's that, Miss Betty?"

"Why, it's this way," said Miss Betty—"that nobody was here in the parlour but Sam when the box vanished. It is my brother Charles who had done it all; he is so passionate, you know. John has properly quarrelled with him for it."

'It is not possible, you know, Miss Betty, that Sam Dene could have done it," struck in Tod, who was boiling over with rage at the whole thing. "Some thief must have stolen in at the street door when Sam had left the room."

"Well, no, that could hardly have been, seeing that Charles never left the street door after that," returned Miss Betty, mildly. "It appears to be a certain fact that not a soul entered the room after the young man left it. And there lies the puzzle of it."

Putting to be as Miss Betty put it—and I may as well say here that nothing turned up, then or later, to change the opinion—it looked rather suspicious for Sam Dene. I think the Squire saw it.

"I suppose you are sure the box was on the table when you left the room, Miss Betty?" said he.

·"Why, of course I am sure, Squire," she answered. "It was the last thing my eyes fell on; for, as I went through the door, I glanced back to see that I had left the table tidy. Susan can bear witness to that. Dutton, the police-sergeant, thinks some demon of mischief must be in that box—meaning the deuce, you know. Upon my word it looks like it."

Susan came in with some glasses and ale as Miss Betty spoke, and confirmed the testimony—which did not need confirmation. As she closed the parlour-door, she said, after her mistress had passed out, she noticed the box standing on the table.

"Is Sam here to-day—in the office?" asked Mr. Jacobson.

"Oh, my goodness, no," cried Miss Betty in a fluster. "Why, Frederick, he has not been here since Thursday, when they had him up at the Guildhall. He couldn't well come while the charge is hanging over him."

"Then I think we had better go out to find Sam, and hear what he has to say," observed Mr. Jacobson, drinking up his glass of ale.

"Yes, do," said Miss Betty. "Tell poor Sam I'm as sorry as I can be—pestered almost out of my mind over it. And as to their having found one of the guineas in his pocket, please just mention to him that I say it might have slipped in accidentally."

"One of the guineas in Sam's pocket!" exclaimed Mr. Jacobson, taken aback.

"Well, I hear so," responded Miss Betty. "The police searched him you see."

As the Squire and Mr. Jacobson went out, Mr. Cockermuth was coming in. They all turned into the office together, while we made a rush to Sam Dene's lodgings in Edgar Street: as much of a rush, at least, as the Saturday's street would let us make. Sam was out, the young servant said when we got there, and while parleying with her Mrs. Parslet opened her sitting-room door.

"I do not suppose Mr. Dene will be long," she said. "He has to appear at the town hall this morning, and I think it likely he will come home first. Will you walk in and wait?"

She handed us into her parlour, where she had been busy, marking sheets and pillow-cases and towels with "prepared" ink; the table was covered with them. Tod began telling her that Mr Jacobson was at Worcester, and went on to say what a shame it was that Sam Dene should be accused of this thing.

"We consider it so," said Mrs. Parslet, who was a capable, pleasant-speaking woman, tall and slender. "My husband says it has upset Mr. Cockermuth more than anything that has occurred for years past. He tells his brother that he should have had it investigated privately, not have given Mr. Dene into custody."

"Then why did he let him do it, Mrs Parslet?"

She looked at Tod, as if surprised at the question. "Mr. Cockermuth knew nothing of it; you may be sure of that. Captain Cockermuth had the young man at the Guildhall and was preferring the charge, before Mr. Cockermuth heard a word of what was agate. Certainly that is a most mysterious box! It seems fated to give trouble."

At this moment the door opened, and a young lady came into the parlour. It was Maria. What a nice face she had!—what sweet, thoughtful eyes!—what gentle manners! Sam's friends in the town were accusing him of being in love with her—and small blame to him.

But Sam did not appear to be coming home, and time was getting on. Tod decided not to wait longer, and said good-morning.

Flying back along High Street, we caught sight of the tray of Dublin buns, just put fresh on the counter in Rousse's shop, and made as good a feast as time allowed. Some people called them Doubling buns (from their shape, I take it), and I don't know to this day which was right.

Away with fleet foot again, past the bustle round the town hall, and market house, till we came to the next confectioner's and saw the apple-tarts. Perhaps somebody remembers yet how delicious those apple-tarts were. Bounding in, we began upon them.

While the feast was in progress, Sam Dene went by, walking very fast. We dashed out to catch him. Good Mrs. Mountford chanced to be in the shop and knew us, or they might have thought we were decamping without payment.

Sam Dene, in answer to Tod's hasty questions, went into a passion; swearing at the world in general, and Captain Cockermuth in particular, as freely as though the justices, then taking their places in the Guildhall, were not as good as within earshot.

"It is a fearful shame. Todhetley!—to bring such a charge against me, and to lug me up to the criminal bar like a felon. Worse than all, to let it go forth to the town and county in to-day's glaring newspapers that I, Sam Dene, am a common thief!"

"Of course it is a fearful shame, Sam—it's infamous, and all your friends know it is," cried Tod, with eager sympathy. "My father wishes he could hang the printers. I say, what do you think has become of the box?"

"Become of it!—why, that blundering Charles Cockermuth has got it. He was off his head with excitement at its being found. He must have come into the room and put it somewhere and forgotten it: or else he put it into his pocket and got robbed of it in the street. That's what I think. Quite off his head, I give you my word."

"And what fable is it the wretches have got up about finding one of the guineas in your pocket, Sam?"

"Oh, bother that! It was my own guinea. I swear it—there! I can't stay now," went on Sam, striding off down High Street. "I am due at the town hall this minute; only out on bail. You'll come with me."

"You go in and pay for the tarts, Johnny," called back Tod, as he put his arm within Sam Dene's. I looked in, pitched a shilling on the counter, said I didn't know how many we had eaten; perhaps ten; and that I couldn't wait for change."

Crushing my way amidst the market women and their baskets in the Guildhall yard, I came upon Austin Chance. His father held some post connected with the law, as administered there, and Austin said he would get me in.

"Can it be true that the police found one of the guineas about him?" I asked.

Chance pulled a long face. "It's true they found one when they searched him—"

"What right had they to search him?"

"Well, I don't know," said Austin, laughing a little; "they did it. To see perhaps whether all the guineas were about him. And I am afraid, Johnny Ludlow, that the finding of that guinea will make it rather hard for Sam. It is said that Maria Parslet can prove the guinea was Sam's own, and that my father has had a summon's served on her to appear here to-day. He has taken Sam's case in hand; but he is closer than wax, and tells me nothing."

"You don't think he can have stolen the box, Chance?"

"I don't. I shouldn't think him capable of anything so mean; let alone the danger of it. Not but that there are circumstances in the case that tell uncommonly strong against him. And where the deuce the box can have got to, otherwise, is more than mortal man can guess at. Come along."

Not for a long while had Worcester been stirred as it was over this affair of Samson Dene's. What with the curious discovery of the box of guineas after its mysterious disappearance of years, and then its second no less mysterious loss, with the suspicion that Sam Dene stole it, the Faithful City was so excited as hardly to know whether it stood on its head or its heels.

When the police searched the prisoner on Thursday morning, after taking him into custody, and found the guinea upon him (having been told that he had one about him), his guilt was thought to be as good as proved. Sam said the guinea was his own, an heirloom, and stood to this so indignantly resolute that the police let him have it back. But now, what did Sam go and do? When release upon bail by the magistrates—to come up again on the Saturday—he went straight off to a silversmith's, had a hole stamped in the guinea and hung it to his watch-chain across his waistcoat, that the public might feast their eyes upon it. It was in this spirit of defiance—or, as the town call it, bravado—that he met the charge. His lodgings had been searched for the rest of the guineas, but they were not found.

The hour for the Saturday's examination—twelve o'clock—was striking, as I struggled my way with Austin Chance through the crush round the Guildhall. But that Austin's father was a man of consequence with the door-keepers, we should not have got in at all.

The accused, arraigned by his full name, Samson Reginald Dene, stood in the place allotted to prisoners, cold defiance on his handsome face. As near to him as might be permitted, stood Tod, just as defiant as he. Captain Charles Cockermuth, a third in defiance, stood opposite to prosecute; while lawyer Cockermuth, who came in with Sam's uncle, Mr. Jacobson, openly wished his brother at Hanover. Squire Todhetley, being a county magistrate, sat on the bench with the City magnates, but not to interfere.

The proceedings began. Captain Cockermuth related how the little box, his property, containing sixty golden guineas, was left on the table in a sitting-room in his brother's house, the accused being the only person in the room at the time, and that the box disappeared. He, himself (standing at the front-door), saw the accused quit the room; he went into it almost immediately, but the box was gone. He swore that no person entered the room after the prisoner left it.

Miss Betty Cockermuth, flustered and red, appeared next. She testified that she was in the room nearly all the morning, the little box being upon the table; when she left the room, Mr. Dene remained in it alone, copying a letter for her brother; the box was still on the table. Susan Edwards, housemaid at Lawyer Cockermuth's spoke to the same fact. It was she who had fetched her mistress out, and she saw the box standing upon the table.

The accused was asked by one of the magistrates what he had to say to this. He answered, speaking freely, that he had nothing to say in contradiction, except that he did not know what became of the box.

"Did you see the box on the table?" asked the lawyer on the opposite side, Mr. Standup.

"I saw it there when I first went into the room. Miss Betty made a remark about the box, which drew my attention to it. I was sitting at the far end of the room, at Mr. Cockermuth's little desk-table. I did not notice the box afterwards."

"Did you not see it there after Miss Cockermuth left the room?"

"No, I did not; not that I remember." answered Sam. "Truth to say, I never thought about it. My attention was confined to the letter I was copying, to the exclusion of everything else."

"Did any one come into the room after Miss Cockermuth left it?"

"No one came into it. Somebody opened the door and looked in."

This was fresh news. The town hall pricked up its ears.

"I do not know who it was," added Sam. "My head was bent over my writing, when the door opened quickly, and as quickly shut again. I supposed somebody had looked in to see if Mr. or Miss Cockermuth was there, and had retreated on finding they were not."

"Could that person, whomsoever it might be, have advanced to the table and taken the box?" asked the chief of the magistrates.

"No, sir. For certain, no!"—and Sam's tone here, he best knew why, was aggravatingly defiant. "The person might have put his head in—and no doubt did—but he did not set a foot inside the room."

Captain Cockermuth was asked about this: whether he observed any one go to the parlour and look in. He protested till he was nearly blue with rage (for he regarded it as Sam's invention), that such a thing never took place, that no one whatever went near the parlour-door.

Next came up the question of the guinea, which was hanging from his watch-guard, shining and bold as if it had been brass Sam had been questioned about this by the justices on Thursday, and his statement in answer to them was just as bold as the coin.

The guinea had been given him by his late father's uncle, old Thomas Dene, who had jokingly enjoined him never to change it, always to keep it by him, and then he would never be without money. Sam had kept it; kept it from that time to this. He kept it in one pocket of an old-fashioned leather case, which contained some letters from his father, and two or three other things he valued. No, he was not in the habit of getting the guinea out to look at, he had retorted to a little badgering; had not looked at it (or at the case either, which lay in the bottom of his trunk) for months and months—yes, it might be years, for all he recollected. But on the Tuesday evening, when talking with Miss Parslet about guineas, he fetched it to show to her; and slipped in into his pocket afterwards, where the police found it on the Thursday. This was the substance of his first answer, and he related it now.

"Do you know who is said to be the father of lies, young man?" asked Justice Whitewicker in a solemn tone, suspecting that the prisoner was telling an out-and-out fable.

"I have heard," answered Sam. "Have never seen him myself. Perhaps you have, sir." At which a titter went round the court, and it put his worships's back up. Sam went on to say that he had often thought of taking his guinea into wear, and had now done it. And he gave the guinea a flick in the face of us all.

Evidently little good could come of a hardened criminal like this; and Justice Whitewicker, who thought nothing on earth so grand as the sound of his own voice from the bench, gave Sam a piece of his mind. In the midst of this a stir arose at the appearance of Maria Parslet. Mr. Chance led her in; her father, sad and shrinking as usual, walked behind them. Lawyer Cockermuth—and I liked him for it—made a place for his clerk next to himself. Maria looked modest, gentle, and pretty. She wore black silk, being in slight mourning, a dainty white bonnet.

Mr. Dene was asked to take tea with them in the parlour on the Tuesday evening, as a matter of convenience, Maria's evidence ran, in answer to questions, and she briefly alluded to the reason why. Whilst waiting together, he and she, for her father to come in, Mr. Dene told her of the finding of the ebony box of guineas at Mr. Cockermuth's. She laughingly remarked that a guinea was an out-of-date coin now, and she was not sure that she had ever seen one. In reply to that, Mr. Dene said he had one by him, given him by an old uncle some years before; and he went upstairs and brought it down to show to her. There could be no mistake, Maria added to Mr. Whitewicker, who wanted to insinuate a word of doubt, and her sweet brown eyes were honest and true as she said it; she had touched the guinea and held it in her hand for some moments.

"Held it and touched it, did you, Miss Parslet?" retorted Lawyer Standup. "Pray what appearance had it?"

"It was a thin, worn coin, sir," replied Maria; "thinner, I think, than a sovereign, but somewhat larger; it seemed to be worn thin at the edge."

"Whose image was on it?—what king's?"

"George the Third's. I noticed that."

"Now, don't you think, young lady, that the accused took this marvellous coin from his pocket, instead of from some receptacle above stairs?" went on Mr. Standup.

"I am quite sure he did not take it from his pocket when before me," answered Maria. "He ran upstairs quickly, saying he would fetch the guinea: he had nothing in his hand then."

Upon this Lawyer Chance inquired of his learned brother why he need waste time in useless questions; begging to remind him that it was not until Wednesday morning the box disappeared, so the prisoner could not well have had any of its contents about him on Tuesday.

"Just let my questions alone, will you," retorted Mr. Standup, with a nod. "I know what I am about. Now, Miss Parslet, please attend to me. Was the guinea you profess to have been a perfect coin, or was there a hole in it?"

"It was a perfect coin sir."

"And what became of it?"

"I think Mr. Dene put it in his waistcoat-pocket: I did not particularly notice. Quite close upon that, my father came home, and we sat down to tea. No, sir, nothing was said to my father about the guinea; if it was, I did not hear it. but he and Mr. Dene talked of the box of guineas that had been found."

"Who was it that called while you were at tea?"

"Young Mr. Chance called. We had finished tea then, and Mr. Dene took him upstairs to his own sitting-room."

"I am not asking you about young Mr. Chance; we shall come to him presently," was the rough-toned, but not ill-natured retort. "Somebody else called: who was it?"

Maria, blushing and paling ever since she stood up to the ordeal, grew white now. Mr. Badger had called at the door, she answered, and Mr. Dene went out to speak to him. Worried by Lawyer Standup as to whether he did not come to ask for money, she said she believed so, but she did not hear all they said.

Quiet Mr. Parslet was the next witness. He had to acknowledge that he did hear it. Mr. Badger appeared to be pressing for some money owing to him; could not tell the amount, new nothing about that. When questioned whether the accused owed him money, Parslet said not a shilling; Mr. Dene had never sought to borrow of him, and had paid his monthly accounts regularly.

Upon that, Mr. Badger was produced; a thin man with a neck as stiff as a poker; who gave his reluctant testimony in a sweet tone of benevolence. Mr. Dene had been borrowing money from him for some time; somewhere about twenty pounds, he thought, was owing now, including interest. He had repeatedly asked for its repayment, but only got put off with (as he believed) lame excuses. Had certainly gone to ask for it on the Tuesday evenings; was neither loud nor angry, oh dear no; but did tell the accused he thought he could give him some if he would, and did say that he must have a portion of it within a week, or he should apply to Mr. Jacobsen, of Elm Farm. Did not really mean to apply to Mr. Jacobson, had no wish to do any one an inury, but felt vexed at the young man's off-handedness, which looked like indifference. Knew besides that Mr. Dene had other debts.

Now I'll leave you to judge how this evidence struck on the ears of old Jacobson. He leaped to the conclusion that Sam had been going all sorts of ways, as he supposed he went when in London, and might be owing, the mischief only knew how much money; and he shook his fist at Sam across the justice-room.

Mr. Standup next called young Chance, quite to young Chance's surprise; perhaps also to his father's. He was questioned upon no end of things—whether the accused had shown any guinea to him when he was in Edgar Street on the Tuesday night. Austin answered that he believed Mr. Dene owed a little money, not a great deal, so far as he knew; and that he had not seen the guinea or heard of it. And in saying all this, Austin's tone was just as resentfully insolent to Mr. Standup as he dared to make it.

Well, it is of no use to go on categorically with the day's proceedings. When they came to an end, the magistrates conferred pretty hotly in a low tone amongst themselves, some apparently taking up one opinion, as to Sam's guilt, or innocence, and some the other. At length they announced their decision, and it was as follows.

"Although the case undoubtedly presents grave grounds of suspicion against the accused, Samsom Reginald Dene—'Very grave indeed,' interjected Mr. Whitewicker, solemnly—we do not consider them to be sufficient to commit him for trial upon; therefore, we give him the benefit of the doubt, and discharge him. Should any further evidence transpire, he can be brought up again."

"It was Maria Parslet's testimony about the guinea that cleard him," whispered the crowd, as they filed out.

And I think it must have been. It was just impossible to doubt her truth, or the earnestness with which she gave it.

Mr. Jacobson "interviewed" Sam, as the Americans say, and the interview was not a loving one. Being in the mood, he said anything that came uppermost. He forbade Sam to appear at Elm Farm again ever, as "long as oak and ash grew"; and he added that as Sam was bent on going to the deuce head foremost, he might do it upon his own means, but that he'd never get any more help from him.

The way the Squire lashed up Bob and Blister when driving home—for, liking Sam hitherto, he was just as much put out as old Jacobson—and the duet they kept together in abuse of his misdeeds, was edifying to hear. Tod laughed; I did not. the gig was given over this return journey to the two grooms.

"I do not believe Sam took the box, sir," I said to Jacobson, interrupting a fiery oration.

He turned round to stare at me. "What do you say, Johnny Ludlow? *You do not believe he took the box?*"

"Well, to me it seems quite plain that he did not take it. I've hardly ever felt more sure of anything."

"Plain!" struck in the Squire. "How is it plain, Johnny? What grounds do you go upon?"

"I judge by his looks and his tones, sir, when denying it. They are to be trusted."

They did not know whether to laugh or scoff at me. It was Johnny's way, said the Squire; always fancying he could read the riddles in a man's face and voice. But they'd have thrown up their two best market-going hats with glee to be able to think it true.

Samson Reginald Dene was relieved of the charge, as it was declared "not proven"; all the same, Samson Reginald Dene was ruined. Worcester said so. During the following week, which was Passion Week, its citizens talked more of him than of their prayers.

Granted that Maria Parslat's testimony had been honestly genuine, a theory cropped up to counteract it. Lawyer Standup had been bold enough to start it at the Saturday's examination: a hundred tongues were repeating it now. Sam Dene, as may be remembered, was present at the finding of the box on Tuesday; he had come up the passage and touched the golden guineas in it with the tips of his fingers; those fingers might have deftly extracted one of the coins. No wonder he could show it to Maria when he went home to tea! Captain Cockermuth admitted that in counting the guineas subsequently he had thought he counted sixty; but, as he knew there were (or ought to be) that number in the box, probably the assumption misled him, causing him to reckon them as sixty when in fact there were only fifty-nine. Which was a bit of logic.

Still, popular opinion was divided. If part of the town judged Sam to be guilty, part believed him to be innocent. A good deal might be said on both sides. To a young man who does not know how to pay his debts from lack of means, and debts that he is afraid of, too, sixty golden guineas may be a great temptation; and people did not shut their eyes to that. It transpired also that Mr. Jacobson, his own uncle, he best friend, had altogether cast Sam off and told him he might now go to the dogs his own way.

Sam resented it all bitterly, and defied the world. Far from giving in or showing any sense of shame, he walked about with an air, his head up, and that brazen guinea dangling in front of him. He actually had the face to appear at college on Good Friday (the congregation looking askance, at him and sat out the cold service of the day: no singing, no organ, and the little chorister-boys in black surplices instead of white ones.

But the crowning act of boldness was to come. Before Easter week had lapsed into the past, Sam Dene had taken two rooms in a conspicuous part of the town and set-up in practice. A big brass plate on the outer door displayed his name: "Mr. Dene, Attorney-at-law." Sam's friends extolled his courage; Sam's enemies were amazed at his impudence. Captain Cockermuth prophesied that the ceiling of that office would come tumbling down on its crafty occupant's head: it was *his* gold that was paying for it.

The Cockermuths, like the town, were divided in opinion. Mr. Cockermuth could not believe Sam guilty, although the mystery as to where the box could be puzzled him as few things had ever puzzled him in his life. He would fain have taken Sam back again, had it been a right thing to do. What the captain thought need not be enlarged upon. While Miss Betty felt uncertain; veering now to this belief, now to that, and much distressed either way.

There is one friend in this world that hardly ever deserts us—and that is a mother. Mrs. Dene, a pretty little woman yet, had come flying to Worcester, ready to fight everybody in it on her son's behalf. Sam of course made his own tale good to her; whether it was a true one or not he alone knew, but not an angel from heaven could have stirred her faith in it. She declared that, to her posivite knowledge, the old uncle had given Sam the guinea.

It was understood to be Mrs. Dene who advanced the money to Sam to set up with; it was certainly Mrs. Dene who bought a shutting-up bed (at old Ward's), and a gridiron, and a tea-pot, and a three-legged table, and a chair of two, all for the backroom of the little office, that Sam might go into house-keeping on his own account, and live upon sixpence a-day, so to say, until business came in. To look at Sam's hopeful face, he meant to do it, and to live down the scandal.

Looking at the thing impartially, one might perhaps see that Sam was not swayed by impudence in setting-up, so much as by obligation. For what else lay open to him?—no firm would engage him as clerk with that doubt sticking to his coat-tails. He paid some of his debts, and undertook to pay the rest before the year was out. A whisper arose that it was Mrs. Dene who managed this. Sam's adversaries knew better; the funds came out of the ebony box; that, as Charles Cockermuth demonstrated, was as sure as heaven.

But now there occurred one thing that I, Johnny Ludlow, could not understand, and never shall: why Worcester should have turned its back, like an angry drake, upon Maria Parslet. The school, where she was resident teacher, wrote her a cool, polite note, to say she need not trouble herself to return after the Easter recess. That example was followed. Pious individuals looked upon her as a possible story-teller, in danger of going to the bad in Sam's defence, nearly as much as Sam had gone.

It was just a craze. Even Charles Cockermuth said there was no sense in blaming Maria: of course Sam had decieved her (when pretending to show the guinea as his own), just as he deceived other people. Next the town called her "bold" for standing up in the face of eyes at the Guildhall to give her evidence. But how could Maria help that? It was not her own choice: she'd rather have locked herself up in the cellar. Lawyer Chance had burst in upon her that Saturday morning (not ten minutes after we left the house), giving nobody warning, and carried her off imperatively, never saying "Will you, or Won't you." It was not his way.

Placid Miss Betty was indignant when the injustice came to her ears. What did people mean by it? she wanted to know. She sent for Maria to spend the next Sunday in Foregate Street, and marched with her arm-in-arm to church (St. Nicholas'), morning and evening.

As the days and the weeks passed, commotion gave place to a calm; Sam and his delinquencies were let alone. One cannot be on the grumble for ever. Sam's line's were pretty hard; practice held itself aloof from him; and if he did not live upon the sixpence a-day, he looked at every halfpenny that he had to spend beyond it. His face grew thin, his blue eyes wistful, but he smiled hopefully.

"You keep up young Dene's acquaintance, I perceive," remarked Lawyer Chance to his son one evening as they were finishing dinner, for he had met the two young men together that day.

"Yes: why shouldn't I?" returned Austin.

"Think that charge was a mistaken one, I suppose?"

"Well I do, father. He has affirmed it to me in terms so unmistakable that I can but believe him. Besides, I don't think Dene, as I have always said, is the sort of fellow to turn rogue: I don't, indeed."

"Does he get any practice?"

"Very little, I'm afraid."

Mr Chance was a man with a conscience. On the whole, he felt inclined to think Sam had not helped himself to the guineas, but he was by no means sure of it: like Miss Betty Cockermuth, his opinion veered, now on this side, now on that, like a haunted weathercock. If Sam was not guilty, why, then, Fate had dealt hardly with the young fellow—and what would the end be? These thoughts were running through the lawyer's mind as he talked to his son and sat playing with his bunch of seals, which hung down by a short, thick gold chain, in the old-fashioned manner.

"I should like to say a word to him if he'd come to me," he suddenly cried. "You might go and bring him, Austin."

"What—this evening?" exclaimed Austin.

"Aye; why not? One time's as good as another."

Austin Chance started off promptly for the new office, and found his friend presiding over his own tea-tray in the little back-room; the loaf and butter on the table, and a red herring on the gridiron.

"Hadn't time to get any dinner to-day; too busy," was Sam's apology, given briefly with a flush of the face. "Mr Chance wants me? Well, I'll come, What is it for?"

"Don't know," replied Austin. And away they went.

They lawyer was standing at the window, his hands in the pockets of his pepper-and-salt trousers, tinkling the shillings and sixpences there. Austin supposed he was not wanted, and shut them in.

"I have been thinking of your case a good bit lately, Sam Dene," began Mr. Chance, giving Sam a seat and sitting down himself; "and I should like to feel, if I can, more at a certainty about it, one way or the other."

"Yes, sir," replied Sam. And you must please to note that manners in those days had not degenerated to what they are in these. Young men, whether gentle or simple, addressed their elders with respect; young women also. "Yes, sir," replied Sam. "but what do you mean about wishing to feel more at a certainty?"

"When I defended you before the magistrates, I did my best to convince them that you were not guilty: You had assured me you were not: and they discharged you. I believe my arguments and my pleadings went some way with them."

"I have no doubt of it, sir, and I thanked you at the time with all my heart," said Sam warmly. "Some of my enemies were bitter enough against me."

"But you should not speak in that way—calling people you enemies!" reproved the lawyer. "People were only at enmity with you on score of the offence. Look here, Sam Dene—did you commit it, or did you not?"

Sam stared. Mr. Chance dropped his voice to a solemn key, his head pushed forward, gravity sat on his face.

"No, sir. No."

The short answer did not satisfy the lawyer. "Did you filch tht box of guineas out of Cockermuth's room; or were you, and are you, as you assert, wholly innocent?" he resumed. "Tell me the truth as before Heaven. Whatever it be, I will shield you still."

Sam rose. "On my sacred word, sir, and before Heaven, I have told nothing but the truth. I did not take or touch the box of guineas. I do not know what became of it."

Mr. Chance regarded Sam in silence. He had known young men, when under cloud, prevaricate in a most extraordinary and unblushing manner; to look at them and listen to them, one might have said they were fit to be canonized. But he thought truth lay with Sam now.

"Sit down, sit down, Dene," he said. "I am glad to believe you. Where the deuce could the box have got to? It could not take flight through the ceiling up to the clouds, or down to the earth through the floor. *Whose hands took it?*"

"The box went in one of two ways," returned Sam. "If the captain did not fetch it out unconsciously, and lose it in the street, why, somebody must have entered the parlour after I left it and carried off the box. Perhaps the individual who looked into the room when I was sitting there."

"A pity but you had noticed who that was."

"Yes, it is. Look here, Mr. Chance; a thought has more than once struck me—if that person did not come back and take the box, why has he not come forward and openly and honestly to avow it was himself who looked in?"

The lawyer gave his head a dissenting shake. "It is a ticklish thing to be mixed up in, he may think, one that he had best keep out of—though he may be innocent as the day. How are you getting on?" he asked, passing abruptly from the subject.

"Oh, middling," replied Sam. "As well, perhaps, as I could expect to get on at first, with all the prejudice abroad against me."

"Earning bread and cheese?"

"Not quite—yet."

"Well, see here, Dene—and this is what I cheifly sent for you to say, if you could assure me on your conscience you deserved it—I may be able to put some little business in your hands. Petty matters are brought to us that we hardly care to waste time upon. I'll send them to you in future. I dare say you'll be able to rub on by dint of patience. Rome was not built in a day, you know."

"Thank you, sir; I thank you very truly," breathed Sam. "Mr. Cockermuth sent me a small matter the other day. If I can make a bare living of it at present, that's all I ask. Fame and fortune are not rained down upon black sheep."

Which was so true a remark as to need no contradiction.

May was nearing its close then, and the summer evenings were long and lovely. As Sam went forth from the interview, he thought he would take a walk by the river, instead of turning in to his solitary rooms. Since entering upon them he had been as steady as Old Time: the accusation and its attendant shame seemed to have converted him from a heedless, youthful man into a wise old sage of age and care. Passing down Broad Street towards the bridge, he turned to the left and sauntered along beside the Severn. The water glittered in the light of the setting sun; barges some of them bearing men and women and children, passed smoothly up and down on it; the opposite fields, towards St. John's, were green as an emerald: all things seemed to wear an aspect of brightness.

All of a sudden things grew brighter—and Sam's pulses gave a leap. He had passed the grand old red-stoned wall that enclosed the Bishop's palace and was close upon the gates leading up to the

Green, when a young lady turned out of them and came towards him with a light, quick step. It was Maria Parslet, in a pretty summer muslin, a straw hat shading her blushing face. For it did blush furiously at sight of Sam.

"Mr. Dene!"

"Maria!"

She began to say, hurriedly, that her mother had sent her with a message to the dressmaker on the Parade, and she had taken that way, as being the shortest—as if in apology for having met Sam.

He turned with her, and they paced slowly along side by side, the colour on Maria's cheeks coming and going with every word he spoke and every look he gave her—which seemed altogether senseless and unreasonable. Sam told her of his conversation with Austin Chance's father, and his promise to put a few things in his way.

"Once let me be making two hundred a year, Maria and then—"

"Then waht?" questioned Maria innocently.

"Then I should ask you to come to me, and we'd risk it together."

"Risk what?" stammered Maria, turning her head right round to watch a barge that was being towed by.

"Risk our luck. Two hundred a year is not so bad to begin upon. I should take the floor above as well as the ground-floor I rent now, and we should get along. Any way, I hope to try it."

"Oh, Mr. Dene!"

"Now don't 'Mr. Dene' me, young lady, if you please. Why, Maria, what else can we do? A mean, malicious set of dogs and cats have turned their backs upon us both; the least we should do is to see if we can't do without them. I know you'd rather come to me than stay in Edgar Street."

Maria held her tongue, as to whether she would or not.

"Mamma is negotiating to get me a situation at Cheltenham," she said.

"You will not go to Cheltenham, or anywhere else, if I get any luck," he replied dictatorily. "Life would look very blue to me now without you, Maria. And many a man and wife, rolling in riches at the end, have rubbed on with less than two hundred a year at the beginning. I wouldn't say, mind, but we might risk it on a hundred and fifty. My rent is low, you see."

"Ye—es," stammered Maria. "But—I wish that mystery of the guineas could be cleared up!"

Sam stood still, turned, and faced her. "Why do you say *that*? You are not suspecting that I took them?"

"Oh dear, no," returned Maria, losing her breath. "I *know* you did not take them: could not. I was only thinking of your practice: so much more would come in."

"Cockermuth, has sent me a small matter or two. I think I shall get on," repeated Sam.

They were at their journey's end by that time, at the dressmaker's door. "Good-evening," said Maria, timidly holding out her hand.

Sam Dene took it and clasped it. "Good-bye, my darling. I am going home to my bread and cheese supper, and I wish you were there to eat it with me!"

Maria sighed. She wondered whether that wonderful state of things would ever come to pass. Perhaps no; perhaps yes. Meanwhile no living soul knew aught of these treasonable aspirations; they were a secret between her and Sam. Mr. and Mrs. Parslet suspected nothing.

Time went on. Lawyer Chance was as good as his word, and put a few small matters of business into the hands of Sam Dene. Mr Cockermuth did the same. The town came down upon him for it; though it let Chance alone, who was not the sort of man to be dictated to. "Well," said Cockermuth in answer, "I don't believe the lad is guilty; never believed it. Had he been of a dishonest turn, he could have helped himself before, for a good deal of cash passed at times through his hands. And, given that he was innocent, he has been hardly dealt by."

Sam Dene was grateful for these stray windfalls, and returned his best thanks to the lawyers for them. But they did not amount to much in the aggregate; and a gloomy vision began to present itself to his apprehension of being forced to give up the struggle, and wandering out in the world to seek a better fortune. The summer assizes drew near. Sam had no grand cause to come on at them, or small one either; but it was impossible not to give a thought now and again to what his fate might have been, had he stood committed to take his trial at them. The popular voice said that was only what he merited.

The assizes were held, and passed. One hot day, when July was nearing its meridian, word was brought to Miss Cockermuth—who was charitable—that a poor sick woman whom she befriended, was worse than usual, so she put on her bonnet and cloak to pay her a visit. The bonnet was a huge leghorn, which shaded over her face well from the sun, its trimming of straw colour; and the cloak was of thin black "taffeta," edged with narrow lace. It was a long walk on a hot afternoon, for the sick woman lived but just on this side Henwick. Miss Betty had got as far as the bridge, and was about to cross it when Sam Dene, coming over it at a strapping pace, ran against her.

"Miss Betty!" he cried. "I beg your pardon."

Miss Betty brought her bonnet from under the shade of her large grass-green parasol. "Dear me, is it you, Sam Dene?" she said. "Were you walking for a wager?"

Sam laughed a little. "I was hastening back to my office, Miss Betty. I have no clerk, you know, and a client *might* come in."

Miss Betty gave her head a twist, something between a nod and a shake; she noticed the doubtful tone in the "might". "Very hot, isn't it?" said she. "I'm going up to see that poor Hester Knowles; she's uncommon bad, I hear."

"You'll have a warm walk."

"Aye. Are you pretty well, Sam? You look thin."

"Do I? Oh, that's nothing but the heat of the weather. I am quite well, thank you. Good-afternoon, Miss Betty."

She shook his hand heartily. One of Sam's worst enemies, who might have run in a curricle with Charles Cockermugh,as to an out-and-out belief in his guilt, was passing at the moment, and saw it.

Miss Betty crossed the bridge, turned off into Turkey, for it was through those classical regions that her nearst and coolest way lay, and so onwards to the sick woman's room. There she found the blazing July sun streaming in at the wide window, which had no blind, no shelter whatever from it. Miss Betty had had enough of the sun out-of-doors, without having it in. Done up with the walk and the heat, she sat down on the first chair, and felt ready to swoon right off.

"Dear me, Hester, this is bad for you!" she gasped.

"Did you mean the sun, ma'am?" asked the sick woman, who was sitting full in it, wrapped in a blanket or two. "It is a little hot just now, but I don't grumble at it; I'm so cold mostly. As soon as the sun goes off the window, I shall begin to shiver."

"Well-a-day!" responded Miss Betty, wishing she could be cool enough to shiver. "But if you feel it cold now, Hester, what will you do when the autumn winds come in?"

"Ah, ma'am, please do not talk of it? I just can't tell what I shall do. That window don't fit tight, and the way the wind pours in through it upon me as I sit here at evening, or lie in my little bed there, passes belief. I'm coughing always then."

"You should have some good thick curtains put up," said Miss Betty, gazing at the bare window, which had a pot of musk on its sill. "Woolen ones."

The sick woman smiled sadly. She was very poor now, though it had not always been so; she might as well have hoped to buy the sun itself as woolen curtains—or cotton curtains either. Miss Betty knew that.

"I'll think about it, Hester, and see if I've any old ones that I could let you have. I'm not sure; but I'll look," repeated she—and began to empty her capacious dimity pockets of a few items of good things she had brought.

By and by, when she was a little cooler, and had talked with Hester, Miss Betty set off home again, her mind running upon the half-promised curtains. "They are properly shabby," thought she, as she went along, "but they'll serve to keep the sun and the wind off her."

She was thinking of those warm green curtains that she had picked the braid from that past disastrous morning—as the reader heard of, and all the town as well. Nothing had been done with them since.

Getting home, Miss Betty turned into the parlour. Susan—who had not yet found leisure to fix any time for her wedding—found her mistress fanning her hot face, her bonnet untied and tilted back.

"I've been to see that poor Hester Knowles, Susan," began Miss Betty.

"Law, ma'am!" interposed Susan. "What a walk for you this scorching afternoon! All up that wide New Road!"

"You may well say that, girl: but I went Turkey away. She's very ill, poor thing; and that's a frightfully staring window of hers, the sun on it like a blazing fire, and not as much as a rag for a blind; and the window don't fit, she says, and in cold weather the biting wind comes in the and shivers her up. I think I might give her those shabby old curtains, Susan—that were up in Mr. Philip's room, you know, before we got the new chintz ones in."

"So you might, ma'am," said Susan, who was not a bad-hearted girl, excepting to the baker's man. "They can't go up at any of our windows as they be; and if you had'em dyed, I don't know as they'd answer much, being so shabby."

"I put them—let me see—into the spare ottoman, didn't I? Yes, that was it. And there I suppose they must by lying still."

"Sure enought, Miss Betty. "With all the trouble that got into our house at the time, I couldn't give my mind to seeing after the old things, and I've not thought about them since. Come upstairs with me now, Susan; we'll see what sort of a state they are in."

They went up; and Miss Betty took off her bonnet and cloak and put her cap on. The spare ottoman, soft, and red, and ancient, used as a receptacle for odds and ends that were not wanted, stood in a spacious linen-closet on the first-floor landing. It was built out over the back-door, and had a skylight above. Susan threw back the lid of the ottoman, and Miss Betty stood by. The faded old brown curtains, green once, lay in a heap at one end, just as Miss Betty had hastily flung them in that past day in March, when on her way to look at the chintzes.

"They're in a fine rabble, seemingly," observed Susan, pausing to regard the curtains.

"Dear me?" cried Miss Betty, conscience-stricken, for she was a careful housewife, "I let them drop in any way, I remember. I did mean to have them well shaken out of doors and properly folded, but that bother drove it all out of my head. Take them out, girl."

Susan put her strong arms underneath the heap and lifted it out with a fling. Something heavy flew out of the curtains, and dropped on the boarded floor with a crash. Letting fall the curtains, Susan gave a wild shriek of terror and Miss Betty gave a wilder, for the floor was sudenly covered with shining gold coins. Mr. Cockermuth, passing across the passage below at the moment, heard the cries, wondered whether the house was on fire, and came hastening up.

"Oh," said he coolly, taking in the aspect of affaris. "So the thief was you, Betty, after all!"

He picked up the ebony box, and bent his head to look at the guineas. Miss Betty sank down on a three-legged stool—brought in for Philip's children—and grew as white as death.

Yes, it was the missing box of guineas, come to light in the same extraordinary and unexpected manner that it had come beofre, without having been (as may be said) truly lost. When Miss Betty gathered her curtains off the dining-room table that March morning, a cumbersome and weighty heap, she had unwittingly gathered up the box with them. No wonder Sam Dene had not seen the box on the table after Miss Betty's departure! It was a grievous misfortune, though, that he failed to take notice it was not there.

She had no idea she was not speaking truth in sayng she *saw* the box on the table as she left the room. Having seen the box there all the morning she thought it was there still, and that she saw it, being quite unconscious that it was in her arms. Susan, too, had noticed the box on the table when she opened the door to call her mistress, and believed she was correct in saying she saw it there to the last; the real fact being that she had not observed it was gone. So there the box with its golden frieght had lain undisturbed, hidden in the folds of the curtains. But for Hester Knowles's defective window, it might have stayed there still, who can say how long?

Susan, no less scared than her mistress, stood back against the closet wall for safety, out of reach of those diabolical coins; Miss Betty, groaning and half-fainting on the three-legged stool ,sat pushing back her cap and her front. The lawyer picked up the guineas and counted them as he laid them flat in the box. Sixty of them: not one missing. So Sam's guinea *was* his own! He had not, as Worcester whispered, trumped up the story with Maria Parslet.

"John," gasped poor Miss Betty, beside herself with remorse and terror, "John, what will become of me now? Will anything be done?"

"How 'done'?" asked he.

"Will they bring me to trial—or anything of that—in poor Sam's place?"

"Well, I don't know," answered her brother grimly; "perhaps not this time. But I'd have you take more care in future, Betty, than to hide away gold in old curtains."

Locking the box securely within his iron safe, Mr. Cockermuth put on his hat and went down to the town hall, where the magistrates, after dispensing their wisdom, were about to disperse for the day. He told them of the wonderful recovery of the box of guineas, of how it had been lost, and that

Sam Dene was wholly innocent. Their worships were of course charmed to hear it, Mr. Whitewicker observing that they had only judged Sam by appearances, and that appearances had been sufficient (in theory) to hang him.

From the town hall, Mr. Cockermuth turned off to Sam's office. Sam was making a great show of business, surrounded by a table full of imposing parchments, but with never a client to the fore. His old master grasped his hand.

"Well, Sam, my boy," he said, "the tables have turned for you. That box of guineas is found."

Sam never spoke an answering word. His lips parted with expectation: his breath seemed to be a little short.

"Betty had got it all the time. She managed somehow to pick it up off the table with those wretched old curtains she had there, all unconsciously, of course, and it has lain hidden with the curtains upstairs in a lumber-box ever since. Betty will never forgive herself. She'll have a fit of the jaundice over this."

Sam drew a long breath. "You will let the public know, sir?"

"Aye, Sam, without the loss of an hour. I've begun with the magistrates—and a fine sensation the news made amidst 'em, I can tell you; and now I'm going round to the newspapers; and I shall go over to Elm Farm the first thing tommorow. The town took up the cause against you, Sam: take care it does not eat you now in its repentance. Look here, you'll have to come round to Betty, or she'll moan her heart out: you won't bear malice, Sam?"

"No, that I won't," said Sam warmly. "Miss Betty did not bear it to me. She has been as kind as can be all along."

The town did want to eat Sam. It is the custom of the true Briton to go to extremes. Being unable to shake Sam's hands quite off, the city would fain have chaired him round the streets with honours, as it used to chair its newly returned members.

Captain Cockermuth, sent for post haste, came to Worcester all contrition, beseeching Sam to forgive him fifty times a day, and wanting to press the box of guineas upon him as a peace-offering. Sam would not take it: he laughingly told the captain that the box did not seem to carry luck with it.

And then Sam's troubles were over. And no objection was made by his people (as it otherwise might have been) to his marrying Maria Parslet by way of recompense. "God never fails to bring good out of evil, my dear," said old Mrs. Jacobson to Maria, the first time they had her on a visit at Elm Farm. As to Sam, he had short time for Elm Farm, or anything else in the shape of recreation. Practice was flowing in quickly: litigants arguing, one with another, that a young man, lying for months under an imputation of theft, and then coming out of it with flying colours, must needs be a clever lawyer.

"But, Johnny," Sam said to me, when talking of the past, "there's one thing I would alter if I made the laws. No person, so long as he is only suspected of crime, should have his name proclaimed publicly. I am not speaking of murder, you understand, or charges of that grave nature; but of such a case as mine. My name appeared in full, in all the local newspapers, Samson Reginald Dene, coupled with theft, and of course it got a mark upon it. It is an awful blight upon a man when he is innocent, one that he may never quite live down. Suspicions must arise, I know that, of the innocent as well as the guilty, and they must undergo preliminary examinations in public and submit to legal inquiries: but time enough to proclaim who the man is when evidence strengthens against him, and he is committed for trial; until then let his name be suppressed. At least that is my opinion."

THE ADVENTURE OF THE FALLEN ANGELS

by Percival Wilde

First published in 1925

The atmosphere in the little room was electric. The explosion, one sensed rather than felt, would come soon.

From outside, far below in the street, came the occasional clatter of a belated taxi-cab. From above came the steady, unwinking glare of high-powered lights. The clock on the mantel, and the overflowing ash-trays, indicated the hour of two in the morning. Yet the men seated about the bridge table in the Himalaya Club, cutting in and out at the end of each rubber, played with a concentration that was apparently regardless of everything else.

Straker, so he asserted afterwards, had been on the verge of an apoplectic stroke since midnight. Billings clutched his cards in a nervous hand, and impatiently awaited the moment when the accusation would be made. Chisholm, who could watch the ticker spell out fluctuations which meant tens of thousands to him without turning a hair, bit the ends of his straggly moustache from time to time, and hoped that his exterior did not betray his excitement.

Like the others, Chisholm had absolute confidence in Anthony P. Claghorn—"Tony" Claghorn to his inmates—who, by his own admission, was an expert on everything having to do with games of chance; but, as the minutes stretched into hours, and as Claghorn, with not a wrinkle in his lofty brow, confined himself to smoking the best cigars that the Himalaya Club—and his hosts provided, and refrained from uttering a word, Chisholm's worries multiplied.

He could not assert that Tony had been an inattentive spectator. At nine, promptly, the game had begun. At nine, promptly, Tony had pulled up the most comfortable chair, and had anchored in it. At half-hourly intervals or thereabouts rubbers had ended, and the six players, cutting to determine the four to play next, had changed seats. Af half-hourly intervals or thereabouts Tony, without moving, had called for a fresh cigar.

At ten Chisholm had glanced at Tony questioningly. Tony had repied with an innocent stare. At intervals from then on to midnight, Straker, Billings, Hotchkiss, and Bell had glanced questioningly at the silent young man. He had given them glance for glance—but no satisfaction. Yet during the preceding afternoon Tony had discoursed eloquently upon the ease with which he would solve the mystery.

To be sure, it had been a mystery of Tony's own creating. Roy Terriss, the suspect, had not been looked upon as such until Tony, by a few well-chosen words, had called the attention of his club-mates to the fact that Roy was a remarkably consistent winner. Before that time it had been admitted that Roy was generally successful at bridge; that he enjoyed playing in an expensive game; and that the game was rarely, if ever, expensive for him. It was Tony who pointed out that Roy's gains, during a winter's play, probably mounted well up into five figures; and it was Tony who, without making direct accusations, had raised his eyebrows significantly at moments when that simple act was not altogether beneficial to Roy's reputation.

Having created the mystery, he had been invited to solve it. With becoming modesty he had accepted the task, and, after sitting solemnly through one five-hour session, had expressed a desire to sit through another. This wish granted, he had declared his intention of being present on yet a third occasion. The results had been painful to his friends, who, expecting they hardly knew what, had thrown caution to the winds, and had been divested of large sums by Terriss, who, knowing nothing at all of what was afoot, had played calmly, coldly, and with deadly precision.

Chisholm, indeed, had explained his own mistakes to Tony that very afternoon. "I'm a conservative player," he had asserted earnestly. "I follow the book. I know the rules, and I don't try to improve on them. I don't overbid, and, if the other fellow overbids, I'm a sharp at doubling. But when I'm expecting the whole game to blow up any minute, I can't put my mind on it, and I don't play like myself."

"Even at twenty-five cents a point?"

"What does twenty-five cents a point matter when I'm waiting for you to start the fireworks? Take that hand last night: it was good for three odd. I bid up to five. That wasn't like me, was it? Then Terriss doubled—that's what any sane, level-headed player would have done, holding his cards; and, instead of shutting up and taking my medicine like a little man, what did I do but re-double! Claghorn, I put it to you: was that the act of a normal man? Was that the kind of play you'd look for from me? Then the finesses didn't hold, and I got set for eight hundred pounds."

Tony smiled reminiscently. "That was a most instructive hand," he commented. "Now, if you had doubled his four instead of going up yourself——"

Chisholm cut him short with a growl.

"Look here," he pointed out succinctly, "we didn't get you into this to give us bridge lessons, you know. If we wanted lessons, we could get them for about a tenth of what his performance is costing us. You said there was something queer about the game. We're waiting to be shown, that's all."

At two o'clock, ten hours later, Chisholm was still waiting.

Billings, neat and dapper, a stickler for etiquette, had, upon this third evening, to his everlasting embarassment, been detected in a revoke. He had paid the penalty promptly—graciously; had, indeed, insisted upon its being exacted. But the look which he had given Tony had explained more eloquently than could any number of words how he had come to be guilty. And Hotchkiss, fumbling his cards nervously, had failed to cover an honour with an honour—with results which bulked large when the score was added.

And, at two o'clock, Billings and Hotchkiss, as well as Straker, Bell, and Chilsholm, were waiting—waiting.

The great moment, the long-anticipated moment, came when it was least expected. At two-fifteen the men had adjourned hopelessly. Chisholm was balancing the score; his confederates had already opened their cheque-books; Terriss, with folded arms, was waiting to learn the exact amount of his gains.

It was then that Tony flicked the ash from the tip of his cigar, and spoke. "Mr. Terriss is again the only winner," he murmured, as if to himself. "I wonder what he would say if I mentioned that the cards with which he has been winning are marked."

In an instant Terriss was on his feet.

"What did you say, Claghorn?" he thundered. "What did you say?"

Tony stood his ground stoutly. "I made the statement," he declared, "that you have been winning with marked cards." He took up the two packs that had been used in the bridge game, and balanced them in his hands. "I still make that statement."

"You——!" shouted Terriss, and dashed at him.

Chisholm thrust his bulk between.

"Take it easy, Terris," he suggested, "we all know what's been going on. Mr. Claghorn has been looking into things for us."

Terriss gazed around the circle of faces.

"What's this? A conspiracy?" he demanded.

Chisholm shook his head. "Terriss, you know us better than that. Bell, Hotchkiss, Straker, Billings—they've all got reputations to lose, not to mention me. We've asked Mr. Claghorn to investigate. That's all."

"And how is Mr. Claghorn qualified to pass upon such matters? What right has Mr. Claghorn to make accusations against me?"

A chorus answered him. Straker, it appeared, had been present upon a certain occasion when Tony had unmasked one Schwartz. Billings, who had been another witness of that feat, contributed details of the manner in which Tony had exposed a sharper at Palm Beach. Chisholm, a third witness, had half a dozen stories at his finger tips.

Tony Claghorn's career, it was evident from their testimony, had been one long succession of triumphs. His wake was dotted with discomfited cheats, prestidigitateurs, and imposters. Once put upon the scent, he had never failed to bring down his man.

With appropriate modesty Tony bowed his head while his friends detailed his triumphs. To be sure, the credit for each victory was wholly due to one Bill Parmelee, an unassuming countryman whose acquaintance Tony had made one summer; and Tony, not once, but a dozen times, had explained how his own contribution to the various episodes which had since become famous was of the slightest. But Tony's explanations must have lacked the convincing note, for his friends did not hesitate to trumpet his praises to the four corners of the earth.

That they should forget the quiet young man who had played the leading rôle was not unnatural; Parmelee, farmer and reformed gambler, cared nothing for advertising, and chose to remain out of sight. Almost mechanically his laurels descended upon Claghorn, who, despite his protestations, found the eminence thus forced upon him far from unpleasant.

When Terriss's monotonous success at bridge had come to Tony's attention, he had attempted to interest Parmelee in the matter. He had failed. Parmelee, Cincinnatus of gamblers, cared more for his blooded cattle than for fresh laurels. And he had not agreed entirely with Claghorn's conclusions.

"Tony, because a man's a winner, it doesn't follow that he's a cheat," he had pointed out.

"No, but in this case——"

"In any case," Parmelee had interrupted, "you must remember that for every dollar won by dishonest gambling, a thousand are probably won by honest play."

"You don't believe that!"

"I don't know whether I do or not. But that's what I like to think."

Tony's enthusiasm had been dampened, but not extinguished. After revolving the subject in his mind overnight, he had decided that he himself was entirely competent, and that Bill's confidence in human nature was, to say the very least, exaggerated. Wherefore, Tony had gallantly launched himself into the breach.

He smiled at Terriss across the table. Success was his, and its taste is sweet.

"Marked cards, Mr. Terriss," he repeated, "marked cards."

Terriss glanced at the set faces about him, and his assurance decreased visibly.

"I suppose," he flatered, "that it will be quite useless for me to say that I didn't know the cards were marked."

"Quite useless," said Tony.

"I won fairly and squarely, I played the game according to the rules."

"What's the good of arguing?" enquired Straker icily.

Terriss gazed about helplessly. "No; there's no good in arguing if you're all against me," he assented. "What do you expect me to do?"

"Make good."

"How?"

"Give back what you won."

Terriss snorted. "I'll be damned if I do," he declared.

"If you don't," said Chisholm, "you will forfeit your membership in this club."

And if I do," challenged Terriss, "will I hold on to it? Am I the kind of man whom you want to remain? What's the difference whether I give back my winnings or not—except me? I've been caught cheating, haven't I? that makes me an undesirable member by itself, doesn't it? Of course, I say that I played honestly: that's what you'd expect me to say. But, even if I give back my winnings, you won't believe me."

"It's the correct thing to do, Terriss," said Straker quietly.

"What does the correct thing matter to a man who has been caught cheating? No; if I'm to be hanged, I'd rather be hanged as a wolf than as a lamb." He took up the score, and surveyed the totals. "Gentlemen, you owe me money. Write your cheques."

"What?" gasped Chisholm.

"You've lost. Pay me."

"What about the marked cards?"

"Well, what about them? If there are marked cards, you may have profited by them yourself. Try and prove you didn't."

"I lost!" spluttered Chisholm, nearly speechless.

"What of that? If the cards hadn't been marked you might have lost still more. And that applies to all of us." With supreme self-confidence he beamed upon the players. "Pay me," he invited; "pay me, or I'll bring suit against every man jack of you. You see, I no longer have a reputation to lose, and it won't hurt me to go to court. But if you fellows think you will enjoy the publicity, if you look forward to seeing your names decorating the front pages of the newspapers, just try getting out of your debts."

Helplessly the conspirators turned to Tony. "What do you advise?" they asked as one man.

Tony shrugged his shoulders. "This is out of my department," he said modestly.

Straker glanced about keenly. "You know," he said brightly, "Terriss may be bluffing."

Terris grinned. "If that's what you think, why don't you call his bluff?"

There was a pause. Then Billings seized his pen and dashed off a cheque.

"Here you are," he said ungraciously, "I have a wife and two daughters. I can't afford to get mixed up in a scandal."

"Quite so," said Terriss. "I thought you'd see the point after I'd explained it to you."

One by one the men wrote cheques, and passed them to the lone winner. He pocketed them carefully, rose, surveyed the conspirator. "Gentlemen," he murmured, "I am about to leave you, to return to my poor but honest domicile. And I have one last request to make of you: don't tell anybody what happened in this room to-night; don't breathe a word of it to your closest friend."

Straker laughed aloud. "Won't we?" he cackled, "Oh, won't we? I'll make it my business to see that every man in this club knows just what took place in twenty-four hours!"

Terriss smiled ominously. "In that event, Straker," he warned, "don't pretend you're suprised when I bring suit for criminal libel."

"What?"

"Against each and every one of you." At the threshhold he paused. "I can't stop you from blackening my reputation among yourselves; you seem to have done that pretty thoroughly, anyhow. But let me hear that any one of you has dared to say a word against me outside of this room, and I'll hit back? By George, I will! I'll hit back, and I'll hit back hard! Marked cards! Who brought them into the game? Who profited by them? Who didn't profit by them?" A mocking smile hovered upon his lips as he opened the door. "Gentlemen, think it over! Before you do anything, think it over—and then don't do it!"

The latch clicked, and he was gone.

It was Billings who first broke an agonised silence. "Another such victory," he soliloquised, "and we'll all be broke. What do we do next, Claghorn?"

But that worthy, pausing only to light a fresh cigar, had prudently retreated to the threshhold.

"What do we do next, Claghorn?" Hotchkiss echoed.

Tony shrugged his shoulders. "This is out of my department," he said modestly.

Long, long after he had left, gently closing the door behind him, the conspirators sat round the table, comparing notes, exchanging advice, and sympathising with each other's misfortunes. But that, however interesting in itself, has nothing to do with this story.

II

There are always several ways of looking at a matter. A disinterested judge, for example, might hesitate to characterise the episode which we have recounted as a triumph for Mr. Anthony P. Claghorn. But Claghorn himself spoke of it as a triumph without question. He had set out to expose a sharper; he had succeeded. That the operation had been monstrously costly to his friends was not so important as the fact that it had attained its object. Tony, indeed, did not use stronger terms than "triumph" only because stronger terms did not occur to him.

To his pretty wife he related his exploit with gusto. She understood nothing of cards, but Tony wanted admiration, and her admiration was better than none. But the approbation which mattered most was that of Bill Parmelee, and to that Tony looked forward eagerly. Half a dozen times Tony had been a mystified spectator while Bill, moving along curious lines, had laid the foundations of one of his many victories. It had been Tony's part to observe, to wonder, and to applaud at the conclusion of each carefully planned campaign.

Now, Tony felt modestly, the roles were reversed. Without help from his friend, acting entirely upon his own initiative he—Tony—had brought his attack to a successful conclusion. It would be Bill's turn to listen while Tony condescended to explain. In the anticipation it was all very pleasant, and Tony lost no time in scurrying to the little town in which Parmelee had immured himself.

"I was satisfied that something was wrong," Tony began magisterially, "oh, long ago; ever so long ago."

"In spite of what I said?" Bill enquired.

"What did you say?" asked Tony tolerantly.

"I tried to convince you that a man can be a winner without being a cheat."

"Oh, yes; I remember that."

"I said that for every dollar won by dishonest gambling, a thousand are probably won by honest play."

"I remember that also," Tony admitted, and lighted a cigar, "but your faith in human nature is—shall we say—exaggerated? In this case the suspect—I'd rather not tell you his name—broke down and admitted everything."

"Well! Well!" said Bill. "Go on with your story."

"I investigated the case carefully. I used a process of elimination. The game was bridge. Certain methods of cheating were, therefore, useless."

"Quite correct."

"A hold-out, for example, would be of no value," said Tony, and went on to explain the nature of a hold-out to the man who had initiate him into its mysteries. "By a hold-out," he volunteered graciously, "I mean a device which can be used for the purpose of keeping one or more cards in concealment until the player wants them in his own hand."

Not a vestige of a smile was visible on Bill's placid countenance.

"I have heard there were such devices," he murmered.

"Quite so; but as I have explained to you, the suspect—whom I prefer not to call by name—could not possibly have used one. It would have meant introducing a fifty-third card into a complete deck, and that would have been detected at once. You see, if Ter— the suspect had introduced a fifth ace into his hand it would inevitably have duplicated an ace in some other hand. Whenever all the cards are dealt out, a hold-out becomes worthless."

Bill stared at the carpet intently. "Not altogether worthless," he qualified.

"Altogether worthless," Tony insisted.

"A hold-out might be used on the deal itself," murmured Bill, as if to himself. "The—ahem!—suspect might put all four aces and all four kings as well into a hold-out, offer the pack to be cut without them, and pass them into his own hand on the deal."

"What?" gasped Tony.

Bill continued unemotionally. "Of course, that would be pretty raw. Nobody but a beginner would try to get away with anything like that. A really sharp player, playing bridge, would pass the top cards into his partner's hand. His partner, you see, wouldn't have to be a confederate: give him more than his share of aces and kings, and he'd go a no-trumper, wouldn't he? In all innocence he'd make the correct bid. It would be quite enough for the sharper, sitting accross the table, to give him the cards warranting it."

"By George!" ejaculated Tony. "I never thought of that!"

"There are still other ways in which a hold-out might be used without duplicating any one of the fifty-two cards in the deck, but it's not necessary to discuss them. Go on, Tony."

It was with a sensation that the wind had been taken out of his sails that the young man continued. "Rightly or wrongly, I decided that the suspect was not using a hold-out. You don't think he was, Bill?" he interjected anxiously.

"No."

"I continued with my process of elimination. There are many cheating devices. In bridge most of them are useless. But one cheating device is useful in every card game." He paused, to aim a long forefinger at his friend. "I refer, of course, to marked cards."

"Ah-ha!"

"I examined the cards carefully. They were not marked. But I risked everything on a bold bluff," chortled Tony, "and it worked. I made one heap of all my winnings," he misquoted, 'and I risked it all on one pitch—on one pitch—I forget how it goes on."

"Cut out the poetry and tell me what happened."

"I picked the psychological instant. I've always been good at that—picking the psychological instant—and I boldy accused Ter—the suspect of using marked cards. I knew well enough he wasn't using them. Here"—and Tony produced the cards themselves from capacious pockets—"here they are—unmarked. But I understand human nature, and I felt sure that if I accused a cheat of cheating he would—ahem!—collapse. Whether or not I happened to mention the exact method he was using did not matter; the accusation would be enough."

"Did it work?"

"To perfection. Ter—the suspect was silent, and silence is confession."

Bill smiled. "Is it?" he queried. "If so, a sleeping man is guilty of anything and everything."

"The suspect knew the game was up."

"Perhaps he felt you were carrying too many guns for him. What was the use of pleading innocence when you—and your friends—were convinced he was guilty?"

"I made it a point to treat—ahem!—the suspect with scrupulous fairness."

"Why not call him by his name? Roy Terriss?"

"How did you know?" gasped Tony.

"That's neither here nor there. Go on."

But Tony was too astonished to continue. "How did you know?" he demanded. "How on earth did you know?"

Billy shook his head. "We'll skip that for the time being. Finish your story."

Tony gazed at his friend with some bewilderment. He had looked forward to this moment of triumph. In the realisation it was not so satisfactory as in prospect. He passed a shaky hand over his brow. "Perhaps you can finish the story yourself, Bill?"

"Perhaps I can. Terriss admitted nothing. Terriss denied nothing. He refused to give back the money he had won. That took nerve, and I admire him for it. He knew he had no chance of vindicating himself. He decided to wait for a better opportunity."

Tony nodded reluctantly. "Most of that's quite correct," he admitted grudgingly.

"You accused Terris of playing with marked cards. He replied that if the cards were marked he hadn't benefited by it. And he added what was, after all, a logical conclusion; that the marks might have been a value to your friends."

"Absurd on the face of it," commented Tony "The cards aren't marked."

"Not so absurd as you think," qualified Bill and his face set in stern lines. "The cards *are* marked."

Sometimes the word "surprise" is too feeble fully to express a state of mind. Indeed, to picture Tony's reaction to his friend's simple announcement in reasonably accurate terms, it would be necessary to overhaul, refurbish, and expand the English dictionary.

Tony gazed at Bill with eyes that popped out of his head, opened his mouth two or three times, wetted his lips, and sputtered, "Wh-what did you say?"

"I said," repeated Bill, "that these cards are marked."

"But they can't be!" exploded Tony. "Don't you see? That was the whole beauty of my bluff—that the cards were what they should be, and that I made him believe they were something else."

Bill smiled grimly. "Sometimes a bluff isn't a bluff. Sometimes a man shoots in the dark and hits the bull's-eye. Sometimes a well-meaning blunderer like you, Tony, tells the truth when he least suspects it."

"But it's impossible! I've examined those cards with a magnifying glass! I've gone over them not once, but a dozen times! I haven't found a thing!"

"Tony, you didn't know what to look for." Bill spread half a dozen cards on a convenient table. "In the first place, the cards are of an uncommon pattern. You notice the two little angels in the centre? They're what is known as 'Angel-Backs!'"

"They're the cards that the club supplies."

"I don't doubt that."

"For the last eight months no other cards have been used at the Himalaya."

"Then how about these?" Bill spread half a dozen cards from the second pack on the table.

Tony gave the cards, decorated with a conventional geometrical design, only a glance. "Oh, those? Those are poorer-class cards which the club laid in when it began to run short of the better ones."

"The Angel-Backs being the better class?"

"Of course. Your can see that in a minute."

Bill half-closed his eyes reminiscently.

"When I made my living as a gambler—when I was just beginning to learn the ropes—Angel-Backs were fairly common. They were good cards. They were high-priced, but they were worth it. They gradually dropped out of use; cheaper cards took their place. To-day people don't care about quality; it is price that matters. In fact, this pack of Angel-Backs is the first that I have seen in some years. I was under the impression that they were no longer being manufactured."

Tony could not restrain his impatience.

"Come back to the subject, Bill," he begged. "You said the cards were marked. Which pack? And how are they marked?"

"The Angel-Backs, of course. Look at the angels closely."

"I see nothing."

Bill smiled. "This angel, for example, must have gone walking in the mud. His right foot is not as clean as it might be."

"What of that?"

"This other angel evidently put one hand into the mud. You'll notice it's dirty. This third angel knelt in it: there's some on one of his knees. And this fourth angel must have been doing somersaults; you'll notice his complexion has become decidedly swarthy."

"By George!" ejaculated Tony.

"Go through the pack," invited Bill, "and you'll find that there isn't an angel in it who wouldn't be the better of a bath. And you'll find—it's a pure coincidence, doubtless—that the kings have marks on their right shoulders, the queens marks on their left shoulders, the jacks marks at the waist-line, and so on throught the lot. The angels are small—and the marks are still smaller—but they're very evident when you're looking for them."

Without a word Tony whipped ot a magnifying glass, and bent over the cards. "You're right!" he said excitedly; "you're right. And that proves my case beyond a doubt."

"What do you mean?"

"Terriss was using marked cards. My guess hit the nail on the head. Terris marked the cards while the game was under way."

"Marked them as delicately as this? As accurately? Tony, don't you believe it!"

"But cards can be marked during the progress of a game."

"Yes—with a prick, or with a spot of colour. But to mark cards like this? To select a minute speck on the back of each, and dot is as neatly as these are dotted? That takes time, skill, and privacy. The man who marked those cards did it in his room."

"You mean Terriss brought the marked pack with him, and substituted it for one we were using?"

"Not likely."

"Why not? It could have been done."

"It's most improbable. You'll notice that every card in the pack is marked—not the high cards alone."

"What of that?"

"What would be the object—in bridge? Really fine players place the cards as far down as the sevens and eights. But who ever heard of taking a finesse against a three-spot? Or a four? Or a five? Why should any sane man take the trouble—and the risk—to mark them?"

Tony corrugated his brow. "Perhaps," he hazarded, "perhaps the man who marked the cards who keen on doing a thorough job. Having begun, he didn't know when to stop."

Bill shook his head decisively.

"It won't do, Tony. It won't do at all. An amateur might have done that—you might have done that at a first attempt—but the man we are looking for is a professional, or I know nothing about gambling and gamblers. Look at the colour of the backs! And, remember, if he marked the twos and threes there was a good reason."

Tony shrugged his shoulders. "Reason or no reason, I can't see that it's of any particular importance."

But Bill was already studying a time-table. "The next train for town leaves in forty minutes," he mentioned. "I'm going to pack my bag."

Tony gazed at him with surprise.

"Going to town because the twos and threes are marked? Really, I think you're exaggerating their importance."

"It would be difficult to do that," said Bill. He rose and glanced keenly at his friend. "In the first place, they prove that Roy Terriss is innocent."

"How so?"

"I have been given to understand that he plays no other game than bridge."

"Yes; that's so."

"Well, the man who marked these cards didn't expect to play bridge at all. That's my second point, Tony. The man who marked these cards didn't neglect the little ones for the soundest reason in the world."

"And what's that?" asked Tony scornfully.

Bill opened his valise, and began to jam articles of clothing into it. He glanced at his friend and smiled, opened his mouth to speak, closed it, and smiled again. "Tony, hasn't it struck you yet?" he demanded at length. "The man who marked these cards expected to play poker!"

Upon every other occasion that Parmelee had accompanied him to town Tony had been filled with happy anticipation. It had meant, invariably that the man-hunt was on in earnest; that a pursuit which would end only with the exposure of the guilty individual was under way. In the past Tony—a privileged spectator, knowing enough to whet his curiosity to the utmost, but never knowing quite as much as he wanted to—had enjoyed a long succession of happy thrills.

Not once, but half a dozen times, had he observed Parmelee picking up a scent like a well-trained bloodhound, disentangling it from others, following it to a surprising conclusion. Tony had watched, wondered, admired; here was drama, hot off the griddle, served in the most appetising fashion, and the clubman, whose chief entertainment, in earlier days, had been provided by the headlines of the senational newspapers, had come to learn that a thrill at first hand was worth a dozen relayed through print. It had all been most enjoyable—yet Tony, upon this particular occasion, was conscious of no pleasurable feelings.

He gazed gloomily out of the window and gave himself up to unhappy reflections. the cards had been marked; Terris was not the guilty man. Both facts, Tony was compelled to admit, were crystal clear. It followed, as night follows day, that the criminal must be one of his own particular cronies: Chisholm, Billings, Hotchkiss, Bell, or Straker. Tony reviewed the list to the accompaniment of the click of the wheels. Man-hunting, he admitted, was a sport which eclipsed all other sports; but somehow it lost its zest when the prospective victim was one of his own friends.

After half an hour's gloomy meditation he turned to the quiet countryman at his side. "Bill," he ventured tentatively, "I take it that when you reach town you will want to go to the Himalaya Club."

"You take it correctly."

"It's not necessary, you know."

"Why not?"

"Well, really, I haven't asked you to investigate anything."

"That's all right, old fellow," Bill responded heartily; "I haven't waited to be asked."

Tony's voice carried a gentle tinge of reproof. "Don't you think," he enquired tactfully, "that you should wait until you are asked?"

Bill laughed. "Meaning, I suppose, that I'm butting in——"

"I wouldn't say that."

"No: but it's what you're thinking." He glanced shrewdly at Claghorn. "Tony, old fellow, you shot in the dark, and you brought down the wrong man. You have branded Roy Terris a crooked gambler—a cheat, a thief—a man unfit to be received in decent society. Do you want him to rest under that cloud?"

"No, no, indeed," began Tony vociferously, "that's not what I mean at all——"

"Of course not," Bill chimed in; "you're too fair and square to tolerate anything like that. You want Terris cleared—cleared triumphantly—only"—and Bill smiled shrewdly—"only you're rather scared that I'm going to fix the blame on one of your very best friends. Isn't that so?"

Tony nodded.

Bill grinned. "That's what might happen, no doubt. I'm not denying it. If I merely wanted to bag a man, and didn't care how I did it, I think I could convict any one of your friends—or you yourself, for that matter."

"Convict me?" gasped Tony.

"It could be done. How did you come by those marked cards?"

"Why, why, I took them from the table."

"How did they get there? How do I know you didn't mark them yourself? How do I know that you and your friends weren't banded together to rob Terriss?"

It was Tony's turn to grin. "Well, we lost."

"To Terriss, perhaps. But the night before the same crowd won pretty heavily from somebody else—what?"

"How did you know that?"

"It doesn't matter," said Bill; "I know it—that's enough. I'm simply trying to show you how easy it would be to find a victim if I were after no more than that. You and your friends have touched pitch, Tony, and you can't touch pitch without being defiled."

Tony's brain whirled. "You mean, then," he sputtered, "you mean that the guilty man is Chisholm—or Billings—or Straker—or Bell—or Hotchkiss—or—or me?"

Bill laughed. "If it will comfort you—and I think it will—I'll let you into a secret, and tell you that I don't suspect any of them—or you, I mean," he corrected gravely.

Tony felt a crushing weight rising buoyantly, easily, happily. "Do you mean that?" he cried.

"We're looking for a professional cheat," said Bill. "Remember that. Hold fast to that. It's the only thing, Tony, between you yourself and the deep sea. You've been worrying about your friends so much that you've completely overlooked what a suspicious character somebody else is."

"Who?" begged Tony.

"Tony Claghorn," said Bill—he smiled at his friend's consternation—"Tony Claghorn has been running around with me so much that he has acquired a first-hand knowledge of cheating devices. How do you know he hasn't used that knowledge? How do you know he hasn't tried to covert theory into practice? It would be profitable—very profitable—and he might get away with it. No, Tony," said Bill, "Roy Terriss is safe. It's Tony Claghorn we have to look after now. And if I'm going to town it's because I think I see a chance to save his skin."

Tony was to completely dumbfounded that he was silent for the rest of the trip.

It was between hours at the Himalaya Club when the two men walked in. The regulars, who ate their lunch in the raftered dining-hall every day, had departed, and the even-more regulars, who experimented with games of chance in its card-room from late afternoon until early morning, had not yet arrived.

"We'd better go away and come back later," said Tony.

"Why not wait here?" suggested Bill. He seated himself at a table. "Tony, how would you like to play some cold hands?"

Tony gazed at his friend with a suspicious eye. "What stake?" he enquired.

"Why any stake at all?' countered Bill. "We'll play for nothing—and the fun of it."

Tony assented doubtfully. Ordinarily filled with implicit trust in his friends, his adventure on the train had sadly shook his equilibrium. He—Tony—was under suspicion. Any move of Bill's might therefore be dangerous to him. In some vague, incomprehensible manner disaster threatened—with the most innocent exterior.

With noticeable lack of enthusiasm he seated himself at the table and rang for cards.

Bill glanced at the box and did not open it. "I don't care for these cards," he announced. "Can't we have some Angel-Backs?"

"I'll see, sir," said the man.

Tony's suspicions redoubled. "What's the matter with the cards," he inquired.

"I like to play with cards of better quality," the countryman alleged. His eyes shone as the waiter returned with a pack of the required pattern.

He broke the seal, opened the box, and riffled the cards throughtfully.

"Do you like these better?" Tony asked.

"Much better. Very much better." He dealt the cards, face down, with amazing speed. "king of hearts. Two of diamonds. Eight of hearts. Ace of spades. Three of clubs. Seven of spades. Ten of hearts. Seven of clubs. Five of hearts. Seven of hearts."

"What's this?" demanded Tony—"legerdemain?"

Bill shrugged his shoulders. "Call it what you like. But if you will look at your cards you will find that you have a four-flush in hearts. You will fill on the draw. The card on top of the pack is another heart."

"And you?" gasped Tony.

"Triplets; nothing but triplets," smiled Bill; "three sevens."

"And they'll be four of a kind on the draw?"

"That would be too raw, old fellow. No, a full house will be enough. That will beat your flush."

Tony broke into a roar of laughter. "I see it!" he cried. "Of course I see it!"

"What do you see?"

"You stacked the cards!"

"That's pretty evident."

"And they weren't hard to stack because you substituted the marked pack—the pack I brought up to the country—for the new pack the waiter handed you!"

"Is that so?" challenged Bill.

"These cards are marked!"

"They must be the same pack, unless—unless——"

"Well, say it."

"Unless," faltered Tony, with cold seat breaking out suddenly on his brow, "unless every pack of Angel-Backs in the club is marked!"

Bill smiled. "That's what I'm trying to find out," he granted. "They may all be—shall we say?—Fallen Angels."

Without a word Tony rang for the waiter. "We want another pack—two more packs—of Angel-Backs,"he snapped.

The waiter shook his head. "Sorry, sir, I can't do it."

"Why not?"

"We're running very short of the Angel-Backs, and the members prefer them to the other cards. They're better quality.The steward instructed me not to give out more than one pack to a party."

Tony extracted a banknote from his pocket. "I want two packs of Angel-Backs,"he repeated. "Do you understand?"

"I'll do what I can," said the waiter. He was back in a few minutes with a single pack. "I couldn't get you two,"he apologised. "There's not a gross left, sir. I'm breaking orders as it is, sir."

In silence Tony passed the unopened box to his friend. "Open it, Bill."

Parmelee put his hands behind his back. "Open it yourself. You might accuse me of substituting another pack."

Without a word Tony broke the seal, inverted the box, and allowed the cards to cascade upon the table.

"Well?" bill enquired.

"Marked—marked; every blamed one of them!"

"Fallen Angels!" murmured Parmelee, "Fallen Angels! Tony, don't you think we might have a chat with the steward?"

Tony clenched his fists. "If he's the man who marked them I'll see that he's out of a job in ten minutes!"

"Why so excitable?" soothed Bill. "What would the steward have to gain by trickery? He isn't the man we want, you can depend upon that."

He listened quietly while his explosive friend summoned the steward, and explained the state of affairs to that worthy. The man examined the cards, paled, bit his lips. "Really, sir," he stammered, "this is most surprising—most surprising——"

"It is!" asseverated Tony.

"I wouldn't believe it if I didn't see it with my own eyes. It's monstrous—incredible!"

"How do you explain it?"

"I—I don't."

"How do we know that you're not the guilty man?"

"Oh, sir, I've been in the employ of this club for twenty-eight years! It would be late in life for me to turn round and become a common cheat. Really, sir, you don't think that I could be capable of such a thing?"

Bill broke into the conversation. "How many more packs of Angel-Backs have you?"

"Less than a gross?"

"Why didn't you order more?"

"I did. The jobber couldn't fill my orders."

"Oh!" Bill half closed his eyes. "When did you first buy Angel-Backs?"

"About a year ago, sir. Shall I tell you about it?"

"I wish you would."

"A sample pack was sent us by a mail-order house. The International Supply Company, they called themselves."

"What was their address?"

"A post-office box at Times Square Station, New York City, sir."

"Go on."

"Samples are sent to us frequently, but this sample was unusually good."

"Angel-Backs—I should think so!"

"Not only that, but the cards were remarkably cheap; so cheap, in fact, that the club could sell them at the same price as inferior cards and still make money."

"Didn't that make you suspicious?"

"The International Supply Company explained that the pattern was about to be discontinued, and that they had a large quantity on hand. If we would take them all, they would make us a special price, sir. I didn't make the purchase on my own responsibility. I referred the matter to the House Committee. They told me to go ahead."

"What else?"

"That's all, sir. The members liked the cards, as I explained they would. We used nothing else for many months. Then the Angel-Backs began to run short. I tried to buy more."

"Your letters to the International Supply Company were returned unclaimed?"

"Yes sir. They had gone out of business."

Bill smiled. "The scent becomes more interesting as we follow it." He turned to his friend. 'Tony, what's the next move?"

"To examine the rest of the cards, of course."

Bill's eye twinkled, but he nodded soberly. "Suppose you do that, Tony. There are over a hundred packs left, so it will take time. But be thorough about it: go through every pack, and tabulate your results in writing."

After his volcanic friend had departed Bill motioned the steward to a chair at this side. "I have a good many questions to ask you," he began, "but Mr. Claghorn is safely out of the way for at least an hour. He will examine every pack of Angel-Backs in the store-room, and he will find every card marked." The steward waited for him to continue. "In the first place, the membership of this club changes rapidly, doesn't it?"

"What do you mean, sir?"

"New members are elected—old members resign, or become inactive."

"More frequently than I like. Yes, sir."

"At a rough guess, how many members, very active a year ago, are inactive to-day?"

"Twenty, perhaps," said the steward."

"Write their names on a piece of paper."
The man did so.

"Play for high stakes is common here?" pursued Bill.

"It is a rule, sir."

"But not all of the twenty played poker."

"No, sir."

"Scratch out the names of those who played other games. That leaves how many?"

"An even dozen, sir."

"Now let us take another angle. There have been big winners in the club during the past year?"

"Yes, sir. At least eight or ten."

"How many of them did their winning at poker?"

"Five or six."

"Write down their names. Compare the two lists. How many of the big winners—at poker—do you find among the inactive members?"

"Only one, sir."

"That's easy to explain, isn't it? A big winner doesn't become inactive. A big winner sticks to the game just as long as he continues winning."

"Naturally, sir."

"Yet one man who was a big winner—at poker—didn't wait for his luck to change. He stopped coming to the club."

The steward nodded. "That always puzzled me, sir. He played poker, and he had the reputation of being the strongest player that ever sat down to a table in these rooms. He played nearly every night for six months——"

"And then?"

"I never could understand it, sir, but he simply stopped coming."

Bill looked keenly at the other. "Was this man—by some curious coincidence—elected to membership just about a year ago?"

The steward nodded with dawning comprehension. "He was, sir. Mr. Ashley Kendrick was proposed one week after I had purchased the Angel-Backs. the Membership Committee has always been notoriously lax; it's easy to get into the Himalaya. Mr. Kendrick was elected five days after his name had been posted."

"He played poker?"

"Yes, sir."

"With the Angel-Backs?"

"Yes, sir."

"And he won?"

"Then, six months later, when the cards began to run short, he stopped coming?"

"Oh, no sir."

"What do you mean?"

"He stopped coming; that part's correct, sir. But at the tme we hadn't begun to run short of Angel-Backs."

Bill whistled. "This gets more interesting as we go along!"

"We were using nothing but Angel-Backs at that time; the supply was very plentiful. Mr. Kendrick simply failed to show up one evening—that was all."

"You had his address?"

"Yes, sir, but it was an address which won't help. His address was right here—in care the Himalaya Club."

"No forwarding address, I suppose?"

"None needed, sir. From the moment he joined until the last evening he spent here Mr. Kendrick never received a letter."

It was at this juncture that Tony Claghorn thrust his exuberant self into the picture. "Bill" he announced, "I've examined the Angel-Backs."

"All of them? So soon?"

"It wasn't necessary to look at ore than a card or two from each pack. They're all marked."

He had expected his announcement to produce a sensation. He was disappointed.

"Yes; I expected to hear that," said Bill camly. "In the meantime, I've been busy."

Tony, I've run up a blind alley. I've found out something, but it doesn't help—not a darn bit. I'm stumped. I found the trail getting hotter and hotter, and I followed it. I fetched up against a blank wall."

"If you had allowed me to help you," Tony declared, "that wouldn't have happened."

"Perhaps not. Perhaps not."

"It's not too late now," invited Tony.

Bill grinned ruefully. "All right, Tony. Show me how to lay my hands on a fellow named Ashley Kendrick."

"Ashley Kendrick? Ashley Kendrick? Why, he hasn't been in here for months."

"I know that already."

"I can't tell you how to reach him, but I can put you in touch with his best friend."

"Also a member of this club?"

"He used to be," said Tony. "He's a chap by the name of Venner; a nice chap, but the unluckiest there ever was."

Bill glanced at the steward. "Is his name on your list of inactives?"

"Yes, sir."

"But not on the list of winners?"

"No, sir. As Mr. Claghorn says, Mr. Venner was—unfortunate."

Bill sucked on his breath sharply. "I wonder . . . I wonder . . . if by any chance his misfortunes began bout the time that the Angel-Backs started to run short."

The steward started. "Come to think of it, they did, sir."

Bill leaped to his feet and flung his arms above his head with excitement unusual for him. "What a fool I was! What a dunderhead! What a numbskull! I should have seen it at once! I should have guessed it right off! Why, it's as plain as the nose on a man's face!"

Tony neither understood nor shared his enthusiasm. "I don't see what you're driving at."

"Don't you see how Venner explains everything?"

Tony fixed a lok of mild reproach upon him. "Bill," he cautioned, "don't let me hear you say a word against Venner! He's a fine a fellow as there ever was—even if his luck turned—and I don't see how he explains anything."

By a superhuman effort Bill composed his face, and seated himself again. "Sorry, Tony. Perhaps I was too enthusiastic. But tell me about Venner; tell me all about him."

Tony stood on his dignity. "I don't see what Venner has to do with this case."

"All right, you don't see," said Bill, controling his impatience with difficulty, "but tell me what I want to know, anyhow."

Tony had acknowledged his friend's authority too long to shake it off easily. "If you insist——"

"I do."

"Then I'll tell you; though I warn you in advance that it won't help you at all." He bent a searching look on the steward. "This must go no further," he warned. "This is to remain a secret among the three of us."

"I shan't say a word, sir. But if you'd prefer to have me go away——"

Magnanimously Tony shook his head.

"Inasmuch as I suspected you, you have a right to listen." He turned to Parmelee. "Bill," he began, "Venner joined the club something less than a year ago—a fine fellow—a gentleman every inch of him."

"Go on."

"He played poker. I played with him myself any number of times. He rarely played for high stakes—that is, in the beginning. He played a fair game—broke a little better than even. Then, to his misfortune, he met Kendrick.

"Of course, I needn't tell you about Kendrick, one of the best poker players I ever saw; a man who could almost read you mind; who always played in the biggest game, and kicked because it wasn't bigger. Venner met Kendrick, and was fascinated by him. He gave up laying himself to watch Kendrick play: he said he had never seen anything so wonderful. And Kendrick used to like it; Kendrick always saved a chair near him for Venner.

"The two came to be close friends. You'd never see one without the other. Kendrick seemed to like teaching Venner; and Venner's eyes never left Kendrick. And when the game broke up they'd go away together. Kendrick used to live here in the club. For a time, I believe, Venner shared Kendrick's rooms.

"Then, one night Kendrick didn't show up, and Venner acted as if he had lost the best friend he had in the world. He hovered round the table at which Kendrick used to play; he kept his eyes on the door as if Kendrick might come through in any minute; he asked every man he met if he had seen Kendrick.

"For a week Venner watched. He told more than one of us that he suspected Kendrick had met with foul play. Then he gave him up for lost."

Parmelee's eyes were fixed on vacancy.

"It was then that Venner took Kendrick's place in the game—the big game?"

"Yes, it was an asinine thing to do, but Venner thought he had learnt enough from Kendrick to fill his boots. He did—for a night or so. He won—won heavily—and then his luck turned. He'd win one evening. He'd lose twice as much the next. He'd win a thousand—and lose three. He'd win two thousand—and lose five.

"I urged him to stop. I urged hm any number of times, but he always explained that out of ordinary courtesy he couldn't. He had won from the other fellows. He had to do the fair thing by giving them a chance for revenge."

Tony paused and nodded gravely.

"That's what Venner did; a chivalrous, gentlemanly, insane performance. Don't you think so?"

Bill turned to the steward. "What do you think?" he enquired.

"After twenty-eight years in the employ of this club I have learnt that there are times when it is wiser not to think."

Bill nodded. "I can understand how you lasted twenty-eight years." He turned to Tony. "Finish your story."

Tony lowered his voice. "I'm coming to the part I want kept secret. Venner lost. Venner lost every cent he had. Venner had to stop coming to the club. He was posted for non-payment of dues."

"Where is he now? And what is he doing?"

"Never tell a soul, will you? Venner's down and out. He's had to take a job as a waiter in a cheap restaurant, and I have to ruin my digestion by having a meal there every once in so often."

Parmelee grinned and cast a grateful glance at his friend. "Tony, you've helped! You have no idea how you've helped!" He rose and deliberately winked at the steward. "Are you good at riddles?"

"What's the riddle, sir?"

"This is a hard one. See if you can guess it." Gravely he propounded: "if a farmer, twenty-five years old, lives in Connecticut, goes to New York on the midday train, spends the afternoon at the Himalya Club, and then, because he has a cast-iron digestion, has his dinner at a cheap restaurant, what—what is the waiter's name?"

"Venner, sir," said the steward promptly.

"Go to the head of the class," said Bill.

While Parmelee and his much-mystified friend proceed to a frowsy, second-class eating-place on lower Eighth Avenue, there to be served by one Venner, there to corral the said Venner in an untidy, private dining-room, there to tempt the said Venner with promises of immunity and gradually increasing amount of currency until his silent tongue becomes exceedingly loquacious, let us turn back the pages of time two years to the very beginning of an exceedingly strange story.

The day was unbearably hot and sultry. Layers of heated air, writhing and twisting like heavy oil in their ascent, floated lazily upwards from the broiling streets. The aspehlt itself was soft and gummy; choking dust, the accumulation of a rainless week, lay in ambush to take suffering humanity by the throat; and in innumerable windows sickly geramiums dropped and wilted under the merciless rays of the sun.

A thermometer, hung at street level, would have indicated a temperature well into the nineties. The same thermometer, carried up five flights of stairs in any one of the nearby tenements would gradually have registered higher and higher figures, until, under the metallic roof, assailed from above by the burning glare of the win, and from below by the out-pour of scorching air, it would actually have indicated a temperature in excess of one hundred. Yet the man who bent over a little table in the inferno known as a hall bedroom, in the topmost storey of one of the most dilapidated buildings in the section, was too intent upon his labours to notice such minor matters as the weather.

His single window was closed, its inside covered with soap, so that no observer across the street might peer through it. His door was locked—not merely locked, but barricaded by pieces of furniture which had been moved against it. And, despite the heat, for not a breath of air travelled through the room, a kettle, placed on a portable oil-stove, boiled briskly at the man's elbow.

On the table below before which he sat, paper cartons—dozens and scores of them—were stacked in orderly fashion until they rached the ceiling. At this right-hand was a saucer containing a reddish liquid with an alcoholic odour. At his left-hand was a second saucer containing a bluish liquid. Half a dozen minute camel's hair brushes were carefully ranged before him. And, as if the weather and the stove and the tightly closed openings had not made the room hot enough, a high-powered electric light was suspended from a cord, casting a blinding glare upon the man's hands, and upon the objects which were engrossing his attention.

He rose, removed a carton from the huge pile, and, holding it dexterously, allowed the stream from the boiling kettle to hiss upon the paper seal. The carton flew open. With delicate care he set it upon the floor and emptied it of its contents: an even gross of individually sealed small paper boxes. Each steel in turn was held for an instant in the jet of escaping steam; each gave way almost instantly.

The man placed the open boxes at one side, seated himself again, and, wiping his hands carefully so that no moisture from them might make a mark, shook one of the boxes, and removed from it a new pack of playing-cards. He spread them out on the table, took up one of his brushes, dipped it in the coloured liquid, and, with the expertness gained by long practice, placed a microscopic dot on the back of each card.

Had an observer been present he would have noted that the colour applied matched the back of the card perfectly; stranger yet, he would have noted that after the minute spot of moisture had dried the closest scrutiny would have been required to show that the card had been tampered with. While moist, the tiny speck of liquid was visible; when dry, it blended with the surrounding colour so excellently that no person unacquainted with the secret would have been able to discover a mark.

During his manipulations the man had been careful not to disturb the order of the cards: factory-packed playing-cards are always arranged in the same manner. He examined six or eight cards closely, satisfied himself that the marks which he had made were indistinguishable, levelled the pack, and returned it to its box. For a second time he held the seal in the jet of steam. Then he closed the flap, pressed the seal so that it adhered again, and laid the box to one side.

A dozen cartons under the table represented the labour of several weeks. Working at the greatest speed which he would permit himself, his output did not exceed ten packs an hour—and each carton contained a gross of packs—and the huge pile before him numbered at least several hundred cartons. Had he paused to calculate he might well have been terrified at the result: ten packs an hour; eighty to a hundred a day; at the very best, not more than five gross a week. And nearly a year would elapse before he might reach the completion of his gigantic task.

Presumably, the man had made his calculations before commencing; had estimated the expenditure of time, and had decided that it was worth his while, for he paused not an instant upon finishing one pack before beginning on another. He worked rapidly yet carefully, with a concentration which might have been explained only had a slave-driver, with a ship, been standing behind him. Practice had brought him surprising skill. There was no waste motion; no misdirected energy. Little by little the pile of unfinished work diminished; little by little the pile of finished work grew.

At seven o'clock, or thereabout, he extinguished the oil-stove, drew a clean white sheet over the mountain of cartons, washed, and made himself presentable, and went out, padlocking the door of his room behind him. Other tenants of the building, gathered at the entrance for a breath of air, nodded to him as he strode by them. "Good evening, Mr. Kendrick," they choroused.

"Good evening," said Kendrick, and went on his way—to a lunch-room round the corner.

"What's he do for a living?" enquired one of the neighbours.

"He's a literary man," said one better informed."

"A which?"

"A literary man. He writes novels and books and stories. Locks himself in his room from morning till night, and writes—just writes. He told me so himself. Keeps regular hours, just like a working man, too."

"That ain't work—just writing," commented a listener, and broke off to enquire. "Have you ever read anthing he's wrote?"

"Not yet. He says there'll be nothing of his published for a year. But he's going to let me now when something comes out."

Let us dive headlong for the end of that year. The pile of unfinished work had shrunk—finally vanished. The little room was filled with neatly stacked cartons, which one might have examined and sworn had never been opened. And the International Supply Company—alias Kendrick—having offered samples of superior quality playing-cards at ruinous prices to three clubs, equally notorious for the size of the games played under their roofs, and for the ease with which a stranger might secure membership, had arranged to sell the entire quantity to the Himalaya.

The following day a horse-drawn truck, specailly hired for the occasion, and personally drive by the International Supply Company—alias Kendrick— delivered several hundred gross of marked cards to the Himalaya club.

Within a week Mr. Ashley Kendrick was proposed for membership in the notorious organisation. He was elected five days later.

Within less than a month he was voted the best poker-player who had ever seated himself at one of the Himalaya's card-tables, and his former neighbours, who had looked forward to reading his books, novels and stories, waited a while—and then forgot him.

A gambler's paradise: a place where the play in continious, where the stakes are high, where the players are liberal, and where every card is marked. It was in such an unbelievably blissful spot that Kendrick now found himself. For a whole year he had worked and planned; for a whole year he had lived economically on his savings; if he was a length to be rewarded, he felt that he deserved it.

Yet he did not make the mistake of playing too well. An infallible player discourages his opponents, wheras an occasional loss is not expensive, and greatly heartens the victim. Kendrick, who knew every card in the pack, who could read his opponents' hands as readily as if they had been exposed, who could tell every time whether or not it was worth while to draw, could have won far more than he actually permitted himself to. Hardly an evening went by without Kendrick sustaining at least one sensational loss; hardly a session without his going down to defeat on at least one well-advertised hand. But never did the gambler rise from his seat poorer than when he had settled himself into it; never did the end of a session make it necessary for Kendrick to produce his cheque book.

He limited himself strictly to a maximum winning, and his self-control was such that he never exceeded the fixed amount. yet the maximum was a liberal maximum, for at the end of ten days he had recouped himself for the expenditure of the proceding year, and at the end of three months his bank account had begun to assume formidable proportions.

At the end of four months he increased his maximum liberally, and doubled his bank account, and at the end of five months he began to fling off all restraint. He began to play poker of a brand unheard of even at the Himalaya,where fine players abounded. He had put by a gigantic nest-egg; and it was his programme to win as much as possible against the day when the Angel-Backs would begin to run short.

It was at this juncture that Venner, so he confessed to Parmelee, projected himself into the situation.

Venner, a shiftless ne-er-do-well of pleasing personality, had dissipated a modest inheritance, and was fast nearing the end of his slender resources. He played poker tolerably; upon occassion he had not hesitated to cheat, and, in the hope of extending his dishonest operations enough to make a killing, he had purchased half a dozen packs of cards at the club, and had taken them home with him with the laudable intention of marking them. Once marked, he would find opportunities to substitute them for the club's cards.

He had marked two or three packs before he made the astounding discovery that the cards were already marked. He could not believed the evidence of his eyes. Feverishly he broke open the sealed boxes, to find that some pioneer in knavery had been before him. More cards, covertly examined at the Himalaya itself, confirmed the amazing truth.

Venner had intended to indulge in cheating on a small scale. His discovery of the existence of a swindle of such gigantic dimentions left him simply thunderstruck. For an instant he reflected that, knowing the secret, he, too, could win as he pleased. But upon second thought it occurred to him that there would be quite as much gain, and far less risk, were he to make a cat's-paw of the daring sharper who was doubtless at work this instant.

For months Kendrick had been a sensational winner. Within twenty-four hours after penetrating his secret Venner confronted him.

"You can't prove anything," Kendrick said.

"I know it," said Venner.

"I'm the most surprised man in the world to learn that the cards are marked," Kendrick alleged.

"Then you won't object if I pass the word on to the other members, and see that other cards are used?"

Kendrick's eyes narrowed. Venner was easy for him to see through. "What's the alternative?" he demanded.

"Divvy up with me," murmered Venner. "Pay me half of whatever you win, and I'll be silent as the grave."

He paused. "If you don't, I'll expose you. I'll say that you confessed everything—"

"Nobody will believe it."

"If that's what you think, turn down my offer."

Kendrick was in an unpleasant position, and was fully aware of it. The solution—the solution that flashed upon him at once—was to pretend to accept Venner's terms, and to disappear for ever from the scene. But the weak point was painfully obvious: Venner, out of spite, might set the authorities upon his trail. It would be better, Kendrick decided instantaneously, to wait until Venner, too, was thoroughly besmirched; to make Venner an accomplice who dared not open his mouth without imperilling his own freedom. And then, also, even if he had to divide his future winnings, a great deal of money might be amassed in a short time—say, two or three weeks.

He shook Venner's hand heartily.

"You're a man after my own heart," he said. "I accept your proposition."

Then began the short but interesting period during which Venner, according to Tony's description, sat at Kendrick's side and ostensibly studied his game, but during which Venner, according to his own confession, followed the play with an eagle eye to make sure that his partner in crime did not win more than he would admit, and thus defraud him of his share.

After a few days Venner invited himself to live in Kendrick's rooms; he could keep a closer watch on him in that manner, and for two brief but happy weeks Venner's income was exceedingly large. He treated himself to a new outfit of clothing, and began to sport small but costly scarfpins. He even looked at automobiles; his improved circumstances would warrant him in purchasing one.

Then, upon the evening of the day that Venner, after convening himself in executive session, had voted that Kendrick should henceforth pay him three-quarters and not merely half of his winnings, the astute gambler disappeared. Venner was worried; honestly believed that his partner had met with foul play. At the end of a week a letter, mailed en route to Mexico City, told Venner the truth. Kendrick had disappeared for good. He had won enough to support him in comfort for the rest of his life. He did not propose to share his winnings, even with so likeable a chap as Venner. Nevertheless, he gave Venner his blessing, and mentioned that he admired Venner's collections of scarfpins, which he had taken to Mexico with him.

At once Venner found himself in straitened circumstances. His income had vanished; his expenditure continued. But the Angel-Backs promised relief.

He took Kendrick's place in the big game, and won heavily for two nights. On the third night, to his unutterable horror, cards of a strange pattern were used, and Venner, compelled to play honest poker against men who qualified as experts, lost more than he had won in the two preceding sessions.

On the fourth night the Angel-Backs returned, and Venner did well. But on the fifth and sixth nights other cards were supplied, and the results were harrowing.

What followed partook of the nature of a nightmare. Venner had run into debt; willing or unwilling, was compelled to play. And he was suddenly confronted with a situation far more dangerous than any that had ever faced Kendrick: the Angel-Backs were running short, other cards were being substituted, and, if Venner invariably won with the Angel-Backs and lost upon all other occasions, it would not be long before some astute observer called attention to the circumstance.

He used to lie awake at night, summoning up hideous pictures, visioning the possibilities. It occurred to him that he might purchase more Angel-Backs, mark them and introduce them into the play. He found that cards of that pattern were not obtainable at any price. Even had they been obtainable, he could not bring them to the table without inviting suspicious comment.

He thought of marking the cards which the club had substituted for the Angel-Backs; but he realised that the sleight-of-hand necessary to exchange them for the pack in use was far beyond him. In his petty cheating in the past he had occasionally indulged in the form of dishonesty known as ringing in a cold pack. That was possible, save for some sharper for more expert than he, in a big game closely watched by twenty or more men.

For a ghastly week Venner endured the tortues of the damned. Like Kendrick, he found it well to limit his winnings when the gods were good to him, and when chance brought a deck of marked cards to the table. But, unlike Kendrick, he was compelled too often to play with strange cards—and he found it quite impossible to limit his losings.

For all his sins in the past the cheat paid a thousand times over during that week. To put in an appearance each night, smiling and jovial, while his soul writhed in torment; to forego pot after pot when the Angel-Backs offered it to him, because to win too much might create suspicion; to lose upon other nights, and lose heavily—disastrously—because he dared not change his style of play; no wonder the man cracked under the strain.

He began to play wildly, recklessly. His opponents, shrewd students of psychology, sensed the change in the wind. In two consecutive sessions they stripped him.

Courtesy prohibits a man from taking another's last cigarette, but it does not prohibit a man from taking another's last dollar. His opponents showed him no mercy. When Venner left the Himalaya Club for the last time, he had borrowed as much as his friends would lend, he owned nothing, and his pockets were empty.

This, coming by driblets in the beginning, coming faster and faster as the man's emotions mastered him in the end, was the story that Parmelee and Claghorn heard him from the lips of one Venner, a waiter in a frowsy, second-class eating-place on lower Eighth Avenue.

IX

It was not until half an hour after they had left the restaurant, on their walk uptown, that Bill opened his mouth. Tony, completely floored, for once in his life, had marched at his side in silence.

"We started, didn't we," said Bill, "to find out whether or not Roy Terriss cheated at bridge? It's funny over what a long trail it has led us! Terriss—the Angel-Backs—the Himalaya—Kendrick—Venner—"

"Don't mention that man's name to me!" interrupted Tony.

"Why not?"

'When I think of what I've been doing to my digestion on his account: eating in that miserable restaurant at least once a week because I sympathised with him! Ugh!"

"Venner is a whole lot worse off, isn't he? You have been a guest of the restaurant; he is the waiter in it."

"Serves him right!"

"Perhaps. Perhaps. Something—call it what you will—has a great way of getting even with the man who doesn't play fair. Venner is paying—Venner is paying heavily. If you're a real man, Tony, you might go on eating a meal in that restaurant once in a while."

"Why?"

"Some day you may be able to set Venner on the right path, and that would be your way of paying whatever you owe. How about it Tony?"

"Er—I'll think about it."

Bill nodded his approval. "Pay! Pay! Pay! You can't get out of it!"

"No? How about Kendrick?"

"He'll be no exception. Think of the year's slavery he endured before he could bring off his coup! Think what he could have done—where he could have been to-day—had he applied the same energy to any honest pursuit!"

"He's living in luxury, in Mexico."

"Yes for six months, perhaps."

"He won enough to support him the rest of his life."

"Lots of gamblers have done that, but somehow the money doesn't last. Money made that way never lasts. Like the angels—the fallen angels—it has wings! An honest man can call on the law to protect his property. Kendrick can't. The moment the others find that out—in Mexico—what chance will he have? Bill shook his head vigorously. "No, of the two, I think Venner is the lucky one. He's alive, and I'll bet two to one this minute that Kendrick isn't. He worked too hard for his money to give it up alive; and in Mexico life is cheap—very cheap."

"Maybe," said Tony; "maybe." He thought hard for a minute. Then he turned to his friend. "From the very beginning I've never understood why you've been so keenly interested in this affair. What was it? Love of adventure?"

"Not after six years of drifting about the country, old fellow."

"Then what was it?"

Bill permitted himself the luxury of a smile. "As I told you this morning—it seems so long ago, doesn't it?—it was nothing but a friendly desire to save your reputation."

"My reputation," repeated Tony incredulously.

"That was all. You see, after you had exposed Terriss, it occurred to him that you were a pupil of mine, and he came straight to headquarters, with his troubles."

"He went to you?" gasped Tony.

"That is the thought I am trying to convey," Bill assented. "Terriss was innocent. You know that now. He knew it then, and he convinced me like a shot. He wanted to be vindicated, but that wasn't all; he was dead sure that if the cards were marked you had marked them yourself, and he wanted to see you—you and your friends—behind the bars! He is a clever man, a mighty quick-thinking man, and I'm pretty sure that if I hadn't taken the case he'd have turned the tables on you before now!"

Tony's face became purple. "But I'm innocent! You know I'm innocent!"

"Sometimes it's very hard to prove, Tony. Terriss was innocent, but he couldn't make you see it."

Tony swallowed hard. "My friends and I owe Terriss a handsome apology."

"You do!"

"I shall see that it is forthcoming. And, by the way, whatever fee you charge Terriss will be paid by me."

"Fair enough."

"Your expenses, too. Whatever they were. I will reimburse you."

Bill smiled. "Well, you heard me promise Venner a hundred dollars if he'd tell his story."

"I'll pay that."

"When you make out your cheque to Venner, make a mistake and slip an extra nought before the decimal point."

"Why on earth should I do that?" protested Tony.

"No reason at all," said Bill, "except that I'm sentimental. For a hundred dollars—a contemptible hundred dollars—Venner turned his soul inside out. I'm going to improve his self-respect by convincing him that his soul is worth at least a thousand."

Tony nodded. "I get your point. The cheque will read a thousand. And now, your fee."

"That will come high."

"I expect that."

"Terriss expected it too, the quick-thicking devil! He insisted on your friends paying up because he wanted plenty of ready money on hand to satisfy me."

Tony smiled. His finances had taken a turn for the better since he had followed his friends' example and had become merely a spectator, and not a participant, in games of chance. His bank account had become plethoric, and the knowledge was pleasant.

"Bill," he said, "you can't frighten me. Name what you want."

"It will come hard."

"If it does, it's worth it."

"All right, Tony, here goes." Bill stretched out his hand. "Pay me fifty-two Angel-Backs—fifty-two marked cards—fifty-two Fallen Angels. I'm going to nail them to the walls of my bedroom as a souvenir!"

AUTHOR'S NOTE:

The central episode of this story, extraordinary as it is, is founded on facts recounted by the celebrated Robert Houdin.

Bianco, a Spanish sharper, marked an immense number of playing-cards, resealed them in their original boxes, and sold them to clubs in Havana at bargain-counter prices. Following his cards to Cuba, he won large sums of money.

Everything went well until a second sharper, Laforcade, a Frenchman, wishing to mark cards for his own uses, took home a quantity, and, to his astonishment, discovered that they were already marked. Knowing of Bianco's sensational successes, Laforcade quickly satisfied himself that the Spaniard was the guilty man, and, instead of exposing him, invited him to share his winnings.

To this proposal Bianco reluctantly acceded, but, tiring of it after some months, disappeared. Laforcade, left to shift for himself, lacked Bianco's expertness, was detected cheating, and was arrested. At his trial it was proved that Laforcade had not marked the cards, and that he had not imported them; it was impossible to prove that he was aware the cards were marked. The prosecution broke down, and Laforcade was acquitted.

In his turn, Laforcade vanished, and neither he nor Bianco was ever heard of again.　　P. W.

THE GHOST AT MASSINGHAM MANSIONS

by Ernest Bramah

First published in 1923

"Do you believe in ghosts, Max?" inquired Mr. Carlyle.

"Only as ghosts," replied Carrados with decision.

"Quite so," assented the private detective with the air of acquiescence with which he was wont to cloak his moments of obfuscation. Then he added cautiously: "And how don't you believe in them, pray?"

"As public nuisances—or private ones for the matter," replied his friend. "So long as they are content to behave as ghosts I am with them. When they begin to meddle with a state of existence that is outside their province—to interfere in business matters and depreciate property—to rattle chains, bang doors, ring bells, and predict winners, and to edit magazines—and to attract attention instead of shunning it, I cease to believe. My sympathies are entirely with the sensible old fellow who was awakened in the middle of the night to find a shadowy form standing by the side of his bed and silently regarding him. For a few minutes the disturbed man waited patiently, expecting some awful communication, but the same profound silence was maintained. 'Well,' he remarked at length, 'if you have nothing to do, I have,' and turning over went to sleep again."

"I have been asked to take up a ghost," Carlyle began to explain.

"Then I don't believe in it," declared Carrados.

"Why not?"

"Because it is a pushful, notoriety-loving ghost, or it would not have gone so far. Probably it wants to get into the *Daily Mail*. The other people, whoever they are, don't believe in it, either, Louis, or they wouldn't have called you in. They would have gone to Sir Oliver Lodge for an explanation, or to the nearest priest for a stoup of holy water."

"I admit that I shall direct my researches towards the forces of this world before I begin to investigate any other," conceded Louis Carlyle. "And I don't doubt," he added, with his usual bland complacence, "that I shall hale up some mischievous or aggrieved individual before the ghost is many days older. Now that you have brought me so far, do you care to go on round to the place with me, Max, to hear what they have to say about it?"

Carrados agreed with his usual good nature. He rarely met his friend without hearing the details of some new case, for Carlyle's practice had increased vastly since the night when chance had led him into the blind man's study. They discussed the cases according to their interest, and there the matter generally ended so far as Max Carrados was concerned, until he casually heard the result subsequently from Mr Carlyle's lips or learned the sequel from the newspaper. But these pages are primarily a record of the methods of the one man whose name they bear and therefore for the occasional case that Carrados completed for his friend there must be assumed the unchronicled scores which the inquiry agent dealt capably with himself. This reminder is perhaps necessary to dissipate the impression that Louis Carlyle was a pretentious humbug. He was, as a matter of fact, in spite of his amiable foibles and the self-assurance that was, after all, merely an asset of his trade, a shrewd and capable business man of his world, and behind his office manner nothing concerned him more than to pocket fees for which he felt that he had failed to render value.

Massingham Mansions proved to be a single block of residential flats overlooking a recreation ground. It was, as they afterwards found, an adjunct to a larger estate of similar property situated down another road. A porter, residing in the basement, looked after the interests of Massingham Mansions; the business office was placed among the other flats. On that morning it presented the appearance of a well-kept, prosperous enough place, a little dull, a little unfinished, a little depressing perhaps; in fact faintly reminiscent of the superfluous mansions that stand among broad weedy roads on the outskirts of overgrown seaside resorts; but it was persistently raining at the time when Mr. Carlyle had his first view of it.

"It is early to judge," he remarked, aftger stopping the car in order to verify the name on the brass plate, "but, upon my word, Max, I really think that our ghost might have discovered more appropriate quarters."

At the office, to which the porter had directed them, they found a managing clerk and two coltish youths in charge. Mr. Carlyle's name produced an amiable flutter.

"The governor isn't here just now, but I have this matter in hand," said the clerk with an easy air of responsibility—an effect unfortunately marred by a sudden irrespressible giggle from the least overawed of the colts. "Will you kindly step into our private room?" He turned at the door of the inner office and dropped a freezing eye on the offender. "Get those letters copied before you go out to lunch Binns," he remarked in a sufficiently loud voice. Then he closed the door quickly, before Binns could find a suitable retort.

THE GHOST AT MASSINGHAM MANSIONS

So far it had been plain sailing, but now, brought face to face with the necessity of explaining, the clerk began to develop some hesitancy in beginning.

"It's a funny sort of business," he remarked, skirting the difficulty.

"Perhaps," admitted Mr. Carlyle; "but that will not embarrass us. Many of the cases the pass through my hands are what you would call 'funny sorts of business.' "

"I suppose so," responded the young man, "but not through ours. Well, this is at 11 Massingham. A few nights ago—I suppose it must be more than a week now—Willett, the estate porter, was taking up some luggage to 75 Northanger for the people there when he noticed a light in one of the rooms at 11 Massingham. The backs face, though about twenty of thirty yards away. It struck him as curious, because 11 Massingham is empty and locked up. Naturally he thought a first that the porter at Massingham or one of us from the office had gone up for something. Still it was so unusual—being late at night—that it was his business to look into it. On his way round—you know where Massingham Mansions are?—he had to pass here. It was dark, for we'd all been gone hours, but Willett has duplicate keys and he let himself in. Then he began to think that something must be wrong, for there, hanging up against their number on the board, were the only two keys of 11 Massingham that there are supposed to be. He put the keys in his pocket and went on to Massingham. Green, the resident porter there, told him that he hadn't been into No. 11 for a week. What was more, no one had passed the outer door, in or out, for a good half-hour. He knew that, because the door 'springs' with a noise when it is opened, no matter how carefully. So the two of them went up. The door of No. 11 was locked and inside everything was as it should be. There was no light then, and after looking well round with the lanterns that they carried they were satisfied that no one was concealed there."

"You say lanterns," interrupted Mr. Carlyle. "I suppose they lit the gas, or whatever it is there, as well?"

"It is gas, but they could not light it because it was cut off at the meter. We always cut it off when a flat becomes vacant."

"What sort of light was it, then, that Willett saw?"

"It was gas, Mr. Carlyle. It is possible to see the bracket in that room from 75 Northanger. He saw it burning."

"Then the meter had been put on again?"

"It is in a locked cupboard in the basement. Only the office and the porters have keys. They tried the gas in the room and it was dead out; they looked at the meter in the basement afterwards and it was dead off."

"Very good," observed Mr. Carlyle, noting the facts in his pocket-book. "What next?"

"The next," continued the clerk, "was something that had really happened before. Whey they got down again—Green and Willett—Green was rather chipping Willett about seeing the light, you know, when he stopped suddenly. He'd remembered something. The day before the servant at 12 Massingham had asked him who it was that was using the bathroom at no. 11—she of course knowing that it was empty. He told her that no one used the bathroom. 'Well', she said, 'we hear the water running and splashing almost evey night and it's funny with no one there.' He had thought nothing of it at the time, concluding—as he told her—it must be the water in the bathroom of one of the underneath flats that they heard. Of course he told Willett then and they went up again and examined the bathroom more closely. Water had certainly been run there, for the sides of the bath were still wet. They tried the taps and not a drop came. When the flat is empty we cut off the water like the gas."

"At the same place—the cupboard in the basement?" inquired Carlyle.

"No; at the cistern in the roof. The trap is at the top of the stairs and you need a longish ladder to get there. The next morning Willett reported what he'd seen and the governor told me to look into it. We didn't think much of it so far. That night I happened to be seeing some friends to the station here—I live not so far off—and I thought I might as well take a turn round here on my way home. I knew that if a light was burning I should be able to see the window lit up from the yard at the back, although the gas itself would be out of sight. And, sure enough, there was the light blazing out of one of the windows of No. 11. I won't say that I didn't feel a bit home-sick then, but I'd made up my mind to go up."

"Good man," mumured Mr. Carlyle approvingly.

"Wait a bit," recommended the clerk, with a shame-faced laugh. "So far I had only to make my mind up. It was then close on midnight and not a soul about. I came here for the keys, and I also had the luck to remember an old revolver that had been lying about in a drawer of the office for years. It wasn't loaded, but it didn't seen quite so lonely with it. I put it in my pocket and went on to Massingham, taking another turn into the yard to see that the light was still on. Then I went up the stairs as quietly as I could and let myself into No. 11."

"You didn't take Willett or Green with you?"

The clerk gave Mr. Carlyle a knowing look, as of one smart man who will be appreciated by another.

"Willett's a very trustworthy chap," he replied, "and we have every confidence in him. Green also, although he has not been with us so long. But I thought it just as well to do it on my own, you understand, Mr. Carlyle. You didn't look in at Massingham on your way? Well, if you had you would have seen that ther is a pane of glass above every door, frosted glass to the hall doors and plain over each of those inside. It's to light the halls and passages, you know. Each flat has a small square hall and a longish passage leading off it. As soon as I opened the door I could tell that one of the rooms down the passage was lit up, though I could not see the door of it from there. Then I crept very quietly through the hall into the passage. A regular stream of light was shining from above the end door on the left. The room, I knew was the smallest in the flat—it's generally used for a servant's bedroom or sometimes for a box-room. It was a bit thick, you'll admit—right at the end of a long passage and midnight, and after what the others had said."

"Yes, yes," assented the inquiry agent. "But you went on?" "I went on, tiptoeing without a sound. I got to the door, took out my pistol, put my hand almost on the handle and then——"

"Well, well," prompted Mr. Carlyle, as the narrator paused provokingly, with the dramatic instinct of an expert raconteur, "what then?"

"Then the light went out; while my hand was within an inch of the handle the light went out, as clean as if I had been watched all along and the thing timed. It went out all at once, without any warning and without the slightest sound from the beastly room beyond. And then it was as black as hell in the passage and something seemed to be going to happen."

"What did you do?"

"I did a slope," acknowledged the clerk frankly. "I broke all the records down that passage, I bet you. You'll laugh, I dare say, and think you would have stood, but you don't know what it was like. I'd been screwing myself up, wondering what I should see in that lightened room when I opened the door, and then the light went out like a knife, and for all I knew the next second the door would open on me in the dark and Christ only knows what came out."

"Probably I should have run also," conceeded Mr. Carlyle tactfully. "And you, Max?"

"You see, I always feel at home in the dark," apologised the blind man. "At all events, you got safely away, Mr.——?"

"My name's Elliott," responded the clerk. "Yes, you may bet I did. Whether the door opened and anybody or anything came out or not I can't say. I didn't look. I certainly did get an idea that I heard the bath water running and swishing as I snatched at the hall door, but I didn't stop to consider that either, and if it was, the noise was lost in the slam of the door and my clatter as I took twelve flights of stairs six steps at a time. Then when I was safely out I did venture to go round to look up again, and there was that damned light full on again."

"Really?" commented Mr. Carlyle. "That was very audacious of him."

"Him? Oh, well, yes, I suppose so. That's what the governor insists, but he hasn't been up there himself in the dark."

"Is that as far as you have got?"

"It's as far as we can get. The bally thing goes on just as it likes. The very next day we tied up the taps of the gas-meter and the water cistern and sealed the string. Bless you, it didn't make a ha'peth of difference. Scarcely a night passes without the light showing, and there's no doubt that the water runs. We've put copying ink on the door handles and the taps and got into it ourselves until there isn't a man about the place that you couldn't implicate."

"Has anyone watched up there?"

"Willett and Green together did one night. They shut themselves up in the room opposite from ten till twelve and nothing happened. I was watching the window with a pair of opera-glasses from an empty flat here—85 Northanger. Then they chucked it, and before they could have been down the steps the light was there—I could see the gas as plain as I can see this ink stand. I ran down and met them coming to tell me that nothing had happened. The three of us sprinted back up again and the light was out and the flat as deserted as a churchyard. What do you make of that?"

"It certainly requires looking into," replied Mr. Carlyle diplomatically.

"Looking into! Well, you're welcome to look all day and all night too, Mr. Carlyle. It isn't as though it was an old baronial mansion, you see, with sliding panels and secret passages. The place has the date over the front door, 1882—1882 and haunted, by gosh! It was built for what it is, and there isn't an inch unaccounted for between the slates and the foundation."

"These two things—the light and the water running—are the only indications there have been?" asked Mr. Carlyle.

"So far as we ourselves have seen or heard. I ought perhaps to tell you of something else, however. When this business first started I made a few casual inquiries here and there among the tenants. Among others I saw Mr. Belting who occupies 9 Massingham—the flat direcly beneath No. 11. It didn't seem any good making up a cock-and bull story, so I put it to him plainly—had he been annoyed by anything unusual going on at the empty flat above?

" 'If you mean your confounded ghost up there, I have not been particularly annoyed,' he said at once, 'but Mrs. Belting has, and I should advise you to keep out of her way, at least until she gets another servant.' Then he told me that their girl, who slept in the bedroom underneath the little one at No. 11, had been going on about noises in the room above—footsteps and tramping and a bump on the floor—for some time before we heard anything of it. Then one day she suddenly said that she'd had enough of it and bolted. That was just before Willett first saw the light."

"It is being talked about, then—among the tenants?"

"You bet!" assented Mr. Elliot pungently. "That's what gets the govenor. He would't give a continental if no one knew, but you can't tell where it will end. The people at Northanger don't half like it either. All the children are scared out of their little wits and none of the slaveys will run errands after dark. It'll give the estate a bad name for the next three years if it isn't stopped."

"It shall be stopped," declared Mr. Carlyle impressively. "Of course we have our methods for dealing with this sort of thing, but in order to make a clean sweep it is desirable to put our hands on the offender in *flagranti delicto*. Tell your—er—prinicpal not to have any further concern in the matter. One of my people will call here for any further details that he may require during the day. Just leave everything as it is in the meanwhile. Good-morning, Mr. Elliot, good-morning. . . . A fairly obvious game, I imagine, Max," he commented as they got into the car, "although the details are original and the motive not disclosed as yet. I wonder how many of them are in it?"

"Let me know when you find out," said Carrados, and Mr. Carlyle promised.

Nearly a week passed and the expected revelation failed to make its appearance. Then, instead, quite a different note arrived:

"MY DEAR MAX,—I wonder if you formed any conclusion of that Massingham Mansions affair from Mr. Elliott's refined narrative of the circumstances?

"I begin to suspect that Trigget, whom I put on, is somewhat of an ass, though a very remarkable circumstance has come to light which might—if it wasn't a matter of business—offer an explanation of the whole business by stamping it as inexplicable.

"You know how I value your suggestions. If you happen to be in the neighbourhood—not otherwise, Max, I protest—I should be glad if you could drop in for a chat.

"Yours sincerely,
"LOUIS CARLYLE."

Carrados smiled at the ingenuous transparency of the note. He had thought several times of the case since the interview with Elliot, chiefly because he was struck by certain details of the manifestation that divided it from the ordinary methods of the bogy-raiser, an aspect that had apparently made no particular impression on his friend. He was sufficiently interested not to let the day pass without "happening" to be in the neighbourhood of Bampton Street.

"Max," exclaimed Mr. Carlyle, raising an accusing forefinger, "you have come on purpose."

"If I have," replied the visitor, "you can reward me with a cup of that excellent beverage you were able to conjure up from somewhere down in the basement on a former occasion. As a matter of fact, I have."

Mr. Carlyle transmitted the order and then demanded his friend's serious attention.

"That ghost at Massingham Mansions——"

"I still don't believe in that particular ghost, Louis," commented Carrados in mild speculation.

"I never did, of course," replied Carlyle, "but, upon my word, Max, I shall have to very soon as a precautionary measure. Triggett has been able to do nothing and now he has as good as gone strike."

"Downed—now what on earth can an inquiry man down to go on strike, Louis? Note-books? So Trigget has got a chill, like our candid friend Elliot, eh?"

"He started all right—said that he didn't mind spending a night or a week in a haunted flat, and, to do him justice, I don't believe he did at first. Then he came across a very curious piece of forgotten local history, a very remarkable—er—coincidence in the circumstances, Max."

"I was wondering," said Carrados, "when we should come against that story, Louis."

"Then you know of it?" exclaimed the inquiry agent in surprise.

"Not at all. Only I guessed it must exist. Here you have the manifestation associated with two things which in themselves are neither usual nor awe-inspiring—the gas and the water. It requires some association to connect them up, to give them point and force. That is the story."

"Yes," assented his friend, "that is the story, and, upon my soul, in the circumstances—well, you shall hear it. It comes partly from the newpapers of many years ago, but only partly, for the circumstances were successfully hushed up in a large measure and it required the stimulated memories of ancient scandalmongers to fill in the details. Oh yes, it was a scandal, Max, and would have been a great sensation too, I do not doubt, only they had no proper pictorial Press in those days, poor beggars. It was very soon after Massingham Mansions had been erected—they were called Enderby House in those days, by the way, for the name was changed on account of this very business. The household at No. 11 consisted of a comfortable, middle-aged married couple and one servant, a quiet and attractive young creature, one is led to understand. As a matter of fact, I think they were the first tenants of the flat."

"The first occupants give the soul to a new house," remarked the blind man gravely. "That is why empty houses have their different characters."

"I don't doubt it for a moment," assented Mr. Carlyle in his incisive way, "but none of our authorities on this case made any reference to the fact. They did say, however, that the man held a good and responsible position—a position for which high personal character and strict morality were essential. He was also well known and regarded in quiet but substantial local circles where serious views prevailed. He was, in short, a man of notorious 'respectability.'

"The first chapter of the tragedy opened with the painful death of the prepossessing handmaiden—suicide, poor creature. She didn't appear one morning and the flat was full of the reek of gas. With great promptitude the master threw all the windows open and called up the porter. They burst open the door of the little bedroom at the end of the passage, and there was the thing as clear as daylight for any coroner's jury to see. The door was locked on the inside and the extinguished gas was turned full on. It was only a tiny room, with no fireplace, and the ventilation of a closed well-fitting door and window was negligible in the circumstances. At all events the girl was proved to have been dead for several hours when they reached her, and the doctor who conducted the autopsy crowned the convincing fabric of circumstances when he mentioned as delicately as possible that the girl had a very pressing reason for dreading an inevitable misfortune that would shortly overtake her. The jury returned the obvious verdict.

"There have been many undiscovered crimes in the history of mankind, Max, but it is by no means every ingenious plot that carries. After the inquest, at which out gentleman doubtless cut a very proper and impressive figure, the barbed whisper began to be insinuated and grow in freedom. It is sheerly impossible to judge how these things start, but we know that when once they have been begun they gather material like an avalanche. It was remembered by someone at the flat underneath that late on the fatal night a window in the principal bedroom above had been heard to open, top and bottom, very quietly. Certain other sounds of movement in the night did not tally with the tale of sleep-wrapped innocence. Sceptical busybodies were anxious to demonstrate practically to those who differed from them on this question that it was quite easy to extinguish a gas jet in one room by blowing down the gas-pipe in another; and in this connection there was evidence that the lady of the flat had spoken to her friend more than once of her sentimental servant's extravagant habit of reading herself to sleep with the light full on. Why was nothing heard at the inquest, they demanded, of the curious fact that an open novelette lay on the counterpane when the room was broken into? A hundred trifling circumstances were adduced—arrangements that the girl had been making for the future down to the last evening of her life—interpretable hints that she had dropped to her acquaintances—her views on suicide that the best means to that end: a favourite topic, it would seem, among her class—her possession of certain comparatively expensive trinkets on a salary of a few shillings a week, and so on. Finally, some rather more definite and important piece of evidence must have been conveyed to the authorities, for we know now that one fine day a warrant was issued. Somehow rumour preceded its execution. The eminently respectable gentleman with whom it was concerned did not wait to argue out the merits of the case. He locked himself in the bathroom, and when the police arrived they found that instead of an arrest they had to arrange the details for another inquest."

"A very convincing episode," conceded Carrados in response to his friend's expectant air. "And now her spirit passes the long winter evenings turning the gas on and off, and the one amusement of his consists in doing the same with the bath-water—or the other way, the other way about, Louis. Truly, one half the world knows not how the other half lives!"

"All you cheap humour won't induce Triggett to spend another night in that flat, Max," retorted Mr. Carlyle. "Nor, I am afraid, will it help me through this business in any other way."

"Then I'll give you a hint that may," said Carrados. "Try your respectable gentleman's way of settling difficulties."

"What is that?" demanded his friend.

"Blow down the pipes?" repeated Carlyle.

"At all events try it. I infer that Mr. Trigget has not experimented in that direction."

"But what will it do, Max?"

"Possibly it will demonstrate where the other end goes to."

"But the other end goes to the meter."

"I suggest not—not without some interference with its progress. I have already met your Mr. Trigget, you know, Louis. An excellent and reliable man within his limits, but he is at his best posted outside the door of a hotel waiting to see the co-respondent go in. He hasn't enough imagination for this case—not enough to carry him away from what would be his own obvious method of doing it to what is someone else's equally obvious but quite different method. Unless I am doing him an injustice, he will have spent most of his time trying to catch someone getting into the flat to turn the gas and water on and off, whereas I conjecture that no ones does go into the flat because it is perfectly simple—ingenious but simple—to produce these phenomena without. Then when Mr. Trigget has satisfied himself that it is physically impossible for anyone to be going in and out, and when, on the top of it, he comes across this romantic tradegey—a tale that might psychologically explain the ghost, simply because the ghost is moulded on the tragedy—then, of course, Mr. Trigget's mental process is swept away from its moorings and his feet begin to get cold."

"This is very curious and suggestive," said Mr. Carlyle. "I certainly assumed——But shall we have Trigget up and question him on the point? I think he ought to be here now—if he isn't detained at the Bull."

Carrados assented, and in a few minutes Mr. Trigget presented himself at the door of the private office. He was a melancholy-looking middle-aged man, with an ineradicable air of being exactly what he was, and the searcher for deeper or subtler indications of character would only be rewarded by a latent pessimism grounded on the depressing probability that he would never be anything else.

"Come in, Trigget," called out Mr. Carlyle when his employee diffidently appeared. "Come in. Mr. Carrados would like to hear some of the details of the Massingham Mansions case."

"Not the first time I have availed myself of the benefit of you inquiries, Mr. Trigget," nodded the blind man. "Good-afternoon."

"Good-afternoon, sir," replied Trigget with gloomy deference. "It's very handsome of you to put it in that way, Mr. Carrados, sir. But this isn't another Tarporley-Templeton case, if I may say so, sir. That was plain as a pikestaff after all, sir."

"When we saw the pikestaff, Mr. Trigget, yes, it was," admitted Carrados, with a smile. "But this is insoluble? Ah, well. When I was a boy I used to be extraordinarily fond of ghost stories, I remember, but even while reading them I always had an uneasy suspicion that when it came to the necessary detail of explaining the mystery I should be defrauded with some subterfuge as 'by an ingenious arrangement of hidden wires the artful Muggles had contrived,' etc., or 'an optical illusion effected by means of concealed mirrors revealed the *modus operandi* of the apparition.' I thought that I had been swindled. I think so still. I hope there are no ingenious wires or concealed mirrors here, Mr. Trigget?"

Mr. Trigget looked mildly sagacious but hopelessly puzzled. It was his misfortune that in him the necessities of his business and the proclivites of his nature were at variance, so that he ordinarily presented the curious anomaly of looking equally alert and tired.

"Wires, sir?" he began, with faint amusement.

"Not only wires, but anything that might account for what is going on," interposed Mr. Carlyle. "Mr. Carrados means this, Trigget: you have reported that it is impossible for anyone to be concealed in the flat or to have secret access to it——"

"I have tested every inch of space in all the rooms, Mr. Carrados, sir," protested the hurt Trigget. "I have examined every board and, you may say, every nail in the floor, the skirting boards, the window frames and in fact wherever a board or a nail exists. There are no secret ways in or out. Then I have taken the most elaborate precautions against the doors and windows being used for surreptitious ingress and egress. They have not been used, sir. For the past week I am the only person who has been in and out of the flat, Mr. Carrados, and yet night after night the gas is cut off at the meter is lit and turned out again, and the water that is cut off at the cistern splashes about as the grave and everything is exactly as I left it. It isn't human, Mr. Carrados, sir, and flesh and blood can't stand it—not in the middle of the night, that is to say."

"You see nothing further, Mr. Trigget?"

"I don't indeed, Mr. Carrados. I would suggest doing away with the gas in the room altogether. As a box-room it wouldn't need one."

"And the bathroom?"

"That might be turned into a small bedroom and all the water fittings removed. Then to provide a bathroom——"

"Yes, yes," interrupted Mr. Carlyle impatiently, "but we are retained to discover who is causing this annoyance and to detect the means, not to suggest structural alterations in the flat, Trigget. The fact is that after having put in a week on this job you have failed to bring us an inch nearer its solution. Now Mr. Carrados has suggested"—Mr. Carlyle was not usually detained among the finer shades of humour, but some appreciation of the grotesqueness of the advice required him to control his voice as he put the matter in its baldest form—"Mr. Carrados has suggested that instead of spending the time measuring the chimneys and listening to the wall-paper, if you had simply blown down the gas-pipe——"

Carrados was inclined to laugh, although he thought it rather too bad of Louis.

"Not quite in those terms, Mr. Trigget," he interposed.

"Blow down the gas-pipe, sir?" repeated the amazed man.

"What for?"

"To ascertain where the other end comes out," replied Carlyle.

"But don't you see, sir, that that is a detail until you ascertain how it is being done? The pipe may be tapped between the bath to the cistern in the attic above, a distance of only a few feet, and I have examined it. The gas-pipe, it is true, passes through a number of flats, and without pulling up all the floors it isn't practicable to trace it. But how does that help us, Mr. Carrados? The gas-tap has to be turned on and off; you can't do that with these hidden wires. It has to be lit. I've never heard of lighting gas by optical illusions sir. Somebody must get in and out of the flat or else it isn't human. I've spent a week, a very trying week, sir, in endeavouring to ascertain how it could be done. I haven't shirked cold and wet and solitude, sir, in the discharge of my duty. I've freely placed my poor gifts of observation and intelligence, such as they are, sir, at the service——"

"Not 'freely', Trigget," interposed his employer with decision.

"As I am speaking under a deep sense of injury, Mr. Carlyle," retorted Mr. Trigget, who, having had time to think it over, had now come to the conclusion that he was not appreciated. "I am alluding to a moral attitude such as we all possess. I am very grieved by what has been suggested. I didn't expect it of you, Mr. Carlyle, sir; indeed I did not. For a week I have done everything that it has been possible to do, everything that a long experience could suggest, and now, as I understand it, sir, you complain that I didn't blow down the gas pipe, sir. It's hard, sir; it's very hard."

"Oh, well, for heaven's sake don't cry about it, Trigget," exclaimed Mr. Carlyle. "You're always sobbing about the place over something or other. We know you did your best—God help you!" he added aside.

"I did, Mr. Carlyle; indeed I did, sir. And I thank you for that appreciative tribute to my services. I value it highly, very highly indeed, sir." A tremulous note in the rather impassioned delivery made it increasingly plain that Mr. Trigget's regiment had not been confined entirely to solid food that day. His wrongs were forgotten and he approached Mr. Carrados with an engaging air of secrecy.

"What is this tip about blowing down the gas-pipe, sir?" he whispered confidentially. "The old dog's always willing to learn something new."

"Max," said Mr. Carlyle curtly, "Is there anything more that we need detain Trigget for?"

"Just this," replied Carrados after a moment's thought. "The gas-bracket—it has a mantle attachment on?"

"Oh no, Mr. Carrados," confided the old dog with the affectation of imparting rather valuable information, "not a mantle on. Oh, certainly no mantle. Indeed—indeed, not a mantle at all."

Mr. Carlyle looked at his friend curiously. It was half evident that something might have miscarried. Furthermore, it was obvious that the warmth of the room and the stress of emotion were beginning to have a disastrous effect on the level of Mr. Trigget's ideas and speech.

"A globe?" suggeste Carrados.

"A globe? No, sir, not even a globe, in the strict sense of the word. No globe, that is to say, Mr. Carrados. In fact nothing like a globe."

'What is there, then?" demanded the blind man without any break in his unruffled patience. "There may be another way—but surely—surely there must be some attachment?"

"No," said Mr. Trigget with precision, "no attachment at all; nothing at all; nothing whatsoever. Just the ordinary or common or penny plain gas-jet, and above it the whayoumaycallit thingamabob."

"The shade—gas consumer—of course!" exclaimed Carrados. "That is it."

"The tin thingamabob," insisted Mr. Trigget with slow dignity. "Call it what you will. Its purpose is self-evident. It acts as a dispirator—a distributor, that is to say——"

"Louis," struck in Carrados joyously, "are you good for settling it to-night?"

"Certainly, my dear fellow, if you can really give the time."

"Good; it's years since I last tackled a ghost. What about——?" His look indicated the other member of the council.

"Would he be of any assistance?"

"Perhaps—then."

"What time?"

"Say eleven-thirty."

"Trigget," rapped out his employer sharply, "meet us at the corner of Middlewood and Enderby Roads at half-past eleven sharp to-night. If you can't manage it I shall not require your services again."

"Certainly, sir; I shall not fail to be punctual," replied Trigget without a tremour. The appearance of an almost incredible sobriety had possessed him in the face of warning, and both in speech and manner he was again exactly the man as he had entered the room. "I regard it as a great honour, Mr. Carrados, to be associated with you in this business, sir."

"In the meanwhile," remarked Carrados, "if you find the time hang heavy on your hands you might look up the subject of 'platinum black.' It may be the new tip you want."

"Certainly, sir. But do you mind giving me a hint as to what 'platinum black' is?"

"It is a chemical that has the remarkable property of igniting hydrogen or coal gas by mere contact," replied Carrados. "Think how useful that may be if you haven't got a match!

To mark the happy occasion Mr. Carlyle had insisted on taking his friend off to witness a popular musical comedy. Carrados had a few preparations to make, a few accessories to procure for the night's work, but the theatre spanned the interval between dinner at the Palm Tree and the time when they left the car at the appointed meeting-place. Mr. Trigget was already there, in an irreproachable state of normal dejection. Parkinson accompanied the party, bringing with him the baggage of the expedition.

"Anything going on, Trigget?" inquired Mr. Carlyle.

"I've made a turn round the place, sir, and the light was on," was the reply. "I didn't go up for fear of disturbing the conditions before you saw them. That was about ten minutes ago. Are you going into the yard to look again? I have all the keys, of course."

"Do we, Max?" queried Mr. Carlyle.

"Mr. Trigget might. We need not all go. He can catch us up again."

He caught on, sir," he reported.

"Do we use any special caution, Max?" asked Carlyle.

"Oh, no. Just as though we were freinds of the ghost, calling in the ordinary way."

Trigget, who retained the keys, preceded the party up the stairs till the top was reached. He stood a moment at the door of No. 11 examining, by the light of the electric lamp he carried, his private marks there and pointing out to the others in a whisper that they had not been tampered with. All at once a most dismal wail, lingering, piercing, and ending in something like a sob that died away because the life that gave it utterance had died with it, drawled forebodingly through the echoing emptiness of the deserted flat. Trigget had just snapped off his light and in the darkness a startled exclamation sprang from Mr. Carlyle's lips.

"It's all right sir," said the little man, with a private satisfaction that he had the diplomacy to conceal. "Bit creepy, isn't it? Especially when you hear it by yourself up here for the firt time. It's only the end of the bath-water running out."

He had opened the door and was conducting them to the room at the end of the passage. A faint aurora had been visible from that direction when they first entered the hall, but it was cut off before they could identify its source.

"That's what happens," muttered Trigget.

He threw open the bedroom door without waiting to examine his marks there and they crowded into the tiny chamber. Under the beams of the lamps they carried it was brilliantly though erratically illuminated. All turned towards the central object of their quest, a tarnished gas-bracket of the plainest description. A few inches above it hung the metal disc that Trigget had alluded to, for the ceiling was low and at the pont it was brought even nearer to the gas by corresponding with the slant of the roof outside.

With the prescience so habitual with him that it had ceased to cause remark among his associates Carrados walked straight to the gas-bracket and touched the burner.

"Still warm," he remarked. "And so are we getting now. A thoroughly material ghost, you perceive, Louis."

"But still turned off, don't you see, Mr. Carrados, sir," put in Trigget eagerly. "And yet no one's passed out."

"Still turned off—and still turned on," commented the blind man.

"What do you mean, Max?"

"The small screwdriver, Parkinson," requested Carrados.

"Well, upon my word!" dropped Mr. Carlyle expressively. For in no longer time than it takes to record the fact Max Carrados had removed a screw and then knocked out the tap. He held it up towards them and they all at once saw that so much of the metal had been filed away that the gas passed through no matter how the tap stood. "How on earth did you know of that?"

"Because it wasn't practicable to do the thing in any other way. Now unhook the shade, Parkinson—carefully."

The warning was not altogether unnecessary, for the man had to stand on tiptoes before he could comply. Carrados received the dingy metal cone and lightly touched its inner surface.

"Ah, here, at the apex, to be sure," he remarked. "The gas is bound to get there. And there, Louis, you have an ever-lit and yet a truly 'safety' match—so far as gas is concerned. You can buy the thing for a shilling, I believe."

Mr. Carlyle was examining the tiny apparatus with interest. So small that it might have passed for the mummy of a midget hanging from a cobweb, it appeared to consist of an insignificant black pellet and an inch of the finest wire.

"Um, I've never heard of it. And this will really light the gas?"

"As often as you like. That is the whole bag of tricks."

Mr. Carlyle turned a censorious eye upon his lieutenant, but Trigget was equal to the occasion and met it without embarrasment.

"I hadn't heard of it either, sir," he remarked conversationally. "Gracious, what won't they be getting out next, Mr Carlyle!"

"Now for the mystery of the water." Carrados was finding his way to the bathroom and they followed him down the passage and across the hall. "In its way I think that this is really more ingenious than the gas, for, as Mr Trigget has proved for us, the water does not come from the cistern. The taps, you perceive, are absolutely dry?"

"It is forced up?" suggested Mr Carlyle, holding towards the outlet.

"That is the obvious alternative. We will test it presently." The blind man was down on his hands and knees following the lines of the different pipes. "Two degrees more cold are not conclusive, because in any case the water has gone out that way. Mr Trigget, you know the ropes, will you be so obliging as to go up to the cistern and turn the water on."

"I shall need a ladder, sir."

"Parkinson."

"We have a folding ladder out here," said Parkinson, touching Mr. Trigget's arm.

"One moment," interposed Carrados, rising from his investigation among the pipes; "this requires some care. I want you to do it without making a sound or showing a light, if that is possible. Parkinson will help you. Wait until you hear us raising a diversion at the other end of the flat. Come, Louis."

The diversion took the form of tapping the wall and skirtingboard in the other haunted room. When Trigget presented himself to report that the water was now on Carrados put him to continue the singular exercise with Mr. Carlyle while he himself slipped back to the bathroom.

"The pump, Parkinson," he commanded in a brisk whisper to his man, who was waiting in the hall.

The appliance was not unlike a powerful tyre pump with some modifications. One tube from it was quickly fitted to the outlet pipe of the bath, another trailed a loose end into the bath itself, ready to take up the water. There were a few other details, the work of moments. Then Carrados turned on the tap, silencing the inflow by the attachment of a short length of rubber tube. When the water had risen a few inches he slipped off to the other room, told his rather mystified confederates there that he wanted a little more noise and bustle put into their performance, and was back again in the bathroom.

"Now, Parkinson," he directed, and turned of the tap. There was about a foot of water in the bath.

Parkinson stood on the broad base of the pump and tried to drive down the handle. It scarcely moved.

"Harder," urged Carrados, interpreting every detail of sound with perfect accuracy.

Parkinson set his teeth and lunged again. Again he seemed to come up against a solid wall of resistance.

"Keep trying; something must give," said his master encouragingly. "Here, let me——" He threw his weight into the balance and for a moment they hung like a group poised before action. Then, somewhere, something did give and the sheathing plunger "drew."

"Now like the blazes till the bath is empty. Then you can tell the others to stop hammering." Parkinson, looking round to acquiesce, found himself alone, for with silent step and quickened senses Carrados was already passing down the dark flights of the broad stone stairway.

It was perhaps three minutes later when an excited gentleman in the state of disrobement that its tacitly regarded as falling upon the *punctum càecum* in times of fire, flood, and nocturnal emergency shot out of the door of No. 7 and bounding up the intervening flights of steps pounded with the knocker on the door of No.9. As someone did not apear with the instantaneity of a jack-in-the-box, he proceeded to repeat the summons, interspersing it with an occasional "I say!" shouted through the letter-box.

The light above the door made it unconvincing to affect that no one was at home. The gentleman at the door trumpeted the fact through his channel of communication and demanded instant attention. So immersed was he with his own grievance, in fact, to notice the approach of someone on the other side, and sudden opening of the door, when it did take place, surprised him on his knees at his neighbour's doorstep a large and consequential-looking personage as revealed in the light from the hall, wearing the silk hat that he had instinctively snatched up, but with his braces hanging down.

"Mr. Tupworthy of No. 7, isn't it?" quickly interposed the new man before his visitor could speak. "But why this—homage? Permit me to raise you, sir."

"Confound it all," snorted Mr. Tupworthy indignantly, "you're flooding my flat. The water's coming through my bathroom ceiling in bucketfuls. The plaster'll fall next. Can't you stop it. Has a pipe burst or something?"

"Something, I imagine," replied No. 9 with serene detachment. "At all events it appears to be over now."

"So I should hope," was the irate retort. "It's bad enough as it is. I shall go round to the office and complain. I'll tell you what it is, Mr. Belting: these mansions are becoming a pandemonium, sir, a veritable pandemonium."

"Capital idea; we'll go together and complain: two will be more effective," suggested Mr. Belting. "but not to-night, Mr. Tupworthy. We should not find anyone there. The office will be closed. Say to-morrow——".

"I has no intention of anything so preposterous as going there to-night. I am in no condition to go. If I don't get my feet into hot water at once I shall be laid up with a severe cold. Doubtless you haven't noticed it, but I am wet through to the skin, saturated, sir."

Mr. Belting shook his head sagely.

"Always a mistake to try to stop water coming through the ceiling," he remarked. "It will come, you know. Finds its own level and all that."

"I did not try to stop it—at least not voluntarily. A temporary emergency necessitated a slight rearrangement of our accommodation. I—I tell you this in confidence—I was sleeping in the bathroom."

At the revelation of so notable a catastrophe Mr. Belting actually seemed to stagger. Possibly his eyes filled with tears; certainly he had to turn and wipe away his emotion before he could proceed.

"Not—not right under it?" he whispered.

"I imagine so," replied Mr Tupworthy "I do not conceive that I could have been placed more centrally. I received the full cataract in the region of the ear. Well, if I may rely on you that it has stopped, I will terminate our interview for the present."

"Good-night," responded the still tremulous Belting. "Good-night—or good-morning, to be exact." He waited with the door open to light the first flight of stairs for Mr. Tupworthy's descent. Before the door was closed another figure stepped down quietly from the obscurity of the steps leading upwards.

"Mr. Belting, I believe?" said the stranger. "My name is Carrados. I have been looking over the flat above. Can you spare me a few minutes?"

"What, Mr. Max Carrados?"

"The same," smiled the owner of the name.

"Come in, Mr. Carrados," exclaimed Belting, not only without embarrassment, but with positive affection in his voice. "Come in by all means. I've heard of you more than once. Delighted to meet you. This way. I know—I know." He put a hand on his guest's arm and insisted on steering his course until he deposited him in an easy-chair before a fire. "This looks like being a great night. What will you have?"

Carrados put the suggestion aside and raised a corner of the situation.

"I'm afraid that I don't come altogether as a friend," he hinted.

"It's no good," replied his host. "I can't regard you in any other light after this. You heard Tupworthy? But you haven't seen the man, Mr. Carrados. I know—I've heard—but no wealth of the imagination can ever really quite reconstruct Tupworthy, the shoddy magnifico, in his immense porcine complacency, his monumental self-importance. And sleeping right underneath! Gods, but we have lived to-night! Why—why ever did you stop?"

"You associate me with this business?"

"Associate you! My dear Mr. Carrados, I give you the full glorious credit for the one entirely successful piece of low comdey humour in real life that I have ever encountered. Indeed, in a legal and pecuniary sense, I hold you absolutely responsible."

"Oh!" exclaimed Carrados, beginning to laugh quietly. Then he continued: "I think that I shall come through that all right. I shall refer you to Mr. Carlyle, the private inquiry agent, and he will doubtless pass you on to your landlord, for whom he is acting, and I imagine that he in turn will throw all the responsibility on the ingenious gentleman who has put them to so much trouble. Can you guess the result of my investigation in the flat above?"

"Guess, Mr. Carrados? I don't need to guess: I *know*. You don't suppose I thought for a moment that such transparent devices as two intercepted pipes and an automatic gas-lighter would impose on a man of intelligence? They were only contrived to mystify the credulous imagination of clerks and porters."

"You admit it, then?"

"Admit! Good gracious, of course I admit it, Mr. Carrados. What's the use of denying it?"

"Precisely. I am glad you see that. And yet you seem far from being a mere practical joker. Does your confidence extend to the length of letting me into your object?"

"Between ourselves," replied Mr. Belting, "I haven't the least objection. But I wish that you would have-say a cup of coffee. Mrs. Belting is still up, I believe. She would be charmed to have the opportunity——No? Well, just as you like. Now, my object? You must understand, Mr. Carrados, that I am a man of sufficient leisure and adequate means for the small position we maintain. But I am not unoccupied—not idle. On the contrary, I am always busy. I don't approve of any man passing his time aimlessly. I have a number of interests in life—hobbies, if you like. You should appreciate that, as you are a private criminologist. I am—among other things which don't concern us now—a private retributionist. On every side people are becoming far too careless and negligent. An era of irresponsibility has set in. Nobody troubles to keep his word, to carry out literally his undertakings.

In my small way I try to set that right by showing them the logical development of their ways. I am, in fact, the sworn enemy of anything approaching sloppiness. You smile at that?"

"It is a point of view," replied Carrados. "I was wondering how the phrase at this moment would convey itself, say, to Mr Tupworthy's ear."

Mr Belting doubled up.

"But don't remind me of Tupworthy or I can't get on," he said. "In my method I follow the system of Herbert Spencer towards children. Of course you are familiar with his treatise on 'Education'? If a rough boy persists, after warnings, in tearing or soiling all his clothes, don't scold him for what, after all, is only a natural and healthy instinct overdone. But equally, of course, don't punish yourself by buying him other clothes. When the time comes for the children to be taken to an entertainment little Tommy cannot go with them. It would not be seemly, and he is too ashamed, to go in rags. He begins to see the force of practical logic. Very well. If a tradesman promises—promises explicitly—delivery of his goods by a certain time and he fails, he finds that he is then unable to leave them. I pay on delivery, by the way. If a man undertakes to make me an article another—I am painstaking, Mr Carrados: I point out at the time how exactly like I want it—and it is (as it generally is) on completion something quite different, I decline to be easy-going and to be put off with it. I take the simplest and most obvious instances; I could multiply indefinitely. It is, of course, frequently inconvenient to me, but it establishes a standard."

"I see that you are a dangerous man, Mr Belting," remarked Carrados. "If most men were like you our national character would be undermined. People would have to behave properly."

"If most men were like me we should constitute an intolerable nuisance," replied Belting seriously. "A necessary reaction towards sloppiness would set in and find me at its head. I am always with minorities."

"And the case in point?"

"The present trouble centres round the kitchen sink. It is cracked and leaks. A trivial cause for so elaborate an outcome, you may say, but you will doubtless remember that two men quarrelling once at a spring as to who should use it first involved half Europe in a war, and the whole tragedy of *Lear* sprang from a silly business round a word. I hadn't noticed the sink when we took this flat, but the landlord had solemnly sworn to do everything that was necessary. Is a new sink necessary to replace a cracked one? Obviously. Well, you know what landlords are: possibly you are one yourself. They promise you heaven until you have signed the agreement and then they tell you to go to hell. Suggested that we'd probably broken the sink ourselves and would certainly be looked to to replace it. An excellent servant caught a cold standing in the drip and left. Was I to be driven into paying for a new sink myself? Very well, I thought, if the reasonable complaint of one tenant is nothing to you, see how you like the reasonable complaints of fifty. The method served a useful purpose too. When Mrs. Belting heard that old tale about the tragedy at No. 11 she was terribly upset; vowed that she couldn't stay alone in here at night on any consideration.

"My dear,' I said, don't worry yourself about ghosts. I'll make as good a one as ever lived, and then when you see how it takes other people in, just remember next time you hear of another that someone's pulling the string.' And I really don't think that she'll ever be afraid of ghosts again."

"Thank you," said Carrados, rising. "Altogether I have spent a very entertaining evening, Mr. Belting. I hope your retaliatory method won't get you into serious trouble this time."

"Why should it?" demanded Belting quickly

"Oh, well, tenants are complaining the property is being depreciated. The landlord may think that he has legal redress against you."

"But surely I am at liberty to light the gas or use the bath in my own flat when and how I like?"

A curious look had come into Mr. Belting's smiling face; a curious note must have sounded in his voice. Carrados was warned and, being warned, guessed.

"You are a wonderful man," he said with upraised hand. "I capitulate. Tell me how it is, won't you?"

"I knew the man at No. 11. His tenancy isn't really up till March, but he got an appointment in the north and had to go. His two unexpired months weren't worth troubling about, so I got him to sublet the flat to me—all quite regularly—for a nominal consideration, and not to mention it."

"But he gave up the keys?"

"No. He left them in the door and the porter took them away. Very unwarrantable of him; surely I can keep my keys where I like? However, as I had another . . . Really, Mr. Carrados, you hardly imagine that unless I had an absolute right to be there I should penetrate into a flat, tamper with the gas and water, knock the place about, tramp up and down——"

"I go," said Carrados, "to get our people out in haste. Goodnight." "Good-night, Mr Carrados. It's been a great privilege to meet you. Sorry I can't persuade you . . ."

THE LONG
BARROW
by H.C. Bailey

First published in 1925

Mr. Fortune came back from the Zoo pensive. He had been called to the inquest on Zuleika the le-mur—a strange, sad case.

He rang for tea, and was given a lady's card. Miss Isabel Woodall, who had no address, wished to consult Mr. Fortune: she had been waiting half an hour. Mr. Fortune sighed and went into the ante-room.

Miss Isabel Woodall stood up, a woman who had been younger, still demurely handsome. She was large and fair, but so plainly and darkly dressed that she made little of herself. "Mr. Fortune?" she said with a pleasant shy smile.

"Yes. I'm afraid you didn't know that I'm not in practice now."

"But I didn't come to see you—er-medically. I'm not a patient, Mr. Fortune. I'm not ill. At least I don't think so. I wanted to consult you about a mystery."

"Oh! I never go into a mystery except with the police, Miss Woodall."

"The police won't do anything. They laugh at us." She twisted her handkerchief in her hands. "I'm frightfully worried, Mr. Fortune. And I don't know what to do." She looked at him with large, anxious eyes. "Do you mind hearing about it?"

Reggie Fortune decided that he did not mind. She was good to look at. He opened the door of his consulting-room.

"I'm Mr. Larkin's secretary," she explained. "Mr. Joseph Larkin: do you know him?"

"The antiquary?" Reggie Fortune murmured.

"Archaeologist." Miss Woodall corrected him sharply. "He's the greatest authority on the Stone Age in England, Mr. Fortune. He has a house down in Dorsetshire, just on the border of the New Forest country, Restharrow, Stoke Abbas." As she seemed to expect it, Reggie made a note. "I've been working with him down there. But lately it's been horrible, Mr. Fortune." Her voice went up. "As if somebody wanted to drive me away."

"Yes. Now suppose we begin at the beginning. How long have you been Mr. Larkin's secretary?"

"Oh, more than six months now."

"And nobody was ever horrible to you before?"

She stared at him. "Of course not. Nothing ever happened to me before. What do you mean, Mr Fortune? You don't think it's Mr. Larkin, do you?"

"I haven't begun to think," said Reggie. "Well, you lived a peaceful life till you became Mr. Larkin's secretary. And then?"

"Oh, yes, and long after that. It was all quite peaceful while we were in London. But in the spring Mr. Larkin took his house at Stoke Abbas. It's a very lovely place, where the moors meet the downs. Mr. Larkin wanted to study the prehistoric remains about there. There's lots of them, ancient earthworks and burial places."

"Yes. Several long barrows on the hills."

She leaned forward clasping her hands. "That's it, Mr. Fortune," she said in a low, eager voice. "Mr. Larkin has been making plans to excavate the long barrow above Stoke Abbas. Did you know about it?"

Reggie smiled. "No. No. I'm afraid Mr. Larkin hadn't attracted my attention."

She flung herself back in her chair. She gave a little cry of irritation. "Do please be serious! That's just like the stupid police down there. They only make fun of it all as if I was a nervous fool. But it's horrible, Mr. Fortune."

"Why not tell me what it is?" Reggie suggested.

"That is what is so difficult." She looked down at herself, arranged the blouse at her bosom. "You see, there isn't anything definite. It's as if some one was working against me; as if some one wanted to hurt me. I'm being followed, Mr. Fortune. Whenever I go out alone I'm followed."

Reggie sighed. Many people have made that complaint to patient doctors, and incredulous policemen. "Who follows you?" he said wearily.

"But I don't know! Only I'm sure there is somebody. I'm being watched."

"Why should anybody watch you, Miss Woodall?"

"That's what I want to know," she cried. "But somebody does, Mr. Fortune. I've heard him. I've seen his shadow."

"Oh, you are sure it's a man," Reggie smiled.

"You don't believe me, do you?" Miss Woodall was growing angry with him. "That isn't all. When I go out alone I find dead animals."

Reggie sat up. "Do you though?"

She thought he was still satirical. "Yes, I do, Mr. Fortune. Real ones. I've found two crows and another bird—a jay, I think it was—and a weasel. Horrible." She shuddered.

"Extraordinary mortality among the animals of Stoke Abbas," Reggie murmured. "How did they die, Miss Woodall?"

"Good gracious, I don't know. They were very dead. Just on the path where I was walking."

"Yes, that's very interesting," said Reggie.

"It frightens me, Mr. Fortune. What does it mean?"

"I should rather like to know," Reggie admitted. "Yes, I'll look into it, Miss Woodall."

"You yourself? Oh, thank you so much. If you would! I do so want it cleared up." She was effusively grateful. She fumbled in her bag. "I really don't know what your fee is, Mr. Fortune."

"There isn't one, Miss Woodall." He got rid of her. He consulted a book of reference upon Mr. Joseph Larkin. "I wonder," he said, and rang again for tea.

On the next day, he sat down to lunch in that one of his clubs where they understand the virtues of the herring. The chief of the Criminal Investigation Department saw him, and tripped across to his table. Both men love the simple life. They engaged upon a profound discussion whether the herring when pickled is the better for cloves. "In the delights of your conversation, Reginald," the Hon. Sidney Lomas protested at last, "I'm forgetting that I wanted to speak to you. A quaint old bird came to me this morning, one Joseph Larkin, an archaeologist. He said——"

"He said," Reggie interrupted, "that he wanted to excavate a long barrow at Stoke Abbas and somebody was interferin' with the progress of science and nobody loved him, and what are the police for, anyway? Is that right sir?"

"How do you do it, Reginald? Messages from the spirit-world, or just though-reading?"

Reggie smiled. "Satan's Invisible World Displayed: by R. Fortune. No, Lomas, old thing. No magic. The fair Isabel told me her sorrow."

"That's Miss Woodall, the secretary? She came to you, did she? The old boy didn't tell me that."

"Well, the fair Isabel didn't tell me Joseph was going to you."

The two men looked at each other. "Curious lack of confidence about them," said Lomas.

"Yes. several curious points. Well, what's Joseph's story? Is he followed when he goes out alone? Find dead animals in the path?"

"No carcasses for him. They're kept for Miss Woodall. He's followed. He hears strange noises at night. They come from outside the house. He's quite clear about that."

"Isabel didn't mention noises," Reggie murmured.

"No. The old boy said she hadn't heard them, and he didn't want to worry her, she was worried quite enough. That's his chief trouble. He seems rather gone on his fair secretary. What did you make of her, Reginald?"

"She's got the wind up all right. And she wasn't born yesterday. Queer case."

"Simple enough," Lomas shrugged. "The old boy goes down to this lonely place and wants to dig up an old grave, and the country people don't like it, and put up practical jokes to scare him off. That's what the local police think. I've been talking to them on the 'phone this morning."

"And the local police don't want to have a fuss with the local people over a couple of strangers."

"I sympathise," Lomas smiled. "Anyway, there's nothing for us."

"I wonder," Reggie said. "Why did one come to me and the other to you?"

"Oh, my dear fellow! They're both scared, and each of them wants to hide it from the other, and wants protection without making the other more scared."

"Yes. All very natural. Do you know anything about 'em?"

"Joseph is a man of means. Isabel came to him six months ago. Very highly qualified, he says. Classical scholar. Woman in a thousand for his job."

Reggie smiled. "His job! My dear fellow, he hasn't got a job. He's only a crank. He's always fussing round here, there, and everywhere. Why is he so mighty keen on this particular long barrow? Why is Isabel so mighty nervous about being followed? She's no chicken and no fool."

"I don't know what your're getting to, Reginald," Lomas frowned.

"Nor do I. That's what worries me. I want to go and look at Stoke Abbas. Let me have Underwood."

"But what are you thinking of?" Lomas objected.

"I think is isn't as natural as it looks," said Mr. Fortune.

In the morning his car picked up Sergeant Underwood and bore that officer away on the Southampton road. Sergeant Underwood, who looks like a nice, innocent undergraduate, lay back luxuriously enjoying the big car's purring speed. Reggie was studying an ordnance map of large scale. They were rushing the hill to Bagshot before he put it away and smiled at Underwood. "Well, my child, do you think you'll like it?"

"I like working under you, Mr. Fortune. But I don't know what I have to do."

"You have to catch butterflies. You're a promisin' young entomologist lookin' for rare species round the New Forest." He proceeded to give a lecture on English butterflies and moths. "Entomology in one lesson: by R. Fortune. Got that?"

Sergeant Underwood gasped a little. The labours of his intellect were betrayed on his comely face. "Yes, sir. Some of it. But Mr. Lomas said something about a long barrow. I don't rightly know what a long barrow is. But how does that come into butterflies?"

"It doesn't. A long barrow is the mount over an old grave. Thousands of years old." He opened the ordnance map. "This is our long barrow. Mr. Larkin and Miss Woodall—who live in that house—want to dig it up. And funny things have been happening. You're going to find a room in a nice pub somewhere near, but not too near, and watch the barrow and watch them and watch everybody—while catching butterflies."

In Southampton he bought Sergeant Underwood the complete equipment of a butterfly hunter, and put him on the train to find his own way to Stoke Abbass. The car bore Mr. Fortune on through the green glades of the New Forest to the bare heath country.

It was a day of cloud, and the very air over the moors was grey, and the long waves of heather were dark as the black earth, the distant woodland had no colour, the form of the chalk hills to northward was vague and dim. Mr. Fortune stopped the car and looked about him. Some grey smoke hung in a hollow from unseen houses. As far as he could see there was no man nor any of the works of man. The moor carried no cattle. There was sign of life but the hum of bees, and the chirp of grasshoppers, and the flies and butterflies in the heavy air.

"Empty, isn't it, Sam?" said Mr. Fortune, and got our of the car.

"Brighter London!" said Sam the chauffeur.

Mr. Fortune took a track across the heather. It was heavy going, rather like a ditch than a path, an old track long disuses and overgrown, but its depth showed that many feet must have passed that way once. It passed by a grey hovel lurking in a dip of the moor where a shaggy donkey was tethered, and some fowls of the old game-cock breed scratched in the sand. The thatch of heather was ragged, the mud walls crumbling here and there showed the wattle framework, the little windows were uncurtained.

The track led on to a bluff hill. Mr. Fortune groaned (he does not love walking) and set himself to climb. The hill-side was seared by a long scar. When he came to it he found the double ditch and bank of an old fort. He scrambled in and out and reached the flat hill-top. There rose the mound of the long barrow of Stoke Abbass.

Mr. Joseph Larkin had done no digging yet. Nor anyone else. The mound was clothed in heather and old gnarled gorse. The black sods beneath had not been turned for many a year.

Reggie looked over miles of bare moor and saw no one between him and the horizon. But on one side the hill was scooped out like a bowl, and down in the depths a rabbit scuttered to its burrow. Mr. Fortune went down that way. A man was squatting in the heather, binding bunches of it into little brooms, far too busy to look at him. "Oh, good day," said Mr. Fortune, and stopped. "What's the name of that thing up there?"

The man lifted his bent shoulders and showed a dark, beardless face, wide across the cheekbones, a big head for his small size. He stared like a startled animal.

"Do you know the name of that thing up there?" Reggie said again.

"Dragon Hill, 'tis Dragon Hill," the man cried, gathered up brooms and slid away through the heather. His legs were short, he was broad in the beam, his speed was surprising.

Mr. Fortune trudged back to his car and was driven to the house of Mr. Joseph Larkin. It stood beyond the village in a shrubbery of rhodonendrons, a plain red-brick box. Mr. Larkin was out. Miss Woodall was out too.

The conventional furniture of the drawing room was dismal. It seemed to contain no book but *Paradise Lost*, illustrated by Gustave Dore. Mr. Fortune shuddered and wandered drearily to and fro till he found on the writing-table the catalogue of a second-hand bookseller.

Mr. Larkin seemed to have an odd taste in books. Those which he had chosen to mark were a mixed lot—somebody's sermons, a child's picture book. Mr. Smiles on Thrift, a history of aviation, Izaak Walton. He marked them in a queer way. A line was drawn under one letter. Reggie Fortune pondered. The letters underlined were SKUTHAI: probably more farther on in the catalogue. But some one was talking outside. Reggie put the catalogue back.

A chubby old fellow came in smiling. "Mr. Reginald Fortune? I don't think I have the pleasure—"

"You called on Scotland Yard, Mr. Larkin."

"Oh, you've come from Mr. Lomas! That's very good of you, very good indeed." He smiled all over his rosy face. "Now let's just go into the study and I'll tell you all about it."

He did. He told at great length, but he did not say anything new, and in the midst of it Miss Woodall arrived in a hurry. "Mr. Fortune! You've come down yourself! But how very kind." While she took Reggie's hand she smiled on Joseph Larkin.

He needed it. He had been much disconcerted. "Oh, do you know Mr. Fortune, my dear?" he said, frowning.

"I didn't. But he is the great expert, you know. I went to him to ask his advice about this horrible business."

"But, my dear child, you didn't tell me."

"I couldn't bear you to be so worried, Mr. Larkin," she laid her hand on his arm.

"There, there. But you shouldn't, you know. You really shouldn't my dear. Leave everything to me."

"You are kind," she murmured.

"I have arranged it all," Mr. Larkin chirped. "I went to the fountain head, Mr. Sidney Lomas. And here is our expert." He beamed on Reggie. "Now—now I think I've told you everything, Mr. Fortune."

"Well, not quite," Reggie murmured. "Why are you specially keen on his long barrow, Mr. Larkin?"

Mr. Larkin began to explain. It took a long time. It was something about Phoenicians. The Phoenicians, Reggied gathered, had been everywhere, and done everything before the dawn of time. Mr. Larkin had given his life to prove it. He had found evidence in many prehistoric remains in many countries. When he came down to Stoke Abbas to complete his great book on *The Origins of Our World* he found this fine barrow at his very door. Miss Woodall very properly suggested to him that—

"Oh, Mr. Larkin, I'm afraid it wasn't me." Miss Woodall smiled, "I'm not expert enough to advise."

"Well, well, my dear, you're a very capable assistant. We decided that when we'd finished the book we must excavate the barrow on Dragon Hill, Mr. Fortune."

"And that's how the trouble began," Reggie murmured. "Yes. Any particular reason why you came to Stoke Abbas?"

Mr. Larkin looked at Miss Woodall. "I—I really don't know. I think this house was the most suitable of any that you saw, my dear."

"Oh, much the most suitable. Mr. Larkin must have quiet, you see, Mr. Fortune."

"And this is charmingly quiet, my dear." They purred at each other, and Reggie felt embarrassed. "Charming—if only Mr. Fortune can stop this annoyance. I hope you'll stay with us, Mr. Fortune."

They went to bed early at Restharrow. About midnight Mr. Fortune, just dropping off to sleep, was roused by an odd whistling roaring noise, such a noise as a gale might make. But there was no gale. He went to the window and peered out. The moon was rising behind clouds, and he could see nothing but the dark mass of rhodondendrons. There was a tap at the door and Mr. Larkin came in with a candle showing his pale face. "That's the noise, Mr. Fortune," he said. "What is it?"

"I wonder. Miss Woodall sleeps on the other side of the house?"

"Yes. I don't think she has ever heard it. It only comes and goes, you know. There! It's stopped. It'll come again. Off and on for half an hour or so. Most distressing. What can it be, Mr. Fortune?"

"I should rather like to know," Reggie murmured. They stood and listened and shivered, and when all was quiet at last he had some difficulty in getting Mr. Larkin to bed.

Reggie rose early. He saw the post come in, but Mr. Larkin and Miss Woodall were both down to take their letters. There was some mild fun about it. Mr. Larkin took the whole post by playful force, and sorted it with little jokes about "censoring your correspondence, my dear." It appeared to.

Reggie that the old gentleman was jealous in the matter of his fair secretary. But the only thing for her was a bookseller's catalogue.

After breakfast the two shut themselves into the study to work. Mr. Fortune went walking, and upon the moor found Sergeant Underwood in pursuit of a cabbage butterfly. His style with the net was truculent. "Game and set," Mr. Fortune smiled. "Fierce fellow. Don't be brutal, my child. No wanton shedding of blood."

Sergeant Underwood retrieved his net from a bramble. "I never hit the perishing things," he said, and mopped his brow.

"Never mind. You look zealous. Keep an eye on the hut over ther in the hollow. I want to know who comes out and what he does."

After lunch Mr. Larkin and Miss Woodall rested from their labours. The old gentleman withdrew to his bedroom. The lady sat in the garden. Reggie went out. To the west of the grounds of Restharrow a clump of lime and elm rose to shelter the house from thc wind. Reggie went up into one of the elms and climbed till he was hidden and high. He saw Miss Woodall leave the garden alone. She turned off the road by a footpath which led across the moor. Reggie took binoculars from his pocket. She went some way, looked about her and sat down in the heather. Her back was towards him, but he could see that she bent over a paper. Ahead of her a little dark shape moved in the heather, came near the path, and turned away and was lost in the folds of the moor. Miss Woodall rose and walked on more quickly. Reggie steadied his binoculars on the bough. She was going into the village, and among the houses he lost sight of her.

He slid to the ground and met her on her way back. "Alone, Miss Woodall? That's very brave."

"Isn't it?" She was flushed. "Do you know what I found on the path?"

"Yes. I've seen it. A dead stoat."

"Oh, horrible! What does it mean, Mr Fortune?"

"I shouldn't worry about that," said Reggie. He went on. He saw a butterfly net waving.

"This is a rum business, sir," Sergeant Underwood protested. "A little fellow came out of that hut, kind of gipsy look, and he mooched about over the heath. Seemed to be looking at snares he had set. He found a beast over that way, and sat down there from making brooms. Then a woman came down from the house, and he scuttled along and chucked the beast on to the path and cut off. Very rum game."

Nothing in it," said Reggie sadly. "Well, we'd better deal with him. Go to your pub, my child, and have some food and a nap. I want you outside that hut after dark."

Soon after dinner that night, Mr. Fortune professed himself sleepy and went to his room. He smoked a cigar there, heard the household go to bed, changed into his flannels and rubber shoes, and dropped unostentatiously out of the window. Among the rhododendrens he waited. It was a calm, grey night; he could see far, he could hear the faintest sound. Yet he had seen and heard nothing, when from behind the headge which marked off the kitchen garden came that whistling, roaring noise. Mr. Fortune made for it, stealthily, as it seemed to him, silently. But he only caught sight of a little man whirling something at the end of a string when the noise ended in a whiz and the fellow ran off. Mr. Fortune followed, but running is not what he does best. The little man was leaving him from the start, and soon vanished into the moor. Mr. Fortune at a sober trot made for the hovel under the hill, and as he drew near whistled.

He arrived to find Sergeant Underwood sitting on a little man who wriggled. "I'm a police officer, that's what I am," Underwood was saying. "Now don't you be nasty, or I'll have to be harsh with you."

Reggie flashed a torch in the wide, dark face of the broom-maker and signed to Underwood to let him sit up. "You've given me a lot of trouble," he said sadly. "Why do you worry the lady? She don't like dead stoats."

"Her don't belong on the moor," said the little man sulkily. "Her should bide in her own place."

"The old gentleman too. You've worried him with your nasty noises. It won't do."

"He should leave the land quite. 'Tis none of hisn."

"They are quiet. Quite quiet. They've never done any harm."

"Fie, fie! That they have surely, master. They do devise to dig up old Dragon's grave. 'Tis a wicked, harmful thing."

"It don't hurt you if they see what's inside the old mound."

"Nay, it don't hurt Giles. Giles was here before they come, me an mine, ten thousand year and all.

Giles will be here when they be gone their way. But 'tis evil to pry into old Dragons' grave. There's death in it, master."

"Whoever died there in your time?" Reggie said quickly.

"Nay, none to my time. But there's death in it, for sure. bid 'em go their ways, master, and leave the moor quiet."

"They'll do you no harm, my lad. And you mustn't bother them. No more of these tricks of yours, Giles, or we'll have to put you in gaol."

The little man squeaked and took hold of his knees and stroked them. "Ah, you wouldn't be so hard. I do belong on the moor, me and mine. I don't break no laws."

"Oh, yes, you do, hunting these folks. You ought to be in gaol now, my lad. You've made a lot of trouble. If there's any more of it you'll be shut up in a little close cell, not walking in the wind on the moor."

'Nay, master, you wouldn't do it to a poor man."

"You be good, then. I know all about you, you know. If the Restharrow folks have any more trouble it's gaol for Giles."

The little man breathed deep. "The old Dragon can have them for Giles."

"Don't forget. By the way, where's the thing you made the noise with?"

The little man grinned, and pulled out of his coat a bent piece of wood at the end of a cord. When he whirled it round his head it made the whistling roar of a gale.

Mr. Fortune came back to his bedroom by the window, and slept the sleep of the just. He did not reach the breakfast table till Joseph and Isabel were nearly finished. "All my apologies. I had rather a busy night." Miss Woodall hoped he had not been disturbed. "No, not disturbed. Interested." Mr. Larkin quivered with curiosity. He thought Mr. Fortune had gone out.

"Out on the moor at night?" Miss Woodall shuddered. "I wouldn't do that for anything."

Mr. Fortune tapped his third egg. "Why should you? But no one will meddle with you. Miss Woodall. The fellow that made the trouble won't bother you any more."

"Who was it?" she said eagerly.

"Well, I shouldn't worry. One of the local people suffering from superstition. He thought it was dangerous to dig up the old barrow. He wanted to scare you off. But I've scared him, and he's seen the evil of his ways. I think we'll give him a free pardon. He wouldn't have hurt you. You can rule him out and get on with the excavation."

"But that's magnificent, perfectly magnificent," Mr. Larkin chirped. "How quick too! You've really done wonderfully well." He twittered thanks.

"You're quite sure about it. Mr. Fortune?" said Miss Woodall.

"Nothing more to be afraid of, Miss Woodall."

"How splendid!" She smiled at him. "Oh, you don't know what a relief it is."

Mr. Larkin plunged into plans for the excavation. Old White at the Priors had promised to let him have men at any time before harvest. No time to lose. Better see the old man at once. Why not that morning? He did hope Mr. Fortune would stay and watch the excavation. Most interesting. Mr. Fortune shook his head. Perhaps he might be allowed to come down and see the result.

"That's a promise, sir. An engagement," Mr Larkin cried. "We shall hold you to that, shan't we, my dear?"

"Of course," said Miss Woodall.

They went off together to see old White—it seemed impossible for Mr. Larkin to make any arrangements by himself. Reggie was left in the house waiting for his car. He wandered into the study. Everything had been tidied away. Everything but the books was locked up. "Careful souls," Reggie murmured, and paused by a waste-paper basket. It had some crumpled stuff in it. He smoothed out the catalogue of a draper's sale. Some articles had been marked by a line under a letter. He ran his eye over the pages. T A P H O N O I G E I N he read, and heard the horn of his car. He dropped the catalogue back in the basket, and slid out of the study as the door bell rang. The maid coming to tell him his car was at the door, found him in his bedroom writing a letter.

The big car purred over the heath, passed a man pursuing butterflies, slowed and stopped. The chauffeur went to examine his back tyres. The passenger leaned out of and watched. When the car rolled on again there was something white by the roadside. The butterfly hunter crossed the road and picked up a letter. The passenger glanced back. "Now let her out, Sam," he said.

In the late afternoon, the Hon. Sidney Lomas, making an end of his day's work in Scotland Yard, was surprised by the arrival of Mr. Fortune. "Oh, Reginald, this is so sudden," he complained. "Finished already? Has Isabel no charms?"

"Some of your weaker tea would do me no harm," said Mr. Fortune. "Isabel's a very interestin' woman, Lomas. Joseph also has points of interest. They're both happy now."

"Cleared it up, have you? What was it?"

"It was a son of the soil. Very attractive person. Bushman type. Probably a descendent of some prehistoric race. You do find 'em about in odd corners. Family lurking on that moor for centuries. He had a notion if anybody opened the old Dragon barrow, death came out of it. Probably a primeval belief. So he set himself to scare off Joesph and Isabel—tokens of death for 'em—the bull-roarer at night."

"What in wonder is a bull-roarer?"

"Oh, a bit of wood rather like a boomerang. You twirl it round on the end of a string and it makes a deuce of a row. Lots of savages use them to scare off outsiders and evil spirits. Very curious survival is Giles. Well, we caught him at it and bade him desist. He's in a holy funk of Prison, and he's going to be good. And Joseph and Isabel are getting on with the excavation."

Lomas smiled. "So it was just the local rustic playing the fool. Reginald, my friend, I enjoy the rare and exquisite pleasure of saying I told you so."

"Yes." Reggie drank his tea. "Yes. Tell me some more, Lomas. Why did Joseph and Isabel go down to this place off the map and get keen on excavating its barrow? Lots of other nice barrows."

"No. I think there's something special in Joseph and Isabel. I found in the house a second-hand bookseller's catalogue. Some letters in it were undlined: SKUTHAI. Probably more. I hadn't time to go on. Joseph came in, and afterwards the catalogue vanished.

"Losts of people mark catalogues," Lomas shrugged.

"Yes. But not so that the marks make a word."

"Word?"

"Lomas, my dear old thing, I though you had a classical education. SKUTHAI is Greek for scythians, and in Athens the policemen were Schythians."

"Oh this is fantastic."

"Well, to-day I found a draper's catalogue in a waste-paper basket. Letters marked as before. TAPHONOIGEIN. Probably more, again. But that's two words. Taphon oigein. To open the tomb. Either Joseph or Isabel is making very secret communications with somebody about excavating that barrow. Why?"

"You do run on," Lomas protested. "But what are you starting from? These people have been doing their damnedest to get the police to look into their affairs. If either of them was up to anthing shady, that's the last thing they'd want."

"There's about a dozen answers to that," said Reggie wearily.

"Have some. Suppose something suspicious happen later. Mr. Lomas will say 'Oh, nothing in it, these people must be all right, they came and asked us to look into their affairs.' Why, you're saying that already. In the second place, both of them may not be in it; perhaps one of them knew the other was going to the police and played for safety by going too. Thirdly, they were both rattled, one of them may have thought somebody knew more than was convenient, and wanted to make sure. Fourthly and lastly, my brethren, whatever the job is, it has something to do with opening this barrow. They're both dead keen on that. They wanted to make sure they could do it without bother."

"Very ingenious, Reginald. And partially convincing," Lomas frowned. "If you'll tell me what they can get by exavating a barrow, I might begin to believe you."

"Nothing," said Reggie, "nothing. That's why it's interesting."

"My dear fellow! You have to much imagination."

"Oh lord, no. None. I'm the natural man. I get nerves when things aren't nice and normal. hence my modest fame. But imaginative! Oh, Mr. Lomas, sir, how can you?"

"Well, well. Time will show," Lomas rose. "If any corpses lie out on the shinning sand, I'll let you know."

"That'll be alright," said Reggie cheerfully. He did not move. "I left Underwood down there."

"The deuce you did!" Lomas stared and sat down again. "And what's he doing?"

"He's catching butterflies. He's also finding out whether Joseph or Isabel posts any catalogues and where they go to."

"Confound you, he mustn't do that on his own. If you want postal correspondence examined we must apply to the Postermaster-General. You ought to know that, Fortune."

"My dear old thing, I do. I also know country post offices. Don't be so beastly official."

"This is a serious matter."

"Yes. Yes, that's what I've been trying to indicate," Mr. Fortune smiled. "Look here. These beauties go down to a place off the map for no decent reason but that it's off the map. Joseph could write his silly books anywhere. Did Isabel take Joseph, or Joseph take Isabel? Their stories don't agree. Joseph is affectionate and Isabel coy. Joseph watches her jealously and Isabel is meek. When they've been there some time they get might keen on digging up a barrow. Lots of barrows in lots of places, but they must have the lonely one at Stoke Abbas. Then we find them dealing in messages too secret for a letter in plain English. One message something about the police, another about opening the barrow. Well there's going to be dirty work at the cross road, old thing."

"But it's all fanciful, Fortune. Why the deuce shouldn't they write letters? What's the use of putting a message in Greek?"

"They're all alone. Each of 'em can see all the letters the other gets, perhaps all the letters the other posts. But a catalogue wouldn't be noticed. If one of 'em don't know Greek the marked letters would be absolutely secret. S K U T H A I didn't suggest anything to the Chief of the Criminal Investigation Department."

"But what do you suppose the game is?"

"No dear"; Mr. Fortune smiled. "I have no imagination. You've got all the facts. Oh, not quite. I did a little distant snap-shot of Joseph and Isabel." He laid a roll of film on the table. "Get the faces enlarged big. Some of your fellows might know 'em. Good-bye. I've got to dine with my young neice—the one that married a gunner. Always merry and bright. Very exhausting."

After which nothing happened for a couple of weeks. Lomas when he met Mr. Fortune in their clubs made sarcastic remarks about the Greek language and the use of the imagination. Then Joseph Larkin wrote to Mr. Fortune that the excavation was nearly complete, urging him to come and see the result. Mr. Fortune told Lomas over the telephone and Lomas made scornful moises. "I'm going," said Mr. Fortune.

"You've got a lot of time to waste," said the telephone.

But three days afterwards, while the car stood at his door to take him to Stoke Abbas, the telephone spoke again, "Hallo, Fortune. Are you up? Marvellous. Just come round here."

Lomas was in an early morning temper. "Some more crazy stuff about the Stoke Abbas case." He stared at Reggie with a bilious eye. "I put the post office people on to it, more fool me. Here's a report. A bookseller's catalogue was posted on Monday with a number of letters from Restharrow. It was addressed to Miss George, 715 Sand Street, Bournemouth. In it a number of letters were marked, a, b, four e's, g, h, two i's, l, m, n, p, r, two s's, t and u."

"As you say," Reggie groaned.

"What do you mean?"

"You said more fool you. Quite so. Why didn't you leave it to Underwood? He'd have got it all right. And I told him to give us the letters in order."

"Confound you, we can't tamper with the mail."

"My dear old thing, you're too good for this world," Reggie took pen and paper. "Say it again, A, b—" He wrote down ABEEEEGHIILMNPRSSTU, lit a cigar and pondered. "You moral men give me a lot of trouble. Here you are. PRESBUS GAMEIN THELEI. And very interesting too. That clears up several points."

"What the deuce does it mean?"

"What did you learn at school, Lomas? I've often wondered. It means 'The old man desires to marry.' Yes, I thought so. I told you you had all the facts. You remember Joseph said Isabel had had a classical education. Not like you, Lomas. She's sending the messages. She's caught Joseph. It's opening out. Now tell your priceless post office folks to report the order of the letters in future. I don't want to work cryptograms because you've got a conscience. And send somebody to look into Miss George, of 715 Sand Street, good and quick. I'm going down to Stoke Abbas. They've opened the barrow. Oh, by the way, what about the snapshots?"

"They enlarged well enough. Nobody here knows the people."

Not known to the police? Well, well. Get a snap of Miss George. Good-bye."

That evening Mr. Fortune stood on Dragon Hill with Joseph and Isabel. Half a dozen labourers rested on their spades and grinned. The long mound of the barrow was gone. It lay in scattered heaps of grey sand around the cromlech which it had covered, three upright stones supporting one flat. Under that flat stone, as a man might lie under a table, lay a skeleton. Reggie knelt down and took up the skull. "Ah, genuine antique," he gave sigh of relief.

Miss Woodall shuddered. "He looks like a monkey."

"No, I wouldn't say that," said Reggie gently, still intent on the bones.

"I am convinced he was a Phoenician," Mr. Larkin announced.

"Oh, lord, no," said Reggie. He was not interested in Mr. Larkin's theory that everything old was Phoenician. He was thinking that this man of the barrow with his long head and his big cheekbones and his short wide body must have been much like Giles of the hovel on the moor. An ancestor perhaps; five thousand years ago the family of Giles the broom-maker were kings on the sandhills. But Mr. Larkin went on talking about Phoenicians. . . . "Yes, very interesting," said Reggie wearily, and stood up.

"Poor dead man," Miss Woodall sighed. "He looks so lonely."

"My dear," said Mr. Larkin affectionately. "What pretty thoughts you have." They walked back to Restharrow, and he proved again that the skeleton was Phoenician, and it was most gratifying, and he was going to give it to the British Museum, and Reggie was bored.

In that condition he remained for the duration of his visit to Restharrow. When Mr. Larkin was not talking about Phoenicians, or (worse still) reading extracts from his new book on *The Origins of Our World*, he was (worst of all) being affectionate with Miss Woodall. A mawkish little man. But there was no mystery about them. The great book was published, the barrow was open. Mr. Larkin was going to write a pamphlet about it, close it down again, marry Miss Woodall, and take her off to South Africa, where he meant to find many more traces of the Phoenicians. Reggie wished them joy, and as soon as he decently could, went back to London.

Two days afterwards Lomas found him having breakfast in his bedroom, a rare thing, a sure sign of depression. "My dear fellow, are you ill?"

"Yes, very ill. Go away. I don't like you. You look distressin'ly cheerful, and it's very bad for me."

"There's been another message. TUCHEAPELTHE."

"Don't gargle, spell it," said Mr. Fortune peevishly. "Yes TUCHE APELTHE. Two words. 'Fortune has gone away.' Very kind for her to notice it."

Lomas smiled. "So Isabel wanted Miss George to know Mr. Fortune had gone away. That's intereting. And we've got something about Miss George, Reginald. She isn't a woman. Oh no. She's a middle-aged man, who calls himself George Raymond. He don't live at 715 Sand Street. That's a little shop where they take in letters to be called for. George Raymond has lodgings the other end of the town, and lives very quite. My fellows have a notion he's American."

"Fortune has gone away," Reggie murmured. "I wonder if Fortune ought to have stayed. No. Nothing would happen with me in the house. I wonder if anything will happen."

"What, are you giving up the case?" Lomas laughed.

"No. There's a case all right. But I don't know whether we'll ever get it. Joseph and Isabel are going to marry, and be off to South Africa."

Lomas was much amused. "and that's the end of it all! My poor Reginald? What a climax! Mr. Fortune's own particular mystery. All orange blossom and wedding cake."

"Yes. With Miss George as best man. I hope your fellows are looking sharp after Miss George."

"He's giving no trouble. They won't miss him. We've got a photograph too. Nobody knows him, but we'll have it enlarged."

"Well, watch him."

"Oh, certainly; anthing to oblige. Have they asked you to the wedding, Reginald? You really ought to send them a present."

Lomas says that Reggie then snarled.

Two weeks passed. Reggie received an angry letter from Mr. Larkin stating that the British Museum had refused the skeleton, and he was replacing it in the barrow, and publishing the full facts to inform the public of the blind prejudice of the official world against his work. He was leaving immediately for South Africa, where he had no doubt of obtaining conclusive proof of the theory of the Phoenician origin of all civilisation. Mrs. Larkin sent Mr. Fortune kind thoughts and best wishes.

Mr Fortune moved uneasily in his chair. "And they lived happily ever after," said Mr. Fortune. "Kind thoughts and best wishes. Dear Isabel. "He rang up Lomas to ask how Miss George was getting on.

"Many thinks for kind enquiries," said the voice of Lomas. "Nothing doing. Not by George. He lives the life of a maiden lady. What did you say?"

"I said damn," said Mr. Fotune.

That evening came a letter from Sergeant Underwood. He was plaintive. He thought Mr. Fortune ought to know there seemed nothing more to do at Stoke Abbas. The barrow was being covered up. The servants were leaving Restharrow. Mr. Larkin and Miss Woodall were going to be married at the registry office to-morrow, and the next day sailing from Southampton. Mr. Fortune spent a restless night.

He was fretting in the library of his dreariest club next morning, when the telephone called him to Scotland Yard. Lomas was in conference with Superintendent Bell. Lomas was brisk and brusque. "They've lost George Raymond, Fortune. He left Bournemouth this morning with a suit-case. He went to Southampton, put in the cloakroom, went into one of the big shops, and hasn't been seen since. When they found they had lost him they went back to the station. His suit-case was gone."

"Well, well," Said Mr. Fortune. "You have been and gone and done it, Lomas." But he smiled.

"What do you want us to do now?"

"Oh, you might watch the Cape boat. Make sure G. Raymoind isn't on the Cape boat when she sails. If you can."

"I've arranged for all that. Anything else?"

"You might give him a time-table," said Mr. Fortune. "I'm going down to the long barrow."

"Good gad!" said Lomas.

As darkness fell on the moors that night, Mr. Fortune and Superintendent Bell stopped a hired car a mile away from Stoke Abbas, and walked on through the shadows. When they came near the shrubbieries of Restharrow, a voice spoke softly from behind a clump of gorse. "Got your wire sir. All clear here. They were married this morning. Both in the house now. Servants all gone. No one else been here."

Reggie sat down beside Sergeant Underwood. "Seen anyone strange about?"

"I did fancy I saw some one going up towards the barrow a while ago."

"Work up that way quietly. Don't show yourself."

Sergeant Underwood vanished into the night. Bell and Reggie sat waiting while the stars grew dim in a black sky. The door of Restharrow opened; and a bar of light shot out. They heard voices. "A beautiful night," said Larkin. "The most beautiful night that ever happened." said Mrs. Larkin. They came out. "Let us go up to the dear old barrow," she said. "I shall always love it, you know. It brought us together my dearest."

"My dear child," Mr. Larkin chirped. "You are full of pretty thoughts."

They walked on arm in arm.

A long way behind, Reggie and Superintendent Bell followed. When they came to the crest of the hill, where the turned sand was white in the gloom, "Dear place," said Mrs. Larkin. "How sweet it is here. I think that old Phœnician was lucky, don't you, Joseph dearest?"

A man rose up behind Joseph dearest and grasped his head. There was no struggle, no noise, a little swaying, a little scuffle of feet in the sand, and Joseph was laid on his back and Isabel knelt beside him. The other man turned aside. There was the sound of a spade. Then Sergeant Underwood arrived on his back. They went down together. Bell charged up the hill to catch Mrs. Larkin as she rushed to help. But Underwood already had his man handcuffed and jerked him on to his feet.

Reggie came at his leisure and took a pad of cottonwool from Mr. Larkin's face. "Who is your friend with the chloroform, Mrs. Larkin?" he said gently.

"You devil," she panted. "Don't say a word, George."

"Oh yes, I know he's George," said Reggie, and flashed a torch on the man.

Sergeant Underwood gasped. Sergeant Underwood stared from the man in hancuffs to the man on the ground. "Good Lord! Which have I got, sir?" for the man who stood was of the same small plump size as Mr. Larkin, grey-haired, clean-shaven too, dressed in the like dark clothes.

"Yes, a good make up. That was necessary, wan't it, Mrs Larkin? Well, we'd better get the real Mr. Larkin to hospital." He whistled across the night and flashed his torch and the hired car surged up to the foot of the hill. Mr. Larkin was carried to it, it bore him and Reggie away and behid them. Mrs. Larkin and George, handcuffed wrist to wrist, tramped long miles to a police station.

A little man lying in the heather on the hill watched them go. "Old Dragon hath taken her," and he capered home to his hut on the moor.

Superintendent Bell coming into the coffee-room of an inn at Wimborne next morning, saw Mr. Fortune dealing heartily with grilled salmon. "You had a bad night, sir," he said with sympathy.

"Yes. Poor Joseph was very upset. Spiritually and physically. Can you wonder? It's disheartening to a husband when his wife attempts murder on the wedding night. Destroys confidence."

"Confidence! They're a pair of beauties, the woman and this chap George. I suppose they were going to bury poor Larkin alive."

"Yes. Yes. He wouldn't have been very lively of course."

"I should say not. What do you think that fellow had on him, sir?"

"Well, chloroform, of course. A pistol, I suppose. Probably some vitriol."

"That's it." Superintendent Bell gazed at him with reverent admiration. "It's wonderful how you know men, Mr. Fortune."

Mr. Fortune smiled and passed Bell his plate of nectarines. "I knew they'd think of everything. That's their weakness. Just a little too careful. But it's a beautiful plan. Grave all ready, nice light soil, spades handy, chloroform the old man, pour vitriol over him, bury him. Not likely anyone would open that barrow again in a century. If they did, only an unknown corpse inside. Nobody missing. No chance anybody would think the corpse was Mr. Larkin who sailed for South Africa alive and kicking. And George and Isabel are Mr. and Mrs. Larkin and live happy ever after on the Larkin fortune. If only she hadn't taken such pains about a grave, if only she hadn't bothered about Giles, if only they hadn't bee so clever with their secret messages, they'd have brought it off. Poor old Joseph, though. He's very cut up. He fears Isabel never really loved him. But he don't want to give evidence against her, poor old thing."

"I don't wonder," said Bell. "He'll look a proper fool in the witness-box."

"Yes. Yes. Not a wise old boy. But human, Bell, quite human."

There was a sprightly noise without. Lomas came tripping in, and on the heels of Lomas a solid man with the face of a Roman emperor. "Reginald, dear fellow, all my congratulations," Lomas chuckled. "You told me so. You really did. Splendid case. This is Mr. Bingham Jackson of the American service."

"I want to know you, sir," said Mr. Bingham Jackson magisterially. "This is right good work. We wanted those two and we wanted 'em bad."

"When Mr. Jackson saw your photographs of George and Isabel he called for champagne," Lomas chuckled.

"Yes. I though somebody ought to know them," said Mr. Fortune. "I though they weren't new to the business."

"No, sir." Mr. Jackson nodded impressively. "Not new. Isabel and George Stultz are American citizens of some reputation. We shall be right glad to have them back. They eliminated Mrs. Stanton Johnson of Philadelphia and got off with her collection of antique jewels. They used morphia and cellar then. One of our best crimes."

"This is going to hush up Joseph's trouble," said Mr. Fortune with satisfaction. "You'll claim their extradition for murder?"

"Sure thing. We didn't get in on our case early like you. They brought the murder off our side. You always had 'em on a string. But I want to say, Mr. Fortune, I do admire your work. You have flair."

"Not nice people, you know," said Reggie dreamily. "I get nerves when people aren't nice and ordinary."

"Some nerves," said Mr. Jackson.

APPENDIX

THE following is the solution of the end-game referred to in the chess story entitled *A Happy Solution.*

I . . . . P to K6 ; 2.

Q to R6 (a), Q to R5, ch. ; 3.

Q (or B) takes Q, B to B5 ; 4. Kt to Kt3, B takes Kt and mates, very shortly, with R to R8.

(a) 2. Kt to Kt4, Q takes Kt ; 3. Q (or P) takes Q (b), B to B5 as before.

(b) If 3. Q to R6, Q to R5, ch., as before.

If 2. P to K Kt4, B to Kt6 ; 3. Kt takes B, Q takes Kt and wins.

The following is the proof, from the position of the pieces, that a white queen must have been taken by the pawn at Q Kt3 : All the black men except two are on the board ; therefore White made only two captures. These two captures must have been made with the two pawns now at K5 and B3, because they have left their original files. White, therefore, never made a capture with his Q R P, and therefore it never got on to the knight's file. Therefore the black pawn at Q Kt 3 captured a *piece* (not a pawn). The game having been played at the odds of queen's rook, the white Q R was off the board before the game began, and the white K R was captured on its own square, or one of two adjacent squares, there being no way out for it.

Now, since Black captured a *piece* with the pawn at Q Kt 3, and there are no white *pieces* off the board (except the two white rooks that have been accounted for), it follows that whatever piece was captured by the pawn at Q Kt 3 must have been replaced on the board in exchange for the white Q R P when it reached its eighth square. It was not a rook that was captured at Q Kt3, because the two white rooks have been otherwise accounted for. The pawn, on reaching its eighth square, cannot have been exchanged for a bishop, or the bishop would still be on that square, there being no way out for it, nor can the pawn have been exchanged for a knight for the same reason (remembering that the capture at Q Kt 3 must necessarily have happened *before* the pawn could reach its eighth square).

Therefore the pawn was exchanged for a queen, and therefore it was a queen that was captured at Q Kt3, and when she went there she did not make a capture, because only two captures were made by White, both with pawns. Q.E.D.